The Lady and the General

The pretty lady had come through the Confederate lines by way of the Corinth Road and delivered her information to the stocky, rather homely and rumpled-looking Yankee general named Grant.

"Madam, I think you are a patriot," said the General, with a surprising amount of courtesy for a man Liberty Lee had heard described as a monster. "I insist on providing you an escort to a safe area on the other side of the river."

She protested, but the General was firm. "Oh, here comes one of my aides now ... Captain?"

Liberty looked up and felt a sudden sinking in in the pit of her stomach and she felt for a moment she'd faint. For there, coming toward her in the uniform of a Union officer was her former lover, the one man who could unmask her— Dan O'Lee.

"Captain O'Lee," General Grant said, "Allow me to introduce you to ..."

"My name is ... Jane Roberts," Liberty said, looking at the ground, hoping the wide brim of her hat would shield her.

"Good afternoon, Miss Roberts," Dan said eagerly, but with a hint of menace in his voice ...

HEARTS DIVIDED

Paula Moore

A DELL/BRYANS BOOK

Published by
Dell Publishing Co., Inc.
1 Dag Hammarskjold Plaza
New York, New York 10017

Dell ® TM 681510, Dell Publishing Co., Inc.

ISBN: 0-440-03917-7

Printed in the United States of America

First printing—September 1979

HEARTS
DIVIDED

1

Dan O'Lee shifted in his seat, the better to restore the circulation in his sore and cramped legs, and pulled the curtain back to peer through the stagecoach window. The snow, which had started as a light powder when they boarded this morning in Springfield, Missouri, was now coming down in large, heavy flakes. It was falling so steadily that the line of woods to either side of the road was all but obscured.

It was January 23, 1862, and Dan was twenty-three-days out of San Francisco, with just two more days to go before he reached St. Louis. Twenty-three days of bone-jarring stages, high mountain passes, wide-open spaces, and now the woods and hills of Missouri. He had come nearly two thousand miles since saying goodbye to Lady Pamela Buttle-Jones.

If Dan had learned one thing in the last twenty-three days, it was the best way to get comfortable in the cramped confines of the stage. He stretched his long legs out, folded his arms across his chest, pulled his hat low over his eyes, and cast his thoughts back . . . back to New Year's Eve, and the going-away dinner Pamela had given him.

"I really feel I should stay," Dan had told her.

"Whatever for?" Pamela asked.

Dan laughed. "I don't know. Maybe it's just that I feel that I'm deserting you in your hour of need."

This time it was Pamela's time to laugh. "My dear boy, it is not *my* hour of need we are concerned with here. It is yours. You are the one who suffered a broken heart."

"It wasn't broken," Dan insisted. "It was only bent. Besides, you've helped me to get over it quite nicely."

"Dan," Pamela said gently, placing her hand on Dan's cheek. "I am flattered that you would find me desirable enough to assuage the hurt you felt. But I am also much older than you."

"That means nothing," Dan insisted.

"Shh," Pamela said, putting her finger to her lips. "Hear me. I am much too vain a woman to sit by gracefully, should your eyes ever wander to a younger woman."

"Pamela, how could you suggest . . ."

"Shhh," Pamela said again, still smiling. "Perhaps you're right. Perhaps your eyes never would wander. But mine might. Don't you see, darling? I love you, I truly do, but I don't want the responsibility of your heart on my hands.

8

That's why I think it is best that you go to St. Louis."

Dan took Pamela's hands in both his, and held them tightly for a moment. Finally he spoke, surrendering to her logic. "You're right," he agreed. "There are too many memories here."

"Exactly," Pamela said. "If you go to St. Louis, soon all the unpleasant memories will fade, and there will be only the pleasant ones. I want to be remembered fondly, Dan, not lost in the morass of bitter reminders."

"So I'll go to St. Louis," Dan agreed, smiling at her persuasiveness.

"Wonderful. And I have some news for you. I've had some detective work done by my friend Allen Pinkerton. Your brother is currently employed by the Mississippi Transportation Company, as a loading foreman. He's working on the levee in St. Louis."

"You've located Burke?" Dan asked, surprised.

"Located him yes, and written to him as well, though I've received no answer to my letter as yet. But that doesn't matter. What matters is we've found him. How long has it been?"

Dan ran his hand through his thick, reddish-brown hair as he thought. He looked up. "It's been twelve years," he said. "He was a ten-year-old kid when I left him with my aunt and uncle—to come out to California to make my fortune, you know." He grinned ironically. "Well, came to California, anyway."

"That will make him twenty-two now. Do you think you'll recognize him?" Lady Pamela asked.

"I . . . I really don't know," Dan shrugged. "Fact is, I'm not sure if he would want to see me again. He was pretty upset by my leaving him there. He couldn't seem to understand that a twenty-one-year-old had no business raising the little tyke he was. At least that's what I told myself. But I've often wondered if I wasn't just being selfish. I could have kept him with me if I had worked at it. Maybe I should have."

"Never mind that now," Pamela said. "That's water under the bridge. It's only important that you're going to see him again."

"Guess you're right," Dan said. He smiled. "Damn, I do believe I'm looking forward to this."

"As well you should," Pamela said. She slid her arms around his neck, then leaned into him and brought her lips just a kiss away from his. "And I, my handsome young traveler, am looking forward to telling you goodbye, and wishing you a happy new year, in a very special way."

"What about you?" someone asked Dan. The memories suddenly popped out of Dan's mind as if someone had burst a balloon, and he realized that he was on the stage, being spoken to.

Dan slid his hat back and looked into the face of a red-faced, fat-cheeked drummer by the name of Quimby. He'd met the salesman just that morning; he was in cookware.

"Beg your pardon," Dan said. "Did you say something to me?"

"Yes. I said this here war is all but over, but these fellas don't seem to agree."

"I'm afraid I haven't been following the news as closely as I should. I'm only recently arrived from California."

"Well, I'll tell you what I know," the drummer said. He leaned forward confidentially, as if sharing a war secret with Dan and the other two passengers, one a Union army officer, the other a preacher. "I was in General Halleck's office myself last week, and I seen dispatches that said that the Federal troops were pushing the Secesh all over the place. Why, General Thomas run them plumb outta Mill Springs, Kentucky where they fought a battle, and the Rebel general, a fella named Zollicoffer, he was kilt."

"Zollicoffer was an amateur," the Union officer said. "He had no more business in a uniform than you do."

Dan and the preacher laughed.

"Just 'cause you got that soldier's suit on, that don't make you no military expert, sonny," Quimby said, piqued. "I'm tellin' you the Secesh don't have no officers worth a tinker's dam."

"What about Beauregard, and Albert Sidney Johnston?" the Union officer asked.

"Or Sterling Price, Jeff Thompson, or even Quantrill?" the preacher added.

"Beauregard and Johnston are cowards," the drummer said resolutely. "Price, Thompson, and Quantrill? Incompetents, hardly worth mentioning."

"If I see Quantrill I'll tell him of your high regard for him, sir," the preacher said.

The Union officer smiled, then peered through the window again, for perhaps the hundredth time since they'd left St. Joseph. At first Dan had thought the officer was concerned with the weather, but there was a nervousness in his manner now not brought on by the snow. Dan watched him curiously, but without question.

Quimby went on, a bit angrily. "You fellas are talking like a couple of Secesh. It's a good thing you're a wearin' that blue uniform, elsewise I might wonder just whose side you're on. 'N I could ask the same thing of you, preacher."

"I'm a man of the cloth, sir," the preacher said, smiling. "I will preach the word of the Lord to whoever shall heed it, be he Union or Confederate."

"That's a dangerous position to take in Missouri," the drummer said. "You've got to assert yourself here. Elsewise in this state, nobody will know who is for what."

"On the contrary," the preacher replied wryly. "I would say that this is the safest position to take in a border state."

"And you, sir? You've just arrived from California. How stands that state?"

"I can only speak for myself, not for California," Dan said. "Me, I sure don't want to see the Union dissolved. But I've no wish to take up arms against my fellow countrymen either. I still have hopes of a peaceful solution."

"All such hopes are gone, I fear," the Union officer said. "The drummer is at least right on that point. By the way, we haven't met. My name is Thomas Ward. I'm a lieutenant in the regular army."

"Dan O'Lee," Dan said, taking the hand offered him. It was a firm and friendly handshake. "Are you on leave?"

"No. I'm on special orders," Ward said. "I'll be joining General Halleck's staff in St. Louis. Is St. Louis your destination as well?"

"Yes," Dan said. "I've a brother there whom I haven't seen in many years. And I've a bit of business to attend to."

Dan was truthful in telling the officer he had business in St. Louis. Lady Pamela Buttle-Jones had given him a bank draft for ten thousand dollars, with instructions to buy a piece of land. The land was owned by Hiram Dempster, an old acquaintance of Lady Pamela's, and he had promised to sell it to her if the ten thousand dollars was "personally delivered" to his hands.

"If I can be of any assistance in any way," Ward said, "please look me up."

"Thanks for your offer, lieutenant," Dan said.

The conversation died down, each man seemingly lost in his own thoughts. Outside the stage slipped and slid through the blinding snowstorm, its forward motion now reduced to a speed no faster than a man could walk.

2

Under a cluster of trees near the stage pike, a group of horsemen waited. They wore sheepskin coats, and scarfs wrapped around their necks, and hats which were brimful of snow.

"I don't think he'll be a-comin' out in this kind of weather," one of the men said. He squirted a stream of tobacco juice toward the snowbank, where it browned for just a moment, then was quickly buried by new snow so that it wasn't visible.

"The chief said it would be here, it'll be here," another answered.

"You think the chief cain't do nothin' wrong," the first said. "What's he got for you, boy? A pocket full o' sugar titties?"

The boy who had defended his chief unbuttoned his coat, and faced his taunter. The man's gun hand was clearly visible, and the boy moved his hand to hover menacingly over it.

"Pull your gun, you son of a bitch, or ride out of here," the boy said.

"Jesse, come on, he didn't mean nothin' by it," one of the other men said.

"I said pull your gun," Jesse said again, looking at the man with cold, calm, blue eyes.

A third man moved in between the two. "Dingus, we got us enough Yankees to kill, without havin' to shoot up our own," he complained. He was using Jesse's nickname as a placating gesture, but Jesse wasn't put off by it.

"Burke, get out of the way," the boy said coldly. "I don't want to shoot you."

"Then call this thing off," Burke said. "Leastwise 'till we get somewhere where you two can settle it between yourselves without putting the rest of us in danger. Frank, talk to your brother."

Frank James rode over to his younger brother and put his hand on Jesse's arm. "Close up your coat, Dingus," he said. "You're gonna catch your death with a chill."

There was a tense moment, then Jesse relented. "Sure, Frank," he said. "Whatever you say." He buttoned his coat back up, then stuck his hands in his pockets to warm them.

"I don't know why he got so mad. All I said was . . ." the other man started, but the rider nearest him, the one called Burke, twisted in his saddle and cuffed him on the jaw, stopping him in mid-sentence.

"Hey, what'd you do that for?" the man asked.

"Figured I'd save your life, you damn fool,"

Burke said. "We don't want to hear what you said. Just shut up, and listen for the stage."

Burke O'Lee settled back in his saddle and tried to fight off the cold. He had made a decision to support the South and had joined up with the guerilla William Clarke Quantrill because he thought that was the quickest way to get into the war. Quantrill, who often used the alias Charley Hart, was thus called Charley, had the deadliest gang of cutthroats and brigands ever assembled in one company. Burke O'Lee could hold his own with most men, had in fact been in a few duels in his young life, and the fact that he was still around attested to his success in them. But men like Frank and Jesse James and Jim, Bob, and Cole Younger were little more than cold-blooded killers and thieves, and Burke was becoming disaffected with his association with them.

Quantrill wasn't with them for this mission. He had left Frank James in charge. It was a relatively simple mission. They were to stop a stage and recover a document which was being carried by a Yankee courier.

"Listen up," Frank suddenly called, holding a hand high. "I think I hear 'em comin'."

Burke strained to hear. In the softness of the snowfall, he could hear the driver whistling and shouting at his team to urge them on.

"Burke, you ride out into the road and try'n stop the driver. Tell him you want to buy passage to the next town, and you aim to tie your horse on back. We'll have the drop on him that way, and we might can pull this off without any gunplay."

"It would be simpler just to shoot him," Jesse said easily.

"We'll try it my way," Frank insisted.

The rest of the gang melted back into the woods to wait for Burke to do his job. Burke rode out onto the road and stood there with his hand raised.

The plan may have worked, but the rider who had been braced by Jesse earlier got a little nervous and dashed out of the woods too quickly. The driver saw him out of the corner of his eye, and, realizing something was up, raised his rifle and shot Burke.

Burke felt a searing pain tearing into his shoulder, and his breath left him as the bullet knocked him off his horse. Almost as soon as he fell into the snow, he heard the guns of the others open up. He saw the driver pitch off the high seat, then land spreadeagled in the snow, his blood staining red on the pristine white.

From Burke's vantage point on the ground, he saw, despite his pain, a peculiar thing. The rider who had compromised their position suddenly tumbled out of his saddle, shot dead, though not one bullet had been fired from the stage.

The riders reined up alongside the stage, their

horses prancing about in excitement and breathing clouds of steam into the cold air.

"You folks in the stage, climb down outta there," Frank shouted.

Cole Younger rode over to where Burke lay in the snow and looked down at him.

"Help me onto my horse, Cole," Burke said, keeping his voice calm. He wasn't sure but that they might shoot him if they thought he was hurt badly enough to slow them down, so he was underplaying his wound as much as possible.

"Are you bad hit?"

"No," Burke said. "It's just a flesh wound." The bullet was in fact buried deep in his shoulder. He could feel the weight of it and the heat of it, as if someone were holding a hot poker to his flesh.

Burke followed the action near the stage as best he could, while Cole helped him mount. Four men stepped out of the coach.

"Boy, am I glad to see you gentlemen of the South," the drummer said nervously. "I've been expressing my Southern sentiments to these fellas, but they are all Union to the core, and they've given me a pretty rough time of it."

Frank laughed. "Is that true, Charley? Have you fellas been giving this Southern patriot a hard time?"

The preacher stroked his Vandyke beard for just a moment, then smiled and removed his

19

long, black coat. Beneath it he wore the gray and gold tunic of a Confederate captain. "Oh, yes," he said. "We've really been giving him a rough time."

"You!" the drummer said, his face reflecting his fear. "You're a Rebel!"

"Gentlemen, my name is William Clarke Quantrill, at your service," the man said, smiling at them. He dropped the black coat and wrapped himself in a grey officer's coat, provided him by one of his men who also brought up a spare horse. "I regret the inconvenience, but it is a necessity of war. Lieutenant Ward, I do believe you have a dispatch which would interest us."

"I have nothing of the sort," Ward said stiffly.

"Please, just give it to us and we'll be on our way," Quantrill said. "I don't want to have to shoot you."

"I don't know what you are talking about," Ward said again.

"I'm sorry, lieutenant. You are a brave man, and it is a shame to have to kill you," Quantrill said. He signaled to the young, beardless boy, and the boy raised his gun and fired without a second's hesitation.

There was a loud, unexpected boom. The impact of the heavy .44 caliber bullet slammed Lieutenant Ward against the wheel of the stage. Then he slid down to the ground, holding his hand over the wound in his chest. Blood spilled over his fingers and ran down the front of his coat.

"Search him," Quantrill ordered, and two of the riders swung off their horses and began stripping the lieutenant. Within moments the young officer was lying naked in the snow, his body already turning blue, the blood from his wound coagulating in the cold.

"There ain't nothin' on him, Charley," one of the searchers said.

"Are you positive?"

"Well, hell, look for yourself. There ain't nothin' in his clothes, 'n he's as nekkid as the day he come into the world. Where would it be at?"

"Damn," Quantrill swore, striking his fist into his hand. "We must have been given the wrong information. Well, mount up. We've got us a long ride ahead."

"May I attend to the lieutenant now?" Dan asked.

"Yeah," one of the riders said. He was the one who had shot Ward. "But he's gonna die, 'cause I shot him in the heart. You can try'n get him warm if you want."

One of the other riders laughed. "Dingus, I allus did say your heart was too soft for serious killin'."

"I do my job," Jesse replied.

Quantrill shouted an order and the riders rode away into the snowstorm. Dan noticed that one

21

of them was wavering in the saddle, obviously seriously wounded.

Dan took the coat Quantrill had discarded and used it and Lieutenant Ward's own coat to try and make the lieutenant comfortable.

The lieutenant barely had the strength to raise his hand to his mouth. He pointed, then opened his mouth and raised his tongue. Dan saw a rolled-up piece of white paper in his mouth, and, realizing that the lieutenant wanted him to get it, reached in and pulled it out.

"I'll get this to General Halleck for you," Dan promised.

"Liberty," the lieutenant said, the word barely audible.

"What? What did you say?"

The lieutenant coughed, and the spasms shook his body so that he had difficulty breathing. Finally, he was able to speak again. "Liberty," he said, struggling to get the word out. Then his head rolled to one side, and a final, rasping breath escaped from his mouth.

"He's dead," Dan said.

"What was he sayin'?" the drummer asked. "Sounded like liberty."

"Yes," Dan said, standing up and looking down at the dead officer.

"The poor fella must'a been delirious," the drummer suggested. "I guess he was tryin' to tell us that he died for liberty."

"I guess so," Dan said. "Come on, help me get him into the coach."

"What? You mean he's gonna ride inside with us?"

"He's going to ride inside with you," Dan said. "He, and the driver both. I've got to drive this thing. I'll be on top."

"I don't want to ride inside with a couple of dead men," the drummer complained. "Why'nt we just leave 'em out here 'n send somebody back for 'em? They're dead now. It won't make no never mind to them."

"I have a better idea," Dan said.

"What?"

"I'll leave you here, and send someone back for you."

"No," the drummer said. "I don't want to stay out here all alone."

"You won't be alone," Dan sugegsted. "You'll have him for company." He pointed at the dead guerilla, lying perhaps twenty yards from the stage, his body now nearly covered with snow.

"You wouldn't really leave me out here, would you?"

"I'm considering it, if you don't help me get these two inside," Dan said. "We'll leave him for whoever wants him," he added, pointing to the raider's body.

The drummer complained mightily, but he helped Dan load the bodies of the driver and the lieutenant. Then he got inside with them, and Dan climbed up on the high seat to take the reins of the horses.

It was a fifteen-mile run to the next way station. Though the snow finally quit falling, it still took them the better part of three hours to make it. When they got there, Dan was relieved to see a detachment of Federal troops also at the station, and he turned both bodies over to them.

Dan considered surrendering the paper he had taken from Lieutenant Ward's mouth to them as well, but at the last minute, he decided to keep it himself and deliver it personally to General Halleck. After all, he was going to St. Louis anyway. This way he would be satisfied that Lieutenant Ward's mission, whatever it was, would be completed.

3

The terrible pain stopped and a warming numbness set in. It was that numbness which allowed Burke to keep up with the others on their mad ride away from the scene of the hold-up. But with the numbness came also a weakness from loss of blood, and by the time they rode into Rolla, Missouri just before dawn the next morning, Burke was staying in his saddle only by supreme effort of will.

"Hey, chief, Burke's about to keel over here," Jesse called. Jesse had taken it on himself to ride beside Burke, and for the last three hours it had been he who held the reins to Burke's horse, while Burke used both hands on the pommel, just to stay up.

How like Jesse James that was, Burke managed to think, despite the befuddling haze of pain he was in. Dingus, who could kill a man without blinking an eye, could also be moved to acts of extreme kindness and gentleness. By far the youngest of Quantrill's band, he was clearly the most fascinating.

"I know a doctor in this town who'll patch him up," Quantrill said.

"Do we have the time?" one of the other riders asked.

"We won't wait for him. We'll just drop him off and ride on our way."

"What if the sawbones turns him into the Yankees?" Jesse asked.

"We'll pay him enough to buy his silence," Quantrill said. "Dingus, you and Burke come with me. Frank, you and the rest of the boys ride down to that farmhouse there. It belongs to a fella name of Matthew Poe. Tell him you're with Charles Hart and that we've come to Rolla to buy cattle. He'll have his woman fix you some hot grub. Me'n Dingus'll take breakfast at the doc's house."

"Let's go boys," Frank said.

As they left, Quantrill, Jesse and Burke headed for the doctor's house. Though it was still pre-dawn dark, the snow on the ground made it appear light. As the three rode through the street, they could see squares of golden light on the snow, cast there through the windows of the houses where early risers were already beginning to set to breakfast.

Quantrill halted them when they reached the end of the street.

"What is it, chief?" Jesse asked.

"That's the house down there," Quantrill said, pointing to a low, single-story building which sat nearly half a block away from the others. A wisp of wood smoke rose from the chimney, carrying with it the aroma of frying bacon. "I just want to make sure there's no one around."

The saddle squeaked as Jesse twisted in it to look around. Burke held on, telling himself there was only a short time left and then he could lay down and rest in a warm house.

"It looks clear," Jesse said calmly.

Quantrill clicked to his horse, and the three of them slowly crossed the distance. They stopped just in front of the doctor's house.

SAM COYLE, M.D., the sign read by the door. Quantrill didn't bother to knock, he just pushed it open. Then he and Jesse half-carried, half-supported Burke inside.

"What the—? What is this?" the surprised doctor asked, looking up from his breakfast table. His wife was standing at the stove frying bacon, and she looked around in alarm as well.

"Don't get fretted none, doc," Quantrill said quietly. "It's just me. One of my men got hisself shot up yesterday afternoon. He needs some doctorin'."

The doctor moved quickly to the door and looked around nervously before he shut it. "Did anyone see you bring him here?" he asked anxiously.

"No," Quantrill said. "We know it ain't healthy to be Secesh in this town."

Jesse lay Burke on the bed. Doctor Coyle sat beside him and opened his coat, then his shirt.

"He's lucky," he said. "The cold stopped the bleeding, and I don't think there's any festering. But the bullet is going to have to come out."

Quantrill sat at the breakfast table without asking and began helping himself. Jesse stood by the bed for a moment longer, then, when the doctor's wife invited him to breakfast, he too sat at the table.

"Here's a little laudanum," Dr. Coyle said to Burke, handing him a small bottle. "Take it. You'll need it when I start probing for the bullet."

Doctor Coyle's wife assisted him. They removed Burke's shirt and then the doctor began digging into the wound for the bullet. Quantrill and Jesse ate their breakfast as if totally unconcerned with what was going on over on the bed. A few minutes later, when Coyle announced that he had the bullet and then dropped it with a clink into the pan of warm water, neither of the two made a comment.

"Can he ride out with us now?" Quantrill asked, when he and Jesse finished their breakfast.

"Are you serious? I should say not. It'll be a few hours before he'll even wake up."

Quantrill tugged at his beard for a moment, then reached into his coat pocket and pulled out a gold coin. "Here, doc, this is for fixin' up the boy and feedin' us breakfast. Tell Burke he's on his own when he wakes up. We can't wait around for him."

"I can't keep him here," Doctor Coyle protested.

"You don't have to keep him here. Send him on his way."

"He should have at least a day's rest," Doctor Coyle said.

"Then give it to him," Quantrill said. "You've been paid handsomely enough. Come on, Dingus, we've got to be on our way."

Quantrill and Jesse left the small house, and Coyle and his wife stood there, looking at the door as if unable to believe what had happened to them this morning. They waited for a moment, and when they heard the horses leave, Doctor Coyle walked over to look through the window to make sure they had gone.

"Sam, you knew those people?" Coyle's wife said. She brushed a wisp of errant brown hair out of her eyes, and looked at the young man who lay on their bed, bare from the waist up and now sleeping peacefully.

"That was Quantrill," Doctor Coyle said.

"Quantrill! The murderer?"

"Molly," Dr. Coyle said from the window. "If

anyone comes by today, you tell them I was called to Jefferson City, do you have that? I'm going to Jefferson City."

"What for?"

"Unless I miss my guess, there'll be a reward out for this man. I aim to bring a couple of soldiers back with me."

"Sam, you're going to leave me with him, alone?" Molly asked, surprised by his statement and frightened by the prospect.

"Don't worry none. He'll mostly be out of it for the next twelve hours, and I figure to be back by nightfall. If anyone asks who he is, why, you just tell them he's your nephew, wounded in the war."

"Sam, what will they do to him?" Molly asked, looking at Burke.

"Hang him, most likely."

"Hang him? But he's just a boy."

"That ain't none of our concern, Molly," the doctor said, already slipping into his coat. "You just do like I told you, and I'll see you tomorrow mornin'." He smiled. "Countin' the gold piece old Quantrill gave me, 'n the reward this boy's sure to bring, why this'll be a pretty profitable day, don't you think?"

Molly put the "doctor out of town" sign on the front door after Coyle left, then cleaned up the breakfast dishes, and then the house. But throughout the morning, her eyes kept wandering over to the boy on the bed. His hair was blond, and he had a thin, blond mustache over lips which were almost too full for a man's. There was a dimple in his chin. His chest, though adorned with only the sparsest blond hair, was full and muscular. The skin was clear and smooth.

Whenever Molly caught herself looking at him, she would scold herself mentally, and look away. After all, the boy couldn't have been much over twenty, and she was thirty-eight years old . . . a married woman who had no right to think about how handsome a man might be.

But she couldn't keep the disturbing thoughts of him from creeping into her mind, and before she knew it, she would be looking at him again.

Molly stoked up the fire in the fireplace, not because it was cold in the house—in fact, it was quite warm—but just to keep herself occupied so that she wouldn't look at him.

But it didn't work. Once more she turned to see him, and this time as she stared she could feel a warmth in her body which wasn't brought on entirely by the fire she had built. She took off her sweater. She felt some respite from the increased temperature but no relief from the heat building within. The heat drove her to unbutton the top six buttons of her dress, and she folded the collar back, almost all the way down to the swell of her breasts. She knew it was a scandalous move, but as she was alone, she didn't care.

No, she thought, she wasn't alone. The young man on the bed was with her. But he's sleeping, she decided, thus justifying her scandalous action.

Molly walked over to the stove and poured a kettle of hot water into a basin, then carried the basin over to the bed and sat on it. She began giving the young man a bath. She was doing no more than administering to a patient, she told herself. But her breathing began to be more labored, and felt such a churning within that it could scarcely be contained.

The man's eyes opened.

He started to sit up, but so abrupt was his movement that it sent a searing stab of pain into his shoulder, and he fell back down on the bed.

"Lie still, sir, and you will be more comfortable," Molly instructed.

"Who are you?" Burke asked. He looked around. "What is this place?"

"Don't you remember coming here, earlier this morning?"

Burke looked into the face of the woman who was bathing him. It was a pleasantly attractive face, he decided, and it eased some of the fear which shot through him.

"No," he finally said. "I remember only the cold. The cold, and the riding. Where am I?"

"This is the house of Dr. Coyle in Rolla."

"Where are the others?"

"Your friends have gone," Molly said. "They left you here to mend."

Burke looked up at the ceiling. Molly thought she had never seen eyes so clear a blue. They looked like the afternoon sky on the sharpest, sunlit day.

"Where is the doctor?" Burke asked.

"He's . . . gone . . . on business," Molly said. "There are just the two of us here."

As Molly talked, she continued to bathe Burke, and now the cloth was on Burke's stomach. The action caused Molly to bend over and as she did her unbuttoned dress fell forward slightly, exposing the curve of her breast. She felt a heat there, then looked up to see that Burke was staring at the scene she had thus presented.

"I . . . I'm sorry," she mumbled, and she reached up to close the buttons.

"No," Burke said, putting his hand on hers, gently. "You don't have to close the buttons if you don't want to."

"I'm a silly old woman," she said. She turned her head away from him, closing her eyes tightly and biting her lower lip.

"You are a lovely woman, without age," Burke said easily. He reached down and unfastened his breeches, then pushed them down and guided her hand, the hand which was now

33

mindlessly bathing in a circle on his stomach, down further, until she felt his bulging manhood.

"No," she said, "please no." She was trembling now, like a frightened bird. Tears streamed down her face. "Help me to fight this evil want that's come over me."

Burke put his hand behind her neck, then gently pulled her head down to his, pressing her lips to his.

She let out a small whimper, and returned his kiss with surprising ardor. Her skin was incredibly warm, and he could feel the pulse in her neck beating rapidly. Finally, with a gasp of breath, she sat up. "I beg of you," she said. "Don't you know what you are doing to me?"

Burke smiled, and pulled her back to him for another kiss. This time he began unbuttoning the remaining buttons. Without mind or will of her own, Molly helped him, so that within a moment, she lay beside him on the bed . . . the bed she shared with her husband . . . as naked as was this beautiful young man.

Molly tried to fight against the terrible need which was consuming her body, but she was too weak, too invested with desire, to be effective. The warmth spread through her with dizzying speed, and she surrendered herself to it, no longer putting up the pretense of fighting.

Burke tried to change positions, to move over her, but the pain in his shoulder stabbed at him again. When Molly saw that, she smiled gently, put her cool fingers on his shoulders to indicate that he should stay where he was, and moved over him, taking him into her, orchestrating the unfolding events on her own.

Molly felt Burke beneath her, thrusting up against her, helping her as she continued to make love to him. Then, finally, she felt the jolts of rapture which racked her body and caused her to fall across him with a groan of ecstasy, even as he was spending himself in her in final, convulsive shudders.

They lay that way for several moments, with Molly on top, allowing the pleasure to drain from her body slowly, like heat leaving an iron. Finally, she got up and looked down at him.

Burke smiled at her. "Your husband is a lucky man, madam," he said.

Molly gasped and put her hand to her mouth. "Oh," she said. "I nearly forgot. You can't stay here, you have to leave."

"Why? Are you afraid he can see it in our faces?" Burke asked.

"No, it isn't that at all," she said. "But my husband has gone after the Union soldiers. He intends to turn you in for the reward money."

Burke sat up, and felt a wave of dizziness and nausea overtake him. He sat on the edge of the bed for several moments until the feeling passed. "How much time do I have?" he asked.

"He said he wouldn't be back until tonight,

but if he finds soldiers between here and Jefferson City, he'll be back much sooner than that. I really can't say when he'll be back."

Burke reached for his pants. "Help me get dressed," he asked, and Molly, still naked herself, bent down beside him to help him into his clothes.

After Burke was dressed, Molly dressed quickly, then made him several sandwiches and wrapped them in a cloth to give to him. "Here's lunch and dinner," she said.

"Thanks," Burke replied, taking the proffered package. "Is my horse still here?"

"Yes, Sam took him to the barn."

"Still saddled?"

"I'm sure it is. He didn't stay out there long enough to unsaddle it."

"That's bad for ole' Poke," he said. "But good for me. I don't know if I could get him saddled myself."

With Molly's help, he put his coat on, then started out the back door. Just before he opened it, he looked at her and smiled. "Thanks," he said.

Molly kissed him goodbye, then watched him walk through the snow to the small lean-to which served as a barn. When Burke swung onto his horse and rode away, his last sight was of Molly standing in the doorway watching him.

4

Dan O'Lee stood at the window of the Federal Building in St. Louis, waiting to talk to General Halleck. From where he stood he could see the Mississippi River as it flowed by. Chunks of ice joined the other debris which floated downstream. The cobblestone levee, where several boats were tied up, was slick with winter ice, and there were several men working there, loading and unloading the boats.

Burke O'Lee, Dan's brother, wasn't one of the men. That was the first place Dan went to when he reached St. Louis, thinking his reunion with his brother should take precedence over all else. But the reunion didn't take place, for the simple reason that Burke no longer worked on the river front, and no one could give Dan a hint as to where he had gone.

"Mr. O'Lee, General Halleck will see you now," a staff officer said. Dan thanked him and followed him into the general's office. This was the second place Dan had come to after reaching St. Louis, feeling that the message he took from the dead lieutenant would be of great importance.

General Halleck greeted Dan with a smile of welcome. The general had a very high forehead, bushy, nearly white, mutton-chop whiskers, dark eyebrows, and large, rather pleasant looking eyes. He was known as a man of brilliance: a West Point graduate who once resigned his commission to study law and enter into mining in California, but returned to the military at the outbreak of war due to his devotion to the Union cause.

"General, it was good of you to see me," Dan said.

"You said that you were a friend of Lady Pamela Buttle-Jones," General Halleck said. "I have a great deal of respect and admiration for that lady, and any friend of hers is certainly worth a few moments of my time. Tell me, how is she?"

"She is very well, General. In fact, one of my reasons for coming to St. Louis is to fulfill an errand for her."

"Oh? And how may I help?"

"General, my asking to see you has nothing to do with that errand," Dan said. "But rather with an incident which occurred on the stage while enroute to St. Louis."

General Halleck offered a seat to Dan, which Dan accepted gratefully, then told of the stage being waylaid by Quantrill's gang. He told of the driver being killed, and of the lieutenant's brave death.

General Halleck pinched the bridge of his nose as Dan finished the story. "Ah, such a fine young man," he said sadly. "It is always tragic for me to have to write the parents of our boys who are killed, but it will be particularly so for me to write to Tom's parents, for I have known them a long, long time."

"General, there is more to the story," Dan said, taking the paper from his pocket. He handed it to the general. "Lieutenant Wade somehow managed to conceal this in his mouth just before he got out of the stage. The bushwhackers overlooked it."

"What is it?" General Halleck asked.

"Well, I . . . I really don't know. I was hoping you would. It is obviously important, since the lieutenant died protecting it."

General Halleck unrolled the paper and looked at it. "It's in code," he said. He picked up a bell on his desk and shook it, summoning the same officer who had escorted Dan into the general's office. "Have this decoded and returned to me immediately," the general said.

"Right away, sir," the officer replied.

"Tell me about Lady Pamela," Halleck said, as they were waiting for the decoding of the message. "Is she still as beautiful as ever?"

"Amazingly so," Dan replied.

"You may be interested in an amusing, and somewhat ironic incident which occurred just before I left California," Halleck said. "I was pleasantly surprised one morning to find in my mail an invitation to one of Lady Pamela's dinner parties. To be honest, I was quite busy, and had another engagement, but one doesn't spurn the opportunity to attend one of Lady Pamela's celebrated dinners, so I rearranged my schedule to allow me to go. When I arrived there, I saw an old friend of mine had also been invited. We had known each other for many years, though we had drifted apart somewhat after I left the army. We had a most entertaining visit that evening, recalling old times, catching each other up with the latest news in our own lives." Halleck chuckled. "Do you know who that old friend was?"

"No, sir," Dan said. "Though I do recall the party you are speaking of. I was out of town that evening, I believe."

"That old friend was Albert Sidney Johnston. Now I am Commanding General of the Union Army of the West, and General Johnston is Commanding General of the Confederate Army of the West. So here we have two old friends facing each other."

"General, here is the decoded message," the officer said, returning at that moment.

"Good, good," Halleck said. He opened the drawer to his desk and pulled out a pair of wire-rim spectacles, then put them on, hooking them carefully, one ear at a time. He used his forefinger to slide them up his nose, then read the decoded message.

"Well, Mr. O'Lee, you'll be interested in knowing that you have indeed brought us a message of great importance."

"I am glad, sir."

"Have you ever heard of a place called Sikeston?"

"Sikeston? No, sir, I'm afraid not."

"Well, there's no reason you should, really. It's so tiny that it isn't even on most of the maps. But it could be a crucial spot for us now. You see, there is a railroad which runs from Bird's Point on the Mississippi River to the tiny town of Sikeston. There, the railroad ends. But from Sikeston to New Madrid, there is a fine plank road, over which we could transport men and material through the swamps. The Rebels realized the importance of Sikeston as well, and they put several pieces of artillery there to defend the railhead. But, according to this message, Jeff Thompson has pulled his guns away from Sikeston and turned them over to General McCown to use in fortifying Island Number Ten, at New Madrid."

"And that is good news to you?" Dan asked.

"That is very good news to me," Halleck replied. He smiled, and put his hand on Dan's shoulder. "And it is all thanks to you."

"No, sir," Dan replied. "It is thanks to Lieutenant Ward. It is a shame he had to die to get the information to you, though."

"Yes it is," Halleck agreed. "But when one must die, it is at least good to have one's death be meaningful. Tom Ward didn't die uselessly. He died for liberty."

Suddenly the lieutenant's dying word came back to Dan. He started to say something, thinking it ironic that General Halleck would express the same sentiment. But General Halleck was already starting for the door to summon the next in a long line of visitors, and Dan, knowing that the general's time was valuable, let the thought die before giving it tongue.

Dan was glad that this mission had been successful. Earlier, he had failed in trying to find his brother. That left only his business for Lady Pamela to accomplish, and in that, at least, he was reasonably certain of success.

Dan took a room in the Boatman's Hotel and later waited in the lobby, having sent a message to Hiram Dempster that he was at his disposal. While waiting, he read the *St. Louis Democrat*. Though the major papers of the east were already beginning to talk of the war as a phony war, with little significant action thus far, all over Missouri, Kentucky, Tennessee and Arkansas, men were fighting and dying, and the paper had one entire column listing casualties in the Western skirmishes.

Dan was about to put the paper down, when, as it sometimes will, a word seemed to leap from the page to arrest his attention. The word was liberty.

LIBERTY SPEAKS FOR LIBERTY, the head of one of the articles stated.

Miss Liberty Welles is well noted for her ability to hold sway over a crowd by the power of her elocution, but never was she in better form than she was last night when she told of the bravery of Verity Eternal.

Verity Eternal's resolute course and trying ordeal have given this sturdy lady of color a strong hold upon public attention. She is welcomed in the loyal States with a degree of warmth consonant with her own sanguine temperament.

One day a crowd in Tennessee threatened to tear down the Stars and Stripes which flew in front of her house, she being a free woman and able to have a home of her own. But, like a lioness in defense of her lair, Miss Eternal threatened to shoot the first man to touch her flag.

"Miss, you won't shoot, will you?" asked the leader.

"You had better try the experiment," said Verity Eternal.

"Go on, go on!" shouted the crowd. "She daren't shoot."

With that, Miss Eternal instantly drew from her pocket one of Colt's revolvers and, cocking it, leveled it at the man's head.

"Never mind her, she's but a colored woman," cried the mob.

"My God! Look at her eye!" responded the man. He made a bow, scraped the ground and toddled off, followed by the whole crowd.

This story was related before a meeting of the St. Louis Abolitionist Society by Miss Liberty Welles, and so well was it told by the beautiful lady that she was often interrupted by hurrahs and cheers, and afterwards warmly applauded.

There was that word liberty again, Dan thought, folding the paper and laying it to one side. At that precise moment, he was approached by a uniformed bellboy.

"Mr. O'Lee, there is a gentleman in the bar who wishes me to escort you to him," the bellboy said. "He says you summoned him for a meeting."

"Ah, yes," Dan said, standing. "That would be Hiram Dempster. Please, lead on," he added, handing the boy a coin.

The bar was crowded with uniformed men and well-dressed women. St. Louis was a military city, and most of her men wore uniforms, whether of the regular army or fighting reserves, or even the colorful 'Home Guards', whose gaudiness of uniform was inversely proportional to the likelihood of their ever seeing action.

The bellboy pushed through them with the self-appointed importance of being on a hotel errand, and introduced Dan to a man who sat at a table near the rear.

The man was tall and thin, with a drooping handlebar mustache and dark bags under pale blue eyes. He smiled a greeting, but his eyes did not, and his handshake was like a dead fish. Dan was placed on immediate guard with him.

"So, Mr. O'Lee, what can I do for you?" Dempster asked.

Dan reached into his inside jacket pocket and removed the envelope containing the bank draft. "I represent Lady Pamela," he said. "She wishes to buy the piece of land you have offered, and has adhered to the requirements of the deal, namely that ten thousand dollars be delivered to you by hand."

Dempster waved the money away. "The deal was that it be delivered by *her* hand," he said. "It is not acceptable, coming from you."

"You did not so stipulate in your agreement, sir," Dan said.

"It was implied," Dempster said.

Dan sighed and returned the draft to his inside pocket. "I'm sorry," he said. "It would appear that my trip for Lady Pamela has been in vain. I will send her a telegram to that effect, and ask further instructions."

"I remember Lady Pamela . . . from the old days," Dempster said. His eyes grew deep, and were glazed with a lustful tint. "I would like to see her again. Tell her that if she wants this property, she must come to St. Louis personally, and ask me for it."

"No, Mr. Dempster, I don't think I will do that," Dan said. "Lady Pamela is most happy in California, I assure you. Besides, with the unsettled conditions of the war, I would protest vigorously should she even consider it."

"You would protest? By what right would you protest?" Dempster asked.

"By the right of one who has been, and is still, very close to her."

"Close?" Dempster said. "What do you mean close? Are you her lover?"

The corners of Dan's mouth drew back into a tight line, and a vein on his temple throbbed in anger. He forced himself to remain quiet for a moment before he spoke, and when he did, his words fell like ice.

"Mr. Dempster, there was a time when I would have killed you for that remark. The relationship between the lady in question and myself is none of your business."

"Lady?" Dempster snarled. "She's a lady in name only. If you ask me, she's a . . ."

Dempster was unable to finish his sentence, because Dan suddenly whipped a vicious backhand slap across his face, bringing blood to the corner of Dempster's mouth. The sound popped loud, even over the noise of the crowded room, and many turned to look at the table, anxious to see what happened and what would happen next.

Dan was nearly as surprised by his action as the others in the room were. He had acted in a flash of anger, without thinking, and now had to prepare himself for anything Dempster might try.

Dempster jerked the tablecloth from the table, tipping over his drink and the centerpiece and sending them crashing to the floor. He patted the tablecloth against the cut on his lip, and looked at Dan. He smiled a small, wicked smile. "You will rue the day you met me, Mr. O'Lee," he said.

47

"I already count meeting you as one of my more unpleasant experiences," Dan replied evenly.

"Good day to you, sir," Dempster said, moving quickly through the crowd.

After Dempster left, Dan took a seat at the table and sat there for a moment while a waiter replaced the cloth and centerpiece. The crowd, seeing that the excitement had ended, returned to their own conversations, leaving Dan alone.

"Mr. O'Lee, may I join you, sir? I come bearing beer, as you can see," a man said.

Dan looked up to see a man dressed in a Union offier's uniform, carrying a mug of beer in each hand. One of them he set before Dan.

"Thank you," Dan said, blowing away the foam and taking several welcome swallows. Finally, he put the mug down, wiped his mouth with the back of his hand, and looked across the table at the officer who had joined him.

"Who are you?" Dan asked.

"I am Captain Andrew Todd. The gentleman you have just angered, Hiram Dempster, is a most influential man."

"Is he a friend of yours?"

Todd laughed. "Hardly, as I am a Union officer, and he is one of the biggest firebrands for the Secesh in St. Louis."

"He's a Rebel?"

"No, Mr. O'Lee. He's a bigot. He backs his

prejudices with money. Rebels back their sentiments with blood. Whether you can agree with
them or not, you can at least respect a man who
has enough strength of conviction to fight for
what he believes in."

"I'm glad to see that you confirm my first
impression of the man," Dan said.

"What was your business with him, Mr.
O'Lee?"

"I was going to buy a piece of property for . . .
just a minute, what business is it of yours anyway? And how do you know my name?"

"Oh, I know a great deal about you, sir. You
arrived in St. Louis this morning from California, where, among other things, you were a
mining engineer."

"Prospector," Dan corrected him.

"But with enough experience in mining pro-
cedures to qualify as a mining engineer," Captain Todd said. "You are thirty-three years old,
your parents died when you were twenty-one,
leaving you with a ten-year-old brother to care
for. You deposited your brother with Dr. and
Mrs. Jebediah Hornung, of this city, both now
deceased, and you proceeded to the California
gold fields. Your brother's name is Burke, and
you haven't seen him in twelve years. You hoped
to find him this morning, but you were disappointed."

Dan looked at Captain Todd, first with

amused interest, and then with disquieting concern. Finally, as Todd finished his dissertation, Dan spoke.

"Todd, what the hell is all this? How do you know so much about me, and why?"

"Oh, believe me, Mr. O'Lee, I know even more than I have told you," Todd said easily. "It is my business to find out about people. Especially people we feel may be helpful to us."

"Helpful? Helpful to who?"

"Why, to the Union cause, of course," Todd said easily.

"I'm not interested," Dan said, dismissing him with another swallow of his beer. "Right now my only concern is in finding my brother."

"We are both interested in finding your brother, Mr. O'Lee. Perhaps we can help each other."

"What do you mean? Why do you want to find him?"

"Mr. O'Lee, the last word we had about your brother put him with Quantrill."

"What? Impossible."

"Why do you think it's impossible? Because you didn't see him when Quantrill and his men stopped the stage? Tell me, Mr. O'Lee, would you have recognized him?"

"I . . . I don't know," Dan said.

"Then it isn't impossible that he was with Quantrill, is it?"

"I guess not," Dan said. "But why should I help you find him?"

"You are a good citizen, Mr. O'Lee. If you weren't, you would never have delivered Lieutenant Ward's message. You'll tell us if you hear from your brother, because it is your duty."

"What about duty to my brother? Don't I have a duty to him as well?" Dan asked.

"You should have asked yourself that question twelve years ago, Mr. O'Lee," Captain Todd replied. "Oh, by the way. Did Lieutenant Ward say anything to you before he died?"

"Like what?"

"I don't know. His mission was supposed to be secret. Somehow it was compromised. He may have realized that, and tried to tell you. Did he mention a name?"

Dan thought a moment, then decided that he would not mention the lieutenant's dying words. "Uh, no," he said. "I don't think so."

"Think very hard, Mr. O'Lee," Captain Todd insisted. "The least thing might be significant."

"I can't think of anything," Dan lied. "Besides, if your intelligence is all that good, why don't you find out who the drummer was who was on the coach with us, and ask him?"

"His name was Orville Quimby," Captain Todd said. "And I'm afraid he is unable to tell us anything. We found him murdered this morning, his throat having been cut."

51

5

Dan had taken the address from the newspaper, and now he checked it against the number on the building. Satisfied that it was the same, he climbed the concrete steps and went inside. A sign stood on the easel in the entry hall of the building, inviting interested guests to Room 104 to hear the "eloquent and instructive Liberty Welles."

Dan proceeded to the room, and stood in the hallway, looking through the double doors. There were several people seated inside. Their attention was being held by a woman speaker who stood in front of the room. Dan caught his breath when he saw her. He had read in the newspaper article that she was beautiful, but he had thought that was standard newspaper rhetoric. The woman he was looking at now was one of the most beautiful he had ever seen.

"If you care to hear the lecture, sir, I'm afraid it will cost you ten cents."

So entranced was Dan by the unexpected good

looks of the lady in front of the room that he didn't hear the question the first time, and it had to be repeated.

Dan looked at the questioner, a small, nearly bald man, wearing wire-rim glasses. "Oh, uh, yes," Dan said. "Tell me, is that Miss Liberty Welles?"

"Yes it is," the man said, smiling proudly. "We are proud to have her as a member of our Society. The lecture will cost ten cents, I'm afraid."

"Ten cents?"

"The money goes to further the goals of our abolitionist society," the man explained.

"And what are those goals?" Dan asked, pulling the money from his pocket.

"Why, to see every man, woman, and child in this country be free," the man answered.

Dan took a printed program from the man, then stepped inside and settled into a chair. Liberty Welles was just finishing a poem:

"And not unblessed they come; their brows
Were kissed by saintly mothers;
Fond wives will for their husbands pray,
And sisters for their brothers.

Then speed them forward! they shall write
Our country's proudest story,
Or, if they die, their falling place
Will be the field of glory!"

Liberty finished the poem on a grand scale, and the audience applauded and cheered enthusiastically.

Liberty bowed, then raised up, smiling at her reception. She had flashing green eyes, ringlets of dark brown hair, rosy cheeks, and white, evenly spaced teeth. She wore a green ribbon tied in a bow around her neck, and a white and green dress, the green in both cases seeming to pick up the color of her eyes.

"Thank you," Liberty said. "That poem was written by Marian Douglas of Boston, and I feel it best expresses the way we feel about our brave soldiers in this war. Thank you so much for coming tonight, and for your generous donations to our cause. Good night."

The audience applauded again, then stood as one as Liberty took her final bows. Finally, the applause died, and the audience started for the door, but Dan remained in his seat. Soon everyone was gone except the man who had collected his money, and that man began to sweep the room.

"Sir, are you angry because I collected the fee and she was just finishing?" the man asked Dan.

"No, I'm not angry," Dan said.

"Then why are you still here?"

"I want to see Miss Welles," he said. "I must talk to her."

"I'm afraid she's already gone," the man said.

"Gone? How could she leave? I've been sitting right here all the time?"

"She left through another door, I'm afraid. I'm sorry, I'm afraid you've missed her."

"Do you know where she lives?" Dan asked.

"I'm afraid I don't," the man said.

Dan cursed his luck, and got up from his chair and walked outside, slowly, angrily. Then, just as he reached the street, he saw her getting into a carriage.

"Wait!" he called, starting toward the carriage on the run. "Miss Welles, wait a minute, won't you?"

Liberty looked at him with a puzzled expression on her face, but waited as Dan requested.

Dan ran up to the carriage, then stopped, breathing a little harder from the exertion.

"Yes?" Liberty asked. "What can I do for you?"

Dan felt like a fool. He had yelled for her to stop, and yet he had no idea what he would say to her. He couldn't ask her if the last word on a dying man's lips had been her name. What could he say?"

"It was an inspiring speech," he finally said, foolishly, self-consciously.

Liberty laughed. "How do you know? You

didn't arrive until the last two stanzas of the poem. In fact, I thought you were accosting me to return your money."

"You . . . you noticed me?" Dan asked, amazed that she had.

"Of course. The audience wasn't that large, and you did come in at the very last."

"I had a difficult time finding the place," Dan said. "I'm new to the city and don't know my way around."

Liberty looked at him, as if studying him. "You say you are new to the city?"

"Yes."

"That's funny. I feel that we've met before. Have we met?"

"No," Dan said. He smiled. "If we had met, Miss Welles, I would not have forgotten it, I'm certain of that. Oh, please forgive me for not introducing myself. My name is Dan O'Lee."

"O'Lee?" Liberty asked rather sharply.

"Yes. Why, is something wrong?"

Liberty smiled. "No, of course not. It's just an unusual name, that's all. You don't hear it too often."

"No, I don't suppose you do," Dan said. "Though I have a brother here in St. Louis, named Burke O'Lee. Or rather, I did have. He seems to have disappeared."

"Disappeared?"

"In a manner of speaking," Dan said. "I

wanted to see him when I reached the city, but when I inquired after him where he worked, I was told he was gone."

"I'm sorry to hear that," Liberty said. She reached into her reticule and pulled out a small card. "Mr. O'Lee, I shall be giving another lecture here tomorrow night. Please return, as my guest. I feel it unfair that you arrived too late tonight."

Dan put the card in his jacket pocket. "Thanks," he said, smiling broadly. "I'll be here . . . you can count on that."

Liberty smiled and waved goodbye to Dan, then climbed into the carriage and settled against the seat for the ride back to the boarding house where she lived. She thought of the man she had just met as the carriage rolled along. Perhaps she should have told him that she knew Burke. It's funny that Burke had never mentioned him. Maybe he wasn't really Burke's brother. Maybe he was just pretending to be, in order to get information on Burke. But no, she reasoned. He was Burke's brother, she could look at him and tell that. That was why she thought she had seen him before. But on the other hand, in this war where nobody knew where the other person stood, one couldn't be too careful.

When Liberty reached the rooming house and paid the driver, she climbed the dark steps which led up to her private entrance. Once inside her room, she found a match and lit the lantern which was mounted on the wall just inside the door. She turned it up, spreading a soft, yellow light through the room.

"Hello, Liberty girl," a man said quietly.

Liberty gasped, then spun around toward the sound of the voice. There, sitting on the edge of her bed, was Burke O'Lee. His shirt was off, and he had a bandage around one shoulder. The bandage was soaked red with blood.

"Burke! What are you doing here?" she asked.

"I had to come somewhere, Liberty girl. I got myself shot up a couple of days ago." Burke winced, and put his hand up to his wound.

"Have you seen a doctor?" Liberty asked, moving to him and looking at the bandage.

Burke smiled, the wry, boyish grin which had won Liberty over so many months ago. "Yeah, I saw one," he said. "He got the bullet out, then decided to sell me to the highest bidder. I had to leave. I guess the ridin' busted open the wound again."

"Oh, Burke, that dressing has to be changed," Liberty said. "You lie down. I'll make a new bandage."

"Thanks," Burke said. He lay back on the bed, heaving a sigh of contentment.

"Is it hurting much?"

"A little," Burke admitted. He lay there, unprotesting, as Liberty cut the old bandage off, washed the wound, then started tearing strips from a petticoat to make a new dressing. "Your friend was killed," he finally said.

"Who?"

"Lieutenant Ward. Quantrill had him killed."

"Oh, no, Burke, why? What happened?" Liberty cried. "Did something go wrong?"

"No," Burke said. "He just refused to part with the paper, so Quantrill had him shot."

"You didn't do it, did you?" she asked quickly.

"No," Burke replied, wincing as she wrapped the bandage. "I was lying on my butt in the snow. Jesse James shot him. It's probably just as well, Liberty girl. Pretty soon he would have been able to put two and two together, and figure out that you were the only one he told about the courier mission. When he figured that out he would have come for you."

"I was prepared to cross that bridge when I came to it," Liberty said. She finished the dressing. "There," she said, "now if you don't go out and break it open again, that should hold you for a while."

"Are you upset because Ward was killed?" Burke asked.

"Of course I'm upset. If I had known he would be killed, I would never have sent Quantrill to intercept the message."

"Liberty girl, there's a war on," Burke said. "Folks get killed in a war, and when you give away confidential information, you contribute to it."

"It's different when it is in battle. There, everyone faces equal danger. But to set someone up, especially a nice young man like Tom Ward, that's very different, and it bothers me. It bothers me a great deal."

"I thought you said all you and Ward did was have dinner together a few times," Burke said. "You're talking like maybe there was something more."

"Nothing more happened," Liberty insisted. "And if I had known he was going to be killed, I would have never met with him in the first place."

"I have to admit, Liberty, that I find it difficult to understand you."

"Why?"

"Well, here you are, making speeches at the abolitionist society, being friends with Verity Eternal, and yet all the time you've been spying for the South."

"I'm a southerner by birth," Liberty replied. "The Welles family is one of the oldest families in Mississippi. I feel a deep sense of loyalty to my state, and to the new nation it has joined. But I am against slavery and always have been. Slavery isn't the central issue of this war, states' rights are. Slavery has just been made so by the agitators up north. In fact, after the South has won her independence, we shall move to abolish the peculiar institution of slavery."

"Doesn't it bother you that most of your fellow southerners are bigots?" Burke asked.

"Bigotry is not an exclusive franchise of the South," Liberty reminded him. "I give you Hiram Dempster as a case in point. He is northern born, but supports the South for no reason, other than his hatred of Negroes. And you. You aren't a southerner by birth, yet you have espoused our cause. Why?"

"Why indeed?" Burke replied, smiling at her. "Could it be because I have fallen for the charms of a delightful, if not to say, delicious temptress?"

"You mean you have no true allegiance to the South?" Liberty asked.

"Liberty girl, if you wanted me to fight for the Mexicans, I would," Burke said, laughing. And in that statement, Burke was truthful, for he had been inspired to enter into the fray by his sheer zest for adventure, and the genuine love he felt for Liberty. If she asked him now to switch sides and fight for the North, he would cheerfully comply.

"You have no allegiances, and no loyalties," Liberty said. "Do you have any family?"

"Nope."

"No one? Not even a sister or a brother?" she asked, trying to find out about the man who had identified himself as Dan O'Lee.

"I guess I have a brother," Burke said.

"Really? You've never mentioned him. Why?"

The smile left Burke's face, and he lay back on the pillow agan, looking up at the ceiling. "I've got a brother, all right. His name is Danny O'Lee. Our parents died in a riverboat accident when I was a child. Danny was older and didn't want to be saddled with me, so he dumped me off with my aunt and uncle and went to California to the gold fields."

"Do you blame him, Burke? After all, you were probably quite a responsibility for a young fellow to take on."

"Yeah, I blame him," Burke said. "You see, Uncle Jebediah wasn't that enthused over having me either. He was a doctor." Burke gave a short, bitter laugh. "But the only medicine he knew for me was a dose of the whip."

"Oh, Burke, you mean he beat you?"

"Yeah, he beat me. Every day, until I grew big enough to take the whip away from him and give him a taste of his own medicine. I hated him, and I hated Danny for leaving me with him." Burke suddenly smiled. "But let's not talk about Danny," he said. "Let's talk about me."

Liberty grinned. "You don't want to talk, Burke O'Lee." She lay her cool palms on Burke's chest, feeling his smooth muscles, and experiencing a warm shiver in her body. She leaned over to kiss him with moist lips, feeling herself grow weak as the kiss deepened.

It was always like this with Burke O'Lee, she thought. From the moment she had first seen him, sitting in the back row of a lecture hall, listening to her give a speech against the evils of slavery, she had been attracted to his easy, boyish charm. Later, as they became friends, and then lovers, she discovered that he was able to bring her to heights of passion that she had not thought possible, and she was unable to deny him her bed, anytime he sought her favors.

She even fancied that she loved him. But Burke was a rash young man, given to outbursts of temper, and quick to fight, and she felt that he was just too immature for her to even consider marriage. Sometimes she laughed when she thought of that, for though she considered him immature, he was in fact, at twenty-two, two years older than she.

The musings fled from Liberty's mind, and she lost touch with time and space as she felt herself being loved by her handsome young warrior. He was a man of great strength and surprising tenderness, caressing her without subtleties but with great passion. Finally, Liberty could feel Burke's tightly muscled thigh against the smooth skin of her own naked legs, and she could see him above her, moving down to her. After that all sights, sounds and textures blended together, to carry her to rapture's door.

They lay in each other's arms after they had made love, and Liberty studied the shadows cast on the wall by the flickering gold light of the lantern. Finally she spoke.

"Burke, I don't want you to go back to Quantrill."

"All right," Burke said easily. "But Quantrill won't care much for that. He doesn't like deserters."

"Go somewhere else. Go where he can't find you," Liberty suggested.

"Do you have any ideas?"

"How about Jeff Thompson?" Liberty suggested. "He's down in southeast Missouri, and what he's doing is important to our cause, Burke. He's keeping the Yankees from using the river to strike into the heart of the South."

"I might prefer fighting against soldiers instead of bank clerks and stage guards at that," Burke said. "Besides, I hear there's a big battle shaping up down there. It might prove to be the crucial battle of the war and I'd hate to miss out on it just because I was chasing around in Kansas or someplace with Quantrill."

"I'll make the necessary arrangements tomorrow," Liberty said.

"Are you that anxious to get rid of me, Liberty girl?" Burke teased.

"Of course not," Liberty replied. "But darling, every day you stay here increases the danger for you. What if you are discovered? Especially wearing that Confederate uniform."

"I thought about taking it off," Burke said. "But I figured it would be better to be captured

65

as a Confederate soldier than be shot as a Rebel spy."

At the mention of the word spy, Liberty flinched, and Burke, seeing the quick spasm of fear cross her face, quickly put his arms around her to comfort her.

"I'm sorry Liberty girl," Burke said, hugging her tightly. "I wasn't thinking when I made such an unkind remark."

"I knew the risks I was taking when I started," Liberty said, still trembling. "It's just that I try and keep them out of my mind, because it's too late to turn back now."

6

Dan used the pass Liberty had given him and attended the lecture the next night. On this night Liberty shared the dais with Verity Eternal, and in truth, Dan was hard pressed to say which of the two ladies had made the more inspired talk.

Or for that matter, which of the two was more beautiful.

Liberty's beauty had been striking enough to cause Dan to think of her often in the last twenty-four hours. He had committed her brown hair, green eyes, and glowing pink skin to his memory. But now he felt himself, inexplicably just as taken with the loveliness of Verity Eternal.

When Verity was introduced, she glided to the podium with a movement that was as graceful as a swan on the water. She was slender as a lily, with long, blue-black hair and large, liquid brown eyes. Her skin was the color of creamed coffee, and so clear and lovely that Dan wanted to just touch it.

Finally, Verity's talk was concluded, and she and Liberty received the applause of the audience then retired backstage. This time as the crowd started to leave, however, the man who had taken Dan's ticket the night before came over to speak to him.

"Are you Mr. O'Lee?" he asked.

"Yes, I am."

"Miss Welles asks if you will come backstage to see her."

"Yes, yes of course I will," Dan said, smiling at the unexpected invitation. "How do I get there?"

"Follow me, please," the man said, leading the way.

A moment later Dan was standing outside a door as the man knocked. "Miss Welles, I have the gentleman here with me," he said.

The door opened and Liberty stood there, smiling broadly. "Thank you, John, that was nice of you. Won't you please come in, Mr. O'Lee?"

Dan stepped into the room and saw that it was occupied not only by Liberty, but Verity Eternal as well. Liberty introduced them.

"I must say, Miss Eternal," Dan said, after the introductions were made. "Your talk tonight was absolutely inspiring."

Liberty laughed. "And you can believe him

tonight," she said. "For he was here the entire time. Last night I managed to inspire him with but two stanzas of *Our Mountain Soldiers.*"

"I'm sorry," Dan apologized. "I did want to meet you, and I couldn't think of anything else to say last night. I must confess, however, that events tonight have borne me out. You are an inspiring speaker."

"You flatter me, sir," Liberty said.

"I have taken the liberty of reserving a table for us for dinner," Dan invited. "I hope you'll do me the honor?"

"Why, I would be delighted to join you for dinner," Liberty replied.

"And, Miss Eternal. You will join us as well, I trust?"

Verity smiled, a slow, sad smile. "That's most kind of you Mr. Lee. But I would not be welcome at such a place."

"Of course you would be welcome," Dan said not understanding her meaning.

"Verity means she would not be welcome by the establishment of the restaurant," Liberty explained.

"Why not?" Dan asked. Then, realizing what he was saying, he put his hand to his mouth. "Oh, forgive me," he said. "For a moment I forgot that . . . uh . . . I forgot."

"That I am colored?" Verity asked.

"Uh, yes," Dan said. "I'm sorry."

"Oh, don't be sorry, Mr. O'Lee. I'm not in the

least sorry that I am black. I hope the day comes when everyone can be proud of their color. Pride, without prejudice. That is a worthy goal, don't you believe?"

"Yes, of course I do," Dan said. "I didn't mean to imply that I was sorry about your color. I just meant that I was sorry I was so awkward."

Verity smiled. "Now it's my time to apologize, Mr. O'Lee. I knew what you meant, but I just used it to make a point. Won't you forgive me?"

"Of course, though I feel there is nothing to forgive."

"Liberty, I like your gentleman friend," Verity said, touching Dan lightly on the hand. "Treat him well."

"I promise I will," Liberty said. "Would you get my wrap, please?" she asked, looking at Dan.

Dan left to get Liberty's coat, and when he returned, Verity had already left.

"She is a beautiful lady, isn't she?" Liberty asked.

"Yes," Dan said. "Strikingly so."

"I'm glad you like her. And I'm glad you came tonight. I wasn't sure you would."

Dan laughed. "I came down almost an hour early, just to make sure I would be on time. I waited in a tavern across the street until the others started arriving, because I didn't want to come in first."

Dan hailed a hack, and fitted the lap robe

70

around the two of them as they drove off. The closeness of the seat, and the use of the lap robe necessitated that they sit very close, and he could feel the heat of her body, even through their clothes. It was a somewhat giddy feeling, and he enjoyed it while he could, even finding excuse to press more tightly against her whenever the hack made a turn.

"Here we are, sir," the driver called back a few moments later.

"That's a shame," Dan said quietly, thinking that the excuse to be close to Liberty was now removed. Liberty looked at him with a quick smile which told him she knew what he was thinking about, and that shared intimacy warmed Dan.

They spoke in generalities at dinner, then, over dessert, Dan asked Liberty how she became involved in abolitionist work.

"I was born into it," Liberty said. "What I mean was, I was born on a slave-holding plantation, and I saw with my own eyes the misery one human being can visit on another. Husbands and wives were separated, children torn from their mother's arms—there was a complete stripping away of dignity. Not on my father's plantation, for he was at least a good-hearted man and long ago set our people free. Oh, they still live and work on Trailback Plantation, but they are there now of their own free will."

71

"Is that in Missouri?" Dan asked.

"No," Liberty said. "It is in Corinth, Mississippi."

"Then the freedom they now enjoy is a matter of degree, isn't it?"

"You might say that," Liberty replied. "Anyway, it made an abolitionist of me, and I swore to pursue that goal until slavery was ended."

"But why did you choose St. Louis?"

"Because St. Louis is the largest city of any slave-holding state. And because the abolitionists are active in St. Louis. And because the Dred Scott trial happened here, and was a setback for the abolitionist movement."

"This is an indelicate question," Dan said. "But do you feel like a traitor to your own people?"

"Because I'm an abolitionist?" Liberty replied. "No, I don't feel like a traitor. There are others in the South who feel just as I do."

"Oh? I would have thought that such a feeling would be very rare among southerners."

"Not as rare as it would seem," Liberty said. "But most of those who share my point of view have no voice. The monied factions, and the politicians who speak out the loudest for the South are strong proponents of slavery. Therefore the official position of the South is proslavery. But, I hope that changes one day."

"It will change, as soon as this war is over,"

Dan said. "Once the North shows the South that they can't pull out of the Union at their own whim, it will establish the supremacy of the federal government once and for all, and the slave question can be settled in Washington as it should be."

Dan thought he saw a look of disagreement flash across Liberty's face. Not her face, really, but a subtle change of her eyes. Whatever it was, it happened so quickly and was so soon controlled that he couldn't be sure. Liberty smiled then, as if in total agreement, and answered: "It would make this awful war worthwhile. Though, with so many young men being killed, I sometimes wonder if it wouldn't be better to let the South go in peace."

"Speaking of young men being killed," Dan said, "I had a rather tragic circumstance happen to me on the way to St. Louis." He went on to relate the story of Quantrill's raid on the stage, and told of the murder of the driver and the young Union officer. "His name was Ward," Dan said. "Lieutenant Thomas Ward. Did you know him by any chance?"

"Know him?" Liberty replied. "No, I don't think I did. Why? Did he speak of me?"

"Not exactly," Dan said. "Though he mentioned your name."

"He mentioned my name?" Liberty asked, this time showing some concern.

"Yes," Dan said, purposely not going into detail as to how her name was mentioned, or even if it really had been her name Ward spoke.

"Thomas Ward, you say? I'm sorry, Mr. O'Lee, but I don't believe I knew the young man. Though, it some vanity I must confess that it would not be all that unusual for my name to be mentioned. I am often written about in the newspapers of this city, and I have given lectures for more than one year now. I have achieved a modest degree of fame."

"And well-earned too," Dan said. He signaled for the check. "Miss Welles, do you have a previous engagement for Friday evening?"

"I . . . I don't think so," Liberty replied.

"General Halleck is giving a dinner for his staff officers, and I have been invited for some reason. It would be a pleasure to go if you went as my guest."

"With General Halleck, you say?" Liberty asked, smiling broadly. "My, you have moved up quickly since arriving in St. Louis. He is the Commanding General for the entire Department of the West."

"I assure you, it is not due to any achievement of my own," Dan said. "The general and I have a mutual acquaintance, and I feel he is anxious to hear more news of her."

"Her? My, this is getting more interesting. Who is this mysterious her, Burke?"

The sound of his brother's name hit Dan like

a slap in the face, and he stared at Liberty in total shock. For her part, Liberty looked down quickly and flushed a deep red. The silence grew longer and more awkward. Finally Dan spoke.

"What did you call me?"

"I . . . I must have called you Burt. I'm sorry, he's an old beau of mine. It's terribly embarrassing, I can't tell you how sorry I am. Please, you must tell me you forgive me."

Dan was silent for several seconds before he spoke. He smiled easily. "Of course," he said. "But only if you agree to come to the general's dinner with me."

"Of course I will go with you," Liberty said. "If only to make up for my *faux pas*."

"Good, good. Oh, and the next time you see Burt, you must thank him for me."

"Thank him?"

"Certainly. By saying his name, you felt obligated to accept my invitation."

Liberty laughed good-naturedly and quickly changed the subject, pointing to the chandelier which hung in the foyer of the restaurant and commenting that a similar fixture was in the dining room of her home in Corinth.

Dan gracefully allowed the subject to be changed, and followed her lead in conversation as they rode in the hired carriage to return Liberty to her home.

"It's getting late," Liberty said, when the carriage stopped on the street in front of her boarding house. "You'd better take this carriage on back to your hotel while you can, for at this hour there are few hacks in this neighborhood."

"The lady's right, sir," the driver said, hoping to double his fare by taking Dan back with him.

"Very well," Dan said. He stepped out of the carriage and helped Liberty to alight.

Liberty looked up at the driver and saw that he was watching them. "Driver, would you kindly look to your horse?" she said.

"Yes, ma'am." The driver responded, looking away quickly.

Liberty looked up at Dan, smiled, and then planted a cool kiss on his lips. Dan was surprised by her action and suddenly started to put his arms around her. But she backed away daintily, smiling at him, then shook her finger in mock disapproval.

"Mr. O'Lee, I feel I have already overstepped my bounds as it is. Please do not compromise me with my neighbors." Even as she spoke, though, her flashing eyes told Dan that under other circumstances she would not have disapproved of his move.

"Uh . . . no, of course not," Dan said. "Then it's goodnight, I suppose."

"Goodnight . . . Dan," Liberty said. She turned quickly and started up the sidewalk toward the stairs which led to her apartment.

Dan stood by the carriage and watched her until she reached her door. She turned and waved to him, then stepped inside, and Dan got back into the carriage and signaled the driver on. He leaned back to be with his own thoughts.

Liberty was on his mind.

7

With Liberty at General Halleck's dinner party, Dan was keenly aware of being the envy of nearly everyone present, and he was also cognizant of the possessive way she clung to his arm when he offered it to her as they went into the dining room.

It was a small party, with no more than ten guests, so they were able to sit around one long table and listen to General Halleck as he told them how the war should be fought. Halleck was well known as a military theorist. He had taught at West Point for several years, and had written a highly regarded textbook on military strategy, which was being used not only by the United States Army but by European armies as well.

"My biggest fear," Halleck said, as he spread butter on a roll, "is that the Eastern press will get too impatient and force us into a large, set-piece battle with the Rebels. That would be a great mistake."

"Why is that, general?" a reporter for one of the St. Louis newspapers asked. "Surely you don't believe the Rebels can stand up to us in a classic battle?"

"Oh, but they can, sir," Halleck replied. "In fact, that is their only chance for victory. If they could engage us in a few large battles, the casualties would be so high on both sides that the mood of the public would quickly turn to one of peace at any cost . . . even if that cost was the disunion of our nation."

"Then how do you propose this war be fought, if not in the classic manner?"

"We must obtain several strategic positions and hold them," Halleck said. "Right now, for example, there is a position on the Mississippi River which is vital to us. It is an island in the river, just at the bottom of the New Madrid bend. The Confederates hold that island now. With it, they are maintaining tenuous control of the river. We must take that island, and when we do, we will have the Mississippi River, all the way to Memphis. That leaves only Memphis and Vicksburg to prevent us from controlling the entire Mississippi. Thanks to General Grant, we already have the Cumberland and the Tennessee. With the waterways under our control, I propose to start dismembering the South's railway system, so that all means of transportation is effectively shut off. Blockading the seaports means that no supplies can come in, and we'll have the Confederacy trapped in a bag. All we have to do is close the neck, and hold it until the South quits struggling."

As Halleck spoke, he demonstrated with a napkin, forming it into a sack, then drawing the neck tight and squeezing it.

"General, the plan you propose is a brilliant one, to be sure," Liberty said. "But what about people like Johnston, Beauregard, Lee, and Longstreet? Do you think they haven't considered the very thing you are speaking of?"

Most of the other dinner guests looked at Liberty, surprised that she would offer any comment at all in this, a strictly male conversation, and shocked that her comment would seem to be one which questioned the great general.

Halleck laughed easily. "I'm certain they have thought of it," he said. "Indeed, I would be upset if they hadn't, because this is just the type of concept I have preached in my lectures and advocated in my books. I would hope I have had some influence on them. But the trick, my dear lady, is to accomplish this, while they know it, but can do nothing about it. And to do that, we must avoid a set-piece battle at all costs."

"At all costs, general? Even if it means fleeing to avoid a battle?" the reporter asked.

"Yes," Halleck said. "Though in this case I wouldn't say we are fleeing to avoid the battle. I prefer to say we are merely strategically repositioning our forces."

"What is your next objective after Island Number Ten?" the reporter asked.

"There is one very strategic railroad junction which should be taken out," Halleck said. "If we control it, we have cut off all transportation between Memphis and Charleston, and from Mobile to the Ohio. In fact, within a triangle of about twenty miles, we can totally disrupt nearly one third of the South's railway system. That will be our next objective."

"Where is that, general?"

Halleck laughed. "That is information which I am sure Beauregard would like to have as well. Better that I keep it to myself for now."

The general conversation continued in a military vein for a while longer, but as Dan was not a military man, he didn't participate in it. He was amused to see that Liberty was a spirited participant, and amazed at her grasp not only of the situation but of military concepts. He mentioned it to her as they left the dinner that night.

"I have to stay abreast of all the war news, because of my speaking engagements," Liberty explained. "I know it may not be considered a 'woman's place,' but the cause of abolition recognizes no sexual lines."

"Liberty, if it isn't too presumptuous of me, could I invite you to my room for a quiet drink?"

"To your room?" Liberty asked.

"I'm sorry," Dan said. "It was presumptuous of me. But it would be unseemly to go to your room, as you might be embarrassed before your neighbors. In my hotel, however, such things are frequently done, and done in innocence, so you need have no fear for your reputation. And I very much want to spend some time with you."

Liberty smiled. "It's sweet of you to concern yourself for my reputation, Dan. But the truth is, I fear I jeopardized my reputation long ago, when I began speaking out on behalf of abolition. Yes, I will join you in your room, though I don't wish to drink."

Liberty's voice had been throaty, almost husky, as she accepted the invitation, and it sent a small shiver of anticipation coursing through Dan. Was her voice a promise of something? Maybe so, he thought. It would certainly be worth exploring. He leaned forward to inform the driver of their destination.

The Boatman Hotel was equipped with Mr. Otis's elevators, and as the doors closed to take them up to Dan's fourth floor room, Dan was aware of Liberty's perfume. It was subtle, though effective enough to titillate his senses. He moved a step closer to her, and when she felt him move she looked up at him and smiled. Their gaze held for just a moment, then, a sudden, almost overpowering feeling made Dan want to take her in his arms and kiss her. Only the presence of the elevator operator prevented him from doing so. Liberty's face flushed, and Dan knew that she knew exactly what he was thinking.

"Oh, my," Liberty said as the elevator stopped on Dan's floor. "I shouldn't ride elevators. They addle my senses and make my head spin." She was covering up her own reaction, for she was as fully attracted to Dan as he was to her.

The doors were cranked open, and they stepped into the fourth floor hallway. "My, uh, room is just down here," Dan said, leading the way.

They walked quickly and silently down the hall to Dan's room, then stopped as Dan extracted his key.

"408? This is your room?" Liberty asked, the tone of her voice showing some surprise.

"Yes, why? Don't you not like the numbers 408 for some reason?" Dan asked, with a small laugh.

"No, nothing like that. I'm just making nervous conversation," Liberty said.

"There's no reason to be nervous, Liberty," Dan said easily. He opened the door and they stepped inside. Liberty didn't move on into the room; instead she stopped just inside, and when Dan closed the door and turned around, she was there before him, in as close proximity as she had been in the elevator. The overpowering urge to kiss her came over him again, and this time he did not have the restraint of the elevator operator to prevent him from doing so.

"Dan?" Liberty said softly, looking deep into his eyes and reading his very thoughts.

Dan put his arms around her and pulled her to him. It was not a hesitant kiss, soft and apologetic as it had been in the carriage the other evening, but a deep kiss, joined in with a fervor which surprised them both. Dan's hands began to move through the folds of Liberty's dress, bunching up the material of the skirt until the way was opened to give him access to her bare leg. He put his hand on her warm flesh.

"No," Liberty finally managed to say, twisting away from him suddenly. "Dan, not like this. I don't want to be some casual wartime romance . . . a woman you use like a trollop."

"Do you think you are?" Dan asked, surprised by her sudden move.

"I don't know. I don't know what to think. I . . . I shouldn't even be here."

"I'm sorry," Dan said. "Liberty, I don't want to hurt you."

"Please try to understand," Liberty said.

"I do understand," Dan said. "Look, if you'd rather go now, I'll take you back."

"No," Liberty said. "I don't have to go . . . just yet. I just don't want you to have the wrong impression of me."

Dan smiled. "Then you'll stay?"

"For a while."

Dan kissed her again, and, as before, the kiss deepened. This time Dan's hands were in Liberty's hair, and he tilted her head back, and kissed her on the lips, the cheeks, the throat, and up to one ear.

"No," Liberty moaned deep in her throat, but even as she protested, she tightened her embrace and pressed her body against his.

Dan's hands moved from her hair down her neck, then, easily and naturally, the buttons of the high neck-dress were opened and he found the palm of his hand slipping along the smooth, incredibly warm skin until he cupped one of her breasts in his hand. It was warm and alive, and he took her hard, button-like little nipple between his thumb and forefinger.

"Oh, oh," Liberty said, almost in a whimper. She searched for Dan's mouth with her own, and when she found it, opened her lips to his deep, penetrating kiss.

Dan swept her up then, and carried her to his bed. Her protests had stopped now, and she matched his kisses, and opened her dress, offering her body to him, to use as he wished.

Dan's hands were busy, taking advantage of her assistance. He freed her breasts, then, a moment later, removed her dress, so that she lay on the bed, her naked skin pink and glowing in the soft gaslight.

As Liberty lay on the bed, feeling the silken caress of the air against her naked skin, she looked up at the man who was now removing his clothes to join her. She couldn't believe she was doing this. All sanity and reason seemed to have deserted her. It was as if he had cast some sort of spell over her. Almost from the beginning, she had known this moment would come. She knew about it and was thus forearmed . . . but still was defenseless against it.

Why? She cried out inside herself. Why was she as helpless as a kitten before him? But even as she asked the question, the answer came to her. Here was the same sensual attraction she felt in Burke . . . but in a more mature, more sensitive man. It was a combination against which she had no defense . . . and indeed, wanted none. She knew that such things were not to be enjoyed by women; in fact, some believed it was sinful even for married women to enjoy their husbands. But Liberty didn't always conduct her life in accordance with the dictates of society. She was an abolitionist among southerners, and a Confederate among abolitionists—two prime examples of contradictory, even paradoxical behavior. And add to her fight for the emancipation of slaves, the fight to emancipate women, she thought. For if it is no sin for a man to enjoy sex, then it should be no sin for a woman to enjoy it. And she was enjoying it. As she waited for him, the air sensitized her naked, splayed legs, and it was a good feeling, a grand and glorious feeling.

She felt Dan's weight come down on her, and she breathed the maleness of him. Her legs were downy soft and creamy white, beneath his muscle-hard and swarthy dark ones. When she felt him enter her, she thrust against him, feeling a pleasure so intense that she cried out from the joy of it.

Their movements established an easy rhythm, and they matched each other, move for move, until finally, with a powerful shudder, she felt an explosion of pleasure inside her that completely engulfed her, wrenching a sob of ecstasy from her throat. So lost was she in her own release that she scarcely noticed Dan's own frenzied climax.

Liberty lay beneath him for a while, feeling his weight on her, enjoying the warm and pleasant dampness that filled her. She stroked his shoulder with her hand, and he kissed her again, then rolled over and lay beside her. They were both silent, save for their breathing, which was just beginning to return to normal.

"Dan," she finally asked. "Do you think I'm an evil woman?"

Dan raised up and leaned on his elbow, looking down at her. "Of course not," he said. "Why would you ask such a thing?"

"Because of this," she said. "I enjoyed what

we did. I can't begin to tell you how much I enjoyed it."

"I enjoyed it too. Does that make me an evil man?"

"But women aren't supposed to enjoy it," Liberty said. "At least, that's what everyone says."

Dan laughed. "Liberty, somehow I have the feeling that you don't give a fig what everyone says."

Liberty laughed with him. "Maybe you're right," she said. She sat up, then leaned over to kiss him, the nipples of her breasts brushing him lightly as she did so. Then she looked at him with a serious expression on her face.

"We mustn't see each other again," she said.

"What? What are you talking about?" Dan asked, puzzled by her remark.

"Just what I said. We mustn't see each other again. It can only cause pain."

Dan raised his hand and ran his fingers along her cheek. "No," he said. "Not pain, joy. Liberty . . . this is much too early for me to say it, I know. But I can't help it. I—"

"No," Liberty interrupted quickly, placing her fingers across his lips. "No, don't say it, please."

"But why not?"

"Because . . . because it would be too easy for me to fall in love with you."

"What's wrong with that?"

"Everything," Liberty said heavily. "I have

no right to fall in love with you, or with anyone. Especially not with you."

"Why especially me?" Dan asked.

"Because I have very strong convictions about what I believe in," Liberty said. "You won't understand those convictions, and you would feel betrayed. It would cause painful misunderstandings."

"Why would that cause misunderstandings?" Dan asked. "Liberty, we're at war now. This is a time that calls for convictions and honor." He laughed, self-deprecatingly. "In fact, it is I who should be apologizing to you, for here I lie with no clear convictions to guide me. But though I have no convictions of my own, Liberty, I have respect for those who do. Who cannot respect honor?"

"Sometimes the line between honor and dishonor may be thinly drawn," Liberty said, her voice and expression reflecting the torment of self-doubt. "Even I have difficulty in drawing the distinction. But I am embarked upon my course, Dan, and I have no choice but to follow it to the end, or admit that I have been wrong. And I can't admit I've been wrong—I fear I couldn't live with the ghosts of the realization."

"Whew," Dan said, frowning, "That's pretty serious stuff."

"Then perhaps you can see what I am burdened with," Liberty said. "Now, I think I'd better get home."

"I'll take you," Dan said, swinging his legs over the edge of the bed and reaching for his clothes.

"You don't have to."

"I know I don't have to," Dan said. "But I very much want to. And, despite what you say, I do want to see you again. Very soon."

"No," Liberty said. "Please, Dan, don't make it harder on me than it already is. Try to understand."

"I'm sorry," Dan said. "But I can't understand."

"Then please forgive me," Liberty said quietly. "For this is the way it must be."

They rode out to Liberty's boarding house in comparative silence. Beneath the lap robe they held hands, not in an intimate, sensual way, but in a way which suggested their hopelessness for a situation which could not be.

When they reached the boarding house, they kissed the long, sad, desperate kiss of lovers who saw their world together ending, before it ever had a chance to start.

8

Dan could still feel the heat of Liberty's body and taste the bittersweetness of her kiss as he stepped out of the carriage in front of the Boatman's Hotel. He paid the driver, then stood in front of the hotel and watched the carriage as it slipped off into the darkness. Behind him, and up a set of foot-polished steps, were the glass doors which led into the bright lights of the hotel lobby. In a town dizzy with war fever, such places were golden promises of excitement. Now the golden promise seemed to mock Dan.

What had gone wrong? There had been a mutual attraction between them, he knew. He hadn't forced himself on her; she had responded willingly, even eagerly. And yet, though she had shared her body with him, she had preserved, kept back, the mingling of souls which he yearned for.

Dan thrust his hands in his pockets, and started up the steps. What he needed was a little drink. No, what he needed was a lot of little drinks. Perhaps then he would be able to figure things out.

"Mr. O'Lee, hello to you, sir," a familiar voice called. Dan looked toward the sound of the voice, and saw Captain Todd just rising from one of the many overstuffed chairs which were scattered about on the floral carpet. Todd was carrying a newspaper under his arm, as if he had been waiting for some time and had passed that time by reading. He walked across the lobby toward Dan.

"Well, Captain Todd. I see you're here. This couldn't just be coincidence, could it?"

Todd smiled. "Not exactly," he said. "Miss Welles is a lovely girl, isn't she? I don't blame you for inviting her to your room. I trust your efforts were rewarded?"

Dan's face showed a quick irritation. "Captain Todd, why do you see fit to pry into every aspect of my private life?"

"Mr. O'Lee, you must appreciate the fact that we are at war," Captain Todd said. "And I have a job to do."

"Assuming I can accept that, captain, why must your job always involve me? What do I have to do with the war?"

Todd pulled a small box of cigars from his breast pocket, offered one to Dan, and when Dan declined, took one for himself and lit it, wreathing his head in smoke before he answered.

"You seem to be right in the center of things, Mr. O'Lee."

"What do you mean, right in the center of things?"

Captain Todd smiled, then pulled the cigar from his mouth.

"Consider my perspective, Mr. O'Lee. You were on the stage when it was jumped by Quantrill's bushwhackers. You spoke with Lieutenant Ward, and delivered what was purported to be his message to General Halleck."

"Purported to be?" Dan asked. "What do you mean by that?"

"I'll tell you what I mean by that, Mr. O'Lee. Suppose you aren't who you represent yourself to be."

"You already know I am Dan O'Lee. Surely your spies have told you that," Dan replied hotly.

"Oh, I don't doubt that you are Dan O'Lee," Captain Todd said easily. "But I may doubt that you are the patriot you claim to be. You see, Mr. O'Lee, what if you wanted to strengthen the Rebel position at Island Number Ten in New Madrid? What better way than to lure our men and material to Sikeston, then fall upon them with massed artillery? We would not only lose several men, we would in all likelihood lose many cannons, much ammunition, powder, food, clothing, and other stocks of war. Stocks badly needed by the Confederacy."

"I see," Dan said. "So what you are saying is that I faked the message, hoping to draw the supplies into Sikeston. Is that it?"

"I'm not overlooking that possibility, Mr. O'Lee."

"Why would you think such a thing?"

"You were on the coach, Mr. O'Lee. You had the opportunity to fake the message, and no one would be any wiser."

"There were others on the stage," Dan said.

"But they're dead, Mr. O'Lee. Except for Quantrill himself. We have only your word that what you say is true, and as there is no one to dispute your version, that puts us in a precarious position."

"Why would you doubt my word?"

"Well, sir, there is the matter of your brother," Captain Todd said. "He is a known Confederate. He was riding with Quantrill, but he was wounded during the stage hold-up. He was treated for his wound by Dr. Coyle, a physician known to have Secesh leanings, in Rolla, Missouri. But Dr. Coyle is also a greedy man, so he attempted to turn Burke in for the reward. By the time he returned to Rolla with a prisoner escort, though, Burke had managed to give the good doctor's wife the slip. Now, we don't know where he is. But we do have an idea."

Dan blinked. Burke with Quantrill? He'd had difficulty assimilating Todd's news; he just hadn't seen or recognized Burke in the band, one or the other.

"You think you know where Burke is?" he said. "Where?"

"We believe he is with Liberty Welles."

"Impossible," Dan said quickly.

"Oh? And why do you think it is impossible? Because you made love to her?"

Dan felt his face burning. "No," he said. "That has nothing to do with it. It's just that she knows I am looking for my brother. She wouldn't hide it from me . . . she wouldn't deceive me."

"Lieutenant Ward thought that she wouldn't deceive him, either," Captain Todd said dryly, "You see, he was also Miss Liberty Welles' lover. But his trust in her was so misplaced that it got him killed."

"I don't believe that," Dan insisted. "I asked Miss Welles if she knew Lieutenant Ward, and she said she did not."

"She would hardly admit it under the circumstances, would she?" Captain Todd replied. "Tell me, Mr. O'Lee. Was there any particular reason you asked her? Did the lieutenant mention her name, by any chance?"

"No, of course not," Dan said. He paused for a moment. "At least . . . I don't think he did."

"Aha! You have remembered something," Captain Todd said triumphantly. "Please, tell me what it is."

"I haven't just remembered it," Dan said. "But I was sure that it was of no consequence. Still, I had to be sure, so I checked myself."

"What did he say, Mr. O'Lee?"

"His dying word was liberty," Dan said.

"And you thought *that* insignificant?" Captain Todd said.

"I thought it merely a testimony to the lieutenant's patriotism."

"I see. But now you realize that it was Miss Welles' name the lieutenant spoke . . . perhaps as a warning."

"I don't know that," Dan said. "As I said, Miss Welles told me she didn't know the lieutenant."

"I can easily get dozens of witnesses who will swear that they saw them together, including the desk clerk of this very hotel, who often arranged a room for their trysting places. Ironically, they once used room 408. Your room, I believe?"

Suddenly Dan remembered Liberty's strange reaction to room 408, and the memory gave him pause for a moment. Could there be something to Captain Todd's accusation?

But Dan thrust the thought away as being disloyal, and continued to challenge Captain Todd's statements.

"Suppose what you say is true," Dan suggested. "How would Liberty get word to Quantrill?"

"Through your brother."

"Ah, yes," Dan said, sarcastically. "And I suppose you have evidence that my brother is also her lover."

"As a matter of fact, we do, Mr. O'Lee," Todd said firmly.

The cumulative effect of all Todd's information now hit Dan in the face like a slap, and he pressed the knuckles of his fist against his forehead. "Then she did call me Burke," he finally said quietly.

"I beg your pardon?"

"The other evening she called me Burke," Dan muttered. "She covered it up by telling me she had called me Burt, and explained that he was an old beau. I know now, though, that it was Burke's name she said." He laughed a short, bitter laugh. "And to think I was about to tell her . . . that I thought I . . ." He broke it off and looked at Captain Todd with hurt, embarrassed silence.

"Mr. O'Lee, you are not the first man to be taken in by the lady's charms. But if we can put her out of business, you will be the last," Captain Todd said.

"This is what she was talking about," Dan said. "She was trying to warn me."

"What?"

"Nothing," Dan said. "It has nothing to do with the information you are trying to discover. Captain Todd, I assure you that the message is genuine if Lieutenant Ward was genuine. I

99

merely did what I perceived to be my duty in delivering it to General Halleck."

"I would very much like to believe you, Mr. O'Lee. For if the message you handed General Halleck is authentic, it will provide our forces with a great advantage. If, however, it is a false message, planted only to lure us into a trap, then I fear it could have disastrous results should we follow through on it."

"I did not fake that message," Dan said.

"We will proceed on that assumption, Mr. O'Lee, but we shall proceed with caution."

"I'm sure you will," Dan said. "And now, if you will excuse me, I must be going." Dan turned to walk toward the door.

"Mr. O'Lee, are you going out again?"

"Why?" Dan asked. "Have you already let your spies off for the night?"

Todd smiled. "We never sleep, Mr. O'Lee."

"Well, for your information, I feel the need to think about a few things. I would like to be alone."

"Have a pleasant evening, sir," Captain Todd called cheerily as Dan pushed, angrily, through the front door.

A carriage had just deposited a passenger at the hotel, and as the driver started to pull away, Dan hailed him.

"I'm sorry, sir," the driver replied. "I'm goin' home to the wife 'n kids now. I'm through for the day."

"But I have some place I must get to quickly," Dan said.

"I'm sorry sir."

"I'll double your fare," Dan offered.

The driver hesitated. "I'd like to help you, sir, really I would. But . . ."

"I'll give you three times your fare."

"Three times?"

"Yes."

"You want to get there awful bad, don'cha'?"

"Yes," Dan agreed. "Will you do it, man?"

"Sure'n for that much I'd carry you on my back," the hack driver said. "Get in."

Dan returned to the block where Liberty lived, paid the driver the agreed-upon price, and stepped out of the carriage. The driver, afraid that Dan would want him for further duty, snapped the reins at the horse, and the horse stepped off at a brisk trot.

The night air was cold, and as Dan walked along the edge of the street, his breath blew clouds of fog. Finally he reached the boarding house, sneaked up the same stairway he had seen Liberty use, and listened quietly through the door.

"It has to be Corinth," Liberty's voice was saying. "Burke, I heard General Halleck say that within a twenty-mile triangle, he could capture critical railroad junctions which would disrupt one third of the South's railroad system. I was born and raised at Corinth, and I know what he's talking about. He wouldn't say where it was, but it has to be there."

"Then we've got to get word to General Beauregard," a man's voice said. "If he's in time, he can gather enough forces to stop Halleck."

"You must tell him yourself, Burke. Don't trust the message to anyone else."

"I'll leave first thing in the morning."

"Are you going to see Dan before you leave?"

"I think not," the man's voice answered.

"But Burke, he *is* your brother," Liberty's voice said.

"He stopped being my brother twelve years ago."

It *was* Burke! Dan could no longer restrain himself, and he began pounding on the door.

"Who is it?" Liberty called.

"Liberty, it's me, Dan. Let me in, please!"

"Dan! It's terribly late, Dan, can't you come back tomorrow?"

"Liberty, I know Burke is in there. Please let me in. I must talk to him."

The door opened then, and Liberty stepped back to allow Dan to enter. He brushed by her quickly, then looked on the bed. There, naked from the waist up, and covered by bedcovers from the waist down, sat his brother. Even though Burke had been only ten the last time Dan had seen him, the features were unmistakable, and he had an urge to rush to him and embrace him. Something in Burke's face stopped him though. Then, with a short gasp of surprise, he recognized what it was. It was hate.

"Well, well, well," Burke said coldly. "If it isn't the long-lost gold hunter."

"Burke, it's good to see you," Dan said.

"I'm sorry I can't say the same of you," Burke replied.

"What are you doing here?" Liberty asked.

Dan looked at Liberty for the first time. She was in a dressing gown, and she pulled it tightly about her, modestly shielding from his gaze that which she had so willingly opened to him only a few hours earlier.

"I see," Dan finally said. "I'm sorry if I arrived at an inopportune time."

"Oh, my, aren't you the wounded brother though?" Burke asked, laughing shortly. "Did you think that by sleeping with her once, you had staked claims to her? Well, how do you think I feel? I've loved her for over a year. At least you can say she's keeping it in the family."

"Burke!" Liberty said, the exclamation coming out almost as a sob. "How could you say such a thing?"

"So this is your little speech of honor," Dan spat.

"I told you, you wouldn't understand," Liberty said. She began crying. "I told you not to try to see me again. I knew this would happen."

103

"Oh, spare me your tears of remorse, Miss Welles. Let's be honest, shall we? For you, I was merely a means of getting to General Halleck to learn some valuable information. And for me? Well, you were . . . how did you put it? A wartime romance? A woman I could use like a trollop?"

"Dan, it's not like that, believe me," Liberty cried. "I . . . I'm trapped into doing this . . . bound by honor to . . ."

"Honor?" Dan said. "You don't know the meaning of the word." Dan looked at his brother, and noticed the bandage on his shoulder. "It's true, isn't it?" he said, looking at the wound. "You were one of the gang of bushwhackers who jumped the stagecoach and killed the driver and the lieutenant."

"I didn't kill anyone in that raid," Burke said. "I was flat on my butt in the snow, if you recall. I was lucky to get away alive. I got treated by some sawbones in Rolla, and made it here to Liberty's place."

"Yes," Dan said. "The doctor who treated you is named Coyle. I heard all about it."

"Coyle? Yeah, I think that's his name. How did you know?"

"You aren't safe here, Burke," Dan said. "They know all about you. And you, too, Liberty."

"Me? How do they know about me?"

"I don't know. Perhaps some of the men you've slept with were Union spies."

Liberty blinked back the tears.

"Liberty, we've got to get you outta here," Burke said.

"But I can't leave," Liberty said. "My work is too important for the Confederacy."

"Go down to Corinth," Burke advised her. "You carry the message to General Beauregard yourself."

"How will I get there?"

Burke swung his legs over the edge of the bed and started pulling on his pants, wincing as he did so. It was only then that Dan realized that his brother had been holding a gun on him from the moment he stepped into the room. "I can get you there," Burke replied. He looked at Dan. "The only thing, I don't know what to do with 'brother' here."

"That is a problem, isn't it?"

"Would you give us your word to say nothing to the authorities until we've had time to make good our escape?" Liberty asked.

"My word of 'honor'?" Dan replied, twisting the word so that it became almost obscene.

"Would you rather I just shoot you?" Burke replied, raising his pistol menacingly.

"Burke, you wouldn't really do it?" Liberty sounded shocked.

"I don't see as we have any choice," Burke said quietly. He held the pistol steady, unwaveringly, pointed right at Dan's head. He was so calm, and so cool, that Dan was certain he was about to die. He stood there, rooted in shock, waiting for his brother's bullet to crash into him.

Burke slowly lowered the gun. He looked at Dan with an expression of hurt and anger on his face.

"Why did you leave me?" he finally asked.

"Burke, be reasonable. I wasn't much more than a kid myself. I couldn't have taken care of you."

"You mean you didn't want to."

"I mean I couldn't," Dan said firmly. "I had to do what I felt was best for you. I left you with Aunt Zelda and Uncle Jebediah."

"You would have been better off abandoning me in the street somewhere," Burke said bitterly. "I would have had an easier time of it on my own, than with that sadistic bastard of an uncle."

"Burke . . . Burke, I'm sorry," Dan said, genuinely struck by Burke's revelation. "I had no idea that you wouldn't be well treated."

"What difference did it make to you?" Burke asked. "You had what you wanted. What did you care if a ten-year-old kid had to put up with a beating now and then? After all, it was no skin off your back." Burke laughed bitterly at his metaphor. "That's pretty good, don't you think?"

"Burke, believe me, I'm sorry," Dan said. "I am truly very sorry. If I had only known, I would have come back for you no matter what it took. And I would have gotten you out of there."

"Yeah? Well you never even bothered to

check in to see how I was doing all those years. And now you come around telling me how sorry you are. That's supposed to make it all right, is it? You make a confession of guilt, and I, like a priest, am supposed to grant you absolution. Well, it isn't that easy, brother. I can't forgive and forget after what I've been through."

"I don't blame you for being angry," Dan said. "But what can I say now?"

"There is nothing you can say now," Burke said. "And there's nothing you can do. The damage has been done."

There was a sudden knock at the door, and it startled them all. Burke raised the pistol again, and pointed it toward the door.

"Who is it?" Liberty called.

"It's me, Hiram Dempster," a voice replied.

"He has a letter of introduction for you to General Jeff Thompson," Liberty told Burke swiftly.

"Well, he's just going to have to put one more name in it," Burke replied. "You'll be going with me, Liberty girl. Oh, if that's all right with you, Danny," he added, sarcastically.

"I don't care where she goes, or what happens to her," Dan said, forcing a coolness to his voice. He looked at Liberty, and was surprised to see a hurt reflected deep in her eyes.

"Good," Burke said softly. "Now, Liberty girl, show Mr. Dempster in. He's going to keep an eye on big brother here until after we're gone."

9

"So, we meet again, do we?" Dempster said, after Burke and Liberty had left. He was holding a pistol leveled at Dan, and his thumb played, almost lovingly, with the hammer.

"This is a boarding house, Dempster," Dan said. "If you shoot now, you'll have everyone in here banging on the door, wanting to know what happened."

"Oh, don't you fret about that, dear fellow. I could quite easily explain that my firearm discharged accidentally. But, just to avoid any such embarrassing moments, might I suggest that we go somewhere else?"

"I'm quite comfortable here, thank you," Dan replied.

"You don't understand," Dempster said. The easy smile left his face, and he motioned toward the door with the business end of his pistol. "That wasn't really a suggestion, it was an order. Now move, or I will be forced to shoot you here and try my luck at explaining it later."

Dan reluctantly, but wisely, chose to step through the door into the cold night air. As he descended the steps in front of Dempster, he ran through possible escape plans in his mind. He considered whirling around and trying to grasp the gun away before Dempster could react, or trying to leap over the rail, or even shouting out loud for help. But he discarded each plan as soon as it came to mind, as being unworkable.

There was a carriage sitting at the curb, and a Union officer stepped out as the two men approached.

"Captain!" Dan said happily, calling the officer by rank. "Am I glad to see you! This man is a Rebel spy! You'd better—" Dan stopped abruptly.

The Union officer had shrugged. He opened the holster flap and pulled out his pistol.

Dan turned toward Dempster and was crestfallen to see him laughing.

"Is the fella giving you any trouble, Hiram?" the Union officer asked.

"Not anything I can't handle," Dempster replied. "Mr. O'Lee, may I introduce Colonel Blackie Beauregard?"

"Colonel?"

The man in the Union officer's uniform smiled and preened his mustache and Van Dyke beard. "Don't let this Yankee uniform fool you," he said amicably. "It's merely an expediency. I am,

110

in fact, a colonel in the Confederate Army, in St. Louis on confidential assignment."

"I'm certain you've heard of Blackie's illustrious uncle," Dempster went on. "He's is General P.G.T. Beauregard."

"I see," Dan said.

"Yes, unfortunately, you do see," Dempster drawled. "And that brings up a most regrettable point."

"What are we going to do with him, Hiram?"

Dempster pondered. "Unfortunately, colonel, we're going to have to find some way to dispose of him."

"Hell, that's not hard." The man who called himself Blackie Beauregard drew back the hammer on his pistol, and once again Dan found himself a breath away from instant death.

"No," Dempster said quickly. "I have a better idea. I have an idea that will make Mr. O'Lee's demise useful to the Confederacy."

"What are you thinking?" Beauregard asked.

"We'll take him down to the river and put him on board the *Delta Star*. When the boat blows up, Mr. O'Lee will go with it. And, if they manage to find enough of him to identify, he'll be considered responsible for the blast."

Blackie smiled broadly in the moonlight. "Yeah," he said. "Yeah, that sounds like a real good idea. Come on, you, get in the carriage."

It was a private carriage, and the driver, whoever he was, was obviously in the employ of the

111

two who held Dan captive, so Dan realized that he could expect no help from that quarter. And as both Hiram Dempster and Blackie Beauregard held their pistols on him, escape was impossible by his own devices. So there was little Dan could do but ride quietly through the streets of St. Louis, bound for the riverfront.

"There she is," Dempster said grimly, pointing out a side-wheeler paddleboat as the carriage stopped on the levee. "The *Delta Star*. Used to carry cotton from Memphis to St. Louis before the Federals got hold of her and impressed her into service."

"That pirate, Commodore Foote, stole her," Blackie said darkly.

"Ah, yes," Dempster added. "I forgot to tell you, O'Lee, that the *Delta Star* once belonged to Colonel Beauregard."

"She still belongs to me," Blackie said. "I'll not see her in Yankee hands."

"So we are going to destroy her," Dempster said.

"That doesn't make sense," Dan objected. "You'll get her back after the war. Why would you want to destroy her?"

"I will gladly destroy her to serve the Confederacy," Blackie said narrowly.

"Don't get it," Dan said, fighting for time. "How will destroying her serve the Confederacy?"

Dempster laughed. "Oh, dear fellow, didn't we tell you? The *Delta Star* is loaded with ammunition and supplies for General Grant, in Cairo. She leaves tomorrow morning. Grant is desperately in need of those supplies, if he is to have any success in capturing Island Number Ten. I have it on good authority that he has twice petitioned General Halleck for permission to conduct the operation."

"He needs the ammunition almost as badly as he needs the whiskey the *Delta Star* is carrying," Blackie said derisively.

"Unfortunately for General Grant, he's going to get neither," Dempster said to Dan. "You are going to prevent it, by blowing up the boat."

"We've talked enough," Blackie said impatiently. "Let's do it, and be done."

Still covered by the two guns, Dan had no choice but to walk down the cobblestone levee and step onto the loading gangplank.

"Who's there?" a voice called from the darkened deck of the boat.

"Hello, Carl, is that you?" Blackie said.

Carl came forward into the light.

"Oh, cap'n. What are you doin' down here?"

"I thought I'd take a look at the engine," Blackie said. "The boiler hasn't been holding pressure like it should. It may be being used by the government, but it still belongs to me. Is anyone else aboard?"

113

"No, sir. They won't be comin' on board 'till six o'clock in the mornin'. I drew the graveyard watch."

"Well, you're a good man for it."

"You can believe it. If any of them Sesesh bastards try anything on this boat, I'll let 'em have what for. If I had my way we'd hang ever' one of the Rebel bastards," Carl said bitterly.

"These two gentlemen are boiler inspectors," Blackie said. "They'll be with me."

Dan wanted to speak out, to deny Blackie's easy lie, but he knew that if he did, it would only put Carl's life in danger as well, so he remained quiet as the four of them went below into the engine room.

The engine room smelled of burning wood, steam and oil. There was also the lingering odor of sweating human bodies, a kind of signature of the toiling firemen who kept the tender stoked. It was warm, and Dan could hear the water bubbling inside the boiler, and see an orange glow from the firebox.

"I see you're keeping some pressure up," Blackie said.

"Right on thirty, just like I'm supposed to," Carl replied. "That way it won't take us long to get underway in the mornin'."

"There," Blackie said, pointing to a maze of pipes behind the boiler. "That's what I'm talking about right there. Isn't that a steam leak?"

"I don't see nothin'," Carl said.

"Get your head down here so you can see," Blackie suggested.

Carl bent down and leaned around behind the boiler, trying to see the leak Blackie had mentioned.

"No, Carl, look out!" Dan shouted, suddenly realizing what Blackie intended to do. But his warning came too late, for by the time Dan perceived Blackie's intent, he had already taken a water-pipe wrench from the worktable and brought it crashing down on Carl's head.

Carl dropped to the deck without uttering a sound, and when Dan looked at the back of his head he could see that the skull was crushed. Blood and brain tissue gushed out of the wound.

"My God, you killed him!" Dan said.

"What difference does it make?" Blackie replied. "He would have died in the explosion anyway. Same as you're going to."

Seeing the lifeless body of Carl lying in his own ooze sharply brought home to Dan his immediate danger, and whereas he had considered and rejected all escape plans earlier, this time he reacted without thought. He shoved Blackie out of the way and started running for the ladderway which led back to the main deck.

He didn't make it. Before he had gone two steps, he felt a crashing blow to his head and saw brilliant pinpoints of light flashing before him. Then, the lights went out.

* * *

When he awakened sometime later, Dan
didn't know how long he had been out. For the
first few seconds he just lay where he was, feeling a tremendous pain emanating from the back
of his head. When he tried to sit up nausea
overcame him, and he had to lay back down for
a moment.

He suddenly realized where he was and how
he got there. He looked around quickly and
saw that he was alone, except for Carl's body,
which lay in the same place. Dan knew that
he had been very fortunate. It had been Dempster who hit him, and Dempster was neither as
strong as Blackie, nor did he use as heavy an
instrument. Dan had only been stunned. He
could have been killed.

And still might be, he suddenly realized! He
remembered then that Dempster and Blackie
intended to destroy this boat!

Dan stood quickly, and when the wave of
dizziness and nausea overwhelmed him, he
grabbed onto an overhead beam for support,
hanging on until he was sure he wouldn't pass
out again. Finally, his reeling senses stabilized,
he began to move around on the boat.

He climbed the ladder and walked out on the
deck. He was surprised to see that instead of
being tied to the levee, the boat was now in the
middle of the river, floating downstream. Evi-

dently, the mooring lines had been slipped by Dempster and Blackie as they left the boat, and the current of the river was all that was needed to carry him out here.

The river was chocked with floes of ice, and the current was swift. From this point, Dan was more than a thousand feet from the bank. Even under the most ideal conditions, a swim to shore in the swiftly moving current would be extremely hazardous. Tonight, in his weakened state, and with the temperature of the water at freezing, such a swim would be impossible. So he gave up the idea of diving into the river, deciding instead that his only chance lay in discovering where the explosive bomb was planted. Somehow, he would have to try and defuse it.

Sure that the bomb would be set in the powder locker, in order to take advantage of the remaining powder and thus completely destroy the boat, Dan summoned his courage and ran into the cargo hold to look for it. It was dark inside the hold, and he didn't dare light a lamp for fear of setting off the powder. Still, with no light, it was impossible to see where a bomb might be set.

He stood there, frustrated, freezing, and frightened. There was a bomb set to explode right under him, and he had no idea where it was. His breath was coming in painful rasps now, and he could hear his own heart beating, but though he looked as hard as he could, he could see no tell-tale sign of a sparkling fuse. He held his breath and tried to listen, to see if he could hear a slow burning fuse sputtering, but he heard nothing. Nor did he smell the cordite burning.

Perhaps they were unable to plant the bomb, he thought. But no, that couldn't be. There was nothing to prevent them. Carl had been killed, and he had been unconscious. The very fact that the boat had been slipped from its mooring was proof enough to Dan that the bomb had, indeed, been planted.

But where? he wondered. And how?

He started walking slowly back to the warmth of the boiler room, where he hoped to be able to figure it all out.

Compared to the icy blast of wind on deck, the boiler room was like the hottest summer day. In fact, it seemed to Dan unusually warm even for a boiler room, and almost as he thought that, he realized how Blackie intended to destroy the *Delta Star!*

He ran to the boiler, to check the steam pressure gauge. It had been maintained at a steady 30 PSI when Carl had pointed it out to them as they came aboard. Now the needle was beyond 200, well into the red danger mark, and still moving up.

Dan looked up at the safety valve and saw

that it had been wired tightly shut. When he tried to unwire it, he found the wire was much too hot to touch. Besides, it was so intricately wound that it would take him several minutes to release it, even if he could touch it. And a quick glance at the gauge told Dan that he no longer had several minutes. In fact, he might not even have several seconds.

By now the water in the boiler was roaring, and wisps of steam were escaping from any place that would allow it. The needle hit the peg at the top of the gauge, then began clicking as it bounced against it, trying to go still further.

Dan, tasting the bile of panic in his throat, started for the ladder, determined to take his chances in the icy river. Then, just before he reached it, he saw the heavy wrench Blackie had used to kill Carl, and he grabbed it and returned to the safety valve. He began pounding on the valve, praying aloud, and cursing the valve for being stuck. Finally, with one last, desperate swing, he knocked the entire valve off the pipe. A stream of scalding steam shot straight up, roaring as it poured through the hole and filling the entire boiler room with a hot, moist white cloud.

Dan let out a yelp of pain, dropped the wrench, then ran for the ladder to regain the deck.

Steam poured up through the hatch. It rolled across the deck of the boat and drifted across the river in a billowing white puff. All the while, it was giving off a tremendous roar as it issued from the rent he had put in the system.

Dan looked at his hands in the moonlight. Already the pain of the steam burn was subsiding, and he realized how lucky he had been, for he might have prevented the boiler explosion only to be scalded to death. Fortunately, the pressure had been so high that the steam had shot up in a tight jet before dissipating throughout the entire room. Dan had not been directly exposed to it, and was thus spared a severe burn.

"Ahoy, *Delta Star!*" Dan heard someone shouting. He looked back in surprise to see a small, fast, stern-wheeler boat approaching him.

"Here!" Dan yelled, running to the stern of the boat and waving both arms over his head. "Here, I'm adrift!"

The approaching boat closed with Dan, and a sailor on it tossed a line across. "Make the line fast," he called, and Dan wrapped it several turns around a stanchion.

The sailor on the small steamboat began hauling in on the line, and the boats closed together. Two men stepped from the other boat onto the *Delta Star.*

"It's all right now, Mr. O'Lee," one of them said. "We'll take care of the *Delta Star.* You hop over and they'll take you back to the bank."

Dan was so grateful for the rescue that he

didn't inquire as to how they knew who he was. But the mystery was answered for him when he stepped onto the small boat.

"Hello, Mr. O'Lee," Captain Todd said, smiling broadly. "Did you have a nice trip?"

"Well, if it isn't you," Dan said, his gratitude mixed with irritation. "Where the hell were you when I needed you?"

"I was around, Mr. O'Lee," Todd replied.

"You were around? I was nearly killed, do you know that? Why didn't you do something to stop it?"

"I had to know if the message was genuine," Todd said easily.

"You had to what?"

"You were aware that there was some question about the authenticity of the message," Captain Todd said. "I had to be absolutely positive that it was. The best way to validate the message was to validate you."

"Validate me, or kill me?" Dan asked.

"It's the same thing, really. If they had killed you, I would know that you weren't working for them. The fact that they tried is enough."

"Well, thank God for that, at least," Dan said. "I mean I wouldn't want to spoil your plans by living, or anything."

"Why are you so upset? We saved you, didn't we?"

"No, Captain Todd. All you did was give me a ride. I saved myself."

"Well, all's well that ends well, they say. You'll be interested to know that we captured Hiram Dempster. He'll spend the rest of this war languishing in a Federal prison for treason. Unfortunately, we weren't as lucky with Blackie Beauregard. He got away."

"I see," Dan said.

"Aren't you interested in what happened to your brother? Or Miss Welles?"

"I'm sure you'll tell me," Dan said.

"You're right, I will. They both got away too. I'm sure you are equally happy about that."

"Yes, I am glad," Dan said. "I'm glad they are out of my life. Especially Liberty Welles."

"Ah, look at it this way," Captain Todd said. "You met an attractive woman, and you had a fine time. There was no damage done."

"No," Dan agreed. "There was no damage done. Oh, wait a minute! She knows. We've got to tell General Halleck! Liberty knows where Halleck intends to strike!"

Captain Todd laughed. "Corinth, right?"

"Yes. He has to be warned. She's going to tell Beauregard, and he'll have the entire Confederate Army there!"

Captain Todd was still laughing, and he laughed so hard the tears came to his eyes. He wiped them with a handkerchief. "Excuse me," he said, barely able to get the words out. "Oh, you must excuse me, but this is so funny."

"Funny? What's funny about it?" Dan asked.

"I just told you that Liberty knows General Halleck's plans. She's going to have the whole Rebel army there to meet Halleck."

"Mr. O'Lee, that is exactly what General Halleck *wants* them to do," Todd said.

"What? No, he mentioned at the dinner that the very thing he didn't want to do was to meet the Confederates in a major battle."

"He said that for Liberty's ears only," Captain Todd explained. "Don't you see? This is perfect. She thought she was using you, but all along, you were using her. With our help, of course."

"I don't understand," Dan said.

"It's quite simple, really. Lieutenant Ward believed Liberty was a spy, and was working on her case when he was killed. But he passed along enough information for us to have our suspicions. Then, when we learned that she was to be your guest at the general's dinner, we simply set it up. The General gave her just what information we wanted her to have, hoping thereby to lure the entire Rebel army into one major battle. And Miss Welles fell for it, hook, line and sinker."

"I see," Dan said quietly.

Captain Todd began laughing again. "So, Mr. O'Lee. You have achieved your revenge over her, much sooner than you thought. It's really very funny, isn't it?"

"Yeah," Dan said. "So why am I not laughing?"

10

The Mississippi River starts as a clear stream, no more than eighteen feet wide, in northern Minnesota, and by the time it reaches St. Louis, where it is joined by the Missouri, its chief tributary, it has grown to be nearly a mile across. It was at that point that Dan O'Lee was rescued from the *Delta Star*.

As Dan stood on the deck of the little rescue craft, he looked back across the wide Mississippi, and at the ice floes he would have had to contend with had he elected to jump into the river. He watched one large floe as it floated south at a steady two miles per hour, matching the speed of the river current.

Had Dan been able to follow the ice floe on south, he would have passed such places as Sainte Genevieve and Cape Girardeau, in Missouri, towns whose names still bore the mark of their original French settlers. Then he would have seen Cairo, Illinois, the point at which the Ohio River joins the Mississippi, and the headquarters for General Grant's field command. By the time the ice floe reached New Madrid, far down in the boot-heel of Missouri, it would have nearly melted, and there, Dan would have gotten a glimpse of Island Number Ten.

Major islands in the river were numbered from north to south, and Island Number Ten, just north of New Madrid, was one of the larger and more dominating ones. There, the Confederates had built a fort which they called the Confederate 'Rock of Gibraltar.' The fort helped make Island Number Ten a cork in the mouth of a bottle; it kept the Union forces from going any further downriver.

Past that point the ice floes have melted, and their water becomes one with the river, continuing south, passing Kentucky, Tennessee, Arkansas, and forming most of the western border of the state of Mississippi.

The lower course of the Mississippi is between wide, flat shores, mostly mud carried and deposited there by the river itself. This has formed a valley as fertile as that of the Nile River in Egypt, and through this valley the river meanders through bayous, lakes and swamps, depositing rich, black dirt which is the stuff of great plantations.

One such plantation is Calvert Hills, located just north of Natchez, Mississippi. Calvert Hills was founded by Jesse Calvert in 1810, and when Jesse Calvert was buried in his land, he passed control over to his son, Amon. Except that on the afternoon of February 10, 1862, Amon Calvert, a major and the executive officer of the 2nd Mississippi Horse Regiment, fired a ceremonial cannon in salute to the Stars and Bars of the Confederacy. The breech of the gun had been double-charged, in order to make a more fitting salute, and it burst upon firing, killing Major Amon Calvert instantly.

The mythical ice floe had by now reached this point on its steady two-mile-per-hour course toward the Gulf, and was silent witness to the funeral scene unfolding on Calvert Hills.

The rain had fallen steadily all morning long, and the black dirt of the delta land of Calvert Hills had turned to mud. The horses struggled through the mire, pulling their hooves free only with effort.

The preacher who was conducting the funeral had dragged the eulogy on and on while the mourners were in the church, hoping the rain would stop. But the point had been finally reached when the mourners preferred the rain to the sermon, so the great oaken doors were swung open, and the pall bearers bore Amon Calvert's casket to the wagon.

Tamara Calvert sat in that wagon, beside her father's body. She was a striking girl with long, flowing black hair, deep blue eyes, and a flawless complexion. She held an umbrella which did nothing to stop the slashing rain, and her black dress hung heavy with water. She looked at the train of wagons and buggies following them, noting with some pride the many neighbors had turned up for her father's funeral.

The Negroes who had belonged to Amon Calvert struggled through the mud on both sides of the road. They made up a pathetic little army of blacks. They were singing some hymn which, with their own embellishments, was barely recognizable; nevertheless, it was mournful and hauntingly beautiful.

"Miss Tamara," Colonel Putnam said, clearing his throat. Tamara lifted her head and looked at him. It was the first word spoken to her since they had left the church. "I want to express the regrets of the Second Mississippi Horse Regiment about the unfortunate accident which took your father from us. We consider his death to have as much honor and meaning as if he had fallen on the field of battle." The colonel was riding close to Tamara, and he lay his hand on her leg.

"Do you, Colonel Putnam?" Tamara asked indifferently, taking her leg away, not sharply but resolutely.

"Absolutely," Colonel Putnam said, noticing neither the expression in Tamara's voice nor the reaction to his intimate gesture. "In fact, we're leaving soon for an encampment way upriver— I'm not at liberty to tell you just where—and we aim to put your father's name on our flag. It will be carried into combat with honor."

"I am sure I shall take great comfort from that," Tamara said, her voice just short of sarcastic. She was against this war, and had tried to talk her father out of it. But he had insisted, and his insistence had cost him his life. Tamara could not now be bought off with a sham show in his honor.

The grave where Tamara's father was to be laid had been dug by two Negroes while the funeral service had been going on in the church. Now they stood by the hole as the cortege approached, leaning on their shovels and peering at the procession with eyes that looked out from mud-caked faces.

The grave was half-full of water. When the coffin was lowered, it floated, as if Amon Calvert were reluctant to leave the land he and his father before him had built into one of the finest plantations in Mississippi. Colonel Putnam motioned to the two gravediggers, and they began to shovel dirt on top of the casket, which finally forced it down.

"Miz Tamara," one of the blacks said, approaching the wagon respectfully. "I've carved out a headpiece for your papa, 'till you gets a fancy rock one. Do you s'pose it'd be all right if I put it on the grave?"

The man held up a marker inscribed simply:

Amon Calvert—Born March 5, 1814—Died February 10, 1862.

"Thank you, Troy," Tamara said. "I think it is beautiful, and I'd be proud to have it marking papa's grave."

"What are you aiming to do now, Miss Tamara?" Colonel Putnam asked.

"Do?" Tamara replied. "Why, I'm going to continue on here at the plantation of course."

"Miss Tamara, now that your pa is gone, you don't have anyone to look after things," Colonel Putnam said. "Don't you think it would be best if you come to live with the missus and me, and let us handle the plantation for you?" Putnam put his hand on her again, and looked at her with eyes that were very deep, with red dots far at the bottom. "I'd treat you like one of my own."

"No," Tamara said. She shivered, from the suggestion and from the touch. "Besides, I do have someone to look after things. In less than a month I shall be Mrs. Blackwell Terrence Beauregard. Blackie is coming home soon. Have you forgotten about him, Colonel Putnam?"

"Blackie is away at war," Colonel Putnam said, pulling his hand back. "And operating behind enemy lines like he does, it would be difficult for him to get home frequently enough to take care of you the way he should. The way I could," he added.

"Then I've got Alva and Troy."

"Alva and Troy are both black, Miss Tamara," Putnam said slowly, as if trying to explain something to a child.

"I *know* they are black, Colonel Putnam. But they will watch out for me until Blackie returns."

"Well, don't you fret none about it," Putnam said, as if not hearing a word Tamara was saying. "We'll work something out for you." He reached his hand over to squeeze Tamara's leg a third time, and she pulled it away from him again, this time sharply.

The wagons and buggies were once more filled with people as the procession started back to the big house which dominated Calvert Hills. The house servants had been working all morning, and by the time the mourners reached the house they found food prepared and plates set out on every available table and sideboard.

From the conversation at the table it was hard to realize that the people were gathered for the purpose of mourning. But funerals ranked right behind weddings as social events, and the families who saw each other only occasionally were now able to exchange all the latest gossip. The dinner was gay and noisy, and now and then a trill of laughter rent the air, only to be cut off by a quick, embarrassed shush as someone realized that the mood was supposed to be solemn.

After the dinner, Colonel Putnam stood up and called for the attention of the men.

"Gentlemen, I gave my word to Miss Tamara that the name of Major Amon Calvert would be inscribed on our battle flag and carried in honor. I would now like to propose a toast, to be drunk by all, which binds us to uphold this flag of honor at all times. May it never fall into Yankee hands!"

"Here, here!" one of the other officers shouted, and there was a cheer by all the men, followed by the draining of their glasses.

"Colonel, when are we gonna see some action?" another asked.

"I was waiting for the opportunity to tell you," Colonel Putnam replied. "And I guess now is as good a time as any. We are moving up the Mississippi tomorrow, and my guess is, we will be joining General McCown on Island Number Ten."

"Where is that?"

"It's a large island in the river, just above a place called New Madrid, in Missouri. The river makes a big bend there, and whoever controls that island, controls the river. We aim to make sure that the South controls it. Gentlemen, we'll be standing in the front door of the Confederacy!"

Again there were cheers.

"And now, gentlemen, I think it is time we came to some agreement about Miss Tamara."

"What agreement?" Tamara said quickly.

"There, there, Tamara, honey. Don't you wor-

ry about it any. The men folk will think of
something," Ellen Putnam said, as she patted
Tamara's arm. Ellen was Colonel Putnam's wife.
Where Putnam's features were bony and hawkish, Ellen's were full and round.

"I don't want them to think of something,"
Tamara protested. "I don't need their help."

"Don't worry about it, child," Ellen said.
"You won't be a bother to them at all. Come
on with us. I had your girl, Alva, fix us up some
sassafrass tea. There's nothing like a little sassafrass to keep the chill from settin' in on a body."

Tamara was coaxed away by the good-neigh-
bor ladies and given a seat in a rocking chair.
A cup of tea was put in her hand and she sipped
it absently, straining to hear the conversation of
the men who were across the hall in the library.

The ladies pulled out knitting and embroidery
and talked among themselves, while their hands
moved about their work. To Tamara, their hands
looked like dirt daubers, birds flitting along a
fence row.

By ignoring the banal gossip of the women,
Tamara was able to overhear snatches of conversation from the men. Colonel Putnam's voice
was the loudest, and she could hear him clearly:
". . . and the county clerk told me himself that
Miss Tamara approached him on the very day
her father was killed and told him of her fool
idea for setting all her niggers free. If she sets
her niggers free, and with us all gone off to the

war, what do you think is going to happen? There won't be a white woman safe on any of the plantations, that's what. I tell you, we've got to do something about it."

Tamara got up from her chair and went into the library. It was full of smoke and the men stood clustered together chewing their cigars and waving their glasses. Tamara stood in the doorway watching them.

"Why, Miss Tamara," Putnam said as he saw her. "You shouldn't come in here. This is just man-talk."

"It's man-talk about me, Mr. Putnam," Tamara said, purposefully disdaining his military title. "I have every right to be in here."

"Let her stay, colonel," one of the others called. "Tamara, I'm going to be honest with you. Your papa would spin in his grave if he knew you were planning on setting all the niggers free."

"I'm doing more than planning," Tamara said resolutely. "I'm going to do it.'

"But think about what you are doing, girl! If you set your niggers free, they'll be wanting to be free on the other plantations too. The next thing you know, they'll start revolting, and then we'll have two wars on our hands. One against the Yankees, and one against our own niggers."

"If you would free your people, we wouldn't have any problem," Tamara said.

There was a rush of protesting voices, some

of them raised in anger, until Colonel Putnam raised his hand to silence them. "It isn't as simple as all that," the colonel said. "There are questions here, far too complex for you to understand."

"I understand the cruelty of keeping another human being in perpetual bondage," Tamara replied evenly. "And I understand the Christian brotherhood that would set them free."

Tamara walked over to the window. It was still raining, and the two little black boys who sat minding the visitor's horses were huddled beneath a piece of canvas, trying unsuccessfully to keep dry. Tamara looked up the long driveway and saw a rig approaching. Whoever it was, she thought, he was too late for the funeral, and if he was going to agree with the others, she'd just as soon he did not come at all.

Tamara started to look away when she noticed something about the driver, a familiar way of his sitting at the reins, which made her heart skip a beat with joy. She let out a little whoop of excitement.

"It's Blackie!" she said, shouting at the others. She turned to look at them with a smile of victory on her face. "What I do now is no one's business. Blackie has come home to marry me!"

Tamara ran from the library and out the front door, down the front steps, through the rain, and out into the driveway, arriving just as Blackie pulled his horse to a halt.

"Oh, Blackie, you've come!" she said excitedly. "Oh, darling, I am so happy to see you. Those awful men in there, they—"

"Is Colonel Putnam in there?" Blackie asked, cutting her off.

"Yes," Tamara said. "He's the worst of the lot, Blackie. They keep saying they want to come to some sort of agreement about me."

Blackie stepped out of the rig and started toward the house without so much as a perfunctionary kiss for Tamara. Considering that he had been away for over six month, Tamara found his indifference to her perplexing. She was also hurt by it.

Tamara hurried after him, thinking that perhaps he was so intent upon righting the wrong that had been done her that he had let the greeting slip by for the moment. Such thoughts poured balm on her hurt feelings. But then, with a quick fear, she thought that he might be angry enough to do something unwise.

"Blackie, you won't do anything that might be dangerous?" she asked.

"What do you mean?"

"Like challenge Putnam to a duel or anything like that."

"Don't be foolish, Tamara," Blackie said. "I have no intention whatever of fighting a duel."

"That's good," Tamara said with a relief. "For a moment, I thought—"

"Don't think," Blackie interrupted.

Blackie stepped into the library, and when the others saw him, they greeted him warmly.

"How was St. Louis?" one of them asked him.

"Seething with support for our cause," Blackie answered. "I honestly believe that if my uncle were commander of the West instead of Johnston, I could raise an army in St. Louis that would capture the city, then descend down the river to Cairo and crush General Grant."

"Colonel Beauregard." Putnam spoke. "Did you have an opportunity to check on that little matter we spoke of yesterday?"

"Yesterday?" Tamara asked, quickly. She looked at Blackie in confusion. "You were back yesterday, and yet you didn't come to see me? Why not?"

"I had business to attend to," Blackie said. He looked at Putnam with a set expression on his face. "You were right, colonel. You have my undying gratitude, sir, for informing me of the situation before I made a fool of myself."

"It was the honorable thing to do," Putnam said. "That's why I informed you of it, as soon as I discovered it." Putnam looked at Tamara, and Tamara saw the same strange look in his eyes again.

"Blackie, Colonel Putnam, what are you talking about?" Tamara asked, a nervousness rising in her. She looked from one to the other.

Blackie didn't answer. Instead, he looked at the other men gathered there in the library.

"Gentlemen, there will be no niggers freed from Calvert Hills. I can promise you that."

"What?" Tamara asked, stunned. "Blackie, how can you make such a promise? Calvert Hills belongs to me now, and I'll do as I wish with it."

"That's just it," Blackie said easily. "Calvert Hills doesn't belong to you, it belongs to me. So do you, by the way."

"So do *I*? What are you talking about? What do you mean Calvert Hills belongs to you? And how can you say I belong to you? We aren't married yet, Blackie Beauregard, and if this is to be your attitude, we never shall be!"

Blackie smiled. "On that point, my dear, you are one hundred percent correct. I will never marry you."

"What?" Tamara asked in a small voice. She felt her head spinning, and a quick nausea in her stomach. "Blackie, what are you saying?"

"I have no desire to marry you, Tamara, and, according to the laws of this state, I couldn't marry you if I wished."

"But . . . but we are engaged!" Tamara said. "Blackie, don't you remember the night before you left for St. Louis? You asked my father for my hand in marriage, and he said yes. He even made you the executor of his will."

"I remember," Blackie said flatly. "And I am grateful to him for that, for in the same act he made me the ultimate heir, should you be unable to inherit Calvert Hills. By a codicil of the will, Calvert Hills now belongs to me, land and chattel. And, as you are part of the chattel, you too belong to me."

Tamara couldn't believe her ears.

"What do you mean, I'm part of the chattel?" she demanded.

Blackie removed an envelope from the inside pocket of the gray-and-gold Confederate officer's tunic he was wearing, pulled a paper from the envelope and began reading.

"I, Amon Calvert, do hereby attest and affirm that the following property, herein listed as collateral for a loan . . . and so on and so forth," Blackie said. "Ah, here's the interesting part. Calvert Hills, located north of Natchez where the Mississippi River makes the first large bend to the west, said land to encompass all ground within such bend. In addition to the land there is the main house, stable and outbuildings, a row of ten slaves' shacks, twenty mules, and sixty-five slaves, as of this date, this date being August 10th 1861. The slaves are here below listed by name: Tamara Calvert, my issue by the slave Tricia, now deceased, Alva Morris, housemaid, Troy Parnell, overseer," Blackie looked up at Tamara. "Do I need to go on?"

"I don't understand," Tamara said in a weak voice.

"There's nothing to understand," Blackie said. "Your father was strapped for money, so he borrowed against what he owned. He had to list all his assets, and he listed you among them. Once he made his crop he paid the money back, but the statement he made was still in the bank vault. You are a nigger, Tamara."

There was a stunned silence from the men in the library, and Tamara stood there for a moment, trying to regain her breath. Once, as a child, she had fallen from a tree and lay on the ground for several seconds, unable to breathe. She felt the same way now.

"Isn't that true, Alva?" Blackie called out.

Tamara turned to see that Alva had been hiding behind the door. Now she stepped out into plain view, with tears burning her eyes. "Mr. Amon done give Tricia his word that this girl don't never find out."

"Well, Mr. Amon is dead, and so is Tricia," Blackie said. "And since Tamara is a nigger, and a slave, she can't inherit this plantation. That makes it mine, and I have no obligation to honor any promise made by Amon Calvert. Besides, it serves him right for trying to marry me off to his nigger whelp."

"Alva, is this true?" Tamara asked in a small voice.

Alva hung her head in sorrow. "It's true, girl. I'm sorry," she said. "The Lawd knows I'se tried to pertect your secret."

Alva turned slowly and started to leave.

"No, Alva, wait, please," Tamara said.

Alva stopped. "I know you hates me now, child, for deceivin' you all these years."

"Hate you? How could I hate you?" Tamara asked. "I love you, Alva, and I always have. Now, more than ever." Tamara ran to Alva and threw her arms around her neck.

"So, gentlemen, we'll leave the two nigger women to themselves, and get down to business. As I said, the niggers here will not be freed, and any future dealings with Calvert Hills will come through its new owner . . . me."

"Congratulations," Colonel Putnam said, smiling broadly and offering his hand to Blackie. The others joined in offering congratulations. Tamara and Alva walked back into the kitchen.

"Sit there, child," Alva said, pointing to a chair near the table. "I'll fix you some coffee and tell you a story."

11

Tamara was stunned by the news that she was herself a slave and not the white mistress of Calvert Hills. In the library, the voices of the men could still be heard, though now their conversation was spiced with ribald laughter. She heard a few shocked comments from the women who sat in the parlor, and though she may have imagined it, she thought she could feel the women slipping quietly in ones and twos down the hall to peek into the kitchen, to stare at her and reassure themselves that her skin hadn't suddenly turned coal black.

Troy came into the kitchen and poured himself a cup of coffee, then settled into a chair quietly, as Alva comforted Tamara.

"Alva, all I remember about mama was that she was so very pretty," Tamara said. "And her skin was as white as mine. I had no idea she was not white."

"Your mama was the smartest and the prettiest woman who ever drew a breath in her body," Alva said. She picked up a brush and began to stroke Tamara's hair. Tamara had very long hair, which was almost blue-black. It had been the pride of her father, and Alva spent many hours brushing it so that it would shine.

"Where did mama come from, Alva?"

"I was with your mama at a fashionable house for ladies in N'Orleans," Alva said. "Your mama was so beautiful that folks would come from miles around just to see her."

As Alva talked, Tamara closed her eyes to listen. The soothing tone of Alva's voice and the relaxing feeling of the brush allowed her to drift off, and she could almost see the fashionable house for ladies, where Alva and her mother lived. Troy picked up the story in those places where he could add his account:

The river packet *Isabelle Queen* had pulled into the slip at New Orleans amidst the ringing of bells and occasional stomach-shaking blasts from the deep whistle.

"Captain Reynolds," Amon said as he approached the wheelhouse. "I would like to thank you for the hospitality you have shown me during this voyage. It has been most pleasant."

"Mr. Calvert, I'm mighty proud to offer you any comforts that this old boat has. You are one of my best customers, and many's the time your cotton's been the only paying freight," Captain Reynolds answered.

"Come on, Troy," Amon said to the big man with him. Troy was handsome, tall, and vigorous. A light-skinned, half-caste Negro, he was actually Amon Calvert's half-brother, sired by Amon's father out of a pure Ibo named Harau. Troy had been a childhood companion to Amon, and had grown up to be his personal servant, accompanying him wherever he went.

Although Troy and Amon knew they were related, they never mentioned it. In fact, whereas Amon often spoke of his "father," Troy spoke of the man always as "Masta Jesse."

Troy picked up the baggage and followed Amon down Canal Street until they reached the hotel where they would stay. Amon had a room, to be shared by Troy, though Troy would have to sleep on a pallet on the floor.

"Mr. Amon, where do you know this fella we are goin' to meet from? What's his name? Cap'n Mason?"

"Captain Tom Mason," Amon answered. "He was a classmate of mine at the College of William and Mary. You remember that time that I was gone up to Virginia to go to school?"

"Yes, suh, I 'members," Troy answered. "You was gone a long time."

"Captain Mason was there at the same time, and he is from New Orleans. He wrote me a letter last month, telling me about a plan for shipping cotton direct to England on his own ship. In fact, he wants to sell me half of it."

"Can't you just put your cotton on the boats what stops at Calvert Hills?"

"No," Amon laughed. "Those are just riverboats. They can't go in the ocean. Captain Mason has a large ship that can sail right across the ocean. A big ship like the one your mama come over on."

"For the Lawd's sake, Mr. Amon, you ain't gonna make Troy ride on that thing, are you?" Troy asked, fearfully. Troy's only knowledge of sailing vessels had been garnered from his mother. She had told him of the journey she had made in a slaver's brig.

"Don't worry, Troy. This ship is strictly for cotton. No niggers on it, except maybe some of the crew."

Captain Mason met with Amon and they spent the next few hours discussing the business arrangements and methods of profit-sharing. Finally, after coming to a mutual agreement, they decided to "do the town".

"Amon, there's a place down here that you have got to see. It's the finest sportin' house in N'Orleans, and that makes it about the finest in the world—and I oughta know," Captain Mason said with a wink. "I've been in whorehouses from Frankfurt to Hong Kong, and this one tops them all."

Amon had never been in a whorehouse. He

had never even been away from Calvert Hills, except for the time he was away in school. Williamsburg, Virginia didn't have anything in the way of a sporting house, so he was inexperienced. Oh, he had the run of wenches on his and most neighboring plantations. But this was to be a new experience for him.

"Welcome, Captain Mason. Welcome to Harmony House," a woman said as she greeted the two men.

"Good evening, Mrs. Drew. This is my friend from Natchez, Mississippi, Mr. Amon Calvert, Esquire."

"*Enchanté,* Mr. Calvert. Welcome," Mrs. Drew said, extending her hand.

"*Merci beaucoup, madame,*" Amon answered. He took her hand and kissed it.

"Oh, Captain Mason, your friend is so gallant and charming," Mrs. Drew cooed.

"He wasn't like me, Mrs. Drew. He paid attention to his studies. He was a whiz at college. He never even played hooky with me to go to Norfolk—not even once."

"Will your pleasure be the same tonight, captain?" Mrs. Drew asked.

"Yes, ma'am. I would like to see Fifi, if you please."

"Yes, of course. Go into the Parisian Room. She will be with you shortly. And you, Mr. Calvert. How does your taste run?"

Amon stood there stupidly for a few moments.

He was a little embarrassed and didn't know quite what to say or do.

"You're gonna have to excuse my friend. He's never been to one of these places before. Send him the nicest girl you've got."

"Very well, Mr. Calvert, I understand," Mrs. Drew said with a pleasant smile. "You just wait in the Rose Room. Someone will be in shortly."

Amon walked down the carpeted hallway until he got to the Rose Room. He was alone because Harmony House made provisions for entertainment for the body servants of the gentlemen callers, and Troy was, at this moment, with a girl provided just for that purpose.

"Are you Mr. Amon, suh?" a tall, light-skinned and very pretty Negro girl asked.

"Yes, yes, I am."

"Go right on in, suh. It'll just be another moment."

"Are you the one?"

"Lawd, no, suh! I'se Alva, Miss Tricia's lady-in-waitin'."

Amon eagerly began to look forward to his encounter. If the lady-in-waiting was this pretty, then the lady must be beautiful.

She was. She moved through the door and into the room an effortless glide. Her skin was alabaster, and her eyes were a cool deep, deep green.

"Mister Calvert, my name is Tricia Cote. I've

been selected as your companion, and may I say that it is an honor, sir?"

Tricia's voice fell on Amon's ears like the tinkling of wind chimes stirred by the breeze. He was thunderstruck. Never in his life had he seen anyone so beautiful, or heard a voice so soft. He fell instantly in love.

Tricia walked over to the bed and stood quietly beside it, while Alva turned down the covers. She turned her back to Amon, and Alva began undressing her.

Amon watched, spellbound, as the girl's shoulders, then the smooth expanse of skin on her back, and finally the delightfully formed buttocks were exposed. Within moments, Tricia stood nude, though Amon had not yet seen any more than her back.

Amon felt like a field hand; he felt rude, uncouth, clumsy. He knew that the girl he was watching was a prostitute, a common whore. No—not a common whore, an uncommon whore! He should feel superior. He was wealthy, educated, and born of one of the finest families in Mississippi, yet in the presence of this beautiful girl, he felt like the lowest field hand on his plantation.

The girl nodded at Alva, and Alva held the sheet so that she could slip modestly into bed. Never, during the entire episode, had she presented any view to Amon that was immodest or ill-chosen.

"Mr. Calvert," Tricia said softly. "If you will pull out the top drawer of that dresser, you will find a robe. Please step into the dressing room and remove your clothes."

Amon wanted to answer, but his tongue grew thick, and his mouth was dry. He took the robe and left without a word.

Amon spent the night with Tricia. Their love-making was not the frenzied wild thrusting that Amon had experienced with the wenches in the quarters. It was tender and sensitive, yet a passionate and complete affair. Amon would have given his life for her by the next morning.

Alva was able to relate the story, because she had spent the night with them in the same room, napping in the chair, always present for her mistress's beck and call. With the coming of dawn's light, Alva began the morning ministrations for her lady.

"Well, Amon," Captain Mason laughed, when they met the next morning. "What did I tell you? Is this a nice place?"

"It's very nice, captain. I enjoyed myself," Amon answered. He kept looking in the back, hoping for another glimpse of Tricia. "I must see Mrs. Drew."

"Not on your life, sir," Captain Mason said. "You were my guest, and I will pay for the services."

"No, you don't understand. I want to inquire about the lady I was with last night."

"You were taken with her, were you? Well, I don't blame you. These women are the highest-class whores in the world. They are all quadroons—only one-fourth nigger. Just enough nigger blood to sex 'em up, but the rest is white, to make 'em ladies."

"You mean she was a Negro girl?"

"The law says one sixteenth is enough to make you a nigger," Mason answered. "I know she is in bondage, and can be bought. The price is awfully high, though. Probably a lot higher'n you'd be willin' to pay."

Amon was struck dumb by the revelation. He had no idea that Tricia was legally a Negro. And he had thought he was in love with her. "I guess you're right, captain. Maybe we'd better go," Amon answered.

But Amon couldn't stay away. Later that same day, he returned to Harmony House, this time without Captain Mason. He was greeted at the door by Mrs. Drew.

"Bonsoir, je suis heureuse de vous voir encore."

"Mon plaisir," Amon answered. "I am happy to see you again too."

"Mr. Calvert, what a gentleman you are!" Mrs. Drew said, beaming. "Now, what can I do for you this evening?"

"I'd like to see Miss Cote, please."

"Oh, dear me. I'm terribly sorry. I'm afraid that Miss Cote is occupied at the moment.

Your French is superb, however. Perhaps Fifi?"

"No. Only Miss Cote."

"I'm terribly sorry, really I am," Mrs. Drew replied.

Amon turned to leave, but as he reached the door he looked back at Mrs. Drew.

"Mrs. Drew, do you own this place?"

"Yes, I do. Is there something I can do for you?"

"I want to buy Miss Cote."

"I beg your pardon?"

"I was led to believe that I could—uh—buy any of your girls if the price were right. I want to buy Miss Cote, and you can name your own price."

"Oh, Mr. Calvert, there is much more than the price. If I were to sell Miss Cote, or any of my girls, I would have to know beyond the shadow of a doubt that they would never, never under any circumstances, be mistreated. And you may have noticed that Tricia has a maid-servant, Alva. She would never go anywhere without Alva."

"Your price, Mrs. Drew. I won't haggle."

"Eight thousand dollars for Miss Cote, and two thousand for Alva. Ten thousand dollars total."

Amon opened his jacket pocket and pulled out a bank draft. "Have someone take this draft to the bank. I'll make it out to you for eleven thousand dollars. I want Miss Cote, and Alva, and I want both women to have complete wardrobes. I intend to take Miss Cote with me tonight."

"But the gentlemen who is with her will be offended. He paid one hundred dollars in good faith," Mrs. Drew said.

Amon opened his billfold and took out two hundred dollars in cash. "Give him one hundred dollars in cash, and offer him his choice of any other girl."

"You are most generous," Mrs. Drew answered.

Amon sat on the big overstuffed sofa in the lobby of Harmony House for perhaps fifteen minutes. He picked up a copy of *Harper's Weekly*, and was thumbing through it when he heard his name called.

Again, the tinkling of a breeze through wind chimes.

"Mr. Calvert?"

Amon stood quickly and looked over at her. "You may call me Amon," he said.

"I will be happy to belong to you, Amon," she said, smiling.

"And she was happy," Alva said, as she completed brushing Tamara's hair. "She was happy right up 'till the day she die. Your papa never told a soul that Tricia wasn't a white girl, 'n wasn't his wife."

"You mean papa and mama never were married?" Tamara asked.

"No'm, they wasn't," Alva said. "But they loved each other, same as if they was married. When the big sickness come in 1853, it killed hundreds of folks here 'bouts, both black and white. And your mama, child, was one of the first to go. Now, your papa is buried out there right beside her, and they'll lie together in the hereafter, just like they did in this life, with no nevermind that one was white and one was black."

Colonel Putnam stepped into the kitchen at that moment, and Alva and Troy both grew quiet and reserved. Tamara had noticed this subtle but ever present reaction of blacks to the presence of whites before. But now, for the first time, she understood, and realized with sudden insight, that *she had reacted just as Alva and Troy had.*

"Tamara," Putnam said, looking at her with that strange, almost frightening expression she had seen in his eyes earlier. "Under the circumstances, Colonel Beauregard felt it would be best if you didn't stay at Calvert Hills. Therefore, he offered you for sale, and I have bought you. Get some of your things together. I'll be taking you home with me."

Tamara stood woodenly and walked up the stairs to her bedroom. She took a suitcase from the trunk and began packing her clothes, moving mechanically, still too numbed by all that was happening to show any reaction.

The door opened and closed.

"Alva, would you help me . . ."

"It's me," Putnam said.

"Colonel, you've no right to come into a young lady's room without knocking," Tamara said.

Putnam smiled, an evil smile, and now Tamara recognized the expression in his eyes for what it was. It was lust. She realized that he wanted her, and she was frightened by the realization.

"You are no longer a young lady," Putnam said. "You are a slave girl. My slave girl, Tamara, and I can do anything with you I wish."

"What?" Tamara asked, putting her hand up to her mouth. She stepped back, her fear growing to panic.

Colonel Putnam slipped his tunic off, then began unbuckling his belt. "Don't be frightened, Tamara," he said. "This is something all the nigger girls have to go through. Especially the pretty ones."

"What are you doing?" Tamara said angrily. "Get away from me!"

Putnam reached out to grab Tamara, but she jumped back. His hand caught the front of her dress, and he ripped it down the middle, opening it up and revealing her small but perfect breasts. The nipples, reacting to the sudden exposure of air, tightened into tiny rosebuds.

"Look at that," Putnam said. His eyes grew glassy, and he opened his trousers, exposing himself to her. He reached out again and grabbed her, and threw her on the bed. She tried to fight against him, but he was too strong for her, and she was unable to ward him off.

Putnam made no effort to remove her dress. He just tore it from her, ripping it all the way down the front, then laying it open, so that she presented him with her naked body. She tried to hold her legs together, but the effort was futile, and he loomed over her, looking like an apparition from hell.

When she felt his full weight on her, Tamara wanted to scream, but knew to do so would be useless. He entered her brutally, and she felt a searing, shameful pain. It was so acute that she cried out with the agony of it, and wondered how such a thing could happen to her in her own home. That it occurred in her very bed was the final degradation.

Finally Putnam let a grunt escape from his lips, and shuddered once as he finished. He withdrew from her then, and turning his back to her, began dressing quietly.

As Tamara lay on her bed, used, degraded, and injured, she saw a pair of scissors on the bedside table. When she looked up, Putnam was still standing with his back to her, now pulling on his pants. He was talking to her.

"I know you didn't like it much that time,"

Putnam said. "It's always painful the first time. But you'll get used to it like all the others, I reckon, and then . . ."

Putnam never finished his sentence, for Tamara brought the scissors down right in the side of his neck. The scissors severed an artery, and a thick, gushing spurt of blood squirted out. Putnam turned to face her with a look of surprise on his face. He made one or two futile efforts to withdraw the scissors. That failed, and he collapsed to the floor. He lay there, jerking convulsively, until he died, never uttering another sound.

Alva stepped into the room a few moments later and saw at once what happened. She gasped quietly, but she didn't scream.

"Tamara, get dressed and get out of here quick," she said. "You mustn't be here when the white folks find out."

"Alva, I . . . I had no choice," Tamara said. "He *raped* me."

"No'm, honey, he didn't rape you. Nigger men rapes white women, but white men pleasures nigger women. Leastwise, that's the way they'll tell it, and you'll hang, girl, sure as Nat Turner. You've got to get out of here."

"But where will I go?" Tamara asked.

"Go north, honey. Go north."

12

North of Calvert Hills, but still in the state of Mississippi, was Trailback Plantation, owned and farmed by Mr. A.G. Welles. Mr. Welles' real name was Alexander Grace Welles, but he hated the name Alexander and refused to be called Alex. Grace was his mother's maiden name and, as she was an only child and her father, Charles Grace, had wanted to see the family name carried on, it had been tacked on to Mr. Welles as a middle name. Grace was, of course, too feminine to be used, so Alexander Grace Welles had simply been called A.G. from the time he was old enough to express a preference.

A.G. was sixty years old. His crisp curly hair was silver-white, but his face was unlined, his eyes were sparkling and young, and he wore proudly the uniform of a colonel in the Mississippi militia. He was wearing it now, as he waited at the depot to meet the night train.

Meeting any train was exciting, but night

trains were even more so. There was always a carnival atmosphere about the crowd: laughter, good-natured joking, the constant cry of drummers hawking their wares and, since the war had begun, music from a military band. For Colonel A.G. Welles, though, meeting this particular train would be even more exciting, because it would be bringing his daughter, Liberty, back home to Trailback Plantation.

"Here she comes!" someone yelled, and the band struck up a brisk, military aire.

The train pounded into the station, its great driver wheels flashing by in a blur, while glowing embers tumbled from the firebox and wisps of steam vented from the cylinders. Finally, the train ground to a stop, and through the windows and into the yellowed interiors of the cars, A.G. could see the passengers starting for the doors to disembark at the Corinth station.

"Father, hello!" Liberty called, stepping down onto the platform.

"Daughter!" A.G. replied, running to her with the enthusiasm of a man much younger in years. Liberty had been a late blessing, born when A.G. was already forty and had given up on children. She was an only child, and the absolute apple of her father's eye. And now, she was even more important to him, for she had grown to be a woman who was the exact image of her mother, now dead these many years. To look upon his daughter was a bittersweet experience for A.G., for in her he saw his wife again.

"Father, what is that uniform?" Liberty asked when she saw how her father was attired.

"Do you like it? I am the commanding officer of the Welles' Home Guards. I raised my own regiment, daughter, equipped them, furnished uniforms, horses, everything."

"Good Lord, that must have cost a fortune!" Liberty said.

"I don't mind telling you, daughter, it was no small amount," Welles admitted. "But it is for the Confederacy."

"It is no such thing," Liberty scolded. "It is so you can play soldier and be a colonel."

A.G. Welles looked crestfallen and embarrassed at being subjected to Liberty's perceptive insight. Liberty, not wishing to hurt his feelings, eased the moment by laughing warmly. "Father, if this is something you feel you must do, you'll hear no guff from me. But you must promise me that you won't volunteer your regiment for field duty."

"We are a home guard regiment," Welles said. "If our very homes are threatened, then I shall fight to the last breath in my body."

"I hope such an occasion never presents itself," Liberty said.

There had been a young man hovering near Liberty for the duration of their conversation, and A.G. finally noticed him. "Why is that man staring at us?" he asked.

"Father, I'd like to introduce Burke O'Lee. He saw me safely out of St. Louis, and will be returning to Missouri tomorrow to join with General Jeff Thompson's army."

"Have you been fighting with Thompson?" A.G. asked.

"No, sir," Burke said, now stepping up to join them, having been invited to. "I have been with Quantrill."

"With Quantrill, you say? Well, now, I guess you've seen some action then, haven't you?" A.G. said, obviously impressed.

"Not the type I wanted to see," Burke replied. "Colonel Welles, Quantrill is nothing but a common criminal, using the Confederacy as a cover. I have no pride in my association with him."

"Acts of war can sometimes be cruel, son. Perhaps you shouldn't be so quick to judge."

"I make the judgment against myself," Burke said. "For I have been as guilty as the rest. But I hope with Jeff Thompson to participate in a way which will have more relevancy to the southern cause."

"Father, is General Beauregard still in Corinth?"

"Yes," A.G. said.

"I must speak to him."

"I'll invite him over tonight," A.G. said. "He

has been a frequent house guest. I'm sure he will come."

"Good."

"And you, Burke. Will you stay with us tonight? I'm sure we can offer much more comfortable arrangements than would the hotel."

"I'd be happy to," Burke said. "If it won't be any trouble."

"It won't be any trouble at all," A.G. said. "Liberty, take the carriage. I shall invite Beauregard and ride out with him when he comes."

"Impress upon him that it is important," Liberty said.

"I shall, daughter, I shall," A.G. promised. "You take your young man on home now."

Liberty kissed her father again, then, as a porter appeared with her bags, she pointed to the carriage. After the bags were loaded, she climbed onto the seat, handed the reins to Burke, and showed him which way to go.

Burke was quiet for several moments, concentrating more than necessary on driving, speaking only when they were well on the road to Trailback.

"Am I?" he asked.

"Are you what?" Liberty asked, puzzled by the odd statement.

"Your father said take your young man on home now. Am I your young man?"

"Well, you are here with me, aren't you?"

"But you aren't with me."

"Of course I'm with you. What are you talking about?"

"You aren't really with me, Liberty. You're thinking about something else. You're thinking about *somebody* else."

"Suppose I am?" she said. "It's just that I can't get over how badly Dan must be hurt."

"What about me? Have you no sympathy for my feelings?"

"Burke, I haven't hurt you. Besides, I haven't forgotten that comment you made about sharing me with everyone. How could you say such a thing? That made it sound as if I'd been an easy mark for anyone to sleep with . . . and I've never slept with anyone but you."

"And Dan," Burke said.

Liberty was silent for a long time.

"You did sleep with Dan," Burke said again. "Didn't you?"

"Yes," Liberty said quietly.

"And you say you've never hurt me."

"You've been chaste, I suppose?" Liberty replied hotly.

"No, of course I haven't. But it's different with a man."

"How well I know," Liberty said. "Though I hope the time will one day come when men and women are equal."

Burke laughed. "That day will never come."

They were quiet for several minutes more, then Liberty spoke again. "I'm sorry I hurt you,

Burke," she said quietly. "I didn't want to hurt anyone . . . and it seems I've hurt everyone."

General Pierre Gustave Toutant Beauregard, known as the Great Creole, was a dashing and argumentative figure who already, in the short war, had clashed with Jefferson Davis. But he was the hero of Bull Run, and had been in charge of the southern troops which had fired on Fort Sumner, so he was highly regarded throughout the South, despite his difficulty with the President of the Confederacy.

Beauregard arrived with A.G. Welles and listened attentively as Liberty related the conversation which had taken place at General Halleck's dinner.

"I believe you are correct," Beauregard said. "He intends to strike at Humboldt, or Corinth. At any rate, it will be somewhere in this area."

"General, I can have the home guards out in a moment's notice," A.G. offered hopefully.

Liberty looked at her father sharply, but was relieved to hear that Beauregard had other plans.

"I thank you for your offer, colonel," Beauregard said. "But I fear your home guards won't be up to the task. In fact, my entire army is insufficient to defend the junctions, without reinforcement." He smiled. "But we have been anticipating just such a move somewhere. We just had no idea where the major push would come. Miss Welles, I thank you very much for your information. I shall contact General Johnston immediately. This is just the break we've been looking for. And you, young man, I appreciate your contribution as well. Will you be joining us here?" he asked Burke.

"No, general," Burke replied. "I'm going over to join General Thompson tomorrow."

"Ah, yes, the Swamp Fox. Give him my regards, and inform him of my appreciation for his job in holding New Madrid. I have overall command of the Mississippi River, you know, and right now, Island Number Ten is one of the most important points in the entire Confederacy. As long as we hold it, we are keeping the front door shut and locked, so to speak."

"Then we shall hold it forever," Burke said.

"Let us pray that we do. And now, Miss Welles, colonel, Mr. O'Lee, if you will excuse me, I must return to camp. Due to the information you have brought us, I have much work to do."

Colonel Welles escorted the general to his horse, then returned to spend the rest of the evening in conversation with Liberty and Burke. They talked long into the night, and only when Burke began yawning openly did A.G. realize how late it was.

"You must forgive me," he said. "You have to

leave early to catch the return train tomorrow, and here I've kept you up. Liberty, show the young man his room." A.G. yawned, then smiled. "I guess I'm sleepy too," he said.

A.G. kissed Liberty goodnight, then went off to his own room. Liberty led Burke up the stairs, then down the hall to the room which would be his.

"I can get you a few extra pillows if you'd like," she said, after turning down the covers to his bed.

"It's not pillows I want," Burke said. "It's you." He reached for her, but Liberty turned, ostensibly to fluff the bed, but in reality to avoid his embrace.

"I thought you were sleepy," she said.

"I just let on that I was sleepy, in order to get an excuse to come to bed." He reached again, and this time Liberty didn't try to avoid him. But she didn't help him either. After a brief kiss, Burke let her go, then stepped back and looked at her. "What's wrong?" he asked.

"Nothing," Liberty said. "I suppose I'm just tired. It's been a long trip."

"Yes, it has," Burke admitted. "I'm sorry. Of course you're tired. I'm tired myself." He leaned forward and kissed her lightly. "You go on to bed. I'll see you in the morning."

"Goodnight," Liberty said, returning his kiss.

* * *

Too many things were on Liberty's mind. Though she was very tired, she was unable to sleep. She tossed and turned, fluffed up her pillows, smoothed her covers, and nothing helped. Finally, after laying in bed for nearly an hour, she got up and walked over to the window and pulled the curtain to look outside.

Under the full moon, the well-kept lawn was very bright, and a large magnolia tree, its leaves shining like silver ingots, kept the same patient vigil over the house that it had since long before Liberty was born.

Liberty slipped into a robe and decided to take a walk, thinking that perhaps the fresh night air would help her to sleep.

The stars were incredibly bright. Some of them seemed to be hung so low that she could reach up and grab them. Even the black of the night sky itself was dusted with so many tiny stars that it looked as if a star-blue powder had been spread through the heavens.

"I saw you from my window," Burke's voice suddenly said, and Liberty turned with a start. Burke laughed softly. "I'm sorry, I didn't mean to frighten you."

"It's all right," Liberty said. "I was just lost in my own thoughts and didn't hear you."

Burke looked up at the sky, then out across the gently rolling fields. "It's so quiet out here," he said. "It's hard to even imagine there is a war on somewhere."

"The war is coming here," Liberty said.

"Yes, I know."

They were silent for a moment longer, then Burke started to ask a question. But even as he drew the breath for his comment, Liberty interrupted him.

"Don't ask, Burke. Please don't ask."

"Don't ask what?"

Liberty looked at him, and her eyes were brimming with tears. "You *know* what you were going to ask. If I was in love with Dan."

"I have to ask," Burke said. "Can't you see that?"

"Oh, I am, Burke. What am I going to do?" Liberty asked. She began crying and Burke took her in his arms. He held her close to him and she cried against his chest, letting the tears of despair flow freely, undammed at last.

"There, now," Burke said, stroking her hair gently. "There, you go ahead and cry. Let it all out. It'll do you good."

Liberty cried until she could cry no more. Then, when the tears would no longer come, she just leaned her head against Burke's chest and let him hold her. After a moment, Burke put his finger under her chin and gently turned her face up toward him. He kissed her, and she put her arms around his neck and pressed her body tightly against him. Burke began to fumble with the tie of her robe.

"No," Liberty suddenly said. She pulled back

away from him and looked into his face, her eyes pleading with him.

"Liberty," Burke said. "I just . . ."

The tears were flowing freely down Liberty's face again. "No, Burke, please don't."

"All right," Burke said quietly.

Liberty took his hands in hers. "I'm sorry."

"I understand," Burke said.

"Do you? Do you really understand? Because, God help me, Burke, I don't understand at all."

Burke smiled, the same, boyish smile which had so endeared him to her. "Liberty, believe me, I know what it's like to love someone with your heart, and not with your head. My head has always told me that the day would come when you would tell me you were in love with someone else, but my heart wouldn't listen." He laughed. "I just never thought it would be my brother, that's all."

"Forgive me, Burke."

"Oh, I forgive you, Liberty girl," Burke said easily. "And, whether you believe me or not, I hope it works out for you."

Liberty smiled at him through her tears. "It can't possibly work out," she said. "But you're sweet for wishing so."

13

Article appearing in a St. Louis newspaper:

The streets of this city are full
of passing troops. Until the last
two or three weeks, the impression has prevailed that the forces
of this department were all in
the field, but day by day one
column arrives and another de-
parts, until the reserve seems to
be inexhaustable. And still they
come. Of the numbers and direction, we may not speak. Stalwart
thousands march through our
streets; and one thinks each regiment must be the last, but tomorrow brings another. The phy-
sique of the men in the newly
arrived regiments is remarkable.
One new member of these regiments is Second Lieutenant Dan

O'Lee, most recently noted for his bravery in thwarting an attempt by Rebel spies to destroy the *Delta Star,* and the valuable arms and powder she was carrying. Lieutenant O'Lee has been assigned to General Halleck's staff.

Dan folded the newspaper and lay it aside, then looked up at the others in the lobby of the Boatman Hotel. As usual, the lobby was exceptionally busy, and as usual, the majority of the men wore uniforms. Now Dan had become one of them, wearing the dark blue and gold uniform of an Army lieutenant. Because of his mining background, he had been commissioned in the Engineers, and he wore the Engineers' castle emblem on his collar. As second lieutenants did not wear any insignia of rank, there was only the cut of the uniform and the castle to identify him as an officer.

All around Dan, conversations were going on about the war. They spoke of the war in the east, the war in the west, and the war in Missouri. It seemed clear to everyone that a battle was shaping up further south, for control of the river. Ideas and plans curled and seeped through the group as very senior officers advanced their pet theories as how best to accomplish the upcoming mission. Dan smiled to himself. There would be little risk involved, he decided, for a Rebel spy to just sit in the lobby and listen to the conversation.

But then, there was such confusion as one plan seemed to supercede another that Dan decided that confusion was itself the best security against unwanted information leaks to the Confederacy.

A carriage pulled to a stop at the curb in front of the hotel. Dan, sitting next to the window, looked out and saw a woman sitting in the shadows of the back seat. He watched as she passed money across to the driver. When she stepped out of the carriage, Dan recognized her as Verity Eternal.

Dan watched as she approached the entrance. He guessed her age as around twenty-five. She had high cheekbones, not prominent but well accented. Even at this distance, Dan could see that her eyes sparkled like set jewels, and were framed by eyebrows as beautiful as the most delicate lace. Her movements, as she walked toward the hotel entrance, were as graceful as a willow in a breeze, and Dan was struck again by her beauty, moved by it as greatly as he had been the first time he had seen her.

Dan found himself standing up and moving toward the front door to meet her as she entered.

"Miss Eternal, it is a pleasure to see you again," he said, offering his hand.

Verity looked at him, puzzled for just a moment, then smiled broadly. "You are Mr. O'Lee, aren't you? Liberty's friend. Only I see you are a lieutenant now."

"Yes," Dan said, flattered that she remembered him. "But I'm not exactly a friend of Liberty Welles."

A shadow came across Verity's eyes. "Yes, I heard what happened with her. I'm terribly sorry. I'm sorry for Liberty, but I'm especially sorry for the cause of abolition. She was a powerful force for good here."

"A force for good?" Dan asked, as if unable to believe what he had heard. "Miss Eternal, didn't you hear that Liberty Welles is a spy? She is a southern sympathizer."

"Well, she is, after all, from Mississippi," Verity said, being charitable in her appraisal of Liberty.

"Then how can you say she was doing good?"

"Oh, but she was, Mr. O'Lee," Verity insisted. "The fact that she was a southerner . . . even the fact that she has now, evidently, gone back south to help the confederacy, doesn't mean that she meant the movement any harm. Liberty Welles was, and is, an abolitionist, as dedicated to the cause of freedom for all slaves as I am."

Dan laughed, a short, disbelieving laugh. "I must say, I admire your loyalty," he said. "I am unable to remain so loyal to people who fail me."

"That's just it, Mr. O'Lee," Verity said. "Liberty hasn't failed me. But, what are you doing here, in this hotel?" she asked, changing the subject.

"I live here," Dan said.

"Oh? I would have thought you would have to live in a barracks somewhere."

"Not yet. Quarters have grown scarce in the city. Besides, as a member of General Halleck's staff, I can pretty much live where I please. Do you live here as well?"

Verity laughed, and the laughter fell from her lips like the musical trill of a bubbling brook. "No, Mr. O'Lee, I don't live here," she said. "I am here to make arrangements for a talk I shall be giving later. I can come to such places as this to give a speech, but I must choose another place to live."

"Oh," Dan said, awkwardly. "I'm sorry." He laughed self-consciously. "I guess that eliminates my next question as well."

"And what would have that next question have been?"

Dan cleared his throat. "I was going to invite you to dinner," he said. "Again."

Verity laughed again. "You seem determined to take me to dinner, Mr. O'Lee," she said.

"I can't help it. I find you a fascinating woman, and I would like to get to know you better."

"Then I have a proposal. Since it is not possible for me to go to dinner with you . . . how would you like to come to dinner with me?"

"What? Are you serious?" Dan asked. "Yes . . . I'd love it. But . . . how, I mean, where could we go?"

Verity opened her purse and removed a card. "Be at this address tonight at eight," she invited. "You won't disappoint me now?"

"Disappoint you? No, what are you talking about? Of course, I'll be there. I'll be there at eight . . . sharp."

"Good," Verity said. "Now, I must see the gentleman at the desk, and explain my presence to him. Already, he is beginning to wonder why a Negro woman has come into the lobby."

"Well, you just let me . . ." Dan started.

"No, Dan, please," Verity said, using Dan's first name for the first time. She put her hand on his arm, and though her fingers felt amazingly cool, they seemed to generate a heat within him. "I'm used to this sort of thing," she said. "I'll handle it."

"Very well, if you insist," Dan said, wondering how she could generate such heat with such cool fingers. "I'll see you at eight tonight, then."

"You've got three blocks to go yet, before you reach that address," the hack driver said, stopping his carriage.

"Then why are you stopping here?" Dan asked.

"Look down that street, lieutenant. What do you see?"

"I don't see anything. What are you talking about?"

"I see niggers," the driver said. "Nothin' but freed niggers, and freed niggers is the worst kind. Like as not, most of them ain't free anyhow, they's just runaways."

"What difference does that make?"

The driver spit a chew of tobacco over the rim of the wheel, and pushed the hat back on his head.

"I don't like niggers," he said. "And I ain't gonna drive my hack down a street where that's all there is. Now you pay me what you owe me, and walk the rest of the way. Unless, now that you've seen where you was goin', you've changed your mind, and'll be headin' back."

"I've done no such thing," Dan said. He stepped out of the hack, and handed the driver some money.

"Hey, this isn't the right amount," the driver said, looking at the fare.

"This isn't the right place, either," Dan replied easily. "Take me the rest of the way, and I'll give you the rest of the fare."

The driver looked at the money for a second, then put it in his pocket. "I'll settle for this," he said, flicking the light whip against the horse's hide.

Dan started down the street, and a small, black child started following him.

"Is you Marse Link?" the boy asked.

"I'm Lieutenant O'Lee," Dan replied.

"Marse Link," the boy said again.

The young black boy was joined by another, and then another, and still another, until by the time Dan reached the address given him by Verity, there were dozens of kids, laughing and shouting at him, all calling him "Marse Link."

"Here, you children," Verity said, stepping out to meet Dan and escort him the rest of the way. "Scat. Go home now, you hear me?"

"Marse Link," they called as one. "Marse Link, Marse Link, Marse Link."

"What are they saying?" Dan finally asked.

Verity laughed. "They think you are Abraham Lincoln," she said.

"Oh, Lord, no, I'm not that ugly, am I?" Dan replied, laughing.

"No, but you are a white man in the uniform of Lincoln's army. They don't fully understand, but they know that a war is being fought which may mean the end of slavery. They know that Lincoln is the President, and they just make the natural connection, that's all. Please, come in, Mr. O'Lee."

"You called me Dan earlier," Dan said. "I think I liked that better."

"Then I shall call you Dan," Verity said. She touched him, and again he was amazed by the coolness of her fingers, and the heat her fingers spread.

Inside the small house, Dan saw that Verity had taken great pains to prepare a fine dinner for him. A table was laid with china and silver, and she led him to it.

"It looks beautiful," Dan said.

"Thank you. It isn't exactly the dining room at Antoine's, I'm afraid."

"No, it isn't," Dan replied. "It is much better than that." He held the chair for Verity, then sat across from her. They were served by another black woman, darker and older than Verity.

"Thank you, Mandy," Verity said, as the older woman withdrew. "Mandy came to St. Louis six months ago," she said. "She ran away from her owner in Arkansas. I'm actually violating the law by sheltering her, you know. She is a fugitive slave, and Missouri is a slave-holding state. You won't turn me in, I hope?"

"No, of course not," Dan said.

Verity laughed. "I was teasing. I knew you wouldn't, or I would have never mentioned it to you in the first place."

"Are you a runaway?" Dan asked.

"No. I was free-born, in Memphis, Tennessee. But even though I was free-born, I could not enjoy my freedom. Just seeing so many of my people in bondage . . . that was in itself a sort of bondage. I began agitating for freedom for my people as soon as I could speak, and I've never stopped."

"You are an amazing woman, Verity Eternal," Dan said. "And a beautiful one as well."

Verity looked down in modesty as Dan complimented her, then looked up once, raising her eyelids as though they were exquisite fans. Her eyes shone gold in the candlelight.

"Have I embarrassed you?" Dan asked.

"No," Verity replied. "But . . ."

"But what?"

"I am a Negro," she said.

"What difference does that make?"

"It makes a tremendous difference," Verity said.

Dan reached across the table and took her hand. He held it for a moment, then raised it to his lips and kissed it lightly. At first, she tried to pull her hand away, but Dan held it more firmly and kissed it again. Finally he released her.

"Are you turned away by the fact that I am white?" Dan asked. "Is that the tremendous difference you speak of?"

"No," Verity said. "That's not it at all."

"Then you will not be offended if I call on you again?"

"I would be honored," Verity said. "If you really want to."

"I really want to."

180

Mandy interrupted their conversation with the second course of the meal, and though they spoke of many things that night, exchanging anecdotes of their past, discussing their philosophies of life, they never reopened the subject of their own relationship with each other. But though the words were unspoken, a deeper and more meaningful communication took place between them that night. They exchanged intimate glances, looking at each other with eyes which were windows to their souls. They touched, lightly, lingeringly, over wine and dessert. When Dan left later that evening, he offered a kiss which she accepted. Before either of them could control it, the kiss began to deepen, until finally Verity pulled away with a gasp of breath.

"You'd . . . . . you'd better go now," she said.

"Goodbye," Dan said, making no effort to leave.

"You must go," Verity replied.

"I'm going," Dan said. He kissed her again.

"No," Verity said, but she found that she was speaking into his mouth as his lips closed over her own, and this time as they kissed, she knew that it was too late. There would be no turning back.

Now time and circumstances hung suspended as Dan and Verity came together. They were not principals in one of the world's major conflicts—they were not black and white—they were not representatives of opposing cultures. They were a man and woman, complete within themselves.

Verity took Dan's hand and led him into her bedroom. There she lit a candle, and began removing her clothes for him. Behind her was a window, opening onto the Mississippi River, and in the dark the black water twinkled with reflected light as it flowed, ever, ever southward.

Dan removed his clothes as Verity did, and when both were nude, they went to bed, not in a hot-blooded rush of desperate lovers taking sex from each other, giving nothing in return, but in the tender and passionate way of people who care for each other and are capable of sharing.

When they made love it was rich and fulfilling. It was strongly physical and immensely satisfying, as if their passions were perfectly orchestrated to move in harmony, so that there was a tremendous sense of mutual need and attainment.

Afterward, they both slept.

Dan awoke once in the middle of the night. The moon was shining brightly, sailing high in the velvet sky. It spilled a pool of iridescence through the window and onto the bed. It bathed Verity in a soft, shimmering light.

Verity was asleep, breathing softly. Dan reached over gently and put his hand on her naked hip. He could feel the sharpness of her hip bone and the soft yielding of her flesh. The contrasting textures were delightful to his sense of touch. He let his hand rest there, enjoying a feeling of possession, until finally sleep claimed him once again.

Dan awoke the next morning to the smell of bacon sizzling in the pan. A moment later Verity came in to tell him that breakfast was ready.

"When I accepted your dinner invitation, I had no idea that breakfast would be part of the deal," Dan said, smiling.

"No, but you hoped it would, didn't you?" Verity asked, laughing at her own ribald jest.

"*Touché, madame,*" Dan said, buttering a steaming hot biscuit.

"Dan, there's something that needs to be said," Verity ventured a moment later.

Dan held his hand out, as if to stop her. "Verity, if you're going to bring up the fact that you are a black woman and I am a white man, it is obvious, and doesn't need to be discussed. We will be who we are, and the color line will not come between us."

"It isn't the color line that's between us, Dan O'Lee," Verity said plainly.

"I don't understand. What are you talking about?"

"Liberty Welles," Verity said.

"Liberty Welles?" Dan gave a weak laugh. "Why would you mention that Rebel spy?"

"Why indeed?" Verity said.

"I told you what she did . . . or rather, what she tried to do. As it turned out, she was hoist by her own petard, and I say fair enough."

"Say what you really think," Verity said.

"I don't understand," Dan said.

"Yes, you do," Verity insisted. "You understand perfectly. Dan, do you think a woman can let a man make love to her, and not know that his heart is with another?"

"No, that's not true," Dan said. "I don't love Liberty Welles. I don't."

Verity smiled, a slow, understanding smile. "Keep talking, brother, maybe you'll convince yourself. You certainly won't convince me."

Dan sighed. He lay his biscuit down, then looked at Verity, his face displaying the hopelessness of it all.

"It's true," he finally said. He gave a short, unconvincing laugh. "I don't think I had even admitted it to myself, until this moment. I don't know how it can be true, Verity, but it is. I do love her, even though a love between her and me is as impossible as a love betwen you and me."

"No," Verity said. "Love between you and me is not impossible. It is just forbidden. But forbidden fruit is always sweetest, so we'll take what we can, Dan O'Lee, while we can. And when the time comes for us to part, we shall do so without looking back, and with no regrets."

"You're willing to do that?" Dan asked.

"I *want* to do that," Verity said.

"You are an amazing woman."

"And Liberty Welles is a lucky one," Verity said.

14

The snows of February were blown away by brisk March winds. During the last two weeks of February and the first two weeks of March, Dan spent all his spare time with Verity Eternal. He knew that their love affair was star-crossed and destined to be short-lived, but he determined to make the most of it, for in the words of an old Chinese philosopher he had met in San Francisco: "It is not the time granted a love, but the love granted a time which is important. The flower that buds, blooms and dies in a single day does not differ at heart from a tree that lives a thousand years."

Thus it was, that when General Halleck told Dan that he would be sending him south to Sikeston the next day, Dan was prepared for it. After all, he had already enjoyed more time than he expected.

"What do we know of Sikeston, general?" Dan asked.

"Very little, I'm afraid," General Halleck answered. "It doesn't even show up on most maps, the town was only begun two years ago. It's important to us though, because it sits at the western terminus of the railroad which starts at the river, and there is a good road through the swamp south from Sikeston to New Madrid."

"I see," Dan said, looking at the map General Halleck spread before him.

"I have a man here who does know the town," Halleck said. "I've asked him to brief you."

"How well does he know it?"

Halleck smiled. "About as well as anyone, I reckon. His name is John Sikes, and he started it."

Dan looked up a moment later as a tall, thin man stepped into the room. He had piercing brown eyes, and rather prominent cheekbones, and he extended his hand in a perfunctory, businesslike way when Dan offered his.

"Major Lathrop will be in command of the detachment at Sikeston," General Halleck continued. "It will be his job to supervise the off-loading and assembly of the artillery. Your job will be to secure the road south from Sikeston, protect it against Confederate raiders, and effect such construction as is necessary to allow cannon caissons and wagons to pass across it."

"Would you tell me something about that road, Mr. Sikes?" Dan asked.

"It's part of the old El Camino Real," Sikes said. "King's Highway, we call it now. It's a road that stretches from St. Louis to New Madrid, and though much of it has fallen into disrepair, the stretch from Sikeston to New Madrid is quite good."

"Is it surfaced?"

"Yes, sir," Sikes said. "It is a plank road, made of crossed logs."

"The trouble is, we don't know whether or not the Rebels have torn it up," Dan mused.

"The road was in good repair as of two days ago," Sikes commented. "I rode it myself then."

"As you can see, Lieutenant O'Lee, speed is important," General Halleck said. "You must get down to Sikeston immediately, lest the Rebels decide to cut the road."

"I'll arrange for transportation," Dan said.

"That's already taken care of," General Halleck said. "You'll leave at once aboard the ironclad, *Cairo*. Mr. Sikes will be returning to Sikeston with you."

"General, will I have time to tell someone goodbye?" Dan asked.

General Halleck pulled his watch from his pocket and looked at it. "I'm afraid not, lieutenant," he said. "If you wish, you may write a note and I'll have it delivered."

Dan thought about it for a moment, then decided that it would be better not to send a message to Verity by someone else. It might lead to embarrassing questions being asked of her and he had no wish to complicate her life. They had both realized that the time would come when he would have to leave St. Louis, and he knew that Verity would understand that they had said their goodbyes.

"No, sir, thank you," Dan said. "That won't be necessary." Dan looked at John Sikes. "Are you ready, Mr. Sikes?"

"Quite ready, thank you," Sikes answered. "I am looking forward to returning home."

One hour later, Dan was leaning over the railing looking at one of the huge paddle wheels, now lifeless in the water. He studied a twig as it floated along the waterline of the boat, then got caught in the wheel. John Sikes was standing beside him.

"Has there been much action around Sikeston?" Dan asked, wondering if he was about to see any.

"Well, the actual fighting has been going on down around Island Number Ten," Sikes said. "But we've suffered terribly from the bushwhackers. Raiders ride through the town, terrorizing our citizens, robbing and burning. In truth, lieutenant, more than two thirds of the townspeople have abandoned Sikeston."

"And yet you're staying on?"

"I will as long as I can," Sikes said. "But if this war continues much longer, I fear there will be little to stay for."

The boat sounded its whistle and started reversing the paddle wheel on the left while going forward with the one on the right. The boat turned, then, both paddles slapping at the water together, bubbled up a frothy white wake as it moved majestically into the center of the river before turning downstream.

Though the *Cairo* would ultimately be going into battle as a gunboat—and indeed cannon protruded from both sloping, iron-clad sides—it was now being used as a troop boat. In addition to Dan, there were nearly one hundred other soldiers on board the vessel. They sat, or lay around where they could find space, playing cards, writing letters, talking, or just staring off into space, lost in their own private thoughts.

Facing them was a twenty-four hour trip downriver. Dan sought out a small corner where he could stretch out during the long, cool night. Though he had figured on getting in only a few hours' sleep, when he was awakened by the heavy blast of the ship's whistle, he saw the red smear of an early morning sky through one of the gun-ports. He stood up, stretched, and walked out on a small afterdeck which was unprotected by the iron plate.

He'd no sooner reached the deck when he heard a pinging sound against the plate behind him. He turned, curiously, to see what had made the noise.

"Get down, lieutenant!" a voice called, and

someone ran quickly across the deck, crashing into him and knocking him down, just as a large splinter of wood was torn from the rail near where he had been standing.

This time Dan heard the unmistakable sound of a rifle shot, a flat sound that echoed across the water.

"Raise up ag'in, Yank, 'n give me another potshot at ye," a voice called from the shore. The voice rolled, amazingly clear, across the river, aided by the sound-carrying property of the water.

Dan looked over to see who had saved his life by knocking him down. It was a young, handsome, rather small soldier. He smiled broadly at Dan.

"Sorry I had to bowl you over like that, lieutenant, but there are Rebel sharpshooters all along the river, just waiting for an opportunity like you gave them." The soldier's voice was soft, with an unmistakable southern drawl.

"Don't apologize to me, soldier," Dan said quickly. "I should apologize to you for being such a damn fool as to make you expose yourself to danger in order to save me. And I thank you for it."

"No thanks needed, lieutenant. I was only doing my job. I'm Private Cote. Cal Cote, now of the 24th Missouri, though a Mississippian by birth." Cote stuck out his hand, and Dan shook it, knowing that wasn't protocol for an officer meeting an enlisted man but not caring. This man had saved his life; he couldn't help but be thankful, as well as drawn to his friendly ways.

"Dan O'Lee," Dan said.

"I know who you are," Cote smiled broadly. "Fact is, when I saved you just then, I was saving my own commanding officer. I'm in the company that's been assigned to work on the road leading down to New Madrid."

Dan laughed. "I guess news gets around fast," he said. "I wouldn't be surprised if everyone on the boat knows about me."

"Everyone does know," Cote said. "And you can bet the Rebels know too."

"Then I expect we'll get a welcome from them."

By mid-afternoon of the second day, the boat reached its destination, and most of the soldiers, weary now, were ready for anything, even immediate action, if it meant relief from the cramped voyage. They were mustered into squads by the N.C.O.'s, and now stood around anxiously, as the boat's captain and crew members shouted landing instructions to each other.

The boat was putting ashore at Bird's Point, Missouri, just opposite Cairo, Illinois. The paddle wheels stopped as it glided up to a mooring. There was a small scrape as the boat rubbed against the bottom, then a rush of steam and a frantic beating of paddle wheels as the captain "pegged her to the bank" by running the bow slightly aground.

"Well, hello, John," a Union major greeted Sikes as he and Dan stepped off the boat. "And you must be Lieutenant O'Lee."

"Yes," Dan said. "You are Major Lathrop?"

"Right you are, lieutenant. The artillery pieces are already loaded on the train. I need only you and your men, and we're ready to go."

"They are loading now, sir," Dan replied. He looked over toward the standing box cars and saw the soldiers, Cal Cote among them, climbing on, handing up their long rifles, jostling and joking with each other to take the edge off their nervousness.

"Mr. Sikes, I honestly didn't think you would return after that hanging," Major Lathrop commented.

"Hanging? What hanging?" Dan asked.

John Sikes put his hand to his throat in an unconscious move as Lathrop told the story.

"It happened about two months ago," Lathrop said. "John, and in fact, most of the good citizens of Sikeston, were asleep, when a group of bushwhackers rode into town. They burned a couple of houses, then threatened to burn John's if he didn't come out. When he did, they strung him up to a tree and left him hanging there. They meant to kill him, but a young black girl who knew where John hid his money offered to tell the bushwhackers where it was if they would cut him down. So they did, just in time."

"You mean you would let them hang you, without telling them?" Dan asked.

"I didn't have any choice," Sikes replied grimly. "You can't talk with a rope around your neck."

The whistle on the train sounded a warning.

"Come on, we'd better get," Lathrop said, starting toward the train.

The cattle cars were loaded with soldiers, and the flatcars with equipment. Dan, Major Lathrop and John Sikes climbed into the engine cab as the train got underway, puffing loudly and throwing great pillars of smoke into the sky.

Riding in the cab, Dan kept his face in the wind, trying to overcome the excitement that was brewing inside of him. When he looked back along the string of cars, he could see that the men were all as excited as he. They were cheering and shouting at each other, trying to be heard over the sound of the train.

The train approached a long trestle, which stretched out over swampland, and it roared and clacked out onto it. Suddenly Dan's heart leaped to his mouth, because the opposite end of the trestle exploded and erupted in a sheet of flame!

"Engineer! Back this thing down!" Dan yelled. "The Rebels have the other end . . . it's on fire!"

The engineer threw the lever into reverse and opened the steam valve full. The wheels began reversing, throwing up a shower of sparks that bathed the inside of the cab in a glow of orange.

The sudden stopping of the train threw many of the soldiers against each other, cursing and shouting. Some of those riding in the open doors fell out, and Dan saw one unfortunate soldier get crushed by the car wheels.

A mounted band broke out of the woods and raced toward the train, firing and yelling as they approached. Bullets began crashing against the engine cab, and Dan and the others ducked down. One bullet hit the steam gauge, and a hissing rush of white steam spurted out. Dan pulled his pistol and began returning fire.

The Rebels only made one pass, then broke away and rode off into the woods, still shooting and yelling. Dan raised up and looked in the direction they had gone for a moment, then realized that the troops were still firing into the woods, now just wasting ammunition.

"Cease firing!" he yelled, finally leaving the engine cab and waving his arms at them until they heard his order. Their guns fell silent.

Major Lathrop and Dan walked down the track to inspect the damage. They were surprised to see that there was practically no damage at all.

"Whoever laid the charge didn't know what the hell he was doing," Lathrop commented, kicking at a singed but still intact railroad tie.

"Luckily for us," Dan replied.

Lathrop waved the engine on, and with he and Dan walking the track in front of the train, it proceeded slowly across the trestle. Sikeston was now less than a mile ahead, and with Dan and Lathrop back aboard, that last mile was turned quickly.

Major Lathrop wasted no time in assembling the artillery, and Dan formed up his company to inspect the road from New Madrid. They began moving down it, and were approximately one mile south when one of Dan's outriders came galloping back, his horse's hooves drumming on the plank road like the beating of a drum.

"Lieutenant, it's Thompson's raiders!" the rider warned. "They're comin' up fast!"

Dan yelled at the men who were working with pick and shovel, and the tools were quickly cast aside in favor of rifles. The men spread out along both sides of the road and waited for the Rebels.

Dan took a position behind their line, watching down the road. His heart was in his stomach, for here would be his first actual battle.

They could feel the vibrations of the approaching cavalry in the road planks before they could hear them, and they could hear them before they could see them. Then, finally, they saw them, moving up the road in mass, a tiny dot of red waving above the column.

Dan felt a slight thrill as he realized that he was seeing an enemy flag in battle for the first time. He stared at it until it was close enough to make out . . . a circle of white stars in a field of blue, and three broad, horizontal bars of red, white and red.

The approaching riders halted approximately five hundred yards away. Dan heard the tinny blast of a distant bugle and saw the column spread out into a wide front.

"Get ready, men," he said, forcing a calmness to his voice which he did not feel.

There was another faint, tinny sound from the bugle, and then the riders started toward them.

At first Dan could hear only the beat of the hooves, then the jangle of the gear and the rattle of sabers. Finally he heard the Rebels themselves, shouting and screaming at the top of their lungs as they approached his line of soldiers.

Dan knew that his men had the more favored position. They had cover behind trees, logs, and mounds of earth. But he also knew that his men were raw recruits, seeing combat for the first time. The riders advancing toward them had many battles under their belt.

"Hold your fire, men, until I give the word," Dan called. He pulled his pistol out of his holster, and leveled it at the approaching army.

Closer and closer they came, until the great, gray mass became distinguishable as horses and riders, then closer yet until even the Rebels' faces were visible.

"Now, men, fire!" Dan yelled, shooting even as he spoke.

There was a deafening rattle of musketry as Union and Confederate soldiers opened fire. A soldier standing less than two feet from Dan suddenly spun around with blood spurting from his forehead, and Dan saw one of the Rebels he had shot pitch forward from his saddle.

The Rebels came close enough to cut down a few of Dan's men with saber slashes, then, just as Dan was afraid some of his men might turn and run, the Confederates suddenly, and inexplicably, wheeled and started back down the road.

Dan's men began cheering.

"Lieutenant," one of his sergeants shouted. "Lieutenant, let's mount up and chase the bastards down! We'll give them a thrashing they won't soon forget!"

"Right you are, sergeant!" Dan yelled, now caught up in the same infectious excitement that swept over his men.

With a shout Dan's men leaped into their saddles. Seconds later, they were pounding down the road in hot pursuit.

Dan kept up the pursuit for nearly an hour, until he suddenly realized what he was doing. He wasn't chasing the enemy! He was being led by them! They were taking him right into New Madrid, where all the Confederate forces were concentrated!

He held his arm up, signaling for his men to stop.

"Don't stop now, lieutenant, we've nearly caught them!" his sergeant yelled.

"Sergeant, we've got to get out of here," Dan said. "Do you know how many of us there are?"

"About eighty," the sergeant said. "And I didn't count more'n fifty of them."

"But in New Madrid, and around Island Ten, there are nearly ten thousand Rebels," Dan said.

"My God, lieutenant, you mean we're ridin' into a trap?" The sergeant's eyes grew wide with fear.

"Not if I can help it," Dan said. "Let's get out of here."

Dan turned his company around and led them back up the road toward Sikeston, feeling very exposed and very foolish.

But he had accomplished one thing. He had reconnoitered the road almost all the way to New Madrid, and he could report to Major Lathrop that the cannons could be brought down and put into position immediately.

And, small though it had been, he had fought his first battle. And he had survived.

15

Burke O'Lee rode across the water to Island Ten in a small skiff. Large cannon protruded from earthen works on the island, pointed upstream to turn back the gunboat flotilla of Union Commodore Foote. Thus far they had been successful.

The guns were heavy and mounted in fixed positions, commanding the river approach only. That had made Burke feel uneasy, but when he commented on it, his apprehension was laughed off.

"We control the Tennessee side of the river," General McCown said. "There is absolutely no way heavy artillery can be brought through the swamps to threaten us at New Madrid. And as for the river . . . now we can hardly expect an attack from the southern approach, can we? Your fears, captain, are unfounded, though I appreciate your interest. You just do your duty in harassing the enemy with your cavalry raids. And leave the fortifications up to us."

Burke, who had been appointed a captain by General Jeff Thompson in recognition of his experience with Quantrill's raiders, had accepted General McCown's assurance when he first arrived at Island Number Ten. But having seen with his own eyes Union artillery being assembled in Sikeston, he knew that heavy guns could indeed be brought to New Madrid. The only thing that would prevent it would be to destroy the road. Though he had petitioned to do this several times, General McCown had refused to grant permission. Now, with the guns in Sikeston, General McCown had no choice. The road, Burke thought, would have to be destroyed.

The Confederate soldiers on Island Number Ten were composed of troops from General Polk's regular army, which included the Second Mississippi Horse Regiment, now commanded by Colonel Blackwell Beauregard. Blackie had succeeded Colonel Putnam in command after Putnam's murder by the runaway slave, Tamara Calvert. Blackie, from having spent some time in St. Louis disguised as a captain in the Union army, knew Burke and welcomed him warmly when he stepped off the skiff onto the island.

"Blackie, we've got to cut the road," Burke said.

"Impossible," Blackie replied. "It would not be politically expedient to do so."

"Politically expedient? What the hell are you talking about?" Burke asked.

"Governor Jackson has announced his intention to convene the Missouri state legislature in New Madrid in one week," Blackie said. "There are only two roads coming into New Madrid now, one from Charleston and one from Sikeston. The Charleston road is controlled by Yankee troops. If you cut the Sikeston road, New Madrid will be cut off from the rest of the state, and none of the legislators will be able to get here."

Burke ran his hand through his hair in exasperation. "Governor Jackson is a damned idiot! He's been run out of Jefferson City, and the state government has been taken over by the military. Who the hell does he think he is kidding?"

"Nevertheless, it is Governor Jackson's government which is recognized by the Confederacy, and it is important that he hold a meeting of the general assembly."

"If I don't cut that road, colonel, the only people who will come to his meeting will be Yankees," Burke stormed angrily. "Now, please step aside and let me speak with General McCown."

"I'll do better than that," Blackie said easily. "I'll take you to see the general."

Burke followed Blackie through the breastworks of the Island, then down an excavated stairway until they reached General McCown's bunker. The General was sitting behind a small field desk, looking at a map. He glanced up when Burke and Blackie entered.

"Hello, Blackie," General McCown said. "And, O'Lee, isn't it? You're with Thompson?"

"Yes, sir," Burke said.

"General, Captain O'Lee wants permission to cut the Sikeston road," Blackie said. "I told him it was quite impossible."

"Quite right," General McCown replied. "I'm afraid that we can't cut that road."

"But, general, I just returned from a raid at Sikeston," Burke said. "The Yankees have brought in a whole trainload of supplies and equipment, including heavy guns. If you don't let me cut that road, we're going to be dodging cannon balls around here in less than twenty-four hours."

General McCown laughed. "Oh, I hardly think so. At any rate, I'm leaving the Island shortly, and it will be the responsibility of General Gantt. You'll have to get permission from him."

"Where is General Gantt now?"

"He won't be here until midnight," General McCown said. He rolled the map up and handed it to Blackie. "Colonel, I've marked all the known positions of Union forces on the map. Please see that General Gantt gets the information immediately when he arrives."

"Yes, general," Blackie said.

General McCown looked around the bunker. "I'd like to stay here," he said absently. "I think this is truly the Gibraltar of the South."

Burke swore under his breath. After receiving

permission to withdraw, he returned by skiff to Fort Thompson, as the Confederate works on the Missouri side had been named.

"What about it, cap'n? Have we got permission to cut the road?" Sergeant Chism, his first sergeant, asked.

"Yeah," Burke said, in a sudden decision to disobey specific orders. "Yeah, let's get out there and get it done."

There was a sudden rushing noise, then a loud explosion, followed immediately by another rushing noise, and another explosion.

One of the men who had been posted as a picket came running back into the encampment. "Cap'n O'Lee!" he yelled. "My God, cap'n, there's Yankees out there, and they've got the biggest goddamn cannons I've ever seen!"

By now the night was raining shot and shell. Flashes lit up the sky and explosions shook the ground. Burke ran for shelter in the earthworks of the fort.

So, he thought. Events had proved him right after all. But the distinction of being right left a bitter taste in his mouth.

By the time Dan and his troops had returned to Sikeston, Major Lathrop had already assembled the cannon. Dan reported to him that the road was intact as far as he had gone—which was within a mile of New Madrid—so Major Lathrop

moved his entire command out in force. Though
they expected to be jumped by Confederate
raiders at every turn of the road, they proceeded
unmolested all the way to the Rebel's advance
picket lines, from which point they were well in
range of Fort Thompson, though not within
range of Island Number Ten itself.

The fire from Major Lathrop's guns was the
first notice General Gantt, who was in Fort
Thompson preparing to assume command of the
island, had of the proximity of Union batteries.
He ordered that Fort Thompson return fire with
all its guns, and Commodore Hollins of the Confederate navy brought his gunboats in close
enough to shore to aid.

General McCown visited Commodore Hollins
on his flagship, and, after a brief conference, decided to order Fort Thompson abandoned. Under cover of the commodore's gunboats, the
Confederate troops fled from Fort Thompson,
crossing the river to the Tennessee shore.

The Union troops, unaware that the fort had
been abandoned, continued to pour artillery fire
into it through the rest of the night. They were
receiving return fire from the gunboats, and mis-
takenly assumed that some of it was coming
from the fort. To make matters even more difficult for them, it began to rain, a cold, drenching
rain, which filled the shelters with water and
turned the ground into near quicksand.

Dan had his troops in position to repel any

Rebel advance against their batteries. He shivered in the cold, and pressed himself down into the mud to avoid the flying shrapnel of the incoming fire. It was one of the longest and most miserable nights of his life.

The rain stopped just before dawn, but daybreak itself was masked with a very thick fog, which rolled in off the river and lay its oppressive wet blanket about everything. The fog was so thick that Dan could see no more than fifty feet in front of him. This would be a perfect time, he thought, for the Rebels to counterattack.

"Cote," he called quietly. The soldier who had saved his life on board the riverboat a few days earlier now seemed always to be nearby.

"Yes, sir?"

"Pass the word to all the men to be especially watchful of a counterattack. I couldn't think of any better time to do it than right now."

"Yes, sir," Cote replied, and Dan heard the young soldier pass the word down to the next man in line, and so forth, until his entire company had been alerted.

Strange, muffled sounds floated up to Dan's ears distorted by the fog, until even his own breathing sounded like the approaching footsteps of an army. Finally the fog began to roll away, and he could see trees and bushes and, finally, after nearly two hours, the river itself.

And the fort.

All was quiet in the fort. There were no flags flying. From his vantage point, Dan could see no sign of life.

"Cote," he yelled.

"Yes sir?"

"Tell Major Lathrop I believe the Rebels have abandoned the fort."

"I'll find out, sir," Cote said, raising up quickly and starting toward the fort in a low, crouching run.

"No, Cote, come back here!" Dan called, but it was too late. Cote had gone. "Sergeant, have the men cover Private Cote!" he shouted, when he realized he wasn't going to return.

An anxious moment later, Cote was standing on the parapet of the fort, signaling for Dan to come down.

"All right," Dan shouted happily. "Sergeant, send word to the major that the fort has been abandoned. Men, to the fort, on the double!"

Dan ran down to the fort with the others from his company, and Cote met him, smiling broadly.

"What are you trying to do, get your fool self killed?" Dan scolded.

An expression of hurt passed across Cote's handsome features, and Dan upbraided himself silently for speaking so sharply. After all, it had been a brave and important act, and Cote deserved praise, not reprimand. It was just that he had grown attached to the little soldier and was solicitous for his welfare.

"Ah, don't mind me," Dan said, smiling. "I guess I'm just angry because you've made more work for me."

"I've made more work for you? How?" Cote asked, confused.

"Now I'll have to mention you in the dispatches," Dan said.

Cote rewarded him with an even broader smile.

Major Lathrop's artillery and Dan O'Lee's engineer and recon company were both part of General Pope's army. On word that the fort was abandoned, General Pope moved his Union forces quickly to take up positions inside it and bring their guns to bear on the river. Five Confederate gunboats steamed upriver, and moved into position to try and destroy the Union batteries. They started steaming in a big circle, each boat, as it arrived in position for firing, delivering a broadside that rent the air with its thunder. The fort returned the fire, and the battle continued for an hour and a half, resulting in the sinking of one of the gunboats and severe damage to the others.

But Fort Thompson also received damage, and casualties, as one shell exploded not ten feet from Dan, killing two of his men.

And wounding Calvin Cote.

"Cote!" Dan shouted, when he saw the brave little soldier trying to crawl away from the carnage the shell had caused.

He ran out of his shelter toward Cote to help him. A quick glance at the other two told him that they were beyond help.

"How badly are you hit?" he asked Cote.

"Not too bad," Cote said. "I'll be all right, I just . . ." Cote passed out. Another shell burst nearby, and Dan had no recourse but to pick up the small soldier and carry him out of the field of fire. He scooped Cote up in his arms, then ran back across the open ground until he returned to his own position. There, he lay Cote gently on the ground and looked at the blood-stained tunic.

Much of the blood looked like it might have been splashed onto Cote from his two dead comrades. The tunic wasn't heavily soaked, and there didn't seem to be any fresh blood pumping out of his chest, but Dan knew that he had better check more carefully, so he opened Cote's tunic to examine the extent of the wound.

Then he was staring disbelievingly.

Cote was a woman!

For a moment, Dan stood stock-still in a surprise bordering on shock. Then, confusedly, he checked the severity of the wound and saw, thankfully, that it wasn't critical, though it was serious enough to require immediate attention.

Dan began administering to the wound. Cote, whoever she was, had been struck just below her right breast by a shell fragment. The fragment was still imbedded in her flesh, and, after first checking to ensure that its removal wouldn't cause immediate hemorrhaging, Dan pulled it out. The wound, he saw, wasn't too deep, though it was of the type which could easily fester if not properly attended to.

Cote's eyes fluttered open as Dan was working. At first she lay there dazedly, then realizing what was happening, tried to sit up.

"No," Dan said sharply, holding her down gently, but firmly. "You've been wounded."

"But I . . ." the girl said, trying to pull her tunic closed.

"Shh," Dan said. "So far your secret is safe with me." He looked at her face more closely, and saw that the features which he had thought were the young, handsome lines of a boy were in fact, the beautiful lines of a clear-skinned woman of about twenty-one or so. She winced once as he began applying the bandage, and he made an effort to be more gentle.

"Who are you?" Dan asked quietly.

"My name is Tamara Calvert," the girl replied. "I'm a . . . a runaway slave."

"A what?" Dan asked in surprise. "But you're. . ."

"White?" Tamara said bitterly, finishing Dan's statement.

"Yes."

"Ah, but that's only my skin. Look at my blood, for there is the true test. My blood is black. Or at least, one-eighth black, and that's enough to make it all black."

"From what I can see of it . . . and at the moment I see a great deal of it, your blood is red, like everyone else's," Dan said. "How could anyone say . . ." he started, but when he looked into Tamara's face, he saw that she had passed out again.

Dan stood up and looked around the fort. The bombardment was still going on, and everyone had taken cover, so that he was, for the moment, unobserved.

He wondered what to do about Tamara. As a woman, she would be turned out of the service, and once turned out, she would technically be a fugitive from justice, and thus enjoy no special protection from the government.

Dan knew he would have to sneak her off the battlefield. And that presented a problem of what to do with "Cal Cote." Suddenly, he saw the body of a Rebel soldier about thirty yards away. The dead Rebel was about the same size as Tamara, and, as he had been the victim of an exploding shell, was not easily identifiable. Looking around to make certain he wasn't being observed, Dan removed Tamara's tunic entirely, then ran to put it on the dead man. Then he put the Rebel's body alongside the two men who had been with Tamara when the shell exploded, so that it looked as if the shell had killed all three. Now, Cal Cote was dead. And Dan had only Tamara Calvert to contend with.

16

Shortly after two in the morning, while the Confederates were abandoning Fort Thompson, General Jeff Thompson, after whom the fort was named, sent for Burke O'Lee. When Burke reported to him, General Thompson was just getting around to having his supper.

"They tell me you warned General McCown of this," Thompson said. He was sitting on a log, eating a piece of cornbread, shielding it from the rain which had already started by holding it under the apron of his poncho.

"Yes, sir, I warned him," Burke replied. "I warned him at least two times."

"Well, he's a hard man to figure out sometimes," Thompson said. "Like, you take now, for instance. He's determined to make a fight for Island Number Ten, when any fool can see the writing on the wall." Thompson pointed to the island. "He's sendin' half of his troops over there, and the other half over to the Tennessee side. He's wanting to send my men as well."

"Are we going?"

"I don't know," Thompson said. He finished his cornbread, wiped his hands on his pants, then went on with his explanation. "I'm trying to talk him into freeing my men and let them slip away to act as raiders. Like I said, though, McCown is a hard man to figure out. He may let us go, he may not. Truth is, I get the impression that he's just about written Missouri off. If he knew about the money I had, I think he would take it for his own troops."

"Money?"

"Yeah." Thompson grinned. "I got nearly one hundred thousand dollars from Governor Jackson, to be used for equipping my men. All in gold," he added. "It's not going to do me much good now, so I want you to take the money to General Sterling Price. Tell him where ole' Jeff Thompson and the boys are. Tell him we need more guns and ammunition, maybe a few horses and some staples too. There's a lot depending on you now, Burke. You've got to get out of here on your own. Get through, for the Confederacy in Missouri."

"When you reckon would be the best time to go?" Burke asked.

"I don't know. I've got the two best horses ready for you, one to ride and one to pack with. I'd say go ahead and get ready to make a getaway whenever you think you can."

"And leave you fellas to do all the fighting?" Burke asked.

Thompson smiled. "My friend, I have a feeling you'll be seeing all the fighting you want when you get out of here. Grant has an entire army moving this way. They'll have patrols out on both sides of the river, and you're more'n likely gonna be running into them."

"I'll get through, general."

"I figured I could count on you," Thompson said.

"General Thompson, sir, his respects, and General Gantt would like a word with you," an approaching officer said. The new officer was dressed in the gray and gold-trimmed uniform of Gantt's regular troops and he looked with ill-concealed contempt at Thompson and Burke in their homespun denim clothes.

Thompson stood up and pointed to a pair of saddlebags. "Take care of that for me, will you?" he asked, pitching his voice in a careless inflection which told the visiting officer nothing of the contents of the bags.

"Yes, sir, right away," Burke replied.

After General Thompson and the staff officer left, Burke hefted the saddlebags, surprised at their weight, then went to the remuda and took the two horses General Thompson had ready.

"Wait," another voice called.

Burke turned to see Sergeant Chism, his first sergeant.

"Cap'n, let me go with you," Chism said. "I know what you're doin' 'n bein' as I was born down here, I think you'd have a better chance with me along."

"You'd be safer staying here," Burke said.

"And I'd be safer yet back home plowin' the field for spring plantin'," Sergeant Chism answered, smiling wryly.

Burke had learned to trust Chism since joining with Thompson's irregulars, and he returned Chism's easy smile with one of his own. "All right," he said. "Let's go."

They mounted their horses and rode through the abatis construction out into the dark, rainy night. They rode north along the Missouri side of the river. Mingled with the sounds of the night were the occasional sounds of Federal troops. On the opposite side, they could make out a few campfires, although they didn't know whether they were northern or southern fires. Occasionally they would hear a shout, or a guttural laugh. Once a skiff moved down the river quickly, a dark shadow slipping through the night rain.

"You're crazy. Grant ain't half the gen'rl Fremont is," a strange voice said loudly.

Burke held up his hand and the two riders stopped. "There's a Yankee patrol comin' in," he hissed at Chism.

The two men moved into the shadows of the trees and waited while the patrol moved

216

through. Burke and Chism were veterans of a hundred raiding campaigns. They knew how to use the night to mask their moves, how to strike and then melt back into the trees before the advancing Federal troops. The Yankee patrol they had just encountered had spent their entire period of service in a garrison. They marched as if on parade, talking in loud voices.

There was no way out of the woods, for the entire Union attacking force had landed on the Missouri side by then, so Burke and Chism had to slow their horses to a walk through the thick, tangled undergrowth, picking their way around swollen sloughs and patches of quicksand.

Always as they moved, they heard the constant sound of artillery fire as the duel between the Union and Confederate cannoneers continued. Then they heard an explosion so close that they were sure a cannon ball had landed right between them. To their surprise they discovered that they had blundered into a Union battery. The gun had just been fired, and one of the soldiers was swabbing the barrel with water to prevent premature detonation of the next charge. The soldier looked up just as Burke and Chism burst onto them. The two men weren't in uniform, and the soldier didn't realize who they were.

"Hey, you two civilians get the hell out of here! There's a battle going on!"

"We're sorry," Chism answered, exaggerating the flat southeast Missouri twang. "We'uns is a lookin' for some stray hawgs."

The battery commander came toward them. "We haven't seen any pigs around here," he said. "You'd best get on out of harm's way."

"Thank'ee. We'll be goin' then," Chism said.

"Who the hell ever heard of goin' out at night in a rainstorm, in the middle of a battle, just to look for some damn pigs?" one of the soldiers commented suspiciously.

"Hey!" the battery commander said. "Wait a minute. That's right. Maybe you two fellas better climb down off those horses."

Burke and Chism slapped the reins of their horses and darted away. The Union soldiers yelled at them to stop, but as they were working the cannon, none were armed with sidearms, so they had no way of stopping them.

Burke and Chism managed to get away from the Federal battery, then rode north along the riverbank. The riverbank was badly overgrown, and the established roads were full of Union soldiers, so the progress was very slow. Finally they halted for a break.

"There's only one way we're going to make it out of here," Burke said. "We're going to have to bury the money somewhere. Lugging it around is going to get us caught."

"But that's the only reason we left Fort

Thompson," Chism protested. "We've got to get that money through to Price."

"And we will," Burke promised. "But right now it's pulling us down. Which would you rather have, the money hidden safe so we could come back for it, or have it captured by the Yankees?"

"I guess you're right," Chism said.

"We'll bury it right here."

"No," Chism said. "This section is being farmed—it might get dug up before we can get back to it. I have a place in mind not far from here. It's right near the river and can't be farmed. It'll never be discovered."

Burke followed Chism to a place on the river that Chism indicated would be the best spot, then stood guard while Chism buried the money. Once or twice Burke glanced down by the river-bank and saw Chism by the light of a lightning flash, busily shoveling the wet sand. After a while Chism came back, brushing his hands together.

"If a person didn't know exactly where to look, he couldn't find that money in a hundred years," Chism said. "Let's go."

The two men continued north trying to avoid the roving bands of soldiers as they headed for their rendezvous with Price.

Just at dawn, their luck ran out. They blundered into another Union column and were challenged by the pickets. The two men spurred their horses in an attempt to run away, but the terrain was so badly undergrown that the horses couldn't run much faster than a man on foot. The pickets fired, and Chism fell from his horse, mortally wounded. Burke's horse was shot out from under him, and he pitched over the animal's head onto the ground. When he came to a moment later, there were four bayoneted rifles pointed at him.

"Easy, boys," Burke said. "I know when it's foolish to keep on running. You got me."

"He's alive, sarge," one of the Union soldiers yelled. "What should we do with him?"

"Take him to New Madrid," the sergeant answered. "General Pope will know what to do with him."

Burke was jerked roughly to his feet and prodded in the rear with one of the bayonets, just enough to make him wince and elicit a bit of laughter from the soldiers who were guarding him.

"You just keep it movin' right along there, Reb, and I'll try'n keep my bayonet outta your ass."

The others laughed, and the soldier, enjoying being the center of attention, added a bit to hold the limelight as long as possible.

"Mind you now, I'll just try. But my arms is itchy, and ever' now'n then I'm liable to lose control, 'n the next thing you know, somethin' like this will happen."

The soldier jabbed Burke again, this time more painfully than before. But Burke refused to give them the pleasure of watching him wince a second time.

Back in New Madrid, Dan had commandered an empty cabin for his personal quarters. He attended to Tamara himself, intending to explain her presence away by saying she was a wounded civilian, should her presence be discovered. In the meantime, the casualty report he turned in included Private Calvin Cote among the killed.

Tamara responded to treatment well. Within a short time, she had told Dan her entire story: how she had been raised as a southern belle, only to discover that she was not who she thought she was, but the illegitimate child of a black slave. And she told of being raped, and then murdering her rapist.

"No, Tamara, that wasn't murder," Dan said softly, brushing her hair away from her face tenderly.

"I killed him, Dan," Tamara said. "I stabbed him in the neck with a pair of scissors. If that wasn't murder, what was it?"

"It was self-defense if nothing else," Dan said. "Whatever it was, it was certainly justifiable. Any court in the land would defend your right to do what you did."

"Any court?" Tamara asked. "Even a Mississippi court, if the murdered man was the owner of the slave who did the killing?"

Dan looked at Tamara, and his heart suddenly went out to her. So this was what Verity had been telling him about? Here, right before him, was a helpless victim of the evils of slavery. He felt a quick, burning rage, and knew now, more than at any time before, the fundamental right of the cause of abolition.

"That's what we're fighting for," he said.

"That's what I'm fighting for," Tamara replied. "Or was . . . until this happened. Dan, please, you must let me get back into the fight."

"There, now, Tamara, your fighting days are over. Besides, it shouldn't have to be your fight."

"But I want it to be my fight," Tamara insisted. "You don't understand. I can know no peace until I know I have done everything I can do to change the way things are. I must fight."

"You must also see that I can't allow it," Dan said quietly. "Please, Tamara, let's not speak of it again."

Tamara looked up from the pillow and smiled, a small, conspiratorial smile. "Dan, I know what we could do," she said. "You could make me your aide. I would always be by your side. That way you could keep an eye on me, and satisfy yourself as to my safety."

"I don't know," Dan said.

Tamara's smile broadened. She reached up

and took Dan's hand in hers, kissed the end of his fingers, then brought it down to her breast. "There would be other advantages too," she said.

"Tamara, I . . . I couldn't take advantage like this," Dan said. But even as he spoke, he felt the heat of her breast burning his hand even through the thin nightgown he had found for her to wear.

"It is an advantage I would gladly give," Tamara said.

Dan felt his breath quicken, then, before he could stop himself, found himself kissing her. His arms went around her, and he pressed her down into the mattress.

Tamara felt his weight upon her. For an instant she wished she could call back what she had started. She meant only to play the game with him, entice him with a promise of things to come, not offer him herself. But his hand on her body roused unexpected passions, and soon she was so caught up in the rising tide of pleasure that she was scarcely aware of Dan removing her nightgown, exposing her naked skin to the cool air. When he began removing his own clothes, she lay on the bed silent and unprotesting, still riding the cresting wave of pleasure which had begun to sweep over her. Then she felt him return to her, and she opened to him, welcoming him into her with a small groan of pleasure.

Dan took her with amazing tenderness, as

different from the brutal pounding she had been subjected to under Putnam as a gentle shower is from a ripping thunderstorm. And yet, though he was as tender as a gentle shower, the passions he released in her flashed through her like charges of lightning.

Tamara had never before felt such jolts of pleasure, and she cried out in ecstasy as they occurred, once, twice, three times in rapid succession, then a fourth time which was as great as the first three combined and lasted for several seconds, causing her to arch her body up to him, holding him in her for as long as possible, then feeling him join her as he spent himself in her.

Finally a last shudder of ecstasy convulsed both of them, and they collapsed back to the bed, lying in each other's arms for a long moment before Dan rolled away from her. Tamara lay with her eyes closed for a long while, listening to the sounds from outside . . . the occasional crump of distant artillery, a sergeant shouting impatient orders to his squad, a group of men laughing over some shared joke.

Finally she opened her eyes and looked into Dan's face. He was on one elbow, looking down at her. Somewhat hesitantly, he spoke to her.

"Forgive me," he said. "I had no right to do that."

"You had the right of my consent, sir," Tamara replied. She smiled. "Dan, other than the rape I spoke of, this has been my only experience."

Dan returned her smile. "And tell me, madam," he teased. "Was it a pleasurable one?"

"Uhmmm," Tamara replied, rolling her eyes impishly. "You have no idea. Let's do it again."

"What? You mean now?" Dan asked in surprise.

"I mean right now," Tamara replied, reaching her arms up for him.

Suddenly the door to Dan's cabin burst open and slammed shut. Tamara let out a small scream, and Dan whirled in anger.

"So, brother, we meet again."

Burke O'Lee, wild-eyed and wounded, stood just inside the door, holding a pistol.

"Burke, what the hell are you doing here?" Dan asked.

Burke coughed, and when he did, blood came from his mouth. The gun he was holding lowered, and he grabbed his chest with his free hand. Blood spilled between his fingers.

Dan started toward him, but Burke recovered. He brought the pistol up again. "No," he said. "Stay where you are."

"I . . . Burke, may the lady and I get dressed?"

Burke looked toward the bed, seeing Tamara for the first time. He smiled a small, strained, smile. "Excuse me, ma'am," he said to her. Then to Dan: "I didn't know you were engaged. I would have knocked."

As they hastily pulled their clothes on, Dan questioned Burke again.

"I asked you what you are doing here?"

"I was a prisoner," Burke said. "And I escaped." He coughed again, and more blood came up. "But not before your brave boys in blue tried to get me to answer a few questions."

"Burke, are you saying we did that to you, just to get military information?" Dan asked in surprise.

Burke gave a short, bitter laugh. "No, brother, military information didn't have anything to do with it. It seems some of your soldiers discovered that I rode away from here last night with one hundred thousand dollars in gold. They wanted to know what I did with it, and they tried to prod the answer from me with their bayonets. I managed to grab a pistol from one of them, and I killed the son-of-a-bitch who was asking all the questions. I got away, and intended to steal a boat to make it to the other side, but the bayonet jabs started bleeding and I had to take a rest. While I was hiding, I heard someone mention your name, and saw them point out this cabin, so here I am."

"Burke, I've got to get a doctor for you."

"A Yankee doctor?" Burke asked.

"That's the only kind around," Dan said.

"No, thanks."

"But you'll die!"

"I'm going to die anyway," Burke said. He laughed. "It's funny, isn't it?"

"What?"

226

"You left me twelve years ago to look for gold. Now I'm about to leave you and I know where gold is. All the gold you could ever use." Burke laughed again. "And I'm not going to tell you, any more than I would those sons-of-bitches who were torturing me."

"I wouldn't ask you, Burke," Dan said quietly.

"I know you wouldn't," Burke said. He coughed again, and this time he dropped his pistol. Dan rushed to him quickly and caught his brother just as he collapsed. He held him and lay him gently on the floor.

"Dan, I want you to know why I won't tell you about the gold," Burke said weakly.

"It doesn't matter," Dan replied. "I understand."

Burke waved his hand. "No. No, you don't understand," he said. "You think it's because I want to get even with you, but that's not the reason. S'funny, but I don't have any hate left in me. But if I tell you, it'll wind up in Yankee hands, I know it will. I can never get it to General Price now . . . but at least I can keep the Yankees from usin' it. I've not done a lot of things to be proud of in my life, Dan." He smiled, weakly. "But I'm going to die a noble death. I'm not sure I'm fightin' for the right side, or the right reason. But I aim to be loyal to the side and the reason I've chosen. I hope you can understand that."

"I think maybe I do," Dan said.

"Dan, I hope you do. There's somebody else who is true to a cause too, and you know who I'm talkin' about. I'm talkin' about Liberty. You've got her all wrong, brother. She's a good woman. And what's more, she's in love with you."

"What makes you say a thing like that?" Dan asked.

"Believe me, brother, I don't want to say it. But she told me herself, and I know it's true." Burke paused for a moment to get his breath. He looked up at Tamara, who was now standing over them, looking down. "Excuse me, ma'am, I know it's indelicate to be talkin' about another woman in front of you, but it needs sayin', 'n I don't have that much time left."

"You're talking about Liberty Welles?" Tamara asked.

Dan looked up in amazement. "*You* know her?" he asked.

"Yes," Tamara said. "She's a good woman."

"There," Burke said. "You see? Even your lady friend agrees with me. She is a good woman. She's torn between two loyalties, Dan. She's a true abolitionist . . . but she's a southerner. It's not easy for her. If you see her again, and I hope that you will, remember that. And tell her I died with her name on my lips." Burke smiled, one last time. "It's a pretty name, isn't it? Liberty."

Burke broke into another convulsion of coughing, and this time when he finished, he made a last, rattling gasp for breath, then died.

"Burke! Burke!" Dan shouted, pulling his younger brother to him and cradling him in his arms. "Burke, no, don't die!"

Dan had an eerie feeling as he realized that, for the second time, someone had died in his arms with Liberty's name on his lips.

His door burst open again, and this time there were four armed soldiers standing there.

"Lieutenant, did you see . . ." one of them, a sergeant, started to ask, then stopped as he saw Burke lying on the floor.

"That's him," one of the other soldiers said, pointing at Burke. " I told you I seen him run in here."

Dan looked up at the sergeant. "Are you the one who did this to him?" he asked coldly.

"No, sir. We just knew that there was an escaped Rebel prisoner somewhere here'bouts, and Marty here seen this fella come runnin' into your cabin. We thought you might be in danger, that's all."

"I'm in no danger," Dan said, looking sadly into Burke's face. He took his fingers and gently closed Burke's eyes.

"Is he dead, lieutenant?" one of the others asked.

"Yes," Dan said. "He's dead."

"I wonder who he was?"

"His name was Burke Patrick O'Lee," Dan said.

"O'Lee? But see here, ain't that your name too?"

"Yes. Burke was my brother."

The sergeant paused awkwardly, "I know how you feel, lieutenant," he said then. "I got me a brother who is a Secesh hisself." He turned to the other men. "Let's go, men."

The detail left. Dan stood there, looking down at the lifeless body of his brother for a long moment. He had forgotten all about Tamara, who finally spoke.

"I'm sorry, Dan," she said. "I'm truly very sorry."

Dan sighed, then turned to walk back and sit on the bed with her. He looked back at Burke again.

"Was he in love with Liberty too?"

"Yes," Dan said.

"Then he did die a noble death, telling you how she felt. I hope you won't let his death be in vain."

"What are you talking about?"

"I'm talking about Liberty Wells," Tamara said. "I know her, and I know she is a fine woman. You are a lucky man to have her love."

"Tamara, you needn't be self-sacrificing," Dan said. "I'm not about to go to her."

Tamara smiled. "I'm not being self-sacrificing in the least," she said. "What we have just had,

Dan O'Lee, is all I can ever give you. There will never be room for love in my heart again. There is too much hate. Too much pain."

"You don't have a patent on pain, Tamara," Dan said resolutely. "You'll learn that pain is a universal human experience."

17

Island Number Ten fell under constant bombardment for the next week, but despite the terrible rain of shells upon the defenders, the island held fast, accomplishing its avowed purpose of keeping the Union fleet bottled upriver, above the New Madrid bend.

Commodore Foote made several sorties against the island with his gunboats, but each attack was driven back by deadly accurate cannon fire. Finally, in frustration, Foote withdrew his gunboats and asked for a conference with General Pope, commanding general of all New Madrid forces.

"I can't knock that island out with gunboats," the commodore said. He had just come to Pope's headquarters from one of the boats, and had gratefully accepted a cup of coffee.

"We have to capture that island," Pope replied. "It is beginning to stick in my craw. Grant wants it, Halleck wants it, McClellan wants

it . . . even the Secretary of War has sent a telegram asking when we can expect it to fall."

"General, if I could sink that damn island for
you, I would readily do so," Foote said. "It
won't sink, but my boats will. I've already lost
eleven, and a goodly number of men. I'm telling
you, I can't take that island with a frontal
attack."

"We've captured Fort Thompson," General
Pope replied. "We've at least relieved the pressure from you on the Missouri side of the river."

"The guns at Fort Thompson won't reach the
island," Foote said. "What I need is a few batteries on the Missouri shore, just opposite the
island. Perhaps the combined effect of your
shore batteries and my gunboats would reduce
it."

General Pope unrolled a map on the table in
his tent, and held the corners down with a pistol,
his coffee cup, field glasses and a book. "Then
you are asking the army for help, is that it?" he
asked with a superior air in his voice.

"If it is within your power to do so, then
please help," Foote said.

"What about this?" Pope asked, pointing to
the map. "I propose to build a road from the
Sikeston-New Madrid road, stretching over to
the riverbank at this point. If we erected batteries here, we could aid in the bombardment."

Foote put the cup down and looked at the
map where indicated. "I agree, it would be a

great help," he said. He rubbed his chin. "The question is, how are you going to build a road across the swamp?"

"Simple, my dear fellow," Pope replied, smiling. "I am going to order it done. That is the way we do things in the Army."

"Ordering it and doing it are two different things," Dan said a bit later, after he heard of General Pope's comment. Dan was assigned to Colonel Bissel of Pope's engineers, and to the two men fell the task of examining the area where Pope wanted his road built.

"Perhaps we could fell enough trees to lay a foundation," Bissel suggested. "We could build a corduroy road like the one from Sikeston."

"That road follows a ridge line of high ground," Dan said. "Look at this swamp, colonel. It is absolutely impassable. A man on foot would do well to make it to the river. There is no way we can build a road good enough to haul in cannons and ammunition. The only thing we can do is disassemble the artillery, and pack it in by hand."

"I suppose you're right," Bissel said. "But that limits us to the smaller guns, and I don't know how effective that will be against the island."

Dan stood alongside a winding slough of water, looking at it, lost in thought. "Colonel," he said, "let me look at that map for a moment."

"Sure," Bissel answered easily. "Do you think you've found a route for the road?"

"Not a road," Dan replied. "A canal."

"A canal?" Bissel mused. "You may have something, Dan." Bissel looked at the map with him. "Of course. Why didn't I think of it? We could just follow the St. John's here . . . damn, that would take a lot of digging though, wouldn't it?"

Dan laughed. "Colonel, you're looking at the most experienced digger of all diggers. I've moved enough dirt looking for gold to change the course of this damned river."

"So, you were a gold digger, huh?"

"Mostly I was a dirt digger," Dan answered, and both men laughed.

"Let's get this idea to General Pope," Bissel suggested.

When the two returned to Pope's headquarters, they found him posing for Mr. Simplot, a staff artist from *Harper's Weekly*. He was sitting stiffly in a chair, gazing off into space, holding one hand thrust inside his tunic jacket, in a pose that was considered very appropriate for military pictures.

"Well," Pope said, not looking at the two men as he spoke. "My two road-builders. What have you come up with?"

"General, there's no way a road can be built through that swamp," Bissel said.

"What?" Pope said, jerking his head toward them.

"General, please, just a moment longer," Mr. Simplot pleaded.

General Pope returned to the original pose. "What do you mean, a road can't be built?" he barked.

"General, what we are dealing with is swampland, pure and simple. We'd have to lay a roadbed fifteen feet thick just to keep it from sinking," Bissel explained.

"Then build the road fifteen feet thick," Pope said, taking a sidelong glance at the artist's sketch to see if Simplot was capturing the look of authority he wanted to portray.

"General, I think Lieutenant O'Lee has a better idea," Bissel suggested.

"How can a lieutenant have a better idea than a general?" Pope wanted to knew.

"It is merely a recommendation, for your action, general," Bissel corrected. "Lieutenant O'Lee wants to build a canal."

"Why would you want to build a canal?" Pope asked.

"General, a canal would allow the boats to pass through the swamp and approach the island from the rear. As the island's guns are all pointed upriver, that would put Commodore Foote's gunboats in an excellent position to rout the enemy."

"And give credit for the victory to Foote and the navy?" Pope replied. "Absolutely out of the question. Foote has already admitted defeat, and

I'll be damned if I'll hand him victory on a silver platter."

"But General, it could shorten this campaign by . . ." Dan started.

"Lieutenant, I have made my decision, and until such time as I am overruled, that decision will stand. You will proceed to Cairo at once, secure the tools you need, then return here and build that road."

"Yes, sir," Bissel replied. "Let's go, Dan."

"Oh, colonel, before you leave, check my likeness, will you? This picture is going to appear in *Harper's Weekly*. People all over the country will read of this battle, and about me. Does the picture do me justice, do you think?"

Bissel looked at the drawing, a highly romanticized rendering of General Pope. "It is one you will appreciate, general, I'm sure," he said dryly.

"Ah, excellent, excellent. This war is going to create some powerful political personages you know, colonel. People like McClellen, Halleck, Grant and, if I may say so in all modesty, even myself, are going to be touted by many as possible presidential material. It doesn't hurt to start getting a little advance publicity . . . and it's wise to make sure that you don't miss out on every opportunity that presents itself by foolishly squandering it away. That's what I would be doing if I allowed Commodore Foote to reap the rewards of my victory."

Dan and Colonel Bissel left Pope's headquarters, frustrated that their idea hadn't fallen on favorable ears.

"At least we'll get a chance to spend one night in Cairo," Bissel said. "One good meal, and a clean, dry bed before we come back to this God-forsaken swamp."

"Colonel, there is someone I would like to take to Cairo with me," Dan said. "A civilian."

"A civilian?"

"Yes, sir. It's a girl. She was wounded in the fighting when we took Fort Thompson. I've been tending to her in my cabin, but as she's getting along nicely now, I feel that it wouldn't be proper to keep her any longer."

Bissel laughed. "Why you sly old dog, you. You can find a girl even on the field of battle."

"Well, she was wounded, sir, and . . ."

"And you never thought to report her to the division surgeon," Colonel Bissel interrupted. "Ah, never mind. Perhaps I would have done the same thing, had I the opportunity. Don't worry. I'll talk to General Pope and get him to issue her a pass through the lines. But you must promise to tell her that I came to her rescue."

"I promise, colonel," Dan said, laughing easily.

Tamara, as Dan knew she would, protested when she discovered that he intended to take her to Cairo. But her protests went unheeded. When Dan and Colonel Bissel stepped on board Commodore Foote's flag vessel later that day, Tamara Calvert was with them.

Dan couldn't help but notice the several side-long admiring glances the soldiers gave her. Colonel Bissell was as obvious in his attentions as the others, and Dan chuckled to himself, thinking of how many of these man had served with Tamara when they thought she was a soldier like them. It was amazing that she hadn't been discovered by virtue of her beauty alone, but as women never affected men's clothing, they could often pass just by their sheer audacity in dressing as one.

The steamer on which they took passage was also carrying the dead and wounded back to Cairo, and the bodies of the soldiers who had been killed during the Fort Thompson fighting were wrapped in canvas bags and laid on the deck. There were some Confederate dead among them, one of whom was Dan's brother. It had been Dan's unpleasant duty to verify the identity of Burke in the casualty letter which was exchanged with the Confederates, and, as he was Burke's next-of-kin, he had authorized the return of the body to St. Louis, to be buried in the same cemetery as their parents.

When the steamer reached Cairo, Dan placed Tamara in the only available boarding house, then joined Colonel Bissel in securing the equipment they would need to build the road.

"It's a shame," Dan said as they acquired the floating steamshovels, saws, axes, etc. "These same tools could be used much more effectively in building a canal."

"I agree," Bissel said. "But Pope is in command." Bissel rubbed his hands together. "Now, my boy, we've done all that we can do tonight. The Little Egypt Hotel has been converted into an officers' dining hall, and the food is delicious. Suppose we try it out?"

Dan smiled. "The biscuits and salt pork are getting a little tiresome," he said. "I would be most happy to join you."

They went to the officers' dining hall, anticipating their first good meal in weeks. They were still studying the menu, when Bissel suddenly pulled Dan's menu down and looked at him with a conspiratorial expression on his face.

"Dan, how serious are you about that canal?"

"What do you mean?" Dan replied, puzzled that the subject had been introduced anew.

"Are you positive that you can do it?"

"Of course I can. Why do you ask?"

"Because if you are really serious, I think I know how to get permission to build it."

"What? How?"

Colonel Bissel pointed to a table on the far side of the room. "That man over there is General Grant," he said. "Do you know him?"

"No, sir."

"Well, I do," Bissel said. He smiled dryly. "The fact is, when he was a captain, I was a major in the same regiment, and so was his superior. Come over with me. I'll introduce you."

"Should we disturb him? I mean after all, he is the top commander of all forces in the field. He has more important things to do than talk to us."

"Trust me, Dan," Colonel Bissel said. "Sam is as approachable as they come. And if he likes your idea, he'll authorize it."

"Are you going to tell him about it?"

"No. You are," Bissel replied.

"I think you should. You're senior in rank, and you know him."

"But it's your idea, and it'll be better coming from you," Bissel said. "We'll wait until he's finished his meal, then we'll talk to him."

Dan studied General Grant as they were eating. Until a few months ago, Dan had never heard of Grant. In fact, there were few in the country who had. He had been a captain, and he was a veteran of the Mexican War, but his military career had been undistinguished. He'd resigned his commission in 1854, but when the war started, he'd managed to be appointed to the rank of colonel in an Illinois regiment. He was advanced to the rank of brigadier general during the general mobilization, was posted to Cairo, Illinois, then was catapulted to national prominence with his twin victories at Ford Henry and Fort Donnelson, opening up the Cumberland

and Tennessee Rivers. Now he needed only a victory at Island Number Ten to open up the Mississippi as well, and thus own every waterway leading into the south.

General Grant was a very short man, with a full beard and mustache. His beard was a little long, unkempt and irregular, of a sandy, tawny shade. His hair matched his beard. At first glance he seemed to be a very ordinary sort of man. Indeed, he was a little below average attractiveness in appearance. But as Dan sat watching him, the general's face grew on him. Grant's eyes were gentle, with a kind, thoughtful expression. He was listening to his table guest with quiet attention, and was smoking a pipe which he often had to relight. Finally he signaled the waiter to remove his plate.

"Now," Bissel said. "If we don't see him now, I feel we will lose our opportunity."

Bissel stood up and walked toward the general's table. Dan had no recourse but to follow him.

"Hello, Sam," Bissel said. "It's good to see you again."

Dan was surprised by Bissel's familiarity, but Grant showed no displeasure at the lack of respect. On the contrary, his face lit up in genuine appreciation of seeing an old friend again.

"Harry, well, you are looking very well. Won't you join me?"

"Thank you, general, I will. This is Lieutenant Dan O'Lee. He has an idea that I think is worth listening to."

"I'm always open to ideas," Grant said. "What is it?"

Dan looked at Bissel nervously, then cleared his throat. "General, I would like to build a canal at Island Number Ten."

"A canal, you say?"

"Yes, sir," Dan said. "As you know, the New Madrid bend forms a large letter 'U.' Island Number Ten sits in the bottom of the U, with all its guns pointing north, keeping our gunboats away. But if we cut a canal across the top of the U, we could run gunboats through that way and attack the island from the rear."

"Good heavens, what a good idea," Grant said quickly. "But tell me, is such a canal possible?"

"Yes, sir," Dan said. "There is no doubt that I could build it."

"Then do so, lieutenant. Do so at once."

"There's a catch, Sam," Bissel said.

"What's that?"

"General Pope wants a road."

"A road?"

"Yes, sir," Dan said. "He wants a road built down to the river, so he can put artillery on the Missouri side."

"That sounds feasible," Grant said. "If you can build a road, perhaps you should do it."

"We can built it, general, but it would take at

least two months to get a solid enough foundation to move cannons through that swamp."

"I see," Grant said. "How long would the canal take?"

"Less than thirty days, I'm certain," Dan put in.

"Then why in blazes would Pope want a road?"

"Because Foote can't run his gunboats down a road," Bissel said dryly.

Grant chuckled. "I see. He wants the credit, is that it?"

"Yes, sir," Bissel answered.

Grant drummed his fingers on the table in silence for a long while, puffing on a curved-stem meerscham pipe which wreathed his head in blue smoke. Finally he spoke. "Build your canal, Captain O'Lee."

"I'm a lieutenant, sir," Dan corrected him.

"You were a lieutenant when you were in Pope's command. Now you are on my staff and you are a captain. Build the canal, then return to Cairo." Grant chuckled again. "I'm about to go into the railroad business down south, and I want you to come along."

"Are you talking about the railroad junctions in and around Corinth, general?"

"Yes," Grant replied.

"I would be glad to join you. I have a personal interest in that campaign."

"Oh?"

"Dan is the man who set up the Rebel spy to draw the Confederate forces into Corinth," Bissel said. Bissel had heard the story, first from General Halleck himself, and then had it confirmed by Dan during the long night duty-hours he and Dan had spent together.

"That's not entirely true, sir," Dan said quickly. "I was involved, but I didn't set Miss Welles up. In truth, she set me up."

"You sound as if there was some personal betrayal involved," Grant said.

"There was," Dan said. "She was a person who thought nothing of trifling with a man's affections, if in so doing she gained her objective. She was a woman totally without honor."

"Don't be so harsh on her," General Grant said. "After all, didn't you do the same thing to her?"

"Not knowingly, general. Not knowingly," Dan insisted.

"But you used her, none the less. I fear that the line between honor and dishonor is thinly drawn here, and you should not be so quick to cast stones."

Dan felt a sudden chill pass over him. It was a touch of *déja vu*, for those were the same words he had heard Liberty speak.

"I'm sure you're right, general," he said. "I must confess to my own confused emotions when dealing with this. Liberty Welles was a woman

246

who made a lasting impression in my heart. And now that heart is divided as to loyalty and love."

"There are many hearts divided by this terrible war," Grant said. "But if fortune smiles upon us, we may be on the verge of an engagement which could hasten the end of it."

"Do you think the fighting to come will be significant?' Dan asked.

"Yes," Grant answered. "We have information that General Johnston is joining forces with General Beauregard. That should bring a sizeable portion of the Confederate army together, and it will give us the opportunity to deal them a terrible blow."

'But what if they defeat us in battle?" Dan asked.

"They cannot win," Grant said simply. "If we are better armed, which we are, if we have more men, which we do, and if we can sustain the greater losses, which we can, then it is a question of mathematics, pure and simple. Masses of men and materiel against masses of men and materiel, and the side with the most surviving men and materiel will be victorious. We shall be the survivors, Mr. O'Lee."

"And what of the losers?" Dan asked. "What is to become of them?"

"That I shall leave in the hands of the politicians who shall come after this war," Grant said. "Our duty, as soldiers, is merely to fight the war. I have resolved myself to the conduct of that duty."

"As have I, general," Dan said resolutely. "As have I."

18

"Gentlemen are not allowed beyond the lobby, sir," a rather plump, frumpy looking woman said. She was the registration clerk at the Ladies' Temperance Boarding House, the hotel where Dan had left Tamara.

"Yes, I know," Dan said. "I would like to call on Miss Calvert. She checked in earlier today. Would you notify her that Captain O'Lee is here to see her?"

"Have a seat," the unsmiling woman said. "I'll send for her."

"Thank you," Dan replied. He walked over to one of the hard, uninviting chairs and sat down. The room was very spartan. Dan didn't know whether it was to maintain the image of temperance or to discourage men visitors. This would not have been his choice as a hotel for Tamara, but the population of Cairo was swollen by the war, and rooms were at a premium—even rooms in such uninviting establishments as this.

Tamara came to the door a moment later,

looked toward Dan and smiled. "Well, is it visiting day already?" she asked, walking toward him.

"Visiting day?"

"As you have placed me in a jail, sir, I thought perhaps you were now coming to visit me."

"Tamara, be fair," Dan said. "You know this was the only place we could find. What other choice did I have?"

"You had the choice of leaving me as you found me," Tamara said. "I managed to carry off my deception until you discovered my identity. Were you to say nothing, I could no doubt continue the charade indefinitely."

"No," Dan said. "That is absolutely out of the question. I won't allow you to return to the battlefield. I want you to stay here in Cairo, where it is safe for you."

"You forget, sir, I am a runaway slave," Tamara said. "I'm not safe anywhere until this war is won."

"You are safe here, and you know it," Dan said. "Besides, I've been assigned to General Grant's staff, Tamara. After I complete the project I'm working on, I'll be able to return to Cairo. When I do, I shall request a furlough to see you safely to St. Louis."

"I don't want to go to St. Louis," Tamara said. "I want to return to the battlefield."

"There are other ways of fighting which are

just as effective as risking your life on the battle-field," Dan said.

"Those ways do not suit me," Tamara said. "I am a simple girl who has been wronged. I know only the simple solution to right that wrong."

"Tamara, believe me, I am only doing what is best for you. You've let your emotions blind your reason."

"And you have not, sir?" Tamara challenged.

"What do you mean by that?"

"You were hurt by Liberty Welles, and now everything you do is colored by your reaction to that hurt. If that is good enough for you, why shouldn't it be good enough for me?"

"I . . . I don't have an answer for that," Dan said. "And I shan't try. But you must promise me that you'll be here when I get back."

"I'll see you again," Tamara said. "I promise you that."

"Good," Dan said. "In the meantime, you get plenty of rest. Your room and board is paid for two months. That should give you plenty of time to recuperate."

Dan left, smiling and waving at Tamara, who was smiling and waving back at him. She laughed at her little joke. He had asked her if she would be here when he got back, and she had answered only that she would see him again. That she could do on the field of battle.

Tamara remained in the lobby until she saw

Dan hail a carriage and drive away. Then she hurried back up to her room and closed the door, locking it behind her. Then she reached under the bed and pulled out a box, removing the contents and laying them on the bed.

The box contained the uniform of a captain in the Union Army. It was among the stores carried by the steamer, and Tamara had managed to move it into the pile of her personal luggage. Dan himself had seen to the transfer of her luggage to her room, and once, when he dropped some of the boxes, part of the uniform had come out. Tamara had held her breath for a moment, but Dan had stuffed it back into the box without paying attention to what it was, and she'd breathed easier as they continued toward her hotel.

Getting the uniform on the steamer had been easy. But when she'd looked into the box during an unguarded moment and saw that she had acquired the uniform of a captain, she'd feared that identity papers might be difficult to obtain. Then she'd remembered the bodies being returned to Cairo. It was a gruesome task, but Tamara had managed to search them until she found the body of a captain with identity papers. Distasteful though it was, she'd removed the papers. Now, armed with them, and the uniform, she was ready to rejoin the army.

Tamara modified the uniform to fit. A short time later, she climbed through the window and down the back of the hotel. When she saw a transport being loaded with soldiers, she stepped easily into the group and boarded with them.

"You, captain," a colonel said, noticing Tamara a moment later. "What is your name?"

"Savage, sir," Tamara replied, taking the name from the identity papers. "Captain Bill Savage."

"What is your assignment?"

"Replacement pool, unassigned."

"Good. You will take command of G Company. I've just sent the previous commander to St. Louis under arrest for being drunk on duty."

Tamara felt a quick beat of fear. Passing herself off as a private was one thing, since she could lose herself in the crowd. But to become a commanding officer of a company was something entirely different. She would be highly visible, and the least mistake might compromise her identity.

Well, she decided resolutely, she just wouldn't make any mistakes.

"Colonel, I've just arrived in Cairo. Where is this boat going?"

"Up the Ohio until we reach Paducah, then down the Tennessee to Savannah."

"Then there is a chance that we are going to see some fighting?" Tamara asked, enthusiastic at the prospect.

"Not much chance, I'm afraid," the colonel said. "It'll probably just be guard duty. There aren't any Confederates there. They're all down at Island Number Ten. That's where the fighting is."

On the night of the day that Tamara started toward Pittsburgh Landing, General McCown and General Gantt left the Confederate works on the Tennesee side of Island Number Ten, taking ten regiments with them. They proceeded down-river to Fort Pillow, then overland to Corinth, Mississippi, there to join the growing army of General P.G.T. Beauregard. The Confederate force left on the island was greatly reduced. Numbered among its units was the Second Mississippi Horse Regiment.

"Colonel, it isn't fair," Major Owens, one of Blackie's staff officers argued. "We're havin' to stay here to fight in Missouri, when there is likely to be a big battle fought in Mississippi. We are Mississippians, by God, 'n by rights that's where we ought to be."

"Major Owens is right," another put in. "General Beauregard is your uncle, sir. Don't you think he'd rather have the Second Mississippi Horse Regiment at Corinth than here in New Madrid?"

"We've received no orders to that effect," Blackie said.

"Well, hell's bells, colonel, you give the orders. The men want to fight for you and Mississippi, not MacKall and Missouri. Besides, what right

did McCown and Gantt have in making Mac-
Kall a general over you anyway? You were senior
to him," Owen said.

Upon that point, Owen had struck a telling
blow, for Blackie had been offended that Mac-
Kall, not he, had been selected to assume command of the island.

"All right," Blackie said. "Alert the men. We'll
leave tonight."

"Yes, sir!"

Less than thirty minutes later, newly appointed General MacKall came to see Blackie,
who was now gathering the personal belongings
he intended to carry with him.

"Sir, I have been informed that you intend to
quit the island. Is that true?" MacKall asked.

"Yes," Blackie said.

"Colonel, I consider that desertion under fire,
and I will personally carry the report to General
Beauregard."

Blackie smiled. "I'm sure my uncle will see
things my way. Besides, we will be of some use
to the South in Mississippi. We are of no use to
them here."

"That is not true, sir," MacKall replied. "We
are keeping the Yankees bottled up. It is my intention to erect batteries facing south, and thus
render the island impregnable from all sides.
But I can't do that without your men and equipment."

"You're going to build batteries facing south?"

Blackie asked, laughing. "And whom do you expect to drive off? Admiral Semmes?"

"No," MacKall said. "Yankees. They now own New Madrid and Fort Thompson and may devise some means of putting floating batteries below us. We would be highly vulnerable to such an attack."

"*General* MacKall," Blackie said, twisting the word general as he spoke, so that his face looked like an image in a distorted mirror. "I feel that you are trying to keep my men here merely to swell the numbers of your command and thus inflate your importance. Well, sir, I have no intention of remaining on this island while my home state is being threatened. I am taking my men out of here tonight."

"And I will personally carry my report of your disgrace to General Johnston when he arrives to take command of the combined armies."

General MacKall refused to authorize the transports which were under his command to carry Blackie and his regiment to the Tennessee shore, so they made the trip across in skiffs, carrying four and five men at a time. It took almost three hours before the entire regiment had abandoned the island. Blackie then led them straight toward Reelfoot Lake, where he hoped to catch a ferry the rest of the way.

Blackie was unfamiliar with the country, and, unknowingly, led his men right into the middle of the swamp. All pretense of command and order failed. His regiment disintegrated from a military unit to a band of nearly one thousand fugitives, each man on his own, fighting the forces of nature inherent in the swamp. A journey which on the map appeared to be a distance of no more than an hour's duration stretched through the whole night, until finally, cold, drenched with water and caked in mud, the men began to straggle in the next day. It was after noon before the forlorn band had completely traversed the swamp. Without knapsacks or blankets, many of them without arms, they began their weary march toward Corinth.

19

Armed with information supplied them by Liberty Wells, Generals Albert Sidney Johnston and P.G.T. Beauregard brought their two armies together under the command of the former and prepared to defend the critical railroad junctions in and around Corinth, Mississippi. Thus far, there were thirty thousand Confederate troops in position, and the numbers continued to grow as new regiments came in daily.

General Beauregard, who had command responsibility for the defense of the Mississippi River, was less than enthusiastic when he learned that his nephew had quit Island Number Ten at a time when its defense was most critical. But short of a general court martial, an action he was loath to take against his only brother's son, there was nothing he could do but accept the Second Mississippi Horse Regiment into his command.

The soldiers of the Second Mississippi Horse Regiment, having been exposed to battle at Island Number Ten, swaggered around the camp grounds, lording it over those troops who were as yet untested. There were few now who had seen no action. Most of the soldiers gathered by Johnston and Beauregard were veterans of a string of campaigns, from Bull Run to Fort Donnelson and Island Ten, and they bore the bragging of the Second Mississippi stoically, knowing that a few more campaigns would make the Second Mississippi as jaded as the rest of them. They were young men who were aged long before their time, who had seen and smelled death far too often to find any degree of glory in war.

Colonel Blackie Beauregard was invited to dine at Trailback Plantation by Colonel A.G. Welles. Generals Johnston and Beauregard would also be guests, the invitation noted, as would Colonel Welles's daughter, Liberty.

Blackie found his freshest tunic. When he appeared at the Welles home, he was greeted by Liberty.

"Liberty, you are as beautiful as you were the last time I saw you in St. Louis," Blackie said, removing his hat and bending low in a sweeping bow.

"And you as gallant, sir," Liberty replied.

Blackie looked around. "Has General Johnston or my uncle arrived?"

"They sent word they would be detained on some military business," Liberty said. "But they will be here shortly."

Blackie smiled. "Good. That means that I, as

a result of my punctuality, will be able to enjoy the full measure of your company all alone for a brief time."

"Why, colonel," Liberty said, smiling coyly. "Is that any way for an engaged man to talk?"

"Engaged? But I'm not engaged," Blackie said.

"Oh, forgive me," Liberty apologized. "I thought you were engaged to Miss Tamara Calvert, of Calvert Hills."

The smile left Blackie's face, and a dark mask descended over his eyes. "No," he said. "But I shall live with the shame of having been engaged to her for the rest of my life."

"The shame?"

"You mean you haven't heard?"

"No."

"I wish I could keep my silence, and thus spare myself the embarrassment," Blackie said. "But as the matter has been raised, I feel I owe you an explanation." Blackie drew a deep breath. "I discovered, just in time, I might add, that Tamara Calvert is a nigger."

"What?" Liberty asked.

"Yes, I can see you are surprised, as I'm sure you can appreciate I was."

"Surprised? I'm more than surprised," Liberty said. "I know Tamara very well, have known her for years. She is not a Negro. Where did you get such an idea?"

"Her mother was one-fourth nigger, bought and paid for by Tamara's father as his slave

261

girl," Blackie said. "That makes Tamara one-eighth nigger."

"It also makes her seven-eighths white, and eight-eighths a person, so what difference does it make? Did she tell you this?"

"Did she tell me? No, she didn't tell me. She didn't even know. It came out after her father was killed. Tamara was due to inherit Calvert Hill, and she tried to free all the slaves. I'm sure you can well imagine what a dangerous thing that would be . . . it could start a general uprising. Then Colonel Putnam discovered that while negotiating a loan last year Amon Calvert had to list all his holdings, and he listed Tamara as one of his slaves."

"Oh, how awful," Liberty said.

"Yes, that's what I thought. Here I was engaged to a girl, and all the time she was a nigger slave. Fortunately, Calvert had placed a codicil in the will leaving the place to me, should Tamara be unable to inherit. She, being a slave, cannot hold property by Mississippi law, so the property became mine, and I put a quick end to the idea that the niggers would be freed."

"I meant how awful for Tamara," Liberty said. "To discover that she was no more than property."

"Well, I thought of that too," Blackie said. "And I figured that it would be best if she left the place. So, for her own good, I sold her to Colonel Putnam. And now, here's the really terrible part, Liberty. She *murdered* Colonel Putnam. She stabbed him in the neck with a pair of scissors."

"Why?" Liberty asked. "Did he abuse her?"

"Abuse her? He owned her. He could do as he liked with her."

"What happened to her?" Liberty asked.

"I don't know. I do know that the girl, Alva, had something to do with helping her get away. But even though I tore the hide off her back with a whipping, she never told me where Tamara went. She's a fugitive, all right, and right now there's a warrant out for her arrest on the charge of murder."

"Oh, the poor thing," Liberty said. "What she must be going through."

"She's not going through half what I'll put her through if I ever find her," Blackie said. His eyes narrowed menacingly. "If I find her, I'll kill her."

"Then I pray that you never find her," Liberty said quietly.

"I will find her, Miss Welles. You may count on that."

There was a noise in the entry foyer as Generals Johnston and Beauregard arrived. They came into the parlor, escorted by Colonel Welles.

"Miss Welles," General Johnston said, bowing before her. "May I say that it is an honor to see you again? Allow me once more to give you my thanks, and the thanks of the entire South for your services."

"It is a privilege to serve, general," Liberty said. Her eyes got a troubled look about them. "Though it is not always an easy thing to do. I am as dedicated to the cause of abolition as I am to the cause of the Confederacy. It is only because I hope eventually to serve the abolitionist cause in the new South that I am able to abandon my work in St. Louis."

"You mean you were *serious* about freeing the niggers?" Blackie asked. "I thought you were just using that as a cover."

At that moment a black servant walked in, carrying a tray of drinks. Blackie took one, then smiled. "But, I see, you have niggers of your own here."

"I have no slaves," Colonel Welles put in quickly. "Those who work for me work for wages."

"Well, if you'll excuse me, sir, that's a very dangerous precedent to be establishing," Blackie said. "I don't approve of it at all."

"I would hope that there will be room in our new nation for diversity of thought," General Johnston put in. "I feel no threat from such beliefs. General Lee himself has freed his slaves."

"Nevertheless, it doesn't set well with me, and I feel it won't set well with many others," Blackie said.

"Then they shall have to accommodate themselves to it," Liberty said resolutely. "For I shall continue the fight for abolition with all my energies."

General Johnston laughed. "And colonel, as you have seen, she is a person of immense energies. Her service to us in the past is witness to that."

"General, will the Yankees attack anyway, now that we have brought in more troops?" Colonel Welles asked.

"They will attack all right. In fact, I think the biggest battle of the war is about to take place here within a matter of a few weeks."

"How big?" Blackie asked.

"Very big," General Johnston answered. "General Halleck is putting as many divisions together as he can to make his demonstration here, and we have nearly as many men assembled to meet him."

"Will we win the battle?" Colonel Welles asked.

Johnston got a faraway look in his eyes. "Yes," he finally said. "I think we will. Our chances improve each day we continue to hold Island Number Ten. You see, that not only ties up General Pope's army but it keeps the river open to us, and as long as the river is open we can move men over here. But I'll tell you this. The creeks and streams are going to run red with the blood that will be shed in this battle. There will be a carnage such as this continent has never before witnessed. And all of us must accommodate ourselves to our own mortality. The angel of death may be waiting for me, as well as for any of my command, and I must be prepared to accept this."

"General, I pray that isn't true," Liberty said. "The South needs you badly. Not only as a great general, but as a statesman who will help in establishing our new society."

"I shall give my all for the South, my dear, but I fear I shall not live to see our new society established," Johnston said.

There was a moment of awkward silence. Then Johnston smiled, dispelling the mood. "However, we must not dwell on such things," he said. "The purpose of this dinner is to honor one of our genuine heroines. If we are successful, it will be due to Liberty Welles." Johnston held his drink out in a toast. "May we drive the Yankees out of Mississippi."

"General, I look forward to the small part I shall play in serving Mississippi," Blackie said, holding up his own glass.

General Johnston looked at Blackie with narrowed eyes. "You would have served Mississippi better by helping in the defense of Island Number Ten. By leaving it, you may have cost us thirty-five thousand men."

General Beauregard cleared his throat in embarrassment, and Blackie looked at the floor, his cheeks burning in shame. Liberty smiled a small smile of satisfaction. Blackie had gotten his comeuppance.

20

To General Pope's credit, he responded to General Grant's directive that a canal be built by offering immediate cooperation in all ways. He authorized Colonel Bissel, his chief engineer, to set his entire command to work and even got assurances from Commodore Foote that he would provide manpower too, if need be.

It was a formidable task to build the canal. Dan had to cut through the forest a channel fifty feet wide, four-and-a-half feet deep and twelve miles long. In order to accomplish this, he and his men waded through mud and stood waist deep in icy water to saw through the trunks of trees. The trees, once felled, had to be cut up and disposed of. The overhanging boughs of other trees which were standing outside the channel had to be lopped off, and their limbs cleared away. Shallow places were excavated, and men worked around the clock in three shifts. Dan drove himself and his men relentlessly, often working two full shifts himself, then showing up to oversee a portion of the third.

On the seventeenth of March, General Grant moved his headquarters from Cairo to Savannah, Tennessee. He checked on the progress of the canal before he left Missouri. Dan was standing chest deep in water, straining with nineteen of his men to dislodge a fallen tree from the mud and thus clear away a portion of the channel.

"Cap'n, we're gettin' a current from the river now," one of his sergeants said, after they had tried unsuccessfully to dislodge the large trunk. "That's fightin' us."

Dan scratched his cheek, leaving a smear of mud there as he did so, and examined the problem. "All right," he said finally. "Let's clear a little path out that way, and we'll use the current to help us carry it out."

The sergeant looked in the direction Dan had indicated, then spit a chew of his tobacco and smiled. "Well, now, I reckon that's why you're a cap'n 'n I'm a sergeant," he said.

"He's a captain because I made him a captain," General Grant grunted, and the men, who had not heard Grant approach, looked around in surprise.

"General Grant, sir," Dan said. "I didn't know you were coming, or I would have come to meet you." He climbed out of the water and reported to the general.

"That's precisely why I didn't let you know I

was coming," Grant said. "You would have come to meet me, and we would have lost your services here for a few hours. The canal is much more important than protocol, Dan, believe me. How is it coming along?"

"It's coming along fine, sir," Dan said. "We'll meet our deadline, with time to spare."

"The sooner the better," Grant replied. "If we can control this river, we'll have a waterway that leads right into the heart of the South. But we'll have something else, which right now is even more important."

"What's that, general?"

Grant put both hands behind his back and looked southeast. "There's a big battle brewing down there, Dan. The biggest of this war. Johnston and Beauregard have been fortifying Pittsburgh Landing and the railroad junctions around Corinth, thanks to the information Miss Welles carried to them. They're pulling in troops from all over. But if we can control this river, we'll have some thirty-five thousand Confederates trapped west of the Mississippi. That would be thirty-five thousand people that Johnston won't be able to use. You can see, then, the importance of taking out Island Number Ten and establishing control of the river."

"Yes, sir," Dan said.

"Fire in the hole!" someone yelled. The yell was repeated down the line until one of the men in Dan's party picked it up and passed it on.

"Watch yourself, general," Dan said. "We're about to blast away some trees." He put his hand on General Grant's arm and led him back a little way. Seconds later there was a deep, stomach-jarring explosion, and water, mud, smoke, ad small pieces of tree flew into the air where the blast had occurred.

General Grant chuckled. "It's too bad we can't get the Confederates to fire a few explosive shells this way. They might do some of our work for us."

"They might at that," Dan agreed.

"Captain, I'm most impressed with your work here. Keep it until the canal is opened, then report to me at Pittsburgh Landing."

"Yes, sir," Dan replied.

Grant waved goodbye, then began walking slowly, picking his way back through the swamp. Within a few moments he was swallowed up by the twisted tangle of trees and vines. Dan thought how easy it would be for a lone Rebel soldier to sneak into the swamp, hide and kill General Grant, then escape without ever being caught. It would be a small act, but one with a tremendous consequence. He shuddered at the thought.

"Hey, cap'n, was that feller really Gen'rul Grant?" one of Dan's men asked.

"He sure was, Charlie," Dan said.

"I'm gonna write my pa' that I seen him,"

Charlie replied. He looked at his rope-burned hands. "That is, if I got anything left to write with after diggin' this here damn canal." Charlie's eyes suddenly brightened, and he smiled broadly. "Hey, fellers, did you hear what the gen'rul said? What we're 'a doin' here is important! Come on, let's get with it. We can't stand around here 'n lollygag all day long!"

Dan laughed, but appreciated the fact that General Grant's visit had instilled in his men an understanding of the degree of importance of the canal. It would make the task of motivating them a little easier.

If motivation was easier, the actual work was not. There were twelve tortuous miles to be completed. The canal was dug, chopped and blasted through for twenty-four hours a day, in every condition of weather, without letup. Finally, on the twenty-eighth of March, thirteen days after Dan had turned the first spade of dirt, the way was free and clear. He reported to General Pope and Commodore Foote that the canal was open.

"We have your guarantee that safe passage can be effected through your canal now, is that it, captain?" Commodore Foote asked, pulling on his chin whiskers.

"No, sir," Dan replied.

"What? You don't feel your canal is safe?"

"The canal is passable, sir," Dan answered easily. "And it will allow your boats to be put

271

into position behind the enemy. But I don't guarantee that it has not been mined with floating torpedoes, or that some enterprising Confederate officer hasn't found a way to move cannons into position to bear on its mouth."

Colonel Bissel, who had gone with Dan to make the report, threw his head back and laughed richly. "Dan," he said. "Let's hope that the Confederates don't have an officer as enterprising as you are."

"I would not wish to underestimate them, colonel," Dan replied.

"Nor I," Pope agreed. "But decisions have to be made, and risks must be taken. Based on Captain O'Lee's report, it is my decision that the canal be declared open. Commodore Foote, I suggest that you try and effect a passage as soon as possible."

"Of course, general," Foote replied. "Though I can't help but notice that it is your decision, and my risk. Or, rather, the risk of Commander Walke, who has already volunteered to take the first boat through."

"Balls of fire, commodore!" Pope exploded. "What do you want? We've done all the work for you now, and you stand to reap the glory. Were it my risk to take, I would gladly take it!"

"I'm thinking of Commander Walke and his men," Foote said. "They must face this alone."

"Commodore, I have already spoken with

Commander Walke," Dan said. "I intend to be on the boat with him."

"We don't need an army officer to give us courage," Foote replied rather stiffly.

"Courage has nothing to do with it, sir," Dan said. "Who better knows the canal than I?"

"The captain has a point, commodore," Pope said.

Foote stroked his chin whiskers again, striking a thoughtful pose for a moment. He was clean-shaven around his mouth, and he pursed his lips. Finally he spoke. "Very well, I have no objections. But I want it clearly understood that Commander Walke is in command. From here on out, it is a naval operation."

"I appreciate that fact, commodore," Dan said. "And now, if I may be excused, I promised to help Commander Walke prepare the *Carondelet*."

The *Carondelet* was a beehive of activity by the time Dan returned to the boat. Its crew, along with Dan's men, were covering the decks with heavy planks. Chains were coiled over the most vulnerable parts of the boat, and an eleven-inch hawser was wound around the pilot-house, as high as the windows. Barriers of cordwood were built around the boilers. Finally, protected in every way possible, the boat was ready to make the passage.

"Dan," Walke said. "Are you absolutely positive you want to go with us? It will be dangerous, and you did your part when you cut the canal."

"I'm ready to go," Dan said.

"All right. It's your funeral."

"Thanks," Dan said, grinning dryly. "But couldn't you have chosen another metaphor?"

Walke returned the grin, then added, with another touch of grim humor, "I'll make you an honorary member of the United States Navy," he said. "If you get killed, we'll bury you at sea . . . in the swamp."

"That'll make me the first sailor in history to have dug my own grave at sea," Dan replied, laughing.

"Commander Walke, Commodore Foote says you may proceed at your discretion," a sailor reported, coming aboard the *Carondelet* with the message.

"Very well, tell the commodore we will get underway just after sunset," Walke replied.

Clouds had been building all day. By the time the sun set, the sky was hazy and overcast. Walke called for the guns to be run back, and he closed the ports. The sailors were all armed with handguns and put in strategic positions to be used in resisting any attempted boarding. Men were also put in position to open the petcocks and sink the boat if she appeared likely to fall into enemy hands. Walke signaled the pilot, and the boat was cast loose to steam slowly downriver, heading toward the mouth of the canal.

By now a storm was gathering, and the boat was little more than a dark shadow against the night, practically invisible as it moved down-river.

"Damn," Dan said, shortly after they got underway. "Listen to the noise this son-of-a-bitch is making. I never paid any attention to how loud these things were before. We might as well have a brass band on board."

"You're right," Walke said. "But I know how to take care of it. Phillips," he called to the pilot, a man who had plied the river as a civilian pilot for many years and was now offering his services to the Union. "Pull the flue-caps shut. That'll keep the steam from puffing up through the stacks."

"Cap'n, that could be dangerous," the pilot replied.

"I hope you're not doing anything that might make the boiler explode," Dan put in quickly. He remembered his experience on the *Delta Star*, and the prospect was more frightening to him than the possibility of coming under Rebel cannons.

"No, nothing like that," Walke said. "The steam'll just vent through the cylinder ports; it won't build up an explosive pressure. But Phillips is right about being concerned, because the steam is the only way we have of keeping the soot wet. If the soot dries out, there could be a stack fire."

"There will be a stack fire, cap'n. I've seen it happen too many times," Phillips said.

"We've got to take that chance," Walke said. "Pull the caps shut."

The valves were pulled shut, and the puffing noise ceased almost immediately, so that the boat, in addition to being practically invisible, was now nearly noiseless as well.

"Here we are," Walke said quietly, as if even his voice could give them away. "The first Rebel position is right over that point. The gun they have there can throw a ball four miles."

Suddenly a sheet of flame, five feet high, shot up from the stack.

"Open the flue caps!" Walke shouted.

A rocket darted skyward from the riverbank.

"It's too late! They've seen us!" Walke shouted. His shout was followed by the explosions of heavy cannonading.

As if on cue, the storm which had been threatening broke. Streaks of lightning flashed through the sky, commingling the flashes and thunder of the heavens with the flashes and thunder of men.

Shrapnel from exploding shells crashed through the window of the pilothouse. One of the armed sailors let out a scream, then crumpled to the floor.

"What is that?" Phillips shouted during one of

the lightning flashes. "Cap'n, there's an obstruction ahead!"

Dan strained to look through the broken window. Then he could see it too, a long, low-lying mass stretched across the river in front of them.

"It's a chain!" he shouted. "They've stretched a chain across the water!"

"Phillips, back down!" Walke shouted.

A cannon ball passed through the wheelhouse at that moment, not exploding but crashing through with a ripping, smashing sound. The ball cut right through Phillips. When Dan looked, he saw the macabre sight of the top half of a man hanging from the wheel, still holding on tightly, while the bottom half was torn away and flattened against the bulkheads on the other side of the wheelhouse.

"My God!" Dan said, fighting instant nausea. Walke moved quickly to take the wheel. "There's no time to reverse the engine," he shouted. "We're going to hit the chain!"

"Commander, try and hit one of the supporting floats," Dan yelled. "Maybe it'll give way there!"

Walke grabbed the wheel and spun it, heading them toward the nearest float. Seconds later the boat hit it with a jar which was great enough to pitch Dan against the front of the wheelhouse. He put his hand out to brace himself and was painfully cut by the jagged pieces of the remaining glass. The boat shuddered, then continued forward.

"We made it through!" Walke shouted happily.

The storm continued to vent its fury upon the river and combatants, but the fire from the shore batteries was no longer effective as the *Carondelet* passed into the mouth of the canal.

Once the *Carondelet* was through the canal, Walke fired a signal rocket, and the other gunboats of the fleet started through. From the deck of the *Carondelet*, Dan and the others watched anxiously, as the flashes of the batteries competed with the lightning to illuminate the night sky. Finally the first boat appeared, then the second, then another, until the entire fleet had made the passage.

By the break of dawn, in a still pouring rain, the defenders of Island Number Ten saw a ghost fleet materializing out of the swamp, steaming toward their island with all guns firing.

21

At the height of the cannonading, one of the guns burst on the island, killing three men and wounding four others. That left the commander of the artillery, Captain Jeremy Humes, with only seven working guns. He went to General MacKall to make a desperate plea to move some of the guns from the Tennessee side of the river onto the island.

"No," MacKall said. "I don't think that would be practical."

"But, general, with just a few more guns, I feel like we could hold the Yankees off indefinitely," Humes said. "Look what we're doing now with only eight. Seven, now that the *Belmont* is out of action."

MacKall put his hand affectionately on Captain Humes's shroulder. "Captain, you have done an admirable job here. You've stemmed the tide against impossible odds. But the truth is, this island is going to fall, despite all we can do to hold it. And when it does, we'll lose all materiel on it. It would be folly of me to bring more guns into a position where they are likely to fall into enemy hands."

"But, general, with a spirited defense the island need not fall at all," Humes protested.

"It is going to fall," MacKall said flatly. "But we have accomplished our mission thus far. We have kept the Yankees bottled up here while Johnston and Beauregard have gathered their forces at Corinth. Now I'm off to join them with what remains here."

"You mean we are abandoning the island?" Humes asked.

"I'm leaving you in command, Captain Humes. You, and one battalion of artillery. I'll take every remaining unit, slip across to the Tennessee shore under cover of darkness, and try and make it to Johnston's position."

"I wish you luck, sir," Humes said.

"Jerry," General MacKall said, looking at the junior officer with deep, sad eyes. "I wish there was a way we could all get out of here. But I must ask you to stay and hold the enemy off for as long as possible, in order to give us the chance to get away. I'm asking a great deal of you, I know."

"We'll do the best we can, sir."

"I'm not asking for a stand till you die in defense of the island," MacKall said. "After we've slipped away, your conduct will be up to your own discretion. You may slip away if you feel you can . . . or surrender, if need be."

"General, the boats are ready to take us ashore," a colonel called.

"Start the evacuation," MacKall ordered. He looked at Humes for a long moment, then shook his hand warmly. "Good luck, captain."

"Give my best to Pelham, will you?" Humes replied, smiling cheerfully. "He's with General Johnston."

"I'll do that," MacKall promised.

When Captain Humes returned to his batteries, his men started plying him with questions.

"Are we gettin' ready to skedaddle?" one of them asked.

"No, gentlemen, we are going to stay right here and make a fight of it," Humes said. Even as Humes spoke, another volley of shells arched in from the gunboats, which now invested the island from both sides.

"We're gonna stay here 'n fight? What the hell are we gonna fight with?" another said. "Damn it, cap'n, there ain't but seven guns still firin'."

"Then double the rate of fire," Humes said. "That will make seven guns do the work of fourteen."

"We'll burst another breech," one of the men protested.

"Which gun is most likely to go?" Humes asked.

"The MacIntyre, in number three."

"Then I'll thumb the touchhole on the *MacIntyre* by myself," Humes said. "If the breech bursts, I'll be the only one hurt. Let's go, men, we've got some fighting to do."

Captain Humes's talk managed to instill a little spirit into his men, and they let out a cheer of defiance and returned to their guns. Though the rate of fire wasn't doubled, it was increased, and moments later they let out a lusty cheer as one of Foote's gunboats left the line, burning badly.

The increased rate of fire was enough to provide the cover General MacKall needed. He and his men slipped across the water to the Tennessee side, then started south and east to link up with Johnston.

Dan was still on board the *Carondelet* with Commander Walke and determined to stay with him until the island was completely silenced. Commodore Foote had assigned Walke the task of taking out the remaining Confederate batteries on the Tennessee shore. Dan stood behind the iron-plated shields as the guns boomed away, throwing shot and shell at the shore batteries. The shore batteries consisted of three sixty-four pound guns, standing half a mile apart, and they maintained a spirited contest for a couple of hours until they were finally silenced by the gunners on board the *Carondelet*.

"You want to go ashore and have a look around?" Walke asked, after the Confederate guns quit answering the fire.

"Sure," Dan replied, effecting a calm which he didn't feel. "We might as well."

Walke headed the boat into a sandbar and grounded the bow, so that a reconnassiance patrol could disembark. Dan, going ashore with the patrol, found the Rebel guns, two of which had been knocked out by fire from the *Carondelet* and one of which had been spiked by the retreating Confederates. The works were abandoned, though a few bodies had been left behind. One, a boy who couldn't have been over seventeen, sat in an upright position against the gun carriage, his arms by his side, his hands lying on the ground palms up, his mouth hanging slightly open and his eyes wide, as if staring accusing at the men who killed him. The sailors spoke in hushed tones around the body, as if the boy could hear them and would be disturbed by their conversation.

One cannon ball had chopped through a tree, and the tree was akimbo, leading to a great height at an angle that was easy to climb. Dan, on impulse, climbed it. From his position near the top, he could look far up and down the broad, amber-colored river. He could see the gunboats sailing in circles to either side of the island, firing as they came into position, and he could see the island returning the fire. The sounds of the cannons rolled across the flat space like thunder, and though he knew they were sending missiles of death, he was nevertheless thrilled by the sight.

Dan had turned to come back down the tree when he saw something that made him gasp. A large body of troops, the largest he had ever seen assembled in one place, were moving south and east. He looked closer and saw that they were Confederates!

Dan scrambled down the tree quickly. "Come on!" he shouted to the others. "We've got to get word to General Pope! The Rebels are getting away!"

The men ran back to the *Carondelet,* and Walke made a quick run across the river to New Madrid to communicate the news to General Pope.

"We've got 'em!" Pope said, hitting his fist into his hand. "Walke, General Paine's division is on board boats, ready to assault the island. Tell them to land on the other side of the river and go after the Rebs!"

"I'd like to go with General Paine, sir," Dan requested.

"Go ahead," Pope said. "You found them, you earned the right." Pope laughed. "I shall be anxious to see the headlines in the eastern papers after this engagement is concluded."

Dan left General Pope and returned quickly to the *Carondelet* with Walke. The *Carondelet* pushed back into the river and joined with the three transport boats which had on board General Paine's troops. There Dan transferred to the flag vessel, where he told Paine what he had seen and delivered General Pope's instructions.

Paine landed his division in two brigades, one commanded by Colonel Morgan, the other by Colonel Cummings. They passed by abandoned camps and artillery. Straggling prisoners were gathered up. Finally they came in sight of a detachment of enemy cavalry, but the cavalry fled without giving a fight. About nine miles from the landing, the two brigades, in a pincer movement, flanked the fleeing Confederate army, trapping them against the swamp. Now the Confederates had no way out, except through the Union army.

Confederate pickets brought news of the Federal position to General MacKall, just before midnight. MacKall was sitting on a log, wrapped in a blanket, fighting the effects of chills and fever. His troops had lit no fires, for fear of exposing their position, and had eaten no food since before leaving the island.

"What are we gonna do, general? Fight 'em?" his adjutant asked.

"What is their strength?" MacKall asked, shivering in the cold night air.

"I'd estimate two full divisions, maybe more,"

the adjutant replied. "They're fresh troops too, prob'ly just brought down from St. Louis in the last week or so. They look awful healthy."

"Look at our men," MacKall said. "Less than half of them are armed. Most have dysentery or some other ailment. We have no food, no ammunition, and the man who owns a pair of shoes is considered lucky," MacKall sighed. "We've but one recourse."

"I know, sir," the adjutant said.

"Tell the officers I have decided to sue for surrender."

"You tried your damnedest, general," the adjutant said.

But MacKall couldn't answer. He had hung his head, in shame and sorrow, to hide the tears which were now streaming down his face.

During that same night, thinking that by now General MacKall would have effected his evacuation, Captain Humes sent two men across the river in a boat, flying a white flag, offering to surrender the island and all that was on it.

General Pope was elated, and sent the following telegram to General Halleck:

"General, yours to report that on the night of the 2nd, instant, I have succeeded in opening the Mississippi River all the way to Memphis and Fort Pillow. The spoils of my campaign include one general, two hundred and seventy-three field and company officers, six thousand seven hundred privates, one hundred and twen-

ty-three pieces of heavy artillery, thirty-five
pieces of field artillery, all of the very best character and of the latest patterns, seven thousand
stand of small arms, tents for twelve thousand
men, several wharf-boatloads of provisions, an
immense quantity of ammunition of all kinds,
many hundred horses and mules with wagons
and harness, six steamboats, including officers,
crew, laborers and employees."

General Pope was most generous in his appraisal of the spoils, as most of the materiel and
many of the prisoners he mentioned had actually
been in possession of the Union army for as
much as six months previous, and some of it had
been captured by General Grant in earlier campaigns. In fact, General Paine had taken eleven
hundred prisoners when he captured General
MacKall, many of them unarmed. On the island
with Captain Humes there were sixteen officers
and non-commissioned officers, and three hundred and sixty-eight privates. These nineteen
hundred men had kept General Pope's army of
fifteen thousand tied up for three months, while
much of the Confederate army in the area had
slipped away, like quicksilver, to join General
Johnston and Beauregard along the Tennessee-
Mississippi border. The two nations then turned
their eyes toward a small log-house church
known as Shiloh.

22

General Braxton Bragg, with ten thousand battle-proven veterans, reported to General Johnston at Corinth. Bragg's men, joining those who had managed escape from Island Number Ten before the escape route was cut off, thus swelled the Confederate forces at Corinth. The governors of the Confederate states were called upon to recruit new men, and they added still more to the numbers. Then General Beauregard made a personal appeal for volunteers, and as a result of his efforts the army at Corinth grew larger still.

General Johnston inspected this growing army and discovered that if all the soldiers detailed as cooks and teamsters were relieved of these duties, he could muster yet another brigade of effective men, so he sent messengers through the surrounding country urging citizens to provide their Negroes as cooks and teamsters for sixty days. Unfortunately, the messengers returned with the answer that though the planters would freely give their last son, they wouldn't part with a Negro or a mule.

Despite General Johnston's failure to recruit blacks, he still had an effective army of more than forty thousand men. They were poised, ready to strike at the Union army at the moment he gave the word.

Twenty-three miles away, General Grant was also assembling an army. Grant had nearly as many effectives as General Johnston. In addition, only ninety miles away and coming to join him, was General Buell with his army of the Ohio . . . another forty thousand men. News of Buell's advance was provided to Johnston on the night of April third, and he called an emergency war council of his Generals Beauregard, Bragg, Polk, Hardee and Breckenridge.

"Gentlemen," Johnston said when he had them assembled. "While I have guarded against an uncertain offensive, I am now of the opinion that we should entice the enemy into an engagement as soon as possible, before he can further increase his numbers."

"General, I think we should strike at Pittsburgh Landing right now, while the Yankees are landing. They haven't built any fortifications. My scouts tell me they've set up tents like they were on parade," General Bragg said.

"I'm opposed to that," Beauregard put in. "I would prefer the defensive-offensive; that is, we should take up a position that would compel the enemy to develop his intentions, to attack us. Then, when he is within striking distance of us, we should take the offensive and crush him, cutting him off, if possible, from his base of operations at the river."

The others made their comments as well, and finally Johnston held up his hand to quiet them.

"Well, then, we've all had our say, but as I am in command here, gentlemen, the ultimate responsibility rests with me. I feel that it is imperative to strike now, before the enemy's rear gets up from Nashville. We have him divided. We should keep him so if we can."

Johnston's word was final, so there was no further discussion on that subject. The discussion then turned to the plan of battle, and in this, Johnston decided to form the army into three parallel lines, the distance between the lines to be one thousand yards. Hardee's corps was to form the first line, Bragg's the second. The third would be composed of Polk on the left and Breckenridge on the right.

"Gentlemen, I propose that you have your elements in position by seven o'clock Saturday morning, and we shall begin the attack at eight. Now, as I know you will have staff meetings to conduct, I shall let you return to your units."

The corps commanders saluted, then climbed on their horses to return to their positions. Only Beauregard, who was second in command and had no specific corps, remained with Johnston. Johnston remained seated for a long time, with his head hung, as if praying. Beauregard didn't speak during that time, and the only sound was the popping and snapping of the wood burning in the room's small pot-bellied stove. A pot of coffee sat on the stove, and after a few minutes General Beauregard poured two cups, setting one of them in front of Johnston and taking the other himself.

"Thank you," Johnston said. He sucked the coffee noisily through extended lips. "Gus, I've drunk coffee around hundreds of fires in dozens of campaigns, but I tell you now, this will be my last."

"What do you mean?"

"I fear I will not survive the battle which is coming."

General Beauregard tried to dismiss Johnston's statement with a light laugh. "Sid, every man, be he general or private, feels fear before a battle."

"You don't understand," Johnston said. "I am not afraid. I am certain that I shall be killed, and with that certainty has come a sort of peace. I can't explain it to you, Gus. It's something you must feel, though you can't feel it until you are facing the same situation."

"But you can't know with a certainty," Beauregard argued. "The hour of death is known to no man."

"Until it is upon you, Gus, then you know.

Then you know," he said again, quietly, as if talking to himself. He took another drink of his coffee. As Beauregard could perceive that Johnston wanted to be alone with his thoughts, he made an excuse to check on the disposition of the pickets and left the Confederates' commanding general in the small log cabin which was his headquarters.

As he stepped outside, Beauregard saw his nephew Blackie approaching. Blackie swung down off his horse and hailed his uncle.

"General Bragg has just informed us that we will be going on the attack Saturday morning. Is that true, uncle?"

"Yes."

"Uncle, give me a division to command," Blackie said.

"I can't just give you a division," Beauregard said. "To do so would mean that another commander would be deprived. It would be unthinkable."

"You could create a new division," Blackie implored. "I have my own Second Mississippi Horse. Detach two more regiments from two other divisions and you can create one new division. Uncle, it is only right. I was passed over at Island Number Ten. MacKall was made general over me."

"Is that why you abandoned Island Ten?" Beauregard asked sharply.

"I abandoned it because I felt I would be of

more value here. And it is well I did, for General MacKall and his entire force is now in an enemy prison camp. I, on the other hand, am here."

General Beauregard looked at Blackie for a moment, then sighed. "Very well," he said. "Inform General Bragg that you're to be attached to his corps. You will have your division, Blackie, but God have mercy on you if you dishonor the family name a second time."

"I am to be a general?" Blackie asked, hopefully.

"No. That I will not do. You'll have your division, but you'll lead it as a colonel. If you are successful, then, perhaps, you'll be made a general."

"I shall be successful," Blackie said. He returned to his horse, then looked back toward his uncle just before mounting. "You won't regret this, uncle."

"I regret it already," Beauregard muttered under his breath.

Blackie let out a whoop of excitement and slapped his legs against his horse, riding off through the woods. General Beauregard let out a sigh of resignation, then walked over to his tent to write out the necessary orders, transfering two new regiments to Blackie's 'division.'

* * *

"What are you doing, father?" Liberty asked, as she saw him packing a haversack.

"My regiment is taking to the field," Colonel Welles replied.

"What? No, General Beauregard himself told me that your regiment would be held in reserve."

"I know, and I was resigned to that," Colonel Welles said. His eyes were sparkling in excitement. "But now I'm to get a field command. I'll be part of a new division, assigned to General Bragg's corps."

"I'm going to talk to General Beauregard," Liberty said, starting for her coat. "I'll get this changed."

"No, daughter, you are not," Colonel Welles said quickly.

"Father, you are much too old for this. Please, send your executive officer."

"Liberty, what sort of man would I be if I did that?" Colonel Welles asked.

"You'd be alive," Liberty replied.

"Life without honor is no life at all."

"Honor," Liberty said bitterly. "I wish I had never heard the word. Doing the honorable thing has brought me nothing but pain. I would do many things differently if I could do them over, father, and the very first thing I would do would be to redefine the word honor. Now, please, I beg of you, let your executive officer go in your stead, and you remain behind."

"Liberty, I'm going to the field, and that is all there is to it," Colonel Welles said. He looked at his haversack. "I believe that is about all. . . . Oh, the gloves your mother knitted for me that last year before she died. Where are they?"

"They're in your overcoat pocket, father," Liberty said. Tears started welling to her eyes. "Is there no way I can talk you out of this?"

"Absolutely no way at all," Colonel Welles said. He smiled. "But cheer up, Liberty. I shall be with one of your old friends."

"Who?"

"Colonel Blackie Beauregard. He is to be the commander of the new divsion."

Liberty said coldly, "I do not number Blackie Beauregard among my friends."

Colonel Welles looked at her and frowned. "Well, no matter," he said then, shrugging, "This is something which must be done, and I shall do it, daughter, with or without your blessing." He walked over to Liberty and kissed her lightly on the lips. "We begin our march tonight. Take care."

Liberty stood quietly after her father left, fighting back her stinging tears. Her father was sixty years old. Thus far his age had kept him out of the war except for the most perfunctory of duties. He had wanted to participate, and to that end he had raised and equipped a regiment from his own resources.

But the regiment was a home guard regiment, composed in the main of old men and young boys, part-time soldiers whose dreams of glory had been satisfied by the weekly drill meetings. It had never dawned on Liberty that the regiment might really be called to battle.

Blackie, she thought. Surely he doesn't know about her father's regiment. If he knew it was composed of old men and young boys, he would want to leave it behind.

Liberty hurried to get her coat. If they were marching out tonight, she would have to see Blackie quickly, before it was too late.

When she reached the road that passed in front of her house, she was overwhelmed by the sight that greeted her. It was as if the road itself had come alive, rising into one great gray mass, flowing inexorably north. Company after company of men marched by, like giant centipedes. Sometimes there would be a subdued flash of silver, as their bayonets, sticking up like picket-fence posts, caught an errant moonbeam. Their equipment made small, jangling sounds, and their feet rustled against the dirt road like a heavy brushing on cloth.

Occasionally Liberty would hear the sound of rapid hooves coming up the road, and the moving columns of men would give way as an artillery battery rushed by—the caisson wheels spinning rapidly and rooster-tails of dust all but obscuring the cannon, which pointed back down the road, silent now but wicked-looking nonetheless.

Liberty stepped on the road just as one such cannon rushed by. She heard it barely in time to leap back and thus avoid being struck by it.

A soldier from the ranks called to her. "Miss, them cannoneers don't stop for nothin' or nobody. I done seen 'em run down folks. You'd best mind your way there."

"Who are you with?" Liberty called.

"We're with Whitman's brigade."

"Is this General Bragg's corps?"

"No'm. We'uns is with Hardee. Bragg's corps, hit'll be back down the road a mite."

"Thank you," Liberty replied, and she started back against the mainstream of soldiers.

She'd walked less than half a mile when she saw several men sitting and standing on both sides of the road. There were a few low-voiced comments about a lady being here, at night, but she closed her ears to them. Then, seeing an officer, she inquired if this was Bragg's corps.

"Yes'm," the young lieutenant answered. He tipped his hat. "Can I help you, ma'am?"

"I'm looking for Beauregard's division."

"Beauregard? Ma'am, he ain't got no division. He's second only to Johnston for the whole danged army."

"I think she means Colonel Beauregard," a

captain said, walking over to join them. "I just heard that we had a new division join us, and it is to be commanded by Colonel Blackie Beauregard. Would that be it, ma'am?"

"Yes," Liberty said. "Could you tell me where to find Colonel Beauregard?"

The captain pointed into the woods. "I figure he'll be no more'n five hundred yards that way," he said.

Liberty thanked him, then started into the woods.

"Ma'am, there's likely to be Yankee patrols operatin' in these parts," the captain said. "You'd best stay out of the woods."

"I was raised in these woods, captain," Liberty called back over her shoulder. "I'll be all right."

Though she had indeed been raised in the neighborhood, Liberty had not often been in the woods at night, and she found passage exceedingly difficult. The briars formed barriers and the tree limbs reached out to hold her back. The sounds of the moving army grew muffled and distorted. Though she was less than two hundred yards from the main road and no more than a mile from her house, she felt as if she could have been a thousand miles away.

The briars tore at her clothes, pulled at her hair, and slapped her in the face. Her breath started coming in ragged gasps. Then the ground fell off into steep ravines and wide creeks, throwing still more obstacles in her way. But still she went on.

"Well, Angus, what do we have here?" a voice suddenly asked.

Liberty stopped short, feeling a quick chill run through her. "Who's there?" she asked.

"Naw, lady, you tell us who's there?" the voice replied from the dark.

Liberty looked toward the sound of the voice, but she could see nothing. "I'm looking for Beauregard's division," she said.

"So are we, lady," the voice answered dryly. There was the sound of branches and twigs breaking as whoever owned the voice started walking toward her. A second later, three men stepped out of the woods, all holding pistols. One of them smiled broadly. "Fact is, we're lookin' for the whole damned Rebel army, so's we can carry a report back to Gen'rul Prentiss."

"You're . . . you're *Yankees!*" Liberty said, gasping in recognition.

"Yep, we are," the smiling soldier said. "And you must be what they call a 'southern belle.'"

"What . . . what are you doing here?" Liberty asked. She felt a quick fear growing inside, not merely because they were Union soldiers, but because she sensed in them an even greater danger.

"Angus, you've been down south. Is them southern belles as good in bed as they say they are?"

"I don't know," the soldier named Angus answered. "I never had me no chancet ter try one of 'em out."

"Well, grab aholt of this one," the smiling soldier said, unbuckling his belt. "We'll all try it."

Liberty opened her mouth to scream, but no sooner had she done so than it was stuffed with a foul-smelling, awful-tasting rag. "This'll just keep you from screamin' out when you starts enjoyin' it," Angus said.

Liberty felt her dress being pulled off her, and a moment later, she was thrown down onto a bed of wet leaves. They felt cold and clammy on her skin, but concern over the leaves quickly faded away when the grinning soldier descended over her.

His brutal entry into her brought excrutiating pain. Somewhere in the recesses of Liberty's mind, she wondered how this same activity could be so pleasureable under the right circumstances, and so painful under the wrong. She cried out under his assault, but the rag muffled her scream so that it came out as a small, squeaking noise.

"Listen to her squeal," Angus said. "Hell, she's likin' it."

"All these Rebel women likes it," the other soldier who, along with Angus, was holding her, said. "They's all whores, the lot of 'em."

The first soldier finished with her. Liberty

felt his semen running down her thigh. But there was no respite, for Angus was next, grunting and breathing heavily until he, too, was finished. Then he and the smiling soldier held her for the third. Mercifully, before the third had finished with her, Liberty passed out, and when she came to, how much later she didn't know, the three soldiers were gone.

She stood up, fighting the bile of nausea which tore at her throat. Her body was battered, and her mind assaulted, but she knew that if she let herself go, she would scream herself into insensibility. Slowly, deliberately, she got dressed. The dress was torn in several places, but, thankfully, it was basically in one piece and, with her cloak pulled around her, it was almost undiscernible.

Liberty pulled herself together. She would not let this stop her. She would see Blackie Beauregard, and she would beg him to release her father from the battle. If he wouldn't do it, then she would go to General Bragg, and if she got little satisfaction there, she would go to General Beauregard, or Johnston himself if need be.

After she finished making what repairs she could on the dress, Liberty continued on her quest. She reached the place where Colonel Blackie Beauregard had been, only to discover from the handful of rear echelon soldiers that

Beauregard's division, along with Bragg's entire corps, had already moved out.

"I'm not defeated," Liberty said aloud. "I'll follow them into the line of battle if need be."

With determination and courage, Liberty returned to Trailback, there to prepare for the trip up to the front lines. Whatever it took to get her father out of there, she would do.

23

"Watch your head, cap'n, caisson comin' down!" a gruff voice shouted. Dan looked up to see the caisson being swung off the steamer with a rope and tackle. He ducked, then watched it move over to willing hands on shore.

Dan had just arrived at Pittsburgh Landing. He'd made the trip from Island Number Ten in just two days. It was the night of April fourth, and though the air was cool, it was not brutally cold, a fair departure from the month of privation he had put up with at New Madrid.

"Lieutenant," Dan called to one of the officers supervising the unloading of the steamer.

"Yes, sir."

"Where can I find General Grant?"

"Captain, his headquarters is up at Savannah," the lieutenant said. "But he's been spending every day down here, and far into the night as well. Like as not, he's around somewhere."

"Thanks," Dan replied, and he started through

the hustle and bustle of the troops to look for the short, bewhiskered commander.

Everywhere Dan looked there was activity, and the sight of so many men and so much materiel was a thrilling one. But, and this nagged at him a little, it was also a frightening sight, for he saw no signs of defense. Few men that he saw were even carrying arms. Rifles were stacked. Even the cannons which were being unloaded had not yet been assembled. Dan couldn't help but think what a fine target they would make should the rebels decide to launch an attack.

He climbed up the rather steep riverbank and saw what appeared to be a thousand campfires scattered out through the fields and hills, stretching nearly as far as the eye could see. Now he breathed easier, for who could dare attack an army this large, this grand?

There, not fifty feet in front of him, Dan saw General Grant. The general was sitting on a fallen tree trunk, listening to the reports of a couple of cavalry officers. Dan started toward them.

"Well, Captain O'Lee," Grant said, smiling at his approach. "It's good to see you here."

"It's good to be here, general," Dan said, pleased that Grant had recognized him so quickly.

"Gentlemen," General Grant said to the two officers who were with him, "this is Captain Dan

O'Lee. Regardless of what you might hear from General Pope or Commodore Foote, this man is the true hero of Island Number Ten."

"I'd hardly say that, sir," Dan said, laughing self-consciously under the unexpected praise.

"But I would say it," Grant replied. "I believe that that canal you dug is going to go down as one of the engineering feats of genius of this or any other war. Our great grandchildren will tell of it," he added. "I just wish I had assigned you to General Buell."

"General Buell?"

"Yes," Grant said. "It has taken his engineers twelve days to build just one bridge. Twelve days he's been sitting up there, ninety miles from this very spot, waiting to ford one river. God's whiskers, I never saw a slower or more cautious man in my life! He should have been here by now."

"Are we badly exposed here, sir?" Dan asked.

Grant smiled. "Exposed? Of course we are exposed. But I have scarcely the faintest idea of a general attack being made upon us. No, I think they'll be spending their time erecting defenses around Corinth, and while they are occupied doing that, we'll be growing stronger and stronger."

"What is the size of the Confederate army now?" Dan asked.

"Who can say?" Grant replied. "We've had estimates of everything from twenty thousand to seventy thousand. These gentlemen have just returned from a scouting expedition and are in the process of giving me a report. This is Colonel Morris and Colonel Thomas." Grant pointed to the two officers. They were both younger than Dan, and Dan was struck with the fact that both were lieutenant colonels. They had obviously proven their worth in battles before now, to have obtained so high a rank at such a young age.

"General," Colonel Morris said, "I ranged nearly nine miles, and I encountered a pretty large body of cavalry. We skirmished somewhat, killed a few of them, and lost two of our own. They broke off after about half an hour."

"How large a body was it?" Grant asked.

"I'd say battalion size," Colonel Morris said.

"I'd agree, sir," Colonel Thomas put in. "And maybe even regimental size, as they had a battery of artillery with them."

"Any infantry?"

"None that we could see."

"Hmm," Grant mused. "I'd say it was just a nuisance raid. More than likely they were going to unlimber the artillery pieces, throw a little iron our way just to keep us on our toes, then skedaddle on back to Corinth. Nevertheless, advise Generals Sherman and McClernand to be especially watchful."

"Yes, sir," the two colonels said as one, and they rendered a sharp salute before retiring.

Grant returned the salute almost halfheartedly, as if bemused by the whole thing. After they left, Grant pointed to the tree trunk.

"Have a seat," he invited. "Are you hungry? I have some hardtack and jerky here."

"No, sir," Dan said. "I had supper on the boat."

"You don't mind if I have a bite?" Grant asked. He opened his haversack. As he rummaged through it, Dan saw the unmistakable glint of a bottle of whiskey.

"Maybe you'd like a little drink instead?" Grant offered, making no effort to hide the bottle but handing it directly to Dan.

"Don't mind if I do," Dan said. He uncapped the bottle, turned it up for a generous drink, then returned the bottle to Grant. Grant held it up and examined the remaining liquid. "Not much sense in saving that," he said offhandedly, and he turned the bottle up, draining the rest in one long draught. When he finished he wiped his mouth with the back of his hand, then tossed the bottle aside. Dan heard it break with a tinny crash.

"I'm technically in command of Buell," Grant said, bringing that general's name up again. Dan could see from Grant's behavior that Buell was more or less steadily on his mind. "But he's been senior to me until just a couple of weeks ago, and to tell the truth, I'm a little hesitant to make an issue of it. But here it is, the

fourth of April, and he was supposed to be
here no later than the twenty-fifth of March. If
he hasn't shown by the morning of the sixth, I
want you, personally, to go up there and take
charge of that outfit he calls his engineers. I
want you to get them across that damned
river."

"Yes, sir," Dan said.

"You know what the problem is, don't you?"

"No, sir."

"Halleck is supposed to arrive next week to
take overall command. I think Buell wants to
wait for that moment, rather than put his army
under my command. I've still got a cloud over
my name. Halleck even relieved me once, did
you know that?" Grant asked.

Dan did know of it, but he knew that Grant
wanted to talk, needed someone to hear him out,
so he said nothing.

"Halleck sits up there in the Federal Building
in St. Louis, giving fancy dinner parties and
entertaining politicians, and he gets upset if I
don't tell him everytime I blow my nose. Then
he got the idea that I left my command without
proper authority, and he decided to relieve me.
So he relieved me and appointed General Smith
in my stead. Within a week Smith had so
botched up everything that Halleck gave me my
job back. Politics, captain. I hate politics."

"General, the steamer is ready to return to

Savannah," someone said, coming upon the two men.

"Thank you," Grant replied. He stood up, brushed the back of his pants, and smiled. "One of your duties, captain, is not to pay too much attention to what I say at times like this. It's just like a safety valve on a steam engine. I need to let a little of it out every now and then."

"I understand, general," Dan said.

"I thought you would, captain, or I would have never said a word. Oh, find yourself a billet down here somewhere, would you? I think it would be good for me to have someone from my staff stay here all the time."

"Yes, sir," Dan said.

After General Grant left, Dan stopped a passing soldier.

"Where can I find your commanding officer, soldier?"

"He's got him a tent pitched just t'other side o' that ridge, sir," the soldier said.

"What's his name?"

"Savage, sir. Cap'n Bill Savage."

Savage, Dan thought. That's a good name for a warrior, but he hoped it didn't fit the captain's personality, because if there was room for him, he intended to throw his bedroll in with him for the night.

Dan finally reached the tent, then called from outside.

"Savage? Captain Savage?"

"Yes," the voice answered from the dark interior of the tent.

"I'm Captain Dan O'Lee of General Grant's staff. I need a place to throw my roll for the night. Can I come in with you?"

There was a long pause. Finally a muffled voice answered. "Yes. Throw it over in the corner."

Dan opened the tent flap and stepped inside. It was pitch-black. "Do you mind if I light a candle?" he asked.

"You can't throw a bedroll in the dark?"

"Well, I suppose so, but . . ."

"Then do it," the voice answered. "I have an early patrol."

There was something about the voice which Dan found intriguingly familiar. But he couldn't quite put his finger on it.

"Do I know you, Savage?" he asked hesitantly.

"Who'd you say you were?"

"O'Lee. Dan O'Lee."

"I never heard of you," Savage said. The voice, coming from down in the sleeping bag, seemed even more muffled than before. "Will you for chrissake shut up and let me get a little sleep?"

"Sure," Dan said. "I'm sorry I disturbed you."

* * *

In her sleeping bag, Tamara scarcely dared to breathe. Of all the luck! To have Dan O'Lee, of all the men in Grant's command, come into her tent! Fortunately it was pitch-black, and she would be leaving before first light. She would have to be on guard now, for she knew he would recognize her the moment he saw her. Tamara would just have to make sure that Dan O'Lee never got a good look at Captain Bill Savage.

24

The night passed slowly, almost reluctantly from the earth. When the darkness lifted, the slanting bars of morning sunlight revealed an army of gray, stretched out in a line three miles long. The line was composed of soldiers who made up the corps of Hardee, Bragg, Polk and Breckenridge, and the soldier who had been bloodied in previous battles stood side by side with the man who but two weeks earlier held not a musket but a plow.

"Now, listen to me, men," one senior officer was saying, marching back and forth behind the line. "When you aim, aim low. You do nobody any good by getting in so much of a hurry that you discharge your weapon into the trees."

"And you green'uns, be sure'n prime the pan," one old veteran called, and the other veterans guffawed. Truth was, there were few of them who had not, in the heat of battle and pitch of excitement, poured in powder, wad, and shell, then snapped the trigger uselessly against a firing pan which was not primed, and thus would not discharge.

"Don't get afraid," the senior officer went on. "Just keep it in mind that there's more than forty thousand of us. Forty thousand brave and true, and there's no army in the world that can stand up against us."

The soldiers were growing restless now. Why didn't the generals begin the attack? They had been in battle line since before sunup, and now the sun was rising higher. Didn't the generals know that the more time you had to think about it, the harder it became? There were a few with watches, and they passed the word down the line that it was nearly eight o'clock.

"Eight o'clock is when our attack begins," one of the soldiers said. "I heard the officers talkin' about it."

The soldier's rumor spread through the line. As the seconds ticked off toward eight, nervous hands began to squeeze the muskets, and itching fingers to caress the triggers, waiting for the word to move out.

"Why doesn't it come?" the soldiers asked, over and over again. "Don't them damn generals know that the hardest thing is the waitin'?"

"Yeah," another would answer, and then, as if he had just made the observation for the first time: "Don't they know that the hardest part is the waitin'?"

The same question was asked many more times by many more soldiers, each certain that he was expressing an original thought. Slowly, relentlessly, the time passed until the magic hour of eight came and went, and the sun clicked higher in the eastern sky. But, still the long gray lines waited, and now it was nearly nine. As yet, no order to attack had come.

Five hundred yards behind the line, General Johnston was holding a meeting in an open space beneath some trees. There were ten or twelve generals present, and they listened as Beauregard addressed them. He walked about gesticulating rapidly, jerking out his sentences. General Johnston stood apart from the rest, with his tall, straight form standing out like a specter against the sky. The illusion was sustained by the military cloak which he held folded around him. Finally he walked to the middle of the group and spoke.

"Gentlemen, I fear we have now lost the advantage. We were unable to launch our attack on schedule, because of a misunderstanding."

"Misunderstanding?" Beauregard said. "It is more than a misunderstanding, general, it is pure dereliction of duty. And I hold myself responsible for it, as I was the fool who gave him the division."

"What is the difficulty?" Breckinridge asked, arriving at that moment. "Why have we not

begun the attack? My men are growing nervous.

"We have a large gap in the line," one of the
other generals explained. "Colonel Beauregard's
division didn't arrive on time."

"Well, how late were they?"

The general who had explained the difficulty
coughed, then looked up at General Beauregard.
"Actually, he's not there yet," the general said.

"Gus, see here, what's this all about?" Breckinridge asked.

"Believe me, I wish I knew," General Beauregard answered. "But I shall relieve him immediately he shows up."

"No," General Johnston said. "I feel you are
being too harsh on him because he is a kinsman.
Would you similarly relieve any other officer,
without giving him a chance to present his
reason?"

"General, as he is assigned to my corps, I
feel I should come to his defense," General
Bragg said.

"What defense can there be? By his failure
to carry out his command he has cost us many
precious hours," Beauregard said.

"Be fair," Bragg interceded. "After all, he
was only given the command two days ago, and
it is at best a bastard element, never before
on the march. Believe me, we experiencd some
difficulty in getting into line on time with
seasoned troops."

318

"General Bragg is right," Johnston said. "There is, no doubt, a very good reason for your nephew's tardiness. At any rate, it will do no good to remorse over it now. We must make new plans."

"I say we go ahead and hit them," Bragg said.

"Without Beauregard's division?" Breckinridge replied. "That will leave my flank unprotected."

"I think we have completely lost the opportunity to strike today," General Polk said. "We must wait, and strike at dawn tomorrow."

"The Bishop is right," General Johnston said, referring to the fact that General Leonodis Polk was a Bishop of the Episcopal Church. "We have only one recourse now, and that is to reschedule our attack for tomorrow."

"General Johnston, that will give Buell twenty-four hours more to close ranks with Grant," Beauregard argued.

"We have no choice," Johnston said. "We've lost the element of surprise we could have realized by hitting them early this morning. We can only wait and regain it at dawn tomorrow."

"We could also return to Corinth and move into our fortifications there," Beauregard suggested.

"No," Johnston said. "We must hit them while we still have something close to numerical parity. Gentlemen, return to your units. Put them into bivouac, and prepare them for an attack at dawn tomorrow. Oh, and light no campfires tonight. I don't want to alert the Yankees that we are this close, in this great a number."

"What about Beauregard's division?" Bragg asked.

"If Colonel Beauregard hasn't shown up by six o'clock tonight, replace his position on the line with a brigade from Polk's reserves."

"Replace an entire division with a brigade?" Bragg asked, astonished.

"I'll give you my best brigade," Polk offered. "They're proven men, and that should more than make up for an untested division."

"You have a point," Bragg agreed.

General Johnston returned the salute of the assembled generals, then walked over to stand alone, beneath a tree. The bars of sunlight, much higher now, cut through the limbs to highlight the general in a single spot. It gave him the appearance of standing in a cathedral, washed in some holy light.

Beauregard looked at him for a moment, then walked out onto a small hill to gaze back down the Corinth road. Where was his nephew?

"Colonel, I'm sure it wasn't anything more than an advanced patrol," a colonel was saying.

His name was Kelly, and he was commanding officer of the First Alabama volunteers. It had been Kelly's regiment, along with Colonel Welles' home guards, which had helped to form Beauregard's new division. Unlike Welles' group, Kelly's regiment had seen action. More action even than the Second Mississippi Horse.

"Suppose it wasn't merely a patrol?" Blackie Beauregard said. "Suppose it was a reconnaissance in force? Or suppose it is the advance element of the Yankee positions?"

"We know it couldn't be that," Colonel Kelly said. "We've had patrols through this whole area every day for a month. There's no way the Yankees could have adjusted their lines that far without our knowing."

"But if they have and we blunder into them, then we would be chewed to pieces," Blackie mused. "How would that be, our one division launching an attack against the entire Yankee army?"

"We could move in column," Colonel Kelly suggested. "If we encounter stiff resistance, we could pull back to the tree line and send for help."

"No," Blackie said. He rubbed his hands together nervously, then pulled on his Vandyke beard. "Let's fall into fortified positions here, then I'll send out scouts."

"There are no fortified positions here, colonel," Kelly explained patiently.

"Then have the men dig them," Blackie ordered.

"But, colonel, that would take hours. We couldn't possibly make it to the line of attack in time."

"Mind my orders, colonel," Blackie said sharply. "I'll not lead my division one more step, unless I know where the hell I'm going!"

"Yes, sir," Kelly said dejectedly. He started back to his regiment.

"Colonel Kelly may have a point, Blackie," Colonel Welles said. "After all, he's fought the Yankees before."

"I'm not exactly a green soldier myself," Blackie snapped. "I have a few campaigns under my belt. And I led my men through the Reelfoot Swamp, while being pursued by the whole of Pope's army."

"I'm not questioning your experience or your ability," Colonel Welles said hastily. "Heaven knows, I can't offer any of my own. I was just hoping to be of some use as a mediator."

"There's no mediating to be done," Blackie said simply. "I'm the commander, and that's that. Now, you get back to your regiment and tell them to dig in. After we've prepared for a possible Yankee attack, we'll send out a scouting party."

Blackie took out a pair of field glasses and climbed up on a large rock. He looked north, searching the tree lines for any telltale sign of the enemy, but he saw nothing. The fact that he saw nothing didn't mean they weren't there, he knew. He had learned from his experience at New Madrid. They could be right out there, and he'd never know it unless he looked for them.

Blackie did look for them, sending out three separate patrols and getting an all-clear report from each, before he regrouped his men on the road and continued his march toward the position he was supposed to occupy. He finally arrived at three o'clock in the afternoon, seven hours late.

"Where have you been?" General Bragg asked, not raising his voice, though showing his displeasure in his eyes.

"We encountered a Yankee reconnaissance in force," Blackie said. "I was afraid that to fight my way through would compromise the element of surprise General Johnston is trying to achieve."

"Colonel, there have been daily skirmishes for weeks," Bragg pointed out. "One more skirmish wouldn't have caused any problem."

"Perhaps you're right, sir," Blackie said. "I desperately wanted to engage them, but I felt to do so would have been construed as an act of glory-seeking, perhaps at the expense of the overall objective. It was a command decision I was forced into making. If I erred, I'm sorry."

General Bragg sighed. "Well, who knows?"

he said. "You were in the best position to make the determination."

"Is the attack still on?"

"It is set for dawn tomorrow morning," Bragg said. "Cook all your rations during the daylight hours, using small campfires only. There will be no fires tonight."

"Yes, sir," Blackie replied.

"You'd better give your men some rest. Tomorrow will likely be a very long day," Bragg said.

"Tomorrow will be a day of glory, the likes of which the South has never seen," Blackie said.

"Save your speeches for your men, colonel," Bragg said dryly. "I know better."

"Captain Savage to see General Prentiss," Tamara said, swinging off her horse in front of General Prentiss's tent.

The adjutant showed Tamara in, and she looked at Prentiss. He was a veteran of the Mexican War and wore a sash which had been worn by General Hardin, his slain commander in that war. Prentiss was a politician turned general. He had been an unsuccessful candidate for Congress from the fifth district of Illinois. It was his hope that an inspiring military record would promote his post-war political ambitions.

"General, I think the Confederates may be

planning to launch an all-out attack," Tamara reported.

"What gives you that opinion, Savage?"

"I led a patrol this morning, and I encountered a large group of them moving up Corinth road."

"We've had demonstrations on that road for nearly a month," Prentiss said.

"This wasn't a demonstration, general. This was a march. I believe they were coming up to prepare for an attack."

Prentiss laughed. "Captain Savage, General Grant doesn't believe there will be an attack, General McClernand doesn't believe there will be an attack, General Sherman doesn't believe there will be an attack, and I don't believe there will be an attack. Now we can hardly change the entire conduct of this operation, merely because you have been frightened by the sight of a few of the enemy, can we?"

"No, sir," Tamara said. "But I don't believe any of you gentlemen have had the view I had."

General Prentiss tore off a sheet of paper from a note pad and scribbled on it.

"Here," he said. "If this will make you feel any better, I've written a note to General Grant, telling him that one of my patrols spotted Rebel troops marching *en masse* up Corinth road. If there is a significance to that, I'm sure he will see it. Will that satisfy you?"

"Yes, sir," Tamara said.

"Give this note to Captain O'Lee."

"Give it to whom, sir?" Tamara asked, drawing a quick breath of surprise.

"Dan O'Lee. He's a captain on General Grant's staff. He's a tall, sandy-haired man, clean-shaven, about thirty or so. Ask around, someone will show him to you."

"Very good, sir, I shall," Tamara said.

She saluted General Prentiss, then stepped back outside the tent. So, now she was between the rock and the hard place. She wanted General Grant to have this message, but the only way she had of getting it to him was through Dan O'Lee. And if Dan saw her, he would recognize her, and she would be taken from the field before the battle even commenced.

Tamara thought about it for a long time. If she did give the note to Dan, and Prentiss was right and she was just overreacting, she would have compromised her identity for no good reason. On the other hand, if she was right, then General Grant could at least prepare for an attack. But, as a general, wouldn't he have made preparations for the attack anyway? Not that she could see, she decided. But then, how did she know? After all, she was an amateur at this business. Grant, Sherman, McClernand, Prentiss . . . they were the experts. They certainly knew of the possibility, and yet they weren't concerned. So why should she be? And most of all, why should she expose herself just to give voice to that concern?

Tamara wadded the note into a tight ball and tossed it into Lick Creek, a stream which ran nearby. It floated a little ways downstream, became sodden, then sunk to the bottom. Tamara squared her shoulders and returned to her company, determined to avoid being exposed at all costs.

25

The Confederate army was bivouacked in position to launch their attack early the next morning. They were stretched from Owl Creek on their extreme left to Lick Creek on the extreme right, in three parallel lines of battle, with General Breckenridge's corps poised at the center rear, ready to supply reinforcements wherever needed.

Though most of the army was in line, the necessary train of supplies was still in motion up the Corinth Road, and as Liberty moved toward the front, she was able to find General Johnston's headquarters simply by asking directions of the teamsters. She reached the area of General Johnston's encampment at about two o'clock in the afternoon. She approached silently, waiting for the opportunity to speak with Johnston or Beauregard regarding her father's regiment.

"Where is General Buell?" Johnston was asking, as he paced about nervously. "We must know when he is expected, for if he arrives during the night we'll be moving into a slaughter-house."

"All we've been able to determine is that he isn't there yet," Beauregard said.

"I wish we had a balloon," Johnston said sourly. "Or failing that, a daring and accurate spy within their headquarters."

"I will be that spy, general," Liberty said. She stepped out of the trees and walked forward into the clearing in time to hear the generals' discussion.

"Miss Welles!" Johnston said, obviously shocked at seeing her here on the eve of the battle. "What are you doing here? You shouldn't be this close, you will be in danger."

"I've been in danger before," Liberty said simply. "And I would willingly place myself in danger again. I will locate General Buell for you."

"No," Johnston said. "I can't let you do that."

"Why not? Liberty asked. "I feel responsible for this battle. It was my information which has set it up, am I right?"

"Yes, but you've done enough. I'll not risk putting you in further danger."

"General, because of me, forty thousand of my countrymen are going to be placed in danger. If I can do anything which will lessen that danger—even by a small amount—then I will willingly do it. Now, please, allow me to steal into the Yankee camp and find out what you want to know."

"It would be of inestimable value to us," Beauregard said hesitantly.

"Yes, but such information would be better gathered by a man," Johnston said.

"Why?" Liberty wanted to know. "As a woman, I would have the advantage of placing the Yankees off-guard. And, as I am experienced in this endeavour, I will know what and how to gather the needed information."

General Johnston ran his hand through his hair. Finally he sighed in resignation. "Very well, I shall allow you to go. But be very cautious, and return before darkfall."

"I shall," Liberty said.

"And again, may I say that the South owes you a debt they can never repay?" General Johnston said quietly.

"General, there is something you can do for me," Liberty said.

"Name it, and it's yours."

"My father's regiment,' Liberty said. "It has been attached to Colonel Beauregard's division, and is now on the line of battle. I ask that you pull it out, and hold it in reserve."

"An entire regiment?" Johnston said slowly. "Miss Welles, you ask a great deal. But in deference to your past services, and in view of your father's age, I will concede to withdraw

331

him. I will give command of his regiment to another."

"No," Liberty said. "My father would never forgive me if he alone were pulled from the ranks. It must be his entire regiment. Surely, you've a better regiment to put into the line than his home guards. They're nothing but old men and young boys, never before under fire."

"Home guards?" Johnston asked. "Are you serious?"

"Yes, sir," Liberty said.

General Johnston looked at Beauregard in astonishment. "How did we get a home guard regiment on the front lines? If they break under fire, the Federals could pour an entire division through the gap and turn our flank."

"General, I'm sorry," Beauregard said. "I just assigned the regiments to Blackie to make up the new division. I must confess that I paid no attention to their composition."

"Miss Welles, I thank you very much for calling this matter to my attention," General Johnston said. "And you can be sure that I shall replace the entire regiment. But please, don't think it is necessary for you to buy this consideration at the peril of your own life. I would replace that regiment anyway, given its composition, and my knowledge of the fact."

"I will locate General Buell for you," Liberty said, smiling.

"God be with you, girl," Beauregard said.

Liberty returned to the Corinth road. Twenty-two miles behind her was Corinth, issuing forth a steady stream of Confederate soldiers. The road was absolutely deserted for half a mile in front of her, a no-man's-land, as it were. Then, for the final half mile, the road was in possession of the Union troops in and around Pittsburgh Landing.

Liberty squared her shoulders and started up the road. She'd gone less than one hundred yards when she was challenged by the advance pickets of the Confederate lines.

"I wish passage, sir," Liberty answered to the challenge.

"Ma'am, they ain't naught but Yanks up that road."

"I am not a combatant, sir. I do not feel any jeopardy."

"I don't know," the picket said. "Maybe I'd better see the cap'n."

Liberty felt a degree of frustration. She could have General Johnston clear it with the captain, who would then inform the pickets, but that would increase the number of people who would be aware of her mission. She had learned from experience that the fewer people who knew what you were about, the better the chances for success.

"Let er go, Clay," his companion said. "Like as not we go see that fool cap'n, he'll have dreamed up somethin' else for us to do."

"Yeah," the one called Clay said. He scratched his beard and looked at Liberty. "Ma'am, I don't know why you want to go up there, but if you want to, go ahead. Only do me a favor, would you? If you get stopped by any of our rovin' patrol, don't tell 'em you come through here."

"I won't tell them," Liberty promised.

The Rebel soldier, a man in his mid-to-late thirties who sported a long red beard, waved her on with his rifle. Liberty thanked him, then started on up the road, headed for Pittsburgh Landing. She thought of the soldier who had stopped her. He certainly wasn't fighting this war to preserve slavery. She had known his kind all her life, and she could look at him and tell his entire history. He was no doubt a farmer, owning perhaps twenty acres or less. His only help in running the farm came from his wife and perhaps his oldest child. He had no slaves. If he saw fit to fight in this war without a vested interest in slavery, then that should prove that this war wasn't to perpetuate slavery, as so many in the north believed. She could be a Confederate as well as an abolitionist. People like Clay proved it.

As Liberty continued to walk along the road, she was struck by its look of absolute peace. The sun was shining brightly, the temperature in the high sixties. In the woods to either side of the road, birds chirped gaily. A rabbit was frightened from a clump of weeds, and it darted in front of Liberty, leaving little puffs of dust as it ran. A peach orchard bloomed in colorful profusion, and the fragrance of its boughs was carried softly on a light spring breeze.

Why can't men learn from nature? Liberty thought. It was madness to think that by to-morrow, this very area would be the scene of death and destruction the likes of which had never been seen on this continent.

"Halt!" a loud voice called, and Liberty stopped at once. "Who is there?"

"I want to speak with your commanding general," Liberty called out.

"What?" the soldier replied. "Did you say you wanted to talk to the general?" The soldier stepped out from behind a bush. Liberty saw a clean-shaven, handsome young man, no older than she. She smiled at him.

"Yes," she said. "I have information I think he would like to have."

"Whyn't you just give it to me, ma'am?" the young soldier asked. "I'll take it to him."

"No," Liberty said. "I must be satisfied that it gets into the right hands."

"Well, now, ma'am, what general are you talking about? We've got lots of them here."

"General Grant," Liberty said.

The soldier laughed. "I'll tell you what I'll do. I'll take you to my captain, and he can take you to see the colonel, and the colonel can take you to see one of the generals, and maybe that general can take you to see General Grant. That's the best I can do, ma'am, bein' as I'm just a private myself."

"That will do fine. Thank you very much," Liberty said.

"And ma'am, if you do get to see General Grant, well, whyn't you just tell him that Private Frank Gilbert is due a pass? I'd appreciate it, ma'am."

"I'll try and remember that, Private Gilbert," Liberty said, liking the young man's easy sense of humor. She felt a sudden pang. For hard on the realization that she liked him came the further realization that she was even now bound on a mission that could mean his death.

True to his word, Gilbert passed Liberty on, through the captain, the colonel, then General Sherman, so that now she was being taken by one of Sherman's orderlies to see General Grant.

"General, a dispatch from General Buell," a rider said, pounding into the camp at that moment.

"Good, good," Grant said. "Has he crossed Buffalo River yet?"

Liberty strained to hear the dispatch rider's answer, but she was unable to after he and General Grant walked away several feet and stood under a tree and talked in a very low voice. She looked around, trying to see if there was any way she could get closer and thus hear the conversation without being obvious, but she saw no such way. A moment later, the dispatch rider saluted, returned to his horse and rode away, and the opportunity had passed without Liberty being able to take advantage of it.

"Now, madam, what can I do for you?" General Grant asked, returning to talk to the young woman who had entered his camp.

"I have some information for you, sir, concerning the disposition of the Confederate troops in the area."

"Oh? And what is this information?"

"Generals Johnston and Bragg have joined General Beauregard," Liberty said. "I've seen and recognized both of them in Corinth."

Grant smiled. "Thank you very much, madam. I do appreciate that."

"But they are here, now," Liberty insisted, continuing to play the game. Then she stopped and put her hand to her mouth. "Oh, how foolish of me. But of course you must already know this."

"We've had reports," Grand admitted drily. "Your story does serve to verify it, however, and for this we are thankful."

"You must think I'm a silly, foolish girl, trying desperately to serve her country," Liberty said.

"Madam, I think you are a patriot," General Grant said magnanimously. "But you have placed yourself in some danger. Please, allow me to provide you with an escort to some safe area on the other side of the river."

"Oh, no," Liberty said. "I wouldn't dream of tying up one of your men for such a thing. I'll just return to Corinth."

"You mean via the Corinth road?" Grant asked, suddenly taking a greater interest in Liberty.

"Yes, of course."

"Madam, did you come by that road today?"

"Yes," Liberty answered. "Why? Did I do something wrong?"

"No, of course not. Tell me, madam, have you seen any particularly large concentration of Confederate troops along the road?"

"They are all around Corinth," Liberty said.

"But no closer?" Grant said. "You weren't challenged?"

"I was challenged by one of your soldiers, general, a nice young man named Frank Gilbert," Liberty said. "He asked me to give you a message."

"He wanted you to give a message to me?"

"Yes, sir," Liberty said. "He asked me to tell you that he was due a pass."

Grant threw his head back and laughed. "That is good, madam, that is very good. It tells me that the morale of my men is still very high. Oh, here comes one of my aides. I shall have him escort you, at least back through our pickets."

Liberty looked in the direction indicated by General Grant, then felt a sudden sinking in the pit of her stomach. Her head began to spin, and she felt for a moment as if she would faint. For there, coming toward her in the uniform of a Union officer, was Dan O'Lee.

"Captain O'Lee," General Grant said. "Allow me to introduce you to. . . . I'm sorry, madam, I didn't get your name," Grant said, looking at Liberty.

"My . . . uh . . . name is Jane Roberts," Liberty said. She looked down at the ground, hoping the brim of her hat would shield her face.

"Good afternoon, Miss Roberts," Dan said easily.

"I would like you to escort Miss Roberts back through our pickets," General Grant said.

"It would be my pleasure," Dan replied. "Come along, Miss Roberts."

Liberty followed behind Dan, still keeping her head tilted down. Praise be to God, could it be possible that he hadn't recognized her?

But then Dan spoke, and in so doing shattered all her illusions.

"Liberty, I didn't think you'd have the nerve to ever show your face again," he said stonily.

Liberty gasped. "You recognized me?"

"Of course I did. Do you think I could ever forget you?"

"But why? I mean, you said nothing to General Grant. Why didn't you turn me in?"

"I don't know," Dan said. "I truly don't know. Maybe it's just my way of trying to repay my brother for all the hurt I caused him."

"Have you heard from Burke?" Liberty asked.

"Burke is dead," Dan said simply.

They walked on in silence, Dan leading the way, Liberty walking behind him. After a few moments, Dan heard a quiet sobbing, and he turned around to see Liberty crying.

"You're crying?" he asked.

"Is that so hard to believe?"

"But surely Burke meant nothing to you," Dan said. "I mean, wasn't he just one of the many? As Lieutenant Ward was? As I was?"

"What does it matter to you?" Liberty asked, dabbing at her eyes with a handkerchief. "You're going to believe what you wish to believe, no matter what I say."

They had left the road, and were now walking through a ravine. Dan stopped and turned around. "You tell me what I should believe," he said. "You tell me that I wasn't betrayed."

"I tried to warn you," Liberty said. "I told you that I was honor-bound to abide by my convictions."

"And did your convictions include making love with me, and with anyone else who would aid you in your cause?" Dan asked caustically.

"I made love with you, Dan, because I was in love with you. And, despite everything, I still am," she said.

"Liberty, don't," Dan said sharply. "You have no need for subterfuge now. I'm going to set you safely free, regardless of what your mission was here. You needn't toy with me any longer. You've no idea how I've suffered from the heartache you caused."

"I am not toying with you, sir," Liberty said. "And you've not suffered alone. Dan, can't you recognize an honest declaration of love when it's made?" Her voice came out in a sob.

"And did you make that same declaration of love to Lieutenant Ward? And to my brother?"

"I was very fond of your brother," Liberty said. "I may have even loved him, and I did tell him so. But I've never spoken those words to any other man, except you and your brother. Nor have I made love with anyone else."

"Liberty, why torment me with your lies? Captain Todd told me of seeing you entering room 408 with Lieutenant Ward."

"Yes," Liberty said. "I went to his room, but we did nothing except eat dinner together. This is all that happened, I swear!"

"And you swear that no other man has ever known you?"

Liberty looked at the ground again. This

time the tears began sliding down in even greater profusion. "No," she said. "I didn't say that. I said I have never made love with anyone except you and Burke. But there have been others who have known me."

"Just as I thought, madam," Dan said in bitter triumph. "No doubt, as a part of you spying activity?"

"I was raped, sir!" Liberty cried out. "I was raped not two days ago by three Yankee soldiers. They are the only others to know me!" Liberty began crying aloud, and the sobs racked her body so that she shook as with a chill.

"Liberty . . . I . . . I'm sorry," Dan said. At the sight of her genuine despair, he moved quickly and put his arms around her.

Liberty, feeling his arms about her, feeling comfort at long last, leaned into him. The hurt and bitterness fell away as she turned her trembling lips up to receive his kiss. There was a rushing sound in her ears, as a wind whispering through tall pines, and against her breast she could feel the pounding of his heart. Her body seemed to melt against his, and for a brief moment in the continuum of eternity, they were one, fused together, lip to lip, body to body, heart to heart.

"You do love me, Dan," Liberty said, when finally their lips parted. "Say it!"

"Yes," Dan admitted. "I do love you. I've loved you from the first moment I saw you. I've tried in every way possible to get you out of my mind, Liberty, but I can't do it."

Still he held her to him, trembling, as he spoke, with the fervor of the moment. And he looked at her with eyes tormented with struggle.

"Oh," she said. "Oh, if only we could leave this place now, and run away together, back to California."

"And forsake honor?" Dan asked.

"Yes!" Liberty said. "Oh, Dan, I've been so foolish, so self-righteous! I know now that there is only one honor, and that is to oneself. I love you, Dan, and nothing else matters but that love. Come, let's go away."

"No," Dan said. "In a curious way, Liberty, I've just come to see what you've said all along. I can't run away and you can't either. Don't you see? There would always be this between us. It would never let us go, and eventually it would consume us."

He let go of her and walked a few paces away, then turned to look back. Liberty felt for a moment as if she couldn't stand alone. She gripped a tree limb for support. Then she gathered herself, and looked at him with slow, sad eyes.

"I envy you, that you have found what I seem to have lost," she said finally. "Now, if you will be so kind as to guide me through the pickets, I'll be on my way. I won't bother you again."

"Liberty, no, don't say that," Dan said. "I love you, When this war has ended, I want to marry you."

"This war!" Liberty said, with a hollow mocking laugh. "We are on opposite sides, Dan, and yet we speak of love. Sometimes when I think of it, I think we've gone mad!"

"No, we're sane, Liberty," Dan replied. "It's just that in a world gone mad, sanity is no virtue."

26

The sun was low but hadn't set yet when Liberty returned through the forward pickets of the Confederate lines. She managed to get through with no trouble, and she proceeded directly to General Johnston's headquarters.

"Miss Welles," General Johnston said, greeting her. "You've no idea how happy I am to see that you've returned safely. I've scolded myself continually ever since you left for authorizing such a foolhardy errand."

"I experienced no difficulty," Liberty said.

"Did you locate General Buell?" Beauregard asked.

"Yes. That is to say, I know where he is. But I do not know when he will join General Grant."

"Where is he?"

"He is at Duck River," Liberty said.

"Duck River? That's only ninety miles away!" Beauregard said. "General, we must call this attack off! If he marches all night and gets here before we have established our objectives, we'll be swept from the field!"

"On which side of Duck River is he?" General Johnston asked Liberty.

"I don't know," Liberty answered. "I heard a rider report to General Grant that he had a dispatch from Buell. Grant asked, 'Is he still at Duck River?' The dispatch rider answered in the affirmative but then they moved out of hearing range."

"General, we've got to call this attack off before it's too late," Beauregard urged. "Let's withdraw now to Corinth."

Johnston crossed his arms over his chest and pondered the situation for a few moments before he answered. "Gus, I know Duck River. It is in freshet stage now, flooded with the thaws and the spring rains. If he's on the other side, he could well be stuck there for a week, trying to cross."

"But we don't know how long he's been there, or even if he's on the other side."

"Think carefully, Miss Welles," Johnston said. "Did Grant ask if Buell was *still* at Duck River?"

"Yes," Liberty replied.

"That means he's been there a long time," Beauregard said. "He may have already been there for a week."

"It could also mean that he's trapped on the other side," Johnston replied. "Gus, I feel we have no choice. We must make the attack to-morrow."

"Very well, general," Beauregard replied. "I will support in whatever way I can."

"You must promise me one thing," Johnston said.

"Of course, general."

"If . . . if I am not around tomorrow night, and we have seized the advantage, you must press it hard. Drive the Yankees to the other side of the Tennessee and hold them there. If you control this side of the river they will have little chance of recrossing it."

"I promise, general," Beauregard said. "But you will lead us, not I."

"We shall see," Johnston replied. "And now, Miss Welles, I would feel much better if you retired from this area. You've exposed yourself to enough danger without adding to it by be-ing on a battlefield during an engagement."

"My father," Liberty said. "Where is he?"

"Your father's regiment has been taken from the line and placed into Breckinridge's reserves," Johnston said. He laughed. "He wasn't very happy about it."

"No," Liberty replied, sighing with relief. "I'm sure he wasn't."

Liberty left the area where Johnston and Beauregard had pitched their tents, and started toward the area where she knew the reserves would be encamped. As she walked, she could sense the various moods of the Confederate soldiers on the eve of the battle. Some were almost melancholy, as if resigned to dying on the morrow. Others were excited, looking forward to the battle with eager anticipation. Most seemed unaffected, sitting or lying about with faces devoid of any expression save that which could be seen on any soldier's face in any bivouac: They ate their cold rations, or talked of home, or told jokes. Some were singing. Liberty could hear snatches of songs coming from different parts of the campground. The most popular one seemed to be *Home Sweet Home*.

"Miss," one of the soldiers called. "Miss, would you write a letter for me?"

Liberty stopped and looked at the man who called. He was about forty, with a long black beard and close-set coal-black eyes. He was holding a piece of paper and a pencil out toward her. "I got me these writin' implements, 'n I ain't all that good at my letterin'. I was a hopin' you'd help me out."

Liberty smiled at him. "Certainly I'll help you," she said.

"Thankee, ma'am," the soldier said, smiling broadly. "These here other fellers helps me sometimes, but they got their own letters to write, 'n it ain't fittin' of me to be beggin' off them all the time."

The soldier folded his poncho double, then

put it on a log, making an elaborate show of preparing for Liberty a place to sit. She accepted the seat, then the pencil and paper, and prepared to take his dictation. She looked around and saw that several other soldiers had drawn close to listen to the letter as well.

"Would you rather go some place where you can dictate privately?" Liberty inquired of the soldier.

"Oh, no, ma'am. All the boys, they like to listen to the letters I write to Marthy, 'n then they like to listen to the letters Marthy writes me back, 'cause the truth is, I got to have them read to me, same as I got to have them writ fer me."

"Very well," Liberty said. "I'm ready if you are."

"Dear wife," the soldier began. "I take this opportunity to write you again, having as my pen this time a lovely fair young belle of the South, but don't be jealous none, as my love is only for you, as you know. I am well, and I hope these few lines may come safe to hand and find you enjoying the same blessing.

"We are going to fight a big battle tomorrow, and with God's blessing, throw the Yankees back across the river and whip them good. Maybe that will make them think again before they come down here to raid us in our own homes.

"Tell mother I am well and I would like to

see her very soon. Tell her to write to me as soon as you get my letter, dear wife. Tell our son Mark that it is up to him to get the crops in now, and you tell him I don't want to hear any more about his signing up to fight. I'm doing the fighting for both of us, and he has to do all the farming, but as he is fourteen now, he's big enough.

"Kiss little Anne and tell her that her daddy loves her very much. Martha, if you could get into Jackson and have your likeness made at that place that takes the likenesses and send it to me, I would carry it next to my heart forever.

"I must close now, and remain your husband until death. Direct your letters to Hosea's Infantry, D Company. Signed, T.J. Cole."

"Here it is," Liberty said, as she finished the letter and handed it back to Cole.

"Thankee, ma'am. I thankee kindly," Cole said, taking the precious missive from her.

"Miss, would you do one for me too, please?" another soldier asked, and Liberty took a pen and paper from him to write his letter. After his, there was another, and then another, and Liberty wrote letters until the failing light made it impossible to write any longer. Finally, she begged off, explaining that she couldn't see, and explaining that she was looking for her father's regiment.

"I'll take you there, ma'am," Cole offered,

and Cole had plenty of volunteers to help him, so that when Liberty did enter her father's encampment a while later, she was escorted by four of the soldiers from D company of Hosea's Infantry.

"Daughter," Colonel Welles said, when he saw her. "What are you doing here?"

"I wanted to see you," Liberty said, going to him and accepting his affectionate embrace.

"Well, you've got your wish, daughter," Colonel Welles said dejectedly. "I've been pulled off the line of battle."

"I'm glad, father."

"They've pulled my entire regiment," Welles said. He hit his fist into the palm of his hand. "Damn it all, tomorrow is going to be the battle that brings victory to the South and ends this war, and I'm not going to be a part of it."

"We'll be in reserve, colonel," one of his staff officers said.

"Reserve! What does that mean? It means nothing, that's what it means," Colonel Welles said.

"Papa, at least you're here," Liberty said. "If I had my way, you would still be at home, in Corinth."

Colonel Welles looked at his daughter, and the dejection left his eyes. He smiled at her. "You're right, Liberty. I could be at that. I guess we'll both have to settle for this. But if I didn't know better, I'd say you had something to do with getting my regiment pulled off line."

"Why, papa, whatever gave you that idea?"

"Because you're an independent girl, Liberty, and you don't give up easily. You're well-called, daughter, for liberty is your nature as well as your name."

"Colonel Welles, General Johnston has called a meeting for all officers, down to regimental commanders."

"This is it, daughter!" Welles said. Even in the darkness, his eyes shone with excitement. "I'm going now to get the battle plan for tomorrow's operation. I may get into this fight yet!"

Colonel Welles followed the staff officer who had delivered the message to him, and Liberty, quietly and unobserved, followed a short distance behind. If there had been any change in the plans, and her father was going to be used tomorrow, she wanted to know about it now.

It was a little after eight o'clock by the time the officers had all gathered in the clearing near Johnston's tent. In the middle of the clearing was a visible symbol of the adage "rank hath its privileges," for there burned a small campfire. The smell of bacon permeated the area, so that Liberty knew that the generals, at least, had enjoyed a hot meal on this night.

Nearly sixty officers were assembled, all with the rank of colonel or higher. They were talking quietly among themselves, but grew silent when General Beauregard appeared, stepping out of a tent at the far end of the clearing.

"Gentlemen," Beauregard said. "In a few moments, General Johnston will have a few words to say to you. Before he arrives, I have one thing I would like to say."

There was absolute silence, save the crackling of the fire. All the officers strained to hear Beauregard's one remark.

Beauregard pointed toward the river. "Tomorrow night, we sleep in the enemy's camp!"

There was a round of cheers. Then Beauregard held his hand up, calling for quiet. "Gentlemen, our commanding general!"

General Johnston stepped out of the tent then and walked to the middle of the clearing to address his officers. His face had a hawkish appearance, dominated by a handlebar mustache. He had piercing black eyes beneath heavy dark eyebrows, and when he fixed his gaze upon a person, it seemed to penetrate to that person's very soul. Command set well with him. He was well-experienced, having served as a general in the armies of three countries: the United States, the Republic of Texas, and the Confederate States of America.

Johnston enjoyed the absolute confidence of Jefferson Davis and the Confederate government. When, after an earlier setback, there was some outcry for his removal, it was Davis who responded by saying: "If Johnston isn't a general, then we have no generals in the Confederate army, and had best give up this war." The Union thought highly of General Johnston as well. After their unsuccessful attempt to recruit him, they had made an equally unsuccessful attempt to kidnap him as he journeyed east from California to accept his Confederate command.

Now Johnston looked over the assemblage before him, then spoke in a clear, easily understood voice:

"I have put you in motion to offer battle to the invaders of your country. With resolution and disciplined valor, becoming men fighting as you are for all that is worth living or dying for, you can but march to decisive victory over the mercenaries who have been sent to despoil you of your liberties, your property, and your honor. The eyes and hopes of eight million people are resting upon you, and I assure you that I will lead you to victory!" He ended in a shout.

There was a rousing cheer from the officers. Johnston stood there, looking at them for a moment longer, with an expression on his face which Liberty couldn't fathom. It wasn't excitement, or anticipation, or even fear. It was more like sorrow. She stood back in the shadows and studied Johnston's face for several seconds, until the general turned and walked back into his tent.

Liberty breathed a sigh of relief. Nothing had been changed. Her father's regiment was still in reserve. But even with her relief, she realized the grim facts. Tomorrow, nearly one hundred thousand men would be locked in mortal combat.

Dan couldn't get Liberty from his mind. Should he have let her go? Surely her presence in camp, especially as it had been under an assumed name, bespoke of some nefarious activity. And yet, even as he asked himself the question, he knew there could be but one answer.

He'd let Liberty go because he was hopelessly in love with her. Verity Eternal, Tamara Calvert—they had been, at best, surrogates for the woman he truly loved. And, he had to admit, Liberty had been honest with him. She had tried to warn him during their time together in St. Louis that she might have to do something which would make him feel betrayed.

What a fool he was. She'd offered to deny the Confederacy, to deny everything, so they could be together. She wanted to run away to California with him, and he had spurned her offer. Why? He asked himself that over and over again. Why did he reject her? She was willing to admit that there was no honor, save the honor they felt for each other. Why couldn't he say the same? Why must they be caught up in the insanity of this war?

"Captain O'Lee," General Grant called, and the general's summons interrupted Dan's reverie.

"Yes, sir."

"I'm going back to Savannah to spend the night. General Buell's army has finally crossed Duck Creek, and they should be arriving at about dusk tomorrow evening. At that time, I shall move my headquarters here. I'd like you to scout around tonight, and find a suitable place to establish our field headquarters."

"Very well, sir," Dan agreed.

Grant started to leave, then scratched his beard and turned back to Dan. "Oh, while you're at it, you might scout around for a suitable place for General Halleck too, as he will be arriving soon."

"Yes, sir," Dan agreed.

Grant looked back at the river, then over toward Lick Creek. "You know, I haven't fortified our position against an attack, I've had no instructions from Halleck to do so, and besides—I speak frankly—I have so many untried men that I fear fortifying the camp will just make them fearful of an attack. I don't believe we will be attacked, I really don't. But if we are, this position is naturally strong. We have

Snake Creek on our right, and Lick Creek here on our left. I don't see how an attack could come from anywhere except the area immediately to our front, and that would box them in."

"General, would you like me to give word to be especially watchful tonight?" Dan asked quietly.

"Yes. Tell Sherman to . . ." Grant paused. "No, you'd better not. The Rebels have been making constant demonstrations against us. If the men thought there was a real danger of an attack, they might give way at the first feint. I've seen how panic can rout an army. I'd like to put them on their guard, but I fear to."

"Well, there's just one more night, general, then we'll have Buell's troops and the Rebels would never attack," Dan said.

"I'm certain you're right," Grant said. "I'll bet the Rebels would like to know where Buell is. Well, goodnight to you. I'll be back by seven in the morning."

"Good night, general," Dan said.

Dan watched Grant walk down to the landing and step aboard the steamer which would take him the six miles upstream to his headquarters at Savannah. He knew the general was uneasy with good reason tonight. He wished that Buell had been more efficient in bridging Duck River. Grant was right. If the Confederates knew that this was the last night before Buell joined Grant, they would surely

attack to maintain the advantage as long as
. . . "Liberty!" Dan cried aloud. He snapped
his fingers. "My God, that's why she was here!
She was trying to find out about General Buell!"

27

When Dan realized that the purpose of Liberty's visit had to be to gather information concerning General Buell's position, he went at once to see General Prentiss. Prentiss had already retired but agreed to see him, knowing him to be a member of Grant's staff. When Dan was escorted into the tent, Prentiss had put on his trousers, but nothing more. He sat on the edge of his bunk, running his hand through his tousled hair. The tent's interior was dimly lighted by a candle, and great shadows were projected on the canvas walls.

"What is it, captain?" Prentiss asked irritably. "What is so important that it couldn't wait until morning?"

"General, I have strong reason to believe that the Confederates are going to attack us during the night," Dan said.

"What? Does that word come from General Grant?" Prentiss asked, showing more interest.

"No, sir," Dan admitted. "I have my own reasons for believing this."

"And what are those reasons, captain?"

Dan was stuck. He couldn't very well say that he had recognized a Rebel spy and then let her go without reporting her. He didn't know what to say.

"It's just a feeling I have, sir," he said weakly.

"A *feeling*, captain? You've awakened me because of a *feeling* you have?" General Prentiss said with ill-concealed disgust.

"Well, it's more than a feeling, really," Dan tried to explain. "It's a combination of little things, which, taken by themselves, are insignificant, but in concert point very definitely, I think, to the possibility of an attack."

Prentiss stood up and walked over to the tent flap, then looked outside. A large, silver moon floated high in the night sky, and he looked at it for a moment before he turned around to face Dan. Now, Dan saw that Prentiss had a more thoughtful look on his face.

"Then the information Captain Savage gave you fits in with your other information?" General Prentiss asked.

"The information Captain Savage gave me?" Dan asked.

"Captain, are you going to tell me that Savage didn't come to you today with a note from me for General Grant?"

"No, general," Dan said. "I haven't seen Captain Savage since a very brief meeting last night, when we shared a tent."

"That is most unusual," Prentiss said, frowning. "Savage seemed positive on his information, and wanted to transmit it to General Grant. I authorized the transmittal, and told him to have you take him to Grant."

"What information did he have?" Dan asked, puzzled.

"He said he spotted a large body of Confederate troops moving up the Corinth road this morning."

"A patrol?"

"That's what I believed it to be," Prentiss said. "But Savage seemed to think differently. That was why I authorized him to proceed further with the information. I assumed he had already done so."

"He made no such report to me, sir."

"Hmm," Prentiss said, rubbing his chin. "It may be that Savage had second thoughts. But, as you now have the same degree of jitters, why don't you speak to him yourself about what he saw?"

"I will, sir, and thank you."

"Don't thank me," Prentiss said. "If an attack is imminent, then we should thank you and Savage for warning us. Savage is in Colonel Peabody's brigade. Tell Colonel Peabody that if he deems it appropriate, he may send out a scouting party. But be careful not to bring on any unwanted engagements."

"Yes, sir," Dan said. He saluted, then left the tent and walked across the damp, rolling ground, looking for the tent he knew to belong to Captain Savage.

"Cap'n, I moved your gear outa Cap'n Savage's tent, and pitched one for you over by that oak tree," a private said, as Dan approached the bivouac area of Company G.

"Thank you, soldier," Dan answered. "Is Captain Savage in his tent?"

"Yes, sir. I think he went to bed 'bout half an hour ago."

"Captain Savage," Dan called, just outside the tent.

"Yes, who is it?" a voice answered.

"It's me, Captain O'Lee."

"You've got your own tent now, O'Lee. Let me sleep in peace."

"No, that's not it," Dan said. "I have a message for you from General Prentiss."

"What's the message?"

"He wants you to . . . why the hell am I standing here talking to a tent, Savage? Come on out here."

There was a rustle, and a moment later the small figure of Captain Savage stepped outside. The captain had his hat pulled low, and he had a scarf wrapped around his mouth and nose, so that only his eyes showed, and they were covered by the shadow of the brim of the hat.

"I think I'm coming down with the ague," Savage said, his voice muffled. "Excuse the scarf, but I'm trying to keep away the humors of this damp air."

"The chill and damp can make it worse," Dan agreed. He chuckled.

"What's so funny?"

"It has just come to me that I have known you for twenty-four hours now, and yet I wouldn't recognize you in the light of day."

"If I see you, I'll tell you who I am," Savage replied. "Now, what is this important message?"

"General Prentiss says you were to deliver a message to me for General Grant," Dan said. "But I never received the message."

"It had to do with an idea I had," Savage said. "I decided that my idea wasn't a very good one."

"It may have been better than you thought," Dan suggested.

"Why?"

"Captain Savage, I have every reason to believe that the Confederates are planning an attack on our position this very night."

"Then you mean I did see an army moving *en masse*," Savage said.

"I think you did."

"If Prentiss is concerned, why have we not gone into defensive positions?"

"Prentiss wants Colonel Peabody to send out a patrol," Dan said.

"Very well, I'll pass the word on to Colonel Peabody, then move my company out in force."

"I'm going with you, captain."

"No, you aren't," Savage said.

"Why not?"

"Because I'm going to have enough on my mind without having to play nursemaid to one of Grant's staff officers. I'll handle it, captain."

"I'm a staff officer," Dan admitted. "But I've had a fair measure of exposure to battle."

"You will not ride out with me," Savage said again, resolutely.

"Very well, captain, I won't press the issue," Dan said. "But I must insist that we inform Colonel Peabody at once of General Prentiss's wishes."

Dan followed the feisty little captain over to Colonel Peabody's tent, wondering why he and Savage had become such instant enemies. He couldn't think of anything he had said or done to incur such hostility. But, then, the captain had been exposed to daily patrols and harrassing raids by the Rebels, and was no doubt under a great deal of pressure, so Dan made allowances for his behavior. Still, there was something about Captain Savage which haunted Dan. Why did it seem to him that recognition was there . . . just beyond grasp, dangling tauntingly before him like a half-re-membered melody?

As Tamara led Dan to see Colonel Peabody, she toyed with the idea of telling him who she was. Surely, now on the eve of battle, he wouldn't expose her! But even as the idea surfaced in her mind, she knew that now, more than ever, he *would* expose her. It would be his idea of chivalry, she knew, to try and protect her from the battle that was to come.

Oh, how she wanted to tell him! If only he could understand her reasons for doing this and could accept her for them! They could have comforted each other now, taking love where they found it.

Love? Tamara thought. No, not really, not in the girlish, romantic sense that she had once imagined love to be. Not even in the true sense of a man and woman, cleaving only unto each other until death do them part, she decided. For the truth was Tamara had abandoned those female concepts when she had abandoned the dress of a woman. The need she felt for Dan now was a physical need. No, it was more than just physical, she decided. It was an emotional need, greater than physical, though less than romantic.

Why couldn't Dan accept that? Why couldn't

he fill the need she had, and allow her to do what she must do? But the question, unasked except in Tamara's mind, needed no answer. Things were as they were because of an inviolable law of society, and there was nothing Tamara could do about it.

Colonel Peabody was standing outside his tent when Tamara and Dan reached his headquarters.

"Hello, Captain Savage," Peabody said in greeting. "Captain O'Lee, isn't it?"

"Yes, colonel," Dan replied.

"What brings you two over here?"

"Colonel, General Prentiss requests that you send out a patrol tonight," Tamara said. "I would like to lead the patrol."

"I send out a patrol every night," Peabody replied gruffly.

"Colonel, I have reason to believe that an attack is probable, tonight or early in the morning," Dan said.

"I agree," Tamara put in. "Do you recall that in my patrol today I encountered a rather large body of men moving up the Corinth road?"

"Yes, but when I spoke to you later, you said that you had changed your mind about its significance."

"I've since spoken to Captain O'Lee, and feel that I was right the first time. So, in addition to the regular patrol you intend to send out, I

366

should like to take one of my own, my entire company."

"All right." Peabody nodded. "If you really feel there is something to it, I'll attach two other companies to you, and you can go out in strength."

"Thank you, colonel."

"Colonel, I would like to accompany Captain Savage," Dan put in quickly.

"I don't have any objections," Colonel Peabody replied.

"No!" Tamara said quickly. "Colonel, forgive me, sir, but this is a very important patrol, and I would rather not have an interloper along."

Peabody raised an eyebrow, then shrugged. "Very well, captain, it's your command," he agreed. "I'm sorry, O'Lee, but I have to honor Captain Savage's wishes on this."

"As you wish, sir," Dan said dejectedly.

Tamara turned to Colonel Peabody's orderly. "Would you pass the word to the other two companies that I shall be ready to proceed in half an hour?"

"Yes, sir," the orderly replied, saluting, then hurried off on his mission.

"And, if you will excuse me, colonel, I've my own company to prepare," Tamara said.

"Good luck to you, captain," Colonel Peabody answered.

"I wish you good luck as well," Dan said.

"I'm sorry I couldn't overrule Captain Savage," Colonel Peabody told Dan after Tamara had left. "But as long as my officers serve me well, and faithfully, I make it a point to back them up."

"I understand, sir," Dan said. "What I don't understand is why Captain Savage was so adamant against my coming along. That puzzles me."

"Perhaps it is just as he said. He feels that a stranger along would make his job more difficult."

"I wish I could believe that," Dan said.

"You mean you don't?"

"No, sir. I've known Captain Savage from somewhere else, but for the life of me I can't place where. Wherever it was, though, I must have done something to incur his dislike, for he has barely said a civil word to me since we met."

"I'll admit he's a strange one," Colonel Peabody said. "He's very quiet, and he stays to himself all the time. But he's a courageous officer who never shirks his duty. I wish I had an entire brigade just like him."

"Has he been long in your brigade?"

"He joined us just before we left Cairo. 'Bout the seventeenth of last month, I guess. But he's found a home with me, I'll tell you that."

Colonel Peabody offered Dan a cup of coffee. They drank and talked as they waited for the patrol to depart. Colonel Peabody had heard of the canal Dan had built at New Madrid, and he asked many questions about it.

"Have you ever been to Vicksburg?" Colonel Peabody asked.

"No, sir."

"You mark my words, the battle at Vicksburg is going to be even harder than the one at New Madrid. Vicksburg is the next major fortress on the river. It sits on a big bend, too. Could be that a canal will be needed there."

"I don't know the terrain around Vicksburg," Dan said. "But if it isn't as swampy as the area around New Madrid, I doubt that a canal could be built."

Colonel Peabody chuckled. "I don't think there's any place that can compare with the swamps around New Madrid, except maybe the Okeefenokee in Georgia, or the Everglades in Florida. Besides, the land around Vicksburg is all good, rich farmland."

"Calvert Hills," Dan said.

"I beg your pardon?"

"I know someone whose father owned a plantation near Vicksburg. It was called Calvert Hills," Dan said, thinking of Tamara.

At that moment, the three companies started out on their patrol, and leading them was Captain Savage. The horse he was riding reared once in the excitement, and Savage had to grab the reins to calm the animal. At that moment,

Dan got his first clear look at the captain's face, lighted as it was from the nearby campfire.

"Tamara!" Dan shouted, taking a step toward her.

Tamara spurred her horse and darted to the front of the column, quickly leading them away.

"What did you say?" Colonel Peabody asked, puzzled by Dan's strange behavior.

"Captain Savage, I know now who . . ." Dan started. He stopped. "I know where I've seen him," he finished lamely.

"I know you feel better about remembering," Peabody said. "Something like that can get in a man's craw and agitate him for a long time." He stretched. "Well, they should be out for a couple of hours. I think I'll grab a few winks of sleep. I'd advise you to do the same thing, captain. If we are about to be attacked, we need all the rest we can get."

"I agree, sir," Dan replied. "Good night, sir," he added, starting for his own tent.

But Dan knew he wouldn't sleep. He could think of nothing, except the fact that Tamara was out there leading a patrol.

Tamara had heard Dan's call just before she rode away. So. He recognized her—and was probably telling Colonel Peabody about it, even now. In all likelihood, that meant that this would be the last chance she would have at inflicting damage against the Confederacy. She hoped she would have the opportunity to fight. She smiled. She would create the opportunity. They were out there, she knew. She would just keep going down the Corinth road until she encountered them.

Tamara led the three-company-sized cavalry force down the road, going in a southwesterly direction, moving the animals at a brisk trot. The road lay out before her, dappled silver by the moonbeams which reached it through the spreading branches of the trees.

As they rode, they were not only advancing toward the Confederate lines but moving parallel with the front of the Federal lines. By now, they had moved into the area immediately in front of General Sherman's sector.

It was at that point that they rode right into Hardee's corps. The surprised Confederates, who were moving into a line of battle preparing for their own attack, opened fire at the Union troops.

Tamara heard the bullets humming about her. Then she saw a puff of dust rise from the tunic of the rider immediately to her left as one of the bullets buried itself into his chest.

"Return fire!" she ordered. "Skirmish line to the right!"

The Union troops moved out into a long skirmish line, exchanging fire briskly with the Confederate troops. The sound of the muskets fired by the Confederates, and the pistols and carbines fired by the Union cavalry, grew from rapid poppings to a low, sustained roar, and a huge cloud of smoke billowed over the battlefield.

General Johnston, at breakfast with his staff and hearing the fire of the encounter, turned to his son Preston and to his aide, Captain Munford. He directed them to note the hour in their log books. It was fourteen minutes after five o'clock in the morning.

"Gentlemen, our hand is played," Johnston said quietly. "Give the order all along the line. Attack at once."

28

By daybreak, the wounded from Tamara's reconnaissance in force were returning to the camp, and Colonel Peabody, seeing that the Confederates had been engaged in strength, ordered the long roll beaten. A young drummer boy, perhaps fourteen years old, ran into the company street beating the call to battle on his drum. His call was taken up by other drummers in adjacent regiments, and shortly it began spreading down the line.

"What of Captain Savage?" Dan asked one of the wounded.

"When last I seen the fiery little devil, he was still mounted, leading a charge against a Rebel gun battery," the soldier said.

At that moment General Prentiss came riding rapidly down the line, looking for Peabody.

"Colonel, my orders to you were quite specific," Prentiss shouted angrily. "You were not to bring on a battle. I shall hold you personally responsible for this engagement."

"General, I am personally responsible for all my official acts," Colonel Peabody said.

"My God, colonel, look at that!" one of the nearby soldiers called, and Dan, along with Colonel Peabody and General Prentiss, looked in the direction the soldier had pointed.

There, coming down a gentle slope just in front of them and already within easy musket range, were the Confederates. They were massed many lines deep. They were moving toward them like an ocean of gray, flowing down the hill, rolling over small shrubs and fence lines and crossing roads as if they were a mighty force of nature.

"What then?" Prentiss shouted, shocked at the sight.

The men of Peabody's brigade had fallen in with weapons at the ready. While Prentiss was staring in open-mouthed shock, the colonel had assessed the situation and now acted quickly.

"Attention, men," he shouted. "Ready, aim, fire!"

The muskets of Peabody's brigade sounded as one. But, though Dan saw a score of the gray-clad warriors go down, the Confederate army continued to move forward, and now they were answering the fire.

Dan carried only a pistol as a weapon. He pulled it from his holster and answered the Rebel shot. Bullets whizzed around him like angry bees, and he could feel the shock waves of those which passed very close.

"Hurrah, boys!" one of the officers shouted. "Here comes a battery up. We'll give them hell now!"

Dan answered the shout with a cheer, as did most of the men. But the cheers soon turned to exclamations of surprise and horror, as they realized that the gun was not Union, but Confederate. Within seconds after it was in position, it opened up on Dan and the others with grape and canister.

"Fall back!" General Prentiss started shouting. "Fall back!"

Dan looked around for Colonel Peabody. He saw his horse running by, riderless, the stirrups flapping in the air. He looked in the direction from which the horse had come and saw the colonel lying on the ground, face up to the sky, eyes and mouth wide open.

"Colonel!" Dan shouted, running to the fallen officer. But as soon as he got there he knew that it was too late to help the colonel.

"Fall back, men," Prentiss shouted again. "Captain O'Lee, assume command of the left flank, sir!"

"Yes, sir," Dan shouted. He ran at a crouch to the left flank, where the shot and shell had already decimated the ranks.

Slowly Peabody's brigade retired from one defensible position after another until they finally reached a roadway termed Sunken Road, for it was cut for some distance through a low hill. Here, nature had provided what General Grant had hesitated to dig, a fortified position.

"Hold at this road!" Dan shouted to his men. He stood behind them, himself exposed to fire, and shoved and cajoled them back into position on the parapet of the road. "Stand here and fight, men!" he shouted.

Several of the officers, themselves as green and new to battle as the men they commanded, sought the cover of the embankment. They lay there as low as they could press their bodies, covering their heads with their arms and hands. But a few of the officers joined Dan in helping to squash the retreat. They forced the men back to the line to take up firing positions against the enemy. Finally, the men heeded Dan's entreaties. The retreat stopped at Sunken Road.

"Cap'n!" one of the men shouted. "Here comes that damned battery again!"

Dan looked toward a cannon being pulled rapidly behind galloping horses. Suddenly he recognized one of the outriders as Tamara!

"Don't fire on the battery, men, it's Captain Savage!" Dan shouted, and as the battery roared into position on Sunken Road, Tamara and the handful of men who were with her were given a rousing cheer.

"Where is Colonel Peabody?" Tamara asked, out of breath from the mad dash.

"Killed," Dan said. He looked up and saw a handful of men coming in on horseback, swinging out of the saddles as their horses hit Sunken Road, then driving for the parapet to add their firepower to that of the men already in position.

"Where are the rest of your men?" Dan asked.

"These are all I returned with," Tamara said. "The rest are dead, wounded or missing."

"My God, from three companies?"

"Yes," Tamara said.

"Cap'n, they're fixin' up for another charge!" someone shouted.

"Hold your places, men!" Dan responded. "Is there any ammunition in the caisson of that gun you stole?" Dan asked Tamara.

"Quite a bit."

"Then let's get it firing. You take command."

Tamara, whose face, like everyone else's now, was black with powder and gunsmoke, smiled broadly. "I'll get right on it," she said. "And thanks for not giving me away."

"Tamara, I swear to God, if there was any way I could give you away now and get you out of here safely, I'd do it. But you, like the rest of us, are trapped."

Dan heard the loud shouts of the attacking soldiers, screaming in what was now known as the Rebel Yell. It was an unnerving sound, issuing from the throats of thousands of men.

"Hold your fire, men," Dan shouted. "Load your weapons and hold your fire!"

Dan heard the cannon go off and watched the canister shell rip into the attacking gray line, cutting down five men. Their places were immediately filled by five others, and Dan thought it was like taking your finger out of a bucket of water and leaving a hole. Nothing seemed to stop them.

"Hold your fire until my command," he said again, and all along the line he could see the men nervously holding their muskets, drawing long and careful aim, and waiting nervously for that command.

Still they came.

Now the Confederates were so close that Dan could see their features. He looked at them in amazement, wondering that they could continue on in such an unbroken line, knowing that they were marching right into musketry fire.

One of the men in front of the advancing gray line held up a sword and shouted something to the others. Dan couldn't hear what he said, but he could hear the sound of his voice, small and tinny over the distance, carried to him because, except for the firing of the cannon, there was a temporary lull in the shooting.

The man was obviously an officer. He had

obviously given the command to advance on the double, because the advancing army suddenly broke into a run. Again Dan heard the Rebel yell.

"Now, men, fire now!" he yelled, and his order was answered with the sustained roar of rifle fire.

Four more cannons moved into Sunken Road. They were from the famous Waterhouse battery, specially designed guns bought with private funds by a Chicago millionaire. They opened up on the Rebel lines almost as soon as they were in position. The cannonading, along with the crunching effect of the rifle fire, finally caused the Rebel lines to falter, hesitate, then break and withdraw.

"We whipped 'em, boys, we whipped 'em!" a jubilant soldier shouted, and the others cheered lustily.

But Dan, though he joined in the cheer, wasn't convinced that the tide had been turned. He walked back and forth behind the line of his men, feeling the sweat pour down his back, aware that a muscle in his leg was jumping uncontrollably, sucking in air in audible gasps.

"Do you reckon they'll come ag'in?" one of the men asked.

"Naw, we whipped them seven ways from Sunday," another said.

"I don't know. I never seen nothin' like it. I mean they just kept on comin' at us, even though we was firin' at them somethin' fierce."

"They ain't comin' ag'in," another said. "They's no way on God's earth they could come ag'in."

"Lis'sen to that," somebody else said. From some distance away they could hear the crashing thunder of artillery and the roar of musketry.

"My God, they're attackin' all along our line! There must be a million of 'em!"

"What'll we do, cap'n? We can't stay here an' fight a million of 'em!" another cried.

"There are as many boys in blue as there are in gray," Dan said. "You just do your part and hold back the Rebs that are coming after us. We'll let the generals worry about the others."

"That's what I'm afraid of," one of the soldiers called back. "I'm not sure the generals know what the hell they're doin'."

"We know, soldier," Prentiss said at that moment. He'd come up Sunken Road from Dan's right.

"General Prentiss. How is it over on your side?"

"We've taken quite a few casualties," Prentiss said. "But we're still holding on. How is it with you?"

"About the same," Dan said. He reached for his canteen, then noticed with some consternation that it was only about one-third full. He normally filled it daily, but the events of last

night and this morning had caused him to forget about it.

"I'm afraid the lack of water may give us
quite a few problems," Prentiss said, noticing
Dan's predicament. "Most of the men are in
the same situation you are. Little or no water."

"Son-of-a-bitch, here they come again!" one
of the men yelled.

General Prentiss looked toward the line of
woods into which the enemy had disappeared on
the last assault. He saw that they were, indeed,
forming for another attack.

"I have to get back to my position," the general said, starting at a crouching run for the
right side of the road. "Give 'em hell, men!" he
shouted.

"We will, general."

"Get ready, men, here they come," Dan said.
The warning was hardly necessary. There wasn't
a man in the whole of Sunken Road, now being
called by some the Hornet's Nest, who didn't
know another attack was shaping up.

This attack began just as the other one had.
First came the slow, steady advance of the men
in gray, then the ear-piercing Rebel yell, and
finally the onslaught of firing.

The yells of the men in gray were answered
by cheers of the boys in blue, and these yells and
cheers rose and fell with the varying tide of
battle. Those sounds, along with the hoarse and

scarcely distinguishable orders of the officers, the screaming and bursting of shells, the swishing sounds of canister, the roaring of volley firing, the death screams of the stricken and struggling horses and the cries and groans of the wounded, formed an indescribable impression which Dan knew he would never erase from his memory.

Dan could hear the orders of the Waterhouse battery commander, sharp and clear, above all other noise: "Shrapnel," "Two seconds," "One second," "Canister." And then, as the Rebels reached the closest point: "Double canister!"

Vainly, courageous Cnofederate leaders attempted to rally their forces in the face of the devastating fire. But their lines wavered, halted, then finally made a mad rush for cover, leaving each cannon's line of fire marked by rows of dead and dying.

But with each advance the Confederates came closer. The defending fire lessened as the ranks were thinned and the ammunition expended. The day wore on, and Dan could see his lines gradually melting away. Then he saw Rebel troops crossing the peach orchard in the rear, threatening to surround what was left of General Prentiss's division.

Dan moved quickly down the line to tell Prentiss of the new danger.

"We've got to get out of here," Dan said tersely.

"There's no way we can make it," General Prentiss replied. "Our only recourse is to surrender."

"Surrender? Never!" Dan said. "General, we can get out of here. I know we can."

"We'll be cut down like wheat," Prentiss insisted.

"Then at least give permission to any who wish to try and escape capture to do so," Dan begged.

"Very well," Prentiss said. "You have my permission. But if you intend to try that, do so at once, before your action places the rest of us in grearter danger."

"Yes, sir," Dan said. He moved quickly back to his position along the line. "Men, listen to me," he called. "General Prentiss intends to surrender, but he has given me permission to try and escape, and to take as many of you as want to go. It will be dangerous, but I've no wish to become a prisoner of war. Now, who is with me?"

There were scarcely a handful of men who took advantage of Dan's offer. One who did was Tamara.

"I think we should try and get the batteries out of here," Tamara said. "I don't want them to fall into Rebel hands."

"Good idea," Dan said. "Are your horses hurt?"

"I've only one left without a wound," Tamara said. "But I think I can get them to pull the gun."

"Then let's get going," Dan said.

Tamara returned to the cannon she had stolen from the Confederates. Within moments she had it ready to leave. But when Dan looked back toward the Waterhouse cannons, he saw, amazingly, that they were not preparing to leave.

"We've got to get these guns out of here!" Dan shouted to the battery commander.

"No, sir," the battery commander answered, his eyes reflecting his fright. "I'm not going anywhere. If General Prentiss is about to surrender, I'm not going to take a chance on getting killed trying to escape. I'd rather be captured and accept a parole, or sit out the war safe in some Rebel prison camp."

"But the guns!" Dan shouted. "The Rebels will get the guns!"

"I don't care," the battery commander said.

"Dan, we've got to go now or it'll be too late," Tamara called desperately.

Dan gave an exasperated sigh. The Waterhouse commander would not even try! Then he looked at the ones who had indicated they would leave with him. "All right, those of you who are going, let's go now!" he shouted. A half-dozen brave men started down the road with him. Tamara, riding one of the horses that was pulling the gun, led the way. Because she was mounted and up front, she became the target for the Rebel muskets drawing fire away from the others so that they could make it.

"Cap'n, look at Cap'n Savage!" one of the men shouted breathlessly. "Every Rebel in Mississippi is shootin' at him."

Tamara, urging her horse on with whip and spur, finally rode behind a small hill which offered cover from the fire. She turned them and quickly put the gun into position to fire one covering charge of cannister. It held the Rebels back just enough to allow Dan and his men to effect their escape.

Man or woman, Dan knew he had never been witness to a more courageous act. He doubted that he would ever see such bravery topped. He vowed to himself at that moment never to betray Tamara's secret. For surely, he thought, she had earned her right to fight her war.

29

The brave stand made by Dan and the men of General Prentiss's division in the Hornet's Nest was, for a time, the only thing which checked the Confederate advance. When Prentiss finally surrendered, the men in gray surged on through, cheering and yelling, and pushed toward the bank of the Tennessee River.

Then, unexpectedly, the right side of the advance faltered as the Federal soldiers took a stand and began fighting back. General Johnston, told of the stiffened resistance, ordered that an attack be launched against the Federal position. A few moments later, the messenger returned with a note from the Confederate commander who had been ordered into the assault.

"General," the note read. "I fear an assault of the kind you have ordered is not possible without first halting and regrouping my men. Also, I shall require the support of at least two additional regiments in order to ensure the success of the attack. Your obedient servant, B. Beauregard, Colonel, Commanding."

"I will not commit my reserves now," Johnston thundered. 'There is no reason Beauregard cannot begin his assault immediately. In fact, he should have already done so!"

"I expressed your wishes to the colonel, general," the messenger said. "But he refused to comply."

General Johnston slapped his reins against his horse and raced behind his attacking army until he arrived at the position occupied by Beauregard's division. There, he was amazed to see that the advance had not only been stopped but that the Confederates' positions were in danger of being abandoned. Colonel Beauregard was even then shouting orders to fall back to the tree line.

"Hold it, men," General Johnston shouted, reaching them at that moment. "Hold your position!" Johnston swung off his lathered horse and walked quickly to Colonel Beauregard, whose personal position was some twenty-five yards behind his men.

"Colonel, what's the meaning of this?" he asked. Even as he spoke, the whine of Union bullets could be heard around them.

Blackie looked at General Johnston, and Johnston could see that his eyes were opened wide with fear, his pupils dilated. He was ashen-faced and sweating, and he could talk only with difficulty.

"Ge . . . ge . . . general," Blackie said. "Th . . . the . . . the Yankees have reinforced their position, and they are turning us back."

"Nonsense, colonel," Johnston answered. "You are turning your own men back through your cowardice. Now you get in front of your men, and you lead them to the attack!"

"I . . . I . . . I can't," Blackie said.

"You are a coward, sir, and I shall deal with you later!" Johnston replied angrily. The general whirled around returned to his horse, then leaped into the saddle. He rode to the front of the lines, exposing himself to galling fire, then, moving slowly back and forth in front of the troops, began speaking words of encouragement to them, urging them to pull themselves together, to fight back.

"My God, look at the general!" one of the men shouted.

"I'll follow a general like that anywhere!" another said, and within moments, a cheer of defiance went along the Confederate lines.

"Let's go, men!" General Johnston shouted, and he led the charge.

The line surged forward. The Union soldiers, seeing the Rebels suddenly rise up and charge, gave way, so that the rout became complete, and victory seemed at hand for General Johnston and the Confederate army.

Blackie, now given confidence by the success of General Johnston, rode quickly to the head of his troops. The conversation with General Johnston, and his charges of cowardice, had taken place out of the range of hearing of his troops, so Blackie knew that if he could re-establish himself, he had not yet lost face. Provided, of course, that General Johnston didn't press charges of cowardice against him after the battle was completed.

He had started toward Johnston to plead with him to give him another chance when he saw the general suddenly slump in his saddle. Blackie reached him just before he fell off his horse.

"General, are you wounded?"

"Yes," Johnston replied.

"I will get you to an aid station," Blackie said. Johnston shook his head. "The bleeding," he said. "I am growing weak from the bleeding. You must stop it at once."

Blackie led General Johnston on his horse to a shallow depression about one hundred yards behind the line of battle. There, he dismounted and took the general off his own horse. He lay him down.

"The bleeding," Johnston said again, his voice very weakened.

Blackie looked at General Johnston's leg. It was soaked with blood now, though the wound itself had not appeared to be too severe. An errant piece of shrapnel had evidently severed an artery.

"General, you won't press charges of cowardice, will you?" Blackie asked.

Johnston opened his eyes and looked into Blackie's face. He licked his lips and tried to say something, but now he was too weak to speak.

"It would be bad for morale," Blackie said. "I mean, how would it look if my men thought I was a coward? And me the nephew of General Beauregard. I think it would be best for all concerned if we just forgot all about that charge, don't you?"

Johnston was unable to answer. He had passed out.

Blackie stood there and looked down at the still form of the general for a moment. Suddenly he heard hoofbeats behind him, and he turned to see Captain Mumford, General Johnston's aide.

"How is the general?" Mumford asked anxiously.

"He has a leg wound," Blackie answered easily. "He's resting now. Perhaps you'd better get a surgeon to look at him."

"Yes, sir," Mumford replied quickly. He didn't leave his horse to check on General Johnston's condition. Instead, he whirled the horse about and went for the surgeon at a gallop.

After Captain Mumford had pounded off on his errand, Blackie strode slowly and nonchalantly to his horse. As if mounting for a leisurely ride, he swung into the saddle. Once mounted, he rode a few steps toward the general, then looked down at the prostrate man.

General Johnson was absolutely still. There was a widening pool of blood below his leg. The pumping, gushing action had stopped.

The pounding of hooves reached Blackie again. He turned to see Captain Mumford returning, this time with the division surgeon in tow.

"I'm glad you're here," Blackie shouted. "He seemed to take a turn for the worse, and I thought I'd better summon you quickly."

"My God, man!" the surgeon said, swinging off his horse and hurrying toward General Johnston. He knelt beside the stricken general, put his fingers on his neck, then opened Johnston's eyes and peered into them. He put his ear on Johnston's chest and listened for a moment. Then he straightened up and looked at Blackie and Captain Mumford with a look of surprise on his face.

"I thought you said the General wasn't badly hurt," the surgeon said to Mumford.

"Well, is he?" Mumford asked, clearly puzzled by the surgeon's reaction.

"He's dead, captain."

Captain Mumford looked at Blackie with an expression of shock and disbelief. "Sir, the impression you gave me was that the general was suffering from a slight leg wound only."

"I did not use the word 'slight,' captain," Blackie said easily. "And I did summon a surgeon, did I not? With the many other wounded soldiers, I would scarcely have summoned him had the need not been urgent."

"My God," Captain Mumford said, in anguished tones. "If the general has died due to my inattention, I shall never forgive myself."

"There, captain," Blackie said generously. "You mustn't blame yourself. It is an act of war. Now, if you gentlemen will excuse me, I must get back to my command. Captain Mumford, you'd best inform my uncle at once. He will have to assume command now."

"Yes, sir," Mumford said sadly. He looked at the dead general for a moment longer, then, with a tear sliding down his powder-blackened cheek, turned to deliver the sad message to General Beauregard.

There were more than two hours of sunshine remaining when Beauregard assumed command. At that moment the Confederate army was drawn up in a magnificent line of battle, extending up and down the river bottom to the right and left as far as the eye could see. The Union army, backed up to the banks of the Tennessee, was awaiting the final push and the summons to surrender.

"General, we've got them where we want them," Beauregard's aide said.

"Exactly," Beauregard replied.

"Shall I pass the message to commence the final advance?"

"No," Beauregard said. "We shall stay right here."

"But, general, we have them!" the captain said, not understanding Beauregard's reluctance to attack.

"They will be there tomorrow," Beauregard said.

"Tomorrow? Why wait until tomorrow?"

Beauregard looked at his aide and smiled. "Because if we continue the attack now, I will have to share the victory with General Johnston. If we attack tomorrow, the triumph will be mine alone."

The word was passed to hold positions and continue to fire at the Union lines. By now the enemy was obscured by the battlefield smoke, which lay over everything like a thick fog, so that the firing was without aim or order.

Over on the Union side, General Grant, who had arrived early in the morning when he heard the intense shelling, had formed a last stand on the ridge which commanded the bank of the river. Grant and Sherman were seemingly everywhere at the same moment, staying the retreat and reforming the lines, directing the artillery fire, urging the men to stand fast. The drama of this day was drawing to a close. Grant had been beaten along his entire front, and he knew it.

Then, just before sundown, a breathless messenger arrived and handed a note to Grant. Grant read it, then smiled broadly.

"What is it, general?" Dan asked anxiously. Dan had returned to General Grant's staff after his narrow escape from the Hornet's Nest.

"General Buell has arrived," Grant said. "The tide of battle has turned."

30

Because of the ebb and flow of the battle, there were dead and wounded scattered over an area of ten square miles. The first day's fighting had left a total of nearly ten thousand, counting the casualties of both sides, and as night fell, the sound of their groans and moans were piteous to even the most hardened ears.

One who could not bear the sounds of the suffering without making some effort to provide aid was the small captain whom most knew as Bill Savage, but who was in reality Tamara Calvert. A couple of hours after sundown, Tamara, without telling anyone what she intended to do, picked up as many canteens as she could carry and started out to help the wounded.

The night was dark and overcast, without moon or stars to light the way. A breeze came up, carrying on it a damp chill. Tamara pulled her coat about her and continued on, picking her way across roads and fields now littered with the discarded materiels of war: weapons, equipment, and the dead and dying.

"Water," a weak voice called, and Tamara halted. "I beg of you sir, be you Union or Confederate, if you're a Christian man, you'll give me water."

"Yes," Tamara said. "I have water." She moved quickly to the soldier, a young Union private wearing the insignia of the 14th Illinois on his collar, and held a canteen to his lips. The boy began to drink deeply.

"No," Tamara said, pulling the canteen back. "You mustn't drink too deeply. It isn't good for you."

"I'm dying anyway," the boy said matter-of-factly. "I'd rather die with my thirst quenched."

Tamara gave him the canteen and let him drink his fill. Finally he gave it back to her, then thanked her.

"I'll tell a surgeon where you are," she said.

"Don't bother none, cap'n," the boy said. "There's others out here need'n a drink too. You carry the water to 'em, 'n when you come back this way, why if I happen to still be alive, I might just want another, if you don't mind."

"I promise to do that," Tamara said, choking back the lump in her throat. She stood up, looked down at the wounded soldier, then went to the next one and gave him water as well.

Tamara passed no one, giving water and comfort to Union and Confederate alike. It was in this way that she recognized one of the Confederate soldiers as a young man who had grown up on a plantation adjacent to her father's. She had known him her entire life, and when she bent to give him water and looked into his face, she gasped.

"Jimmy?" she said. "Is that you?"

The wounded man opened his eyes. Even in the dim light she could see the agony in them.

"Do you know me, sir?" the soldier asked.

"Are you Jimmy Wix of Fairhope Acres?"

"Yes, sir," the soldier said. "Who are you? Why, you're a Yankee. I don't know any Yankees."

Tamara tipped the canteen up and let him drink. She put her hand on his forehead. It was burning hot, and she knew a fever had set in, compounding the wound.

"Do you want me to make you a pillow from your knapsack?" Tamara asked.

"Yes, sir," the boy said. He continued to look at Tamara with intense curiosity. Finally, he spoke again. "I do know you, don't I? But you aren't a Yankee. What are you doing in a Yankee uniform?"

"I'm Tamara Calvert," Tamara finally said.

"I swan, you are!" the soldier said. "But . . . but what are you doing here, Miss Tamara?"

"Surely, you've heard the story by now," Tamara said.

"Oh," the boy said. "Yes, yes I suppose I

have. You were to marry Colonel Beauregard, but . . . uh . . ." He stopped in embarrassment.

"I see you've heard it," Tamara said.

"Colonel Beauregard is here," the boy said. "He's commandin' the Second Mississippi Horse. My regiment," the boy added proudly.

"Blackie is here?" Tamara asked, with quickened interest.

"Yes, ma'am," the boy went on. "He was a hero this afternoon, you know that? The whole Second Mississippi Horse was heroes. We made a charge that pushed the Yankees all the way back to the river."

"Where is Blackie now?" Tamara asked.

"Oh, I 'spects he's with General Beauregard. They'll be plannin' what to do tomorra'. Miss Tamara, do you reckon you could see fit to leave me have another drink of water?"

"Certainly," Tamara said, holding the canteen to the boy's lips.

After making Jimmy Wix comfortable, Tamara went on, picking her way through the battlefield, providing what aid she could. But even as she did so, her mind was now racing ahead, concentrating on what she knew she must do.

There were others out aiding the wounded. Confederate and Union soldiers alike worked together to comfort the fallen, without regard as to the victim's side. Because of that it was not unusual to see northern and southern soldiers walking around in the dark, unarmed, sometimes talking to each other.

That was when Tamara realized that her plan would work.

The battlefield was strewn with bodies, and Tamara began to take a special interest in the Confederate dead. Finally, she found a soldier of about her size. Quickly, she stripped him of his uniform. A few moments later, dressed in the gray of a Confederate private, she started walking toward the Confederate lines. She had no particular plan of action, just a purpose. It was to kill Blackie Beauregard.

Because the Confederate army had carried the battle on the first day's fighting, they were better organized in handling their casualties than the Union army was. The Confederate lines were advanced nearly to the river, so much of the battlefield had been within their control during the day. That meant that though thousands of dead and dying Confederate soldiers were still lying out in the dark, many hundreds had been brought back to the rear areas, where a hospital was functioning.

The wounded were lying shoulder to shoulder, stretched out in rows of fifty to sixty men. Some lay stiff and quiet, but many were writhing in pain, moaning and groaning, occasionally screaming out a curse, or a prayer, screaming it in such a way that one couldn't be sure which it was.

Everywhere there was blood, dirty bandages, the smell of unwashed bodies, purged bowels and emptied bladders. Added to this was a vicious swarm of mosquitoes, gorging themselves upon the pitiful victims.

Volunteers and nurses worked feverishly, and in most cases, futilely, to alleviate some of the suffering of the soldiers. One of the volunteers was Liberty Welles.

When Liberty first arrived, she took one look and one smell, then shrank back in horror. She had to fight against throwing up, so overwhelming was the odor, so terrible was the sight. She had never seen anything like this in her life, nor dreamed it, even in her most horrible nightmare. But this was no nightmare . . . this was real. And buried deep in her mind was the knowledge that she was the cause of this battle. *She* was the cause of all this pain and death. But Liberty allowed that thought to surface for an instant only, then buried it with a will, for to dwell on it, she knew, could drive her insane with remorse.

"Miss," one of the soldiers called, as Liberty stood there, looking out at the mass of suffering humanity.

Liberty put all her queasiness aside, pasted on a smile, and moved quickly to the soldier. "Yes?" she answered.

"Miss, would you see to Tim? He's been sufferin' somethin' fierce, though he's quiet now, 'n I'm worried about him."

"Which one is Tim? Liberty asked.

"He's the feller over to the fence there," the soldier said, raising himself with effort and pointing to a prostrate figure.

"I see him," Liberty said. "I'll see how he is for you."

"Thankee, ma'am," the soldier said, lying back down.

Liberty picked her way through the men, passing those who lay dull-eyed, with hands clutched to wounds, glued there now by coagulated blood, until she reached the soldier named Tim.

Liberty gasped. It was T.J. Cole, the soldier whose letter she had written earlier in the day. She bent down to look at him, but even as she did, she knew that T.J. Cole would never need another letter written, or get back to his farm, or kiss his little Anne, or see the likeness of his wife, Martha. For T.J. Cole was dead.

Liberty couldn't face it any more. She stood up quickly, with tears burning her eyes. She had only one thing on her mind now, and that was to run away.

"*How is he?*" the soldier who had sent her to check called. "*How is he, miss? How is old Tim? Tell me, miss, me 'n Tim, we're good friends, how is he?*"

Feverish hands reached for her, grabbed at her skirt. Though they may have been asking for water, or a blanket, in Liberty's troubled mind they were shouting accusations at her.

"You did this!" they seemed to shout. *"It is all your doing. You, you, you, you!"*

"How is he? How is he, miss? How is old Tim? How is he? How is he?"

"You killed us! You killed us! Murderer! MURDERER! MURDERER!"

Liberty screamed, then ran as fast as her legs could carry her, past the surprised surgeons and officers and nurses who looked at her with shock, until finally, she was far enough away that she couldn't smell the stench, or hear the groans, or feel the accusing eyes. And there, she threw herself to the ground, where, no longer able to hold it back, she vomited in the damp, dark dirt.

Less than one hundred yards from where Liberty lay retching on the ground, a jubilant group of Confederate officers celebrated the day's triumph and contemplated the next day's final victory.

"I must confess, Blackie," General Beauregard said proudly, "I had some reservations about giving you a division of your own. But your inspired leadership, coupled with that of our fallen commander, carried the day for us.

I have mentioned you in the dispatches, and I shall petition Congress to appoint you a brigadier general."

Blackie beamed under his uncle's compliments and proudly accepted the congratulations of the other officers. "I just wish General Johnston could be here with us to accept the just fruits of his efforts today," Blackie said.

"Hear, hear," one of the other officers responded.

"Gentlemen, if you would, let's have a moment of silent prayer for our fallen leader," General Polk recommended.

The officers all bowed their heads in silent reverence, and Blackie could scarcely contain his glee. He was going to be a general! And Johnston wasn't around to stop it.

There was a soldier, just outside the circle of light created by the campfire, who was staring at them. In fact, he seemed to be staring directly at Blackie, and it was making Blackie nervous. Who was he? Was he someone who may have overheard General Johnston's accusations of cowardice? Was he about to say something now?

The soldier started toward the group of generals, and Blackie felt a strange sense of foreboding. Somehow, he sensed, this soldier represented a danger to him.

"Blackie," the soldier called.

The fact that a common soldier would address a general-designate by his first name startled the other generals, and they looked up in surprise. They were also annoyed that the soldier had interrupted their moment of silent meditation. Curious, General Polk asked Blackie who the soldier was.

"I don't know, general," Blackie said, starting toward the soldier. "But I shall soon find out."

The soldier took his hat off, then shook his long hair free.

"You know who I am, Blackie, for you were to have married me," Tamara said.

"Tamara, what the hell? What are you doing here?"

"I think you can guess at that," Tamara said. She drew her pistol and pointed it at Blackie. "Draw your gun, Blackie," she said.

"What? Tamara, don't be crazy!"

"Young lady, I don't know who you are, but I'm ordering you to put that pistol down," General Beauregard said.

"I'm sorry, general," Tamara said. "But I don't take orders from you. My commanding general is General Grant."

There was a gasp from those assembled.

Tamara's pistol was steady and unwavering. "I said draw your gun," she said again.

"Don't be a fool, young lady. You'll never get away with this!" General Beauregard said.

"I don't intend to," Tamara replied. "But I

do intend to kill Blackie first. For the last time, Blackie, draw your gun, or I'll shoot you where you stand."

"You'll shoot me as I start to draw," Blackie protested.

"No, I won't do that," Tamara said. "I'll give you the benefit of an affair of honor." She laughed. "How does it feel to be fighting a duel with a Negress?"

"Tamara, I never meant anything by that," Blackie pleaded. "I was going to get it all straightened out, and then . . ."

"Pull your gun!" Tamara said again, interrupting him.

Resignedly, cautiously, Blackie pulled at his gun, fully expecting a ball to crash into his brain at any moment. He was relieved, and somewhat surprised, when he was able to draw the gun free and raise it into position.

"General Beauregard, would you count to three, please?" Tamara asked.

"I will not sanction a duel," General Beauregard said.

"If you don't count to three, I will," Tamara said. "That would give me un unfair advantage. Do you want that?"

"I will not count the numbers," General Beauregard said again. "To do so would give the illusion of my approval, and I heartily disapprove."

"Then I'll have to count," Tamara said.

"No . . . I'll count," one of the general's aides, a captain, said.

"Thank you," Tamara said.

"Tamara, please, you've gone mad," Blackie said desperately. His tongue had thickened, and his throat was dry. From the corner of his eye he could see the others standing around in horror, helpless witnesses to this bizarre encounter.

"Quiet," Tamara said. "Begin counting, please."

"One," the captain said.

Blackie could feel his heart beating wildly.

"Two."

Blackie, cheating by one count, pulled the trigger. With a sudden surge of joy, he saw that his bullet had struck Tamara in the chest. Tamara was knocked down by the impact. Blackie started to shout in triumph, but Tamara forced herself into a sitting position, raised her gun, and fired once before falling back.

The bullet struck Blackie between the eyes. He spun around, then crumpled to the ground, dead.

"Arrest that woman!" General Beauregard shouted, pointing at Tamara. Two of the officers hurried to where she lay.

"Why did you do such a thing?" one asked.

"It was something that had to be done. And it had to be done by me." Tamara tried to sit up again, but when she did blood gushed from her wound.

"You'd best lie still, miss."

Others came to stand over her. They spoke in hushed tones. To Tamara, it sounded as if the words were coming from deep in a cave. She felt a spreading coldness invading her body, and by degrees, began to lose feeling. She knew without being told that she was dying.

"Send for the surgeon," someone said, as if speaking from a great, great distance.

"It's too late," another replied. "She's already dead."

Tamara wanted to tell them that she wasn't dead. She wanted to shout that she still lived. But even as the words formed in her brain, she knew they were false. She felt herself slipping away, as if sliding head-first down a long, long hill. She knew she couldn't hold onto life, and she wasn't sure she even wanted to.

31

Complete physical, mental, and emotional exhaustion took command of Liberty. She lay where she'd fallen for twelve hours. So she was unaware of the drama which had been played out in General Beauregard's headquarters, in which Tamara and Blackie Beauregard had died at each other's hand. And she was equally unaware of the drama which was being played out right now, as General Beauregard saw his lines being steadily rolled back by the Union troops, now reinforced by General Buell.

In the distance she could hear thunder. In the deep recesses of her mind, she wondered if her window was closed. She knew she should get up and check, but she was just too tired . . . and the bed felt too good.

"Get those damn guns up on the road. You there . . . what are you doing?"

"Colonel, I've got six guns and teams to pull only three."

"Then select the best three guns and spike the others, but get moving!"

"You heard the man, get moving," the second voice called.

At first, Liberty was confused as to why those men were in her bedroom. She lay there, fighting consciousness, until finally, slowly, she awakened.

She was not in bed.

Opening her eyes, she saw that she was lying in the dirt beneath a tree. She could hear voices, just from the other side of a small rise, and she raised up and looked toward them. There, men were working feverishly, hitching teams to cannons.

Liberty had a foul taste in her mouth and very much wanted to wash her face and hands. She knew where she was now. She knew also that a stream ran close by. So she gathered the strength to walk to the stream, where she fell on her hands and knees, drank deeply, then splashed the cool water on her face and hands.

She heard the pounding of hooves and looked up just as the cannons, which had been harnessed, came speeding through the stream. The spokes of the wheels were a blur and the horses sent up silver droplets of water as their pumping legs danced and splashed through the creek in their hasty retreat.

Liberty, somewhat refreshed from the water and the impromptu bath, walked back to the road and stood there, looking on in confusion as the army moved out.

"What are you doing here, miss?" an officer called to her. "General Beauregard sent all the civilians out of here this morning."

"What's going on?" Liberty asked. "Where is everyone going?"

"We're movin' back to Corinth, ma'am," the officer said.

"Moving back? But why? I thought we had the Yankees beaten!"

"Buell's army reinforced Grant," the officer said. He touched the brim of his hat. "You'll excuse me, ma'am, but I've got work to do."

"Where is Beauregard's headquarters?" Liberty asked.

"He's been set up over to the meetin' house, ma'am. It's called Shiloh."

Liberty thanked the officer and watched as he left, spurring his horse into a gallop. Once again, she found herself going one way on a road that was filled with soldiers going in the opposite direction. But this time the soldiers were retreating. . . . And whereas two days ago they had been full of bravado and jokes, today they were solemn, if not dispirited.

When Liberty reached General Beauregard's headquarters at Shiloh, she found it a beehive of activity. Mounted officers were arriving with messages and just as rapidly departing with them.

"Colonel Welles is in position, sir," one of the officers said.

"Good," Beauregard replied. "Tell him to commence his attack at three o'clock."

"Colonel Welles? Attack? What are you talking about?" Liberty shouted, running over to General Beauregard.

"Miss Welles, what are you doing here?" General Beauregard asked, surprised at Liberty's outburst.

"Never mind what I'm doing here. The question is, what is my father doing leading an attack? I thought he was in reserve!"

"That's precisely why he's leading the attack, Miss Welles," General Beauregard said. "I've ordered a general retreat of the entire army, but first, I intend to take the offensive again with vigor and drive back the enemy as far as possible. Your father will lead that attack, then hold his position, while the army withdraws to Corinth."

"But . . . but that's insane! That's a suicide mission!"

"Your father is aware of that. But he has assumed command of the division, and . . ."

"He's commanding the division? What happened to Colonel Beauregard?"

"He's dead," the general said simply. "As is Colonel Kelly. That leaves your father in command."

"No," Liberty said. "I won't allow it. General Johnston promised me . . ."

"General Johnston is dead too, Miss Welles," Beauregard explained. "Now, if you will, please retire from the battlefield. You aren't safe here."

Another rider came pounding into the headquarters area. "General Beauregard, Colonel Welles's compliments, sir, and he says to tell you that he has already been engaged by the enemy. He's been forced to start his attack now."

"No!" Liberty said. She started running toward the sound of battle.

"Lady, wait, there's fighting going on there," the dispatch rider called to her.

"Let her go," Beauregard said. "Deliver the message to all commanders. Fall back to the works around Corinth."

"Yes, sir," the rider said.

It was not difficult for Liberty to find her father's division, for she had only to go to the sound of crashing musketry. She ran, blinded by tears of rage and frustration, and finally burst forth from the woods to find herself in an open field. There, on that field, a long line of gray was advancing steadily against a long, low rock wall. There were cannon set up behind the wall, sprouting flame and death, and every foot of the fence line was occupied by a Union soldier, who held his musket at the ready, waiting for the Confederates to come.

"Oh, God, no!" Liberty said, breathing a prayer. "What are they doing?"

The line of gray continued on a slow, steady, unwavering march toward the rock fence. Even from where she stood, she could hear the roll of the drum as they moved out as on the parade field. In front of the line, regimental colors and the Stars and Bars of the Confederacy snapped in the breeze.

Liberty started running across the field. She was nearly even with the left flank of the attacking army when the Union soldiers opened fire. Fully one third of the advancing Confederates were cut down by the opening volley, yet still they continued, still at a slow, stately march.

It was nearly twenty seconds before the majority of the soldiers who had fired the first volley were reloaded, and though they were now firing without command, the natural timing of the action created a second volley nearly as devastating as the first. Nearly one third of the remaining Confederates went down.

Liberty saw her father, now holding a sword aloft with one arm while the other dangled uselessly at his side. He was covered with blood from a Minié ball. She gave a cry and started running to him, but at that moment a third sustained volley erupted from the Union position, and this time her father, along with half of the remaining attacking force, fell.

Seeing their leader down, the remaining soldiers turned and ran, chased across the field by the cheers of victory of the men in blue.

Liberty reached her father, then fell on her knees beside him. Tears were streaming down her face as she called out to him, beggingly.

"Please, don't die," she cried. "Please, don't die. Just don't die!"

But it was too late. Even as she held him, Colonel Welles breathed his last.

Liberty cradled his head in her lap and looked at him. Then she looked at the others, strewn dead and wounded for as far as she could see. At that moment, she knew she was getting a glimpse of hell. And, she realized, it was a hell of her own making.

"Miss," a Union officer called to her from behind the stone wall. "Miss, you'd best get off the field of battle before they come back and there's more shooting."

Liberty didn't move.

"Miss," the officer called again. As yet he had not left the relative safety of the stone fence. "Miss, you'd better get out of there."

Liberty felt defeated. It was as if she carried the weight of every casualty on her shoulders . . . now more than sixteen thousand. She stood up and walked toward the stone wall.

"Here, miss, come through right here," the officer invited, holding his hand out to help her.

"I want to surrender," Liberty said.

"Surrender? Miss, we don't take civilians as prisoners," the Union officer, who was a captain, said.

"I'm not just any civilian," Liberty said. "I'm a spy. Take me to General Grant. He knows of me. My name is Liberty Welles."

"I don't know," the captain said, scratching his head.

"Cap'n, it looks like the Rebs is about to come back," one of the soldiers called.

"Let's get ready for them," the captain said. "You," he called to a private who was standing near by. "Take this woman to General Grant's headquarters. I don't know what he'll do with her, but I'll not have her on my battlefield."

"Yes, sir," the soldier answered, more than willing to leave before another attack.

Liberty walked along quietly. Even when the soldier offered to make friendly conversation, she remained closed-mouthed. She imagined she would be shot . . . perhaps executed this very day. That was normally what they did with spies, she knew.

At his moment, the prospect wasn't all that unpleasant.

32

General Beauregard had ordered that a heavy artillery barrage be sustained just before the attack of Colonel Welles' division. The purpose of the barrage was twofold. It was, of course, to provide Colonel Welles with as much support as possible, but it was also to mask Beauregard's true intention of withdrawing from the battlefield once he had learned of the arrival of Buell's reinforcements.

The mules of the Union army which had packed the supplies in for General Buell were caught in this last great barrage. Many were killed and many more were wounded. Their screams continued on until after the barrage had finished and then they stopped. Finally, even the quiet moans of the wounded men ended.

The heavy bombardment which had gone on for two hours was reduced now to an occasional bursting shell. One would come in, swooshing like distant, rolling thunder, then detonate in a fiery rose, sending deadly missiles of shrapnel whistling through the forest. After each explosion a plume of smoke would drift lazily up through the early morning bars of sunlight which were just beginning to slash down through the trees.

Dan, who had been exposed to the intense fighting of the Hornets' Nest on the day before, then the heavy artillery bombardment earlier this morning, was able to view the occasional shell with a sort of detached interest. He had come through several engagements without a scratch, and was beginning to believe the myth of personal invincibility. Then, while attempting to move some of the uninjured mules out of the way, one lone shell burst nearby, sending a smoking, jagged piece of shrapnel at him, which tore a large chunk of flesh out of his leg. He let out a sharp cry of pain and surprise, then passed out.

When he woke again he was lying outside a field aid station, very near Grant's headquarters. His leg hurt badly, and in a war in which amputation was nearly always the accepted treatment of injured limbs, he feared that he would lose it. He had been put aside, along with the wounded who could wait and the dead. On both sides of him he saw men with lifeless, open eyes and spilled insides.

"Well, how're we doing?" someone asked. He

was a tall man, and he scratched at his face as he looked down at Dan. He had been working with the dead and the wounded and the blood was on his hand so that he left a smear on his cheek when he scratched.

"My leg hurts," Dan said.

"I imagine that it does," the tall soldier said. He smiled. "But you've a few things to be cheered about."

"Tell me," Dan said. "I would like to be cheered."

"Well, one is, you won't be losing the leg. It's an ugly, painful wound, and it cut away some of your muscle so that you'll be walking with a limp for the rest of your life. But you'll keep the legs God gave you."

Dan breathed a deep sigh of relief. "Thanks," he said. "I don't mind telling you that I was worried about that."

"I don't blame you," the tall soldier said. "Oh, the other good thing is, you'll be getting a surgeon's ticket out of the war. You're being evacuated tonight, with the other wounded."

Dan suddenly realized that the sound of battle was further away, and much less intense than it had been earlier.

"The Rebels?" Dan asked. "Have we beaten them?"

The tall soldier laughed. "I'd say they've high-tailed it all the way back to Corinth by now.

They tried one final charge down at the stone wall, but we stopped them good and we've not heard from them since then."

"Good," Dan said. "That is good."

"Oh, and did you hear about the spy?"

"The spy? What spy?"

"A lady spy. They tell me she's as beautiful as a spring flower. A girl by the name of . . . let's see, what was it?"

"Liberty?" Dan shouted anxiously. "Was it Liberty Welles?"

"Yep," the tall soldier said. "Now that you mention it, I mind that that was the name I heard. Why, have you heard of her?"

Dan sat up quickly, but when he did a wave of pain struck his leg, then swept over him so acutely as to bring on instant nausea and dizziness.

"Easy," the tall soldier said. "You shouldn't try to move."

"I've got to," Dan said. "Where did they take the girl? The spy? Where is she?"

"I just saw her go into General Grant's tent about ten minutes ago," the tall soldier said.

"Get me a crutch," Dan ordered.

"Captain, you're in no condition to . . ."

"I said get me a crutch!" Dan ordered again, this time more forcefully than before.

The tall soldier shrugged his shoulders, as if washing his hands of it, then went over to a cache of supplies to get one. It was only then that Dan noticed that the tall soldier was himself wounded, his left arm wrapped in bandages.

Dan took the crutch from him, then, steeling himself against the pain, half-hopped and half-limped across the open space to General Grant's tent. There were two guards outside, but they recognized Dan as a member of Grant's staff and made no attempt to keep him from pushing on inside.

There, sitting on a chair near General Grant's bunk, Dan saw Liberty Welles. She looked small and helpless, and his heart went out to her then as it had never before.

"Oh, Liberty, no," he finally said. "What are you doing here?"

"No," Grant said sourly. "The question is, what are *you* doing here? Captain O'Lee, it wasn't thirty minutes ago that they were debating whether or not to take off your leg, and here you are walking around on it."

"My leg is fine, sir," Dan said offhandedly. "General, how serious is it? What did she do?"

"I don't know," Grant replied. "I might ask you that same question."

"Ask me?" Dan said, looking at Grant in some surprise.

"This is the same girl who came to see me Saturday night, isn't it? The one who identified herself as Miss Roberts?"

Dan felt his face flushing red. Of course the general would put two and two together and realize that he had recognized her but hadn't turned her in.

"I . . . I couldn't turn her in, General," Dan said.

"As it turns out, you didn't have to. The girl turned herself in."

"You . . . you turned yourself in?" Dan asked. "But why?"

"Do you have to ask that question, Dan O'Lee?" Liberty asked. "Have you any idea how many are dead because of me? Have you any idea how many are laying out there in unspeakable agony, because of me?" Liberty pointed at Dan's wound. "You are crippled, because of me, and yet you ask why I turned myself in."

"Why do you say it's because of you?" Dan asked. "Liberty, you didn't bring on this war."

"No, but I brought on this terrible battle," Liberty said, her voice cut with self-loathing. "I'm the one who transmitted the information to General Beauregard that the Union Army intended to strike at Corinth."

"Of course you did," Dan said easily. "That's just what you were supposed to do."

"You mean I was honor bound to do it? God, spare the dying from my honor."

"No," Dan said. "I don't mean that at all. I mean it was planned for you to carry the word to Johnston and Beauregard. Don't you see?"

"Don't I see?" Liberty asked, clearly puzzled

by Dan's remarks. "No, I don't see. I don't see at all. What are you getting at?"

"He means you were set up, Miss Welles," General Grant said evenly.

"Set up?"

"General Halleck knew you were a spy. He gave you just the information he wanted to give you, hoping you would carry it to Johnston and thus bring on this battle."

"You mean . . . you wanted this terrible battle to take place?" Liberty asked in a small voice.

"Yes."

"But . . . but the casualties. Surely, general, your side suffered as many casualties as the South?"

"Oh, I wouldn't be surprised if we didn't suffer more," Grant replied. "But we could have lost two times as many men and would still have won the battle, Miss Welles. It's all a matter of arithmetic."

"A matter of arithmetic? No, general, it's a matter of blood. Blood. Blood that's on these hands." Liberty held her hands out and looked at them. Then, suddenly, she realized what General Grant had said. She got a look of horror on her face, then turned on Dan. "You!" she shouted. "You did this! You brought on this battle, and then you let me suffer with the thought that I did it!"

"Liberty, believe me, I didn't . . ." Dan started, but before he could finish his statement, Liberty,

in a move of incredible speed, grabbed General
Grant's pistol and swung it toward him. She
pulled the trigger, and the roar of the hand-
gun was deafening inside the tent.

Dan could feel the hot air and hear the angry
buzz of the bullet as it whizzed by his head
and punched through the side of the tent. He
looked at Liberty in shock and fear, then saw
with relief that she wasn't going to shoot at him
again. She lowered the gun until her arm was
hanging straight by her side. She hung her
head and cried.

The guards from outside came running in
with their rifles at the high port, but General
Grant stopped them with a wave of his hand.
Quietly and gently, he reached for his pistol,
then gingerly pulled it from Liberty's unprotesting grip.

As soon as she was disarmed, General Grant
motioned for the guards to take her away.

General Grant and Dan were alone in the
tent for a few minutes after Liberty had gone.

"Where will they take her, general?"

"To the gunboat *Lexington*," General Grant
said. "There is a brig on board. We'll confine
her there."

"Is she to be shot?"

"That will depend on the court-martial,"
General Grant replied.

"General, does she have to be court-martialed?
Couldn't you just let her go?"

"Are you in love with her?" General Grant asked quietly.

"Very much in love with her," Dan replied.

"Even though she tried to kill you?"

"If she had really tried, general, I'd be dead now," Dan said.

"Yes," Grant said, "I suppose you would at that." Grant walked over to the door of the tent and looked outside, standing in pensive silence for a moment or two. Then he turned back to look at Dan. "General Halleck is coming down here soon. Did I tell you that?"

"Yes, sir," Dan replied.

"If he gets here and the girl is still in the brig, it will be he who convenes the court-martial. I fear he will not be of a generous nature."

"I'm afraid you are right."

"On the other hand," Grant mused, "if the girl was gone before he got here, there would be no prisoner to court-martial."

"Gone?" Dan asked.

"I do have the authority to parole her into the custody of an officer," General Grant said.

"General, you would do that?"

"I would, yes," General Grant said. "I would parole her to you."

Dan hobbled out of the tent and looked down toward the river at the gunboat *Lexington*. In the west the sun was sinking in a large crimson ball, as if that heavenly body had been itself bloodied by the terrible strife which had taken place on the battlefield for the last two days. Dan studied it quietly for a moment. Finally he turned to Grant.

"I appreciate it, general, but, perhaps you'd better parole her to another. It would not be honorable of me to leave here with the task as yet undone."

Grant put his hand on Dan's shoulders. "Dan, how many of the dead boys lying out there would have gone to Congress had they lived? How many would be doctors, schoolteachers, writers, farmers, carpenters, architects and bridge-builders? Those are men whose skills will never aid the rebuilding of our nation once this war is over. As a commander, I know the folly of squandering all one's resources, and I say that our nation cannot survive if all our resources are wasted in battle. The surgeon has certified your wound of sufficient seriousness to warrant sending you away from the battlefield, and that's just what I'm doing. You will be needed after this war, Dan, and I want to make sure you are still around. You are one of them."

"One of them?"

"One of the builders," General Grant said.

The whistle blew three times, and Dan looked toward the boat.

"I've already had your things loaded aboard," Grant said. "I did that as soon as the surgeon gave me the warrant on your condition."

Dan sighed. "Then I guess I'll be going."

"Have a good trip," Grant invited.

"Thank you, general. Thank you very much," Dan said.

Dan started toward the boat. Just before he stepped aboard, he looked back at the short, stocky general. He had never known anyone quite like General Grant. He was a common man, who, in an uncommon situation, had risen to greatness.

Dan was helped aboard and shown to a cabin which had been prepared for him. He sat, gratefully, on his bunk, then raised his throbbing leg up to give it a rest. He was massaging it gently when he heard a light knock on his door.

"Come in," he called.

The door opened and closed, and Liberty stepped in. She was looking at him with a puzzled expression on her face.

"I'm told I've been paroled to you."

"That's right."

"And what do you intend to do with me?" Liberty asked.

"I don't know," Dan replied. "That all depends."

"Depends on what?"

"On whether or not you still wish to kill me," Dan said, looking up at her.

Liberty hung her head. "I'm sorry," she said. "It was a foolish thing. I guess I was just upset that you succeeded in turning the tables on me."

"But I didn't," Dan said.

"What do you mean?"

"Liberty, I tried to tell you. I had nothing to do with that. I didn't know you were set up until later. In fact, we were both set up."

"Oh," Liberty said, putting her hand to her mouth. "And to think that I almost killed you."

Dan smiled, a slow, knowing smile. "No," he said. "You didn't even come close."

"What do you mean?"

"You didn't really want to kill me," Dan said. "If you had wanted to, you would have."

"You're right," Liberty admitted. "I didn't want to. I mean, I did want to, but I just couldn't do it."

"Why couldn't you?"

"You know why."

"Yes, I know why," Dan said. "But I want to hear it." He smiled again. "Or, perhaps you'd rather be returned to the brig?"

"No, I . . . I don't want to go back there," Liberty said. She looked at Dan, then realized that he was teasing her. "Oh . . . you weren't serious."

"About as serious as your attempt to kill me," Dan said. He swung his leg off the bed, intending to stand up, but when he did the pain hit again, and he winced against it.

"Dan, oh, darling," Liberty said, seeing his

pain. "How awful of me. Here you are suffering so, and I've been so cruel to you." She crossed the cabin in three quick steps, then, gently, lay him back on the bed. "Are you all right?"

"Liberty, I . . . I . . ." Dan gasped. He breathed hard, as if groping for breath.

"Dan . . . Dan . . . what is it? Is there anything I can do?"

Dan opened one mischievous eye and smiled up at her. "Yeah," he said. "You could give me a kiss."

"Well, I don't know, if you're going to act that way, I might just . . ."

Dan pulled her to him and kissed her with lips which promised much more. Then, after breaking once, he kissed her again before she could regain her breath. Finally, when she was totally breathless, he broke off the kiss the second time.

"Say it," he demanded.

"Say what?" she replied, now teasing him.

"Say it, damn it!" Dan demanded.

Liberty smiled. She put her finger on his lips. "I love you," she said.

"That's more like it. I like the sound of it, Liberty, and you'll be saying it often."

"Whenever you wish, my love," Liberty said, kissing his lips quiet.

Praise for *Memoirs of an Imaginary Friend*

"An incredibly captivating novel about the wonder of youth and the importance of friendship, whether real or imagined. Delightfully compelling reading." —*Booklist*

"A fun read and engaging exploration of the vibrant world of a child's imagination." —*Publishers Weekly*

"Quirky and heartwarming." —*Kirkus Reviews*

"Funny, poignant . . . Budo's world is as realistic as he is imaginary. We would all be lucky to have Budo at our sides. Reading his memoir is the next best thing." —*Library Journal*

"Here is a perfectly crafted treasure! While it is shaped around autism, it deals with much more—courage, loss, love, human development and relationships—the very stuff of real life."
—Carol Kranowitz, bestselling author of *The Out-of-Sync Child*

Praise for *Unexpectedly, Milo*

"Amusing and engaging." —*The Wall Street Journal*

"*Unexpectedly, Milo* will satisfy your every demand for humorous fiction that is also nail-bitingly suspenseful (Will Milo get the girl? Which girl?) and infinitely understanding of the weirdo inside each and every one of us. This is a novel that leads with the heart and settles in your brain. Movingly funny. Deceptively profound."
—James Landis, author of *The Last Day*

"An adventure of a summer read you'll never put down."
—*Daily Candy*

"Filled with humor and sweetness, *Unexpectedly, Milo* reminds us that happiness can be found in the strangest of places." —*BookPage*

Praise for *Something Missing*

"The kind of book that will make you miss your next bus, class, or bedtime." —*Milwaukee Journal Sentinel*

"A splendid novel, written with loving attention to character and detail." —*Booklist* (starred review)

"A funny, suspenseful, and thoroughly original debut that will keep you up to the wee hours flipping pages."
—David Rosen, author of *I Just Want My Pants Back*

MATTHEW DICKS

*Memoirs
of an
Imaginary
Friend*

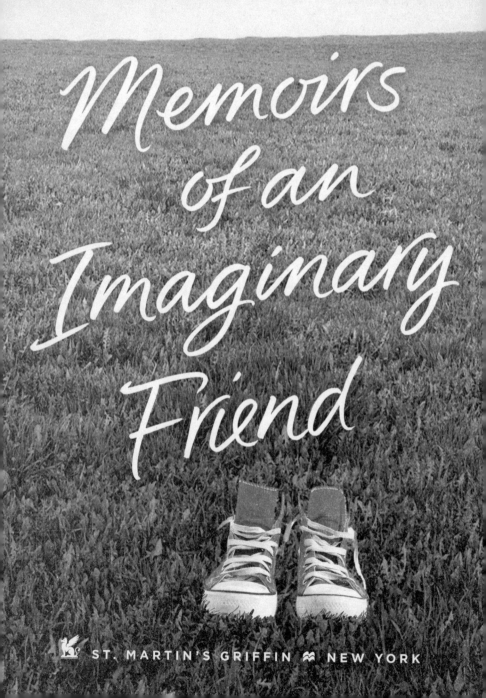

ST. MARTIN'S GRIFFIN ≋ NEW YORK

MEMOIRS OF AN IMAGINARY FRIEND. Copyright © 2012 by Matthew Dicks. All rights reserved. Printed in the United States of America. For information, address St. Martin's Press, 175 Fifth Avenue, New York, N.Y. 10010.

www.stmartins.com

The Library of Congress has cataloged the hardcover edition as follows:

Dicks, Matthew.
 Memoirs of an imaginary friend / Matthew Dicks.—1st ed.
  p. cm.
 ISBN 978-1-250-00621-9 (hardcover)
 ISBN 978-1-250-02400-8 (e-book)
 1. Imaginary companions—Fiction. 2. Psychological fiction. I. Title.
 PS3604.I323 M46 2012
 813'.6—dc23

2012028234

ISBN 978-1-250-03185-3 (trade paperback)

St. Martin's Griffin books may be purchased for educational, business, or promotional use. For information on bulk purchases, please contact Macmillan Corporate and Premium Sales Department at 1-800-221-7945 extension 5442 or write specialmarkets@macmillan.com.

14 13 12 11 10 9 8 7 6

For Clara

one

Here is what I know:

My name is Budo.
I have been alive for five years.
Five years is a very long time for someone like me to be alive.
Max gave me my name.
Max is the only human person who can see me.
Max's parents call me an imaginary friend.
I love Max's teacher, Mrs. Gosk.
I do not like Max's other teacher, Mrs. Patterson.
I am not imaginary.

two

I am lucky as imaginary friends go. I have been alive for a lot longer than most. I once knew an imaginary friend named Philippe. He was the imaginary friend of one of Max's classmates in preschool. He lasted less than a week. One day he popped into the world, looking pretty human except for his lack of ears (lots of imaginary friends lack ears), and then a few days later, he was gone.

I'm also lucky that Max has a great imagination. I once knew an imaginary friend named Chomp who was just a spot on the wall. Just a fuzzy, black blob without any real shape at all. Chomp could talk and sort of slide up and down the wall, but he was two-dimensional like a piece of paper, so he could never pry himself off. He didn't have arms and legs like me. He didn't even have a face.

Imaginary friends get their appearance from their human friend's imagination. Max is a very creative boy, and so I have two arms, two legs, and a face. I'm not missing a single body part and that makes me a rarity in the world of imaginary friends. Most imaginary friends are missing something or other and some don't even look human at all. Like Chomp.

Too much imagination can be bad, though. I once met an imaginary friend named Pterodactyl whose eyes were stuck on the ends of these two gangly, green antennas. His human friend probably thought they looked cool, but poor Pterodactyl couldn't focus on anything to save his life. He told me that he constantly felt sick to his stomach and was always tripping over his own feet, which were just fuzzy shadows attached to his legs. His human friend was so obsessed with Pterodactyl's head and those eyes that he had never bothered to think about anything below Pterodactyl's waist.

This is not unusual.

I'm also lucky because I'm mobile. Lots of imaginary friends are stuck to their human friends. Some have leashes around their necks. Some are three inches tall and get stuffed into coat pockets. And some are nothing more than a spot on the wall, like Chomp. But thanks to Max, I can get around on my own. I can even leave Max behind if I want.

But doing so too often might be hazardous to my health.

As long as Max believes in me, I exist. People like Max's mother and my friend Graham say that this is what makes me imaginary. But it's not true. I might need Max's imagination to exist, but I have my own thoughts, my own ideas, and my own life outside of him. I am tied to Max the same way that an astronaut is tied to his spaceship by hoses and wires. If the spaceship blows up and the astronaut dies, that doesn't mean that the astronaut was imaginary. It just means that his life support was cut off.

Same for me and Max.

I need Max in order to survive, but I'm still my own person. I can say and do as I please. Sometimes Max and I even get into arguments, but nothing ever serious. Just stuff about which TV show to watch or which game to play. But it *behooves* me (that's a word that Mrs. Gosk taught the class last week) to stick around Max whenever possible, because I need Max to keep thinking about me. Keep believing in me. I don't want to end up *out of sight, out of mind,* which is something Max's mom sometimes says when Max's dad forgets to call home when he is going to be late. If I am gone too long, Max might stop believing in me, and if that happens, then *poof.*

three

Max's first-grade teacher once said that houseflies live for about three days. I wonder what the life span of an imaginary friend is? Probably not much longer. I guess that makes me practically ancient.

Max imagined me when he was four years old, and just like that, I popped into existence. When I was born, I only knew what Max knew. I knew my colors and some of my numbers and the names for lots of things like tables and microwave ovens and aircraft carriers. My head was filled with the things that a four-year-old boy would know. But Max also imagined me much older than him. Probably a teenager. Maybe even a little older. Or maybe I was just a boy with a grown-up's brain. It's hard to tell. I'm not much taller than Max, but I'm definitely different. I was more together than Max when I was born. I could make sense of things that still confused him. I could see the answers to problems that Max could not. Maybe this is how all imaginary friends are born. I don't know.

Max doesn't remember the day that I was born, so he can't remember what he was thinking at the time. But since he imagined me as older and more together, I have been able to learn much faster than Max. I was able to concentrate and focus better on the day I was born than Max is able to even today. On that first day I remember Max's mother was trying to teach him to count by even numbers, and he just couldn't get it. But I learned it right away. It made sense to me because my brain was ready to learn even numbers. Max's brain wasn't.

At least that's what I think.

Also, I don't sleep, because Max didn't imagine that I needed sleep. So I have more time to learn. And I don't spend all my time with Max, so I've learned lots of things that Max has never seen or heard before. After he goes to bed, I sit in the living room or the kitchen

5

with Max's parents. We watch television or I just listen to them talk. Sometimes I go places. I go to the gas station that never closes, because my favorite people in the world except for Max and his parents and Mrs. Gosk are there. Or I go to Doogies hot-dog restaurant a little ways down the road or to the police station or to the hospital (except I don't go to the hospital anymore because Oswald is there and he scares me). And when we are in school, I sometimes go to the teacher's lounge or another classroom, and sometimes I even go to the principal's office, just to listen to what's going on. I am not smarter than Max, but I know a lot more than him just because I am awake more and go places that Max can't. This is good. Sometimes I can help Max when he doesn't understand something so well.

Like last week Max couldn't open a jar of jelly to make a peanut butter and jelly sandwich. "Budo!" he said. "I can't open it."

"Sure you can," I said. "Turn it the other way. Lefty loosy. Righty tighty." That is something I hear Max's mom say to herself sometimes before she opens a jar. It worked. Max opened the jar. But he was so excited that he dropped it on the tile floor, smashing it into a million pieces.

The world can be so complicated for Max. Even when he gets something right, it can still go wrong.

I live in a strange place in the world. I live in the space in between people. I spend most of my time in the kid world with Max, but I also spend a lot of time with adults like Max's parents and teachers and my friends at the gas station, except they can't see me. Max's mom would call this *straddling the fence*. She says this to Max when he can't make up his mind about something, which happens a lot.

"Do you want the blue Popsicle or the yellow Popsicle?" she asks, and Max just freezes. Freezes like a Popsicle. There are just too many things for Max to think about when choosing.

Is red better than yellow?

Is green better than blue?

Which one is colder?

Which one will melt fastest?

What does green taste like?

What does red taste like?

Do different colors taste different?

I wish that Max's mom would just make the choice for Max. She knows how hard it is for him. But when she makes him choose and he can't, I sometimes choose for him. I whisper, "Pick blue," and then he says, "I'll take blue." Then it's done. No more straddling the fence.

That's kind of how I live. I straddle the fence. I live in the yellow and the blue world. I live with kids and I live with adults. I'm not exactly a kid, but I'm not exactly an adult, either.

I'm yellow *and* blue.

I'm green.

I know my color combinations, too.

four

Max's teacher is Mrs. Gosk. I like Mrs. Gosk a lot. Mrs. Gosk walks around with a meter stick that she calls her meter-beater and threatens students in a fake British accent, but the kids know she's just trying to make them laugh. Mrs. Gosk is very strict and insists that her students work hard, but she would never hit a student. Still, she is a tough lady. She makes them sit up straight and work on their assignments in silence, and when a child misbehaves, she says, "Shame! Shame! Let all the boys and girls know your name!" or "You will get away with that nonsense when pigs fly, young man!" The other teachers say Mrs. Gosk is old-fashioned, but the kids know that she is tough because she loves them.

Max doesn't like many people, but he likes Mrs. Gosk.

Last year, Max's teacher was Mrs. Silbor. She was strict, too. She made the kids work hard like Mrs. Gosk does. But you could tell that she didn't love the kids like Mrs. Gosk does, so no one in the class worked as hard as they do this year. It's strange how teachers can go off to college for all those years to learn to become teachers, but some of them never learn the easy stuff. Like making kids laugh. And making sure they know that you love them.

I do not like Mrs. Patterson. She's not a real teacher. She's a paraprofessional. This is someone who helps Mrs. Gosk take care of Max. Max is different than other kids so he doesn't spend the whole day with Mrs. Gosk. Sometimes he works with Mrs. McGinn in the Learning Center, and sometimes he works on his speech with Mrs. Riner, and sometimes he plays games with other kids in Mrs. Hume's office. And sometimes he reads and does homework with Mrs. Patterson.

As far as I can tell, no one knows why Max is different from the rest of the kids. Max's father says that Max is just a late bloomer, but when he says that, Max's mom gets so angry that she stops talking to him for at least a day.

I don't know why everyone thinks Max is so complicated. Max just doesn't like people in the same way other kids do. He likes people, but it's a different kind of liking. He likes people from far away. The farther you stay away from Max, the more he will like you.

And Max doesn't like to be touched. When someone touches Max, the whole world gets bright and shivery. That's how he described it to me once.

I can't touch Max, and Max can't touch me. Maybe that's why we get along so well.

Also, Max doesn't understand when people say one thing but mean another. Like last week, Max was reading a book at recess and a fourth grader came over and said, "Look at the little genius." Max didn't say anything to the boy because he knew if he said something, the fourth grader would stay there longer and keep bothering him. But I know that Max was confused, because it sounded like the boy was saying that Max was smart even though the boy was actually being mean. He was being sarcastic, but Max doesn't understand sarcasm. Max knew the boy was being mean, but only because that boy is always mean to Max. But he couldn't understand why the boy would call him a genius, since being called a genius is usually a good thing.

People are confusing to Max, so it's hard for him to be around them. That's why Max has to play games in Mrs. Hume's office with kids from the other classes. He thinks it's a big waste of time. He hates having to sit on the floor around the Monopoly board, because sitting on the floor is not as comfortable as sitting in a chair. But Mrs. Hume is trying to teach Max to play with other kids, to understand what they mean when they sarcasm or joke around. Max just doesn't understand. When Max's mom and dad are fighting, Max's mom says that his dad can't see the forest for the trees. That's like Max except it's with the whole world. He can't see the big things because of all the little things that get in his way.

Today Mrs. Patterson is absent. When a teacher is absent, it usually means that the teacher is sick or her child is sick or someone in her family has died. Mrs. Patterson had someone in her family die once. I know this because sometimes the other teachers will say nice things to her like, "How are you holding up, dear?" and sometimes they whisper to each other after she has left the room. But that was a long time ago. When Mrs. Patterson is absent, it usually means that it is Friday.

There's no substitute for Mrs. Patterson today so Max and I get to stay with Mrs. Gosk all day which makes me happy. I don't like Mrs. Patterson. Max doesn't like her, either, but he doesn't like her in the same way he doesn't like most of his teachers. He doesn't see what I see because he's too busy looking at the trees. But Mrs. Patterson is different from Mrs. Gosk and Mrs. Riner and Mrs. McGinn. She never smiles for real. She's always thinking something different in her head than what is on her face. I don't think she likes Max, but she pretends that she does, which is even scarier than just not liking him.

"Hello, Max, my boy!" Mrs. Gosk says as we walk into the classroom. Max doesn't like when Mrs. Gosk calls him "my boy" because he is not *her boy*. He has a mother already. But he won't ask Mrs. Gosk to stop calling him "my boy" because asking her to stop would be harder than listening to Mrs. Gosk say "my boy" every day.

Max would rather say nothing to everyone than something to one person.

But even though Max doesn't understand why Mrs. Gosk calls him "my boy" he knows that she loves him. He knows that Mrs. Gosk is not being mean. Just confusing.

I wish I could tell Mrs. Gosk not to call Max "my boy," but Mrs. Gosk can't see or hear me and there's nothing I can do to make her see or hear me. Imaginary friends can't touch or move things in the human world. So I can't open a jelly jar or pick up a pencil or type on a keyboard. Otherwise I would write a note asking Mrs. Gosk not to call Max "my boy."

I can bump up against the real world, but I can't actually touch it.

Even so, I am lucky because when Max first imagined me, he imagined that I could pass through things like doors and windows even when they are closed. I think it's because he was afraid that if his parents closed his bedroom door at night I might get stuck outside the room, and Max doesn't like to fall sleep unless I'm sitting in the chair next to his bed. This means that I can go anywhere by walking through the doors and windows, but never through walls or floors. I can't pass through walls and floors because Max didn't imagine me that way. That would've been too strange for even Max to think about.

There are other imaginary friends who can walk through doors and windows like me, and some who can even walk through walls, but most can't walk through anything and get stuck in places for a long time. That's what happened to Puppy, a talking dog who got stuck in the janitor's closet overnight a couple of weeks ago. It was a scary night for his human friend, a kindergartener named Piper, because she had no idea where Puppy was.

But it was even scarier for Puppy, because getting locked in a closet is how imaginary friends sometimes disappear forever. A boy or girl accidentally (or sometimes, *accidentally on purpose*) locks an imaginary friend in a closet or a cabinet or basement and then *poof!* Out of sight, out of mind. The end of the imaginary friend.

Being able to pass through doors can be a lifesaver.

Today I want to stay put in the classroom because Mrs. Gosk is reading *Charlie and the Chocolate Factory* aloud to the class, and I love it when Mrs. Gosk reads. She has a whispery, thin voice, so all the kids must lean in and be absolutely silent in order to hear, which is great for Max. Noises distract him. If Joey Miller is banging his pencil on his desk or Danielle Ganner is tapping her feet on the floor like she does all the time, then Max can't hear anything but the pencil or the feet. He can't ignore sounds like the other kids can, but when Mrs. Gosk reads, everyone must be perfectly quiet.

Mrs. Gosk always chooses the best books and tells the best stories from her own life that somehow relate to the book. Charlie Bucket does something crazy and then Mrs. Gosk tells us about a time when her son, Michael, did something crazy, and we all laugh our heads off. Even Max sometimes.

Max doesn't like to laugh. Some people think it's because he doesn't think things are funny, but that is not true. Max doesn't understand all funny things. Puns and knock-knock jokes make no sense to him, because they say one thing but mean another. When a word can mean a bunch of different things, he has a hard time understanding which meaning to choose. He doesn't even understand why words have to mean different things depending on when you use them, and I don't blame him. I don't like it much, either.

But Max finds other things hilarious. Like when Mrs. Gosk told us how Michael once sent twenty cheese pizzas and the bill to a school-yard bully as a joke. When the police officer came to their house to scare Michael, Mrs. Gosk told the police officer to "take him away" to teach her son a lesson. Everyone laughed at that story. Even Max. Because it made sense. It had a beginning, a middle, and an end.

Mrs. Gosk is also teaching us about World War II today, which she says is not in the curriculum but should be. The kids love it, and Max especially loves it because he thinks about wars and battles and tanks and airplanes all the time. Sometimes it is the only thing that he thinks about for days. If school was only about war and battles and not math and writing, then Max would be the best student in the whole wide world.

Today Mrs. Gosk is teaching us about Pearl Harbor. The Japanese bombed Pearl Harbor on December 7, 1941. Mrs. Gosk said that the Americans were not ready for the sneak attack because they couldn't imagine the Japanese attacking us from so far away.

"America lacked imagination," she said.

If Max had been alive in 1941, things might have been different because he has an excellent imagination. I bet that Max would have imagined Admiral Yamamoto's plan perfectly, with the midget submarines and the torpedoes with the wooden rudders and everything else. He could have warned the American soldiers about the plan because that is what Max is good at. Imagining things. He has a lot going on inside of him all the time so he doesn't worry so much about what is going on outside him. That's what people don't understand.

That's why it's good for me to stick around Max whenever I can. Sometimes he doesn't pay enough attention to the things around him. Last week he was about to get on the bus when a big gust of wind blew his report card right out of his hands and between bus 8 and bus 53. He ran out of line to get it, but he didn't look both ways, so I yelled, "Max Delaney! Stop!"

I use Max's last name when I want to get his attention. I learned that from Mrs. Gosk. It worked. Max stopped, which was good, because a car was passing by the school buses at that moment, which is illegal.

Graham said that I saved Max's life. Graham is the third imaginary friend at the school right now, as far as I know, and she saw the whole thing. Graham is a girl but she has a boy's name. She looks almost as human as I do, except her hair stands up like someone on the moon is pulling on each individual strand. It doesn't move. It's as solid as a rock. Graham heard me yell at Max and tell him to stop, and then after Max was back in line, she walked over to me and said, "Budo! You just saved Max's life! He would've been squished by that car!"

But I told Graham that I saved my own life, because if Max ever died, I think I would die, too.

Right?

I think so. I've never known an imaginary friend whose human friend died before he disappeared. So I'm not sure.

But I think I would. Die, I mean. If Max died.

five

"Do you think I'm real?" I ask.

"Yes," Max says. "Hand me that blue two-pronger."

A two-pronger is a kind of LEGO. Max has names for all the LEGO pieces.

"I can't," I say.

Max looks at me. "Oh, yeah. I forgot."

"If I'm real, then why are you the only one who can see me?"

"I don't know," Max says, sounding irritated. "I think you're real. Why do you keep asking me?"

It's true. I ask him a lot. I do it on purpose, too. I'm not going to live forever. I know that. But I'm going to live as long as Max believes in me. So if I force Max to keep insisting that I'm real, I think he will believe in me longer.

Of course, I know that by constantly asking him if I'm real, I might be putting the idea that I am imaginary in his head. It's a risk. But so far, so good.

Mrs. Hume once told Max's mom that it's "not uncommon for kids like Max to have imaginary friends, and they tend to persist longer than most imaginary friends."

Persist. I like that word.

I persist.

Max's parents are fighting again. Max can't hear because he is playing video games in the basement and his parents are screaming at each other in whispers. They sound like people who have been yelling for so long that they have lost their voices, which is actually half true.

"I don't care what the goddamn therapist thinks," Max's dad says, his cheeks turning red as he whisper-yells. "He's a normal kid . . ."

he's just a late bloomer. He plays with toys. He plays sports. He has friends."

Max's dad is not correct. Max doesn't have any friends other than me. The kids at school either like Max or hate Max or ignore Max, but none of them are his friend, and I don't think he wants any of them to be his friend. Max is happiest when he is left alone. Even I bother him sometimes.

The kids at school who like Max treat him differently, too. Like Ella Barbara. She loves Max, but she loves him in the same way a kid loves a doll or a teddy bear. She calls him "my little Max," and tries to carry his lunchbox to the cafeteria and zip up his coat before recess, even though she knows that Max can do those things for himself. Max hates Ella. He cringes every time she tries to help him or even touch him, but he can't tell her to stop because it's easier for Max to cringe and suffer than speak up. Mrs. Silbor kept Ella and Max together when she sent them onto third grade because she thought that they are good for each other. That's what she told Max's mom at the parent-teacher conference. Max might be good for Ella, because she gets to play with him like a doll, but Ella is most definitely not good for Max.

"He is not a late bloomer and I wish you'd stop saying that," Max's mom says to his dad in the tone she uses when she's trying to stay calm but is having a hard time doing so. "I know it kills you to admit it, John, but that's just the way it is. How could every expert we meet be wrong?"

"That's the problem," Max's dad says, his forehead turning red and blotchy. "Not every expert agrees and you know it!" When he speaks, it's like he's firing his words from a gun. "No one knows what is going on with Max. So how is my guess any worse than a bunch of experts who can't agree on a thing?"

"The label isn't important," Max's mom says. "It doesn't matter what is wrong with him. He needs help."

"I just don't get it," Max's dad says. "I played catch with him in the backyard last night. I've taken him camping. His grades are good. He doesn't get in trouble at school. Why are we trying to fix the poor kid when there's nothing wrong with him?"

Max's mom starts to cry. She blinks and her eyes fill with tears. I hate when she cries, and so does Max's dad. I have never cried before, but it looks awful. "John, he doesn't like to hug us. He can't make eye contact with people. He flips out if I change the sheets on his bed or switch brands of toothpaste. He talks to himself constantly. These are not normal kid behaviors. I'm not saying he needs medication. I'm not saying that he won't grow up and be normal. He just needs a professional who can help him deal with some of his issues. And I want to do it before I get pregnant again. While we can focus on just him."

Max's dad turns and leaves. He slams the screen door behind him on the way out. It goes *whack-whack-whack* before it stops moving. I used to think that when Max's dad walked away from an argument, it meant that Max's mom had won. I thought his dad was retreating like Max's toy soldiers retreat. I thought he was surrendering. But even though he is the one who retreats, it doesn't always mean that he has surrendered. He has retreated lots of times before, slamming that door and making it go *whack-whack-whack,* but then nothing changes. It's like Max's dad has pressed the Pause button on the remote control. The argument is paused. But it is not over.

Max is the only boy I have ever seen who makes toy soldiers retreat or surrender.

Every other boy makes them die instead.

I'm not sure if Max should see a therapist, and to be honest, I'm not exactly sure what a therapist does. I know some things that they do, but not everything, and it's the everything that makes me nervous. Max's mom and dad are probably going to fight about this again and again, and even though neither one will ever say, "Okay, I give up!" or "You win!" or "You're right," Max will eventually go to the therapist, because in the end, Max's mom almost always wins.

I think Max's dad is wrong about Max being a late bloomer. I spend most of the day with Max and I see how he is different from the other kids in his class. Max lives on the inside and the other kids live on the outside. That's what makes him so different. Max doesn't have an outside. Max is all inside.

I don't want Max to see a therapist. Therapists are people who trick you into telling the truth. They can see inside your head and know exactly what you are thinking, and if Max is thinking about me when he's talking to the therapist, then the therapist will trick Max into talking about me. Then maybe he'll convince Max to stop believing in me.

But I still feel bad for Max's dad, even if Max's mom is the one who's crying now. Sometimes I wish I could tell Max's mom to be nicer to Max's dad. She is the boss of the house, but she's also the boss of Max's dad, and I don't think it's good for him. It makes him feel small and silly. Like when he wants to play poker with friends on a Wednesday night but he can't just tell his friends that he will play. He has to ask Max's mom if it's okay for him to play, and he has to ask at the right time, when she is in a good mood, or he might not be able to play. She might say, "I could really use you at home that night" or "Didn't you play last week?"

Or worse, she might just say "Fine," which really means, "It is not fine and you know it and if you go, I am going to be mad at you for at least three days!"

It reminds me of how Max would have to ask permission to visit a friend, if Max ever wanted to play with anyone but me, which he doesn't.

I don't understand why Max's dad has to ask permission, but I really don't understand why Max's mom would want to make him ask permission. Wouldn't it be better if Max's dad just got to choose what he did?

It's doubly worse because Max's dad is a manager at Burger King. Max thinks that this is one of the best jobs in the world, and if I ate bacon double cheeseburgers and small fries, then I'd probably feel the same way. But in the adult world, a Burger King manager is not a good job at all, and Max's dad knows it. You can tell by the way he doesn't like to tell people about his job. He never asks people what their job is, and that's the most popular adult question ever asked in the history of the world. When he has to tell someone what his job is, he looks at his feet and says, "I manage restaurants." Getting him to say the words "Burger King" is like trying to get Max to choose between chicken noodle and vegetable beef soup. He tries everything he can not to say those two words.

Max's mom is a manager, too. She manages people at a place called Aetna, but I can't figure out what they make at her job. Definitely not bacon double cheeseburgers. I went to her job once, to try to figure out what she did all day, but everyone just sits in front of computers in these tiny boxes without lids. Or they sit around tables in stuffy rooms and tap their feet and look at the clock while some old man or woman talks about stuff that nobody cares about.

But even though it's boring and they don't make bacon double cheeseburgers, you can tell that Max's mom has a better job because the people in her building wear shirts and dresses and ties and not uniforms. She never complains about people stealing or not showing up to work like Max's dad does. And sometimes Max's dad goes to work at five o'clock in the morning and sometimes he works all night long and comes home at five in the morning. It's weird because even though Max's dad's job seems a lot harder, Max's mom makes more money and adults think she has a much better job. She never looks at her feet when she tells people what she does.

I'm glad that Max didn't hear them arguing this time. Sometimes he does. Sometimes they forget to whisper-shout and sometimes they fight in the car, where it doesn't matter if you whisper-shout. When they fight, it makes Max feel sad.

"They fight because of me," he said to me once. He was playing with LEGOs, which is when Max likes to talk about serious things the most. He doesn't look at me. He just builds airplanes and forts and battleships and spaceships while he talks.

"No, they don't," I said. "They fight because they're grown-ups. Grown-ups like to argue."

"No. They only argue about me."

"No," I said. "Last night they argued about what show to watch on the television." I had been hoping that Max's dad would win so we could watch the crime show, but he lost and we had to watch some stupid singing show.

"That was not an argument," Max said. "That was a disagreement. There's a difference."

These were Mrs. Gosk's words. Mrs. Gosk says that it's okay to disagree but that doesn't mean you are allowed to argue. "I can stomach a disagreement," she likes to say to the class. "But I can't stand to listen to an argument in my presence."

"They only argue because they don't know what's best for you," I said. "They're trying to figure out what is right."

Max looked at me for a minute. He looked mad for a second, and then his face changed. It got softer and he looked sad. "When other people try to make me feel better by twisting words, it only makes me feel worse. When you do it, it makes me feel the worst."

"Sorry," I said.

"It's okay."

"No," I said. "I'm not sorry for what I said, because it's true. Your parents really are trying to figure out what is right. I meant that I'm sorry that your parents argue about you, even if it's only because they love you."

"Oh," Max said, and he smiled. It wasn't an actual smile, because Max never really smiles. But his eyes opened a little wider and he tilted his head a tiny bit to the right. That's Max's version of a smile. "Thanks," he said, and I knew that it was a real thanks.

six

Max is in the bathroom stall. He is making a poop, which Max does not like to do outside the home. He almost never makes a poop in a public restroom. But it's 1:15 and there are still two hours of school left and he couldn't hold it anymore. He always tries to poop before going to bed every night, and if he can't, he tries again in the morning before he leaves for school. He actually pooped this morning right after breakfast, so this is a bonus poop.

Max hates bonus poops. Max hates all surprises.

Whenever he poops at school, Max tries to use the handicapped bathroom near the nurse's office so he can be alone, but today the janitor was cleaning puke off the floor because when a kid says that he's going to be sick, the nurse always sends him to that bathroom.

When Max has to use the regular bathroom, I stand outside the door and warn him if someone is coming. He doesn't like to have anyone in the bathroom when he is pooping, including me. But he doesn't like to be surprised even more, so I am allowed to come in, but only if it's an emergency.

An emergency means that someone is coming to use the bathroom.

When I tell him that someone is coming, Max lifts his feet up off the floor so no one can see him and waits until the bathroom is empty again before he finishes pooping. If he is lucky, the person never even knows that Max is on the toilet, unless the person has to poop, too, and knocks on the door to the stall. Then Max puts his feet back on the floor and waits until the person leaves.

One of Max's problems with pooping is that it takes him a long time, even when he is sitting on his own toilet at home. He has been in the bathroom for ten minutes already and he is probably not close to being finished. It's possible that he hasn't even started. He could still be carefully arranging his pants on top of his sneakers so they don't touch the floor.

That's when I see trouble come walking down the hallway. Tommy Swinden has just left his classroom at the far end of the hall and is heading in my direction. As he walks, he swipes the maps of the thirteen colonies off the bulletin board outside Mrs. Vera's class. He laughs and kicks the papers across the floor. Tommy Swinden is in fifth grade and he does not like Max.

He has never liked Max.

But now he doesn't like Max even more. Three months ago, Tommy Swinden took his Swiss Army knife to school to show it off to his friends. Tommy was standing at the edge of the woods, whittling a stick to show the other boys how sharp his knife was, and Max saw the knife and told the teacher. But Max doesn't know how to be quiet about these kinds of things. He ran up to Mrs. Davis and shouted, "Tommy Swinden has a knife! A knife!" A whole bunch of kids heard Max, and a few of the little kids screamed and ran in the direction of Tommy, which scared them even more. Tommy Swinden got in a lot of trouble. He was kicked out of school for a week, kicked off the bus for the rest of the school year, and had to go to these after-school classes to learn about being a good person.

That's a lot of trouble for a fifth grader.

Even though Mrs. Davis and Mrs. Gosk and the rest of the teachers all told Max that he did the right thing by reporting the knife (because weapons are not allowed at school and this is a very serious rule), none of them bothered to teach Max about how to tell on a kid without letting everyone on the playground know that you did. I don't get it. Mrs. Hume spends all this time teaching Max how to take turns and ask for help but no one takes the time to teach Max something so important. Don't the teachers know that Tommy Swinden is going to kill Max for getting him in so much trouble?

Maybe they don't because most of the teachers in Max's school are girls, and maybe they never got into any trouble when they were in school. Maybe none of them ever brought a knife to the playground or had trouble pooping in the bathroom. Maybe they don't know what it is like to be a kid in a lot of trouble, and that's probably why they spend their lunch hours saying things like, "I don't know what that Tommy Swinden was thinking when he brought that knife to school."

I know what he was thinking. He was thinking that his friends might stop calling him Tommy the 'Tard for not being able to read if he could show them that he knew how to whittle a stick with his Swiss Army knife. That's the kind of things kids do. They try to cover up their problems with things like Swiss Army knives.

But I don't think the teachers understand this, which is probably why no one taught Max how to tell a teacher that a fifth grader has a knife without telling the entire world at the same time. So now Tommy Swinden, the fifth-grade boy who can't read and owns a knife and is twice as big as Max, is heading for the bathroom while Max is inside, trying to poop.

"Max!" I say as I pass through the door. "Tommy Swinden is coming!"

Max lets out a groan as his sneakers disappear from the crack between the stall and the floor. I want to pass through the stall door and stand alongside him, so he isn't all alone, but I know I can't. He wouldn't want me to see him on the toilet, and he knows that I can be more helpful outside the stall, where I can see what he can't.

Tommy Swinden, who is as tall as the art teacher and almost as wide as the gym teacher, comes into the bathroom and walks over to one of the toilets on the wall. He takes a quick peek under the stalls, sees no feet, and probably thinks he's alone. Then he looks back at the door to the bathroom, looks right through me, and reaches back, pulling his underwear from the crack in his butt. I see people do this all the time, because I spend a lot of time with people who think they are alone. When your underwear is stuck in the crack of your butt, it's called a wedgie and it can't be too comfortable. I've never had a wedgie because Max didn't imagine me with a wedgie. Thank goodness.

Tommy Swinden turns back to the toilet on the wall and pees. When he's done, he shakes his thing a little before buttoning and zipping his jeans. Not the way I once saw a kid shaking his thing in the handicapped bathroom near the nurse's office when Max asked me to check and see if anyone was in there. I have no idea what that boy was doing, but it was more than just a shake. I don't like to peek in on people using the bathroom, especially when they are tugging on their thing, but Max hates to knock on the bathroom door because he never knows what to say when someone knocks on the door when he's in there. He used to say "Max is pooping!" but then he got in trouble when a kid told the teacher what he said.

The teacher told Max that it's not appropriate to say that you're pooping. "Just say 'I'm in here' the next time someone knocks," she told Max.

"But that sounds silly," he said. "The person won't know who *I* am. I can't just say '*I'm* in here.'"

"Fine," the teacher said in a way that teachers tell kids to do ridiculous things when they're frustrated and don't want to talk anymore. "Tell them who you are, then."

So now when someone knocks on the bathroom door, Max says, "Occupied by Max Delaney!" It makes people either laugh or stare at the door with a funny expression.

I don't blame them.

Tommy Swinden is finished at the toilet and is now standing at the sink, reaching for the faucet, just about to turn the knob and fill the bathroom with the sound of running water when he hears a *plop!* from the stall where Max is hiding.

"Huh?" he says, bending down again to see if there are any feet in the stall. He doesn't see any, so he walks over to the first stall and bangs on the door real hard. Hard enough to make the whole stall shake. "I know you're in there!" he says. "I can see you through the cracks!"

I don't think Tommy knows that it's Max behind the door, because the cracks between the door and the wall are too small to see his whole face. But that's what is good about being one of the biggest kids in school. You can bang on a stall door and not worry about who is behind it, because you can beat up just about every kid at school.

Imagine what that must feel like.

Max doesn't answer, so Tommy bangs again. "Who's in there? I want to know!"

"Don't say anything, Max!" I say from my spot by the door. "He can't get in there. He'll have to leave eventually!"

But I'm wrong, because when Max doesn't answer the second time, Tommy gets down on his hands and knees and peeks his head under the door. "Max the Moron," he says, and I can hear the smile on his face. Not a nice smile. A rotten one. "I can't believe it's you. It's my lucky day. What's the matter? Couldn't hold that last one in?"

"No," Max shouts, and I can already hear the panic in his voice. "It was already halfway out!"

Everything about this situation is bad.

Max is trapped inside a public bathroom, a place that already frightens him. His pants are wrapped around his ankles and he probably hasn't finished pooping. Tommy Swinden is on the other side of the stall door, and Tommy definitely wants to hurt Max. They are alone. Except for me, of course, but they might as well be alone for all the help that I can be.

It's the way Max answered Tommy that scares me the most. There was more than panic in his voice. There was fear. Like when people in the movies see the ghost or the monster for the first time. Max just saw a monster peek underneath the stall door and he is frightened. He might already be close to getting stuck, and that is never good.

"Open this door, idiot," Tommy says, pulling his head back and standing up. "Make this easy on me and all I'll do is bowl you."

I don't know what *bowl* means, but I have visions of Tommy Swinden rolling Max's head across the bathroom like a bowling ball.

"Occupied by Max Delaney!" Max shouts, his voice screeching like a little girl. "Occupied by Max Delaney!"

"Last chance, moron. Open it up or I'm coming in!"

"Occupied by Max Delaney!" Max screams again. "Occupied by Max Delaney!"

Tommy Swinden gets back down on his hands and knees, ready to crawl under the door, and I don't know what to do. Max needs more help than most kids in his class, and I am always there for him, ready to lend a hand. Even on the day that he tattled on Tommy Swinden, I was there, telling him to whisper, begging him to "Slow down! Don't rush! Stop yelling!" Max wouldn't listen to me that day because there was a knife at school and that was such an important rule to break that he could not control himself. It was like the whole world was broken and he needed to find a teacher to fix it. I didn't stop him that day, but I tried.

At least I knew what to do.

But I don't know what to do now. Tommy Swinden is about to crawl under the door and enter a tiny bathroom stall where Max is trapped, probably perched on top of the toilet, knees in his chest, pants around his ankles, frozen in place. If he's not crying yet, he soon will be, and by the time Tommy has made it all the way under the door, Max will probably be screaming, a high-pitched, breathless scream that paints his face red and fills his eyes with tears. He will ball his hands into fists, bury his face behind his forearms, close his eyes tight, and scream the wispy, high-pitched, almost silent shriek that makes me think of a dog whistle. Full of air but almost no sound at all.

Before any teacher gets here, Tommy Swinden will bowl Max, whatever that means. Even though I'm sure that being bowled would be bad for any kid, it's going to be a lot worse for Max, because that is how Max is. Things stay with Max forever. He never forgets. And even the tiniest littlest things can permanently change him. Whatever *bowling* is, it's going to change Max forever and ever. I know it and I don't know what to do.

"Help!" I want to scream. "Someone help my friend!" But only Max would hear.

Tommy's head disappears under the stall and I shout, "Fight, Max! Fight! Don't let him in there!" I don't know what makes me say it. I'm surprised by the words as they come out of my mouth. It's not a great idea. It's not smart or even original. It's just the only thing left to do. Max must fight or he will be bowled.

Tommy's head and shoulders are now under the stall and I can see that he is about to pull his hips and legs under in one quick movement, and then he will be inside the stall with Max, standing over his small, shaking body, ready to hurt him. Ready to bowl him.

I stand like a dummy outside the stall. Part of me wants to go in, to stand by my friend, but Max does not like it when people see him naked or pooping. I am as stuck as Max has ever been.

Then there is another scream, and this time it's not Max. This time it is Tommy who screams. It's not Max's terrified, wispy scream. It's a different kind of scream. A more knowing scream. Not panicked or frightened really, but the scream of someone who can't believe what has just happened. As he screams, Tommy starts to say something and he tries to stand up, forgetting the door above him, and he slams his back into the bottom of the door, causing him to scream again, this time in pain. Then the door flies open and Max is standing there, pants nearly pulled up but not buttoned or zipped, his legs straddling Tommy's head.

"Run!" I shout, and he does, stepping on Tommy's hand, causing Tommy to scream again. Max runs past me, yanking his pants up the rest of the way, and then he is out the door. I follow. Instead of turning left toward his classroom, he turns right, buttoning and zipping his pants without stopping.

"Where are you going?"

"I still need a bathroom," he says. "Maybe the nurse's bathroom is clean now."

"What happened to Tommy?" I ask. "What did you do?"

"I pooped on his head," Max says.

"You pooped with someone else in the bathroom?" I ask. I can't believe it. The fact that he pooped on Tommy Swinden's head is unbelievable, but the fact that he managed a poop in the presence of another human person is even more amazing.

"Just a little one," Max says. "I was almost finished when he came in." He takes a few more steps down the hall before adding, "I pooped this morning, so it was a lot less poop this time. Remember? It was a bonus poop."

seven

Max is worried that Tommy will tell on him the same way that he told on Tommy about the Swiss Army knife. But I know that he won't. No kid wants his friends or even his teachers to know that he was pooped on. Tommy will want to kill Max now. Actually kill him. Make his heart stop beating and whatever else it takes to kill a human person.

But we'll worry about that day when it comes.

Max can live with the fear of death just as long as he doesn't get in trouble for pooping on Tommy Swinden's head. Kids are afraid of dying all the time, so for Max, being afraid that Tommy Swinden might choke him to death or punch him in the nose is normal. But kids don't get suspended from school for pooping on the head of a fifth grader. That would only happen in a broken world.

I tell Max not to worry about getting in trouble. He only half believes me, but that's enough for him to stay unstuck.

Besides, Max pooped on Tommy Swinden three days ago and we haven't seen Tommy since. At first I thought he was absent from school, so I went to Mrs. Parenti's classroom to see if he was there, and he was. Sitting in the first row, closest to the teacher, probably so she can keep an eye on him.

I'm not sure what Tommy is thinking. Maybe he is so embarrassed about having poop on his head that he has decided to forget about the whole thing. Or maybe he's so angry that he is planning to torture Max before he kills him. Like the kids who burn ants with magnifying glasses at recess instead of just stepping on them and smearing them on the bottom of their sneakers.

That's what Max thinks, and even though I tell him that he's wrong, I know he is probably right.

You can't poop on the head of a kid like Tommy Swinden and expect to get away with it.

eight

I saw Graham today. I passed her on the way to the cafeteria. She waved to me.

She's starting to fade away.

I can't believe it.

I could see her spiky hair and toothy grin through her hand as she waved it back and forth in front of her face.

Imaginary friends can take a long time to disappear or a short time to disappear, but I don't think Graham has much time left.

Her human friend is a girl named Meghan, and she is six years old. Graham has only been alive for two years, but she is my oldest imaginary friend and I don't want her to go. She is the only real friend I have except for Max.

I am afraid for her.

I am afraid for me, too.

Someday I will raise my hand in front of my face and see Max's face on the other side of it, and then I'll know that I am fading away, too. Someday I am going to die, if that's what happens to imaginary friends.

It must be. Right?

I want to talk to Graham, but I don't know what to say. I wonder if she knows that she is disappearing?

If she doesn't know, should I tell her?

There are lots of imaginary friends in the world who I never get to meet because they do not leave their houses. Most imaginary friends aren't lucky enough to be able to go to school or walk around on their own like me and Graham. Max's mom brought us to one of her friend's houses once and I met three imaginary friends. They were all sitting in tiny chairs in front of a chalkboard. Their arms were crossed and they were frozen like statues while this little girl named Jessica recited the alphabet to them and asked them to answer math problems. But the imaginary friends couldn't walk or talk. When I walked into the playroom, they just blinked at me from their chairs. That was it.

Just blinked.

Those kinds of imaginary friends never last long. I once saw an imaginary friend pop up in Max's kindergarten classroom for fifteen minutes and then just disappear. It was like someone inflated her in the middle of the room. She got bigger and bigger and bigger like one of those people-shaped balloons they sell at parades until she was almost as big as me. A big, pink girl with pigtails in her hair and yellow flowers for feet. But when story time was done, it was like someone popped her with a pin. She shrank and shrank until I couldn't see her anymore.

I was scared watching that pink girl disappear. Fifteen minutes is nothing.

She never even heard the whole story.

But Graham has been around for so long. She has been my friend for two years. I can't believe that she is dying.

I want to be mad at her human friend, Meghan, because it is Meghan's fault that Graham is dying. She doesn't believe in Graham anymore.

When Graham dies, Meghan's mother will ask Meghan where her friend has gone, and Meghan will say something like "Graham doesn't live here anymore" or "I don't know where Graham is" or "Graham went on vacation." And her mother will turn and smile, thinking her little girl is growing up.

But no. That is not what's going to happen. Graham is not going on any vacation. Graham is not moving to another city or country.

Graham is going to die.

You stopped believing, little girl, and now my friend is going to die. Just because you are the only human person who can see and hear Graham doesn't mean that she is not real. I can see and hear Graham, too. She is my friend.

Sometimes when you and Max are in class, we meet at the swing set to talk.

We used to play tag when you and Max had recess together.

Graham called me a hero once when I stopped M̶

out in front of a moving car, and even though I d̶

hero, it still felt good.

And now she is going to die because you don't b̶

more.

We are sitting in the cafeteria. Max is in music class and Meghan is eating lunch. I can tell by the way that Meghan is talking to the other girls at her lunch table that she doesn't need Graham like she used to. She is smiling. She is laughing. She is following the conversation with her eyes. She is even talking every now and then. She is part of a group now.

She's a whole new Meghan.

"How are you feeling today?" I ask, hoping this might get Graham to mention the disappearing first.

She does.

"I know what's happening if that's what you mean," she says. She sounds so sad, but it also sounds like she has given up, too. Like she has already surrendered.

"Oh," I say, and then I don't know what to say for a moment. I stare at her, and then I pretend to look around, over my shoulder and to my left, acting as if a sound in the corner of the cafeteria has caught my attention. I can't look at her because it means looking through her. Finally, I turn back to her. I force myself to look. "What does it feel like?"

"It doesn't feel like anything." She holds up her hands to show me, and I can see her face, no smile this time, on the other side of her hands. It is as if her hands were made of wax paper.

"I don't get it," I say. "What happened? When you talk to Meghan, can she still hear you?"

"Oh, yeah. And she can still see me, too. We just spent the first ten minutes of recess playing hopscotch together."

"Then why doesn't she believe in you anymore?"

Graham sighs. Then she sighs again. "It's not that she doesn't believe in me. She doesn't *need* me anymore. She used to be afraid to talk to kids. When she was little, she had a stutter. It's gone now, but when she stuttered, she missed out on a lot of time talking with kids and making friends. But she's catching up now. A couple weeks ago she had a play date with Annie. It was her first play date ever. Now

Annie are talking all the time. They even got in trouble in
yesterday for talking when they were supposed to be reading.
And when the girls saw us playing hopscotch today, they came over
and played, too."

"What's a stutter?" I ask. I wonder if Max has a stutter, too.

"It's when words don't come out right. Meghan used to get stuck
on words. She knew what the word was but couldn't make her mouth
say it. A lot of times I would say the word really slowly for her, and
then she could say it. But now she only stutters when she's afraid or
nervous or surprised."

"She was cured?"

"Sort of," Graham says. "She worked with Mrs. Riner during the
week and with Mr. Davidoff after school. It took a long time but now
she can talk just fine, so she's making friends."

Max works with Mrs. Riner, too. I wonder if he can be cured. I
wonder if Mr. Davidoff is the therapist who Max's mom wants him
to see.

"So what are you going to do?" I ask. "I don't want you to disappear. How can you stop it?" I'm worried about Graham, but I feel like
I need to ask these questions for me, too, in case she disappears right in
front of me. I need to ask them while I still can.

Graham opens her mouth to talk and then she stops. She closes her
eyes. She shakes her head and rubs her hands over her eyes. I wonder if
she is stuttering now. But then she starts to cry. I try to remember if I
have ever seen an imaginary friend cry.

I don't think so.

I watch as she dips her chin into her chest and sobs. Tears stream
down her cheeks, and when one finally drips off her chin, I watch as
it falls, splashes on the table and then vanishes completely.

Like Graham will do before long.

I feel like I'm back in the boy's bathroom. Tommy Swinden is
crawling under the stall. Max is standing on top of the toilet, his
pants around his legs. And I am standing in the corner, not knowing
what to say or what to do.

I wait until Graham's sobs turn to sniffles. I wait until the tears
stop running. I wait until she can open her eyes again.

Then I speak. "I have an idea." I wait for Graham to say something.
She only sniffles.

"I have a plan," I say again. "A plan to save you."

"Yeah?" Graham says, but I can tell that she doesn't believe me.

"Yes," I say. "All you need to do is be Meghan's friend." But that's not right and I know it as soon as I say it.

"No, wait," I say. "That's not right." I pause. The idea is there. I just have to find a way to say it right.

Say it without stuttering, I think.

Then I know.

"I have a plan," I say again. "We need to make sure that Meghan still needs you. We have to find a way to make it impossible for Meghan to live without you."

nine

I can't believe we didn't think of this sooner. Meghan's teacher, Mrs. Pandolfe, gives her class a spelling test every Friday, and Meghan does not do well on these tests.

I don't think that Max has ever spelled a word wrong, but Graham says that Meghan spells about six words wrong each week, which is about half of the words on her test, even though Graham didn't know that half of twelve is six. I thought it was kind of weird that she didn't know this, because it seems so obvious. I mean, if six plus six equals twelve, how could you not know that half of twelve is six?

Then again, I probably didn't know what half of twelve was when Max and I were in first grade together.

But I think I did.

Graham and I spent Meghan's lunch period making a list of all of Meghan's problems. I told Graham that we needed to find a problem that she could fix, and then after she fixed it, Meghan would see how much she still needed Graham.

Graham thought it was a great idea. "That might work," she said, her eyes wide and bright for the first time since she started disappearing. "That's a great idea. It might really work."

But I think that Graham would think that any idea is a great idea, because she is fading away more and more by the minute.

I tried to make her laugh by telling her that her ears had already disappeared, since she never had any to begin with, but she didn't even smile at my joke. She's scared. She says she feels less real today, like she's going to fall into the sky and just float away. I started to tell her about satellites in space and how their orbits can decay and they can float away, too, to see if that is how she feels, but then I stopped.

I don't think she wants to talk about it.

37

Max taught me about decaying orbits last year. He read about it in a book. I am lucky because Max is smart and reads a lot, so I get to learn a lot, too. That's why I know that half of twelve is six and that satellites can fall out of orbit and float away forever.

I am so glad that Max is my friend and not Meghan. Meghan can't even spell the word *boat*.

So we made a list of Meghan's problems. Of course, we couldn't write the list down on paper, since neither one of us can pick up a pencil, but it was short enough that we were able to memorize it.

Stutters when she's upset.
Afraid of the dark.
Bad speller.
Can't tie her shoelaces.
Throws a temper tantrum every night before bed.
Can't zip up her coat.
Can't kick a ball past the pitcher.

It is not a good list, because Graham can't help her with a lot of these problems. If Graham could tie shoelaces or zip a zipper, she might be able to tie Meghan's sneakers or zip her coat, but she can't. I only know one imaginary friend who could touch and move things in the human world, and he wouldn't help us even if I begged him.

And I'm too afraid of him to go see him, anyway.

I didn't know what a temper tantrum was, so Graham had to explain it to me. It sounds a lot like when Max gets stuck. Meghan doesn't like to go to bed, so when her mom says that it's time to brush her teeth, she starts screaming and stamping her feet, and sometimes her daddy has to pick her up and carry her into the bathroom.

"This happens every night?" I ask Graham.

"Yeah. She turns red and gets all sweaty and eventually she starts crying. She cries herself to sleep a lot of nights. I feel so bad for her. Nothing that her parents or I say can make it any better."

"Wow," I say, because I can't imagine how annoying it must be to listen to someone have a temper tantrum every night. Max doesn't get stuck too often, but when he does, it's like he is throwing a temper tantrum on the inside. He gets quiet and his hands make fists and he shakes a little, but he doesn't turn red or sweat or scream. I think he is doing all of those things on the inside, but on the outside, he just gets stuck. And sometimes it takes a long time before he gets unstuck.

But at least it's not loud or annoying when it happens. And it never happens just because it's time to go to bed. Max likes to go to bed as long as it's the right time.

8:30 P.M.

If it's too early or too late, he gets upset.

I couldn't think of a way that Graham could help Meghan with her temper tantrums, so that didn't leave much else on the list. And that's what brought us back to the spelling tests.

"How can I help her with spelling?" Graham asked.

"I'll show you."

Mrs. Pandolfe keeps the weekly spelling words hanging on chart paper in front of the room, just like Mrs. Gosk does in her classroom. She takes the list down on Thursday afternoon, so Graham and I spend the last hour of the day standing in front of the chart paper, memorizing each word. I've never paid a lot of attention to Max's spelling tests, and I don't really listen to Mrs. Gosk's spelling lessons, so it was harder than I thought it would be. A lot harder.

But after an hour, Graham knew how to spell the words perfectly.

Tomorrow, she'll stand next to Meghan as she takes the test, and when Meghan spells a word wrong, Graham will tell her how to spell it right. It's an especially good plan because Meghan has to take a spelling test every week, so this won't just be a one-time thing. She can help Meghan every week. Maybe she can even start helping Meghan on other tests, too.

I think this might really work, if Graham doesn't disappear tonight. An imaginary friend named Mr. Finger once told me that most imaginary friends disappear when their human friends are asleep, but I think he was probably making that up to impress me. How could anyone know that? I almost told Graham to try to keep Meghan awake tonight, just in case Mr. Finger was telling the truth, but Meghan is only six years old, and little kids like that can't stay up all night. She would eventually fall asleep no matter what Graham did.

So I'm just hoping that Graham makes it through the night.

ten

Max is mad at me because I have been spending so much time with Graham. He doesn't actually know that I've been with Graham. He just knows that I have been someplace else, and he is mad. I think this is good. I always get a little nervous when I don't see Max for a while, but if he's mad at me for not being around enough, that means he's been thinking about me and misses me.

"I had to go pee and you weren't there to check the bathroom," Max says. "I had to knock on the door."

We are riding on the bus now, going home, and Max is hunkered down in his seat, whispering to me so the other kids don't hear us talking. Except they do. They always do. Max can't see what the other kids can see, but I can. I can see the forest for the trees.

"I had to go to pee and you weren't there to check the bathroom," Max says again. Max repeats himself if you don't answer his questions, because he needs an answer before he can say the next thing. Except that Max doesn't always ask his questions like questions. Lots of times he just says something and expects you to know it's a question. If he has to repeat himself three or four times, which he never has to do for me but sometimes has to do for his teachers and his dad, he gets really upset. Sometimes this makes him get stuck.

"I was in Tommy's classroom," I say. "I was trying to figure out what he plans on doing next. I wanted to make sure that he wasn't going to get his revenge this week."

"You were spying," Max says, and I know that this is a question, too, even if he doesn't say it like a question.

"Yes," I say. "I was spying."

"Okay," Max says, but I can tell that he's still a little mad.

I can't tell Max that I was with Graham because I don't want Max

41

to know that other imaginary friends exist. If he thinks that I'm the only imaginary friend in the whole wide world, then he'll think I'm special. He'll think that I'm unique. That is good, I think.

It helps me persist.

But if Max knew that there were other imaginary friends, and he was mad at me, like he is now, then maybe he would just forget about me and imagine a new imaginary friend. And then I would disappear, like Graham is disappearing right now.

It's been hard because I want to tell Max about Graham. At first I wanted to tell him because I thought he could help. I thought that maybe Max could give me a good idea to help Graham because he's so smart. Or maybe he could help us solve one of Meghan's problems, like teaching her to tie her own shoes, and then he could tell Meghan that it was Graham's idea, so Graham would get all of the credit.

But now I want to tell Max about Graham because I'm scared. I'm afraid that I might lose my friend and I don't have anyone else to talk to about it. I guess I could talk to Puppy, but I don't know Puppy very well, and definitely not as well as I know Max or Graham. And even if Puppy can talk, talking to a dog is weird. Max is my friend, and he should be the one I talk to when I'm sad or afraid, but I can't.

I just hope that Graham comes to school tomorrow and we aren't too late.

Max's father likes to tell people that he and Max play catch every night in the backyard, like they are doing tonight. He tells everyone he can, sometimes more than once, but he usually waits until Max's mom isn't around before he says it. Sometimes he says it just after she leaves the room if he knows that she's coming right back.

But he and Max don't really play catch. Max's dad throws the ball to Max, and Max lets it hit the ground and roll, and when it stops moving, he picks it up and tries to throw it back. Except Max's dad never stands close enough for Max to reach him, even though he tells Max to "Step into it!" and "Throw with your body!" and "Give it your all, son!"

Whenever they play catch, Max's dad calls Max "son" instead of "Max."

But even if Max *steps into it* or *gives it his all* (I don't know what either of those things mean, and I don't think Max does, either), the ball never reaches his dad.

If Max's dad wants the ball to reach him, why doesn't he just stand closer?

Max is in bed now. He is sleeping. No temper tantrum, of course. He brushed his teeth, put on his Thursday night pajamas, read one chapter in his book, and laid his head down on the pillow at exactly 8:30. Max's mom is at a meeting tonight so Max's dad gave Max a kiss on the forehead and said goodnight. Then he turned out the light in Max's room and turned on the nightlights.

There are three.

I sit in the dark beside Max's bed, thinking about Graham. Wondering if there is anything left to think about. Wondering if there is anything else I can do.

Max's mom comes home a little later. She sneaks into the room, tiptoes over to Max's bed, and kisses him on the forehead. Max allows his mom and dad to kiss him, but it has to be quick and always on the cheek or forehead, and Max always cringes whenever they do it. But when Max is asleep like this, his mom can give him a longer kiss, usually on the forehead but sometimes on the cheek, too. Sometimes she goes to his room two or three times a night before she goes to bed to kiss him, even if she was the one who put him to bed and had kissed him already.

One morning at breakfast, Max's mom told Max that she had given him a kiss good night after he was asleep. She said, "You looked like such an angel last night when I went to kiss you good night."

"Dad put me to bed," Max said. "Not you."

This was one of Max's questions-that's-not-a question, and I knew it. So did Max's mom. She always knows. She knows even better than me.

"Yes," she said. "I was visiting Grandpa at the hospital, but when I came home, I tiptoed into your bedroom and gave you a kiss good night."

"You gave me a kiss good night," Max said.

"Yes," his mom said.

Later on, while we were riding the bus to school, Max hunkered down and said, "Did Mom kiss me on the lips?"

"No," I said. "On the forehead."

Max touched his forehead, rubbed it with his fingers and then looked at his fingers. "Was it a long kiss?" he asked.

"No," I said. "It was super short." But that wasn't the truth. I don't lie to Max very often, but I lied that time because I thought it would be better for Max and better for his mother if I did.

Max still asks me if his mom gave him a long kiss when she is not home to put him to bed. I always say, "Nope. Super short."

And I've never told Max about all the extra kisses his mom gives him before she goes to bed.

But that's not a lie, because Max has never asked me if she gives him extra kisses.

Max's mom is eating dinner. She heated the plate of food that Max's dad made for her from the leftovers. Max's dad is sitting at the table across from her, reading a magazine. I am not a very good reader but I know this magazine is called *Sports Illustrated* because Max's dad gets it from the envelope and magazine delivery man every week.

I'm annoyed because it doesn't look like Max's mom and dad are going to watch television soon, and I want to watch television. I like to sit on the couch next to Max's mom and watch the television show and listen to them talk about the show during the commercials.

Commercials are tiny little shows in between the big show, but most of them are stupid and boring, so no one really watches them. People use the commercials to talk or go to the bathroom or fill their glass with more soda.

Max's dad likes to complain about the television shows. He thinks that they are never good enough. He says the stories are "ridiculous" and that there were too many "missed opportunities." I'm not really sure what this means, but I think it means that the television shows would be better if he was allowed to tell the people on the show what to do.

Max's mom sometimes gets annoyed at the complaining because she just likes to watch the shows and not look for the "missed opportunities." "I just want to take a break from the day," she says, and I agree. I don't watch the shows to find a way to make them better. I just like the stories. But most of the time Max's mom and dad just laugh at the shows that are funny and bite their nails when the shows are scary or suspenseful. I don't think Max's mom and dad know that they both bite their nails at the exact same time when they watch television.

They also love to predict what will happen on the next show. I'm not sure, but I think that Max's mom and dad must have had Mrs. Gosk as a third-grade teacher, because she is always asking her students to make a prediction about the book that she is reading, and it seems like making predictions is what Max's mom and dad like to do the best. I like to make predictions, too, because then I can wait and see if I'm right. Max's mom likes to predict that good things are going to happen even when everything looks bad. I usually predict the worst possible ending, and sometimes I'm right, especially when we watch movies.

That's why I'm so nervous tonight about Graham. I can't stop thinking about the worst.

Some nights I have to sit in the cozy chair because Max's dad sits next to Max's mom and puts his arm around her, and she squeezes in real close and they smile. I like those nights because I know they are happy, but I feel a little left out at the same time. Like I don't belong. Sometimes on those nights I just leave, especially if they are watching a show without a story, like the one where people decide who sings the best and the winner gets a prize.

Actually, I think it's more fun to figure out who is singing the worst.

Max's mom and dad are quiet for a long time. She is eating and he is reading. The only sounds are the tinkles of the fork and knife on the plate. Max's mom is never this quiet unless she wants Max's dad to talk first. Usually she has lots and lots to say, but sometimes, when they are fighting, she likes to wait and see if Max's dad will talk first. She's never told me this, but I've watched them for so long that I just know.

I don't know what they are fighting about tonight, so it's almost like watching a television show. I know they are going to argue soon, but I don't know what it will be about. It's a mystery. I predict that it will have something to do with Max, because that's what they argue about the most.

When she is finished with her dinner, Max's mom finally speaks. "Have you thought about seeing a doctor?"

Max's dad sighs. "You really think we need to?" He doesn't look up from his magazine, which is a bad sign.

"It's been ten months."

"I know, but ten months isn't a long time. It's not like we had any trouble in the past." Now he is looking at Max's mom.

"I know," she says. "But how long should we wait, then? I don't want to wait a year or two before we talk to someone and then find out that there's a problem. I'd rather know now, so we can do something about it."

Max's dad rolls his eyes. "I just don't think ten months is that long to wait. It took Scott and Melanie almost two years. Remember?"

Max's mom sighs. I can't tell if she is sad or frustrated or something else.

"I know," she says. "But it wouldn't hurt to just speak to someone. Right?"

"Yeah," Max's dad says, and now he sounds angry. "That'd be fine if speaking to someone was all we had to do. But talking to a doctor isn't going to help if we have a problem. They're going to want to do tests. It's only been ten months."

"But don't you want to know?"

Max's dad doesn't answer. If Max's mom was Max, she would repeat the question, but sometimes adults answer questions by not answering them at all. I think that this is what Max's dad is doing.

When he finally speaks, he answers Max's mom's first question instead of her last. "Okay, we can go see a doctor. Will you make the appointment?"

Max's mom nods. I thought she would be happy that Max's dad agreed to go to the doctor, but she still looks sad. Max's dad looks sad, too. Neither one of them looks at the other. Not once. It is like there are a hundred dining room tables between them instead of just one.

I feel sad for them, too.

If they had just watched television, this would never have happened.

eleven

I tell Max that I'm going to check on Tommy Swinden again. He doesn't mind because he made a poop this morning, so he won't need me to check the bathroom until lunch. And Mrs. Gosk has started the day by reading aloud to the class. Max loves it when Mrs. Gosk reads aloud. He becomes so focused on her voice that he forgets everything else, so he probably won't even know I'm gone.

I don't go to Tommy Swinden's class. I go to Mrs. Pandolfe's classroom. I almost don't want to go, because I'm afraid of what I will find. Or what I won't find.

I step into her classroom, which is much neater and more organized than Mrs. Gosk's classroom. All the desks are in perfectly straight rows and there are no sliding mountains of papers on Mrs. Pandolfe's desk. It's almost too clean.

I look from one side of the room to the other and then back again. Graham is not here. I look in the corner behind the bookshelf and in the coatroom. She is not there.

The children are sitting in their rows, staring at Mrs. Pandolfe, who is standing at the front of the classroom. She is pointing at a calendar and talking about the date and the weather. The chart paper with the list of this week's spelling words is gone.

I see Meghan. She sits near the back of the classroom. Her hand is raised. She wants to answer Mrs. Pandolfe's question about the number of days in October.

It's thirty-one. I know that answer.

I don't see Graham.

I want to walk over to Meghan and ask if she stopped believing in her imaginary friend last night.

"Did you stop believing in the pointy-haired girl who kept you

47

company when you didn't know how to talk and everyone made fun of you?"

"Did you forget about your friend when you forgot how to stutter?"

"Did you even notice that she was fading away?"

"Did you kill my friend?"

Meghan can't hear me. I'm not her imaginary friend. Graham is. Graham was.

Then I see her. She's standing just a few steps away from Meghan, near the back of the class, but I can barely see her. I was looking right through her, straight through to the windows, and I didn't even know it. It's like someone painted her picture on the window a long time ago and now it's all faded and worn. I don't think I would have even noticed her had she not blinked. It was the movement that I saw first. Not her.

"I didn't think you'd see me," Graham says.

I don't know what to say.

"It's alright," Graham says. "I know how hard it is to see me. When I opened my eyes this morning, I couldn't see my own hands at first. I thought I had disappeared."

"I didn't know you sleep," I said.

"Yeah. Of course I do. You don't?"

"No," I say.

"Then what do you do when Max is asleep?"

"I hang out with his parents until they go to sleep," I say. "Then I go for walks."

I don't tell her about my visits to the gas station on the corner and Doogies and the hospital and the police station. I have never told any imaginary friends about my visits. I feel like they are mine. My own special thing.

"Wow," Graham says, and I notice for the first time that her voice is starting to fade, too. It sounds airy and thin, like she's talking through a door. "I never knew that you didn't need to sleep. I feel bad for you."

"Why?" I ask. "What good is sleep?"

"When you sleep, you dream."

"*You* dream?" I ask.

"Of course," Graham says. "Last night I dreamed that Meghan and I were twin sisters. We were playing in the sandbox together, and my fingers could touch the sand. I could hold it in my hands and let it run though my fingers, just like Meghan does."

"I can't believe you dream," I say.

"I can't believe you can't."

Neither one of us says anything for a minute. There is a boy at the front of the classroom named Norman, and he is talking about his visit to a place called Old Newgate Prison. I know what a prison is, so I know that Norman is lying about his trip. Kids aren't allowed to visit prisons. But I can't figure out why Mrs. Pandolfe isn't making Norman tell the truth. If Mrs. Gosk heard Norman telling this story, she would say, "Shame! Shame! Let all the boys and girls know your name!" Then Norman would have to tell the truth.

Norman has a rock in his hand, and he says it came from the prison. He says it came from "the mine." That doesn't make any sense, either. A mine is a bomb that soldiers bury in the ground so that when other soldiers pass by, they will step on it and blow up. Max pretends to dig minefields for his toy soldiers, so that's how I know. So how could Norman get a rock from a mine?

But Norman has everyone fooled, because all the kids in the class want to touch the rock now, even though it's just rock that he probably found on the playground this morning. Even if he really did find the rock on a mine or under a mine, it's still just a rock. Why is everyone so excited? Mrs. Pandolfe has to tell the class to "sit back and relax." When Mrs. Gosk wants her kids to relax, she says, "Don't get your knickers in a bunch." I don't know what this means, but it sounds funny.

Mrs. Pandolfe tells all the kids to sit down again. She promises that everyone will get a chance to hold the rock if they are just patient.

It's just a stupid rock, I want to yell.

All this nonsense going on while my friend is dying.

"When is the spelling test?" I finally ask.

"Next, I think," Graham says, and her voice is even thinner than before. It sounds as if she's standing behind three doors now. "She usually gives the test right after show and tell."

Graham is right. After Norman is done lying about his fake trip to the prison and everyone has touched his stupid rock, Mrs. Pandolfe finally passes out the white-lined paper for the spelling test.

I stand at the back of the room during the test while Graham stands beside Meghan. I can barely see her anymore. When she stands still, she almost disappears completely.

I'm standing in the back, hoping that Meghan makes at least one mistake. Even though she is a rotten speller, Graham said that she's also spelled all the words on some tests correctly. If she spells them all correctly today, we won't have time to make a new plan.

I feel like Graham could disappear at any second.

Then it happens. Mrs. Pandolfe says "giant" and Meghan writes the word on her paper. A second later, Graham leans over, points to it, and says something. Meghan has spelled the word wrong, probably with a *j* instead of a *g,* and I feel giddy as I watch her erase the word and rewrite it.

Three words later, the same thing happens again, this time on the word *surprise.* By the time the test is finished, Graham has helped Meghan spell five words correctly and I am just waiting for the fading away to reverse. Any second now, my friend will appear whole again. She will be safe again.

I wait.

Graham waits.

The test is over. We sit at a small table at the back of the room. We stare at each other. I wait for the moment when I can jump up and shout, "It's happening! You're coming back!"

Mrs. Pandolfe has moved onto math and we still wait.

But it's not happening. In fact, I think she's fading away even more. Graham is sitting three feet in front of me and I can barely see her.

I want to doubt my eyes. They must be playing tricks on me. But then I know it's true. Graham is still fading away. She's becoming more and more transparent by the second.

I can't tell her. I don't want to tell her that the plan didn't work because it should have worked. It had to work.

But it didn't. Graham is disappearing. She is almost gone.

"It didn't work," she finally says, breaking the silence. "I can tell. It's okay."

"It had to work," I say. "She spelled all those words right because of you. She needs you. She knows that now. It had to work."

"It didn't," Graham says. "I can tell. I can feel it."

"Does it hurt?" As soon as I say it, I wish I hadn't asked it. I feel bad asking it, because I'm asking it for me. Not for my friend.

"No," Graham says. "Not at all." Even though it's hard to see her, I think she is smiling. "It feels like I'm floating away. Like I'm free."

"There must be something else we can do," I say. I sound frantic. I can't help it. I feel like I am on a ship sinking into the ocean and there are no little boats to save me.

I think that Graham is shaking her head, but I can't tell. It's so hard to see her now.

"There has to be something that we can do," I say again. "Wait. You said that Meghan is afraid of the dark. Go tell her that a monster lives under her bed, and it only comes out at night, and that you're the only reason she hasn't been eaten yet. Tell her that every night, you protect her from the monster, and that if you die, she will be eaten."

"Budo, I can't."

"It's a rotten thing to do, I know, but you're going to die if you don't. You have to try."

"It's okay," Graham says. "I'm ready to go."

"What does that mean you're ready to go? Go where? You know what happens when you disappear?"

"No, but it's okay," she says again. "Whatever happens, I'll be fine and Meghan will be fine."

I can barely hear her now.

"You have to try, Graham. Go over there and tell her that she needs you. Tell her about the monster under the bed!"

"That's not it, Budo. It doesn't have to do with Meghan needing me. We were wrong. Meghan's just growing up. First it's me, and then it'll be the tooth fairy, and next year it will be Santa Claus. She's a big girl now."

"But the tooth fairy isn't real and you are! Fight, Graham. Fight! Please! Don't leave me!"

"You've been a good friend to me, Budo, but I have to go now. I'm going to go sit next to Meghan now. I want to spend my last few minutes with her. Sitting next to my friend. It's the only thing I'm really sad about."

"What?"

"That I won't be able to look at her anymore. See her grow up. I'm going to miss Meghan so much." She is quiet for a moment and then she adds, "I love her so much."

I start crying. I don't know it at first, because I have never cried before. My nose is suddenly clogged with boogers and my eyes feel wet. I feel warm and sad. So very sad. I feel like a hose with a kink in it, just waiting to let go and spray water everywhere. I feel like I am going to burst open with tears. But I'm glad that I'm crying, because I don't have the words to say good-bye to Graham, and I know that I must. Graham will be gone very soon and I am going to lose my friend. I want to say good-bye and tell her how much I love her, too, but I don't know how. I hope that my tears say it for me.

Graham stands up and smiles at me. She nods her head. Then she walks over to Meghan. She sits behind her and speaks in her ear. I don't think Meghan can hear her anymore. Meghan is listening to Mrs. Pandolfe and smiling.

I stand up. I go to the door. I want to leave. I don't want to be here when Graham disappears. I look back one more time. Meghan has her hand raised again, ready to answer another question. To answer without stuttering. Graham is still sitting behind her, perched in a tiny first-grade chair. I can barely see her now. If Mrs. Pandolfe opened the window and let a breeze in, I think that it might be enough to blow away the last little bit of Graham forever. I look one more time before I leave. Graham is still smiling. She's staring at Meghan, craning her neck to see the little girl's face, and she's smiling.

I turn. I leave my friend behind.

twelve

Mrs. Gosk is teaching math. The kids are spread out around the room, rolling dice and calculating with their fingers. It takes me a minute to check all the corners of the room, but Max is not here. This is good. Max hates these games. He hates to roll dice and listen to kids scream when they roll two sixes. He just wants to solve his math problems and be left alone.

I'm not sure where Max is supposed to be right now. He could be in the Learning Center with Mrs. McGinn and Mrs. Patterson, or he could be in Mrs. Hume's office. It's hard to keep track of Max because he sees so many teachers during the day. I'm also not very good at telling time when a clock has hands on it, and that's the only kind of clock that Mrs. Gosk has in her classroom.

I check in Mrs. Hume's office first because it is the closest to Mrs. Gosk's room but Max is not there. Mrs. Hume is talking to the principal about a boy who sounds a lot like Tommy Swinden except his name is Danny and he is in second grade. The principal sounds worried. She uses the word *situation* three times when talking about Danny. When adults use *situation* a lot, it means that things are serious.

The principal's name is Mrs. Palmer. She's an older lady who doesn't like to punish kids or give out consequences, so she talks to Mrs. Hume a lot about *alternative ways* to make the students behave. She thinks that if she makes a kid like Tommy volunteer in a kindergarten classroom, he will learn to behave.

I think that just gives Tommy Swinden a chance to be mean to even smaller kids.

Mrs. Hume thinks that Mrs. Palmer is crazy. I've heard her say it more than once to other teachers. Mrs. Hume thinks that if Mrs.

Palmer would just give a kid like Tommy Swinden detention more often, he might not try to bowl kids like Max in the bathroom.

I think Mrs. Hume is right.

Max's mom says that the right thing is usually the hardest thing. I don't think Mrs. Palmer has learned that lesson yet.

I walk down the hallway and check the Learning Center, but Max isn't here, either. Mrs. McGinn is working with a boy named Gregory. Gregory is a first grader who has a disease called seizures. He has to wear a helmet all the time just in case he falls on his head when he's having a seizure. A seizure is like a combination of a temper tantrum and getting stuck.

Maybe if I had figured out a way for Graham to help Meghan with her temper tantrums, Graham would still be here. Maybe Meghan didn't care about spelling. Maybe we needed to fix something even bigger than a spelling test.

Max is probably in the bathroom near the nurse's office. He probably had a bonus poop after all. If that's what happened, Max is going to be mad. That's two days in a row that he had to knock on the door.

But Max isn't in the bathroom, either. It's empty.

Now I'm worried.

The only other place where Max could be is in Mrs. Riner's office, but Max only works with his speech teacher on Tuesdays and Thursdays. Maybe he's working with her today for some special reason. Maybe Mrs. Riner has to go to a wedding next Tuesday and won't be able to see Max. It's the only place he could be. But Mrs. Riner's room is on the other side of the school, so I'll have to walk by Mrs. Pandolfe's classroom to get there.

I hadn't thought about Graham for three whole minutes and I was starting to feel better. Now I'm wondering if Graham has completely disappeared. If I walk by the classroom, I wonder if I look inside I will see her still sitting behind Meghan. Maybe I will see just a few wisps left of my friend.

I want to wait until Max gets back to Mrs. Gosk's classroom, but I know I should meet him in Mrs. Riner's classroom. It would make him happy to see me, and to be honest, I want to see Max, too. Watching Graham disappear makes me want to see Max more than ever, even if it means walking by Mrs. Pandolfe's classroom.

But I never get there.

Just as I'm passing the gym, which separates the little kid's side of the school from the big kid's side of the school, I see Max. He is walking into the school, passing through a set of double doors that lead to the outside. It doesn't make sense. It's not recess time, and those aren't even doors that lead to the playground. They face the parking lot and the street. I have never seen a kid go through those doors.

Mrs. Patterson walks in behind him. She stops as she enters the building and looks left and right, like she was expecting to see someone waiting by the doors.

"Max!" I say, and he turns and sees me. He doesn't say anything, because he knows if he does, Mrs. Patterson will start asking questions. Some adults talk to Max like he's a baby when they ask him questions about me. They say, "Is Budo with us right now?" and "Does Budo have anything he wants to say to me?"

"Yes," I always tell Max. "Tell him that I wish I could punch him in the nose."

But he never does.

Then there are other adults that look at Max like he's sick when he tells them about me. Like there's something wrong with him. Sometimes they even look a little frightened of him. So we almost never talk in front of people, and when someone sees Max talking to me from a distance, on the playground or on the bus or in the bathroom, he just says that he was talking to himself.

"Where were you?" I ask, even though I know that Max won't answer.

He looks back outside toward the parking lot. His eyes widen to tell me that wherever he was, it was good.

We walk in the direction of Mrs. Gosk's classroom, Mrs. Patterson leading the way. Just before we reach the classroom door, she stops. She turns around and looks at Max. Then she leans down so that she and Max are eye to eye.

"Remember what I said, Max. I only want what's best for you. Sometimes I think I'm the only one who knows what's best for you."

I'm not sure, but I think Mrs. Patterson said that last part more to herself than to Max.

She's about to say something else when Max interrupts. "When you tell me the same thing over and over again, it bothers me. It makes me think that you don't think I'm smart."

"I'm sorry," Mrs. Patterson says. "I didn't mean that. You're the smartest boy I know. I won't say it again."

She pauses for a second, and I can tell that she's waiting for Max to say something. This happens a lot. Max doesn't notice the pauses. Someone will be speaking to him, and when the person stops, expecting Max to say something, he just waits. If there is no question to answer and nothing that he wants to say, then he says nothing. The silence does not make him squirm like it makes other people squirm.

Mrs. Patterson finally speaks again. "Thank you, Max. You really are a smart and a sweet young man."

Even though I think that Mrs. Patterson is telling the truth, that she really believes that Max is smart and sweet, she is talking in that same baby talk that some people use to talk to Max about me. She sounds fake because she sounds like she is trying to be real instead of just being real.

I do not like Mrs. Patterson one bit.

"Where did you go with Mrs. Patterson today?" I ask.

"I can't tell you. I promised I would keep it a secret."

"But you've never kept a secret from me."

Max grins. It's not exactly a smile, but it is as close as Max gets to smiling. "No one has ever asked me to keep a secret before. This is my first."

"Is it a bad secret?" I ask.

"What do you mean?"

"Did you do something bad? Or did Mrs. Patterson do something bad?"

"No."

I think for a moment. "Were you helping someone?"

"Kind of, but it's a secret," Max says, and he grins again. His eyes get wide. "I can't tell you anything else."

"You're really not going to tell me?" I ask.

"No. It's a secret. It's my first secret."

thirteen

Max did not go to school today. It is Halloween, and Max does not go to school on Halloween. The masks that the kids wear during their Halloween parties scare him. In kindergarten Max got stuck after seeing a boy named JP walk out of the bathroom wearing a Spider-Man mask. It was the first time he got stuck at school and the teacher didn't know what to do. I don't think I've ever seen a teacher so scared.

Max's mom and dad sent him to school on Halloween in first grade, hoping that he had grown out of it. *Grown out of it* means that his parents couldn't figure out what to do, so they didn't do anything except hope that things had changed because Max had grown taller and was wearing bigger sneakers.

But as soon as the first kid put on a mask, Max got stuck again.

Last year he stayed home from school on Halloween, and he is doing the same today. Max's dad took the day off, too, so they could spend the day together. He called his boss and said that he was sick. An adult doesn't have to be sick to say that he is sick, but if a kid wants to stay home from school, he has to be sick.

Or afraid of Halloween masks.

We're going to the pancake house on the Berlin Turnpike. Max likes the pancake house. It's one of his four favorite restaurants. Max will only eat at four restaurants.

A List of Max's Four Favorite Restaurants
1. IHOP
2. Wendy's (Max can't eat at Burger King anymore because his father once told him a story about a customer eating a fish

sandwich with a bone in it and now Max is worried that everything at his father's Burger King will have a bone in it)
3. Max Burger (There are actually a bunch of Max restaurants, with
   names like Max Fish and Max Downtown, and Max thinks it's
   great that they share his name. But Max's parents brought him to
   Max Burger first, and now it's the only one where he will eat)
4. The Corner Pug

If Max goes to a new restaurant, he cannot eat. Sometimes he even
gets stuck. It's hard to explain why. To Max, the pancakes at the pancake house on the Berlin Turnpike are pancakes, but the pancakes at
the diner across the street aren't really pancakes. Even though they
look the same and probably taste the same, they are a completely different food for Max. He would tell you that the pancakes across the
street at the diner are pancakes, but not his pancakes.

Like I said, it's hard to explain.

"Do you want to try blueberries in your pancakes today?" Max's
father asks.

"No," Max says.

"Okay," Max's dad says. "Maybe next time."

"No."

We sit quietly for a while, waiting for the food to come. Max's dad
flips through the menu even though he has already ordered his food.
The waitress stuck the menus behind the syrup when Max and his
dad were done ordering, but Max's dad took it back out as soon as she
left. I think he likes to have something to look at when he doesn't
know what to say.

Max and I have a staring contest. We do this a lot.

He wins the first game. I get distracted when a waitress drops a
glass of orange juice on the floor.

"Are you happy to have the day off from school?" Max's father asks
just as we are beginning another staring contest. His father's voice
startles me and I blink.

Max wins again.

"Yes," Max says.

"Do you want to try trick-or-treating tonight?"

"No."

"You wouldn't have to wear a mask," Max's dad says. "No costume at all if you don't want."

"No."

I think that Max's dad sometimes gets sad talking to Max. I can see it in his eyes and hear it in his voice. The more they talk, the worse it gets. His shoulders slump. He sighs a lot. His chin sinks into his chest. I think that he thinks that Max's one-word answers are all his fault. Like he is to blame for Max not wanting to talk. But Max doesn't talk unless he has something to say, no matter who you are, so if you only ask him yes-or-no questions, you're only going to get yes-or-no answers.

Max doesn't know how to chat.

Actually, Max doesn't want to know how to chat.

We sit in silence again. Max's dad is looking at the menu again.

An imaginary friend enters the restaurant. He's walking behind a set of parents and a little girl with red hair and freckles. The imaginary friend actually looks a lot like me. He looks almost like a human person, except his skin is yellow. Not a little yellow. Yellow like someone painted him with the yellowiest yellow they could find. He's also missing eyebrows, which is pretty common for imaginary friends. But otherwise he could pass for a human person, if anyone except for the little redhead and I could see him.

"I'm going to check out the kitchen," I say to Max. "Make sure it's clean." I do this a lot when I want to explore. Max likes it when I make sure places are clean.

Max nods. He's drumming his fingers on the table in patterns.

I walk over to the yellow boy, who has taken a seat beside the girl. They are on the other side of the restaurant. Max can't see me from here.

"Hello," I say. "I'm Budo. Would you like to talk?"

The yellow boy is so startled that he almost falls off the bench. I get this a lot.

"You can see me?" the yellow boy says. He has a little girl's voice, which is also common with imaginary friends. Kids never seem to imagine their imaginary friends with deep voices. I guess it's just easier to imagine a voice like your own.

"Yes," I say. "I can see you. I'm like you."

"Really?"

"Yes."

I don't use the words *imaginary friend* because not every imaginary friend knows this name, and it scares some of them when they hear it for the first time.

"Who are you talking to?" This is the little girl. Maybe three or four years old. She has heard the yellow boy's half of the conversation.

I see the panic in the yellow boy's eyes. He doesn't know what to say. "Tell her that you were talking to yourself," I say.

"Sorry, Alexis. I was talking to myself."

"Can you get up and walk away?" I ask. "Is that something you can do?"

"I have to go to the bathroom," the yellow boy says to Alexis.

"Okay," Alexis says.

"Okay what?" asks the woman sitting across from Alexis. Alexis's mom, no doubt. The two look so much alike. Red hair and freckles times two.

"Okay that Jo-Jo can go to the potty," Alexis says.

"Oh," Alexis's dad says. "Jo-Jo's going to the potty. Huh?"

Jo-Jo's dad is using the baby talk. I don't like him already.

"Follow me," I say, and I lead Jo-Jo through the kitchen, down a set of stairs, and into the basement. I've explored this place before. With only four restaurants, and only three that we go inside, it isn't hard to cover them all. There is a walk-in freezer to my right and a stockroom to my left, though it's not really a room. It's just a space surrounded by a chain-link fence. The fence starts at the floor and goes to the ceiling. I pass through the door, which is also made from chain-link fence, and sit on one of the boxes on the other side.

"Whoa!" Jo-Jo says. "How did you do that?"

"Can't you pass through doors?"

"I don't know."

"If you could, you would know," I say. "It's okay." I pass back through the door and take a seat on a plastic pail in the corner by the stairs. Jo-Jo stands by the wire fence for a moment longer, staring at it. He reaches out to touch it, moving his hand slowly as if he's afraid to be electrocuted. His hand stops at the chain-link. He doesn't touch the fence. He doesn't move the wire with his hand. His hand just stops. It's not the fence that blocks him from entering. It's the idea of the fence.

I've seen this before, too. It's the same reason I don't fall through the floor. When I walk, I don't leave footprints because I'm not actually touching the ground. I'm touching the idea of the ground.

Some ideas, like floors, are too strong for imaginary friends to pass through. No one imagines an imaginary friend who slides through the floor and disappears. The idea of the floor is too strong in a little kid's mind. It's too permanent. Like walls.

Lucky for us.

"Sit," I say, motioning to a barrel.

Jo-Jo does.

"I'm Budo. Sorry to scare you."

"It's okay. You just look so real."

"I know," I say.

I have frightened lots of imaginary friends when they realize that I am talking to them because I look so real. You can usually tell that someone is an imaginary friend by things like their yellow skin or missing eyebrows.

Most of the time, they don't look a human-person at all.

But I do. That's why I can be a little scary. I look real.

"Can you tell me what's happening?" Jo-Jo says.

"What do you already know?" I ask. "Let's start with that, and then I'll fill in the missing pieces that I know." This is the best way to talk to an imaginary friend for the first time.

"Okay," Jo-Jo says. "But what should I tell?"

"How long have you been alive?" I ask.

"I don't know. A little while."

"More than a few days?" I ask.

"Oh, yes."

"More than a few weeks?"

Jo-Jo thinks for a moment. "I don't know."

"Okay," I say. "Probably a few weeks then. Has anyone told you what you are?"

"Mom says that I'm Alexis's imaginary friend. She doesn't say that to Alexis, but I heard her say it to Dad."

I smile. Lots of imaginary friends think of their human's parents as their parents, too. "Okay," I say. "So you know, then. You're an imaginary friend. The only people who can see you are Alexis and other imaginary friends."

"Is that what you are, too?"

"Yes."

Jo-Jo leans closer to me. "Does that mean we aren't real?"

"No," I say. "It just means that we are a different kind of real. It's a kind of real that adults don't understand, so they just assume that we're imaginary."

"How come you can walk through fences and I can't?"

"We can do what our human friends imagined us to do. My friend imagined that I look like this and can walk though doors. Alexis imagined that your skin is yellow and you cannot walk through doors."

"Oh." It's the kind of *oh* that says, "You just explained a gigantic thing to me."

"Do you really use the bathroom?" I ask.

"No. I just tell Alexis that if I want to look around a little."

"I wish I had thought of that."

"Do any imaginary friends use the bathroom?" he asks.

I laugh. "None that I've ever met."

"Oh."

"You should probably get back to Alexis, now," I say, thinking that Max is probably wondering where I am as well.

"Oh. Okay. Will I see you again?"

"Probably not. Where do you live?"

"I don't know," he says. "In the green house."

"You should try to find out your address, in case you ever get lost. Especially because you can't pass through doors."

"What do you mean?" he asks. He looks worried. He should be.

"You have to be careful that you don't get left behind. Make sure that you climb into the car as soon as the door is opened. Otherwise they could drive away without you."

"But Alexis wouldn't do that."

"Alexis is a little kid," I say. "She's not the boss. Her parents are the bosses, and they don't think that you are real. So you have to take care of yourself. Okay?"

"Okay," he says, but he sounds so small when he speaks. "I wish I could see you again."

"Max and I come here a lot. Maybe I'll see you here again. Okay?"

"Okay." It sounds almost like a wish.

I stand. I'm ready to get back to Max. But Jo-Jo is still sitting on the pail.

"Budo," he asks, "where are my parents?"

"Huh?

"My parents," he says. "Alexis has parents but I don't. Alexis says they're my parents, too, but they can't see me or hear me. Where are my parents? The ones who can see me?"

"We don't have parents," I tell him. I want to say something better, but there is nothing better. He looks sad when I say this, and I understand, because it makes me sad, too. "That's why you have to take care of yourself," I say.

"Okay," he says, but he still doesn't stand. He sits on the pail, staring at his feet.

"We have to go now. Okay?"

"Okay." Finally he stands. "I'll miss you, Budo."

"Me, too."

Max begins screaming at exactly 9:28 P.M. I know this because I am watching the clock, waiting for 9:30 when Max's mom and dad will change the channel to my favorite show of the week.

I don't know why he is screaming, but I know that it is not normal. He hasn't woken up from a nightmare or seen a spider. This is not a normal scream. I know that he's probably going to get stuck no matter how fast his parents run up the stairs.

Then I hear it.

Three bangs coming from the front of the house. Hitting the house. There might have been a bang right before Max started screaming, too. The television was on a commercial, and commercials are loud. Then I hear two more bangs. Then the sound of glass breaking. *A window,* I think. A window has broken. Max's bedroom window has broken. I don't know how I know it, but I do. Max's mom and dad are already on the second floor. I can hear them running down the hall toward Max's room.

I'm still sitting in the cushy chair. I'm stuck for a second, too. Not like Max, but the screams and the bangs and the breaking of glass have me stuck in place. I don't know what to do.

Max says that a good soldier is "good under pressure." I am not good under pressure. I am bad under pressure. I don't know what to do.

Then I do.

I get up and go to the front door. I pass through the door and step out onto the front porch. I catch a glimpse of a boy just as he disappears behind the house across the street. It's the Tylers' house. Mr. and Mrs. Tyler are old people. They don't have little boys, so I know this boy is just using their backyard to escape. I think about chasing him for a second, but I don't need to.

I know who it is.

Even if I caught up to him, there is nothing that I could do.

I turn and look at the house. I expect to see holes in the house. Maybe sparks and fire. But it's just eggs. Eggshells and yolk are running down the siding around Max's bedroom window. And his window is broken. The glass on part of the window is gone.

I don't hear Max screaming anymore.

He's stuck.

There is no screaming when he is stuck.

When Max gets stuck, there's nothing anyone can do for him. His mom will rub his back or stroke the hair on his head, but I think that this only helps his mom feel better. I don't think Max even notices. Max eventually gets unstuck on his own. And even though Max's mom is worried that this will be "the worst episode that Max has ever had," Max never gets more stuck or less stuck. He just gets stuck. The only thing that changes is how long he gets stuck. Since Max has never had his bedroom window break and glass land on his bed while he was sleeping, I think he's going to be stuck for a while this time.

When Max gets stuck, he sits with his knees pulled really tight into his chest and he rocks back and forth and makes a whining sound. His eyes are open, but it's like they can't see anything. He really can't hear anything, either. Max once told me that when he's stuck, he can hear the people around him, but it sounds like they are coming from a television in the neighbor's house—fake and far away.

Kind of like how Graham sounded before she disappeared.

So there's nothing I can say or do to help.

That's why I'm going to the gas station. I'm not being mean. I'm just not needed here.

But I waited for the police to show up and ask Max's mom and dad a bunch of questions. The police officer, who was much shorter and skinnier than the police officers on television, took some pictures of the house and the window and Max's room and wrote everything down in a little notepad. He asked Max's parents if they knew why someone might egg our house and they said no.

"It's Halloween," Max's dad said. "Don't lots of people get egged?"

"They don't have their windows broken with rocks," the little police officer said. "And it looks as if the person throwing the eggs was aiming specifically at your son's window."

"How would they know it was Max's window?" his mom asked.

"You told me that the window was full of *Star Wars* decals," the little police officer said. "Right?"

"Oh. Yes."

Even I knew the answer to that one.

"Is Max having trouble with anyone at school?" the police officer asked.

"No," Max's dad said, speaking so fast that Max's mom didn't have a chance to speak. Like he was afraid to give her a chance to speak. "Max does well in school. No problems at all."

Unless you count pooping on a bully's head.

fourteen

The gas station is at the end of the street and six blocks over. It's open all the time. It never closes like the grocery store and the other gas station down the street, and that's why I like it so much. I can go out in the middle of the night and still find people who are awake. If I made a list of my favorite places in the whole wide world, I think Mrs. Gosk's classroom would win, but I think the gas station would be second.

When I walk through the door tonight, Sally and Dee are on duty. Sally is usually a girl's name, but this Sally is a boy.

For a second, I think of Graham, my girl friend with a boy's name.

I once asked Max if Budo is usually a boy's name and he said yes, but he crinkled his eyebrows when he said it, so I don't think that he was sure.

Sally is even skinnier and even shorter than the police officer who visited the house tonight. He is practically tiny. I don't think that his real name is Sally. I think that people call him Sally because he's smaller than most girls.

Dee is standing in the candy bar and Twinkie aisle, putting more candy bars and Twinkies out for people to buy. Twinkies are little yellow cakes that everyone makes fun of but everyone eats, so Dee is always filling up the Twinkie shelf. Her hair is wrapped up in little curls and she is chewing gum. She is always chewing gum. She chews gum like she is chewing with her whole body. Everything moves when she chews. Dee is always happy and angry at the same time. She gets mad at lots of little things but always smiles while she is yelling about them. She loves to yell and loves to complain, but I think the yelling and complaining make her happy.

I just think that she is funny. I love her. If I made a list of all the human persons except for Max who I would like to talk to, I think Mrs. Gosk would win, but I think Dee would win, too.

Sally is behind the counter, holding a clipboard and pretending to count the boxes of cigarettes that hang in a plastic case over his head. He is actually watching the small television on the back counter. He does this all the time. I don't recognize the show, but it has police officers in it, like most of the shows on television.

There's one customer in the store. An older man who is wandering in the back of the store near the coolers, peeking through the glass for the right bottle of juice or soda. He is not a regular. A regular is someone who comes to the gas station all the time.

Every day for some of them.

Dee and Sally don't mind the regulars, but Dorothy, who sometimes works overnights, too, hates the regulars. She says that "of all the places these deadbeats can be spending their time, why would they want to hang out in a Godforsaken gas station?"

I guess I'm a regular here, too. Out of all the places that I could spend my time, I come here.

I don't care what Dorothy thinks. I love this place. This was the first place where I felt safe when I started leaving Max at night.

It was Dee who made me feel safe.

I'm standing over by Dee when she notices that Sally isn't working. "Hey, Sally! You gonna stop playing with yourself and finish inventory?"

Sally holds his hand up and points at Dee with his middle finger. He does this a lot. I used to think that he was raising his hand to ask a question, like Max does when he wants to ask Mrs. Gosk a question or like Meghan was doing when I saw Graham for the last time. But I think it means more than that because Sally never seems to have a question to ask. Sometimes Dee points her middle finger back at him, and when she does it, she sometimes adds the phrase *Screw you,* which I know is inappropriate because Cissy Lamont once got caught saying it to Jane Feber in the cafeteria and got in a lot of trouble for it. It's almost like Sally and Dee are high-fiving each other without touching. But I think it's supposed to be a way of acting rude, like sticking your tongue out at a person when you don't like them, because Sally only does this when Dee is being mean to him. But Sally never does it when a customer is being mean and I've seen customers be ten times meaner than Dee. So I'm still not sure.

I can't ask Max, because he doesn't know that I come here.

Actually, Sally and Dee like each other a lot. But whenever a customer is inside the store, they pretend to fight. Nothing too bad. Max's mom would call it bickering, which means fighting without the danger of hating each other at the end of the fight. That's what Sally and Dee do. They bicker. But as soon as the customer leaves, they go back to being nice to each other. When someone is watching, I think they like to put on a show.

Max would never understand this. He has a hard time understanding that you have to act differently in different situations. Last year Joey came over the house for a play date and Max's mom said, "Do you boys want to play with Max's video games?"

"I can't play video games until after dinner," Max said.

"Oh no. It's okay, Max. Joey is here. You can play."

"I'm not allowed to play video games until after dinner, and for only thirty minutes."

"It's okay, Max," his mom said. "You have a friend over. It's different today."

"I can't play video games before dinner."

Max and his mom went back and forth until Joey finally said, "It's okay. Let's go play catch outside."

That was Max's last play date.

The customer leaves and Sally and Dee switch back to nice.

"How's your ma?" Sally asks. He's back to counting cigarettes, but probably because there's a commercial on the television.

"She's okay," Dee says. "But my uncle had his foot amputated when he had diabetes, and I'm worried that they might have to do that to my mom, too."

"Why would they do that?" Sally asks. His eyes are wide.

"Bad circulation. She's already got it a little bit. The foot sort of dies, and they got to chop it off."

"Damn," Sally says in that way that means he's still thinking about what Dee just said and can't believe it.

I can't believe it, either.

This is why I love hanging out at the gas station. Before I came into the store, I didn't know that a foot could die and get chopped off. I thought if one part of a human person dies, everything dies.

I'll have to ask Max what bad circulation means, and I have to make sure he doesn't catch it. And I want to know who "they" are.

The foot-chopping people.

As they talk some more about Dee's mom, Pauley walks in the door. Pauley is a man who works at Walmart and likes to buy scratch tickets. I love scratch tickets, and I love when Pauley comes in to buy them, because he always scratches them right here on the counter, and if he wins, he hands the money right back to Dee or Sally or Dorothy for more scratch tickets.

Scratch tickets are like tiny television shows, even shorter than commercials but a whole lot better. Every scratch ticket is like a story. Pay one dollar and try to win a million dollars, which is a lot of money. Pauley's whole life could change with just one scratch. In one second he could become rich, which would mean he wouldn't have to work at Walmart anymore and could spend more time here. And when I'm here, I get to watch him scratch. I stand right over his shoulder and watch those little shavings get pushed off the card by his lucky quarter. Pauley has never won more than five hundred dollars, but even that made him very happy. He tried to pretend like nothing big happened, but his cheeks turned bright red and he could barely stand still. He shuffled his feet and rubbed his hands, like a kindergartener who has to pee real bad.

Someday I think Pauley is going to win "the big prize." He buys so many scratch tickets that he has to win eventually.

I worry that he's going to win when I'm not here, and I'll only hear about it later from Dee or Sally.

Pauley says that when he hits it big, we won't ever see him again, but I don't believe him. I don't think Pauley has a better place to be than the gas station. Why else would he come every night, buy scratch tickets and a coffee and stay for an hour? I think Sally and Dee and even Dorothy are Pauley's friends, even if Sally and Dee and Dorothy don't know it.

But I think Dee knows it. I can just tell by the way she talks to Pauley. I don't think she wants to be Pauley's friend, but she needs to be Pauley's friend. For Pauley.

That's why Dee is my favorite person in the world except for Max and his mom and his dad. And maybe Mrs. Gosk.

I watch Pauley scratch ten tickets. He doesn't win anything and now he has no more money. "Tomorrow is payday," he says. "I'm a little low on funds."

This is how Pauley asks for free coffee. Dee tells him to take a cup.

Pauley drinks his coffee slowly, standing near the counter and watching the television with Sally, who isn't even pretending to count cigarettes anymore. It's 10:51, which means that the show must be near the end, and that's the worst time to miss something on a TV show. You can skip the first ten minutes if you want, but you can't miss the last ten minutes, because that's where all the good stuff happens.

"I swear that if you don't turn off that goddamn TV, I'm going to tell Bill to throw it away," Dee says.

"Five minutes!" Sally says, not taking his eyes off the screen. "Then I'll turn it off. I promise."

"Have a heart," Pauley says.

When the show ends (a smart policeman catches a thinks-he's-so-smart bad guy), Sally goes back to counting, Pauley finishes his coffee, waits for two more customers to leave, and then says good-bye. He gives a big wave, stands at the door for a moment as if he doesn't want to leave (and I don't think he ever does), and then tells us that he'll be back tomorrow.

Someday I should follow Pauley. See where he lives.

It's still Halloween, and even though it's late and most kids are in their beds, I'm not surprised when the man walks in wearing the mask. It's a devil mask. Red with two plastic horns on top. Dee is stocking the shelf on the far side of the store with Band-Aids and aspirin and tiny tubes of toothpaste. She is down on one knee, so she doesn't see the man in the devil mask come in. Sally is counting scratch tickets now. The man in the devil mask comes in the door closest to Sally and walks up to the counter.

"Sorry, no masks allowed in the store. It's a . . . ."

It sounds like Sally wants to say something else but he stops. Something is wrong.

"I will blow your fucking head off unless you open your register and give me the money now."

This is the voice of the devil man. He is holding a gun. It's black and silver and looks heavy. He is pointing it at Sally's face. I know that the bullet can't hurt me, but I duck anyway. I'm afraid. The devil man's voice sounds so loud even though it is not.

As I duck, Dee rises up next to me, tubes of toothpaste in her hand. We pass each other at the halfway point, and as our faces flash by one another, I suddenly want to tell her to stop. To duck.

"What's going on?" she asks, her head rising above the shelves.

Then I hear a crash. A bang that is so loud that it would hurt my ears if they could hurt. It makes me scream. Not a long scream but a quick scream. A surprised scream. Even before I finish my scream, Dee falls. It's like she is pushed backward, and she falls into a shelf of potato chips. She falls backward and turns at the same time, and I see the blood on her shirt as she turns. This is not like television. The blood is on her shirt but tiny drops are on her face and arms, too. Red is everywhere. And Dee doesn't say anything. She just falls into the potato chips, face first, little tubes of toothpaste landing around her.

"Fuck!" This is the man. The devil man. Not Sally. It's not an angry *no*. It is a scared *fuck*. "Fuck! Fuck!" He screams these last two fucks. He's still afraid, but he also sounds like he can't believe what he is seeing. Like he was suddenly popped into a television show as the bad guy without anyone telling him that this would happen.

"Get up!" He shouts these words, too. He is back to angry now. I think he's talking to me, so I do. I stand up. But he's not talking to me. Then I think he's talking to Dee, who has slid off the potato chip shelf and onto the floor. But he's not talking to Dee, either. He is shouting at the counter, trying to peek over it, but the counter is tall. It is on a stage, and there are three stairs that you have to climb to get behind the counter. Sally is on the other side of the counter, I think. On the floor. But the devil man can't see him from where he's standing.

"Fuck!" He shouts again and makes a growling sound, and then he turns and runs. He opens the door that he walked through a minute ago before Dee was bleeding and runs into the dark.

I stand for a minute, watching him run away. Then I hear Dee. She's on the floor next to my feet, wheezing, like Corey Topper when he's having an asthma attack. Her eyes are open. It looks like she is looking straight into my eyes, but she can't see my eyes. But part of me swears that she can. I think she is looking right at me. She looks so afraid. This is not like television. There is so much blood.

"Dee has been shot." I say, and somehow this makes me feel a tiny bit better, because being shot is a lot better than being dead. "Sally!" I yell. But Sally can't hear me.

I run over to the counter, climb the three steps, and look behind the counter. Sally is lying on the floor. He is shaking. Shaking even more than Max shakes when Max is stuck. At first I think Sally has been shot, too, but then I remember that I only heard one bang. Sally is not shot. Sally is stuck. He needs to call the hospital or Dee will die. But Sally is stuck.

"Get up!" I shout to Sally. "Hurry! Get up!"

Sally is stuck. He is as stuck as Max has ever been. He's curled up into a ball and he is shaking. Dee is going to die because Sally won't move and I can only watch. One of my most favorite people in the whole wide world is bleeding and I can't do a thing.

The door closest to me opens. The devil man is back. I look, expecting to see his gun and his pointy horns, but it is not the devil man. It's Dan. Big Dan. Another regular. Not as nice as Pauley but more normal. Not so sad. Dan walks in and for a moment, I think he is looking at me, because he is. He's looking straight through me, and he looks confused because he sees no one.

"Dan!" I shout. "Dee's shot!"

"Hello?" Big Dan looks around. "Guys?"

Dee makes a sound. Dan can't see her, because she is on the floor behind the shelves, and for a second, I don't think Dan has heard her. Then he looks in her direction and says, "Hello?"

Dee makes another sound, and suddenly I am happy. So happy. Dee is still alive. I shouted that Dee has been shot because it was better than saying that Dee is dead, and now I know that she is not dead. She is making a wheezing sound, and even better, she's trying to answer Big Dan. That means she is awake.

Dan walks over to the aisle where Dee has fallen. When he sees Dee on the floor, he says, "Oh my God! Dee!"

Big Dan moves fast. He opens his cell phone and presses numbers as he moves into the aisle and kneels down beside Dee. He acts like Big Dan, a guy who stops at the gas station every night for a Dr Pepper to keep him awake on his ride home to a place called New Haven. Big Dan, who doesn't linger in the gas station a moment longer than necessary, but who is friendly just the same. I love Pauley and his scratch tickets and the way he tries to drink his coffee as slowly as possible, but in an emergency, I love Big Dan.

fifteen

The ambulance people took Dee and Sally away in two separate vans. Dee was taken first, but Sally left right after her, even though he wasn't hurt at all. I tried to tell the ambulance people that Sally was just stuck, and no one needs to ride in the ambulance van just because they are stuck, but they couldn't hear me, of course.

An ambulance man with bushy hair used an old-fashioned cell phone with a big antenna to tell someone at the hospital that Dee is in critical condition. This means that Dee might die, especially if she got a good look at the devil man who shot her. It seems like the more you know about the person who shot you, the more likely you are to die.

The police closed the gas station even though it's never supposed to close, so after Dee and Sally were taken away, I went home.

Max is still stuck. His dad has to work at five o'clock tomorrow morning so he went to bed. Max's mom is still awake, sitting in a chair next to Max's bed.

My chair.

But I don't mind. I want to sit with Max's mom, too. I want her to stay in Max's room all night. I just saw my friend get shot with a real gun and a real bullet and I can't stop thinking about it.

I wish that Max's mom would stroke my hair back and kiss me on the forehead, too.

Max wakes up on Saturday morning. He is unstuck. "Why are you sitting there?"

I think he's talking to me. I'm sitting on the end of his bed. I've been sitting here all night, thinking about Dee and Sally and the devil man and staring at Max's mom because it makes me feel better.

But Max isn't talking to me. He's talking to his mother. She fell asleep in my chair, and his voice wakes her. She jumps up like some-one pinched her.

"What?" she says, looking around like she doesn't know where she is.

"Why are you sitting there?" Max asks again.

"Max, you're awake." And then the eggs, and the rocks, and the broken window, and Max getting stuck seem to fall out of the sky and fill her up like air in a balloon. She pops up out of the chair, all inflated and awake, and she quickly answers Max. "I'm sitting here because you were upset last night, and I didn't want you to be alone."

Max looks at the window beside his bed. It's covered with clear plastic. Max's dad tacked it up last night. "I was stuck?" he asks.

"Yes," his mother says. "For a little while."

Max knows that he was stuck, but he always asks if he was stuck anyway. I don't know why. It's not like he has amnesia, which is a disease that turns a person's brain off so it can't record what the person sees or does. It happens a lot on television, and I think it's real, even though I've never met anyone with amnesia before. It's like Max is double-checking, to make sure everything is okay. Max is a big fan of double-checking.

"Who broke my window?" he asks, still looking at the plastic.

"We don't know," his mom says. "We think it was an accident."

"How could someone break my window by accident?"

"Kids do crazy things on Halloween," his mom says. "They threw eggs at our house last night. And rocks, too."

"Why?" From the tone in his voice, I can tell that Max is upset about this. I'm sure that his mom can tell, too.

"It's called a prank," she says. "Some kids think that it's okay to pull pranks on Halloween."

"Pull?"

"Make pranks. Do pranks," she says. "People use the expression *pull pranks* sometimes."

"Oh."

"Do you want breakfast?" his mom asks. Max's mom is always worried about Max eating enough, even though he eats plenty of food.

"What time is it?" Max asks.

Max's mom looks at her watch. It's the kind with hands on it, so I can't read it well. "It's eight thirty," she says, looking relieved. Max can only eat breakfast before 9:00. After 9:00, he must wait until 12:00 to eat lunch.

This is Max's rule. Not his mom's.

"Okay," Max says. "I'll eat."

His mom leaves to make the pancakes and to let Max get dressed. He does not eat breakfast in pajamas. This is also Max's rule.

"Did Mom kiss me last night?" Max asks.

"Yes," I say. "But only on the forehead." I want to tell Max that the devil man shot my friend last night, but I can't. I don't want Max to know that I go to the gas station and the diner and the police station and the hospital. I don't think he would like it if he knew I went to those places. He likes to think that I am sitting beside him all night or at least somewhere in the house in case he needs me. I think it would make him mad to know that I have other friends in the world.

"Was it a long kiss?" Max asks.

For the first time ever, this question makes me mad. I know how important it is for Max to know that his mom's kiss was not too long, but the length of a mom's kiss is not that important. It's a tiny thing compared to guns and blood and friends in ambulance vans, and he shouldn't have to ask me every day. Doesn't he know that a mom's long kiss is not a bad thing?

"Nope," I say, like I always do. "It was super short." But when I say it this time, I do not smile. I frown. I say it through clenched teeth.

Max doesn't notice. He never notices these things. He's still looking at the plastic that is covering the window.

"Do you know who broke my window?" Max asks.

I do, but I don't know if I should tell Max. I don't know if this is like his mom's long kisses and I should lie. I'm still mad at him for worrying about the long kisses, so even though I want to do the right thing for him, I don't want to do the right thing, too. I don't want to hurt Max, but I'm not in the helping mood either.

I take too long to answer.

"Do you know who broke my window?" Max asks again. He never has to ask me questions twice, so now he is angry, too.

I decide to answer honestly, not because I think it's the best thing for Max to hear, but because I am mad and don't want to think about what is right.

"It was Tommy Swinden," I say. "I ran outside after I heard your window break and I saw him running away."

"It was Tommy Swinden," Max says.

"Yes," I say. "It was Tommy Swinden."

"Tommy Swinden broke my window and threw eggs at our house." Max says this to his mother while he is eating his pancakes. I can't believe that he told her. I didn't expect him to say it. How is he going to explain it? Suddenly I'm not angry at Max anymore. I'm worried. Worried about what he will say. Now I'm angry at myself for being so stupid.

"Who is Tommy Swinden?" Max's mom asks.

"He's a boy who is mean to me at school. He wants to kill me."

"How do you know that?" His mom doesn't sound like she believes him.

"He told me."

"What did he say exactly?" She's still washing the frying pan, so I know that she still does not believe him.

"He said he was going to bowl me," Max says.

"What does that mean?"

"I don't know, but it's bad." Max is staring at his pancakes because when Max eats, he stares at his food.

"How do you know it's bad?" his mom asks.

"Because everything Tommy Swinden says to me is bad."

His mom doesn't say anything for a minute, and I think she is going to forget the whole thing. Then she speaks again. "How do you know that Tommy threw the eggs and the rocks?"

"Budo saw him."

"Budo saw him." This time it is Max's mom who is saying something that didn't sound like a question but was still a question.

"Yes," Max says. "Budo saw him."

"Okay."

I feel like the elephant in the room. This is an expression that means there is something two people know that is as big as an elephant but no one wants to talk about it. Max's mom uses this expression a lot when she is talking to Max's dad about Max and his "diagnosis."

It took me forever to figure out what the elephant in the room thing meant.

Max and his mom eat for a little while, and then his mom asks, "Is Tommy Swinden in your class?"

"No, he's in Mrs. Parenti's class."

"Third grade?"

"No," Max says. He sounds annoyed. He thinks that his mom should know that Mrs. Parenti doesn't teach third grade, because in Max's world, knowing who teaches what grade is a big deal. "Mrs. Parenti is a fifth-grade teacher."

"Oh."

Max's mom doesn't say anything else about Tommy Swinden or the eggs or the rocks or getting bowled or me, which is bad. It means she is planning on doing something.

I can feel it.

sixteen

Dee and Sally are not back on Saturday or Sunday night. A man who Dorothy calls Mr. Eisner is working instead. I've never seen Mr. Eisner before but Dorothy seems nervous around him. They barely speak to each other.

Mr. Eisner reminds me of Max's principal. Mrs. Palmer is in charge of the school and dresses in fancier clothing than most of the teachers, but I don't think that she could actually teach kids if she had to take over a classroom.

Mr. Eisner is the same. He wears a tie, and he takes the money from the customers and fills the Twinkie shelf like Dee, but you can tell that he has to think too much about what he is doing instead of just doing it.

Dee is not dead. I know this because the regulars like Pauley and Big Dan came in on Saturday night to ask about Dee. Actually, they would have come in anyway, since they are regulars, but even Big Dan hung around for a little while longer than normal, asking questions about Dee. Mr. Eisner didn't talk to them very much, so it was hard for them to hang around. Everything felt different. Not right.

Dee is in a place called I See You. I think it's a place where they watch you carefully to make sure that you don't die. Dorothy says it is not certain that Dee is going to "make it," which I think means that she could die.

I wonder if she will come back to the gas station and if I will ever see her again.

I hope so. I feel like everyone is disappearing.

seventeen

I'm worried about Max. It's Monday and we are back at school.

I think that Max's mom has something planned for today. She is worried about Tommy Swinden, and I am afraid that she might make things worse. I'm hoping that Tommy Swinden got his revenge on Friday night and now Max is safe again. Max got Tommy in a lot of trouble with the knife even before he pooped on him, so maybe Tommy thinks that Max deserves more revenge. He probably does, but it will just be worse if Max's mom gets involved.

Parents are like Max. They don't know how to do things quietly.

Mrs. Gosk is funny today. She wrote a story about what it's like to be a Thanksgiving turkey and she is reading it to the class. She is walking around the room, making turkey sounds while she reads, and even Max is grinning. Not smiling, but almost. Mrs. Gosk is scratching the ground with her foot and flapping her arms like wings. No one can take their eyes off of her.

Mrs. Patterson arrives at the classroom door and motions Max to join her. It takes her a moment to get Max's attention because Mrs. Gosk is so funny. I'm expecting to see Max frown because Mrs. Gosk is not finished with her story yet, but Max's eyes get wide when he sees Mrs. Patterson. He looks excited. I don't understand.

I want to stay with Mrs. Gosk and see what she will do next. Instead, I follow Max and Mrs. Patterson down the hall in the direction of the Learning Center. Except when we get to the spot where we should turn left, Max and Mrs. Patterson go straight, and Max does not say a thing. This is even more surprising than Max wanting to leave Mrs. Gosk because Max does not like change, and this is a definite change in the way that we go to the Learning Center. It's a silly change, too, because it means we have to walk around the auditorium and by the gym, which makes the walk twice as long.

But then we stop at the same doors that I saw Max and Mrs. Patterson enter through last week. We're behind the auditorium now, in a hallway that doesn't have classrooms or offices, but Mrs. Patterson still looks left and right before she opens the door. Then she places her hand on Max's back to nudge him outside. Max is walking out the door on his own, but Mrs. Patterson wants Max to move faster, and this makes me nervous. It's like she needed him to pass through the doors quickly before someone saw him.

Something is not right.

I try to follow. But as Max walks down the cement path toward the parking lot, he turns and looks at me. I'm standing outside now, too, just on the other side of the doors. He looks at me and shakes his head back and forth. I know what this means. It means *No way, Jose.*

He doesn't want me to follow him. Then he waves me back with his hand.

He wants me to go back inside the school.

I almost always do what Max asks me to do, because that is sort of my job. He needs my help, and so I give it to him. There have been other times when he has asked to be alone, like when he's reading a book or making a poop. Lots of times, in fact. But this time is different. I know it. Max is not supposed to be outside the school, and he is most definitely not supposed to be going out these side doors toward the parking lot.

Something is not right.

I go back inside like Max has told me to, but I stand against the wall beside the doors, so I can peek out. Max and Mrs. Patterson are walking in the parking lot now, in the aisle between the parked cars. I think these are the teachers' cars, since the kids can't drive. They must be. Then I see Max and Mrs. Patterson stop next to a small blue car. Mrs. Patterson looks around again. It's the kind of looking around that someone does when they want to make sure no one is looking. Then she opens up the back door of the car and Max climbs in. Mrs. Patterson looks around again before getting into the front seat. The side with the steering wheel. The side where the person who is driving sits.

She is driving away with Max.

Except she's not. The car isn't moving. They are sitting in the car.

Max is in the backseat. Mrs. Patterson is in the front. Mrs. Patterson is talking, I think, and Max keeps ducking his head down. Not to hide, but to look at something on the seat, I think. He looks busy. He is doing something.

A moment later Mrs. Patterson steps out of the car and looks around again. She is making sure that no one is watching. I know it. I have been around too many people who do not know that I'm watching them to know when someone is being sneaky, and Mrs. Patterson is being sneaky. Then she opens the door for Max and he steps out, too. Together, they walk back to the doors. Mrs. Patterson uses a key to unlock the door and they enter. I take a few steps down the hall, away from the door, and I sit with my back against the wall so that Max will think that I have been here the whole time. Not watching.

I want him to think that I don't know where he and Mrs. Patterson went, and more important, I do not want him to think I care. I do not want him to suspect that I am worried, because the next time Mrs. Patterson takes Max out to her car, I am going, too.

If Mrs. Patterson takes him out to her car again (and I think she will), it won't be the same as this time. I don't know what it will be, but it will be more. It will be worse. I know it. Mrs. Patterson wouldn't break the rules for five minutes in her car with Max. Something else is going to happen.

I can't explain it, but I'm more worried about Mrs. Patterson than I am about Tommy Swinden now.

A lot more worried.

eighteen

We are sitting inside Dr. Hogan's office. Dr. Hogan is smart. Max has been here for a long time and Dr. Hogan has not tried to make him talk once. She has been sitting here, watching him play with these plastic and metal pieces that she called "new-fangled thinker toys." I could tell by the way she said it that *new-fangled* isn't really part of their name, but I don't understand what it means.

I know what *new* means, but what's a *fangled*?

Max loves these toys. Max's mom would say that Max is "engaged," which means that he has stopped paying attention to everything around him. Max gets engaged a lot, which is good because it means that he is happy, but it also means that he forgets everything else. When Max is engaged, it is like only one thing exists. Ever since he sat down on the carpet in front of the coffee table and started playing with these toys, I don't think he's looked up once.

Dr. Hogan is smart enough to let Max play. Every now and then she asks a question, and so far all of her questions have only needed yes-or-no and one-word answers, so Max has been answering most of them.

That's smart, too. If Dr. Hogan had tried to get Max to just talk, without the thinker toys and the quiet time, he would have probably *clammed up,* which is what Mrs. Hume says about Max when he won't talk to her. But Max is slowly getting used to Dr. Hogan and eventually he might be able to talk to her if she waits long enough. Especially if she doesn't make him feel like she's staring at him and recording everything that he says. Most of the time adults start out slow with Max but eventually they lose their patience and mess things up.

Dr. Hogan is pretty. She's younger than Max's mom, I think, and she isn't dressed too fancy. She is wearing a skirt and a T-shirt and sneakers, like she's going for a walk in the park. This is smart, too, because she looks like just another girl. Not a real doctor.

Max is afraid of doctors.

Best of all, she hasn't asked one single question about me. Not one. I was worried that she would be asking Max about me for the whole time, but instead, it seems like she's more interested in Max's favorite food (macaroni) and his favorite flavor of ice cream (vanilla) than his imaginary friend.

"Do you like school?" Dr. Hogan asks. Dr. Hogan told Max that he could call her Ellen, but that is too weird for me. Max hasn't had to say her name yet, so I don't know what he has decided to do, but I bet he will call her Dr. Hogan, too. If he can remember her name. If he was listening when she told him.

"Kind of," Max says. His tongue is sticking out of the corner of his mouth and he is squinting, staring at two pieces of thinker toys, trying to figure out how they go together.

"What's your favorite part of school?"

Max doesn't say anything for ten seconds, and then he says, "Lunch."

"Oh," Dr. Hogan says. "Do you know why lunch is your favorite part of school?"

See how smart she is? She doesn't ask Max why lunch is his favorite until she knows that he knows. If Max can't explain why lunch is his favorite part of school then he can just say no, and he doesn't have to feel dumb for not knowing the answer. If Dr. Hogan asks a question that makes Max feel dumb, she might never get him to talk.

"No," Max says, and Dr. Hogan doesn't seem surprised one bit.

I'm not surprised, either. But I think I know why Max likes lunch best. I think it is because it's the part of the school day when he is left alone. No one bothers him, and no one tells him what to do. He sits at the end of the lunch table, all alone, reading his book and eating the same thing every day: peanut butter and jelly sandwich, a granola bar, and an apple juice. The rest of the school day is unpredictable. You never know what might happen. Things are always changing, and teachers and kids are always surprising Max. But lunch is always the same.

This is only a guess. I don't know why Max likes lunch the best, because I don't think Max knows. Sometimes you can feel something but not know why you feel that way. Like the way I feel about Mrs.

Patterson. I knew I did not like her as soon as I met her, but I can't explain why. I just knew. And now that she and Max have a secret, I like her even less.

"Who is your best friend, Max?" Dr. Hogan asks.

Max says "Timothy" because that is what Max always says when someone asks him who his best friend is, even though I know that I am his real best friend. But Max knows that if he says my name, people will ask him questions and tell him that I don't exist. Timothy is a boy who spends time in the Learning Center when Max is there, and sometimes Timothy and Max work together. Max says that Timothy is his best friend because they don't fight. Neither one likes working with other kids, so when their teachers make them work together, they try to find a way to work alone together.

Mrs. Hume once told Max's mom that it is sad that Max's best friends are the kids who leave him alone, but Mrs. Hume doesn't understand that Max is happy when he is alone. Just because Mrs. Hume and Max's mom and most people are happiest when they are with their friends doesn't mean that Max needs friends to be happy. Max doesn't like other people, so he is happiest when people just leave him alone.

It's like me with food. I don't eat. I've never met an imaginary friend who eats. I was visiting the hospital one night, because the hospital never closes, and I was spending time with Susan, a lady who does not eat food with her mouth anymore. She has a straw that goes straight into her belly, and the nurses feed her pudding through the straw. Susan's sisters were visiting, and when they were in the hallway outside Susan's room, her fat sister said it was sad that Susan could not eat anymore because there is so much joy in food.

"No, there's not!" I said, but no one heard me.

But it's true. I'm glad that I don't eat, no matter what Susan's fat sister says. Eating seems like a pain in the butt to me. Even if the food tastes good, you have to worry about having enough money to buy the food and cooking the food and not burning the food and eating the right amount without getting fat like Susan's sister. Plus, all the time it takes to cook the food and clean the dishes and cut the mango and peel the potatoes and ask the waiter for milk instead of cream. The dangers of choking on food or being allergic to certain foods. It all seems so complicated. I don't care how good the food might taste. It wouldn't be worth all the trouble. Maybe Susan feels this way, too, now that she eats with a belly straw, which seems a lot easier than cooking dinner every night. But even if she doesn't feel this way, I still feel this way. If I was given a chance to eat food right now, I'd say no, because I wouldn't want to get in the habit of eating food and starting all of that rigmarole, which is one of Mrs. Gosk's favorite words.

Even though I don't eat, I'm still happy, even if there is so much joy in food. Because there is joy in not worrying about food, too. More joy, I think.

For Max, there's joy in being alone. He's not lonely. He just doesn't like people very much. But he is happy.

"What is your least favorite food?" Dr. Hogan asks.

Max stops for a moment, his hands sort of frozen in midair, and then he says, "Peas."

I would have guessed zucchini. I bet he forgot about zucchini.

"What's your least favorite part of school?" Dr. Hogan asks.

"Gym," Max says, quickly this time. "And art. And recess. It's a tie."

"Who is your least favorite person at school?"

Max looks up for the first time. His face is pinched.

"Is there anyone at school who you don't like?" Dr. Hogan asks.

"Yes," Max says, and then his eyes go back to the thinker toys.

"Who do you not like the most?"

Now I understand what Dr. Hogan is doing. She's trying to talk to Max about Tommy Swinden, and Max is about to open the door and let her inside. It's bad enough that Max's mom knows about Tommy Swinden. This could make things even worse.

"Ella Barbara!" I say, hoping that Max will repeat what I say.

"Tommy Swinden," Max says instead, not looking up as he says it.

"Do you know why you don't like Tommy Swinden?"

"Yes," Max says.

"Why don't you like Tommy Swinden?" Dr. Hogan asks, and I can see that she is leaning forward ever so slightly. This is the answer she has been waiting for.

"Because he wants to kill me," Max says, still not bothering to look up.

"Oh no," Dr. Hogan says, and it sounds like she really means it, like she's really surprised, even though I think that she knew about Tommy Swinden all along. She probably heard all about him from Max's mom.

This appointment was one giant trap, and Max just fell in.

Dr. Hogan doesn't say anything for a little bit, and then she asks, "Do you know why Tommy Swinden wants to kill you, Max?"

Adults always stick Max's name at the end of their questions when they think their questions are important.

"Maybe," Max says.

"Why do you maybe think that Tommy Swinden wants to kill you, Max?"

Max stops moving again. He has a chunk of new-fangled thinker toy in his hand and he just stares at it. I know the look on his face. It is the look that says he's going to lie. Max is not a good liar, and it always takes him a long time to think of a lie.

"He doesn't like boys named Max," Max says. But he says it too fast, and his voice sounds different, so I'm sure that Dr. Hogan knows it is a lie. Max probably got this idea from a fifth grader who once told Max that he has a stupid name. Even though there was a real kid who didn't like his name, I do not think this is a good lie. No one wants to kill someone because of their name.

"Is there anything else?" Dr. Hogan asks.

"What?" Max says.

"Is there any other reason why you think this boy maybe wants to kill you?"

"Oh," Max says, and then he pauses again. "No."

Dr. Hogan doesn't believe him. I want Dr. Hogan to believe him, but she does not. I can tell. Max's mom has talked to her. I know it. I wonder when Max's mom and dad decided to send Max here. I wonder when Max's dad lost this fight.

Maybe when I was at the gas station last night.

But even if Max's mom didn't talk to her, Dr. Hogan would still know that Max is lying. He is the worst liar on the planet.

And Dr. Hogan is really smart. That scares me even more.

I wonder what she plans on doing next.

I wonder if I can find a way to get her to talk to Max about Mrs. Patterson.

nineteen

I'm following Max. He told me to wait by the doors again, but this time, I am going to sneak up to Mrs. Patterson's car and see what's going on inside. I don't care what he says. Something is not right.

Max and Mrs. Patterson are halfway to the parking lot when I pass through the glass doors and leave the school. There is a tree to the right of the walkway, and I go there first and hide behind it. I don't usually have to hide like this. I can't remember ever hiding from Max, and no one else can see me, so in a way, I am always hiding from everyone except Max.

This is the first time I am hiding from everyone.

There's another tree down the walkway a bit, this one on the left side and a little farther off the path, so I run there next. If I actually touched the ground when I ran, I would be walking instead, tiptoeing so that Max would not hear me. But when I move, I am silent, even to Max, so running is a better idea, because it means I will stay unhidden for less time.

I peek around the tree. Max and Mrs. Patterson have almost reached the car. Mrs. Patterson is moving fast, much faster than adults who don't ask kids to keep secrets and bring them out to their cars in the middle of the school day. From the tree, I am going to have to crawl over to the parking lot. There is a row of cars in front of me, about thirty steps away. If I crawl, I can stay hidden behind the row of cars, especially since Max is so short and cannot see over the tall cars. It's funny because as I crawl, every little kid in the two classrooms behind me should be able to see me, crawling through the grass in front of the school. It feels strange, hiding in front of so many faces.

I hear a car door open. Max and Mrs. Patterson have reached the car. I have an idea. I'm crouched behind a little red car, the first one

93

in the row, and I'm peeking through the windows, trying to see if Max is inside Mrs. Patterson's car yet. I can't quite see Mrs. Patterson's car, which is farther down and in the opposite row of cars across the aisle. But I can pass through the cars in front of me, because they all have doors. This is my idea. Instead of walking down the aisle, I will crawl through the cars.

I climb into the red car and crawl over the seats. This is a messy car. The front seat is piled with books and papers and there are empty soda cans and paper bags on the floor. This is probably Mrs. Gosk's car. It reminds me of her classroom. It is full and messy. I like it. I sometimes think that neat and organized people spend too much time planning and not enough time doing. I don't trust neat and organized people.

I bet that Mrs. Patterson is a neat and organized person.

I pass through the door on the opposite side of the red car and then pass through five more cars until I am crouched over inside a big car with four doors plus a door in the back. I can see Mrs. Patterson's car through the back window. Mrs. Patterson pulled her car in face first, not like crazy Mrs. Griswold who spends five minutes every morning backing into a spot while all the kids laugh at her. This is good because it means that she and Max are looking away from me, which is perfect for me to sneak up on them. I pass through the back door of the big car and run over to Mrs. Patterson's car, crossing the pavement between the two rows of cars. I keep my head low in case Max turns around.

Mrs. Patterson's window is open. It is warm and her car is not running, so she probably opened the window for fresh air. I want to look in the backseat and see what Max is doing, but I can hear Mrs. Patterson's voice from where I am standing. She is talking on her phone. I get down on my hands and knees and crawl over to the side of the car with Mrs. Patterson's door, so I can hear better. I am crouched alongside the car, in between the front and back doors.

"Yes, Mom," I hear Mrs. Patterson say.

Then there is a pause.

"Yes, Mom," she says again. "I love you so much."

Another pause.

"No, Mom, I won't get into any trouble. You're my mom, and I should be able to talk to you during the day. Especially since you are so sick."

Another pause.

"I know, Mom. You're right. You're always right."

Mrs. Patterson laughs a little, and then she says, "I am so lucky to have this young man helping me." Then she laughs again. Neither laugh sounds real. "His name is Max." she says. "He is the kindest, smartest boy I know."

She pauses for a second or two and then says, "Yes, Mom, I will be sure to tell Max how grateful you are about his help. I love you so much, Mom. And I hope you feel better real soon. Bye-bye."

Nothing about the conversation sounds right. I have heard Max's mom and dad talk on the telephone many times, and it never sounded like this. Everything about it was wrong. Her laugh wasn't real. The amount of time that she was listening and not speaking was too short. She said the word *Mom* too many times. Everything she said came out perfect.

No *ums*. No stutters.

It sounded like a first-grade teacher reading a book to her class. It sounded like everything she said was for Max and not for her mom.

I start to move, crawling backward, trying to get to the back of the car again when Max's door opens. I'm on my hands and knees right in front of his door, and the bottom part of the door passes right through me as it opens because it is a door.

Max sees me. His smile turns to a frown. His eyes first widen and then shrink to slits, little wrinkles popping up between them. He is mad. But he says nothing, because Mrs. Patterson's door opens a second later and she steps out of the car. I feel foolish, crouched on my hands and knees between them, but I'm too embarrassed and ashamed to stand up. I just stay there as Mrs. Patterson closes her door and reaches for Max's hand. He takes one more look at me, and then he takes her hand. I have never seen Mrs. Patterson hold Max's hand before and it looks odd. Max hates to hold hands. Max does not look back. I stand up and watch him enter the school. He disappears down the hallway. He never looks back.

I look inside Mrs. Patterson's car. There is a blue backpack on the back seat where Max had been sitting. It is closed, so there's no way for me to see inside. There is nothing else in the car except the backpack. The car is clean and empty.

I was right. Mrs. Patterson is neat and organized.

She cannot be trusted.

twenty

Max won't talk to me. He didn't even look at me for the rest of the school day, and when I try to sit with him on the bus ride home, he shakes his head and gives me his *No way, Jose* look. We have never sat apart on the bus before. I take a seat in front of Max, right behind the bus driver. I want to turn around and look at Max, smile at him, and try to get him to smile at me, but I can't bring myself to do it. Because I know he won't smile back.

I have to talk to Max about Mrs. Patterson when he's not mad at me anymore. I still don't understand what is happening, but I know that it is not good. I am even more convinced of it now. The more I think about Max sitting in that car with that blue backpack in the middle of the school day, and that phone call from Mrs. Patterson that didn't sound like a phone call, and especially the way that she and Max were *holding hands,* the more afraid I become.

For a while, I thought I might be overreacting. I thought that maybe this was like one of those television shows where all the clues point to one killer but then it turns out to be another person. A surprise killer. Maybe Mrs. Patterson is a sweet lady and there is a perfectly good reason why she and Max sit in that car. But I know that I am right. I am not overreacting. I can't explain how I know, but I know. This is probably how those characters on television feel, too. The ones who think it's one killer when it is really another. Except this is real life. There are no television makers sprinkling lots of fake clues for me. This is real life, and real life can't have this many fake clues all in a row.

The only good news is that tomorrow is Friday, and Mrs. Patterson almost never comes in on Friday. It makes the principal, Mrs. Palmer, crazy. I once heard her talking about Mrs. Patterson to a lady who nodded and hummed and said that Mrs. Patterson has a right to use her sick days if she is sick, and that was the end of the conversation. I don't know why Mrs. Palmer didn't tell the suit lady that no one gets sick once a week on the same day, but she didn't. After the suit lady left, Mrs. Palmer blamed it on the *damunion*. I still can't figure out what the *damunion* is, and when I asked Max, he didn't know, either.

So Mrs. Patterson will probably be sick tomorrow, or pretend to be sick, and I'll have the weekend to get Max to forgive me so we can talk.

I was scared for a little while, wondering if Max might stop believing in me since he is so mad and refuses to talk to me. But then I realized that Max couldn't be mad at someone who didn't exist, so I actually think that this is a good sign. He must really, really believe in me to be this mad.

Maybe I should have found a way to make Meghan mad at Graham. Maybe that would have saved Graham's life.

I've been thinking about Graham a lot, lately. I think about how she doesn't exist anymore, and how everything that she ever said or did doesn't mean anything to her anymore. Even if Graham still means something to me and Meghan and maybe even Puppy, none of that matters because she doesn't exist anymore.

That's the only important fact of Graham's nonexistence.

When Max's grandmother died, Max's dad said that Grandma would live on in Max's heart, and as long as they remembered Grandma, she would remain alive in their memories. That is fine for Max, and maybe it made him feel a little better, but it didn't help Max's grandmother at all. She is gone, and even if Max is keeping her alive in his heart, she doesn't exist anymore. She doesn't care what's going on in Max's heart, because she can't care about anything anymore. Everyone gets so worried about the people who are still living when the people who are really hurting are the dead ones. People like Grandma and Graham.

They don't exist anymore.

There is nothing worse than that.

Max hasn't talked to me all night long. He worked on his homework, played his video game for thirty minutes, read about a world war from a book as big as his head and then went to sleep without saying a word. I am sitting in the chair beside his bed, waiting for him to fall asleep, hoping to hear his small voice say, "Budo, it's okay." But he never speaks. Eventually his breathing gets steady and he is asleep.

I hear the door open. Max's mom is home. She had a doctor's appointment so she didn't put Max to bed. She comes into the room and kisses Max, pulls the covers up to his neck, and kisses him three more times.

She leaves.

I follow.

Max's dad is watching a baseball game. He presses the Mute button on the remote control when Max's mom enters the living room, but he doesn't take his eyes off the screen.

"So? What did she say?" Max's dad asks. He sounds annoyed.

"She said that it went well. They talked a little, and Max answered some questions. She thinks she can eventually get him to trust her and open up, but it's going to take a while."

"You don't think Max trusts us?"

"C'mon, Dan," Max's mom says. "Of course he trusts us. But that doesn't mean he tells us everything."

"What kid tells his parents everything?"

"This is different," Max's mom says. "And I'm sorry if you can't see it."

Except she doesn't sound like she's sorry at all.

"Explain to me how it's different," Max's dad says.

"I don't feel like I know my own son. He's not like other kids. He doesn't come home telling us stories from school. He doesn't play with other kids. He thinks that someone in his school wants to kill him. He still talks to his imaginary friend. For God's sake, he barely lets me touch him. I have to kiss him after he's asleep. Why can't you see him for who he is?" Her voice gets louder as she talks, and I think that she is going to either cry or scream or both. I think she is probably already crying on the inside but holding it back so she can keep on fighting with Max's dad on the outside.

Max's dad says nothing. It's that silence that adults use to say stuff they don't want to say.

When Max's mom talks again, her voice is soft and calm. "She thinks he's very smart. Smarter than he is able to show us. And she thinks that there is real progress to be made."

"She could tell all that after forty-five minutes?"

"She sees kids like Max all the time. She's not saying anything absolutely yet. She was just guessing. Based upon what she's seen and heard so far."

"How long will insurance cover it?" Max's dad asks. I'm not sure what this means, but I can tell by his voice that he is not asking to be helpful.

"Ten sessions to start, and then it depends on what she finds."

"What's the co-pay?" Max's dad asks.

"Really? We're getting our son some help and you're worried about the co-pay?"

"I was just wondering," Max's dad says, and I can tell that he feels bad for asking.

"Fine," Max's mom says. "It's twenty bucks. Okay?"

"I was just wondering," he says. "That's all." He pauses a minute, and then he smiles and adds, "But if Max is only seeing her for forty-five minutes and the co-pay is twenty bucks, you have to wonder how much she's actually getting paid an hour. Right?"

"She's not working at a liquor store," Max's mom says. "She's a doctor, for Christ's sake."

"I was just joking," Max's dad says and laughs. This time I believe him. And I think that Max's mom does, too. She smiles, and then after a second, she sits down beside Max's dad.

"What else did she say?" Max's dad asks.

"Nothing, really. Max answered almost all her questions, which she said was good. And he didn't seem nervous being in the office by himself, which she said was unusual. But he still thinks that someone at school is going to kill him. Tommy Swinden. Do you know the name?"

"No."

"Max said Tommy doesn't like his name and that's why he wants to kill him, but Dr. Hogan doesn't believe him."

"She doesn't believe that Tommy Swinden wants to kill him, or she doesn't believe that he doesn't like Max's name?"

"She's not sure." Max's mom says. "But she didn't think that Max was telling the whole truth about Tommy, and it was the only time that she got the sense that Max wasn't being honest."

"What should we do?" Max's dad asks.

"I'm going to call the school tomorrow. Max is probably misinter-preting something, but I want to be safe."

"Helicopter Mom to the rescue?" Max's dad has called Max's mom a helicopter mom before, but I don't get it. I know what a helicopter is, but I've never seen Max's mom drive one or even play with any of Max's toy helicopters, and he has a lot of them.

Max's mom smiles, and this makes me even more confused. When Max's dad tells Max's mom that she is a helicopter mom, it usually makes her angry, but sometimes she thinks it's funny, and I can't figure out why.

"If Tommy Swinden has threatened my son," Max's mom says, "I'll bring the whole goddamn air force down on his ass if necessary. Helicopter Mom and all."

"You're a little crazy sometimes," Max's dad says. "Possibly a little neurotic. And you're capable of overreacting from time to time. But Max is very lucky to have you."

Max's mom reaches over and takes Max's dad's hand and squeezes it. For a moment, I think they're going to kiss, which always makes me feel a little weird, but instead Max's mom speaks.

"Dr. Hogan wants to meet with me again after two more sessions. Do you want to come to the next one?"

"Will that cost us another co-pay?"

This time they do kiss, so I look away. I wish I knew what a co-pay was. The first time Max's dad mentioned it, Max's mom got angry. But now it made her want to kiss him.

This is why I understand Max so well. I am sometimes as confused as he is.

twenty-one

Mrs. Patterson is not in school today. Mrs. Palmer might be mad about it, but I am relieved. Max is still not talking to me, but at least I have the weekend to convince him to forgive me.

It has been a strange day. Max won't even look at me. We started off in Mrs. Gosk's room, working on multiplication tables (which Max memorized two years ago), and then we went to art class, where Ms. Knight showed Max how to weave different colored pieces of paper into a pattern. Max didn't seem to like it very much because he barely paid attention to Ms. Knight's instructions, which is strange since Max usually loves things involving patterns.

He just finished his snack in Mrs. Gosk's room and is now walking to the Learning Center. Even though I'm walking right beside him, he won't even look in my direction. I'm actually feeling a little angry now. He is overreacting, I think.

Like Max's mom sometimes.

All I did was follow him to Mrs. Patterson's car.

"Max, do you want to play army after school?" I ask. "It's Friday. We could set up a huge battle and play all day tomorrow."

Max does not answer.

"This is ridiculous," I say. "You can't be mean to me forever. I just wanted to know what you were doing."

Max walks faster.

We're taking the long way to the Learning Center again, the way that Mrs. Patterson took him the other day. I guess this is the new way, even though it takes longer. Maybe Max thinks it is a better way because it means he has to spend less time in the Learning Center.

When we reach the glass doors that lead to the parking lot, Max stops and looks outside. His face is so close to the glass that the window fogs up from his breath. He's not just looking. He's looking for something. He's searching for something. I look, too, to see what he sees, and then he sees it.

I don't.

I don't know what he sees, but he sees something, because he stands up straighter and pushes his nose right up against the glass. And there's no fog on the glass now. He's holding his breath. He sees something, and he is holding his breath. I look again. I don't see anything. Just two rows of cars and the street beyond.

"Stay here," Max says. It's been so long since he had spoken to me that I jump a little.

"Where are you going?" I ask.

"Stay here," he says again. "I'll be right back. I promise if you stay here and wait here for me, I'll be right back."

Max is lying. I know he is lying just like Dr. Hogan knew that Max was lying in her office the other day. But Max is talking to me again. He's talking to me and he doesn't sound angry, so I am feeling happy again. I want to believe him, because if I do, everything will be alright again. Max won't be mad at me, and even though I don't have Graham or Dee or Sally or a mom or a dad, I will have Max back, and that's good enough.

"Okay," I say. "I'll wait here. I'm sorry I didn't listen to you last time."

"Okay," Max says. Then he looks left and right, checking the hallway to see if anyone is coming. He reminds me of Mrs. Patterson, and I suddenly feel worried. Afraid. Max is lying and something is wrong.

No one is coming, so Max opens the doors and leaves the school. He walks down the cement path toward the parking lot, walking fast but not running.

I look again. What does he see? I look in the direction that he is headed and I don't see anything. Just cars and the street. A few trees with yellow and red leaves. Grass.

Nothing.

Then I see it.

Mrs. Patterson's car. I see it now. It's pulling out of a spot behind a silver truck. It was invisible behind that big truck. And she is pulling out face first. Mrs. Patterson backed her car into the parking spot next to the silver truck so she could pull out face first, and that's when

I know that something is really wrong, because only Mrs. Griswold is silly enough to back into a parking spot. But Mrs. Patterson did today, and it feels wrong and sneaky and planned. And somehow I know that Max knew all about it.

The car pulls in front of Max, and Max opens the back door and climbs in. Max is inside Mrs. Patterson's car.

I pass through the glass doors and run down the cement path. I yell Max's name. I yell for him to stop. I wish I could tell him that he is being tricked. I can't explain how I know it—I just know it way down deep inside—and he can't see it because he is Max, who can't see the forest for the trees, but there is no word that says all this so I just yell, "Max!"

The car is moving now, down the row of cars to the street, and I can't catch up. It is definitely Mrs. Patterson because I saw her before the car turned down the aisle. She is speeding up, as if she can see me coming in her rearview mirror, and I can't catch the car in time. The car reaches the end of the row and turns left onto the street and drives away. I keep running until I reach the street. I turn down the sidewalk and run until I can't see the car anymore. I want to keep running because I don't know what else to do, but finally I stop.

Max is gone.

twenty-two

I sit on the curb and wait. I don't care if Max knows that I tried to follow him. I am going to wait until he gets back, and then I am going to tell him that he should never get in Mrs. Patterson's car again. I am not a teacher, but even I know that teachers are not supposed to drive kids around in their cars in the middle of the school day.

If I knew that Max would be back soon, I would not be so worried. But I am worried. There is so much to make me feel worried.

Mrs. Patterson was absent from school today.
She drove to school just to pick up Max.
She backed her car into the parking spot so that she could drive away quickly.
She parked behind the big truck so no one inside the school would see her car.
She and Max made a plan to meet.
Max knew she was coming.
She was waiting for him.
He held his breath when he saw her.
No one saw them leave.

I keep hoping that I am just overreacting like a character on television, the kind that accuses his friend of a terrible crime and then realizes that he was wrong. I must be overreacting, because Max is with a teacher, and even if she is breaking the rules, she is still a teacher.

But she was absent today and came to pick up Max anyway. I can't stop thinking about that. It's the worst part, I think.

I hear a bell ring. It's the first recess bell. I have been sitting on the curb for more than an hour. Max's class is walking down the hallway to the cafeteria right now. I wonder if Mrs. Gosk knows that Max is missing. Even though she is a good teacher, the best teacher, Max has so many teachers that maybe Mrs. Gosk thinks that Max is with Mrs. Riner, or Mrs. Hume, or Mrs. McGinn, and maybe Mrs. Hume and Mrs. Riner think that Max is with Mrs. Gosk.

Maybe Mrs. Patterson knew that Max's teachers would think like this, and that's why she chose today to pick him up.

This makes me worry even more.

It's hard not to worry because trying not to worry reminds me that I should be worried. And when you're sitting on a curb, waiting for your friend to come back, it is hard to forget why you are sitting on the curb in the first place.

Every time a car drives by, every time a bird chirps, every time a recess bell rings, I get more worried. Each car, each chirp, and each bell is one more in between the last time I saw Max and now. Each one makes it feel more like forever.

Four bells have rung since Max left, which means that Max has been gone for two hours. I'm wondering if there is a back entrance to the school that no one ever told me about. Maybe there is a road through the back woods that ends in the parking lot, and maybe Mrs. Patterson brought Max back on this road, since no one would see them together way back there. I'm wondering if I should get up and go look for a back entrance, or maybe go inside and see if Max has come back when I hear Max's name called on the intercom. The intercom plays inside the school and outside on the playground, which is on the other side of the building, but I can still hear Max's name being called. It's the principal. Mrs. Palmer.

"Max Delaney, please report to your classroom immediately."

Max is not back. Or maybe he is back and is walking to Mrs. Gosk's room right now. I think about staying on the curb, waiting like I swore I would, but now that Mrs. Palmer knows that Max is missing, maybe it would be better if I go inside and wait.

I want to find out what is going on, too.

Mrs. Gosk, Mrs. Riner, and Mrs. Hume are standing in Mrs. Gosk's classroom. There are no kids in the classroom. They are in music class, I think. They have music on Friday afternoons. All three teachers look worried. They are staring at the classroom door, and when I walk in, I think they are looking right at me. For a second, I think they can see me.

I enter the classroom. If I could look in a mirror, if I had a reflection, I think I would have the same worried face as the teachers.

Mrs. Palmer walks in a second later. "He hasn't shown up?" she asks. She looks worried, too.

"No," Mrs. Gosk says. I have never heard Mrs. Gosk sound so serious, and she only said one word. She said "No," and I could tell that she is the worriedest she has ever been.

"Where could he be?" Mrs. Hume asks. She is worried, too.

Good, I think. They should all be worried.

"Okay, stay here," Mrs. Palmer says and she leaves the room.

"What if he's run away?" Mrs. Hume asks.

"Max isn't a runner," Mrs. Gosk says.

"I honestly don't think he's in the building, Donna," Mrs. Hume says. Donna is Mrs. Gosk's first name. Kids can never use a teacher's first name but teachers can use it whenever they want.

"He wouldn't just leave the building," Mrs. Gosk says, and she is kind of right. Max would never leave the building unless a teacher tricked him into leaving, which is exactly what happened.

I am the only one who knows what happened, and I can't tell anyone. Max is the only human person who I could tell, but Max isn't here, because Max is the one who disappeared.

Mrs. Palmer's voice comes on the intercom again. "Staff members, please take a moment and look around you and the area that you are in. Max Delaney from Mrs. Gosk's classroom has lost his way somewhere in the building and we want to be sure that he finds his way back to his classroom. If you see Max, please call the office immediately. And Max, if you can hear me, please go to your classroom. If you're stuck somewhere, please call out and we'll find you. No need to worry, boys and girls. It's a big school and kids can sometimes get a little lost."

Yeah, right, I think.

"I don't think he's in the building. I think we need to call the police," Mrs. Hume says. "He doesn't live too far away. Maybe he walked home."

"That's true," Mrs. Riner says. "We should call his parents. He could be on his way home."

"Max would not leave the building," Mrs. Gosk says.

Mrs. Palmer returns. I can't believe how calm she looks. "I have Eddie and Chris checking the basement and opening all the closets.

The cafeteria staff is searching the kitchen. Wendy and Sharon are doing a sweep of the outside."

"He's gone," Mrs. Hume says. "I don't know how or why, but he's not here. It's been too long. This is Max we're talking about."

"We don't know that," Mrs. Palmer says.

"She's right," Mrs. Gosk says. Her voice is softer. She doesn't sound as certain as she did a second ago. She sounds absolutely terrified. "I can't believe that Max would ignore all these announcements."

"You think he left the building?" Mrs. Palmer asks.

"Yes. I don't know how he disappeared, but I think he's gone."

I told you Mrs. Gosk was smart.

twenty-three

The whole school is in something called *lockdown*. This means that no one is allowed to leave the school until the police officers let them leave. Even teachers. Even Mrs. Palmer. It's weird because I am the only one who knows that Mrs. Patterson took Max, but I'm also the only one who can leave the school. I feel like I should be the one who is locked down, but I am the only one who is not.

Even though I know what happened to Max, I still don't know where Mrs. Patterson took him, and even if I did, I still wouldn't know what to do. There is nothing I can do. So I'm just as stuck as all the people who don't know anything.

Except I'm probably the most worried. Everyone is worried. Mrs. Gosk is worried, and so are Mrs. Hume and Mrs. Palmer. But I think I am more worried than all of them, because I know what happened to Max.

Even the policemen are worried. They look at each other with squinty eyes and talk in whisper voices so the teachers and Mrs. Palmer can't hear. But I can hear. I can stand right next to them and listen to every word they say, but I can't get any of them to listen to a single word I say. I am the only one who could help Max, but nobody can hear me.

When I was born, I tried to get other people like Max's mom and dad to listen to me, because I didn't know that they couldn't hear me. I thought they were ignoring me. I remember one night when Max and his mom went out and I stayed home with Max's dad. I was afraid to go with Max because I had never left the house before, so Max's dad and I sat on the couch together for the whole night. I screamed and yelled at him for the whole time. I thought that if I shouted long enough, he would at least look at me and tell me to be quiet. I begged him to listen to me and talk to me, but he just kept staring at the base-ball game like I wasn't even there. Then, as I was screaming, he laughed. I thought for a second that he was laughing at me, but he must have been laughing at something the man on the television had said, because the other man on the television was laughing now, too. And then I realized that it would be impossible for Max's dad to hear the man on the television because I was screaming so loud and right into his ear. That was when I understood that no one could hear me except Max.

Later on, I met other imaginary friends and eventually figured out that they could hear me. The imaginary friends who could hear, at least. Not all can. I once met an imaginary friend that was just a hair bow with two eyes. I didn't even know that she was an imaginary friend until she started blinking her eyes at me, like she was trying to send me a signal. She just looked like a little bow in a little girl's hair. A pink bow. That's how I knew she was a girl. But she couldn't hear anything I said because the little girl never imagined her that way. Even when kids forget the ears on imaginary friends, most of them still imagine that their imaginary friends can hear, so they can. But not this little bow. She just blinked at me and I blinked back. She was afraid, too. I could tell by the look in her eyes and the way that she blinked, and even though I tried, I couldn't tell her that everything would be okay. All I could do was blink. But even those back-and-forth blinks seemed to make her a little less afraid. A little less alone.

But only a little.

I'd be afraid, too, if I was a little deaf hair bow stuck on a kinder-gartener's head.

Little-pink-hair-bow girl disappeared the next day, and even though I think that not existing is the worst thing that could ever happen to someone, I think that little-pink-hair-bow girl was probably happier after she disappeared. At least she wasn't so afraid anymore.

The police think that Max ran away from school. That's what they say when they stand in a circle and whisper. They don't think that Mrs. Gosk is telling the truth. They think that Max probably left her classroom earlier in the morning than Mrs. Gosk says he did, and that is why they haven't found Max yet. "She just lost track of the kid," one of the policemen said, and everyone in the circle nodded their heads. "If that's the case, there's no telling how far he could've walked," another policeman said, and everyone nodded again.

Policemen are not like kids. They always seem to agree with each other.

The police chief said that he has officers and community volunteers (which is just a fancy word for people) looking in the forest behind the school and walking the neighborhood streets searching for Max. They are knocking on the doors of all the houses to see if anyone has seen Max. I thought about going outside to search, too, but I am going to stay inside the school for now. Even though I am not locked down, I am staying locked down. I am waiting for Max to come back. Mrs. Patterson can't keep him forever.

I just wish the police would figure out that Mrs. Patterson took Max. I keep thinking that the police on television would have already figured it out.

I have seen a lot of police officers over the last few days. First, there was the policeman who came to the house after Tommy Swinden broke Max's window, and then there were the policemen and one policewoman who came to the gas station when Dee got shot and Sally got stuck. And now there are policemen and policewomen all over the school. Bunches of them. But none of them look like the police officers on television, so I'm worried that none of them are as smart. The real-world policemen are all a little shorter, a little fatter, and a little hairier than the ones on TV. One even has hair in his ears. Not the girl policeman, though. One of the boy policemen. I have never seen such normal looking police officers on TV. Who do the television maker people think they're fooling?

Who do they think they're fooling? That's a Mrs. Gosk question. She asks it a lot. Mostly to the bad boys when they try to tell her that they forgot their homework on the kitchen table. She says, "Who do you think you're fooling, Ethan Woods? I wasn't born yesterday."

I would like to ask Mrs. Patterson who she thinks she is fooling, but it looks like she is fooling everyone.

Mrs. Palmer is annoyed that the school is locked down. I heard her say it to Mrs. Simpson after the police finished searching the school. Mrs. Palmer thinks that Max ran away, so she doesn't understand why the whole school has to be locked down for all this time. The police already searched every room and every closet and even the basement, so they know that Max is not here. I think they are just being careful. The police chief said that if one child can disappear from a school, others could, too. "Maybe someone took the boy," he said to Mrs. Palmer when she tried to complain. "If that's the case, someone in the school might know something about it."

I don't think he really believes that someone took Max. He is just being careful. He is playing just-in-case. That's why Mrs. Palmer is mad. She doesn't think there is a just-in-case. She thinks that Max went for a walk and didn't come back. That's what the police chief thinks, too.

I keep thinking that every minute the police search the basement and the forest and knock on doors is another minute that I lose Max forever.

I don't think Max is dead. I don't even know why that idea keeps popping in my head, because I don't believe it. I think Max is alive and just fine. He's probably sitting in the backseat of Mrs. Patterson's car with that blue backpack. I think he is fine, but I also keep thinking that he is not dead. I wish I could stop thinking about him being not dead and just think about him being alive.

But if Max was dead, would I ever know? Or would I just *poof* away without even knowing what happened? I keep holding my breath, waiting to *poof*, but if I was going to *poof*, I wouldn't even know it. I would just *poof*. One second I would exist and the next second I would not. So waiting for it to happen is silly. But I can't help it.

I keep hoping that maybe there is a reason why Mrs. Patterson took Max. Maybe they went for ice cream and got lost, or maybe she is bringing Max on a field trip and forgot to tell Mrs. Gosk, or maybe she took Max to meet her mother. Maybe they will pull into the driveway any second and Max will be back.

Except I don't think Mrs. Patterson was talking to her mother yesterday.

I don't think Mrs. Patterson even has a mother.

I wonder if Max's mom knows yet. And his dad. Probably. Maybe they are searching the forest right now.

Mrs. Palmer comes into the classroom. Mrs. Gosk has been reading *Charlie and the Chocolate Factory* to the kids again, which I usually love, but Max is missing the story now and he loves it when Mrs. Gosk reads to the class. Plus, Veruca Salt just disappeared down a garbage chute and I do not think Mrs. Gosk should be reading stories about disappearing kids right now.

Mrs. Gosk stops reading and looks up at Mrs. Palmer.

Mrs. Palmer says, "Could I speak to the class for a moment, Mrs. Gosk?"

Mrs. Gosk says yes, but her eyebrows rise, which means that she is confused.

"Boys and girls, I am sure that you heard us call Max Delaney to the office a little while ago. And you know that we are in a lockdown. I'm sure you have lots of questions. But there is nothing to worry about. We just need to make sure that we find Max. We think he may have wandered off or got picked up early and forgot to tell us. That's all. So I am wondering if anyone knows where Max might have gone. Did he say anything to anyone today? Anything about leaving the school early?"

Mrs. Gosk already asked these questions to her kids a little while ago, when the kids saw the police cars pull up in front of the school and Mrs. Palmer asked teachers to "begin lockdown protocols until further notice." But she lets Mrs. Palmer ask anyway.

Briana raises her hand. "Max goes to the Learning Center a lot. Maybe he got lost going there today."

"Thank you, Briana," Mrs. Palmer says. "Someone is checking on that right now."

"Why are the police here?" This is Eric, and he did not raise his hand. Eric never raises his hand.

"The police are here to help us find Max," Mrs. Palmer says. "They are good at finding lost children. I'm sure that he will turn up soon. But did he say anything to anyone today? Anything at all?"

Kids shake their heads. No one heard Max say anything because no one talks to Max.

"Okay. Thank you boys and girls," Mrs. Palmer says. "Mrs. Gosk, could I speak to you for a moment?"

Mrs. Gosk puts down the book and meets Mrs. Palmer in the doorway to the classroom.

I follow.

"You're sure he didn't say anything to you?" Mrs. Palmer asks.

"Nothing," Mrs. Gosk says. She sounds annoyed. I would be, too. The police chief has asked Mrs. Gosk this question twice already.

"And you are sure about the time he left the classroom?"

"I'm sure," Mrs. Gosk says, even more annoyed.

"Okay. If the kids think of anything, let me know. I'm going to see about lifting the lockdown. We have a bunch of parents on the street already, waiting to pick up their kids."

"The parents already know?" Mrs. Gosk asks.

"The police have been knocking on doors for two hours, and the PTO is organizing volunteers to search the neighborhood. An Amber Alert went out. There's a news van outside already. There are bound to be more before six o'clock."

"Oh," Mrs. Gosk says, and she sounds a lot less annoyed. She sounds like a little kid who has just been punished. Mrs. Gosk never sounds like this. She sounds scared and confused, and this scares me.

Mrs. Palmer turns and leaves Mrs. Gosk standing in the doorway. I follow Mrs. Palmer down the hallway. I want to hear what she says to the police chief, and I do not want to hear what happens to that nasty Veruca Salt.

I don't care how rotten she is. Disappearing kids don't seem so funny anymore.

As Mrs. Palmer crosses through the lobby and turns toward the office, one of the front doors to the school opens. The policeman standing beside it is holding it open.

Mrs. Patterson walks in.

I stop.

I can't believe it. Mrs. Patterson is walking into the school. I wait for Max to follow behind her, but the policeman closes the door.

No Max.

twenty-four

"Karen, I can't believe the news," Mrs. Patterson says. "What could have happened?"

Mrs. Palmer and Mrs. Patterson hug in the middle of the lobby.

Mrs. Palmer is hugging Mrs. Patterson and Max is not here.

I think about running out to Mrs. Patterson's car to see if Max is still in the backseat, but I decide not to. Mrs. Patterson says that she can't believe the news about Max disappearing, and since she is the one who *disappeared* him, I know she is lying. Max isn't in her backseat anymore.

For a second, I think he is dead, and my whole body fills with sadness. I think that I might be dead for a minute, too. Then I remember that I am still here, so Max must still be alive.

Here's the thing: If Max was dead (which he is not) and I was still alive, that would mean that I won't disappear when Max dies or when Max stops believing in me.

I don't want Max to be dead, and I don't think he is dead (because he isn't), but if he was dead and I wasn't dead, that would mean something. It would be the saddest thing ever in the history of all things, but it would mean something, too. Something important about me. I'm not saying I want Max to be dead, because I do not and he is not. But if he ever was dead and I still existed, that would be an important thing to know.

I only keep thinking that he might be dead because I watch too much television.

Mrs. Patterson and Mrs. Palmer finish hugging just as the police chief comes around the corner. It was a long hug. I think they like each other now, even though they didn't like each other before Max disappeared. And I think Mrs. Palmer has forgotten all about the *damunion.* They look like best friends, standing in the middle of the lobby. Sisters even.

"Kelly Patterson?" the police chief asks. I don't know if he is really a police chief but he is in charge today and he has a big belly, so he looks like a police chief. His real name is Bob Norton, which is not a television show police officer kind of name. It doesn't make me feel good about his chances of finding Max.

Mrs. Patterson turns. "Yes, that's me."

"Can we speak in Mrs. Palmer's office?"

"Of course."

Mrs. Patterson sounds worried. The police chief probably thinks she is worried about Max, but I think she is worried about getting caught. Maybe she is trying to make worried-about-getting-caught sound like worried-about-Max-disappearing.

Mrs. Patterson and Mrs. Palmer sit on one of the couches together, and the police chief sits on the couch on the other side of the coffee table. He has a pad of yellow paper on his lap and a pen in his hand.

I sit next to the police chief. Even though he doesn't know it, I am on his team.

"Mrs. Patterson," the police chief says. "You are Max Delaney's paraprofessional. Is that correct?"

"Yes. I spend a lot of time with Max. But I have other students, too."

"You're not with him all day long?" the police chief asks.

"No. Max is a smart boy. He doesn't need assistance all day."

Mrs. Palmer nods while Mrs. Patterson is speaking. I have never seen her be so agreeable around Mrs. Patterson before.

"Can I ask why you were absent from work today?" the police chief asks.

"I had a doctor's appointment. Two appointments, actually."

"Where was your appointment?"

"The first was just down the street," Mrs. Patterson says, pointing in the direction of the front of the school. "At the walk-in clinic. They have a physical therapy center located in the building. I had physical therapy this morning for a shoulder problem. Then I had an appointment on Farmington Avenue. That's where I was when our secretary called."

"Mrs. Palmer says you miss a lot of work, especially on Fridays. Is it because of the physical therapy?"

Mrs. Patterson looks at Mrs. Palmer for a second, and then she turns back to the police chief and smiles.

She has stolen Max and is sitting in front of a police chief, and she is smiling.

"Yes," she says. "I mean, sometimes I'm ill, and sometimes I have doctor's appointments." She pauses, takes a deep breath, and then says, "No one knows this, but I have lupus, and it's caused me to have some health problems over the past couple years. Sometimes a five day work week is just too much for me."

Mrs. Palmer makes a little gasping sound. "Kelly, I had no idea." She reaches out and touches Mrs. Patterson on the shoulder. It's the kind of touch that Max's mother would like to give to Max when he is upset, if Max would ever let her touch him like that. I can't believe that Mrs. Palmer is touching Mrs. Patterson like this. Max disappears and Mrs. Patterson says she has something called lupus, and suddenly Mrs. Palmer wants to hug her and pat her on the shoulder.

"It's okay," Mrs. Patterson says to Mrs. Palmer. "I didn't want people to worry."

"Is there anything that you can tell us that might help us find Max?" the police chief asks. He sounds a little annoyed, and I am glad.

"I can't think of anything," Mrs. Patterson says. "Max has never been a runner, but he's always been a curious boy, and he asks lots of questions about the forest. But I can't imagine that he would go there alone."

"A runner?" the police chief asks.

Mrs. Palmer speaks this time. "Some of our special needs children have a propensity for running away from us. If they make it to the doors, they will sometimes run for the street. But Max isn't a runner."

"Max has never been a runner?" the police chief asks.

"No," Mrs. Patterson says. "Never."

I can't believe how calm she is. Maybe lupus makes people good liars.

The police chief looks down at his yellow pad. He clears his throat. I don't know how I know, but I can tell that he is about to ask important questions now. Tougher questions.

"Max was supposed to go from Mrs. Gosk's class to the Learning Center today, but he never made it there. Is this a walk he usually does by himself?"

"Sometimes," Mrs. Patterson says, but that is not true. I am always with him when he walks to the Learning Center. "If I'm in school, I'll pick him up, but he doesn't need an escort."

"We are trying to get Max to be more independent," Mrs. Palmer says. "So even when Kelly is here, we will sometimes have Max travel around the building on his own."

"But on Fridays," Mrs. Patterson says, "I am scheduled to work with Max in the Learning Center, so I would normally escort him there because I need to be there, too."

"Do you think it's possible that Max could have left Mrs. Gosk's class early?"

"Maybe," Mrs. Patterson says. "He can't read an analog clock. Did Donna send him on time?"

"She says she did," the police chief says. "I'm just wondering if she could have sent him early by mistake, or if he could've left the class without telling her or without her noticing."

"It's possible."

"She's lying!" I shout, only because I can't stop myself. Mrs. Gosk never sends kids early. If anything, she forgets to send them at all. She gets too busy with her books and her teaching. And Max would never leave the room without permission. Never ever.

The more Mrs. Patterson lies, the more frightened I become. She is so good at it.

"What about Max's parents?" the police chief asks. "Is there anything I should know about them?"

"What do you mean?"

"How are they as parents? Do they get along? Do they get Max to school on time? Does he seem well cared for? Things like that."

"I don't understand," Mrs. Patterson says. "Do you think they did something to Max? I thought he was at school today."

"He was, and it's likely he just went for a walk and he'll turn up any minute, playing on someone's backyard swing set or hiding in the forest. But if Max didn't take a walk, then someone took him, and it's almost always someone who the child knows. Most often a family member. Can you think of anyone who might want to take Max? Could his parents be involved?"

Mrs. Patterson doesn't answer this question as quickly as the others, and the police chief notices. He leans forward at the same time I do. He thinks he is about to hear something important, and I do, too.

But the police chief thinks that he is about to get an important fact. I think it's going to be an important lie.

"I've always worried about Max being here at school." She talks like she is lifting a heavy backpack. All her words sound heavy. "Max is a very sensitive boy and he doesn't have any friends. Kids pick on him from time to time. Sometimes he loses track of what he is doing and is unsafe. Runs out in front of a school bus or forgets that he's allergic to tree nuts. I don't know if I would send Max to public school if I were his parent. I think it's too dangerous. I have a hard time thinking that good parents would send a boy like Max to school."

Mrs. Patterson pauses. She's looking at her shoes. I don't think she realizes what she has been saying, because when she looks back up, she seems surprised to be looking at the police chief. "But I don't think they would do anything to hurt Max," she says.

Too quickly, I think.

Mrs. Patterson doesn't like Max's mom and dad. I didn't know that, but I do now. And I don't think she wanted me to know it.

"But there is nothing specific that would cause you concern about his parents?" the police chief asks. "Other than that they send Max to public school?"

Mrs. Patterson pauses, and then says, "No."

The police chief asks Mrs. Patterson questions about the Learning Center teachers, Max's classmates, and everyone else who Max sees every day, which is not too many people. She says that she cannot imagine anyone at school taking Max.

The police chief just nods.

"I'm going to ask you to walk the path that Max usually takes to the Learning Center with one of my officers, to see if anything jogs your memory. If it does, you'll let me know. And he's going to get some contact information from you, and ask you a few questions about anyone else who Max might come into contact with on a daily basis. Okay?"

"Okay," Mrs. Patterson says. "Would it be alright if I go home, after I answer his questions? At least for a little while. The physical therapy and the doctor's appointment took a lot out of me, and I'd like to rest. Or maybe I could just lie down on a couch in the faculty room if you'd prefer I stay at school."

"No, that's fine. We'll contact you if we need anything. If Max doesn't turn up by this evening, we'll probably need to talk to you again. Sometimes people don't realize what they might know that could help us."

"I'll do whatever I can to help," Mrs. Patterson says. She starts to rise from the couch and then stops. "You think you're going to find him. Right?"

"I hope so," the police chief says. "Like I said, I think he'll probably turn up within the hour, playing in someone's backyard. So yes, I think we'll find him."

I know I will.

I'm going home with Mrs. Patterson.

twenty-five

Max's mom and dad are standing behind the counter in the office. I see them first because I walk out of Mrs. Palmer's office first. Then Mrs. Patterson sees them, but I don't think she recognizes their faces. I don't think she even knows them. She stole their son and told the police chief that they are bad parents and she doesn't even know who they are. I don't think Max's parents know who she is, either. They know her name, but they have never seen her face-to-face until now. They have meetings with people like Mrs. McGinn and Mrs. Riner and Mrs. Gosk.

Not Mrs. Patterson. Never paraprofessionals.

Mrs. Patterson doesn't stop to talk to them. She walks to the left, out the office's side door, where a policeman is waiting for her. He's an old man with a brown spot on his neck, and he doesn't look like he could stop a bad guy even if the bad guy was Mrs. Patterson, which she is.

Then Mrs. Palmer comes out of her office, and she sees Max's parents.

"Mr. and Mrs. Delaney," she says, sounding surprised. She walks over to the counter and opens the swinging door that separates the space where regular people stand from the space where the office people stand. "Come in. Please."

Max's mom is usually the boss, but she does not look like the boss right now. Her hands are shaking, and her face is pale. She looks limp, a little bit like a doll. I know it sounds silly, but even her curly hair looks less curly. She doesn't look sharp like she usually does. She looks scared. Hungry, even. Hungry for news, I think.

It is Max's dad who looks like the boss now. He has his arm around Max's mom, and he is looking around the office like Mrs. Gosk looks when she is taking attendance. Checking to see who is here and who is not.

They move past the counter and toward Mrs. Palmer's office, but I don't think Max's mom would be moving if Max's dad was not pushing her along.

"Do you have any news?" Max's dad asks before they even make it to Mrs. Palmer's office. He sounds like the boss, too. His words are like arrows. They shoot straight at Mrs. Palmer, and you can tell that they are full of extra stuff. He isn't just asking a question. He is yelling at Mrs. Palmer for losing Max even though he is not yelling and all he did was ask if there was any news.

"Come into my office," Mrs. Palmer says. "Chief Norton is waiting, and he can answer all your questions."

"Chief Norton wasn't here when Max disappeared," Max's dad says.

More arrows. Sharp ones.

"Please," Mrs. Palmer says. "Step inside."

We step into Mrs. Palmer's office. This time Max's parents sit on the couch where Mrs. Patterson and Mrs. Palmer were sitting a couple minutes ago. I wish I could tell them that they are sitting in the same place where the person who stole Max was just sitting.

Mrs. Palmer moves over to the couch where the police chief is still sitting. There is no room for me, so I stand beside the couch that Max's parents are sitting on. Even though there are no sides here because there is no bad guy in the room like before, I still feel like there are sides, and something tells me that I want to be on Max's parents' side.

The police chief stands up to shake both parents' hands. He introduces himself and then everyone sits down except me.

"Mr. and Mrs. Delaney, I'm Chief Norton. I've taken charge of the search for your son. Let me tell you where we are so far."

Max's mom nods but Max's dad doesn't. He doesn't move at all. I think he does this on purpose. If he moved, if he even nodded, then there would be no more sides in the room. Everyone would be on the same side. They would be a team.

He doesn't move an inch.

The police chief tells Max's parents about the search of the school and the people who are searching the neighborhood. He says that they are "operating under the assumption" that Max has run away and will be found soon, which sounds like he is hoping that Max has run away and will be found soon; otherwise he will not know what to do.

"Max has never run away before," Max dad says.

"No," the police chief says. "But his teachers think it's possible, and it's more likely than any other scenario."

"Like what?" Max's dad asks.

"I'm sorry?" the police chief says.

"What other scenarios are you talking about?"

The police chief pauses for a moment. When he speaks, his words come slowly. "Well, it's far more likely that he ran away from the school than he was abducted."

Max's mom lets out a tiny whimper when he says "abducted."

"I don't mean to frighten you, Mrs. Delaney. Like I said, I expect my phone to ring at any moment telling me they found Max playing in someone's backyard or lost in a patch of woods behind a neighbor's house. But if he isn't found, we will have to look into the possibility that someone has taken him. I've already started the preliminary work in case this ends up being the situation. We're exploring both possibilities simultaneously, just in case."

"Is it possible that he ran away and then got picked up by someone while he was on the street?" Mrs. Palmer asks this question, and I can tell by the look on her face and the police chief's face that they both wish she had not asked it. At least not in front of Max's parents. She looks at Max's mom, who looks like she is about to cry. "I'm sorry," she says. "I don't mean to frighten you."

"It's not likely," the police chief says. "It would be quite a coincidence if Max decided to run away at the same time a child abductor was driving by the school. But we're looking into all options, interviewing all staff members that come into contact with Max, and trying to see if someone new has recently come into contact with him."

"Why was Max alone?" Max's mom asks. This is a good question. An arrow question that should have hit Mrs. Palmer right between the eyes, but instead, the question sounds like jello. There's nothing behind it. Max's mom even looks like jello. She is all wobbly and weak.

"Max's paraprofessional was out today, and Max had walked to the Learning Center many times on his own," Mrs. Palmer says. "In fact, one of his IEP goals is to become more independent in regards to moving around the building and following a schedule, so it wasn't unusual for him to be traveling from his classroom to the Learning Center alone."

"And that's when you think he disappeared?" Max's father asks. "In between his classroom and the Learning Center?"

"Yes," the police chief says, speaking quickly. I think he wants Mrs. Palmer to be quiet, so he is covering up all the spaces where she could speak. "Max was last seen in his regular classroom. He never made it to the Learning Center, but since his paraprofessional was absent today, the Learning Center teachers didn't notice that Max had never arrived since she is the one who works with him there. And his teacher, Mrs. Gosk, assumed that your son was in the Learning Center, so Max could've been gone for as long as two hours before anyone noticed."

Max's dad runs his hands through his hair. He does this when he is stopping himself from saying something bad. He does this a lot when he argues with Max's mom. Usually right before he slams the screen door and leaves.

"We'd like to get some information from you," the police chief says. "Names of people who come into contact with Max on a regular basis. Anyone new in his life. Daily routines. Any medical information we might need to know."

"You said you thought you'd find him any minute," Max's mom says.

"Yes, I know, and I still believe that. We have more than two hundred people searching the area right now, and the media is spreading the word for us as well."

The police chief is about to say something else when there is a knock on the door and a policewoman pokes her head inside the office.

"Mrs. Patterson is ready to go home unless you need her."

"Nothing on the walk-through?" the police chief asks.

"No."

"And we have her contact information?"

"Yes."

"Fine then," he says. "She can go."

"You're letting the bad guy go!" I shout, but no one hears me. It is like when Max's dad or Sally shouts at the television as they watch a detective let the bad guy go free by mistake, except on TV, the bad guys usually get caught. This is the real world, and I don't think the television rules work here. Bad guys like Tommy Swinden and Mrs. Patterson can win in the real world. All that Max has is me, and I am useless.

"Okay, I'll send her home," the policewoman says.

That means it is time for me to go, too, even though a big part of me wants to stay here with Max's mom. The only way to help her is to help Max, but leaving her now seems wrong. She seems so weak. Like only half of her is here.

Still, I have to find my friend.

I pass through the office door and reenter the main office. I do not see Mrs. Patterson. The policewoman who told Chief Norton that Mrs. Patterson was ready to leave is on the phone now. She is sitting at the desk where the secretary lady usually sits. I don't know where Mrs. Patterson is, but I know where she parks her car, and I'm worried that she might already be walking to the parking lot so I start to run out of the office when I hear the policewoman say, "You can tell her that she can go now. But tell her that she needs to leave her phone on in case we need her." She says this to the person on the other end of the telephone.

Good. Mrs. Patterson hasn't left yet.

Still, I want to be inside her car before she gets there, so I run.

I once knew an imaginary friend who could pop. Instead of walking to a place, he could just disappear from one place and reappear in the other place, as long as he had been to the other place before. I thought this was amazing because it was like he stopped existing for a second and then existed again a second later. I asked him what it was like to stop existing because I wanted to know if it hurt, but he did not understand my question. "I don't stop existing," he said. "I just pop from one place to the other."

"But what does it feel like to stop existing for that second before you reappear?"

"It doesn't feel like anything," he said. "I just blink my eyes and I am in the new place."

"But how does it feel when your body disappears from the place that you start."

"It doesn't feel like anything."

I could tell that he was getting angry so I stopped asking. I was a little jealous of him for being able to pop, except that he was only as tall as a Barbie doll and his eyes were blue. All blue. No white part at all. It was like he was looking through a pair of dark blue sunglasses, so he could barely see, especially on a cloudy day or when the teacher turned out the lights to show a movie. And he had no name, which is not uncommon in imaginary friends but still a little sad. And he is gone now. He stopped existing over Christmas vacation when Max was still in kindergarten.

I wish I could pop right now. Instead, I run through the halls, following the same path that Max and I followed earlier today when Mrs. Patterson stole him. Right back to those glass doors where Max left earlier today.

Mrs. Patterson's car is not in the parking lot. I run up and down the row but I can't find it. But there is only one way to the parking lot, only one hallway and one set of doors, and I know that Mrs. Patterson could not have beaten me here because I ran the whole way and Mrs. Patterson would not run since that would make her look suspicious.

Then I figure it out. She has two cars. She drove a different car back to the school. One without the blue backpack and all the evidence that Max was inside. Like a hair from his head or dirt from his sneakers or his fingerprints. All the stuff that the scientists can use to prove that Max was sitting in the backseat. That must be it. She drove a different car back to school just in case the police wanted to inspect her car. That would be sneaky-smart and I think Mrs. Patterson is the sneakiest-smartest person I have ever met. She will be coming out those doors any second and getting into a different car. One I have never seen before. Maybe the one I am standing in front of right now.

I look around to see if I can find a new car in the parking lot. One I have never seen before. Then I see it. Not a new car that I have never seen before but Mrs. Patterson's old car. The one with the blue backpack and Max's hair and Max's dirt. It is in the circle in front of the school. It is parked in the circle, right in front of the doors to the school, even though it is illegal to park in the circle when kids are in school. I know this because sometimes Mrs. Palmer comes on the intercom and asks for the person who is parked in the circle to move their car *immediately.* She says "immediately" in a way to let the person who parked the car know that she is annoyed. She could just say, "Please move your car from the circle. And whoever you are, I am annoyed that you parked there" but instead she says "immediately," which seems nicer and not so nice at the same time.

But it is always a parent or a substitute teacher who parks in the circle because teachers know better. Mrs. Patterson knows better. So why is she parked in the circle now? There are police cars in the circle, too, but police are allowed to break the rules.

Then I see that Max's parents' car is parked in the circle, too. It is parked behind Mrs. Patterson's car, but then it is not parked behind Mrs. Patterson's car because Mrs. Patterson's car starts moving. It is driving around the back of the circle and toward the street. I run. I run as fast as I can, which is only as fast as Max imagined that I could run, which is not that fast. I want to yell, "Stop! Wait! You weren't supposed to park in the circle!" But she would never hear me, because her windows are up and she is so far away and I am imaginary and only imaginary friends and my friend who she stole can hear me. I cross the driveway without looking both ways or using the crosswalk and then I run across the front lawn to the other side of the circle, but Mrs. Patterson is pulling into the street and turning right. I wish I could pop. I close my eyes and try to imagine the backseat of Mrs. Patterson's car, with the blue backpack and the hair from Max's head and the dirt from his sneakers but when I open my eyes a second later I am still running across the front lawn and Mrs. Patterson's car is disappearing down a hill and around a bend.

I slow down and then I stop. I am standing in the middle of the front lawn, underneath a pair of trees. Yellow and red leaves are falling around me.

I lost Max.

Again.

twenty-six

Chief Norton told Max's mom and dad that he has not given up hope on finding Max somewhere in the neighborhood, but that he is "shifting the focus of the investigation in a different direction."

This means he doesn't think that Max ran away anymore.

He sent Max's parents to the teacher's lounge with a policewoman to answer some more questions. Then he told the police officer with the brown spot on his neck to call Burger King and Aetna to make sure that Max's mom and dad were working when Max disappeared. He has to make sure that it wasn't Max's mom or dad who stole Max. I'm not surprised. The police always have to check out the parents first.

It seems like parents are always the bad guys on TV.

The officer comes back into the office and tells Chief Norton that Max's mom and dad were at work all day and were "in plain sight," which means that they could not have driven to the school, stolen Max, and driven back without someone noticing that they were gone.

The chief looks relieved.

I guess it is better to search for a stranger who steals little boys than to find out that a mom or dad stole their own little boy. But I also know from television that the people who hurt and steal kids are usually not strangers, which is true today, too. Mrs. Patterson is not a stranger. She is just smart.

About twenty minutes before dismissal, the chief ended the lockdown and let the kids put on their coats and line up for the buses. But the lines were short today. Lots of the kids got picked up by parents who were biting their nails and twisting their wedding rings and walking faster than normal, as if the kidnapper was hiding behind the trees on the front lawn, waiting to scoop up even more kids.

I tried to talk to Puppy before he went home on the bus with Piper, but we only had a couple minutes before her bus was called.

"Mrs. Patterson stole Max," I said to him. We were standing in Piper's classroom, watching her move the papers in her cubby to her backpack. Actually, Puppy was standing. I have to sit on the floor when I talk to Puppy, since he is a puppy.

"She stole him?" he asked. It always looks weird when Puppy talks, because dogs are not supposed to talk, and he looks like a real dog. When he speaks, his tongue hangs out of his mouth and it makes him lisp. And he scratches himself a lot, even though as far as I know there is no such thing as imaginary fleas.

"Yes," I said. "Max went out to her car and then she drove away."

"So she didn't steal him. Maybe they went for a ride."

"Yeah, but I don't think Max knew what was going on. I think Mrs. Patterson tricked him."

"Why?" Puppy asked. "Why would a teacher trick a little kid like that?"

This is another reason why I do not like to talk to Puppy. He doesn't understand things like I do. Piper is only in first grade, and Puppy almost never leaves her side, so he does not get to see the adult world. He doesn't go to the gas station or the hospital at night and he doesn't watch television with Piper's parents. He's too much like Piper. He hasn't learned anything, like why a teacher might steal a kid.

"I don't know why Mrs. Patterson would trick him," I said, not wanting to explain bad guys to him. "But I don't think that Mrs. Patterson likes Max's parents. Maybe she thinks they are bad people."

"Why would Max's parents be bad people? They're parents."

See what I mean?

I wish Graham was here right now. I miss her so much. I think I'm the only who misses her. If Meghan missed her, Graham would still be here. I wonder if Meghan even remembers Graham.

No matter what happens, I don't think that anyone will remember me when I disappear. It will be like I was never here. There will be no proof that I ever existed. When Graham was disappearing, she said that the only thing that she was sad about was that she could not watch Meghan grow up. If I disappeared, I would be sad about not being able to see Max grow up, but I would also be sad about not watching me grow up.

Except you can't be sad if you disappear, because disappeared people can't feel sad.

They can only be remembered or forgotten.

I remember Graham, so it still matters that she was here. She was not forgotten. But there is no Graham to remember me.

The police ordered Chinese food for Max's parents. Chief Norton just delivered it.

"We have some more questions, but we should be done soon. Can you hang in for another hour and then we'll send you home with a couple officers?"

"We can stay as long as you need us to," Max's mom says. She sounds like she wants to stay here all night. I don't blame her. As long as she does not go home, she can keep thinking that Max will be found any minute. Going home means that they know they won't find Max tonight.

Unless they go to Mrs. Patterson's house, they are not going to find him.

The police officer with the brown spot on his neck leaves with Chief Norton. Chief Norton says that he wants to give Max's parents a few minutes to eat and be alone.

I do not leave. Without Max, Max's mom and dad are the only people I have.

As soon as the door closes, Max's mom starts to cry. It's not a big cry like the kindergarteners do on their first day of school. Just a little cry. Lots of sniffles and tears but that's it. Max's dad puts his arm around her. He doesn't say anything, and I don't understand why. They just sit there together. Maybe they hurt so much that the only way they can say it, is to say nothing.

I hurt so much, too, but if I could, I would talk.

I would tell them how stupid I feel for letting Mrs. Patterson leave without me. How stupid and guilty and rotten I feel. I would tell them how worried I am that today is Friday and I won't be able to ride in Mrs. Patterson's car until Monday afternoon. I would tell them how afraid I am that Mrs. Patterson won't ever come back to school on Monday and I will never be able to find her or Max again.

If I could talk to Max's parents, I would tell them that Mrs. Patterson tricked Max and stole him from the school and lied about it, and now Max is in trouble. If I could tell them all that, then Max could be saved. If only I could touch their world and let them know.

It's why I've been thinking about Oswald, the man at the hospital. The mean imaginary-friend man who I never want to see again.

I might have to see him again.

twenty-seven

There are two police officers at the house tonight, and they are the kind of police officers who don't sleep. I have seen this kind of police officer at the police station before. They can stay awake all night because the police station never closes.

They are sitting in the kitchen, drinking coffee and watching television. It feels weird to have two strangers in the house with us, especially with Max not here. It must be weird for Max's mom and dad, too, because they went to their bedroom early tonight instead of sitting in the living room and watching television.

Max's dad wanted to go out searching for Max, but Chief Norton told him to go home and get some sleep. "We have patrol cars and volunteers walking the neighborhood, and we need you well rested if you're going to be any help to us tomorrow."

"What if Max is hurt somewhere?" Max's dad asked, and there was anger in his voice, but it was the kind of anger that someone has when they are afraid. It sounded more nervous and rushed. It was like fear dressed up in a loud voice and red cheeks. "What if he slipped and fell and banged his head and now he's lying unconscious under a bush, out of sight of your patrol cars? Or what if he fell through an open sewer grate or even tried to climb down on his own? What if he is lying in a puddle under some street, bleeding to death right now?"

Max's mom is crying again, and it stopped Max's dad before he could say anything else about Max dying or being dead.

"Those are all things that we have considered," Chief Norton said. Even though Max's dad was almost yelling, Chief Norton's voice stayed quiet. He knew that Max's dad wasn't mad at him. He might have even known that Max's dad was not really angry at all but just afraid. His name might be Chief Norton, but I think he is smarter than I thought. "We've actually checked every sewer grate within three miles of the school, and we're expanding that radius now. Yes, it's possible Max has managed to get himself stuck in a place that is difficult for our teams to see him, but I've made sure that everyone who is searching knows this and they are leaving no stone unturned."

Max's dad was right. Max is stuck in a place where nobody can see him. But I don't think it matters how hard they look.

So Max's mom and dad went home, and after they showed the police officers where the coffeepot, and bathroom, and telephone, and remote control were, they said that they were going to bed.

Max's mom and dad have not turned on the television, even though I cannot remember the last time they did not spend the evening watching TV. Max's mom took a shower and now she is sitting on the bed, brushing her hair. Max's dad is sitting on the edge of the bed, too, turning his telephone over and over in his hands.

"I just can't stop thinking about how afraid he must be," Max's mom says. She has stopped combing her hair.

"I know," Max's dad says. "I keep thinking that he's stuck somewhere. Maybe he got himself trapped in the basement of an abandoned house or maybe he found a cave somewhere in the forest and he can't get out. Wherever he is, I keep thinking about how alone and how afraid he must be."

"I keep hoping that he has Budo with him."

I let out a little cry when I hear Max's mom say my name. I know she thinks I'm imaginary, but for that split second, I almost felt like she thought I was real.

"I hadn't thought of that," Max's dad says. "Anything to make him feel better. Feel less scared."

Max's mom starts to cry, and a second later Max's dad does, too. But Max's dad cries on the inside. You can tell that he is crying, but you can also tell that he doesn't think you can tell that he's crying.

"I'm trying to think of what we did wrong," Max's mom says, still crying. "I keep thinking that this is somehow our fault."

"Stop it," Max's dad says, and I can tell that he is done crying. At least for now. "That goddamn teacher lost track of Max, and he probably took a walk and got lost. And then he got curious about something that he saw and got stuck somewhere. We have enough to worry about without blaming ourselves."

"You don't think someone took him?"

"No," Max's dad says. "I can't believe that. No, they are going to find him at the bottom of a well, or trapped inside the basement of some abandoned house somewhere, or locked in some shed in someone's backyard. And you know Max. He's probably heard people shouting his name already but won't answer because he doesn't like to talk to people and he doesn't like to shout. He's going to be cold and wet and scared, but he is going to be fine. That's what I believe. I believe it in my heart."

Max's dad's words sound good. They are bursting with hope and I think he really believes everything he said. I think Max's mom is starting to believe it, too. For a second, I even believe it. I want to believe it.

Max's mom and dad hug and don't let go. After a few seconds it feels weird to be sitting next to them so I leave. They will probably be asleep soon, anyway.

I do not want to go to the gas station tonight. Dee and Sally won't be there, and I can't stand to be reminded of all the people I have lost in my life. Graham. Dee. Sally. Max. The gas station used to be one of my favorite places, but not anymore.

I can't stay here, either. Not all night. I do not feel right sitting in Max's parents' room and I do not want to sit in Max's room alone. And I can't sit in the living room or kitchen because the police officers are there and they are watching one of those shows where a man talks to a bunch of people who think he is funnier than the people watching on television do.

Plus, it feels strange to have these strangers in our house.

I need to talk to someone. And there are not many places where an imaginary friend can go to talk to someone, especially at night.

But I know one place.

twenty-eight

The Children's Hospital is across the street from the regular hospital, but I don't go to the regular hospital anymore. Not since I met the mean-man imaginary friend. Sometimes I get nervous just coming to the Children's Hospital, because it is so close to the adult hospital.

But the Children's Hospital is the best place to find imaginary friends. Even better than school. A school is full of kids, but most of them leave their imaginary friends home because it is hard to talk or play with an imaginary friend when teachers and other kids are around. They might bring them to school on the first day of kindergarten, but unless it is someone like Max, the kids figure out fast that talking to someone who no one else can see is not a good way to make friends. This is the time when most imaginary friends stop existing.

Kindergarten kills them.

But the Children's Hospital has always been a good place to find other imaginary friends. I came here when Max was in first grade because Max's first grade teacher, Mrs. Kropp, told us that hospitals never close. She was teaching the class about 911, which is a number that you can press on a phone if there is an emergency.

I would have pressed that number earlier today when Mrs. Patterson stole Max, if I could press numbers.

Mrs. Kropp said that you can press 911 anytime, because the ambulances and hospitals are always open. So one night I decided to skip the gas station and walk to the hospital instead, which is like six gas stations away.

The kids at the Children's Hospital are always sick. Some are just sick for a day or two. They fall off their bikes and hit their heads or catch something called pneumonia, but there are also kids who have been at the hospital for a long time because they are really sick. And lots of these kids, especially the really sick ones, have imaginary friends, probably because they need them. Some of the kids are pale and skinny and have no hair, and some wake up in the middle of the night crying softly so no one will hear them and worry about them. Sick kids know that they are sick, and really sick kids know they are really sick, and all of them are scared. So lots of them need imaginary friends to keep them company when their parents go home and they are left with the beeping machines and flashing lights.

The elevator in the hospital is tricky for me, because I cannot go through the elevator doors. I can pass through glass doors, and wooden doors, and bedroom doors, and even car doors, but I cannot pass through elevator doors. I think it is because Max is afraid of elevators and never ever goes inside one, so he probably does not think of the elevator doors as regular doors. They are more like trapdoors to him.

I want to go to the fourteenth floor, and it is easier for me to take the elevator. Fourteen floors is a lot of stairs. But that means I need to make sure that there is room in the elevator for me, because even though people can't see me or feel me, they can bump me and squish me into a corner if there are too many of them.

That's not quite right. I don't bump into them. I bump into the idea of them, which means that I feel them but they do not feel me. But there have been times when the elevator fills up with people and I am so squished into the corner of the elevator that I start to feel how Max must feel when he is in an elevator. All tight and trapped and suffocated, even though I don't actually breathe. I look like I breathe, but all I breathe is the idea of air, which is always there.

It's very strange to be an imaginary friend. You can't suffocate and you can't get sick, and you can't fall and break your head, and you can't catch pneumonia. The only thing that can kill you is a person not believing in you. That happens more than all the suffocating and bumps and pneumonia combined.

I wait for a person in a blue costume to press the button. She walked into the hospital right behind me. I have to wait for someone to use the elevator since I cannot press the button that tells the elevator that someone is waiting. And then I have to hope that the person is getting off on a floor close to mine. The woman in the blue costume presses the number 11, which isn't bad. If no one else gets on the elevator, I will get off on the eleventh floor, too, and climb the stairs to the fourteenth floor.

No one gets on the elevator before we reach the eleventh floor, so I step off and climb the last three flights of stairs.

The fourteenth floor is shaped like a spider, with a circle in the center, where all the doctors work, and four hallways stretching out from it. I walk down the hallway, toward the middle circle, past open doors on both sides of the hallway. This is another good thing about the Children's Hospital. The doctors do not close the doors to the kids' rooms all the way, so imaginary friends who cannot pass through doors don't get stuck inside overnight.

It is late so the hallway is quiet. The whole floor is quiet. Most of the rooms are dark. There are a bunch of girl doctors in the middle circle, sitting and standing behind counters, writing down numbers and words in notepads, and going to rooms when buzzers buzz. They are like the police officers that never sleep. They can stay awake all night but they do not look like they want to.

At the other end of one of the spider's legs is a room with couches and cushy chairs and lots of magazines and games. This is where the sick kids have recess during the day. At night, this is where the imaginary friends who do not sleep meet.

I used to think that all imaginary friends did not sleep, but Graham said that she slept at night, so maybe there are imaginary friends sleeping with their friends tonight in their hospital rooms tonight.

I imagine Graham sleeping in bed next to Meghan and it makes me want to cry again.

There are three imaginary friends in the recess room tonight, which is not a lot. All three look like imaginary friends. There is a boy who looks a lot like a person except that his legs and feet are tiny and fuzzy and his head is too large for his body. He looks like one of the Red Sox bobblehead dolls that Mrs. Gosk has on her desk. But he has ears and eyebrows and fingers, so this makes him look more like a person than most imaginary friends. Still, I wonder what he looks like when he walks. His head is so big.

Sitting next to the bobbleheaded boy is a girl who is about as tall as a bottle of soda. She has yellow hair, but no nose or neck. Her head is sitting on her body like a snowman. She doesn't blink.

The third looks like a boy-sized spoon with two big, round eyes, a tiny mouth, and stick-figure legs and arms. He is silver all over and wears no clothes, but he doesn't need to wear clothes because except for his arms and legs, he looks just like a spoon.

Actually, I'm not even sure if it's a he or a she. Sometimes imaginary friends are neither. I think it might just be a spoon.

As I enter, they stop talking and stare at me. But they do not look into my eyes, probably because they think I am a human person.

"Hello," I say, and the spoon gasps. The bobbleheaded boy jumps and his head bobbles just like Mrs. Gosk's bobblehead doll.

The little tiny girl doesn't move. She doesn't even blink.

"I thought you were real," the spoon says. He is so surprised that it sounds like he is choking on his words. He has a boy's voice, so I think it's a he.

"Me, too!" the bobblehead boy says. He sounds very excited.

"Nope. I'm like you. My name is Budo."

"Wow. You look so real," the spoon says. He can't stop staring.

"I am real. As real as you." Every time I talk to imaginary friends I have this same conversation. They are always surprised that I am not a human person and they always say how real I look. Then I have to remind them that they are real, too.

"Sure," the spoon says. "But you look like a real human."

"I know," I say.

After a moment of silence, the spoon speaks. "I'm Spoon," he says.

"I'm Klute," the bobblehead boy says. "She is Summer."

"Hi," the little girl says in a teeny-tiny voice. All she says is "Hi," and I can already tell that she is sad. As sad as I have ever seen someone. Sadder than Max's dad when Max won't play catch right.

Maybe as sad as I still feel about Graham.

"Do you have someone here?" Spoon asks.

"What do you mean?"

"Do you have a human friend at the hospital?"

"Oh, no." I say. "I came to visit. I come here sometimes. It's a good place to find imaginary friends."

"That's true," Klute says, shaking his head and making it bobble around. "Me and Eric have been here for a week and I have never seen so many imaginary friends."

"Eric is your human friend?" I ask.

Klute bobbles a yes.

"How long have you been alive?" I ask.

"Since summer camp," Klute says.

I count back to the beginning of summer. "Five months?" I ask.

"I don't know. I don't count months."

"How about you?" I ask Spoon.

"This is my three year," Spoon says. "Preschool, kindergarten, and now first grade. That's three years. Right?"

"Yes," I say. I'm shocked that Spoon is so old. Imaginary friends who don't look like human people don't usually last very long. "Three years is a long time," I say.

"I know," Spoon says. "I've never met anyone older."

"I'm almost six," I say.

"Six what?" Klute asks.

"Six years," I say. "Max is in third grade now. Max is my human friend."

"Six years?" Spoon asks.

"Yes."

No one says anything for a moment. They just stare at me.

"You left Max?" This is Summer speaking. Her voice is tiny, but it surprises me.

"What do you mean?" I ask.

"You left Max at home?"

"Actually, no. Max isn't home. He's away."

"Oh." Summer is silent for a moment, and then she asks, "Why didn't you go with Max?"

"I couldn't. I don't know where he is." I am about to explain what happened to Max when Summer speaks again. Her voice is still tiny but somehow it is loud, too.

"I could never leave Grace," she says.

"Grace?" I ask.

"Grace. My human friend. I could never leave her. Not even for a second."

I open my mouth again to explain what happened to Max but Summer speaks first.

"Grace is dying."

I look at Summer. I open my mouth to say something but nothing comes out. I do not know what to say.

"Grace is dying," Summer says again. "She has leukemia. That's bad. It's like the worst flu a human person could ever get. And now she is dying. The doctor man told Mommy that Grace is going to die."

I still don't know what to say. I try to think of something to make her feel better or make me feel better, but Summer speaks again before I can.

"So don't leave Max for too long because he might die someday, too. And you wouldn't want to miss out on playing with him when he is still alive."

I suddenly realize that Summer's voice hasn't always been this tiny or this sad. It is tiny and sad because Grace is dying, but there was a time when Summer was smiling and happy. I can see that happy version of Summer now, like a shadow around this sad version of her.

"I mean it," she says. "Human friends don't live forever. They die."

"I know," I say.

I don't tell her that Max dying is all I can think about.

Instead, I tell Summer and Spoon and Klute about Max. I start by describing Max. How much he loves LEGOs and Mrs. Gosk. The way he gets stuck. His bonus poops. His parents. His fight with Tommy Swinden. Then I tell them about Mrs. Patterson and what she did to him. How she tricked Max. How she tricked everyone except for me.

Except she tricked me, too, or I would be with Max right now.

I can tell by the way that they listen that Spoon understands what I say the best, but that Summer understands how I feel the best. She is scared for Max, almost as much as I am, I think. Klute listens, but he reminds me of Puppy. I don't think he understands at all. He is just trying to keep up.

"You have to find him," Spoon says when I'm done explaining. He says it with the same voice that Max uses when he talks to his toy soldiers. He doesn't just say it. He orders it.

"I know," I say. "But I don't know what to do when I find him."

"You have to help him," Summer says. Her voice is not tiny anymore. It's still soft, but it is not tiny.

"I know," I say again. "But I don't know how. I can't tell the police or Max's parents where Max is."

"I didn't say to help the police people," Summer says. "I said to help Max."

"I don't understand," I say.

"First you have to find him," Spoon says.

I watch Klute's head bobble around as he turns from me to Summer and to Spoon and back to me. *He's barely keeping up,* I think.

"You have to help him," Summer says, and now she sounds annoyed. Angry, even. "You have to help him get back to his mommy and daddy."

"I know, but if I can't tell the police or his parents, it's—"

"*You* have to do it," Summer says. It's like she's screaming even though she is talking in her same tiny voice. It sounds the same but it isn't tiny anymore at all. It's huge. Summer seems huge. She is still the size of a soda bottle but she seems bigger now. "Not the police," she says. "You. You have to save Max. Do you know how lucky you are?"

"What do you mean?" I ask.

"Grace is dying. She is going to die and I can't help her. I can sit by her and try to make her smile, but I can't save Grace. She is going to die and be gone forever and I can't help her. I can't save her. But you can save Max."

"I don't know what to do," I say. I'm staring down at this tiny little girl with the tiny little voice but I'm the one who feels tiny now. It's as if Summer has all the answers. I am the oldest imaginary friend maybe in the world but this little girl knows everything and I know nothing.

That's when I realize that she may know the answer to the question.

"What will happen to you when Grace dies?" I ask.

"Are you worried that Max might die?" she asks. "That the teacher will die him?

"Maybe," I say. I feel bad for thinking it, but I know it's true. Not thinking about things doesn't make them not true.

"Are you worried for Max or for you?" Summer asks.

I think about lying but I can't. This tiny little girl with the tiny little voice knows everything. I know it.

"Both," I say.

"You can't worry about yourself," she says. "Max might die, and you have to save him. You might save yourself by saving Max, but that's not important."

"What will happen when Grace dies?" I ask again. "Will you die?"

"It doesn't matter," Summer says.

"Why?" I ask.

"Yeah. Why?" Spoon asks. Klute bobbles in agreement. We all want to know.

Summer says nothing, so I ask again. I'm afraid to ask. I'm a little afraid of Summer now. I can't explain why, but it's true. I'm afraid of this tiny girl with this tiny voice. But still, I have to ask. "Will you die when Grace dies?"

"I think so," she says, looking at her tiny feet. Then she looks up at me. "I hope so."

We stare at each other for a long time, and finally she speaks. "Are you going to save Max?" she asks.

I nod.

Summer smiles. It is the first time I have seen her smile. It lasts for just a second, and then it is gone.

"I'll save Max," I say. And then, because I think it is important to say, especially to Summer, I add, "I promise."

Spoon nods.

Klute bobbles.

Summer smiles again.

twenty-nine

I ride the elevator down with a man who is pushing a machine on wheels. He stops the elevator on the fourth floor and I decide to get out. Just because the elevator was heading down doesn't mean that it won't change its mind and go back up. I have seen elevators do this before. I have seen this elevator do it before.

I step off the elevator and turn right. The stairs are around the corner. As I turn, I notice the sign on the wall. It has a list of words with little arrows pointing left and right. I am not the best reader, but I can read some of the words:

> ▸ **WAITING ROOM**
> ▸ **ROOMS 401–420**
> ◂ **ROOMS 420–440**
> ◂ **RESTROOMS**

And below RESTROOMS, the letters ICU with an arrow pointing right.

I see the letters as a word and say it aloud.

"Ickuh? Ick-you?"

Then I notice that all the letters are capitalized. This means that it is not a word. Each letter stands for a word. They are initials. I learned this in first grade.

I say the initials aloud. "I.C.U." I stare at the letters for a second more, and then I read them again. "I See You."

It takes me a second to remember where I've heard these initials before. Then I remember. Dee went to the I See You when she was shot. Except it wasn't the I See You.

It was the ICU.

Dee could be here. In this building. On this floor. To the right. I go right.

There are doors on the left and right of the hallway. I look at the little nametags next to each one as I pass. I am looking for the letters *ICU,* or three words that start with these letters.

I find the words at the end of the hall. There are two doors blocking the hallway. A name tag on the doors reads INTENSIVE CARE UNIT. ICU.

I do not know what *intensive* means, but I bet it means a room for people who were shot by guns.

I pass through the doors. The room is big. There is a long counter in the middle of the room with three doctors sitting behind it. All ladies. The lights are on over the desk but nowhere else. The rest of the room is not dark but dim. There are lots and lots of machines in this room. They are all on wheels. They remind me of little fire trucks, sitting still and quiet but always ready to move.

On the edges of the room are shower curtains hanging from the ceiling. They wrap halfway around the room. Some are closed. The ones that are open have empty beds behind them.

There are two closed curtains. Dee could be behind one of them.

I walk to the first curtain and try to pass through but cannot. I am stopped by the curtain, even though it doesn't move when I bump up against it.

Max doesn't think of shower curtains as doors. At least he didn't when he imagined me. Even though Max is disappeared, I feel like he is here right now, stopping me at the shower curtain. I feel like we are still together even though we are apart.

It feels like a reminder that he is still alive.

I crouch down and crawl under the space between the shower curtain and the floor. There is a girl in the bed behind the curtain, but she is not Dee. She is a little girl. She looks like she could be in Puppy's first-grade class. She is asleep. There are wires and tubes running from little machines over to her arms and under her blankets. Her head is wrapped in a white towel. Her eyes are black and blue. There is a Band-Aid on her chin and above her eyebrow.

She is alone. No mother or father sitting in the chairs next to her bed. No doctor person checking on her.

I think about Max. I wonder if he is alone tonight, too.

"When will she wake up?"

A little girl who looks almost exactly like the little girl in the bed is sitting in a chair to my right. I did not see her when I crawled under the curtain. She stands up when I look at her.

I am surprised that she did not mistake me for a human person like most imaginary friends do. Maybe she knows that I am imaginary because I crawled under the shower curtain and all the human people step through the curtain.

"I don't know when she will wake up," I say.

"Why won't the other people talk to me?"

"Who?" I ask, looking around. For a second, I think that someone else is behind the curtain. Someone else I didn't notice.

"The other people," she says again. "I ask them when she will wake up but no one will talk to me."

I understand now. "Do you know her name?" I ask, pointing at the little girl in the bed.

"No," the girl says.

"When did you meet her?" I ask, pointing again.

"In the car," she says. "After the accident. After the car hit the other car."

"Where were you before you were in the car?" I ask.

"Nowhere," she says. She looks confused and embarrassed. She stares at her shoes.

"When did the girl go to sleep?" I ask.

"I don't know," she says, still looking confused. "The people took her away. I waited by the doors and when she came back she was asleep."

"Did you talk to her at all?" I ask.

"Yes. In the car. Mommy and Daddy wouldn't answer her, so she asked me to help. I stayed with her. I talked to her. We waited until the men with the machine got her out. It was loud and it made fire."

"I'm glad you got out of the car," I say. I don't want her to be afraid, and I think my questions are making her afraid. But I still have a few more to ask. "Have you seen Mommy and Daddy since you got out of the car?" I ask.

"No," she says.

"What is your name?" I ask.

"I don't know," she says, and now she sounds sad. *She might cry,* I think.

"Listen. You are a special friend. An imaginary friend. That means that she is the only one who can see or hear you. She needed you in the car when she was scared so that is why you are here. But everything is going to be fine. You just need to wait until she wakes up."

"Why can you see me?" she asks.

"Because I am like you," I say. "I am an imaginary friend, too."

"Oh. Then where is your little girl?" she asks.

"My friend is a little boy. His name is Max, but I don't know where he is."

She stares at me. She says nothing so I wait. I don't know what to say, either. We just stare at one another over the beeps and hums from the machines beside the bed. The silence seems like forever. Finally I speak. "I lost him. But I'm looking for him."

She keeps staring at me. This little girl has only existed for a day but I know what she is thinking.

She thinks that I am a bad friend for losing Max.

"I have to go now," I say.

"Okay. When will she wake up?"

"Soon," I say. "Just wait. She will be awake soon."

I crawl back under the shower curtain before the little girl can say anything else. There is another closed curtain a few steps away but I know that Dee is not behind it. This is the Children's Hospital. There is probably an ICU in the grown-up hospital, too, and Dee is probably there.

I wonder if Max is all alone like the little girl behind the shower curtain. She has no Mommy or Daddy sitting in the chairs next to her bed. Maybe they are hurt, too.

Maybe they are dead. But I do not think so because that would be too terrible a thing to think.

At least she has her imaginary friend. She may not have a name yet, but she is waiting by the bed, so the little girl is not alone.

I keep thinking about what Max's mom said. "I keep hoping that he has Budo with him."

I am not.

That little girl has her brand-new imaginary friend with her tonight, but Max is alone somewhere. He is alive because I am still here and Max being dead would be too terrible a thing to think.

But he is alone.

thirty

Max's mom will not stop crying. It is not a sad cry. It is a scared cry. It reminds me of the crying that babies do when they can't find their mothers.

Except this time a mother can't find her baby.

Max's dad holds her. He does not say anything because there is nothing to say. He is not crying but I know that he is crying inside again.

I used to think that these were the three worst things in the world:

1. Tommy Swinden
2. Bonus poops
3. Not existing

Now I think these are the three worst things in the world:

1. Waiting
2. Not knowing
3. Not existing

It is Sunday night, which means that tomorrow I can go to school and find Mrs. Patterson and Max.

As long as Mrs. Patterson goes back to school.

I think she will. Otherwise she would look suspicious. If Mrs. Patterson was a bad guy on a television show, she would definitely go to school on Monday. She might even offer to help the police chief search for Max.

I bet she will. She is sneaky-smart.

I spent the weekend looking for Max, but now I feel like all I did was waste my time. I don't know where Mrs. Patterson lives, but I couldn't just sit at home for two days doing nothing, and I couldn't spend any more time around the police officers because too many of them keep wondering aloud (but never around Max's parents) if Max is dead.

So I started searching for Max inside people's houses, hoping that one of the houses would be Mrs. Patterson's house. I know that Mrs. Grady and Miss Paparazo live close enough to the school that they sometimes walk to work together, so I thought that maybe most of the teachers lived close by (even though I know Mrs. Gosk lives in a faraway place on the other side of the river, which is why she is sometimes late). So I started my search with the houses closest to the school. I made circles through the neighborhood like the ripples that a stone makes when Max tosses one into the lake.

Max doesn't swim, but he loves to throw rocks into the water.

I knew it would be almost impossible for me to find Mrs. Patterson's house like this, but I had to do something. But it didn't do any good. I didn't find Max or Mrs. Patterson. All I found were parents who did not lose a child. Families sitting around dinner tables, and raking leaves in the backyard, and arguing about money, and cleaning their basements, and watching movies on television. All of them seemed so happy. It was like they didn't know that Mrs. Patterson could just drive to school one day and steal their little boy or little girl.

Monsters are bad things, but monsters that do not walk and talk like monsters are the worst.

I thought about going back to the hospital to see Spoon and Summer again, but I am afraid that Summer will be mad because I have not found Max yet.

I don't know why I should be afraid of a little girl the size of a soda bottle, but I am. Not afraid like she will hurt me, but afraid in the same way that Max is afraid to disappoint Mrs. Gosk, even though he does it all the time and doesn't even know it.

I am also afraid to find out that Summer's human friend has died and she has died, too.

Disappeared, I mean. Stopped existing.

Last night I stopped at the gas station to see if Dee was back.

She wasn't. Sally wasn't there, either, but I don't think I will ever see Sally again. Getting shot might kill a person but I don't think it would stop someone from going back to work someday. But getting stuck like Sally might stop a person from ever coming back to work, even to say hello to old friends.

I don't think it will ever be the same at the gas station. There were three people working last night but I didn't know any of them. Pauley came in to buy scratch tickets, and I could tell that he feels the same way. He didn't even stay to scratch his tickets. He stood at the counter for a second, thought about it, and then he just left with his head down.

It's not our place anymore.

But it's not a new place, either.

It's not a special place for anyone anymore. The people who work there now just work. There was a girl working last night who looked like she needed to make two or three bonus poops. Her face was all scrunched up and serious. And the other people, both old men, barely spoke to one another. And everyone works. No more goofing around. No more television behind the counter. No more talking to customers and knowing their names. No more Dee telling Sally to get back to work.

I don't know if I will ever go back to the gas station. I would like to see Dee again. Maybe in the ICU someday, if I ever find the courage to go to the adult hospital. But I don't think even Dee could make the gas station like it used to be.

I have to leave early tomorrow morning. I am worried that the bus will not stop at our bus stop, because Max will not be standing by the tree, touching it with one hand at all times so he doesn't accidentally wander into the street. That was my idea, but when he told his mother the idea so that he could wait by himself, he said that it was his idea.

I didn't care. I was his idea, so in a way, my idea was his idea, too.

I could walk to the school if I had to, like I did this weekend when I was searching for Max, but I have always ridden on the bus to go to school, and I feel like it would be good luck for me to ride it tomorrow. Like I'm telling the world that I am on the bus because I know that Max will be back soon.

I have a list of things to do tomorrow. I've been thinking about them all night. Memorizing them. Sometimes I really, really wish I could hold a pencil and write things down. I have to be much more careful this time. On Friday, I was not careful and Mrs. Patterson drove away without me. So I have to be sure to do exactly the right thing tomorrow.

My things-to-do list is short:

1. Leave the house when Max's mom wakes up.
2. Walk to the Savoys' house and wait with them for the bus.
3. Ride the bus to school.
4. Go straight to the parking lot where Mrs. Patterson parks her car.
5. Wait for Mrs. Patterson.
6. When Mrs. Patterson parks her car, get inside Mrs. Patterson's car.
7. Don't leave the car no matter what.

I just hope that Mrs. Patterson comes to school tomorrow. I tried to make a list of things to do if Mrs. Patterson does not come to school but I could not think of anything to put on the list.

If she does not come back to school, I think Max will be lost forever.

thirty-one

The blue backpack is not in the backseat anymore. I am sitting in the spot where it was the last time I saw it.

Thursday. The last time I saw it was Thursday.

Four days ago. It feels like forty days ago.

Mrs. Patterson pulled into the parking lot before the first bell. She parked her car in her usual spot and walked inside like it was a normal school day. A kidnapper is now walking around the halls of the school and no one knows it except for me. I keep wondering if she is planning on stealing another kid soon. Is she tricking other boys and girls like she tricked Max?

Did she want Max because he is Max or because she is collecting kids?

Both ideas scare me.

My list of things to do says to stay in the car no matter what, but the school day is long and it is still early. The first recess bell hasn't even rung yet. I don't think Mrs. Patterson will leave early because that would look suspicious. And I made the list so I can change it if I want. It is not like the rules about running in the hallways, or staying silent during a fire drill, or not eating peanut butter at the peanut-free table. It's my rule so I can break it if I want. So I will.

I just want to see what is going on inside the school.

I want to see Mrs. Gosk.

There is a man sitting at a desk in the lobby. There has never been a desk in the lobby before, and there has never been a man sitting at a desk in the lobby before. He is not wearing a uniform but I can tell that he is a policeman. He looks serious and bored at the same time, just like those police officers who work overnight at the police station. A lady just walked through the front doors and the police officer is waving her over to his desk. He is asking her to sign her name on a clipboard. While she is signing, he asks her to explain why she is here today.

She is carrying a tray of cupcakes.

He must not be a very good policeman. Even a kindergartener would know why this lady is here.

I walk down the hall to Mrs. Gosk's classroom. She is teaching when I walk in. Just hearing her voice in the hallways makes me feel a little better.

She is standing in front of the class and talking about a boat called the *Mayflower*. She has a map rolled down in front of the chalkboard, and she is whacking it with her meter stick and asking where North America is. I know the answer to this question because Max loves maps. He loves to plan imaginary battles with imaginary armies on real maps, so I know the names of all the continents and oceans and lots of the countries.

Max's desk is empty. It is the only empty desk in the classroom. No one else is absent today. It would be better if someone else was absent today. It would make Max's desk seem less empty.

Someone should have stayed home sick.

I sit at Max's desk. The chair is pulled out enough so that I can sit without feeling squished by the idea of the desk and the idea of the chair. Mrs. Gosk has stopped whacking the map. Jimmy answered the question about North America and a bunch of kids seem relieved that he knew the answer. They were afraid that Mrs. Gosk would ask them where North America was, and they could tell that this is the kind of question that even a dummy should be able to answer. Now she is showing the kids a picture of the *Mayflower*, except it looks like someone has chopped the boat in half. We can see the inside of the boat. Little rooms filled with little tables and little chairs and little people.

The *Mayflower* was a big boat.

Mrs. Gosk looks up from the picture to the class and says, "Imagine that you were leaving your home forever. Just like the Pilgrims. You're sailing to America and all you can bring is one small suitcase. What would you pack inside?"

Hands fly up. This is the kind of question that everyone can answer. No one needs Jimmy for this one. Even someone who hasn't been listening can raise their hand and answer this question without sounding like a dummy. Mrs. Gosk asks these kinds of questions a lot. I think she wants all the kids to have something to talk about, and she loves to make the kids feel like they are a part of the story.

Kids start answering. Mrs. Gosk laughs when Malik says, "Lots and lots of underwear" and Leslyan says, "My cell-phone charger. I always forget it when we go on vacation."

I'm surprised that Mrs. Gosk is laughing. And I'm mad. Mrs. Gosk is acting just like Mrs. Gosk. She is not acting like the Mrs. Gosk who is missing a student and who the police tried to blame two days ago. In fact, I think she is even more like Mrs. Gosk than she ever was. She is like Mrs. Gosk times two. She's practically bouncing around the room. It's like her shoes are on fire.

Then I understand.

Mrs. Gosk is *acting* like Mrs. Gosk. She is smiling and asking good questions and swinging her meter-beater around because she is not the only one who is sad or worried about Max. The kids are worried, too. A lot of them don't know Max very well and a lot of them are mean to him, some on purpose and some on accident, but they all know that Max disappeared and they must be worried and scared. Maybe even sad, too. Mrs. Gosk knows this, so even though she is probably the most worried and most afraid person in the whole school, she is pretending to be Mrs. Gosk times two for the kids. She is worried about Max but she is also worried about the twenty other kids in the classroom, so she is putting on a show for them. She is trying to make it the best, most normalest day that they ever had.

I love Mrs. Gosk.

I might love her more than Max does.

I'm glad I came inside. Just seeing Mrs. Gosk makes me feel better.

I go back to Mrs. Patterson's car. I want to stop in the office and see what Mrs. Palmer is doing today. I want to see if the police chief is still sitting on her couch. I want to see if Max's parents are coming to school today to answer more questions. I want to go to the faculty room and see what the teachers are saying about Max. I want to see if Mrs. Hume and Mrs. McGinn and Mrs. Riner are as worried as I am. I want to find Mrs. Patterson and see if she is acting normal today or if she is lying to kids like she lied to Max. Most of all, I want to spend more time in Mrs. Gosk's classroom.

But if Mrs. Gosk can pretend to be herself today, I can wait inside a car until Mrs. Patterson comes back.

Waiting is one of the three worst things in the world, but the waiting will be over soon.

If I just sit and wait in Mrs. Patterson's car, I will find Max.

thirty-two

Mrs. Patterson opens the door and climbs into the driver's seat. The last bell rang about five minutes ago and there are still buses in the circle, waiting to fill up with children. But Mrs. Patterson is not a teacher who is responsible for kids. She does not have to worry about how they get home or if they are getting picked up by a babysitter or an uncle or a grandmother. She doesn't even have to worry if they have friends to play with or eat enough lunch or have a warm coat for the winter.

Only teachers like Mrs. Gosk can be trusted with this stuff, so teachers like Mrs. Patterson can leave when the last bell rings. This must seem good to teachers like Mrs. Patterson but they don't know how much the kids love Mrs. Gosk.

Kids can't love you if you only teach them for an hour a week.

Or if you steal them.

Mrs. Patterson starts the car and turns left out of the circle so she does not get stuck behind the buses. You are not allowed to pass a bus if it has its little stop sign switched on.

I remember the day when Max ran out between the buses and almost got hit by someone who was driving through the circle and breaking the little stop sign rule.

Graham was there that day. Graham and Max. It seems so long ago.

Mrs. Patterson just drives. She does not turn on the radio. She does not make a phone call. She does not sing or hum or even talk to herself. She keeps both of her hands on the steering wheel and just drives.

I watch her. I think about climbing into the front seat next to her but I don't. I have never sat in the front seat before and I do not want to sit next to her. I want to follow her. I want her to lead me to Max so I can save him. But I do not want to sit next to her.

I was going to save Max even if I never met Summer. I love Max and I am the only one who can save him. But I still think about Summer a lot when I think about saving Max. I think about the promise that I made to her. I don't know why, but I do.

I watch for clues while Mrs. Patterson drives. I wait to hear her speak. I have been alone in the car with Max's mom and dad before, and I have been alone in rooms with lots and lots of people who think they are alone, and they are usually doing something. Eventually, everyone does something. They turn on the radio, or hum, or groan, or fix their hair in the little mirror that is pasted onto the windshield, or drum their fingers on the steering wheel. Sometimes they talk to themselves. They make lists or complain about someone to no one or talk to the other people who are driving in cars around them like the other people can hear them through the glass and metal.

Sometimes people are gross. They pick their noses in the car. This is gross even though the car seems like one of the best places to pick a nose, because no one is around and you can get rid of your boogers before you get home. Max's mom yells at Max for picking his nose, but Max says that some boogers won't come out with a tissue, and I think he must be right because I have seen Max's mom picking her nose, too. But never when someone else is watching.

That's what I tell Max. "Picking your nose is like pooping," I say to him. "You have to do it in private."

Max still picks his nose around people sometimes, but not as much as he used to.

Mrs. Patterson does not pick her nose. She does not scratch her head. She does not even yawn or sigh or sniffle. She keeps her eyes forward and only takes her hands off the steering wheel to switch on the flashing arrow when she turns. She is serious about driving.

Serious about everything, I think. *A serious customer,* Mrs. Gosk would say, and that makes me even more scared. Serious people do serious things and don't make mistakes. Mrs. Gosk says that Katie Marzik is a serious customer because Katie always gets 100 percent on her spelling tests and solves all the math problems without any help. Even the ones that the rest of the class can't solve with help.

If Katie Marzik wanted to be a kidnapper when she grew up, she would be a good one.

I bet Katie Marzik will drive just like Mrs. Patterson someday, with her eyes on the road and her hands on the steering wheel and her mouth closed.

If Mrs. Patterson is driving to her house, and I think she is, I am worried about what she has done to Max. How did she keep him stuffed away for the whole day while she was at school?

She could have tied Max up with rope, and that would be bad. Max does not like to be held still. He will not sleep in a sleeping bag because it is too tight. It squishes him, he says. And he says that turtleneck shirts choke his neck, even though they don't but somehow do at the same time. He doesn't go into closets even if the door is wide open and never pulls blankets over his head. He only wears seven pieces of clothing at one time not counting shoes. Never more than seven, because more than seven is too much. "It's too much!" he yells. "Too much! Too much!"

This means that when it is very cold outside, Max's mother can only get Max to wear underwear, pants, a shirt, a coat, two socks, and a hat. Never any gloves or mittens. And even if she took away the socks or the hat and underwear, which I sometimes think she would if she could, he still would not wear the gloves or mittens because he does not like his hands all bundled up and squished inside a glove. So Max's mom sews fur linings into all of his coat pockets and Max just puts his hands in his pockets to stay warm.

If Mrs. Patterson tied Max up or locked him in a closet or inside a box for the day, that would be very, very bad.

I'm mad at myself for not thinking about this before, but I am glad that I did not think about it before, too, because it would have worried me even more.

Maybe Mrs. Patterson has someone helping her. Maybe Mrs. Patterson is married and her husband is stealing Max, too. Maybe it was his idea. Maybe Mrs. Patterson told Mr. Patterson that they would be better parents for Max than Max's parents, so Mr. Patterson has been pretending to be a dad by watching Max all day, which would be better than tying Max up or locking him in a cupboard, but still bad because Max does not like strangers or strange places or new foods or different bedtimes or anything that is different.

Mrs. Patterson turns on her blinking arrow but there is no street ahead to turn onto. Just houses. One of these houses must be her house. Max is inside one of these houses. I can barely sit still now. I am finally almost there. She drives past three driveways and then finally turns right. There is a long driveway in front of us. At the top of the hill is a blue house. It is small but it looks perfect. Like a picture from a book or a magazine. There are four big trees in her front lawn but not one single leaf is on the grass even though there is not one single leaf in the trees, either. No leaves sticking out of the gutters or bunched around the edges of the house, either. There are two baskets of flowers sitting on the stoop by the front door. The same kind that the parents sell every year at school. Tiny yellow flowers in baskets. Maybe Mrs. Patterson bought them from the parents last week when they were on sale. Every tiny flower in the baskets looks perfect. Her driveway is perfect, too. No cracks or patches at all. There is a pond behind her house. *A big pond,* I think. I can see little bits of it around the corners of the house.

As she drives up the hill, she picks up a remote control and presses a button. The garage door opens. She drives into the garage and turns off the car. A second later I hear the garage door rattling and humming. It is closing.

I am inside Mrs. Patterson's house.

I hear Summer's voice in my head, making me promise to save Max again.

"I know," I say. Mrs. Patterson can't hear me. Only Max can hear me, and soon he will hear me. He is somewhere in this house. He is close by, and I am going to find him. I can't believe I have made it this far.

Mrs. Patterson opens the door and climbs out of the car.

I step out of the car.

It is time to find my friend.

"Time to save Max," I say.

I try to sound brave but I am not.

thirty-three

I do not wait for Mrs. Patterson. She stops in a little room just inside the garage to take off her coat and scarf. There are hooks for hanging things, and a neat row of boots and shoes along the floor, and a washer machine and dryer machine, but no Max, so I walk past her into a living room.

There are chairs and a couch, and a fireplace, and a television hanging on the wall, and a little table with books and photographs in silver frames, but there is no Max.

There is a hallway and staircase to my right so I turn and climb the stairs. I climb them two at a time. I do not need to hurry now because I am finally inside Mrs. Patterson's house, but I do anyway. I feel like every second counts.

There is a hallway at the top of the stairs and four doors. Three of the doors are open and one is closed.

The first door on the left is open. It is a bedroom, but it is not Mrs. Patterson's bedroom. There is no stuff in it. Just a bed and a dresser and a nightstand and a mirror. Furniture but no stuff. Nothing on the dresser. Nothing on the floor. No robe or jacket hanging from the hooks on the door. Too many pillows on the bed. A mountain of pillows. It is just like the bedroom that Max's mom and dad have at the end of the upstairs hall. The guest bedroom, they call it, but Max's mom and dad have never had a guest. Probably because Max would not like a sleepover guest. It's like a pretend bedroom. A bedroom that you only look at but never use. Like a bedroom in a museum.

There is a closet next to the bed so I check it. I pass through the door into a dark space. I can't see anything because it's so dark so I whisper. "Max? Are you here?"

He is not. I know it before I even whisper his name.

I don't know why I whisper his name since Max is the only person who can hear me. Max's mom would say that I have watched too much television, and she is probably right.

The second door on the right is also open. It is a bathroom. This bathroom looks like a pretend room, too. A museum bathroom. There is no stuff in here, either. Nothing on the sink or floor. The towels are all hanging perfectly on the rods and the toilet seat is closed. It is a guest bathroom, I think, even though I have never heard of a guest bathroom before.

I walk down the hall to the door that is closed. *If Max is upstairs, he would be in a room with a closed door,* I think. I pass through the door. Max is not in the room. It is a baby's room. There is a crib and a toy box and a rocking chair and a bureau with a basket of diapers on top. There are blocks on the floor and a little blue train engine and a little plastic farm with little people and little animals.

Max would not like the little plastic farm because the people do not look real. They are little pegs with faces, and he does not like those kinds of toys. He likes realistic toys. But the little farm animals and the little people are standing outside the little plastic barn, so the baby must like it.

Then I realize it. Mrs. Patterson has a baby. I can't believe it.

There is a closet in this room, too. A long closet with sliding doors, but one of the sliding doors is open. There are shelves stuffed with tiny shoes and tiny shirts and tiny pants and tiny balls of socks.

But no Max.

Mrs. Patterson has a little baby. This does not seem right. Monsters are not supposed to have little babies.

I leave the baby's room and walk into the room on the other side of the hallway. This is Mrs. Patterson's bedroom. I know it right away. There is a bed and a dresser and another television hanging on the wall. The bed is made but it is not piled with pillows and there is a bottle of water and a book on the headboard. There is a little table beside the bed with a clock, and a pile of magazines, and a pair of glasses. There is stuff in this room. Not like the guest bedroom.

There is a bathroom attached to the bedroom and a big closet without any doors. The closet is almost as big as Max's bedroom. Lots of clothes and shoes and belts, but still no Max.

I shout, "Max! Are you here! Can you hear me?" Just in case I didn't see him.

No one answers.

I leave Mrs. Patterson's bedroom. I stop in the hallway and look up to see if there is a trapdoor on the ceiling leading to an attic. Max's mom and dad have a trapdoor with stairs attached, so when you pull a cord, the trapdoor opens and the stairs unfold and you can climb up into the attic. There is no trapdoor. No attic.

I go back down the stairs.

Instead of turning back into the living room, I turn left. There is a hallway to the left that leads to the kitchen and there is another living room across the hallway. Couches, and cushy chairs, and little tables, and lamps, and another fireplace and a shelf full of books, but no Max. I walk through the living room and turn left into a dining room. A long table with chairs. A little table with more photographs and a tray of bottles. I turn left again and walk into the kitchen. Lots of kitchen stuff, but no Max.

The first floor is a living room, another living room, a dining room, and a kitchen. That is it. No Max anywhere.

No Mrs. Patterson.

I walk through the house again, faster this time. I find a bathroom, which I did not see the first time because the door was closed, and a coat closet by the front door.

No Max.

Then I find the door that I am looking for in the hallway to the kitchen.

The basement door.

Mrs. Patterson is in the basement with Max. I know it.

I pass through the door and onto stairs. The lights in the stairway and in the room at the bottom of the stairs are turned on. The room at the bottom of the stairs is carpeted and looks like another living room. There is a big, green table in the middle of the room with no chairs around it and a little net stretched across it. It looks like a tiny tennis court. Like a tennis court for dolls. There are couches and chairs and a television down here, too, but not Max.

And no Mrs. Patterson.

There is an open door on the other side of the room. I pass through it into a room that looks like a normal basement. The floor is made of stone and there are big, dirty machines in the corner. One is a fur-nace, which heats the house, and one is a water pipe machine, but I do not know which is which. There is a table with hammers and saws and screwdrivers hanging on the wall above it, all just as neat as Mrs. Patterson's closet and lawn. The whole house is neat. The water bottle on the headboard was the only thing that looked out of place in the whole house.

That's it. There are no closets or stairs or anything.

No Max. And no Mrs. Patterson.

I lost her again. In her own house.

I run upstairs into the kitchen and shout Max's name. I run to the garage to check if Mrs. Patterson's car is still in the garage. It is. The engine is making the ticking sound that cars sometimes make after they are turned off. Her coat is still on the hook next to the washer machine.

Maybe she is outside. I am being silly because I can't lose a person inside her own house, but I still feel like I should panic. Something is wrong. I know it. Even if Mrs. Patterson is outside, where is Max? I hold my hand up in front of my face and look at it closely, checking to see if I can see through it.

It's still solid. I am not disappearing. Max must be okay. He is somewhere and he is okay. Mrs. Patterson knows where Max is, so I just need to find Mrs. Patterson and I will eventually find Max.

I go outside. I pass through the sliding glass doors in the dining room and step out onto a deck at the back of the house. Steps lead from the deck to a small patch of grass and down to another set of steps and the pond. It is a wide, narrow pond. I can see houses on the other side of the pond, and I can see the lights from other houses to the left and right of Mrs. Patterson's house through the trees. Mrs. Patterson's neighbors don't live very close to Mrs. Patterson, but she would never bring Max outside.

There is a dock in the water at the bottom of the steps and a little boat floating next to it. A paddle boat. Max's mom tried to get Max to ride in one when we went to Boston last summer but he would not. He almost got stuck before his Mom finally stopped asking him to give it a try. It was one of those times when I thought Max's mom might cry because all the other little boys and girls were having fun in the boats with their parents but Max would not.

Mrs. Patterson is not on the deck. There is a table with an umbrella and a bunch of chairs, but no Max and no Mrs. Patterson.

I jump off the side of the deck and run around the house. I run and look and run until I have gone all the way around the house and am back on the deck, staring out at the pond again. The sun is low in the sky so all the shadows are long. The sunlight makes sparkles on the water.

I shout Max's name as loud as I have ever shouted anything in my life. I shout again and again and again.

The birds in trees answer my calls, but they are not answering me. Only Max can hear me, and Max is not answering.

I feel like I have lost my friend all over again.

thirty-four

I go back inside the house. I must have missed a room or a closet or a cupboard. I stand in the dining room and shout Max's name again. My voice does not echo because the world cannot hear my voice. Only Max can hear my voice. But if the world could hear my voice, it would repeat it now. It would echo again and again. That is how loud I yell Max's name.

I walk through the downstairs again, slower this time, making a loop from dining room to kitchen to living room and back to dining room. I stop in the living room with the television and look at the photographs in the silver frames. There is a baby boy in all three pictures. He is crawling in one picture and standing up in another, holding on to the side of a bathtub. He is smiling in all three pictures. He has brown hair and big eyes and a chubby face.

I still can't believe that Mrs. Patterson has a baby. A baby boy. I say it aloud to make it seem more real. "Mrs. Patterson has a baby boy." I say it again because I still don't believe it.

I wonder: *Where is Mrs. Patterson's baby? At nursery school?*

Then I have an idea. Maybe Mrs. Patterson's baby stays with a neighbor while she is at work. Maybe Mrs. Patterson walked over to the neighbor's house to pick her baby up.

That is it. I know it. Mrs. Patterson left the house when I was upstairs or in the basement but she did not drive her car. She went to get her baby from a neighbor's house or maybe from a nursery school down the street. Someplace close. Maybe she picks up her baby and walks home every day because fresh air is good for babies and she can ask him questions about his day even though he can't answer because that is what mothers do.

I am feeling relieved now. I do not know where Max is, but as long as I follow Mrs. Patterson, I will find him. As long as I do not lose her, everything will be fine. Maybe Max is in another house with Mrs. Patterson's husband. Maybe Mr. and Mrs. Patterson have a vacation house in Vermont like the one that Katie McCormick likes to talk about whenever someone will listen, and maybe Max is there right now. Far away from where the police would look.

That would be a smart thing for Mrs. Patterson to do.

Take Max so far away that the police would never find him.

Far away from the parents she doesn't trust and the school she thinks he shouldn't go to.

But that is okay. If I stay with Mrs. Patterson, she will eventually lead me to Max. Even if he is in Vermont, I will find him.

I check my hand. I hold it in front of my face. I feel bad for doing it, but I remind myself that I am checking for Max's sake even though I know I am checking for my own sake, too. More for my own sake. My hand is still solid. I am okay. I am not disappearing. And Max is okay. Somewhere Max is okay.

I decide to search the house again while I wait for Mrs. Patterson to get back. I feel like a police person on television, looking for clues, and that is exactly what I am doing. Looking for clues that will lead me to Max.

I notice a closet in the kitchen that I did not notice before, and I look inside even though I know that Max is not inside. It would be a silly place to hide a boy, and besides, Max would have heard me calling if he was in this closet. It is dark inside but I can see the outline of cans and boxes in the gloom. It is a pantry.

I find more pictures of Mrs. Patterson's son, on the mantel over both fireplaces and on the little tables in the living room. I don't find pictures of Mr. Patterson, which seems strange at first, but then I realize that Mr. Patterson is probably the one who is taking all the pictures. Max's dad does the same thing. He doesn't show up in many of Max's photographs because he is always behind the camera instead of in front of it.

There is not a lot of stuff in Mrs. Patterson's house. No piles of magazines. No bowls of fruit. No toys on the floor or baskets of dirty clothes near the washer machine. No dishes in the sink or empty coffee cups on the kitchen table. The house reminds me of our house when Max's parents were trying to sell it. Max was in kindergarten and Max's mom and dad decided that they needed a bigger house in case

Max ever got a brother or a sister, so they stuck a big sign in the front lawn, kind of like a price tag without any price, so people would know that the house was for sale. A lady named Meg would bring strangers into the house when nobody was home so they could look around and decide if they wanted to buy it.

Max hated the thought of moving. He hates change, and switching houses would be a big change. He got stuck a few times when he found out that strangers were coming over, so eventually Max's mom and dad stopped telling him that people were coming over.

I think that is why we never moved. They were worried that Max might get stuck forever if we moved to a new house.

Every time the strangers came over to look at the house, Max's parents would push all of the papers and magazines into a kitchen drawer and throw all the clothes on the floor into a closet. And they would make their bed, which they never do. They had to make it look like no one in the house ever forgot to put anything away so the strangers would see what the house looked like if perfect people lived inside.

That's what Mrs. Patterson's house looks like. It looks ready for strangers to come over. But I don't think that Mrs. Patterson is trying to sell her house. I think that this is just how she is.

I check the upstairs and the basement again, looking for closets that I did not see the first time or any clues about where Max might be. I find more pictures of Mrs. Patterson's baby and a closet in the upstairs hallway. Max is not inside.

In the basement, I find three cupboards, but they are dark and dusty and too small for Max to be inside. I find boxes of nails and a pile of bricks and plastic containers full of clothes and a lawn mower, but no Mrs. Patterson and no Max.

It's okay. Mrs. Patterson will walk through the front door any minute. Even though I know that Max will not be with her, that will be okay. Just finding Mrs. Patterson will be enough. She will lead me to Max.

I am standing in the dining room, looking out the sliding glass doors at the pond when I hear the door finally open. The shadows from the trees are dipping into the pond now and the orange sparkles on the ripples of the water are almost gone. The sun is too low to sparkle anymore today. I turn and walk into the kitchen, toward the hallway that leads to the front door, when I see that it was not the front door that I heard opening.

It was the basement door.

Mrs. Patterson is walking through the basement door. She is coming into the kitchen through the basement door.

I was just in the basement a couple minutes ago, looking at the cupboards and finding boxes of nails. Mrs. Patterson was not in the basement two minutes ago and now she is stepping through the doorway to the basement and closing the door behind her.

I am more scared than ever.

thirty-five

My first thought is that Mrs. Patterson is an imaginary friend and I did not realize it. Maybe she can pass through doors like me and somehow she came home and went into the basement without me hearing her.

I know right away that this is ridiculous.

But she must be something special, because somehow she was in the basement without me seeing her. Maybe she can make herself invisible or maybe she can shrink herself.

I know that this is ridiculous, too.

I watch as she opens the refrigerator and removes some chicken. She places a pan on the stove and begins cooking the chicken. While it sizzles, she starts making rice.

Chicken and rice. Max's favorite meal. Max does not eat many things, but he always eats chicken and white rice. He likes foods that don't have bright colors.

I want to go into the basement again and find the closet or staircase that I must have missed. Maybe Mrs. Patterson has a basement under the basement. Maybe there is a door in the floor that I did not see because I don't usually look for doors in the floor.

But I'm afraid to leave Mrs. Patterson again. I will wait. She is making dinner for Max. I know it. I will follow her when she is done.

Mrs. Patterson does not make a mess when she cooks. When she is finished with the cutting board, she rinses it and puts it in the dishwasher. When she is done pouring the rice into a glass bowl, she puts the box away in the pantry. Max's mom would like Mrs. Patterson if she had not stolen Max. They both like things neat. Max's mom says, "Clean as you go." But Max's dad still piles dishes in the sink and leaves them there overnight.

Mrs. Patterson slides a red tray on the counter. She wipes it with a paper towel even though it looks clean. She puts two paper plates and two plastic forks and two paper cups on the tray.

Max likes to eat from paper plates and paper cups because he knows that they are clean. Max does not trust people or dishwashers to get his plates and forks and cups clean. Max's mom and dad don't always let Max eat from paper and plastic stuff, but sometimes they do, especially if Max's mom is trying to get Max to try something new.

But how does Mrs. Patterson know that Max likes paper plates and plastic forks? She has never come over for dinner. Then I realize that Mrs. Patterson has been with Max for three days. She has learned that Max does not trust dishwashers.

Mrs. Patterson puts rice and chicken on both plates and then pours apple juice into both cups.

Max's favorite drink is apple juice.

She lifts the tray and heads down the stairs to the basement. I follow.

At the bottom of the stairs, Mrs. Patterson turns left into the part of the basement with the carpeting and the green table with the net and the television.

There is a door under the carpet somewhere. I know it. Max is probably right underneath me. In a basement's basement.

Then Mrs. Patterson walks across the room, past the green table and to a wall with a painting of flowers hanging from it and a shelf stretching across the top. I wait for her to bend over to pull back the carpet, but instead she reaches up and pushes a little piece of the shelf into the wall. It clicks and then a part of the wall moves. Mrs. Patterson pushes it until there is space enough for her to enter. She does and then a second later the walls slides back and the shelf clicks again. It has popped back into place. The parts of the wall where the secret door and the wall are invisible. There is wallpaper on the wall and the place where a tiny space between the wall and the door might be is hidden by the design in the wallpaper. It is camouflaged. Even though I know the door is there, I cannot see the outline of the door anymore. It is a super-secret door.

Max is behind that super-secret door.

I walk across the room. I am finally going to see Max. I step into the door but I do not pass through. I bump into the door and fall backward onto the floor. The door in the wall is impossible to see so I must have missed it. I move to the left and try again, walking slower this time in case I miss it again. I bump into the wall again. I try this three more times but bump into the wall each time.

There is a door here, but it is like the elevator doors at the hospital. When Max imagined me, he did not imagine super-secret-doors-that-look-like-walls were doors, so I cannot pass through.

Max is on the other side of this door that is not a door. The only way I can get in is if Mrs. Patterson opens the door again.

I must wait.

I sit on the green table and stare at the wall. I cannot step away and cannot daydream. When Mrs. Patterson opens that door, there will be just enough space for her to exit, which means I have to squeeze into that space as soon as she is clear of it. If I am too slow, I will not be able to get through.

I wait.

I stare at the painting of the flowers, waiting for it to move. I try to only think about the door that is a wall but I start to wonder what it is like behind the wall. There must be a room behind the wall, and it must be big enough for Mrs. Patterson and Max to eat dinner together. But it is underground and has no windows and is probably locked so Max must feel trapped, too. And that means that he might be stuck. Or maybe he was stuck but now he is unstuck.

I want to see Max but I am afraid to see what he looks like after three days behind a wall. Even if he is unstuck, he cannot be good.

I wait.

The wall finally moves. I jump off the edge of the table and step over to it. The wall opens and Mrs. Patterson steps through the opening. She looks back after passing through, giving me plenty of time to pass through the opening.

I think she is looking back to make sure that Max is not trying to follow her, but I am wrong. I take one look at the room behind the wall and know that I am wrong.

Max is not trying to escape.

I cannot believe my eyes.

thirty-six

The light is blinding. Maybe it is just because I have been standing in the dimly lit basement for a long time, waiting for the wall to move, but the room is brighter than any underground room I could have ever imagined.

As my eyes adjust to the light, I can see that the room is painted in yellow and green and red and blue. It reminds me of Mr. Michaud's kindergarten classroom, with his giant caterpillar crawling over the white board and his students' finger-painting spread all over the walls. It reminds me of a box of crayons. The boxes with just eight or ten different colors inside. The room is an explosion of color.

There is a bed in the shape of a race car. It is painted red and gold. It even has a steering wheel sticking out of the headboard. There is a dresser with every drawer painted a different color. There is a door on the far side of the room with the word BOYS written on it in red, squiggly letters. There is a desk with a tall pile of drawing paper and an even taller pile of graph paper, which is Max's favorite kind of paper. Good for drawing maps and planning battles. There are model airplanes hanging from the ceiling on wires. There are toy soldiers and tanks and army trucks and airplanes everywhere. Snipers on a shelf over the bed. A line of tanks atop a beanbag chair. Columns of soldiers marching across the center of the room. An airfield on the bed with anti-aircraft guns on the pillows surrounding it. A battle has taken place recently. I can tell by the way the soldiers and tanks are spaced out.

Green has defeated gray, I think. It doesn't look like gray stood a chance.

The room is bigger than I thought. Much bigger. There are train tracks running all the way around the room, disappearing under the bed and popping out on the other side. I do not see a train. Probably parked underneath the bed.

There are dozens, maybe hundreds of *Star Wars* figures standing on the dresser, and *Star Wars* spaceships on one side of the room, organized like Max would like them organized. The X-wing fighters need a runway to take off, so there are no other spaceships parked in front of them. The *Millennium Falcon* can fly straight up, so it is surrounded by tie fighters and twin-pod cloud cars. There are stormtroopers and Cloud City troopers standing next to each spaceship, waiting for Max's orders to launch.

I've never seen so much *Star Wars* stuff in one place except at the toy store. Neither has Max. He probably has the biggest collection of *Star Wars* stuff of anyone in his class, but this collection makes his collection at home look puny.

There are enough stormtroopers here to make a small army.

There are *six* X-wing fighters. Max has two, and even that is a lot.

There is a television hanging on the wall across from the bed and a pile of DVDs underneath it. A stack almost as tall as Max. It is so tall that it looks like it could fall at any second.

There are three green helicopters parked on top of it with snipers guarding the perimeter. The DVD is *Starship Troopers*. Max loves that movie.

There is a carpet on the floor. It is dark blue with stars and planets and moons everywhere. It is new and thick and I wish I could sink my toes into it like Max can. But my feet only touch the idea of the carpet, so they do not sink in. They stay on top.

There is a gumball machine by the bed.

The blue backpack from Mrs. Patterson's car is sitting on the bed. It is open. I can see LEGOs peeking out from underneath the flap.

LEGOs to keep Max *engaged* while he was in the backseat of the car. To distract him until she got him home.

And in the center of the room, there are more LEGOs. Thousands of LEGOs in sizes and shapes that even I have never even seen before. There are large LEGOs and small LEGOs and mechanical LEGOs, the kind that need batteries and the kind that Max loves the most. There are more here than Max could ever dream of. They have been sorted into piles according to size and shape, and I know right away that Max has made those piles. They look like the kinds of piles that Max makes. Lined up like the soldiers on the floor, all the same distance from one another.

And sitting in front of those piles like a LEGO general, with his back to me, is Max.

I found him.

thirty-seven

I can't believe it. I am standing in the same room as Max. I wait one more second before saying his name, just staring at him like his mom does at night when he is asleep after she has sneaked her kisses. I never understood why she just stares at him like that, but now I do.

I never want to stop staring.

I missed Max but I did not know how much I missed Max until now. Now I know what it feels like to miss someone so much that you can't describe it. I would have to invent new words to describe it.

Finally, I say his name. "Max," I say. "I'm here."

Max screams louder than I have ever heard him scream before.

His scream doesn't last long. Just a couple seconds. I am sure that Mrs. Patterson will come running in any second to see what is wrong, but then I realize that I could not hear Mrs. Patterson and Max while I was waiting on the other side of the wall. And Max couldn't hear me when I was screaming his name earlier.

I think this room is soundproof.

There are lots of soundproof rooms on television. Mostly in movies but sometimes in TV shows, too.

Max does not turn around to look at me as he screams, and this is a bad sign. It means he might get stuck. It means that he is getting stuck right now. I walk over to Max but I keep my distance. As his scream starts to fade, I say, "Max, I'm here." I say exactly the same thing that I said before he started to scream. I speak softly and quickly. I move as I speak so that I am standing in front of him, with his army of LEGO piles between us. I can see that he has been building a submarine, and it looks like the propeller might actually move on its own when it is finished.

"Max," I say again. "I'm here."

Max is no longer screaming. He is breathing hard now. Max's mom calls this *hyperventilating*. It sounds like he has just finished running a thousand mile race and now he is trying to catch his breath. Sometimes this will end with Max getting stuck. I say again, "Max. I'm here. It's okay. I'm here. It's okay."

Touching Max would be the worst thing that I could do, if I could touch him. Yelling at Max would be bad, too. It would be like pushing him into his inside stuck world. Instead, I speak softly and quickly again and again. I reach for him with my voice. It is like throwing him a rope and begging him to grab on. Sometimes it works and I can pull him out before he ends up stuck and sometimes it doesn't. But it is the only thing I know that helps.

And it works.

I can tell.

His breathing is slowing down, but his breathing would slow down even if he was getting stuck. I can tell by his eyes. They see me. His eyes see my eyes. He is not disappearing. He is reappearing. Coming back to the world. His eyes smile at me and I know that he is back.

"Budo," he says. He sounds happy, and this makes me happy.

"Max," I say back. I suddenly feel like Max's mom. I want to leap over the piles of LEGO and grab Max by the neck and squeeze him tight. But I cannot. Max is probably happy that the LEGO piles are separating us. They let his eyes smile at me without having to worry that I might touch him.

Max knows that I can't touch him, but he might think this is different. We have never been separated for three days.

"Are you okay?" I ask, sitting down on the floor in front of Max, keeping the LEGOs between us.

"Yes," Max says. "You scared me. I didn't think I would see you anymore. I am building a submarine."

"Yes," I say. "I see."

I don't know what to say next. I try to think about the best thing to say. The thing that will save Max. I feel like I should be sneaky and try to find out how tricked he is, but then I think that I should just find out what is going on no matter what. This is serious business. Not lies about lost homework or throwing chicken nuggets in the cafeteria.

This is even more serious than Tommy Swinden.

I decide not to be sneaky. I decide not to dance with the devil in the pale moonlight. This is something Mrs. Gosk says when she thinks that a student is lying. She says, "You are dancing with the devil in the pale moonlight, Mr. Woods. Watch yourself."

I am dancing with a real devil in the pale moonlight now and I have no time to waste.

"Max," I say, trying to sound like a Mrs. Gosk. "Mrs. Patterson is bad and we have to get you out of here." I don't actually know how to do this, but I know I can't do anything if Max doesn't agree.

"She is not bad," Max says.

"She stole you," I say. "She tricked you and stole you from school."

"Mrs. Patterson says I shouldn't go to school. She says that school is not a safe place for me."

"That's not true," I say.

"Yes, it is," Max says, and it sounds like he is getting upset. "You know it. Tommy Swinden is going to kill me if I stay in school. Ella and Jennifer are always touching me. Touching my food. Kids make fun of me. Mrs. Patterson knows about Tommy Swinden and the other kids, and she said that school is not a good place for me."

"Your mom and dad think school is a safe place for you. And they are your mom and dad."

"Moms and dads don't always know best. That's what Mrs. Patterson says."

"Max, you are locked up in a basement. That is bad. Only bad people lock kids in basements. We have to get you out."

Max's voice softens. "If I tell Mrs. Patterson that I am happy, then she will be happy."

I don't understand what Max means. Before I can ask him, he speaks again.

"If Mrs. Patterson is happy, she won't touch me or hurt me."

"Mrs. Patterson told you that?"

"No. But I think it," Max says. "I think if I tried to get away she might get real angry."

"I don't think so, Max. I don't think she wants to hurt you. She just wants to steal you." But as I say this, I wonder if Max is right. Max doesn't understand people very well, but there are times when he understands people better than anyone else. He might not see how sucking on his fingers in the middle of class makes him look silly, but he was the only one who knew that Mrs. Gosk was sad on the day her mom died. Max knew right away, even though Mrs. Gosk did a good job hiding it, and the rest of the kids didn't know until the next day when Mrs. Gosk told them. So I wonder if he is right about Mrs. Patterson, too. Maybe she is more of a devil than I thought.

"Don't you want to leave?" I ask.

"This is a good place," Max says. "It has lots of good stuff. And you are here. You promise that you will never leave?"

"Yes, I promise. But what about your mom and dad?"

I want to say more. I want to list all the things that Max will miss if he stayed locked up in this room but I can't. I realize that in all of Max's life, the only things that he might miss are his mom and dad. He has no friends. His grandma died last year, and his other grandma lives in Florida and never sees him. His aunt and uncles are nervous and quiet around him. His cousins avoid him. All he has is his mom and dad and his things and me. And his things might be just as important as his mom and dad. That is a sad thing to say, but it is a true thing to say, too. If Max had to choose between his LEGOs and his army men or his mom or dad, I don't know what he would choose.

I think Max's mom knows this, too. I think his dad probably knows, too, but he lies to himself and says it isn't true.

"I can see Mom and Dad again," Max says. "Mrs. Patterson told me. Someday. But not now. She is going to take care of me and keep me safe and keep me away from school. She calls me 'her little lad.'"

"What about her son?" I ask. "Have you met him?"

"Mrs. Patterson doesn't have a son anymore. He died. She told me."

I do not speak. I wait.

Max looks down at his submarine and tries to fit pieces into the unfinished side. After a minute, he starts speaking again. "He died because his daddy did not take care of him good enough. So he died."

I think about asking where Mr. Patterson is right now, but I do not. Wherever Mr. Patterson is, he is not here. He is not a part of this. I know this now.

"Do you like it here?" I ask.

"It's a good room," Max says. "It has a lot of good stuff. It was a mess when I got here but Mrs. Patterson let me fix it. All the LEGOs were mixed up and the *Star Wars* stuff was in the toy box and all the army men were still in their boxes. All wrapped in plastic and stuff. And those DVDs were in a box, too. Now everything is right. She even gave me a piggy bank and a bunch of pennies, and I got to put the pennies inside. There were so many that they almost didn't fit."

Max points at the desk. There is a small, metallic piggy bank on the corner of the desk. It has tiny metal legs and metal ears and a metal snout. It is tarnished and old. "It was Mrs. Patterson's when she was little," Max says, seeming to read my mind.

I think that Mrs. Patterson was smart to let Max fix the room. I bet that fixing the room helped Max get through the first day. Max can't leave his LEGOs unless they are sorted into the right piles, and in kindergarten, he used to sort the LEGO center before he went home or it would bother him all night. I bet that Max stayed busy during his first day here, if he wasn't stuck.

"Max, if you are afraid of Mrs. Patterson, then this is not a good place."

"I am not afraid of her as long as she is happy. And now you are here. I feel a lot better now. As long as you are here, everything will be fine. I know it. I told Mrs. Patterson that I needed you, and she said that maybe you would come. And you did. Now we can just be together here."

That is when I realize it. I will never disappear as long as Max stays in this room. Max's mom and dad are always pushing Max to grow up, to meet new people, to try new things. Max's dad wants him to join something called Farm League next year and Max's mom wants to see if he can play the piano. They send him to school every day even though Max told them that Tommy Swinden is going to kill him. I never thought about it before, but Max's mom and dad are my biggest danger.

They want Max to grow up.

Mrs. Patterson wants to do the opposite. She wants to keep Max in this room made especially for Max. She wants to keep Max here and keep him safe. She is not going to send a ransom note or chop Max up into tiny pieces. She just wants to keep him here like he belongs to her. All locked up and safe. She is a devil in the pale moonlight, but she is not a movie or television devil. She is a real devil, and maybe I should be dancing with her after all.

If Max stays here, I could live for as long as Max lives. I could live longer than any imaginary friend ever.

Maybe if Max stays here in this room, we could both be happily ever after.

thirty-eight

Max and I are playing with army men when the door opens and Mrs. Patterson comes in. She is wearing a pink nightgown.

I feel embarrassed. I am looking at a teacher in her pajamas.

Max does not look at her. His head stays down. He is staring at the pile of army men in front of him. They were just hit by something called a cruise missile. It was actually just a crayon that Max dropped from a plastic airplane, but it blew up all the neat little rows of men by the time Max was done with them.

"You've been playing with your army men?" Mrs. Patterson asks. She sounds surprised.

"Yes," Max says. "Budo is here."

"Oh, he is? I'm so happy for you, Max." She really does look happy. I think she might be relieved to hear that Max has someone to play with, even if she doesn't think I'm real. She probably thinks that Max is getting adjusted to his new room, and that is why I am back.

She doesn't know how hard it was for me to get here.

"It's time for bed," Mrs. Patterson says. "Did you brush your teeth yet?"

"No," Max says, still looking down. There is a gray sniper in his hand. He turns it over and over in his hand as he speaks.

"Will you brush your teeth?" she asks.

"Yes," Max says.

"Would you like me to tuck you in?"

"No," Max says. He says this fast. He answers her question fast, and he says the word *no* fast, even though it's just the word *no*.

"Okay, but you need to be in bed, lights out, in fifteen minutes."

"Yes," Max says.

"Okay, then. Good night, Max." Her voice gets higher as she says the last three words, as if she is waiting for him to speak. She is waiting for him to say "Good night" in return and to finish the little good-night song. She stands by the doorway for a minute, waiting for Max to answer.

Max stares at his sniper and says nothing.

When she realizes that Max is not going to answer, her face falls. Her eyes and cheeks and head all drop, and for an instant, I feel bad for Mrs. Patterson. She may have stolen Max, but she will not hurt Max. In this tiny moment of sadness, I know this for sure.

She loves Max.

I know you can't just steal a little boy from his parents because you lost your own little boy, and I know that she is probably still a devil and a monster. But in that split second, she looks more like a sad lady than a monster. I think she thought that Max would make her happy, but so far he has not.

She finally leaves, closing the door behind her without saying another word.

"Will she come back to check on you?" I ask.

"No," Max says.

"So why not play all night?"

"I don't know," Max says. "She won't peek through the door, but I think she would still know somehow."

Max walks to the door marked BOYS. He opens it. There is a bathroom on the other side of the door. He takes a toothbrush down off the sink, squeezes some Crest Mint toothpaste onto the brush and begins brushing.

"How did she know to get you Crest Kids gel?" I ask. It is the only toothpaste that Max will use.

"She didn't," he says between brushings. "I told her."

I could ask more about the toothpaste but don't. Either Max got stuck on the first night when she tried to get him to use Colgate or Crest Cool Mint (which happened once when Max's dad tried to change the toothpaste) or she asked him which toothpaste he wanted before he needed to brush.

She probably asked Max. Even though Mrs. Patterson changed every single thing in Max's entire life, she also understands that any change is trouble for Max. Max's dad understands it, too, but he keeps trying to change things anyway, even when he knows that Max will get stuck.

His mom understands, too, but she tries to change things slowly, so Max won't notice. Max's dad just changes things, like the toothpaste.

"This room is nice," I say as Max changes into pajamas. They are camouflage pajamas. They are not the pajamas that he usually wears, but I can tell that he likes them a lot. When he is done putting them on, he walks into the bathroom to look at himself in the mirror.

"This place is pretty nice," I say again.

Max does not answer.

I keep thinking about the way he turned that army man over and over in his hand when Mrs. Patterson was talking to him, and the way he would not look at her. Max said that this was a good room and that we could just stay here together. I believe him, but I think there are words behind those words that Max is not saying.

Max is afraid. Max is sad.

Part of me wants to forget about the way he was staring at that army man. It wants me to wait a few days or a month or even a year because Max will eventually like his new room and maybe even Mrs. Patterson. It wants me to believe that Max will be fine like he said he will because that means that I get to exist forever.

But another part of me wants to save Max right now, before it's too late. Before something that I can't see yet happens. That part of me thinks that I am Max's only chance and I have to do something soon. Now.

And I am standing in between the two parts of me. Stuck like Max. I want to save both of us but I don't know if I can.

I don't know how much of Max I am allowed to lose to save myself.

thirty-nine

Max is finally asleep.

He turned out the lights and climbed into bed after brushing his teeth. I sat in a chair next to his bed and waited for him to arrange the pillows. Just like home.

Except there are nine nightlights in the room, six more than Max has in his bedroom at home, so it isn't very dark.

I waited for Max to say something, but he just lay there, staring at the ceiling. I asked him if he wanted to talk, because we usually talk before he goes to sleep, but he just shook his head. After a little while he whispered, "Good night, Budo." That was it.

After a long time, he fell asleep.

I've been sitting here ever since, wondering what to do. I listen to Max breathing. He tosses and turns a little, but he does not wake up. If I close my eyes and just listen to him, it is almost like we are home again.

If we were home, I would be sitting in the living room by now, watching television with Max's parents.

I already miss them.

I feel trapped inside this room.

I am trapped inside this room. I am a prisoner, just like Max. I stare at the door and wonder how I could ever save Max when I can't even escape myself.

Then I know what to do.

I stand up and walk to the door. I take three steps into and then through the door, and a second later I am standing back in the part of the basement with the little tennis table and the stairs. There are no nightlights in this room, so it is pitch-black.

I passed through the door on Max's side of the wall because it looks like a door. Max even called it a door. He had said that Mrs. Patterson would not peek through the door, which means that it is a door to Max, and if it is a door, I can pass through it. It is his idea of a door.

But the super-secret door on this side of the wall is not a door in Max's mind, so I cannot pass through it. In Max's mind it is a wall. Just to check, I turn and walk back toward the wall. It is so dark that I bump into it even harder than I had expected.

I was right. It's just a wall on this side.

This might not have been a good idea. If Max wakes up, I cannot get back into the room to let him know I am still here. I won't even know if he is awake. I have left Max alone again, and he will know it. I have made another big mistake.

I turn and walk along the edge of the room, feeling the wall to find my way, until I make it to the staircase. I climb the stairs slowly, holding the railing as I do, and then I pass through the door at the top of the stairs into the hallway between the kitchen and the living room. Mrs. Patterson is standing in the kitchen. There are Campbell's soup cans and boxes of Kraft macaroni and cheese on the kitchen table. Mrs. Patterson is packing the cans and boxes into a large cardboard box.

Those are two of Max's favorite foods.

Four other cardboard boxes are stacked on the table. The lids are closed so I cannot see what is inside them. For a second I think these boxes are important, but then I know that they are not. I am looking for clues to save Max, except there are no clues. Max is locked in a secret room in the basement and no one knows that he is here. This is not a mystery. It is just bad.

Mrs. Patterson finishes packing the rest of the soup and macaroni and cheese into the box and closes the lid. She adds it to the pile of boxes on the other side of the table. She moves to the sink to wash her hands. She hums as she washes.

When she is done, she walks past me and heads upstairs. I follow. There is nothing else for me to do. I cannot leave the house. Even though the secret room could not hold me, I am trapped inside this house. I do not know where I am or where anything else is. There are no gas stations or police stations or hospitals to visit. Max is here. I cannot leave without Max. I promised him that I would never leave, though I'm starting to think that if I am going to save him, I will have to.

There are cardboard boxes on the floor in Mrs. Patterson's bedroom that were not here earlier today. Mrs. Patterson opens her dresser and begins moving clothing from the dresser into the cardboard boxes. She is not moving all the clothes. She is picking and choosing. Now I think that the cardboard boxes might be a clue after all. Packing food into a box isn't normal, but it is not as strange as packing clothing into a cardboard box.

After she has filled five boxes with clothing and shoes and a bath-robe, she brings the boxes downstairs and adds them to the pile on the table. Then she goes back upstairs and brushes her teeth. *She is getting ready for bed,* I think, so I leave. She is the bad guy, but I still don't think it is right to watch her floss between her teeth and wash her face.

I go to the spare room and sit down in a chair to think. I need a plan.

I wish Graham was here.

forty

I hear Max's voice. He is calling my name. I stand up and run into the hallway. I am confused. His voice is not coming from the basement. It is coming from Mrs. Patterson's bedroom. I turn and run down the hall. I pass through the bedroom door into her room. The sun is peeking through Mrs. Patterson's bedroom window. I look right at it and am blinded for a second. I close my eyes and see orange spots float past my eyes. I can still hear Max calling my name. The sound is coming from this room, but it sounds far away, too, like he is under a blanket or locked in a closet. I open my eyes and see Mrs. Patterson. She is sitting up in bed, looking at her telephone. Except it isn't a telephone. It is bigger than a telephone and chunkier. It has a screen that Mrs. Patterson is staring at. Max's voice is coming from the not-a-phone.

I walk to the other side of the bed and sit down beside Mrs. Patterson. I look over her shoulder to see the not-a-phone. Max is on the screen. It is black and white and gray, but I can still see Max. He is sitting up in his bed, too, and he is screaming my name.

He sounds so afraid.

Mrs. Patterson and I stand up at the same time, she on one side of the bed and me on the other. She slides on a pair of slippers and leaves the room.

I follow.

She goes straight to the basement. I am right behind her. I can hear Max screaming on the not-a-phone but I can't hear him screaming through the wall. It's strange. He's right behind that wall but I can't hear a peep, even though I know he is screaming.

Mrs. Patterson opens the secret door and steps inside. His screams fill the room.

I stand behind Mrs. Patterson. I don't want Max to see me and say my name. He is screaming my name, but that's okay. I don't want Max to see me and say, "Budo! You're back! Where were you? Why were you with Mrs. Patterson?"

If he does, then Mrs. Patterson will know that I was outside of the secret room, spying on her.

I know this would not happen, because Mrs. Patterson does not believe that I am real, but I forget this in the first few seconds that I am back inside the room. It's easy to forget that people don't believe you exist.

When I first step inside, I am afraid. Afraid of being caught by Mrs. Patterson. Mrs. Patterson is a bad person and I do not want her to be mad at me, even if she does not believe in me.

"Max, it's alright," Mrs. Patterson says, moving toward his bed but stopping a few steps short of it, which is smart. Getting too close to Max when he is upset is the thing that most people want to do but should never do. Mrs. Patterson is one smart cookie.

She really is the devil in the pale moonlight.

"Budo!" Max screams again. It sounds one hundred times worse in real life. It is the worst thing I have ever heard. I feel like the worst friend in the world. As I step out from behind Mrs. Patterson, I wonder how I am ever going to leave Max alone today.

"I'm here, Max," I say.

"I'm sure he'll be back," Mrs. Patterson says, speaking immediately after me and making me think for a second that she can hear me.

"Budo!" Max screams again, but this time it's a happy scream. He sees me.

"Good morning, Max," I say. "I'm sorry. I got stuck outside the room."

"Stuck?" Max asks.

"What's stuck?" Mrs. Patterson asks.

"Budo was stuck," Max says. "Right?" He is looking at me when he asks this.

"Yes," I say. "I can tell you about it when we are alone." One of the things that I have learned is that it is too confusing for Max to talk to me and human persons at the same time, so I try to avoid it whenever I can.

"I'm sure that Budo can get himself unstuck," Mrs. Patterson says. "Nothing to fear."

"He's already unstuck," Max says.

"Oh, good," Mrs. Patterson says. She sounds like she just took a deep breath after being stuck underwater for a long time. "I'm so glad he's back."

"Okay," Max says. It sounds like a strange answer, but Max never knows what to say when people tell him how they feel. Most of the time he doesn't say anything. He just waits for the person to say something different. But "okay" is his safe answer.

"Can you get yourself dressed?" Mrs. Patterson asks. "I haven't even started your breakfast yet."

"Yes," Max says.

"Okay," Mrs. Patterson says. She stands by the door again, waiting. I am not sure if she is waiting for Max to say something or trying to think of something else to say. She looks sad either way. Max does not even notice her. He already has an X-wing fighter in his hands. He is pressing the button that makes the wings spread.

Mrs. Patterson sighs and then leaves.

When the door clicks shut, Max looks up from his toy. "Where were you?" he asks. I know that he is angry because he is looking at me when he asks this question, even though there is a *Star Wars* toy in his hand.

"I left the room last night but I couldn't get back in."

"Why not?" Max says. His eyes have returned to the spaceship.

"It's a door on this side but it's a wall on the other side," I say.

Max says nothing. This means he understands what I said or stopped caring about my answer. Usually I can tell which, but this time I can't.

He puts the X-wing fighter down on his pillow and steps out of bed. He walks over to the bathroom and opens the door. He turns and looks at me again. "Promise you'll never leave me alone again," he says.

I promise even though I know I will be leaving him shortly.

forty-one

I think about not telling Max that I am leaving. I think that it will be easier for him if I just sneak out. Then I realize that sneaking out would be easier for me. Not Max.

But I'm worried that Max might get so angry at me that he'll start unbelieving in me.

I wish I knew what to do.

I thought that Max would be trapped here forever, and that I would have time to figure things out. Make a plan. But now I'm worried that Max might not be trapped here forever, and that I am running out of time to help him before the time even started.

I was hoping that Max would fall in love with this place and maybe we could stay here forever. I know that it would be bad not to help Max, but I know that it would be bad to stop existing, too. Lions eat giraffes so they can survive even though the giraffes didn't do anything to the lions, and nobody thinks that the lions are wrong. Because existing is so important. It's the most important thing. So I know I should help Max and I want to help Max and I want to make the right decision, but I want to exist, too.

That's a lot of stuff to think about, and now I am worried that I will not have any more time to think.

Max finished breakfast and he is playing with the PlayStation. He is driving a car around a racetrack. I watch him play because Max likes it when I watch him play his video games. He doesn't talk to me or ask me any questions. He just needs me to watch.

The door swings open. Mrs. Patterson steps inside the room. She is wearing her school clothes and perfume. I can smell her before I can see her.

Not all imaginary friends can smell, but I can.

She smells like old flowers. She is wearing gray pants and a pink shirt and a jacket. She has a *Transformers* lunchbox in her hand.

"Max," she says. "I have to go to work." She speaks like she is dipping her voice into water to see how cold it is. She is slow and careful.

Max doesn't answer. It is hard for his mom and dad to get him to answer when he is playing a video game, so I am not sure if he is ignoring Mrs. Patterson on purpose.

"I have your lunch packed in your lunchbox," she says. "Soup in your thermos and a yogurt and an orange. I know it mustn't be fun eating the same thing every day, but I can't give you anything that you might choke on when I'm not here."

She waits for Max to say something but he just keeps steering his electronic car around the TV track. "But don't worry," she says. "Pretty soon we'll be together all day. Okay?"

Max is still silent. Still staring at the screen.

"I'll miss you today, Max," Mrs. Patterson says, and it sounds like she is reaching to him with her voice now, like I sometimes do. She is throwing him a rope but I already know that he will not reach for it. He is playing video games. Nothing else matters.

"I miss you every day, Max," she says. "And I want you to know that everything that I am doing is for you. Pretty soon things will be much better. Okay?"

Now I want Max to answer. I want him to ask Mrs. Patterson what she is talking about. How are things going to change? When are they going to change? What is she planning?

Instead, he stares at the screen as his car moves around a track.

"Good-bye, Max. I'll see you soon."

She wants to say "I love you." I know it. I can see those three words hanging on her lips. And I believe that she does love Max. Loves him a lot. I feel bad for Mrs. Patterson again. She has stolen Max, and even though she says that it is for his own good, I know that she wants to have a little boy again. And the little boy she stole talks only a little bit more than her dead little boy.

Mrs. Patterson leaves the room and closes the door behind her. As the door clicks shut, Max looks up. He stares at the door for a moment, and then his eyes return to his game.

I wait by the door, watching Max play his game. I count to one hundred. I open my mouth to speak and then I count to one hundred again.

When I am done counting the second hundred, I finally speak. "I am leaving, too, Max," I say.

"What?" Max says. He looks up from his game.

This is not easy because I have to tell Max something important and make him understand, but I also have no time. I was afraid that if I left the room before Mrs. Patterson was walking out the door, she might hear Max scream in her not-a-phone and come back to the room, maybe stay home from work. I need her to be walking into the garage right now but I have no way of knowing if she is. I am just guessing. But I counted to one hundred twice, so she has had plenty of time to get to the car. Probably too much time. I might already be too late.

"I am leaving, Max," I say. "But only for the day. I am going to school with Mrs. Patterson so I can check on Mrs. Gosk and see if your mom and dad are okay. Then I'll be back with her after school."

"I want to go, too," Max says.

I didn't expect this. I don't know what to say. I stand with my mouth open until the words come back to me. "I know," I say. "But I can't get you out of the room. You can't pass through the door like I can."

"I want to go, too!" Max shouts. "I want to see Mrs. Gosk and Mommy and Daddy! I want to see Mommy and Daddy!"

Max never calls his mom and dad *Mommy* and *Daddy*. When I hear him say these words I think that I will never be able to leave this room. I will never be able to leave Max again because doing so would be too sad and too mean.

"I'll find a way to get you out of this room," I say to Max. I say it to make him happy, but as the words come out of my mouth I realize that I did not need any time to decide what to do. I am not a lion and Max is not a giraffe. I am Budo and Max is my friend, and there was only one right thing to do all along. It doesn't mean that I have to stop existing, but it means that I have to stop thinking only about me existing.

That means I have to leave now.

"Max, I am going. But I'll be back. And I'll make sure you see your mom and dad soon. I promise."

This is the second promise I have made to Max this morning. I am about to break the first.

Max screams as I turn toward the door. *"No, no, no, no!"* he shouts.

Max will get stuck if I leave.

If pass through the door, I will not be able to get back into the room until Mrs. Patterson opens the door again after school.

I step through the door anyway, knowing that the hard thing and the right thing are usually the same thing.

I ask someone who I know is not listening to forgive me for breaking my promise to Max and leaving my friend behind.

Sound returns as I step into the basement. Max's silent room is behind me and the hum of the furnace and the swish and drip of water in the pipes fills this room. I know that Max is screaming. He is probably pounding on the door right behind me but I cannot hear him. I am glad. Imagining him getting stuck behind the wall fills me with sadness and guilt. Hearing the real thing would be worse.

A door slams upstairs. I suddenly remember what I need to do. I run across the room and up the stairs to the first floor. I turn in the hallway and look into the kitchen. The cardboard boxes that were stacked on the table last night are gone. I do not see Mrs. Patterson.

Then I hear the sound of an engine starting, followed a second later by the clankity sound of the garage door opening.

I think about running to the garage but decide that it is too late. I turn right and head to the front door. I pass through it and step outside, tripping on the stoop that I did not know existed. I tumble to the ground, bouncing off a stone walkway that wraps around the house and leads to the driveway. I pull myself up, running before I am even standing upright. My knuckles drag on the ground for my first few steps. I run around the bend to the front of the house and see the driveway that stretches down to the road. Mrs. Patterson's car is already halfway down the driveway. Her car is facing toward the road so she is not driving slowly like people who are backing up do.

I will not make it to the car in time. It is already too far away. Max never imagined that I could run that fast. He never imagined that I would need to run that fast.

But I run anyway. I cannot imagine spending the day in Mrs. Patterson's house, knowing that Max is trapped behind a wall and I cannot reach him. I run as fast as I can down the hill, meeting the driveway halfway down. I am running so fast that I am on the edge of falling, half running and half tumbling, and even so, I will not catch Mrs. Patterson.

Then I see it. A car coming down the road. A green car that will pass by Mrs. Patterson's driveway. Mrs. Patterson will need to slow down and maybe even stop to let the car pass.

I have a chance.

And just as I begin to think that I can make it, I cross over the edge from running into tumbling and I am rolling on the pavement, end over end. I hold my arms against my ears to protect my head, and then somehow, I roll over and push up, and a second later I am running again, still out of control but in the right direction, toward the bottom of the driveway and Mrs. Patterson's car. My feet are flailing and my arms are outstretched, trying to help me keep my balance, but I am on my feet and moving.

Her car has stopped at the end of the driveway and the green car is passing by. I veer left off the driveway and onto the grass. I will not reach the bottom of the driveway in time but maybe I can meet the car as it turns onto the street. I point my body at the far corner of the front lawn, where the grass meets a stone wall and a line of trees. I run as fast as I can to that corner as Mrs. Patterson's car turns and accelerates. I will not make it unless I jump. As I reach the edge of the lawn, where the grass meets pavement, I jump and close my eyes, expecting to bounce off the fender or the wheel of Mrs. Patterson's car.

Instead, I feel the almost silent *whoosh* that accompanies every passing through a door, and a second later, I am lying in the backseat of the car, crumpled on the floor, trying to catch my breath.

I can hear Mrs. Patterson. She is singing about hammering. Hammering in the morning and hammering in the evening.

forty-two

Mrs. Patterson sings the hammer song twice and then turns on the radio. She is listening to the news. I listen to hear if there is news about Max. There is not.

I wonder if she is listening for news about Max, too.

We have been driving on a highway for a long time, which is strange since Mrs. Patterson lives so close to the school. Our ride from the school to her house last night took less than fifteen minutes, and I don't remember driving on a highway to get there.

The clock on the dashboard says 7:36. The first bell rings at 8:30 so we still have lots of time to get there, but this highway driving is making me nervous.

Where are we going?

I try not to think about Max. I try to stop imagining Max trapped behind that wall, all alone. I try not to hear his voice crying for me. I tell myself to pay attention to the road and to try to read the green signs and to watch Mrs. Patterson for clues but my imagination keeps imagining Max, screaming and crying and pounding on the walls for help.

"I am helping," I want to tell Max, but even if I could, I know he wouldn't believe me. It's hard to help when you have to break promises and leave your friend alone behind a wall.

I hear a roar over my head and know that it is an airplane. I have never heard a plane flying so low but I have seen and heard them on television and know that this is a big plane somewhere over our heads. A jumbo jet.

I look out the window. I look up. I want to see the plane but I do not. A green sign above the road reads WELCOME TO BRADLEY INTERNATIONAL AIRPORT. There are other words on the sign but I do not read fast enough to read all the words. I am happy that I was able to read the word *international*, because that is not an easy word. I look ahead and see low buildings and tall parking garages and buses and cars and lots of signs everywhere. I have never been to the airport before but I expected to see airplanes. I see none. I can hear them but cannot see a single one.

Mrs. Patterson turns off the main road and drives down and around to a gate. She stops the car in front of a machine, rolls down her window and reaches out to press a button. There is a sign on the machine that says LONG-TERM PARKING. I do not know what *Long Term Parking* means, but I am starting to wonder if I have made another mistake. Is Mrs. Patterson flying away somewhere? Is she worried that the police are about to find Max? I have seen people arrested in airports on television before. They are always bad guys trying to leave the country. I don't know why the police don't just leave the country, too, and arrest the bad guys in the new country, but maybe this is what Mrs. Patterson is doing. Maybe she knows that Mrs. Gosk or the police chief have solved the mystery and know who took Max, and now she has to escape or end up in jail.

The machine makes a humming sound and then spits out a ticket. Mrs. Patterson drives into a parking lot that is full of cars. There must be hundreds of cars and there is a parking garage right next to the parking lot that is full of cars, too.

We drive up and down the rows. We drive past empty spots but Mrs. Patterson does not park in any of them. She is driving like she has a place to go instead of a place to find.

Finally, she slows down and parks the car in an empty spot. She gets out. I get out, too. I am too far from home to get lost now. Wherever Mrs. Patterson goes, I go. She opens the trunk. The boxes that were stacked on top of the kitchen table are piled inside. She lifts a box from the trunk, turns, and walks across the aisle to the other side of the parking lot. She walks down the aisle past three cars and then stops at a van. A huge van. A bus, really. It's one of those houses on wheels, I think. A house-van-bus thingy. Mrs. Patterson reaches in her pocket and removes a key. She puts the key in a door and opens it. It's like the door on Max's school bus. It's regular-sized. Mrs. Patterson climbs three steps and turns left into the house-van-bus thingy.

I follow.

There is a living room inside, right behind the driver's seat. There is a couch and a cushy chair and a table that is attached to the floor so it won't move around. There is a television hanging on the wall and a bunk bed over the couch. Mrs. Patterson puts the box on the couch and turns around and exits. I follow her back to the car and watch as she removes a second box and brings it back to the bus. She puts the box beside the first and turns to leave again. I do not follow this time. I stay. She has six more boxes to bring over and I want to take a second to look at the rest of the bus. I walk past the living room into a narrow hallway. There is a closed door to my right and a little kitchen to my left. There is a sink and a stove and a microwave oven and a refrigerator. I pass through the door to the right and am standing in a tiny bathroom with a sink and a toilet.

A bathroom inside the bus.

If Max's school bus had a bathroom, he would never have to worry about bonus poops again.

Actually, I don't think Max could ever poop on a school bus, even if it had a toilet.

I step back through the door and into the narrow hallway. There is another closed door at the end of the hallway. I look behind me and see Mrs. Patterson dropping two more boxes onto the couch. Four all together now. Two or three more trips and then she'll be done.

I step through the door at the end of the hallway. As I open my eyes, the first shiver of my life runs down my spine. I have heard this expression before but never understood it until now.

I cannot believe what I am seeing.

I am standing in a bedroom.

It is the same bedroom where Max is trapped right now.

It is smaller, and there are fewer lamps, and there are two oval-shaped windows on either side of the bus that are covered by curtains, but the walls are the same colors as Max's room in Mrs. Patterson's basement and the bed is the same race-car bed with the same sheets and the same pillows and the same blankets. The same rug is covering the floor. And the space is filled with LEGOs and *Star Wars* toys and army men. Just as many as are in Max's room in the basement. Maybe more. There is a television stuck to the wall and another PlayStation and another rack of DVDs just like in the room in Mrs. Patterson's basement. Even the DVDs are the same.

This is another room for Max. A room that can move.

I hear Mrs. Patterson drop another box onto the couch. I turn to leave. I do not know if she is going to drive this bus or her car or take an airplane, but I need to stay with her no matter what. I would never find my way home from this airport.

As I pass back through the door, I notice the lock on it. A padlock with a latch.

Another shiver runs down my spine. My second ever.

Mrs. Patterson moves the last three boxes from her car over to the bus and then she steps off the bus. I follow. She closes the door and locks it. She walks back to her car, climbs in, and starts the engine. I take my spot in the backseat. She pulls out, singing the hammer song again as she weaves her way through the parking-lot aisles to a set of gates at the other end of the parking lot.

She pulls up to a booth and hands a man inside her ticket. "Wrong lot?" he asks when he looks down at her ticket.

"No," Mrs. Patterson says. "My sister asked me to check on her car and leave her a jacket. I think she asked me to leave the jacket just so she didn't feel too silly about having me check on the car. She's a little obsessive compulsive."

The man in the booth laughs.

Mrs. Patterson is a good liar. She is like an actress on a television show. She is playing a character instead of being herself. She is pretending to be a woman with a sister who is obsessive compulsive. She is good at it. Even I would believe her if I didn't know that she is a Max stealer.

Mrs. Patterson hands some money to the man in the booth and the gate in front of her car lifts up. She waves to the man as we drive away.

The clock on the dashboard reads 7:55.

I hope we are on our way to school.

forty-three

Max's desk is still empty. He is the only student absent again today, and it makes his desk seem even emptier. Nothing has changed since I left yesterday, which feels like a million years ago. The police officer is still sitting by the front door. Mrs. Gosk is still pretending to be Mrs. Gosk. And Max's desk is still empty.

I would sit at Max's desk if I could, but his chair is pushed in, leaving me no room to sit. Instead, I sit in a chair at the back of the room and listen to Mrs. Gosk talk about fractions. Even without her spring, she is the best teacher in the world. She can even make kids smile and laugh while learning about something as boring as numerators and denominators.

I wonder if Mrs. Patterson would have stolen Max if Mrs. Gosk had been her teacher.

I don't think so.

I think Mrs. Gosk could even turn Tommy Swinden into a nice boy with enough time.

When Mrs. Patterson went to the Learning Center, I came here, to Mrs. Gosk's classroom, to listen to her teach for a while. I cannot take my mind off how I left Max, but I was hoping that listening to Mrs. Gosk might make me feel better.

It has. A little.

When the kids leave the classroom for recess, I follow Mrs. Gosk to the teachers' room. If I want to know what is going on, this is where I will find it. Mrs. Gosk has lunch every day with Miss Daggerty and Mrs. Sera, and they always talk about good stuff.

There are two kinds of teachers in the world: there are teachers who play school and teachers who teach school, and Miss Daggerty and Mrs. Sera and especially Mrs. Gosk are the kind of teachers that teach school. They talk to kids in their regular voices and say things that they would say in their own living rooms. Their bulletin boards are always a little raggedy, and their desks are always a little messy, and their libraries are always a little out of order, but kids love them because they talk about real things with real voices and they always tell the truth. This is why Max loves Mrs. Gosk. She never pretends to be a teacher. She is just herself, and it makes Max relax a little. There is nothing to figure out.

Even Max can tell if a teacher is playing school. Teachers who play school are bad at making kids behave. They like the boys and girls who sit in their seats and listen carefully and never shoot elastics across the room. They want all the boys and girls to be just like they were in school, all neat and perfect and sweet. Teachers who play school don't know what to do with kids like Max or Tommy Swinden or Annie Brinker, who once threw up on Mrs. Wilson's desk on purpose. They don't understand kids like Max because they would rather be teaching their dolls than real kids. They use stickers and charts and cards to make kids behave, but none of that junk ever really works.

Mrs. Gosk, Miss Daggerty, and Mrs. Sera love kids like Max and Annie and even Tommy Swinden. They make kids want to behave, and they are not afraid to tell kids when they stink. And that makes them the best teachers to sit with at lunchtime.

Mrs. Gosk is eating something called a sardine sandwich. I don't know what a *sardine* is, but I don't think it is good. Miss Daggerty crinkles her nose when Mrs. Gosk tells her what she is eating.

"Have the police talked to you again?" Miss Daggerty asks. She lowers her voice a little when she speaks. There are six other teachers in the room. A bunch of them are teachers who play school.

"No," Mrs. Gosk says, not lowering her voice. "But they'd better do their goddamn jobs and find Max."

I have never seen Mrs. Gosk cry, and I have seen a lot of teachers cry. Man teachers, even, but especially the woman teachers. She is not crying now, but when she said those words, she sounded angry enough to cry. Not sad tears but mad tears.

"It has to be one of the parents," Miss Daggerty says. "Or one of his relatives. Kids just don't disappear."

"I just can't believe that it's been . . . what? Four days?" Mrs. Sera says.

"Five," Mrs. Gosk says. "Five goddamn days."

"I haven't seen Karen all day," Mrs. Sera says. Karen is Mrs. Palmer's first name. Teachers who play school call her Mrs. Palmer, but teachers like Mrs. Sera just call her Karen.

"She's been locked in her office all morning," Miss Daggerty says.

"I hope she's doing something to find Max and not just hiding from everyone," Mrs. Sera says.

"She'd better be working to the death and the dirt to find him," Mrs. Gosk says. There are tears in her eyes. Her cheeks are red. She stands up and leaves her sardine sandwich behind. The room gets quiet as she leaves.

I leave, too.

Mrs. Patterson has a two o'clock meeting with Mrs. Palmer. I know this because she asked to meet with Mrs. Palmer when she came into school today but the secretary lady said that Mrs. Palmer was busy until two. So Mrs. Patterson said, "Fine," in that way that means it isn't fine.

I want to be in the room for that meeting.

I still have an hour before the meeting and Mrs. Gosk's students are in gym class. Mrs. Gosk is sitting at her desk, correcting papers, so I go down to Mrs. Kropp's room to see Puppy. I haven't seen him in five days, which is a lot of days in the imaginary friend world.

That's a lifetime for a lot of imaginary friends.

Puppy is curled up into a ball beside Piper. Piper is reading a book. Her mouth moves but she doesn't say the word. First graders read like this a lot. Max used to read like this.

"Puppy," I say. I whisper the words at first. It's a habit. Not my habit but everyone else's habit, so I do it, too. Then I realize how silly it is to whisper in a room where only one person can hear me, so I speak in a normal voice. "Puppy! It's me, Budo."

Puppy doesn't move.

"Puppy!" I shout, and this time he jumps up and looks around.

"You scared me," he says, noticing me on the other side of the room.

"You sleep, too?" I ask.

"Of course I do. Why?"

"Graham once told me that she slept, but I never sleep."

"Really?" Puppy says, walking over to me on the other side of the room. The kids are silently reading and Mrs. Kropp is reading with four kids at a side table. These are only first graders but they all read without fooling around or staring out the windows because Mrs. Kropp doesn't play school, either. She teaches.

"Yeah," I say. "I never sleep. I don't even know how."

"I sleep more than I am awake," Puppy says.

I wonder if I could go to sleep if I wanted to. I never feel tired, but maybe if I laid down on a pillow and closed my eyes long enough, I would fall asleep. Then I wonder if all that sleeping might make it easier to forget how easy it is for us to stop existing.

For a second, I find myself jealous of Puppy.

"Have you heard anything about Max?" I ask.

"Is he back?" Puppy asks.

"No, he was stolen. Remember?"

"I know," Puppy says. "But I thought that maybe he was back."

"You haven't heard anything about it?"

"No," Puppy says. "Did you find him?"

"I have to go," I say. It's not true, but I forgot how annoying it is to talk to Puppy. Not only is he dumb, but he thinks that the whole world is like one of those picture books that Mrs. Kropp reads to her first graders. The books where everyone learns a lesson and nobody ever dies. Puppy thinks that the world is one big, happy ending. I know it's not his fault, but it still annoys me. I can't help it.

I turn to leave the room.

"Maybe Wooly knows," Puppy says.

"Wooly?"

"Yeah. Wooly." Puppy doesn't have any hands, so instead of pointing, he nods his head in the direction of the coatroom. Standing against the far wall is a paper doll. He is about as tall as my waist, and at first, I think it is one of those body tracings that Max refused to do in kindergarten when the kids were told to lie down on big sheets of paper and trace one another.

Max's teacher tried to trace him and Max got stuck.

But when I look closer, I see the paper doll's eyes blink. Then he nods his head left and right, like he is trying to say hello without using his hands.

"Wooly?" I ask Puppy again.

"Yes. Wooly."

"How long has he been here?" I ask.

"I don't know," Puppy says. "A little while."

I walk over to the coatroom to where Wooly still seems to be hanging on the wall.

"Hi," I say. "I'm Budo."

"I'm Wooly," the paper doll says. He has two arms and two legs but not much body, and he looks like he was cut out in a hurry. *Imagined in a hurry,* I remind myself. His edges are all jagged and uneven, and he has creases all over his body from where it looks like he was folded up a million times in a million different ways.

"How long have you been here?" I ask.

"In this room?" he asks. "Or in the whole wide world."

I smile. He is already smarter than Puppy. "World," I say.

"Since last year," Wooly says. "At the end of kindergarten. But I don't come to school very much. Kayla used to keep me at home or folded up inside her backpack, but she has been taking me out for a bunch of days now. Maybe a month."

"Which one is Kayla?" I ask.

Wooly reaches out to point, but as he does, his whole body curls over and slides to the floor, facedown, in a rustle of paper.

"Are you okay?" I ask, unsure what to do.

"Yes," Wooly says, using his arms and legs to flip himself on his back so he is looking up at me. "This happens a lot." He is smiling. He doesn't have a real mouth like me but just a line that opens and closes and changes shape. But the edges are curled up, so I can tell that it's a smile.

I smile back. "Can you stand up?" I ask.

"Sure," Wooly says. I watch as Wooly curls the middle of his body up and then down like an inchworm, pushing himself back against the wall until his head is touching it. Then he curls the middle of his body again, pushing his head against the wall and sliding it up. He does this twice more, reaching out and grabbing the edge of a small bookshelf as he does, and pulling himself up while the middle of his body pushes. When he is finished, he is standing again, but really he is just leaning against the wall.

"That's not easy," I say.

"No. I can get around okay by scooting on my back or my belly, but climbing up the wall is hard. If there isn't something to grab onto, it's impossible."

"Sorry," I say.

"It's alright," Wooly says. "Last week I met a little boy in the shape of a Popsicle stick with no arms and no legs. Just a stick. Jason brought him to school, but when Mrs. Kropp let him try the new computer game first, he threw the Popsicle-stick boy on his desk and just forgot about him. I stood here against the wall and watched him just fade away and disappear. One minute he was here and the next minute he was gone. Have you ever seen an imaginary friend disappear?"

"Yes," I say.

"I cried," Wooly says. "I didn't even know him but I cried. So did the Popsicle-stick boy. He cried until he was gone."

"I would've cried, too," I say.

We are both quiet for a moment. I try to imagine what it must have been like to be that Popsicle-stick boy.

I decide that I like Wooly a lot.

"Why is Kayla bringing you to school now?" I ask. I know that when a kid starts taking an imaginary friend to new places, it usually means something bad has happened.

"Her dad doesn't live with her anymore. He hit her mom before he left. Right at the dinner table. Right on the face. Then she threw her food in his face and they started yelling at each other. Really loud. Kayla cried and cried, and then she started bringing me to school."

"Sorry," I say again.

"No," Wooly says. "Be sorry for Kayla. I like coming to school. I think it means that I won't end up like the Popsicle-stick boy for a while. She is always coming over to the drinking fountain to get a drink, but really she's just checking to make sure I am here. That's why I'm not stuffed in her backpack anymore. I think it would be a lot easier to forget about me if she still had me stuffed inside that backpack. So this is good."

I smile. Wooly is smart. Very smart.

"I was wondering if you heard anything about a boy named Max," I say. "He disappeared last week."

"He ran away. Right?"

"What did you hear?" I ask.

"Mrs. Kropp had lunch in here with two other ladies and they were talking about it. Mrs. Kropp said that he ran away."

"What did the other ladies say?" I ask. I realize that this is the first time I am talking to someone about Max being stolen who is not Puppy. It feels so good.

"One of the ladies said he was probably kidnapped by someone who knew him. She said that kidnapped kids are always kidnapped by people they know. She said that Max was too stupid to run away and hide for so long without being found."

"He's not stupid," I say. I am surprised by how angry I sound.

"I didn't say it. The lady did."

"I know. I'm sorry. Anyway, she's right about him being kidnapped. Mrs. Patterson stole Max."

"Who is Mrs. Patterson?" Wooly asks.

"She is Max's teacher."

"A teacher?" Wooly sounds as if he cannot believe it. I feel like I finally have someone on my side. "Did you tell anyone?" he asks.

"No. Max is the only human person who can hear me."

"Oh." Then his eyes, which are just circles inside a circle, widen. "Oh no. Max is your imaginer friend?"

I have never heard a human person called this before, but I say yes.

"Maybe I should tell Kayla," Wooly says. "Then she can tell Mrs. Kropp for you."

I had not thought of this, but Wooly is right. Wooly could be my connection to the world of human persons. He could tell Kayla, and then Kayla could tell Mrs. Kropp, and then Mrs. Kropp could tell the police chief. I cannot believe I did not think of this before.

"Do you think Mrs. Kropp would believe her?" I ask.

"I don't know," Wooly says. "Maybe."

It might work. I used to think that Max was my only connection to his world, but every imaginary friend is a connection to Max's world.

Every imaginary friend can touch the world of human persons. Even Puppy.

Every imaginary friend can touch the world, I think.

Then I have a different idea. A better idea and a worse idea all rolled into one.

"No," I say. "Don't tell Kayla." I think about Mrs. Patterson's bus with the bedroom in the back and the lock on the door, and I worry that if she finds out what Kayla said to Mrs. Kropp, she might lock Max up in that bedroom and drive away forever. Mrs. Kropp might tell the police, but maybe Mrs. Kropp would smile at Kayla and say something like, "Oh, did Wooly tell you that?" And then she would tell Mrs. Patterson about the funny thing that Kayla said in class today, and Mrs. Patterson would panic and run away with Max before I ever found a way to save him.

Wooly's idea might work, but I have a better connection to Max's world.

A much better and a much worse connection.

I feel another shiver run down my spine.

forty-four

Mrs. Palmer looks tired. Her voice is scratchy and her eyes are puffy and look like they want to close. Even her clothes and hair look tired.

"How are you doing?" Mrs. Patterson asks her.

I notice that Mrs. Palmer's desk is cluttered with papers and folders and Styrofoam coffee cups. There is a pile of newspapers on the floor beside the trash can. I have never seen anything on her desk except for a computer and a telephone. I can't remember ever seeing a single scrap of paper in this office.

"I'm fine," Mrs. Palmer says, and even those two words sound tired. "I'll be much better once we find Max, but I know we're doing everything we can."

"There's not much that we can do. Is there?" Mrs. Patterson asks.

"I'm helping the police as much as possible, and I'm handling the media inquiries. And I'm trying to help Mr. and Mrs. Delaney anyway I can. But you're right. There's not much we can do now but wait and pray."

"I'm certainly glad that you're in charge and not me," Mrs. Patterson says. "I give you a lot of credit, Karen. I don't know how you do it."

But Mrs. Palmer is not in charge, and Mrs. Patterson knows it. Mrs. Palmer answers the phone and makes the announcements over the intercom and reminds Mr. Fedyzyn to wear a tie at graduation, but she is supposed to be in charge of making sure that kids are safe. That is her real job. But Max is not safe, and the person who stole him is sitting right here in her office, and she doesn't know it.

That is not what I call being in charge.

"This has been the toughest time in my twenty years as an administrator," Mrs. Palmer says. "But God willing, we'll get through this

215

and Max will come back to us safe and sound. Now what can I do for you?"

"I know this is bad timing, but I'd like to take a leave of absence. My condition isn't improving and I'd like to spend some time with my sister out west. But I have no intention of leaving you in the lurch. I'm in no rush. I'll wait until you find a replacement, and I'll make sure I cooperate with the police in any way needed and stay in Connecticut until they no longer require my assistance. But when it's possible, and as soon as it's possible, I'd like to take the rest of the year off."

"Of course," Mrs. Palmer says. She sounds surprised and maybe a little relieved. I think she thought Mrs. Patterson was meeting with her about something else. "I don't know much about lupus, and I feel terrible. I would have done more reading about it had I not been focused solely on Max these past few days. But is there anything we can do?"

"Thank you, but I'm okay. I'm taking several medications that seem to have things under control for the moment, but it's an unpredictable disease. I'd hate to wake up one morning and discover that I don't have the time to see my sister and get to know her kids. Let them get to know their auntie."

"It must be hard," Mrs. Palmer says.

"I didn't think I'd ever stand up again when I lost my Scotty. But this place has been so good for me. It brought me back from the dead. It reminded me that there is still good in this world, and that there are kids who really need me. There isn't a day that goes by that I don't think about my boy, but I've moved on and done some good, I think."

"You have," Mrs. Palmer says.

"But Max's disappearance has really got me thinking again about how unpredictable life can be. I pray every night that Max is okay, but there is no telling what has happened. Here today, gone tomorrow. Just like my Scotty. That could be me someday. I don't want to wait until my life is piled high with regrets before I do something about it."

"I certainly understand," Mrs. Palmer says. "I can call Rich tomorrow and have human resources start interviewing replacements immediately. I'd do it myself but I just don't think I'll have the time. But there are a lot of teachers on the market without jobs, so hiring a qualified replacement shouldn't be difficult. Do you think you'll want to return next year?"

Mrs. Patterson sighs, and it sounds so real even though I know that everything she is saying is a lie. I can't believe how good she is at pretending to be someone else. "I'd like to think that I'll be back," she says. "Would it be alright if I let you know for sure in the spring? It's hard to tell how I will feel in six months. To be honest, it's been hard to come to school each day, knowing Max is not here and knowing that had I been working last Friday, none of this would have happened."

"Don't be ridiculous, Kelly," Mrs. Palmer says. Kelly. It sounds too nice for her. I cannot believe that she is a Kelly.

"It's not ridiculous," Mrs. Patterson says. "If I had been . . ."

"Stop," Mrs. Palmer says, holding her hand out like a crossing guard. "This is not your fault. Max did not run away. Someone took him, and if they didn't take him on Friday, they would have taken him another day. The police say that random abductions are almost unheard of. Someone planned this. This is not your fault."

"I know. But it's still hard. If Max comes back to us, I could see myself coming back next year. But if God forbid he is still missing next September, I don't know how I could bring myself to walk through those doors ever again."

Everything Mrs. Patterson says makes her seem more innocent to Mrs. Palmer and more dangerous to me.

"Just don't blame yourself," Mrs. Palmer says. "You had nothing to do with this."

"When I'm lying in my bed at night, thinking about Max and where he might be, it's hard not to think this is all my fault," Mrs. Patterson says.

"Don't. You are too good to be blaming yourself."

Sometimes I ask Max if I exist just to get him to admit that I exist. To remind him that I exist. Now Mrs. Patterson is doing the same thing. Mrs. Patterson, Max's kidnapper, has walked into Mrs. Palmer's office and tricked her into insisting that she did nothing wrong. The bad guy is sitting right in front of Mrs. Palmer, and all Mrs. Palmer can do is tell her over and over that she is innocent, even when she admits that she is to blame.

Mrs. Palmer is dancing with the devil in the pale moonlight, and she is losing badly.

And now Mrs. Palmer has agreed to let Mrs. Patterson take the rest of the year off so she can head to a place out west, to visit a sister who probably does not exist. I think Mrs. Patterson is planning to leave Connecticut, and she might even be planning to head out west, but it's not to see her sister.

She is going to take Max away, and if she does, I don't think that either one of them will ever come back.

I have to hurry.

I have to break another promise to Max.

forty-five

I ride the school bus home but get off at the Savoys' house again since the bus did not stop for Max. I walk to the house to check on Max's mom and dad, but that is not why I rode the school bus home. I do not know how to get to the hospital from school, so I have to start at the house.

I wish I paid better attention to the streets. Max's dad says that he carries a map inside his head that lets him get anywhere. All of my maps start at Max's house. My map looks like a spider. Max's house is the body and all the places that I go are the legs.

No two legs connect.

I also cannot get to Mrs. Patterson's house without driving in her car, which means that if Mrs. Patterson decides never to come back to school again, I am in big trouble. I will never find Max again.

If everything goes according to my plan, I will be back in Mrs. Patterson's car tomorrow.

Max's parents are home. I saw their cars in the driveway when the bus drove past. Normally, Max's dad would be at work and Max's mom would just be getting home in time to see Max off the bus. But today they are both home.

His mom is in the kitchen. She is baking cookies. The house is quiet. No radio or television. The only sound I can hear is Max's dad's voice coming from his office. He is on the telephone.

It is weird. I did not expect cookies and telephone calls.

The house is clean, too. Cleaner than usual. There are no books or mail piled on the dining room table and there are no dishes in the sink. No shoes piled by the front door.

It reminds me a little bit of Mrs. Patterson's house.

Max's dad comes out of his office and walks into the kitchen.

"You're baking cookies?" he asks.

I'm glad he asked because I wanted to ask the same thing.

"I'm making them to bring to the police station."

"You think they need cookies?" Max's dad says.

"I don't know what else to do, okay?" Max's mom says. She pushes the bowl of cookie batter across the counter. It slides over the edge and falls to the floor. The bowl breaks. It makes a cracking sound but most of the bowl stays together. It is held together by the cookie dough. Only a couple pieces of glass separate from the bowl.

Max's mom begins to cry.

"Jesus Christ!" Max's dad shouts. He stares down at the broken bowl. One of the broken pieces has slid across the linoleum and stopped in front of his shoe. He stares at it and then back up to Max's mom.

"I'm sorry," Max's mom says. "I just don't know what to do. There isn't a book that tells you what to do when your little boy disappears. The police tell you to stay home and wait, but what am I supposed to do? Watch TV? Read a book? You're in there playing amateur detective and I'm stuck in here, staring at the walls and wondering what the hell is happening to Max."

"The police said that it was probably someone who Max knows," Max's dad says. "I'm just trying to figure out who it might be."

"By calling everyone we know and hoping that they will admit to taking him? Did you hope to hear him playing in the background with the Parker boys or with my sister's kids?"

"I don't know," Max's dad says. "I have to do something."

"You really think my sister could've taken Max? She can't even talk to Max without getting nervous. She can't even look him in the eyes."

"It's something, goddamnit! I can't just sit here and do nothing."

"And you think baking cookies is nothing?"

"I don't see how it's going to help us find Max."

"And what happens when you run out of people to call?" Max's mom asks. "Then what? How long do we put ourselves on hold before we go back to work and resume our lives?"

"You want to go back to work?"

"No, of course not. But I keep wondering what will happen if they don't find Max. How long are we going to sit in this house waiting for news? I know it's awful, but I keep thinking about how we will ever move on after the police tell us to give up hope. Because I'm starting to give up hope. God help me, I am. It's been five days and they have nothing. What's going to happen to us?"

"It's only been five days," Max's dad says. "The chief said that people make mistakes. Maybe not in the first week or even the first month, but you can't be careful forever. Whoever has Max will make a mistake and that's when we'll find him."

"What if he is already dead?"

"Don't say that!" Max's father shouts. "Don't you ever say that!"

"Why not? Don't tell me you haven't thought about it."

"I'm trying not to think about it," Max's dad says. "For Christ's sake, why would you even say that?"

"Because it's all I can think about!" Max's mom says. "My little boy is gone and he's probably dead and we're never getting him back!"

Now Max's mom is really crying. She throws a wooden spoon covered with cookie batter across the counter and crumples to the floor, her head dipping into her arms. For a moment, she reminds me of Wooly, sliding off his wall and onto the floor. Max's dad steps forward, stops for a moment, and then goes to her. He eases himself down to the floor and puts his arms around her.

"He's not dead," Max's dad whispers.

"But what if he is?" Max's mom asks. "What then? I don't know how we'll ever go on."

"We'll find him," Max's dad says.

"I can't stop thinking that there was something we did. Or forgot to do. That somehow this is our fault."

"Stop," Max's dad says, but he says it gently. Not like a crossing guard. "That's not how the world works and you know it. Some awful person decided to take Max from us. It doesn't have anything to do with us. It's just an awful thing done by an awful person, and we're going to catch the son of a bitch and bring our son back. He's going to make a mistake. The chief said so. When he does, we'll get him back. I know it."

"But what if we don't?"

"We will. I promise."

Max's dad sounds so sure of himself even though he keeps calling the kidnapper a he.

I suddenly realize that Max isn't the only person who I have to save. I have to save his parents, too.

forty-six

I start at the Children's Hospital. I have no reason to be here, but I want to see Summer. I'm not sure why, but I do. I feel like I need to see her.

I make my way to the recess room. The elevator drops me off on the fourteenth floor this time. No stairs. I decide that this is a good sign. Things are already working out.

I make my way to the recess room. It is after seven P.M. so the kids will probably be in their beds and the imaginary friends who leave the rooms will probably be in the recess room by now.

As I walk in, Klute jumps up out of his chair and shouts my name. His head bobbles uncontrollably as he does so. Three other imaginary friends jump up from their seats in surprise as well. None of them are Spoon or Summer.

"Hello, Klute," I say.

"You look so real!" says a boy who looks like a robot. Shiny and boxy and stiff. I have seen many robot imaginary friends before.

"He really does," says a brown teddy bear about half my size.

The third, a girl who looks like a human person except for missing eyebrows and a pair of fairy wings on her back, sits back down and folds her hands in her lap without saying anything.

"Thank you," I say to the robot and the teddy bear. I turn to Klute. "Is Summer still here? Or Spoon?"

"Spoon went home two days ago," Klute says.

"What about Summer?" I ask.

Klute looks at his feet. I turn to the robot and the teddy bear. They both do the same.

"What happened?" I ask.

Klute shakes his head back and forth slowly, but it causes his head

223

to bobble. He will not look at me except when his bobbling head forces his eyes up for a second.

"She died," the girl with the fairy wings says.

I turn around and face her. "What do you mean, she died?"

"Summer died," she says. "And then Grace died."

"Grace?" I ask. Then I remember.

"Her friend," the fairy says. "Her friend who was sick."

"Summer died *and then* Grace died?" I ask.

"Yes," the fairy says. "Summer disappeared. And then a little while later, the doctors said that Grace died."

"It was sad," Klute says. It sounds like he is going to cry. "She was sitting in here with us and then she just started to fade away. I could see right through her."

"Was she scared?" I ask. "Did it hurt?"

"No," the fairy says. "She knew that Grace was going to die so she was happy that she was going to die first."

"Why?" I ask.

"So she could wait for Grace on the other side," the fairy says.

"The other side of what?"

"I don't know," she says.

I look at Klute. "I don't know, either," he says. "She just said that she and Grace would be together on the other side."

"I wasn't here," the teddy bear says. "But it sure sounds sad. I never want to disappear."

"We all disappear someday," the robot says. He talks like a robot from the movies. All stiff and choppy.

"We do?" Klute says.

"Did you find your friend?" the fairy asks.

"What?" I ask.

"Did you find your friend?" the fairy asks again. "Summer told us that you lost your friend and you were trying to find him."

"I told you, too," Klute says, bobbling his head up and down. "I knew Budo before all of you."

"Yes," I say. "I found him, but I haven't saved him yet."

"Will you?" the fairy asks. She stands up, but the top of her head still doesn't reach my shoulders.

I want to tell the fairy that I'm trying to save Max, but instead I say, "Yes. I promised Summer I would."

"Then why are you here?" she asks.

"I need help," I say. "I need help to save Max."

"Our help?" Klute asks expectantly. Excitedly. His head bobbles again.

"No," I say. "But thank you. You can't help me. I need someone else."

forty-seven

Here is what I know about Oswald:

1. He is so tall that his head almost touches the ceiling. He is the tallest imaginary friend I have ever seen.
2. Oswald looks like a human person. He looks as much like a human being person as I do, except he is so tall. Ears and eyebrows and all.
3. Oswald is the only imaginary friend I have ever met who has a grown-up for a human friend.
4. Oswald is the only imaginary friend I have ever met who can move things in the real world. This is why I am only pretty sure that he is an imaginary friend.
5. Oswald is mean and scary.
6. Oswald hates me.
7. Oswald is the only person who can help me save Max.

I met Oswald about a month ago, so I am not sure if he is still in the hospital, but I think he probably is. His human person is on a special floor of the hospital for lunatics, which Max told me is another word for crazy people. That's what I heard one of the doctors say. Or maybe it was a nurse. She said she hated working on the floor with all the lunatics.

But another nurse person said that it was the floor for head injuries, which I think are people who break their heads. So I'm not sure. Maybe it's both. Maybe a broken head turns people into lunatics.

Oswald's human being person is also in a coma, which Max said means that he is sleeping forever.

A coma person is like the opposite of me. I never sleep but a coma person only sleeps.

I was in the grown-up hospital when I first saw Oswald. I like to go there sometimes and listen to the doctors talk about the sick people. Every sick person is different, so every story is different. Sometimes the stories are hard to understand, but they are always exciting. Even better than watching Pauley scratch lottery tickets.

Sometimes I just like to walk around the hospital because it is so big. Every time I go there, I find a new place to explore.

I was exploring the eighth floor that day, and Oswald was walking down the hall toward me. His head was down and he was looking at his feet. He was tall and wide with a flat face and a thick neck. His cheeks were red, like he had just come in from the cold. He was bald. Not a speck of hair on his big head.

But it was the way that he walked that I noticed the most. He threw each leg forward like he wanted to kick the air in front of him. Like nothing in the whole wide world could stop him. He reminded me of a snowplow.

When he got close to me, he looked up and shouted, "Get out of my way!" I turned around to see who was walking behind me, but the hallway was empty. I turned back around and Oswald said, "Get out of my way right now!"

That was when I realized that he was an imaginary friend. He could see me. He was talking to me. So I stepped to the side and he walked right past me. Plowed right past me without even looking up. I turned and followed him. I had never seen an imaginary friend look so real before, and I wanted to talk to him. "I'm Budo," I said, trying to catch up.

"Oswald," he said. He didn't look back at me. He just said the word and kept plowing forward.

"No," I said. "I'm Budo."

He stopped and turned toward me. "I'm Oswald. Leave me alone." He turned and started walking again.

I was a little nervous, because Oswald was so big and so loud and seemed so mean. I had never met an imaginary friend who was mean before. But I had never seen any imaginary friend look so real before, either, so I couldn't help myself. I followed him.

He walked down the hallway, turned, walked down another hallway, turned again, and then he stopped at a door. The door wasn't closed all the way. It was only open a little crack. The doctors keep the doors open a crack a lot so they can sneak into rooms in the middle of the night to check on people without waking them up. The crack in the doorway was too small for Oswald to fit through, so I thought he was going to pass through the door like I would. But instead, he reached out and moved the door. He pushed it open with his hand just enough to squeeze through.

When the door moved, I screamed. I couldn't believe it. I had never seen an imaginary friend move anything in the real world before. Oswald must have heard me scream because he turned. He ran toward me. I was frozen. I didn't know what to do. I still couldn't believe what I had seen. As Oswald reached me, he threw his hands out in front of him and he hit me. No one had ever hit me before. I went tumbling to the floor.

It hurt.

I had never really known that I could hurt until then. I had never even known what *hurt* really meant until then.

"I said to leave me alone!" he shouted. Then he turned and went back to the room.

Even though Oswald had yelled at me and pushed me and hurt me, I had to know what was in that room. I couldn't help it. I had just seen an imaginary friend touch a door and move it in the real world. I had to know more.

So I waited. I went to the end of the hallway and stood there, peeking around the corner, never taking my eyes off that door. I waited forever and finally Oswald came out of the room through the same crack in the doorway that he had made forever ago. He was walking in my direction, so I went down the hallway a bit and hid inside a closet. I stood in the dark and counted to one hundred and then I came back out.

Oswald was nowhere in sight.

So I went back to the room that Oswald had left and went inside. The lights were off but the light from the hallway gave the room a dull glow. There were two beds in the room. A man was lying in the bed closest to the door. The other bed was empty. No sheets or pillows. I looked around for toys or stuffed animals or little pairs of pants or shoes. Anything that would show me that a little boy or a little girl was staying in this room, too. But I found nothing.

Just this man.

He had a bushy red beard and bushy eyebrows, but his head was completely bald like Oswald's. There were machines next to his bed and wires and tubes connected to his arms and chest. The machines beeped and hissed. Lights blinked and glowed on tiny television screens attached to the machines.

I looked back at the empty bed again, thinking that maybe I missed something. Maybe there were stuffed animals and little pants hanging in the closet and the little boy was in the bathroom. Or maybe the bald man in the bed was a dad, and Oswald was the imaginary friend of his son or daughter (but probably his son). Maybe the bald man's son was sitting in the waiting room right now, waiting for his dad to wake up. Maybe the little boy had sent Oswald to check on his dad to make sure he was okay.

Then I thought that maybe the bald man wasn't anyone's dad. This could be any person. Maybe Oswald was just resting on the extra bed. Or maybe Oswald was looking for a quiet place to sit. Or maybe Oswald is just curious like me.

Then I thought that maybe Oswald is a human person who can see imaginary friends instead of an imaginary friend who can touch the human person world. I was trying to decide which was more likely when three people turned on the lights and came into the room. One was wearing a white coat and the other two were standing behind her, carrying clipboards. They walked over to the man in the bed and the woman in the white coat said, "This is John Hurly. Age Fifty-two. Head trauma caused from a fall. Brought to us on August fourth. Nonresponsive to all treatment. He has been in a coma since he arrived."

"What's the plan for Mr. Hurly?" one of the clipboard people asked.

The people kept on talking, asking questions and answering questions, but I stopped listening.

That was when Oswald walked back into the room.

His eyes fell upon the white coat and clipboard people first. He looked annoyed but not angry. He rolled his eyes and snorted a little. I think he had seen them before.

But then he noticed me. I was standing between the two beds, my back against the machines, trying not to move. Hoping that if I didn't move, he might not notice me. His mouth dropped open when he saw me and he froze for a moment. I think he was surprised to see me standing there. As surprised as I had been to see him move that door.

He couldn't believe it. He took a deep breath, pointed his finger at me, and said, "You!" He didn't run at me, but he was so tall and so quick that he moved from the doorway to the space between the two beds in three or four steps. Before I even had time to think.

I was trapped, and I was scared. I don't think that one imaginary friend can kill another imaginary friend, but I didn't think that imaginary friends could hurt each other, either, and Oswald had already proven me wrong about that.

Oswald lunged at me, so I hopped onto and over the empty bed. Oswald followed, rolling over the bed and landing on the other side even before I had a chance to get my balance. He pushed me again. His hands were so big that his push lifted me right off the ground. I fell backward into a small table in the corner of the room. The table didn't move, of course, but I hit it just the same, and it hurt. The corner of the table dug into my back, and I cried out in pain. The idea of the corner, I mean, but it was just as sharp as the real corner. I was about to lift myself off the table when Oswald grabbed me by the shoulders and threw me back over the empty bed. I bounced once on the mattress and fell off the edge and onto the floor between the two beds. I hit my head on the way down, on one of the machines, I think, so I was slow getting back up. I just lay there for a second, trying to calm down and think. I looked under the bald man's bed and saw six feet on the other side. The white coat and the two clipboard people. They were still talking about the coma man. Asking questions and looking at something called a chart. They had no idea that a fight was happening right in front of them, except it wasn't a fight, because I was not fighting. I was just getting hurt.

I lifted myself onto my hands and knees and was about to stand back up when Oswald's knee came crashing down on my back. That was the worst pain I have ever felt. It was like something exploded in my back. I cried out and dropped back down to the floor. My face smacked the tile and my nose and forehead blew up in the same kind of pain that was still exploding in my back. I thought I was going to cry, and back then I had never cried before. I didn't even know that I could cry back then, but I thought I might. It hurt so much.

Little kids who get hurt on the playground call for their mommys a lot. I wanted to call for my mommy but I have no mommy, and not having a mommy hurt the most at that moment. Not having anyone who could help me. The three doctor people were still in the room, still talking, still staring at their clipboards, but they had no idea that someone else in the room was hurt.

I wondered if Oswald could kill me or coma me like the bald man.

Oswald kicked me in the legs. He kicked me in the arms.

I wanted to cry out for my mommy again. Instead, I thought about Dee. I called out her name.

I think I would have started crying then, but there was no time to cry because Oswald was picking me up and throwing me against the wall on the other side of the room. I bounced off the wall and landed on my still-exploding back. Then he lifted me again and threw me in the direction of the doorway. My head hit the wall next to the door and I saw stars. I couldn't tell up from down. Then he lifted me one more time and threw me out of the room and into the hallway. I rolled a couple times and then I started to crawl away as fast as I could. I had no idea which direction I was crawling. All I knew was that I was crawling away and that was good. And the whole time that I crawled I was just waiting for Oswald to pick me up again. But he didn't. I crawled for about thirty seconds, then I stopped and looked behind me. Oswald was standing in the middle of the hallway, staring at me. "Never again," he said.

I waited for him to say something else.

When he didn't, I said, "Okay."

"I mean it," he said. "Never again."

forty-eight

"Oswald is my only chance," I say. "He is Max's only chance. He has to help."

"He won't," Klute says.

The robot shakes his head in agreement.

"He has to," I say.

I take the elevator to the tenth floor and then I walk down two flights of stairs to the eighth floor.

The lunatic floor.

I walk to the room where I last saw Oswald. The room with Oswald's bald lunatic friend. I walk slowly, keeping my eyes peeled as I turn corners and pass by open doors. I do not want to bump into Oswald by mistake. I still have no idea what I will say to him.

The door to the room is open. I walk toward it. I try not to think about the last time I saw Oswald. The sound of his voice. The way he threw me around the room. The way his eyes doubled in size as he said, "Never again."

I agreed with him that day. I promised to stay away forever. But here I am again.

I step into the doorway, bracing myself for attack.

It comes quickly.

I take in many details before Oswald reaches me.

The curtains are open and the room is bright with sunlight. It surprises me. My memories of this room are dark and scary. In my memory, the room has no corners. Just patches of darkness. The room looks too happy and sunny now for anything bad to ever happen, and yet Oswald is already a few feet away from me and shouting, "No! No! No!"

The bald man with the red beard is still in his bed, machines still whirring and hissing and flashing. There is a man in the second bed, too. He is young and round and there is something wrong with his face. It looks rubbery and sleepy.

There is a third man in the room. He is sitting in a chair at the end of the sleepy face man's bed. He is holding a magazine in his hands and he is reading it out loud to Sleepy Face. I only hear a tiny bit of it before Oswald is on top of me. It's a story about baseball, I think. Someone threw a low hitter. But before I can hear any more, Oswald's hands grab me around the neck. He squeezes and turns, throwing me into the room. My body crashes into the bald man's bed. If I was not an imaginary friend, the bed would have slid across the room. That's how hard I hit it.

But I am imaginary so I bounce off the bed and land in a heap at Oswald's feet. My head and chest and neck hurt. I can't breathe for a moment. Oswald bends over, picks me up by the collar of my shirt and the waist of my pants, and flings me over the bald man's bed and onto Sleepy Face's bed. I bounce off him, too, without him ever feeling a thing, and roll off the side of the bed. I land in another heap on the floor against the far wall.

More parts hurt. Lots of them.

This was a bad idea. Oswald is not like a snowplow. He is like one of those giant cranes with the ball hanging from a chain. The kind that knock down old buildings. He just keeps pounding away at me.

I stand up quickly this time. I know that I must or Oswald will pick me up and throw me again or start kicking me again. The man in the chair, a young man with pale skin, keeps reading. He is in the middle of a fight, and he will never know it. Oswald is moving again, filling the space between Sleepy Face's bed and the wall, blocking my escape. I suddenly wish that I had stayed on the floor and rolled under Sleepy Face's bed and then under Bald Lunatic's bed and then out the door.

Oswald takes two steps forward, closing the distance between us. I still have not said a word to him. I decide that now is a good time to speak.

"Stop," I say, trying to sound like I am begging. I do a good job because I am begging. "Please. I need your help."

"I told you to stay away," Oswald shouts. He shouts loud enough to drown out the baseball story for a second. Then he steps forward and puts his hands on my neck again. I try to block him this time but he swats my hands away like they are made of paper. Like Wooly's hands. Oswald starts squeezing. He is choking me. If I breathed air, I might be dying. I breathe the idea of air, but even that is getting squished out of my throat now.

I think I might be dying.

I feel my feet leave the floor when I hear another voice in the room.

"Let go of him, Oswald."

Oswald lets go, but not because he is obeying the command. He is surprised. No, he is shocked. I can see it on his face. My feet hit the floor and I stumble for a moment, catch my balance and my breath at the same time, then turn in the direction of the doorway. The fairy from the recess room is standing in the doorway, except she is not standing. She is flying. She is hovering in place, her tiny wings moving so fast they are a blur.

I have never seen an imaginary friend fly before.

"How did you know my name?" Oswald asks.

I think about taking advantage of the moment and shoving Oswald to the ground and escaping. Hitting him while he is distracted. But I still need his help, even if he wants to kill me, and I think that this might be my one chance to turn things around.

Might be the fairy's one chance to turn things around.

"Budo is my friend," the fairy says. "I don't want you to hurt him."

"How do you know my name?" Oswald asks again. His surprise is quickly turning to anger. His hands ball up into fists. His nostrils flare.

"Budo needs your help, Oswald," the fairy says.

I don't know how I know, but I am sure that the fairy is avoiding Oswald's question on purpose. I think she might be trying to figure out the best answer.

"How do you know my name?" Oswald shouts the question this time and moves toward the doorway, straight toward the fairy.

I follow.

I will not let him hurt the fairy like he has hurt me. But as I reach out to grab him, to pull him back and give the fairy enough time to escape, the fairy's eyes and my eyes meet, and she shakes her head ever so gently. She is telling me to stop. Or to wait at least.

I obey.

The fairy is right to tell me to stop.

As Oswald approaches the doorway, he stops, too. He does not reach for the fairy with his giant hands. He can throw me around the room and kick me and choke me but he does not touch the fairy.

"How do you know my name?" Oswald shouts again, and this time I hear something in his voice that I missed the first time. Oswald is angry, but I think that he is curious, too. Hopeful, even. Underneath his anger is something else. I think Oswald is hoping that the fairy's answer to his question is a good one. I think he wants help, too.

"I am a fairy," the fairy says. "Do you know what a fairy is?"

"How do you know my name?" Oswald roars the question this time. If Oswald was a human person, every window on the eighth floor would have rattled and every single person in the hospital would have heard his voice.

I have never been more afraid.

The fairy turns and points to the bald man in the bed. "He is your friend. And he's hurt. Right?"

Oswald stares at her and says nothing. I am standing behind him so I cannot see the expression on Oswald's face, but his fists unclench and I can see the muscles in his arms and back relax a little.

"Oswald," the fairy says again. "He is your friend. Right?"

Oswald looks to the bald man and then back to the fairy. He shakes his head up and down.

"And he's hurt?" she asks.

Oswald nods slowly.

"I'm so sorry," the fairy says. "Do you know how it happened?"

Oswald nods again.

"Can we go into the hallway and talk?" the fairy asks. "I can't think straight with that man reading that book."

I have forgotten that Sleepy Face and his pale friend were even in the room. I stopped hearing about the low hitter once the fairy started speaking. It was like watching a lion tamer calm down a lion with a toothpick instead of a whip and chair.

No, not a toothpick. A Q-Tip. But somehow it worked. The fairy has done it.

Oswald agrees to move into the hallway. But as the fairy turns to leave, she notices that Oswald does not move. She turns back.

"What?" she asks.

"He has to leave, too," Oswald says, turning and pointing at me.

"Of course," the fairy says. "Budo is coming with us."

Oswald turns and follows the fairy into the hallway. I follow behind him. We walk down a little ways to a space with chairs and lamps and short tables piled with magazines. The fairy sits on a chair. Her wings stop moving. When they are still, they look small and weak and flimsy. I can't believe that she can fly.

Oswald sits on a chair opposite the fairy.

I take a seat in a chair next to the fairy.

"Who are you?" Oswald asks.

"I'm Teeny," the fairy says.

I feel bad. I never asked her name.

"How do you know my name?" Oswald asks again. Anger has now transformed into pure curiosity.

Teeny pauses. I wonder if I should say something to give her more time to think. She looks uncertain. But then she speaks before I can think of something to say. "I was going to tell you that I am a magical fairy who knows everything in the world, and that you need to listen to me. But I don't want to lie. I know your name is Oswald because Budo told me."

Oswald says nothing.

I open my mouth to talk but it is Teeny who speaks.

"Budo needs your help, and I was afraid that you might be mean to him like the last time you saw him. So I followed him here."

"I told him to leave," Oswald says. "I warned him."

"I know. But he needs your help. He had to come."

"Why?" Oswald asks.

"Because Budo said that you can move things in the real world," Teeny says. "Is that true?" She asks the question like she can't believe it herself.

Oswald's bushy eyebrows come together like two caterpillars kissing. He has the same eyebrows as the bald man, I suddenly realize. He looks a lot like the bald man. It's easier to see the resemblance now that I'm not being thrown around the room.

"I saw you push the door to that room open," I say. "You can move things in the real world. Right? Like this table? Or these magazines?"

"Yes," Oswald says. "But it's hard."

"Hard?" Teeny asks.

"Everything in the real world is heavy. A lot heavier than you," he says, pointing to me.

"You would know," I say.

The caterpillars kiss again.

"Never mind," I say.

"And I could never move a table," he says. "Even a little one like this is too heavy."

"But you can move small things," I say. "Right?"

Oswald nods.

"How long have you been alive?" Teeny asks.

"I don't know," Oswald says. He looks down at his feet.

"What is your friend's name?" Teeny asks.

"Who?"

"The man in the bed."

"Oh," Oswald says. "He is John."

"Did you know him before he was hurt?" I ask. I think about the little girl without a name in the Intensive Care Unit. I wonder if Oswald is like her.

"Only for a second," Oswald says. "He was on the ground. His head was broken. He looked up at me and smiled and then he closed his eyes."

"And you followed him here?" I ask.

"Yes." Oswald pauses, and then he says, "I wish John would open his eyes and smile again."

"Can you help Budo?" Teeny asks.

"How?"

"I need you to help my friend," I say. "He isn't hurt like John, but he is in big trouble, and I can't save him without you."

"Will I have to go down the stairs? I don't like the stairs."

"You will have to go far away," Teeny says. "Down the stairs and outside and far away. But it is important and John would want you to do it. And when you're done, Budo will bring you right back here. Okay?"

"No," Oswald says. "I can't."

"Yes, you can," Teeny says. "You have to. A little boy is in trouble and only you can save him."

"I don't want to," Oswald says.

"I know," Teeny says. "But you have to do it. A little boy is in trouble. We can't say no to little boys in trouble. Right?"

"Right," he says. Oswald doesn't say anything for a long time. I want to say something to fill the space, but I don't. I wait with Teeny while Oswald thinks. Finally, he looks back at Teeny.

forty-nine

"How did you do that?" I ask as we walk down the hallway toward the elevators. I am walking alongside Teeny, who is flying down the hall. Her wings make a humming sound that I did not hear when I was in the bald man's room. Even this close, her wings move so fast that they are nothing but a blur.

Oswald is behind us, head down, looking like a snowplow again.

"How did I do what?" Teeny asks.

"Everything," I say, lowering my voice to a whisper. "How did you know that Oswald wouldn't attack you like he attacked me? How did you convince him to help me? How did you even know where I was?"

"The last question is easy," Teeny says. "You told us what floor you found Oswald on the first time. A couple minutes after you left, I decided that you might need some help. So I came over to the grown-up hospital and flew up the stairs to the eighth floor. By the time I got up here, finding you was easy. The two of you were making such a racket that I knew right where to go."

"That racket was me getting tossed around the room like a doll."

"I know," Teeny says, smiling.

"Okay, how did you know that Oswald wouldn't attack you like he attacked me?" I ask.

"I didn't go into his room," Teeny says. "I stood at the doorway."

"I don't get it."

"You told us that Oswald found you sneaking up behind you the first time you met. Right outside his room. And later on he found you in his room. I thought that if I didn't go into the room, he probably wouldn't hurt me. Plus, I'm a girl. And a fairy. You'd have to be a real stinker to hit a fairy."

"You were imagined smart," I say.

Teeny smiles again.

"How long have you been alive?" I ask.

"Almost three years."

"That's a long time for someone like us," I say.

"Not nearly as long as you."

"No, but it's still a long time. You're lucky."

We turn a corner and pass a man in a wheelchair talking to himself. I look around for an imaginary friend but see none. I turn to check on Oswald. He is about three steps behind us, plowing away. I turn back to Teeny. "How did you get Oswald to help me?" I whisper. "All you did was ask him to help, and he said yes."

"I did what Mom always does when she wants Katie to do something."

"Katie is your human friend?" I ask.

"Yes. She has something wrong in her head that the doctors have to fix. That's why she is in the hospital."

"What does your mom do when she wants Katie to do something?" I ask.

"When Mom wants Katie to do her homework or brush her teeth or eat her broccoli, she doesn't tell Katie to do it. She makes it sound like it's Katie's choice. Like it's Katie's only choice. Like not eating the broccoli would be wrong."

"That was it?" I ask. "That's all you did?" I try to remember everything that Teeny said to Oswald but it all happened so fast.

"It was easy with Oswald, because not helping you was a really wrong thing to do. A lot more wrong than not eating broccoli or not brushing his teeth. And I asked him questions, too. I tried to show him I cared, because I thought that he was probably lonely. There aren't too many imaginary friends in a grown-up hospital. Right?"

"You really were imagined smart," I say.

Teeny smiles again. For the first time since Graham disappeared, I think I may have found an imaginary friend who could be my friend, too.

We reach the elevators and I turn to Oswald. "Do you want to ride on the elevator or take the stairs?"

"I never rode on the elevator before," he says.

"Do you want to take the stairs, then?" I ask.

"I don't like the stairs," he says, looking down at his feet.

"Okay. We'll take the elevator then. It will be fun."

We stand by the elevators, waiting for someone to come along and press the Down button. I think about asking Oswald to press the button, just so I could see him move something in the real world again, but I decide not to. He said that it was hard to move things in the real world, so there is no need to make him work when someone else can do the work for him. He is nervous enough already.

It doesn't take long before a man in a white coat comes along pushing another man in a wheelchair. The man in the white coat pushes the Down arrow and when the door slides open, Oswald, Teeny, and I step in behind him.

"I never rode in an elevator before," Oswald says again.

"It's fun," I say. "You'll like it."

But Oswald looks nervous. So does Teeny.

The man pushing the wheelchair presses the number 3 and the elevator begins to move. Oswald's eyes widen. His hands bunch into fists.

"The men are getting out on the third floor. We will, too. We can take the stairs from there."

"Okay," Oswald says, looking relieved. I want to tell him that riding from the third to the first floor in an elevator would only take an extra five seconds, but I let him feel relieved instead. He doesn't like the stairs, so he must hate the elevator.

I think Teeny does, too.

The door slides open and we follow the man and the wheelchair into the hallway.

"The stairs are around the corner," I say. As I speak, I notice the sign on the wall opposite the elevators. In between the directions for restrooms and a place called RADIATION is this:

◀ INTENSIVE CARE UNIT

I stop.

I stare at the sign for a moment.

"What?" Teeny asks when I do not move.

"Can you and Oswald wait here for a minute?" I ask Teeny.

"Why?"

"I want to check on somebody. I think she is on this floor."

"Who?" Teeny asks.

"A friend," I say. "Sort of a friend, I mean. I think she is down the hall."

Teeny stares at me. She narrows her eyes to slits. I feel like she is trying to look straight through me. "Okay," she finally says. "We can wait. Right, Oswald?"

"Okay," Oswald says.

I turn left. I follow the signs like I did when I found the ICU in the Children's Hospital. After two long hallways and one turn, I find myself standing outside a set of double doors that look a lot like the doors to the children's ICU. The name tag on the doors reads INTEN-SIVE CARE UNIT.

I pass through them.

I am standing in a large room with curtains along the outside edges of the room. Some of the curtains are closed and some are open. There is a long counter and desks and lots of machines in the center of the room. Doctors are moving around, going in and out of the curtains, typing on computers, talking on the telephones, talking to each other, writing things down on clipboards, and looking worried.

All doctors look worried, but these doctors look extra worried.

I start with the curtain closest to me. It is closed. I crawl under it. An old woman is lying in the bed behind it. She has gray hair and lots of wrinkles around her eyes. She has machines with wires and tubes hooked up to her arms and a thin plastic tube stuck underneath her nose. She is sleeping.

I move to the next curtain and then the next. When the curtain is closed, I crawl underneath. Some of the beds are empty and some have people in them. All grown-ups. Mostly men. Two of the curtains have no beds at all.

I find Dee behind the last curtain. I do not realize that it is Dee at first. Her head is shaved. She is as bald as Oswald's bald friend. She is as bald as Oswald. Her cheeks are swollen and the skin around her eyes is black. She has the most machines attached to her of anyone I've seen so far. Tubes and wires run from bags of water and machines with tiny television screens to her arm and chest. The machines make hissing, beeping, clicking sounds.

There is a woman sitting in a chair next to Dee. She is holding Dee's hand. It is Dee's sister. I know this because she looks just like Dee. A younger version of Dee. Same dark skin. Same sharp chin. Same round eyes. She is whispering words into Dee's ear. She whispers the same words over and over again. Words like *God* and *Jesus* and *Almighty* and *Praise*. I can barely hear her.

Dee does not look good. She looks very bad.

Dee's sister does not look good, either. She looks tired and scared.

I sit on the edge of the bed next to Dee's sister. I look down at Dee. I want to cry, except I do not have time to cry. Teeny and Oswald are waiting by the elevators and Mrs. Patterson is packing her secret bus with food and clothes. I have to go. "I'm sorry you are hurt," I say to Dee. "I'm so sorry. I wish I could have saved you. I miss you."

Tears fill my eyes. This is only the second time that my eyes have made tears and they feel strange. Slippery and hot.

"I have to save Max," I tell Dee. "I couldn't save you, but I think I can save Max. So I have to go now."

I stand up to leave. I look back at Dee's ruined face and thin wrists. I listen to her raspy, uneven breath and the whispers of her sister and the steady beep of the machine beside her bed. I look and I listen. Then I sit back down.

"I'm afraid," I say to Dee. "I couldn't save you, but maybe I can save Max. Except I'm scared. Max is in trouble, but I think his trouble is good for me. If he stays in trouble, I stay alive. So I'm confused."

I take a deep breath. I think about what I want to say next, but when nothing comes to my mind, I just start talking again. "It's not like Max is going to be shot by a man in a devil mask. It's not that kind of trouble at all. Mrs. Patterson will take good care of Max. I know it. She is a devil, too, but not the kind that shot you. Max will be fine no matter what I do. But I might not be fine. I don't know what is going to happen to me. And now I have Oswald helping me, so I really might be able to save him. I never thought that Oswald would agree to help, but he has. Now I can save Max, I think. Except I'm afraid."

I sit and stare at Dee. I listen to her sister whisper her words over and over again. They sound almost like a song.

"I know saving Max is the right thing to do," I say to Dee. "But it won't matter if I do the right thing if I stop existing. The right thing is only good if you are here to enjoy it."

I feel more hot, slippery tears in my eyes, but these are not for Dee. They are for me.

"I wish there was a Heaven. If I knew there was a Heaven for me, then I would save Max for sure. I wouldn't be afraid because there would be a place to go after this place. Another place. But I don't think there is a Heaven, and I definitely don't think there is a Heaven for imaginary friends. Heaven is only supposed to be for people who God made, and God didn't make me. Max made me."

I smile, thinking about Max as a god. A god locked up in a basement with a bunch of LEGOs and army men. The god of one. The God of Budo.

"I guess that's why I should save him," I say. "Because he made me. I wouldn't be alive without him. But I'm afraid, and I feel bad for being afraid. I feel even worse for thinking about leaving Max with Mrs. Patterson. Even though I know I will try to save him, I think about not saving him and that makes me feel bad. Like a real stinker. But it's not wrong to be worried about myself, too. Right?"

"No." This is not Dee's sister or a doctor who speaks. It is Dee.

I know she can't hear me because I am an imaginary friend. But the word sounds like an answer to my question. It surprises me. Just Dee speaking surprises me. I gasp.

"Dee?" Her sister says. "What did you say?"

"Don't be afraid," Dee says.

"Don't be afraid of what?" her sister asks. She is squeezing Dee's hand. Leaning in closer and closer.

"Are you talking to me?" I ask.

Dee's eyes are open now, but they are only teeny-tiny slits. I look to see if she is looking at me, but I can't tell.

"Don't be afraid," Dee says again. Her voice is thin and whispery but the words are clear.

"Doctor!" Dee's sister shouts, turning her head toward the counter and the desks in the center of the room. "My sister is awake. She's talking!"

Two doctors stand up and move in our direction.

"Are you talking to me, Dee?" I ask again. I know she is not. She can't be. But it seems like she is.

"Go," Dee says. "Go. It's time."

"Me?" I ask. "Are you talking to me? Dee?"

The doctors arrive. They pull the curtains all the way open. A doctor asks Dee's sister to step aside. The other doctor walks to the opposite side of the bed as an alarm sound begins ringing. Dee's eyes roll back in her head. The doctors move faster, and I am pushed off the bed and onto the floor by another doctor who has just arrived. He shoved me out of the way without even knowing it.

"She was just talking!" Dee's sister says.

"She's crashing!" one of the doctors shouts.

Another doctor takes Dee's sister by the shoulder and moves her away from the bed. Two more doctors arrive. I move to the end of the bed. I can barely see Dee. The doctors are crowding around her. One of the doctors puts a plastic bag over Dee's mouth and starts squeezing it open and shut. Another doctor sticks a needle into a tube that is connected to Dee's arm. I watch as a yellow liquid moves up the tube and disappears under Dee's nightgown.

Dee is dying.

I can tell by the look on the doctors' faces. They are working hard and fast, but they are just doing what they are supposed to do. I see the same look on the faces of some of Max's teachers when Max doesn't understand something and the teacher doesn't think he will ever understand it. The teachers work hard, but you can tell that they are just doing the lesson. Not teaching the lesson. That's what the doctors look like now. They are doing the doctoring but they do not believe in the doctoring.

Dee's eyes close.

I hear her words ringing in my head.

Go. It's time. Don't be afraid.

fifty

We are standing at the front doors to the hospital. Snow is falling outside. Oswald says that he has never seen snow. I tell him that he will love it.

"Thank you," I say to Teeny.

She smiles. I know she can't leave Katie, but I wish she could come with us.

"Are you ready, Oswald?" I ask.

The lobby is busy. It is full of people coming and going. Oswald looks even bigger now that I can compare him to so many other people. He is a giant.

"No," Oswald says. "I want to stay here."

"But you will go with Budo and help him," Teeny says. This is not a question. It is a command.

"Yes," Oswald says. The word is *yes* but the sound is *no*.

"Good," Teeny says, and then she flies over to Oswald and hugs his neck, too. He gasps. His muscles tense. His hands ball into fists again. Teeny keeps squeezing until he finally relaxes. It takes a long time.

"And good luck," she adds. "I want to see both of you again. Soon."

"Okay," Oswald says.

"You will," I say.

But I do not believe it. I think this is the last time I will ever see Teeny or this hospital again.

Oswald spends the first five minutes outside trying to avoid the falling snowflakes. He dodges one while ten other flakes pass through him. He doesn't even notice.

Once he realizes that they will not hurt him, he spends the next

247

five minutes trying to catch snowflakes on his tongue. They pass through his tongue, of course, but it takes him a while to realize this, and he bounces off at least three people and a telephone pole while doing so.

"We have to go," I say to Oswald.

"Where?"

"We have to go home. We have to ride the bus to school tomorrow."

"I have never been on a bus before," Oswald says.

I can see that he is nervous. I decide to tell him as little as possible from now on. "It will be fun," I say. "I promise."

It is a long walk from the hospital to Max's house. I usually enjoy the walk, but Oswald asks questions. Lots and lots of questions.

When do they turn the streetlights on?

Does each streetlight have a separate switch?

Where did all the choo-choo trains go?

Why don't people just draw their own money?

Who decided that red means *stop* and green means *go*?

Is there only one moon?

Are all car honks the same?

How do the police stop trees from growing in the middle of the street?

Do people paint their own cars?

What is a fire hydrant?

Why don't people whistle when they walk?

Where do airplanes live when they are not flying?

The questions never stop, and even though I want them to stop, I keep answering. This giant who was throwing me around a hospital room earlier today needs me now, and as long as he needs me, I hope that he will listen to me and help me.

Ever since we left Teeny behind at the hospital, I have been afraid that Oswald would turn into his old, angry self. That Teeny's magic would wear off after we got far enough away. Instead, he has become more like a preschooler who wants to know everything.

"This is my house," I say to Oswald as we finally turn up the driveway. It is late. I do not know how late, but the lights in the kitchen and the living room are turned off.

"Where are we going?" Oswald asks.

"Inside. Do you sleep?"

"When?" Oswald asks.

"Do you sleep at all?"

"Oh. Yes."

"This is where we will sleep tonight," I say, pointing at the house.

"How will I get in?" he asks.

"Though the door," I say.

"How?"

Then I realize it. Oswald can't pass through doors. In the hospital, when we took the stairs from the third floor to the first floor, we followed two men in blue uniforms through the door to the stairway. When we left the hospital, we followed a man and a woman.

This is why Oswald pushed open the door to the bald man's room. John's room. He had to push it open if he wanted to get in.

"Can you open the door?" I ask.

"I don't know," Oswald says. But I can see that he is looking at the door like it is a mountain.

"It'll be locked," I say, which is true. "Never mind."

"How do you get in?" Oswald asks.

"I can pass through doors."

"Pass through?"

I climb three steps to the front door of the house and then pass through. I actually pass through two doors. A screen door and a wooden door. Then I turn around and pass back through to the outside.

Oswald's mouth is hanging open when I reappear on the other side. His eyes are gigantic. "You're magic," he says.

"No, you're magic," I say. "I know lots of imaginary friends who can pass through doors. But I don't know any imaginary friends who can touch the real world."

"Imaginary friends?"

I realize that I have said too much again. "Yes," I say. "I'm an imaginary friend." I pause for a moment, thinking about what to say next. Then I add, "So are you."

"I'm an imaginary friend?" Oswald asks.

"Yes. What did you think you were?"

"A ghost," he says. "I thought you were a ghost, too. I thought you were going to steal John away from me."

I laugh. "Nope. No ghosts here. What did you think Teeny was?"

"A fairy," Oswald says.

I laugh again, but then I realize that this probably helped Teeny convince Oswald to help me. "I guess you're half right about Teeny," I say. "She's a fairy, but she is imaginary, too."

"Oh."

"You look upset," I say. And he does. He is looking at his feet again and his arms are hanging by his side like wet noodles.

"I don't know which is better," Oswald says. "Imaginary or a ghost."

"What's the difference?" I ask.

"If I am a ghost, that means I was alive once. If I'm imaginary, that means I was never alive."

There is silence between us as we stare at one another. I don't know what to say. Then I do. "I have an idea," I say. I say this because I really do have an idea, but mostly because I want to change the subject. "Do you think you could press the doorbell?"

"Where?" Oswald asks, and I can tell by the question that he does not know what a doorbell is.

"This little dot," I say, pointing at the button. "If you press it down, a bell will ring inside the house and Max's parents will open the door. When they do, we can slip inside."

"I thought you could pass through the door," Oswald says.

"Yes, I can. Sorry. I meant *you* could pass through the door."

"Okay," Oswald says. He says *okay* a lot, and I can't help but think of Max every time he does. Max will be alone tonight, locked in Mrs. Patterson's basement, and the thought of that makes me feel sad and rotten.

I promised him that I would never leave. Now I am here with Oswald.

But tomorrow night Max will be sleeping in his own bed. I say these words in my head, and they make me feel a little better.

Oswald climbs the three steps to the landing. He reaches out to press the doorbell, but before he does, his entire body stiffens. The muscles in his arms and neck pop out. A vein in his forehead appears and throbs. The caterpillars above his eyes kiss again. He clenches his teeth. His hand shakes as he reaches out with his finger. It touches the button, and for a second, nothing happens. Then his hand shakes even more and I hear Oswald grunt. As he grunts, the button disappears under his finger and the bell rings.

"You did it!" I say, and even though I have seen him touch the real world before, I am still amazed.

Oswald nods. There are tiny beads of sweat on his forehead and he is trying to catch his breath. He looks like he just ran twenty miles.

I hear someone moving inside the house. We stand back so the door doesn't knock Oswald off the stoop. The wooden door opens inward. Max's mom steps into the doorway and peers out through the screen door. She cups her hands over her eyes. She looks back and forth, and now I can see that this was not a good idea.

I can see hope in her face.

She was thinking that this might be good news. She was thinking that it might be Max.

She opens the screen door and steps out onto the stoop beside Oswald. It is cold outside. The snow has stopped but I can see her breath in the freezing air. She wraps her arms around her body to stay warm. I nudge Oswald forward as Max's mom says, "Hello? Is anyone there?"

"Go inside," I say. "Wait for me." Oswald does as I say. I watch as Max's mom calls out one more time, and then the hope disappears from her face.

"Who is it?" Max's dad says. He is standing in the kitchen now. Oswald is standing beside him.

"No one," Max's mom says. Her words sound like boulders. She can barely pick them up to say them.

"Who the hell rings a person's doorbell at ten o'clock and then runs away?" Max's dad says.

"Maybe it was a mistake," Max's mom says. She sounds far away even though she is standing right beside me.

"I don't think so," Max's dad says. "No one makes that kind of mistake and then disappears."

Max's mom starts to cry. She would have cried anyway, I think, but the word *disappears* hits her like one of those boulders. Her tears pour out.

Max's dad knows it. He knows what he has done. "Honey, I'm sorry." He puts his arms around her and pulls her back from the doorway, letting the screen door close behind him. No *whack-whack-whack* this time. They stand in the kitchen, holding each other, as Max's mom cries and cries and cries. She cries harder than I have ever heard a person cry before.

———

The door to Max's bedroom is closed, so I tell Oswald to sleep on the couch in the living room. He is so long that his feet hang off the end of the couch. They dangle in the air like two enormous fishing poles.

"Are you comfortable?" I ask.

"When someone is sleeping in the bed next to John, I have to sleep on the floor. This is better than the floor."

"Good. Sleep tight, then."

"Wait," Oswald says. "Are you going to sleep now?"

I don't want to tell Oswald that I don't sleep. I think it will just make him ask more questions. So I say yes. "I'll just sleep in this chair. I do it a lot."

"Before I go to sleep, I always talk to John."

"You do? What do you tell him?"

"I tell him about my day," Oswald says. "What I did. Who I saw. I can't wait to tell him about all the things I saw today."

"Do you want to tell me about your day?"

"No," Oswald says. "You already know about my day. You were with me."

"Oh," I say. "Then do you want to tell me something else?"

"No, I want you to tell me about your friend."

"Max?" I ask.

"Yes," Oswald says. "Tell me about Max. I never had a friend who could walk and talk."

"Okay," I say. "I will tell you about Max."

I start with the easy stuff. I talk about what Max looks like and what he likes to eat. I tell him about the LEGOs and the army men and the video games. I explain how Max is different than other kids because he can get stuck and he lives mostly on the inside.

Then I tell the stories. I tell the story about Max's first Halloween party in kindergarten, and his bonus poops, and his fight with Tommy Swinden in the boy's bathroom, and the rock that Tommy Swinden threw through Max's bedroom window last week. I talk about how Max's mom makes Max try new things and how Max's dad likes to use the word *normal* a lot. I tell him about the games of catch in the backyard and the way I help Max choose between a red or green shirt when he can't decide.

And I tell him about Mrs. Gosk. I tell him about how she is almost perfect except when she calls Max "my boy" but that is close enough to perfect to make her perfect.

I do not talk about Mrs. Patterson. I'm afraid that if I do, Oswald might be too afraid to help me tomorrow.

Oswald does not ask any questions. Twice I think he has fallen asleep. I stop talking and he lifts his head, looks at me, and says, "What?"

"Do you know what I like best about Max?" I ask.

"No," he says. "I don't know Max."

"The thing I like best about Max is that he is brave."

"What did he do that was brave?"

"It's not one thing," I say. "It's everything. Max is not like any other person in the whole world. Kids make fun of him because he is different. His mom tries to change him into a different boy and his dad tries to treat him like he is someone else. Even his teachers treat him differently, and not always nicely. Even Mrs. Gosk. She is perfect but she still treats Max differently. No one treats him like a regular boy, but everyone wants him to be regular instead of himself. With all that, Max still gets out of bed every morning and goes to school and the park and the bus stop and even the kitchen table."

"That's brave?" Oswald asks.

"That's the bravest," I say. "I am the oldest, smartest imaginary friend I have ever met. It is easy for me to go out and meet other imaginary friends because they all look up to me. They ask me questions and want to be like me. When they are not beating me up."

I smile at Oswald.

He does not smile back.

"But you have to be the bravest person in the world to go out every day, being yourself when no one likes who you are. I could never be as brave as Max."

"I wish I had a Max," Oswald says. "I never even heard John talk."

"Maybe he will someday."

"Maybe," Oswald says, but I don't think he believes it.

"Can we go to sleep now?" I ask.

"Yes," Oswald says, and he does not say another word. He falls asleep almost immediately.

I sit in a chair and watch him sleep. I try to imagine tomorrow. I make a list of all the things I need to do to save Max. I try to predict where my plan might go wrong. I think about what I will say to Max when the time comes.

This will be the most important part. I cannot save Max alone. I will need Oswald's help, but most of all, I will need Max.

I cannot save Max unless I can convince him to save himself.

fifty-one

Mrs. Gosk once read a story to the class about a boy named Pinocchio. The kids laughed when they heard that she was going to read the story to them. They thought it was for babies.

It is never a good idea to laugh at Mrs. Gosk.

Once she started reading, the kids realized how wrong they were. They loved the story. They didn't want her to stop reading. They wanted to hear more and more and more. But every day, Mrs. Gosk would stop at the most suspenseful moment in the book and make the kids wait until the next day to find out what happened next. They begged her to read more and she would say, "You can take charge of this classroom when pigs fly!" This made them all so mad. Even Max. He loved the story, too. I think Mrs. Gosk did this on purpose just to punish her students for laughing at her.

Never mess with Mrs. Gosk.

Pinocchio was a puppet who was carved from a magical block of wood by a man named Geppetto. Even though he was supposed to be a puppet, Pinocchio was alive. He could move around on his own and talk and his nose even grew longer when he lied. But Pinocchio spent most of the time wishing that he could become a real boy.

I hated Pinocchio. I think I was the only one in the class who hated him. Pinocchio was alive, but that was not enough for him. He could walk and talk and touch things in the real world, but he spent the whole book wanting more.

Pinocchio didn't know how lucky he was.

I started thinking about Pinocchio tonight because of what Oswald said about ghosts and imaginary friends. I think he was right. Being a ghost would be better. Ghosts were alive once. Imaginary friends are never alive in the real world.

If you are a ghost, you don't stop existing if someone stops believing in you. Or forgets about you. Or finds someone better than you to take your place.

If I was a ghost, I could exist forever.

I forgot about getting Oswald out of the house this morning. My first mistake of the day. Making a mistake before we even leave the house is not a good sign.

I think we will still be okay. Max's mom goes for a run on most mornings, and Max's dad usually leaves for work before the bus comes. Plus, he sometimes goes outside to pick up the newspaper off the front lawn. Sometimes he just picks it up and brings it to work with him, but sometimes he brings it inside to read while he is eating breakfast. We just need someone to open the door once and Oswald will be able to get outside.

Max's mom walks into the kitchen at 7:30. She is quiet. She is wearing her robe. Even though she just woke up, she still looks tired. She brews a pot of coffee and eats toast with jam. She is not my mother, but she is the closest thing to a mom that I will ever have, and I hate to see her so small and tired and sad. I try to picture her screaming with joy when she sees Max tonight. I try to erase the picture of her from right now, all tired and ruined, and replace it with my picture from the future. I will fix her. I will save Max and that will save her, too.

Max's dad finally opens the door at 7:48 according to the clock on the microwave above the stove. He is still wearing sweatpants. I don't think he is going to work. He looks tired. Even though Max's mom and dad were hugging last night, I can tell that there is something wrong between them. Max's dad does not talk to Max's mom. He says, "Good morning" and nothing else. And she does not talk to him. It's like an invisible wall is standing between them. Max always gave them lots of reasons to fight, but I think that Max also gave them a reason to love each other. But now they are losing hope. They are starting to think that they might never see Max again. And without Max, there is nothing to hold them together. It's almost like Max is still here, except now he is just a reminder of what they have lost.

I have a lot of saving to do today.

The bus stops at Max's house at 7:55, but the bus will not stop at Max's house today. We have to go to the Savoys' house, and that means we will have to run as fast as we can. We cannot miss the bus because I am not sure if I can find the school on my own. I might be able to, but I do not pay enough attention to the streets when we drive. I might not.

Oswald starts to ask questions as soon as we step outside. "What is that little box at the end of the driveway?" he asks.

"The mailbox," I say.

"What's a mailbox?" he asks.

I stop and turn. "If we do not catch that bus, we can't save Max. You can ask me as many questions as you want once we are on that bus, but we have to run as fast as we can right now if we are going to catch it. Okay?"

"Okay," Oswald says, and he starts to run. He is a giant but he can run fast. I can barely keep up with him.

The bus passes us when we are two driveways away from the Savoys' house. I am sure that we will never make it to the bus stop in time. But there are three Savoy boys and a first-grade girl named Patty who gets on the bus at this stop, so they might slow down the bus driver a little while they climb aboard. Probably not enough, but there is a chance.

Then I see our chance. As Jerry Savoy is getting ready to step onto the bus, his big brother, Henry, knocks the books out of Jerry's hands and laughs. The books fall to the ground in front of the steps, and one book tumbles under the bus. Jerry has to bend over to collect them, and he has to get on his hands and knees to reach the book that landed under the bus. Henry Savoy is a big, mean jerk, but today he has done me a favor. Henry doesn't know it, and Jerry doesn't know it, but they may have just saved Max. We reach the Savoys' bus stop just in time to squeeze through the door behind Patty.

Ten seconds later and the bus would have already been moving.

I try to catch my breath as I point Oswald to the seat where Max and I usually sit.

"Why do kids ride buses?" Oswald asks. "Why don't their moms just drive them to school?"

"I don't know," I say. "Maybe some people don't have cars."

"I've never ridden on a bus before."

"I know," I say. "How do you like it?"

"It's not as exciting as I thought it would be."

"Thanks for running so fast."

"I want to save Max," Oswald says.

"You do?"

"Yeah."

"Why?" I ask. "You don't even know him."

"He is the bravest boy in the world. You said so. He pooped on Tommy Swinden's head and goes to school every day even though no one likes him. We have to save Max."

Listening to Oswald say these words makes me feel warm inside. This must be how Mrs. Gosk feels when she tells a story that becomes a part of her students.

"Except how are we going to save Max?" Oswald asks. "You didn't tell me that yet."

I decide it is time. I spend the next ten minutes telling Oswald everything I know about Mrs. Patterson.

"You're right," Oswald says when I am finished. "She is the devil. She is a little-boy-stealing devil."

"Yes," I say. "But you know what? I don't think Mrs. Patterson knows that she is the devil. She thinks that Max's parents are the devils. She thinks that what she is doing is right. I still don't like her, but it makes me hate her a little less."

"Maybe we are all somebody's devil," Oswald says. "Maybe even me and you."

As he says these last four words, I notice for the first time that I can see the houses and the last few brightly colored leaves flashing by the windows as the bus moves down the street.

I can see the trees flashing by *through him*.

Oswald is fading away.

It makes no sense. What are the chances that Oswald would start to fade away on the very day I need him? On the day that Max needs him?

It doesn't seem fair.

It seems impossible.

It feels like one of those television shows where too many bad things happen at once and the show feels fake.

Then I realize what has happened. It is my fault. Oswald is dying because of me.

Oswald said that before he went to sleep, he would spend every night talking to John. He would tell John what he did and who he saw, and after he was done telling about his day, he would fall asleep.

This must have been what kept John believing in Oswald. John must have been able to hear Oswald tell his stories every night. Either with his ears or maybe just inside his head. Inside his mind. Maybe this is why Oswald existed in the first place. John is trapped in a body that won't wake up, so Oswald is like John's eyes and ears. His window on the outside world. I thought that Oswald could move things in the real world because John is a grown-up. I never met an imaginary friend whose human person friend was a grown-up, so I thought this is what made Oswald special. This is what gave Oswald his special powers.

But maybe Oswald can move things in the real world because John can't move things anymore. Maybe John is so sad about being stuck in his coma that he imagined Oswald being able to move things because he couldn't. Maybe Oswald is John's window to the world and the way that John can still touch the real world.

Except now I have taken that window away. Oswald was not able to talk to John last night, and now John has stopped believing in his imaginary friend.

Oswald is dying because of me.

Oswald was right. Everyone is somebody's devil, and I am Oswald's devil.

fifty-two

We are sitting in Mrs. Gosk's classroom. Mrs. Gosk is telling a story about her daughters, Stephanie and Chelsea. She is still not herself. I can see the sadness in her eyes. She does not bounce around the room like the floor is on fire. But the kids are still sitting on the edges of their chairs. Oswald is sitting on the edge of his chair. He cannot take his eyes off Mrs. Gosk. I think this is the only reason that he hasn't noticed that he is disappearing. He is disappearing fast. Much faster than Graham. I'm worried that he might be completely gone by the end of the school day.

Oswald turns to me.

I brace myself. He knows that he is fading away. I can feel it.

"I love Mrs. Gosk," he says.

I smile.

Oswald turns his attention back to Mrs. Gosk. She has finished telling the story about her daughters. She is talking about something called a predicate now. I do not know what a predicate is. I don't think Oswald knows, either, but he seems more interested in predicates than anyone else in the room. His eyes are glued to Mrs. Gosk.

I know what I have to do. I don't know how I will do it, but I have to find a way. It is the right thing to do.

It feels impossible to do the wrong thing when Mrs. Gosk is in the room.

"Oswald, we have to go," I say.

"Where?" he asks, still staring at Mrs. Gosk.

"The hospital."

He turns to me. Those caterpillars above his eyes kiss again. "What about Max? We have to save him."

"Oswald, you're disappearing."

261

"You know?" he asks.

"You know?" I ask.

"Yes. I noticed when I woke up this morning. I could see through my hands. You didn't say anything, so I thought that maybe only I could see it."

"No, I can see it, and I've seen it happen before. You're going to disappear completely if we don't get you back to John."

"Maybe," Oswald says, but he does not believe maybe. He believes definitely, just like me.

"Not maybe," I say. "I know it. John believes in you because he hears you talking to him every night. But he didn't hear you last night because you were with me. That is why you're disappearing. We have to get you back to him."

"But what about Max?" Oswald asks. There is a tiny bit of anger in his voice that surprises me.

"Max is my friend, and I know that he wouldn't want you to die saving him. It's not right."

"I want to save Max," Oswald says. "And I get to choose." His fists clench and he glares at me. I can't help but wonder if even Oswald is forced to do the right thing when Mrs. Gosk is in the room.

"I know you want to save him," I say. "But not today. We have to get you back to John. You can save Max tomorrow."

"I might not get back to John in time," Oswald says. "And even if I did, I can't feel John anymore. I think it's too late."

I think so, too. I remember what happened when I tried to save Graham. I'm starting to believe that once an imaginary friend begins to disappear, nothing can stop it. But I don't want to be the one to say it aloud. "You're going to die unless we do something," I say.

"It's okay. I know."

"You're not going to become a ghost if that's what you're thinking. You're just going to disappear forever. It will be like you were never here."

"Not if I save Max," Oswald says. "If I save the bravest boy in the world, it will be like I am here forever."

"That's not true," I say. "You'll be gone and no one will remember you. Max won't even remember you. It will be like you never even existed."

"Do you know why I was so angry when you met me?" Oswald asks.

"You thought I was a ghost. And you thought I was going to steal John."

"Yes, but not really. It was because when I was in that hospital, it was like I didn't exist. I was stuck in that room and in those hallways with no one to talk to and nothing to see or do. Maybe I'm not a ghost, but it was like I was a ghost."

"This is ridiculous," I say. And it is. I feel like Oswald and I have switched places. I am angry and scared and ready to punch someone in the face, and he is so stupidly calm. He is disappearing right in front of his own eyes but he doesn't even care. He doesn't want to fight.

He reminds me of Graham after our plan to save her failed. She quit, too.

Then Oswald does the unbelievable. Oswald reaches out and hugs me. He wraps his giant arms around me and squeezes. He lifts me right out of my seat. It's the first time he has touched me without hurting me, and it makes no sense. Oswald is disappearing but I am the one being hugged.

"I knew I was disappearing this morning when I looked through my hands," he says, still squeezing. "I was scared at first, but I was scared the whole time I was in the hospital, too. And now I got to meet you and Teeny. I rode on an elevator and a bus. I got to see Mrs. Gosk. And I will save Max. That is more than I have ever done in my whole life."

"Just think about all you could still do," I say.

Oswald puts me down. Our eyes meet. "Not if I have to stay in the hospital every day. I'd rather have one good adventure than stay at the hospital forever."

"It's wrong not to try to get you back to the hospital," I say. "I feel like we're giving up."

"It's wrong not to help Max," Oswald says. "He's the bravest little boy in the whole world. He needs to be saved."

"You can save him after you save yourself."

Oswald suddenly looks angry. It's the kind of anger that I saw on his face just before he started throwing me around the hospital room. His muscles tighten and he seems to grow six more inches. Then just as quickly I see him change again. His fists unclench. His muscles relax. His face softens. It is not anger anymore. It is disappointment. Disappointment in me. "Stop," he says. "I want to listen to Mrs. Gosk.

Okay? I just want to sit here and listen to Mrs. Gosk until we have to go."

"Okay," I say. I want to say more but I am afraid. I am not afraid because Oswald is angry or disappointed in me, even though that hurts more than I thought it could. I am afraid because I need Oswald. I cannot save Max without him. I am glad that he wants to save Max instead of himself, but that makes me feel awful inside for wanting it. Like I am the worst imaginary friend who ever lived.

Max is the bravest little boy in the world, but Oswald is the bravest imaginary friend in the world.

fifty-three

Oswald stays with Mrs. Gosk all day. He even follows her into the bathroom. I tell him not to, but I don't think he understands about bathroom privacy.

I stay with Mrs. Gosk for most of the day, too. I keep an eye on Oswald. I am worried that he will disappear before he can help me save Max. I stare at his transparent body and try to guess how much longer he has. It is impossible to tell. It makes me crazy just thinking about it.

I also check on Mrs. Patterson. The first thing I did when we arrived at school was check to be sure that Mrs. Patterson is working today. She is. We saw her getting out of her car as the bus pulled into the circle.

Everything is going according to my plan. Except that the most important person for my plan to work is disappearing before my eyes.

Even though the school day ends at 3:20, Oswald and I leave Mrs. Gosk's classroom at three o'clock. Oswald has to climb into Mrs. Patterson's car when she opens the door, so I want him to be ready.

He says good-bye to Mrs. Gosk before he leaves. He walks up to the front of the room and tells her that she is the greatest teacher in the world. He tells her that sitting in her room was the best day of his life. I am not sure if I will see Mrs. Gosk again, but I know that Oswald will not. Watching him wave to her as he steps out of the classroom is almost as sad as watching Graham disappear. Almost the saddest thing ever. I say good-bye, too, but I make my good-bye as quick as possible.

I can't imagine never seeing her again. I love her so much.

Mrs. Patterson walks out the side door of the school five minutes after the bell rings. She is carrying a large cloth bag with both hands. It looks full. Her purse is slung over her shoulder.

"Don't worry about me," I remind Oswald. "I can pass through car doors just like the front door of my house. Just get inside. When she opens the door, jump in ahead of her. Don't wait a second. You have to be fast."

Mrs. Patterson stops by her car. She puts the bag down on the pavement and opens the back door. She lifts the bag. It looks heavy. I can see books and picture frames and snow boots inside. Other stuff, too, underneath all that. She is going to put the bag on the backseat. Oswald is not in position to enter through this door. He is standing in front of the door as Mrs. Patterson opens it. But he panics. He tries to run around the door and around Mrs. Patterson and sneak in as the door closes but he does not get there in time. He slams into the door and bounces off, landing on the pavement. He grunts, shaking his head.

"Get up!" I yell.

He listens. He pops right back up.

Mrs. Patterson steps forward and opens the front door. The one next to the steering wheel. Oswald is still in position to climb in. He is standing a couple steps back from where I told him to wait, but he is close enough to get in, I think.

"Now!" I yell, and Oswald moves, faster than I think he can move, squeezing in and crawling across the driver's seat just ahead of Mrs. Patterson's body. I am not sure what would have happened had Mrs. Patterson sat on Oswald. Imaginary friends are usually pushed out of the way, like when the elevator gets crowded, but there is always someplace to be pushed into. If Mrs. Patterson sat on Oswald, there would be no place for him to go.

I'm glad we'll never find out.

I pass through the backseat door, climb over the cloth bag, and sit behind Oswald, who is now in the passenger seat.

"Are you okay?" I ask.

"Yes," he says. But his voice sounds far away. After a couple seconds, he adds, "She doesn't look like a bad person. I thought she would look a lot meaner."

"That's probably why no one thinks she stole Max," I say.

"Maybe all the devils look normal," Oswald says. "Maybe that's why they can be so bad." He sounds so far away now that I am worried he won't survive the car ride. "Are you sure you're okay?" I ask.

"Yes," he says.

"Good. We'll be at Mrs. Patterson's house real soon."

Even though we'll be at Mrs. Patterson's house soon, we can't save Max until tonight. Oswald has to exist for another few hours, and I am not sure if he will.

I try to put those thoughts out of my mind and pay attention to the streets as we leave the school. I need to draw a map in my head for my plan to work. First we turn left out of the circle. We drive to the end of the road and stop at a stoplight. It's a long light. Mrs. Patterson starts tapping on her steering wheel while we wait. She thinks it is long, too. Finally, the light turns green and Mrs. Patterson turns left. The radio is on. A man is telling us about the news. Nothing about a little boy disappearing from school. We drive past the park on the left and a church on the right. The front lawn of the church is covered by pumpkins. There is a white tent beside the field of orange. A man is standing underneath the tent. I think he is selling the pumpkins. We pass through two more traffic lights. Then we turn right at another traffic light.

"Left then left then three lights and a right," I say, and I repeat it twice more. I try to turn it into a song because songs are easier to remember.

"What are you saying?" Oswald asks.

"Directions. I need to know how to get back to the school."

"Driving in cars isn't very fun, either," Oswald says. "But a little better than the bus."

I wish I could talk to him but I can't. I am trying to memorize directions. But I feel bad. Oswald is fading away fast. The only imaginary friend who I ever met who could touch the outside world will disappear forever and I do not have time to talk to him.

We drive down a long, dark street. No parks or churches. Just houses and roads on the left and right. We go through two stoplights and then Mrs. Patterson turns left and we drive down a small, windy hill. At the bottom of the hill she turns left again. This is Mrs. Patterson's street. I recognize it. The pond is on the right. Mrs. Patterson's house is down the street on the right, too.

I try to imagine the drive from the school to Mrs. Patterson's street in my mind. Left, left, right, left, left. Traffic lights in between. The park. The pumpkin church. The pond.

I realize that I am not good with directions. I can walk to the hospital and the police station and the gas station because I walk slowly. Cars drive fast. It's hard to notice things when you are driving. And there are more turns to memorize because you go farther.

The car slows down and Mrs. Patterson turns right into her driveway.

"We're here," I say. "The house is at the top of this hill."

"Okay," Oswald says.

We drive up the hill to the house. Mrs. Patterson presses the button on the remote control and the garage door opens. She pulls into the garage and presses the button on the remote control again. The garage door closes.

"Is it time to save Max?" Oswald asks.

"Not yet," I say. "We have to wait a few hours. Do you think you can wait that long?"

"I don't know time. I don't know how long a few hours is."

"That's okay," I say. "I'm going to check on Max first, because I can pass through the door to his room. But you will see him soon."

Mrs. Patterson slams her car door shut. It's the bang that makes me realize that Oswald is still sitting in the passenger seat with no way of getting out of the car.

I have made another mistake.

After spending six years being able to pass through doors, I have forgotten that Oswald can't.

Again.

fifty-four

"What's the matter?" Oswald asks. I have not said a word since Mrs. Patterson closed the door.

"I messed up," I say. "I forgot to tell you to get out of the car."

"Oh."

"It's okay," I say. "I'll think of something." But as I tell Oswald not to worry, I can see a picture of him in my mind. The only imaginary friend who could touch the real world, fading away inside this ordinary car in this ordinary garage, unable to do the last, great thing that he was meant to do.

"I could try to open the door," Oswald says.

"You can't," I say. "I saw how hard it was for you to ring the doorbell at Max's house. You'll never be able to pull the handle and push that door at the same time."

Oswald looks at the handle and the door. He nods. "Maybe she will come back," he says.

It's true. She might. She left the cloth bag on the backseat and she may still need it. But Oswald is fading fast. If she does not come back soon, I am afraid that there will be nothing to come back to.

"Climb back here," I say. "If she comes back, she will come back for this bag. This is the door she will open." I point at the door closest to the bag. "We have to be ready."

Oswald climbs into the backseat. I am still amazed at how easily he moves even though he is a giant. He sits between me and the bag. We sit in silence for a while, waiting.

"Maybe you should go inside and check on Max," Oswald suggests. He sounds a million miles away. His voice is soft and muffled.

I thought about checking on Max but I am afraid to leave the car. I am afraid that Oswald will disappear while I am gone. I look closely at him. I can still see him, but I can also see everything behind him. The bag on the seat. The car door. The rake and shovel hanging on the wall of the garage. When he stops moving, it is easier to see the rake and the shovel than to see him.

"I'll be okay," he says. It's like he was reading my mind. "Just go check on Max and come back."

"You're disappearing," I say.

"I know."

"I'm afraid that you will disappear while I am gone."

"You think that if you leave the car, I will start disappearing faster?" he asks.

"No. I just don't want you to die alone."

"Oh."

We sit in silence again. I feel like I have said the wrong thing. I try to think of the right thing to say.

"Are you afraid?" I finally ask.

"No," he says. "Not afraid. Sad."

"Sad about what?"

"I'm sad that we won't be friends anymore. I'm sad that I won't see John or Teeny again. I'm sad that I won't ride in another elevator or another bus. I'm sad that I won't get to be friends with Max." He sighs and hangs his head. I try to think of the right thing to say again, but he speaks first before I can. "But when I disappear, I won't be sad anymore. I won't be anything anymore. So I'm just sad now."

"Why aren't you afraid?" This is not the right thing to say for Oswald, but it is the right thing to say for me, because I am afraid and I am not even disappearing. I feel bad for not thinking about what is the right thing to say to Oswald, but I can't help it.

"Afraid of what?" he asks.

"Afraid of what happens after you die."

"What happens?" he asks.

"I don't know what happens."

"Then why be afraid?" he asks. "I think probably nothing happens. And if it's better than nothing, that's okay, too."

"What if it's worse than nothing?"

"There's nothing worse than nothing. But if it's nothing, I won't know it because I will be nothing."

In that moment, Oswald sounds like a genius to me.

"But what about not existing?" I ask. "The whole world will go on without you. Like you were never here. And then someday every-one who knows you will be dead, too, and then it will be like you never, ever existed. Doesn't that make you sad?"

"Not if I save Max. If I save Max, I will exist forever."

I smile. I don't believe what he has said, but I smile because I like the idea. I wish I could believe it.

"Go check on Max," he says. "I promise that I won't disappear."

"I can't."

"If I start to disappear, I will honk the horn. Okay? I am sure I can do that."

"Fine," I say, and I turn to leave the car. Then I stop. "You're right. You can honk the horn."

"So?"

"Climb into the front seat," I say. "Honk that horn."

"Why?"

"I think it might be your way out of here."

Oswald climbs into the driver's seat. He places both hands on the horn. I can barely see them. I am worried that his power to touch the real world might be disappearing as he himself disappears.

He presses down, and as he does, the muscles in his arms tighten. His body shakes. Two veins in his neck grow thick and dark, even as they grow transparent. He groans a faraway groan. A second later the horn honks. It honks for about three seconds before stopping.

The moment it stops, Oswald relaxes. He sighs.

"Get ready now," I say.

"Okay," he says between breaths.

We wait for what feels like a long time. Ten minutes. Maybe lon-ger. We stare at the door that connects the garage to the house. It does not open.

"You need to do it again," I say.

"Okay," Oswald says, but the look on his face tells me that he is not sure if he can.

"Wait," I say. "Mrs. Patterson might be in the secret room with Max. Maybe she can't hear the horn from the secret room. Let me go inside and check where she is. I don't want you to honk the horn for nothing."

"Me, either," Oswald says.

I find Mrs. Patterson in the kitchen. She is washing a frying pan with a sponge. She is singing the hammer song again. The dishwasher is open. There are plates and glasses and silverware in the racks. Maybe she just finished eating with Max.

I return to the garage. As I approach the car, I do not see Oswald. He has disappeared. Just as I feared, he stopped existing while I was inside the house.

Then I see him. Almost invisible but still alive. He blinks and I can see his two black eyes and then the outline of his giant body. We can't wait until Mrs. Patterson is asleep, I decide. We have to save Max now.

I climb back into the car. "Okay. She is in the kitchen. Listen. When she comes out, she will open the car door to check on the horn. To see what is making it honk. Get out of the car right away and make sure you get into the house as fast as you can. You can't get stuck in the garage."

"Okay," he says. I can barely hear him and I am sitting right next to him.

Oswald returns his hands to the steering wheel. This time when he presses down, he lifts himself up so his bottom is no longer touching the seat. He is using his weight this time to help him. The muscles in his nearly transparent arms pop out again. The veins in his neck return. He groans. It takes at least a minute before the horn finally honks. It only honks for a second this time, but it is enough.

A moment later, the door connecting the garage to the house opens. Mrs. Patterson is standing in the doorway. She stares at the car. Her brow furrows. She leans forward slightly. But she remains in the doorway.

I stare into her eyes. She is not going to check on the car. I know it. "Do it again!" I shout. "Honk the horn again. Now!"

Oswald looks at me. I can barely see him but I can still see the exhaustion on his face. He does not believe that he can do it.

"Do it!" I shout again. "Honk that horn for Max Delaney! You are his only chance. Do it. You will be gone soon and if you don't get out of this car you will have nothing to show for it. Honk it. Honk it now!"

Oswald rises up. He kneels on the driver's seat and leans over, putting all his weight on the horn. And then he pushes, shouting Max's name as he does. Even though every word he says sounds farther and farther away, Max's name fills the car. He doesn't just shout Max's name. He roars it. The muscles in his back rise up with him, joining those in his arms and shoulders. He reminds me of a snowplow again. An unstoppable snowplow. The horn honks almost immediately.

Mrs. Patterson is pulling the door closed when the sound of the horn stops her. She jumps. She releases the door and allows it to swing open again. She stares back at the car. She scratches her head. Then, just as I think she is going to step back into the house and ignore her self-honking car again, she descends the three steps into the garage.

"Here she comes," I say. "When she opens that door, get out of the car and get into the house."

Oswald nods. He cannot speak. He cannot catch his breath.

Mrs. Patterson pulls open the driver's door and leans in. She is reaching for the horn with her right arm as Oswald twists his way past her and steps onto the concrete floor of the garage. He pauses, still catching his breath, when I tell him to go. "Go now," I say.

He listens. As he passes by Mrs. Patterson, she tests the horn, honking it herself. Oswald flinches at the sound but keeps moving. I don't waste a second waiting for her to finish her test. I pass through the door on my side of the car and follow Oswald into the house. As we pass through the washer machine room and into the gloom of the living room, I stop. The sun has set. It is dark outside. We have been sitting in the car longer than I thought. There are no lights on in this room. I have lost sight of Oswald.

"Oswald," I whisper. "Where are you?" Mrs. Patterson cannot hear me but I whisper anyway.

Television makes you do a lot of dumb things.

"Here," he says, grabbing my arm. Oswald is standing beside me but I cannot see him. And I can barely hear him. Yet his grip is strong. It gives me hope that he can do what must be done.

"Okay. Let's go," I say.

"I think that's a good idea," he says. "I don't think I have much time."

The door to the basement is open. After all that has happened, we deserve this small piece of luck. I did not know how to get Oswald into the basement if it had been closed. As I lead Oswald through the kitchen and down the stairs, I look at the clock on Mrs. Patterson's stove.

6:05.

Later than I thought but still not late enough. Mrs. Patterson will not be asleep for hours. But Oswald has no time left. I have to find a way to make it happen now.

The basement lights are on, but it is still almost impossible to see Oswald. As he steps into the room outside of Max's secret room, I can only see him because he is moving. When he stops beside the green table with the tiny tennis court on top, he disappears.

"Max is behind that wall," I say. "It's a door, but it's a secret door so I can't pass through it. And Max can't open it."

"You want me to open it?" Oswald asks from some faraway land.

"Yes," I say.

"This is where I save Max?" Oswald asks. He sounds relieved. He has made it. He is going to be able to do the one big thing in his life before he disappears.

"This is it," I say. "You are the only one who can open the door. The only one in the whole wide world."

I show Oswald the spot on the shelf where he must press. He places both hands against the shelf. He leans in and pushes. His whole body presses forward. He becomes the snowplow. The section of the shelf moves in almost immediately and the door slides open.

"That was easy," I say.

"Yeah," he says, sounding surprised. "Maybe I'm getting stronger."

I can't see Oswald's smile, but I can hear it in his voice.

I step inside Max's room for what I hope is the last time.

fifty-five

The Problems with Getting Max Home

1. Max is afraid of the dark.
2. Max is afraid of strangers.
3. Max will not talk to anyone who he does not know.
4. Max is afraid of Mrs. Patterson.
5. Max won't admit that he is afraid of Mrs. Patterson.
6. Max does not like change.
7. Max believes in me.

fifty-six

Max is expecting Mrs. Patterson to walk through the door. He does not look up when I enter the room. He is building a train with his LEGOs. The tracks are surrounded by platoons of plastic army men.

"Hi, Max," I say.

"A choo-choo train!" Oswald shouts.

Max drops the LEGO piece in his hand and stands up. "Budo!" He sounds happy to see me. His eyes widen as they meet mine. He takes a quick step forward but then stops. His tone quickly changes. His eyes narrow. He frowns. "You left me."

"I know."

"You broke your promise," he says.

"I know."

"Tell him you're sorry," Oswald says. He has moved across the room and is standing beside Max. He can't stop staring down at him. It is like the God of One has become the God of Two.

I look at Oswald with wide eyes and shake my head. I hope he understands my meaning. I am not afraid that Max will hear Oswald. I am afraid that Oswald will distract me. I feel like one of those police officers on television who has to talk a crazy person out of jumping off a bridge. I can't have any distractions. It's time for me to do my part. I only have one chance to save Max and I don't have much time.

"Why did you leave?" Max asks.

"I had to leave. If I stayed here, I thought you would stay here."

"I did stay here," Max says. His eyes narrow even further. He sounds confused.

"I know," I say. "But I was afraid that if I stayed here, you would stay with Mrs. Patterson forever. You're not supposed to be here, Max."

"Yes, I am. Stop it, Budo. You're not talking right."

277

"Max, you have to leave this place."

"No. I don't," Max says. He is starting to get upset. His cheeks are turning red and he is spitting his words. I have to be careful. I need to get Max just the right amount of upset. If he gets too upset, he could get stuck.

"Yes, you do," I say. "You have to leave. You don't belong here."

"Mrs. Patterson says that I belong here. She said you can stay here, too."

"Mrs. Patterson is bad," I say.

"No," Max says. He shouts the word. "Mrs. Patterson takes care of me. She gave me LEGOs and army men, and lets me eat grilled cheese for dinner every night. She told her mom that I am a good boy. She can't be bad."

"This is not a good place," I say.

"Yes, it is. Stop it, Budo. You're not talking right. You're not being a good friend. Why aren't you talking right?"

"You have to leave, Max. If you don't, you will never see your mom or dad or Mrs. Gosk or anyone else ever again."

"I will see you," Max says. "And Mrs. Patterson said I can see Mommy and Dad again soon."

"She is lying about your mom and dad, and you know it."

Max says nothing. This is a good sign.

"And if you stay here, you will never see me again, either," I say.

"Stop it. You're not talking right." Max's hands clench into tiny fists. For a second, he reminds me of Oswald.

"I mean it," I say. "You'll never, ever see me again."

"Why?" Max asks. There is fear in his voice now. This is good.

"I am leaving. And I am not coming back."

"No," Max says. But this is not a command. It is a request. He is asking me to stay. He is almost begging me to stay. Now there is hope.

"Yes," I say. "I am leaving. I am never, ever coming back."

"Please, Budo. Don't leave."

"I am leaving."

"No. Please don't leave."

"I am leaving," I say, trying to make my voice like cold, hard stone. "You can leave, too. Or you can stay here forever."

"I can't leave." Max says. I hear panic in his voice now. "Mrs. Patterson won't let me leave."

"That is why you have to escape, Max."

"I can't."

"Yes, you can."

"I can't," Max says, and it sounds as if he might cry. "Mrs. Patterson won't let me out."

"The door is open," I say. I point to the open door.

"The door is open?" Max says, finally noticing.

"Mrs. Patterson left the door open," I say.

"Liar liar, pants are on fire!" Oswald says from faraway. I smile, wondering where he learned that.

"Listen to me, Max. This is the only time that Mrs. Patterson will forget to lock the door. You have to go now."

"Budo, please stay with me. We can just stay here and play with army men and LEGOs and video games."

"No, we can't. I am leaving."

"Why are you being so mean?" Oswald asks. His voice is like an old whisper. It is like dust. I want to stop and say good-bye to him. Thank him for what he has done. I feel like he could be gone at any second. But I cannot stop. Max is toppling. I can feel it. I need to finish the job.

I turn and take three steps toward the open door.

"Please, Budo." Max is pleading now. I can hear the tears in his eyes.

"No. I am leaving and never coming back."

"Please, Budo," Max says, and my heart breaks a little to hear him so frightened. This is what I wanted, but I didn't know how hard it would be. The right thing and the easy thing are never the same thing, and this is the truest right now.

"Please don't leave me," Max begs.

I decide that this is the moment to make my stand. I change my voice from stone to ice. "Mrs. Patterson is bad, Max. You are afraid to say it, but you know it. But she is even worse than you know. She is planning on taking you away from this room. Away from this house. Far, far away. You will never see your mom or dad again. You will never see me again. Everything is going to change forever and ever unless you go now. You have to go now."

"Please, Budo." Max is crying now.

"I promise that if you leave now, you will be safe. You will get away from Mrs. Patterson. You will make it home. You will see your mom and dad tonight. Cross my heart and hope to die. But we have to go now. Will you follow me now?"

Max is weeping. Tears are spilling down his cheeks. He can barely catch his breath. But in between the sobs, Max nods.

He nods.

We have a chance.

fifty-seven

Mrs. Patterson is in her bedroom. She is packing another box with things from under her bathroom sink. The clock above the stove reads 6:42. It is time to go.

I go back to the basement. Max is standing by the staircase. Right where I left him. He is holding the locomotive from his LEGO train in his hands. He is clinging to it like a life preserver. His pants pocket is bulging with something, too. I do not ask what.

I wonder if Oswald is still here. I look around but cannot see him.

"I'm here," he says, waving his hand. The movement catches my eye. He is standing behind Max but it sounds like he is on the other side of the Grand Canyon. "Did you think you lost me?"

I smile.

"Mrs. Patterson is upstairs," I say. "In her bedroom. You are going to walk up the stairs and follow me. We are going to try to get out through the sliding glass door in the dining room. The door should open quietly. I watched her open it once. It didn't squeak. Once we are outside, you are going to turn right and run as fast as you can into the woods."

"Okay," Max says. His whole body is shaking. He is terrified.

"You can do this, Max."

"Okay," he says. He does not believe me.

We climb the stairs and enter the hallway. The front door is to the right. I think again about sending Max out this door and decide against it. It is at the foot of the stairs. Mrs. Patterson might hear it open.

"This way," I say, leading Max through the kitchen and into the dining room. "The handle is on the right-hand side. Just give the door a pull."

Max shifts the LEGO train to his left hand and grabs the handle with his right. He pulls. The door moves a teeny-tiny bit and then stops with a thud.

"Oh, no," I say, feeling the first bits of panic race through me. "Max, we have to go to . . ."

Before I can finish my sentence, Max has turned a knob on the door. "It was locked," he whispers. "That's all." He pulls on the door a second time and the glass slides open with a quiet hiss.

For a moment, I am excited. Not only is the door open but Max opened it. He solved the problem. Max does not solve problems. Max becomes trapped inside problems.

This is a good sign.

But as the door slides open, three beeps ring out throughout the house. The alarm has not gone off, but it is the beeps that tell the person who owns the door that the alarm is working but is turned off. Max's parents' doors make the same sound. I don't even notice the beeps anymore because they beep every time someone opens the door. They beep all the time.

I do not think these three beeps will go unnoticed.

As if to prove the point, I hear something drop to the floor directly above us. A second later, footsteps thump quickly across the upstairs floor.

"She's coming!" I shout. "Run!"

Max does not move. He stands in the open doorway, frozen in place. The sounds of Mrs. Patterson's charge across the second floor have stopped him in his tracks.

"Max, if you do not run now, you will never escape." I realize how true this is as I say the words. I have taken a big chance. If Mrs. Patterson catches Max now, she will never give him another chance to escape ever again. This is the one chance I have to get Max home.

And he is still not moving.

I hear Mrs. Patterson. She is on the stairs now.

"Max. Please run now. I am leaving with or without you. I am not staying here. There is no time. Your mom and dad are waiting. Mrs. Gosk is waiting. Run!"

Something I said makes him move. I wish I knew what it was so I could use it again. I think it was maybe the mention of his mom.

Max steps into the night. It is dark and I am worried that this will stop Max again but it does not. Max is afraid of the dark but now he is more afraid of Mrs. Patterson. He has admitted that he is afraid of her, and this is good. He crosses Mrs. Patterson's deck and walks down the three steps onto the grass. He looks out at the pond. The moon is hanging just above the trees on the opposite side. White light shimmers on the still water.

The pale moonlight, I think. Max is dancing with the devil in the pale moonlight for real now.

"Turn right and run!" I scream as loud as I can. As angry as I can.

Max turns and runs into the trees.

I turn to look back at the door. Mrs. Patterson is not there yet. She must have decided to check the front door first.

Oswald is standing in the doorway. He shimmers in the mixing of moonlight and light from inside the house like hot air off a parking lot. He is disappearing. It is happening right now. Right in front of my eyes.

"Run, Budo!" he shouts. The sound coming from his mouth does not sound like a voice anymore. It sounds more like a distant memory. A memory almost forgotten, except now I know that Oswald was right. He will never be forgotten. "Save Max," he says. He is probably shouting these words. Roaring this all-important final command. The words that have ended his life. But they come to me as a whisper's whisper. "I have one more thing to do."

I cannot run. I feel like Max. I am stuck in place. Oswald the Giant, imaginary friend of John the Lunatic, the only imaginary friend to have feet in both worlds, is dying before my eyes.

I am responsible for his death.

Just as I expect him to wink out forever, he turns and looks back inside the house. He waits a second, drops to one knee, and places his hands out in front of him like a boy showing his mother how many fingers make ten. I cannot see the details that once made Oswald real, but I do not need to see them to know that his muscles are popping for the last time. The veins in his neck are pulsing their final pulses. He is Oswald the Giant once again, one more time, preparing for battle. Then he turns back to me, sees me frozen on the lawn, the pale moon hanging behind me, and says, "Good-bye, Budo."

I can no longer hear his words, but they somehow find their way into my mind.

And then, "Thank you."

At that moment, Mrs. Patterson comes into view. She is running from the kitchen into the dining room and toward the open door. She is running faster than I thought she ever could, and in that moment I realize that Max's escape will not end with his disappearance into the trees.

It has just begun.

Oswald was right. Everyone is somebody's devil, and Mrs. Patterson is Max's devil.

And mine.

Then the thought hits me.

Oswald is Mrs. Patterson's devil. Oswald the Giant is the devil in the pale moonlight now.

An instant later, Mrs. Patterson charges into the open doorway and hits the crouching, shimmering, dying Oswald. Her right knee strikes his right hand and she topples over, head first, flying up and over and down onto the deck with a grunt and a bang and a thump. She slides all the way to the edge of the deck and then rolls down the three stairs to the grass, stopping inches before my feet.

I look up. I look to the doorway, looking for my brave and dying friend, and already know that he is gone.

"You saved Max," I say to my friend, but no one is listening anymore.

Then I hear Max shout. "Budo!"

Mrs. Patterson's head rises from the grass. She pulls herself up on one arm. She looks in the direction of Max's voice. A second later, she rises to her feet.

I turn and run.

Max's escape has just begun.

fifty-eight

Max is standing behind a tree. He is hugging his LEGO train like it is a teddy bear. Some of the pieces have broken off but I do not think Max has noticed. He is shaking all over. It is cold and Max is not wearing a coat, but I do not think this is why he is shaking.

"You can't stay here," I say. "You have to run."

"Make her stop," Max whispers.

"I can't," I say. "You have to run."

I listen. I expect to hear Mrs. Patterson crashing through the trees and bushes, but I do not. She is probably walking slowly. Trying to be quiet. She is probably trying to sneak up on Max so that she can grab him.

"Max, you have to run," I say again.

"I can't."

"You have to."

At that moment a beam of light passes through the trees. I look back toward Mrs. Patterson's house. There is a dot of bright light near the edge of the trees.

A flashlight.

Mrs. Patterson went back inside the house for a flashlight.

"Max, if she finds you, she will take you away forever and you will be alone forever."

"I'll have you," Max says.

"No, you won't."

"Yes, I will. You say that you will leave me, but you won't leave me," he says. "I know it."

Max is right. I would never leave him. But this is no time for the truth. I must lie to Max in a way I have never done before. In a way I never thought I would ever, ever do.

"Max," I say, looking him in the eyes. "I am not real. I am imaginary."

"No you're not," he says. "Stop it."

"It's true. I am imaginary. You are all alone right now, Max. You can see me, but I am not really here. I am imaginary. I can't help you, Max. You have to help yourself."

The beam of light passes across the trees to the left. In the direction of the pond. Mrs. Patterson is moving down the hill, slightly away from Max, but there is not much ground between Max and the pond. Even if she is heading in the wrong direction, she will see him soon. The moon is lighting up the forest and Mrs. Patterson has a flashlight.

A second later, we hear the first snap of a branch on the ground. She is getting close.

Max startles and almost drops his train. "Which way?" he asks. "Which way should I run?"

"I don't know," I say. "I'm imaginary. You tell me which way."

Another branch snaps, this one much closer, and Max turns and runs up and to the right, away from the water and away from Mrs. Patterson. But he moves too fast and too loud. The light from the flashlight swerves in his direction and lands on his back. "Max!" Mrs. Patterson yells. "Wait!"

When Max hears her voice, he runs faster. I run, too.

I lose sight of Max as he runs through a tight bunch of pine trees. But he is headed in the right direction. There are five houses on this side of the road before the end of the street, and he is getting close to Mrs. Patterson's closest neighbor. I can see the lights of the neighbor's house through the trees. But somehow I have lost Max. He was twenty or thirty steps in front of me but now he is gone.

I stop running. I walk. I want to listen and look. Mrs. Patterson has stopped running, too. She is walking, not too far behind me and off to my left, doing the same thing I am doing.

We are both looking for Max.

"Budo!" Max calls my name, but this time it is a whisper. The voice comes from my right so I look in that direction. I see trees and rocks and leaves and the glow of streetlights at the top of the hill where the forest meets the road but no Max.

"Budo," he whispers again and I become afraid. Max is trying to be quiet but Mrs. Patterson is too close. He cannot afford to make another sound.

Then I see him.

There is a rock and a tree with leaves piled in between them, probably pushed there by the wind. Max has buried himself in the leaves. I can see his tiny hand waving to me from underneath the pile.

I get down on my hands and knees and crawl to him, leaning against the opposite side of the rock.

"Max, what are you doing?" I whisper as softly as I can so Max will do the same.

"Waiting," Max says.

"What?"

"This is what a sniper does," Max whispers. "He lets the enemy soldiers walk right by them before they attack."

"You can't attack Mrs. Patterson."

"No. I will wait until . . ."

Max stops talking as the sound of footsteps rustling in leaves reaches us. A second later, the flashlight passes over the rock where I am sitting and where Max lies buried under leaves.

I look up. I can see Mrs. Patterson now. I can see her outline in the moonlight. She is close. Fifty steps away. Then thirty. Then twenty. She is walking quickly as if she knows exactly where Max is hiding. If she does not change direction, she may step right on top of Max.

"Max," I say. "Don't move. She's coming."

As I sit and wait for Max to be caught, I think about Max's decision to hide under the leaves. *This is what snipers do,* he said.

Max read a book about war. Actually, he has read a million books about war, but now he is using what he read to save himself. In a strange forest. At night. With someone chasing him. And with his best friend insisting that he is not real.

He is not stuck.

It is almost unbelievable.

Mrs. Patterson is now ten steps from Max. Five steps. Her flashlight shoots ahead. Not at the ground but straight ahead. Two steps before she would have stepped on Max, she turns left and heads up the hill toward the road. It makes sense that she turns. Otherwise she would have had to climb over the rock or squeeze between the rock and the tree, but it was still close. If she had shined her flashlight on the pile of leaves, I am sure that she would have seen Max's shape under those leaves.

"How long are you going to wait?" I ask once Mrs. Patterson is far enough away that I cannot hear her footsteps in the leaves.

"Snipers wait for days," he whispers.

"Days?"

"Not me. But snipers do. I don't know. In a little while."

"Okay," I say. I don't know if this is a good idea or a bad idea, but Max has made a decision. He is solving the problem. He is escaping on his own.

"Budo," he whispers. "Are you real? Tell me the truth."

I pause before answering. I want to say yes, because yes is the truth, and yes will keep me safe. Yes will keep me existing. But Max is not safe, and he cannot afford to believe in me now because I cannot save him. He needs to believe in himself. He has depended on me for too long. He needs to depend on himself now. I can't get him home. This is not choosing between chicken noodle or vegetable beef. Blue or green. This is not the Learning Center or the playground or the school bus or even Tommy Swinden. This is the actual devil in actual pale moonlight. Max has to get himself home.

"No," I say. "Cross my heart and hope to die. I'm imaginary. You imagine me to make things easier for you. So you'll have a friend."

"Really?" he asks.

"Really."

"You're a good friend, Budo," Max says.

Max has never said this to me before. I want to exist forever, but if I had stopped existing at this very moment, I would have at least been happy. The happiest ever.

"Thanks," I say. "But I'm only what you imagine. I'm a good friend because you made me a good friend."

"Time to go," Max says. He says it so fast that I am not sure if he was listening to me. He stands up but stays bent over in a crouch. He starts moving up the hill but to the left of where Mrs. Patterson went.

I follow.

As I step past the leaf pile where Max was buried seconds ago, I see the LEGO train sitting by the rock. Max has left it behind.

In a minute we are on the edge of the neighbor's lawn. The long, stretch of grass is split in two by a gravel driveway. On the other side of the lawn is another patch of forest. Smaller, I think. The lights of the next house look close. They shine through the tree line.

"You should go to that house and knock on the door. The people will help."

Max says nothing.

"They won't hurt you, Max," I say.

He does not answer.

I did not really expect Max to get help from Mrs. Patterson's neighbors or anyone else. I think Max would rather melt every LEGO piece and army man and video game in the world into a pile of gooey plastic before he ever talked to a stranger. Knocking on a stranger's door would be like knocking on the door to an alien spaceship.

Max looks left and right across the lawn. He looks like he is getting ready to cross the street, even though he has never crossed a street alone in his entire life. Then he bursts out of the trees and runs across the lawn. He is visible in the moonlight, but unless Mrs. Patterson is watching, he is going to make it across the lawn to the other side without being noticed.

As he reaches the driveway, spotlights on the house switch on. They light up the front yard like the sun. They are the lights that switch on and off when people move. Max's parents have them in the backyard, and the lights turn on sometimes when a stray cat or a deer passes by.

Max freezes when the lights come on. He looks behind him. I am standing on the edge of the trees. I have been watching Max but not following. I have been standing and staring in amazement at this boy who once needed help deciding on which pair of socks to wear.

Max turns toward the trees on the other side of the lawn and starts running again, and that is when Mrs. Patterson bursts from the trees to my right and runs like lightning across the lawn. Max does not see her at first, so I shout. "Max! Look out! She's behind you!"

Max turns to look but does not stop running.

I start running. I shake off my amazement. I am suddenly filled with fear. I follow behind Mrs. Patterson, who is now closing in on Max. She is faster than Max. She is faster than she should be.

She really is the devil.

Max reaches the trees on the other side of the lawn. He takes two steps into the trees and then jumps over an old stone wall. His foot catches a rock and he tumbles to the ground behind the wall, out of sight. A second later he pops up and begins running again.

Mrs. Patterson reaches the trees about ten seconds later. She jumps over the wall, too, but she clears it, landing and running again in one smooth motion. She pumps her arms, the flashlight turned on but not pointed at Max any longer. She can see him now. She is getting closer and closer. The beam of the flashlight flies wildly through the trees.

"Run, Max!" I scream as I jump the wall. I am seconds behind Mrs. Patterson but I can do no good. I am helpless. Useless. I scream again. "Run!

Max reaches the front lawn of the next house. It is not as wide as the first, and the driveway is made of street stuff instead of gravel, but otherwise it is the same. He sprints across the grass, no spotlights turning on this time, and he disappears into the gloom of the trees on the other side.

Max is running out of houses and trees and pond. Two more houses and he will reach a street that he must cross. A street that he has never been able to cross alone before. Then he will be in a neighborhood with houses and sidewalks and streetlights and stop signs. No more leaf piles and stone walls and tall trees. No more gloom. No more hiding places. He will have to find help or be caught.

But none of that will matter if Mrs. Patterson catches him first, and it looks like she will.

Mrs. Patterson reaches the tree line just seconds after Max. I am about twenty steps behind her when I see a thick, bare branch swing out wildly from the gloom and smash Mrs. Patterson in the face. She cries out and drops to the ground like a rock. A second later I see Max. He has changed direction. He has turned right. He is running through the trees toward the road instead of into the forest toward the next house.

I come to a stop where Mrs. Patterson is lying on the ground. Her nose is bloody. Her hands are pressing down hard on her left eye. She is moaning.

Max has danced with the devil in the pale moonlight, and he has won.

I turn and run in the same direction as Max, not bothering to enter the trees. I can run faster if I stay on the lawn. When I reach the street, I stop and look left and right.

No Max.

I turn left, toward the main road, and run, hoping Max has kept moving in the same direction. A few seconds later I hear him call my name.

"Over here!" he shouts in a whisper. He is on the other side of the street, in a small patch of trees, crouched behind another stone wall.

It takes me a moment to realize that he has crossed a street on his own.

"What did you do?" I ask, climbing behind the wall with him. "Mrs. Patterson is hurt."

"I set a trap," he says, panting and shaking and sweating but grinning, too. Not smiling, but so close to smiling.

"What?" I ask.

"I pulled a branch way back and let it go when she got close," he says.

I stare in disbelief.

"I learned it from Rambo," he says. "*First Blood*. Remember?"

I do remember. Max watched the movie with his dad, and then his dad made Max promise not to tell his mom.

But Max told his mom when she got home because Max is a terrible liar. Max's dad slept in the guest room that night.

"She's really hurt," I say. "Bleeding."

"It wasn't really a Rambo trap. His trap had spikes that stuck in the police's legs. I didn't have any rope or a knife, and I didn't have time even if I had that stuff. But it's where I got the idea."

"Okay," I say. I don't know what else to say.

"Okay," Max says. He stands up and moves along the stone wall, staying low, in the direction of the main road.

He does not wait for me to lead or even ask me for a direction. Max is moving on his own.

He is saving himself.

fifty-nine

Max reaches the end of Mrs. Patterson's street and stops. He has stayed in the woods on the opposite side of the street, walking slowly and quietly between the trees, but when he turns off this street, he will no longer have patches of forest where he can hide. The houses with the long driveways and enormous plots of land along the pond will be gone. He will be on a street with short driveways, bunched-up houses, streetlights, and sidewalks.

If Mrs. Patterson is still chasing Max, he will be easy to see.

"Go right," I tell Max.

He is standing on the corner. His body is pressed against a tree. He looks unsure about which way to go.

"The school is to the right," I say.

"Okay," Max says, but instead of stepping out from behind the tree where he is hiding, he turns into the backyard of the first house on the street.

"Where are you going?" I ask.

"I can't walk on the sidewalks," he says.

"So where are you going?" I ask.

"I'll stay behind the houses."

This is what Max does. We walk for almost thirty minutes this way, crossing from one backyard to another. When the space between the houses is not guarded by fences or trees or garages or cars, Max runs. He stays low to the ground and moves fast. When a backyard is fenced, he walks around the outside edge, pushing his way through bushes and weeds. He scrapes his hands and face on shrubs and soaks his feet in puddles and mud but he keeps moving. He sets off six more spotlights along the way but no one inside any of the houses sees him.

Max is not like the Rambo guy in that movie. He can't swim

through abandoned mines or break into police stations or climb mountains, but that is because there are no mines or police stations or mountains here. Max has houses and backyards and fences and trees and rosebushes, but he uses them just like Rambo would.

When we reach the next intersection, Max recognizes where he is. "The park is across the street," he says. "Over there." He points left in the direction of the park. The school is behind the park. But instead of turning left, he turns right.

"Where are you going?" I ask. He is already moving along a fence, making his way behind another house.

"We can't cross the street there," he whispers. "That's where Mrs. Patterson would expect me to cross."

Max crosses the street two blocks down, and he does not cross at an intersection. Instead, he waits behind a parked car until no cars are coming and then he runs across the street without the help of a crosswalk.

Max just broke his first law, I think.

Unless there is a law against pooping on someone's head.

Once he is on the other side of the street, Max keeps running. He is using the sidewalk this time instead of sneaking behind houses, and he is running as fast as he can. He wants to get to the park as quickly as possible, I think. The park feels safe to me, too. The park is a place for kids, even in the middle of the night.

Max crosses one more side street and then he turns right into the park, running off the footpaths and toward a soccer field between two steep hills. Max's dad once tried to take him sledding on these hills. The hills are made for people to sit on while watching the soccer games, but they are great for sledding, too. There are tons of kids on the hills after every snowstorm. But Max refused to get on the sled and complained the whole time that his mittens were wet. His dad finally drove him home without saying a word.

Max flies down the hill today, faster than a sled, it seems, and runs straight across the soccer field. Near the goalpost he turns right toward the baseball field, but he stays off the footpaths, running on the grass and through the trees on the edges of the trails instead. After he is past the baseball field, Max turns right past the playground toward the trees.

There is a small patch of forest that stands between the school and the park. There are trails covered by woodchips, and the teachers sometimes take the students on these trails in the fall and spring. Mrs. Gosk took her class for a walk a few weeks ago so her students could write some poetry about nature. Max sat on a stump and made a list of all the words that rhymed with *tree*.

There were 102 words on his list. It wasn't a poem, but Mrs. Gosk was still impressed.

Max heads in the direction of the forest. He runs along the edge of a small pond on the edge of the trees, daring to step on the path for a moment before he reaches the entrance of the forest and disappears into the gloom.

Fifteen minutes later, after getting lost on the trails twice, we stand on the other side of the forest. A field stands between us and the school. It is the same field where Max has refused to run and jump and throw softballs on field day. The moon has risen higher in the sky since we left Mrs. Patterson's house. It hangs over the school like a giant, blind eye.

I want to tell Max that he has made it. I want to tell him to crawl into the bushes along the edge of the forest and wait until the morning comes. I want to tell him that once the buses start pulling into the circle at the front of the school, all he has to do is run across this field to the school and go through the front doors like it was a regular school day. He could even walk down to Mrs. Gosk's classroom if he wanted. Once he is inside the school, he will be safe.

Instead, I ask, "What's next?" I ask because I am not in charge anymore. I don't think I could be in charge even if I wanted to be.

"I want to go home," he says. "I want to see Mom and Dad."

"Do you know the way home from here?" I ask.

"Yes," he says.

"You do?"

"Yes," he says again. "Of course."

"Oh."

"When should we go?" I ask, hoping he says that we will wait for morning. Hoping that we will let Mrs. Gosk or Mrs. Palmer or the police bring him home.

"Now," he says, turning and starting to walk along the edge of the field. "I want to go home."

sixty

I do not know how long we have been walking when we pass the Savoys' house. The moon has moved across the sky but it is still hanging over our heads. Max has not said much. But this is Max. He may have turned into Rambo overnight, but he is still Max, too.

We have been walking for a long time, staying behind houses and bushes and trees whenever possible. I have followed Max the whole way, and he has not complained once.

I can't believe that Max will be home in a few minutes. I have stopped imagining the look on Max's parents face when they see him standing on the stoop. It is about to happen for real. I did not think it would ever happen.

I stop just before our driveway and stare at my friend. For the first time in my life, I understand what it feels like to be proud of someone. I am not Max's mom or dad, but I am his friend, and I am bursting with pride.

And then I see it.

Mrs. Patterson's bus. The bus with the room in the back just for Max.

Max is about to turn up his driveway and take the final steps to his house, but he doesn't know that Mrs. Patterson is waiting for him. He doesn't know that parked down the street, a little bit past the house, in the dark space between two streetlights, is Mrs. Patterson and her bus.

He doesn't even know that Mrs. Patterson has a bus.

I open my mouth to shout a warning, but it is too late. Max is four or five steps up the driveway when Mrs. Patterson jumps out from behind the giant oak tree where Max and I have waited for the bus every day since kindergarten. The tree that Max touches until the bus comes. Max hears the footsteps before he hears my voice, but both sounds are too late. He sees Mrs. Patterson closing in on him and he runs. He is more than halfway up the driveway when Mrs. Patterson's arm comes down on Max's shoulder and grabs hold. The force of her arm causes Max to trip and stumble to the ground, and for a second, Max is free. He crawls toward the house on his hands and knees, but Mrs. Patterson is on him in seconds, reaching down and grabbing him by the arm. She lifts him up like he is a doll.

Max screams. "Mom! Dad! Help!"

Mrs. Patterson presses her free hand over Max's mouth to silence him. I do not think that Max's parents would hear him anyway. Their bedroom is upstairs and in the back of the house, and it is late. They are sleeping, I think. But she does not know this. She wants him to be quiet so she can get away with him forever.

Finally I move, running up the driveway, stopping in front of Max. He is wriggling, trying to break free. His eyes are wide. I can see the terror in his face. He tries to scream through Mrs. Patterson's hand but all that comes out is a low hum. He kicks at Mrs. Patterson's shins. Some of his kicks connect, but Mrs. Patterson does not even flinch.

I stand there like a helpless fool. I am inches from my friend, watching him fight for his life, and I can do nothing. Max stares into my eyes. He is pleading for help but there is nothing I can do. I can only watch my friend be dragged away forever.

"Fight!" I yell at Max. "Bite her hand!"

He does. I watch his jaw drop open and then shut. Mrs. Patterson winces but does not let go.

Max's arms flail. His feet continue to kick. He grabs onto the hand that is pressed over his mouth and tries to pull it free. He strains, eyes bulging even more, but he cannot. He pounds his fist on her hand. Then I see something in his eyes change. The panic is replaced by something else for just a second. Max reaches into his pocket and removes the object that has caused his pocket to bulge all night. It is the piggy bank that was sitting on his desk in his room. The tarnished pig, filled to the brim with pennies.

I was wrong. When Max crossed the street without the crosswalk, it was the second time he had broken the law.

He was a thief first.

Max holds the piggy bank in his right hand and brings it down on Mrs. Patterson's arm. The pig's tiny metallic feet bite into her skin. She flinches and cries out this time, but her grip remains in place.

She is not going to let go. I realize this now. Bitten and beaten and stabbed by pig's feet, she knows that she only needs to drag Max back to her bus and then she will be safe again. And that is what she begins to do. With Max hammering on her arm with his piggy bank, she backs up, dragging Max back down the driveway toward the oak tree and her bus.

I want to scream and yell for help. Wake up Max's parents. Let the world know that my friend has made it all the way back to his driveway and just needs a final bit of help to finish his escape. He has made this trip on his own and he just needs someone to step in and save him now.

Then the idea strikes me. "Tommy Swinden!" I yell at Max. And even as he continues to batter Mrs. Patterson's arm with the piggy bank and try to wriggle free, he furrows his eyes and stares at me.

"No, I don't want you to poop on her head," I say. "Tommy Swinden. He broke your window on Halloween. Break a window, Max!"

Max cocks his arm, ready to smash Mrs. Patterson's arm again with the piggy bank, when he stops. Understanding fills Max's eyes. He only has one shot, but he understands.

He looks up at the house. He is halfway down the driveway now and still being dragged on the back of his heels. He will have to throw it now or he will be too far. There is a picture window in the living room. It is big. It is smack in the center of the house. But it will be a difficult throw. It is far away and his feet are barely touching the ground.

And Max can't throw.

"Bite her first," I say. "Bite her *hard*. As hard as you can."

Max nods. While being grabbed and dragged, with his chances of ever seeing his mom dad again disappearing, he nods.

And then he bites.

He must have bitten harder than before because as he does, Mrs. Patterson yells this time and pulls her hand away from his mouth, shaking it like it is on fire. More important, she stops dragging Max down the driveway. She is still holding Max by one arm, but Max's feet are now on the ground. He has a chance.

"Step into it," I say. "Throw with your body. Give it your all."

"Okay," Max says between breaths. He reaches back with the piggy bank and throws it into the night.

Mrs. Patterson sees the piggy bank leave Max's hand and her eyes widen as the pig soars snout up and then down toward the picture window.

When pigs fly, I think.

For a moment, it seems as if the entire world stops. Even the moon's blind eye turns to watch that tiny metallic pig fly through the air.

The piggy bank hits the window in its center. It is a throw that would make Max's dad forever proud. It is a throw that will make me forever proud. A throw better than Tommy Swinden could have ever hoped for. The glass explodes, and seconds later, the alarm screams into the night.

Mrs. Patterson reaches out with her free hand. It is bleeding where Max has bitten her. She wrenches it around Max and grabs him by the neck. Then she lifts him off the ground and runs as fast as she can with a wriggling, screaming boy in her arms. She is now running across the front lawn toward her bus.

Max has made the throw of his life. The picture window is broken. The alarm is screaming. The police are on the way. And still Mrs. Patterson is getting away with Max. She is seconds from escaping forever.

All I see is a blur as Max's dad flies past me and slams his body into Mrs. Patterson's back like a runaway train. She cries out as he drives her body toward the ground. Mrs. Patterson releases Max before she strikes the ground, trying to brace her fall. Max falls forward and rolls to the side, panting, heaving, clutching at his throat, trying to catch his breath.

Mrs. Patterson had been choking him to death.

Mrs. Patterson crashes into the ground with Max's dad still on top of her, his arms wrapped around her body like steel cables. He is wearing boxer shorts and a T-shirt, and his arms are torn and bleeding. Long gashes stretch up his arms and across his shoulders. His T-shirt is torn in the back and already covered in blood. I am confused, but then I look back at the house. The door to the house is still shut. Max's dad jumped through the broken picture window. The broken glass cut him on the way through.

"Max! My God! Are you okay?" Max's dad asks, still not letting go of Mrs. Patterson. He has her pinned to the ground but still he presses all his weight into her back. "My God, Max. Are you okay?"

"I'm okay," Max says. His voice is hoarse and scratchy and weak but he is telling the truth.

Max is okay.

"Max!" It is Max's mom. She is standing in the picture window, looking out at the scene on her front lawn. Her bloody husband. Max's kidnapper. And Max, sitting beside his father, rubbing his neck.

"Max! Oh my God! Max!"

She disappears from the picture window. A few seconds later, the lights come on, brightening the front lawn. The front door flies open and Max's mom runs out of the house, down the stoop and across the lawn. She is wearing a white nightgown and it looks like she is glowing in the moonlight. She drops to her knees and slides the last few feet over to Max, wrapping him in her arms and kissing his forehead one million times. I can tell by the look on Max's face that he does not like this many kisses, but for once, he does not complain. His mom is crying and kissing all at once, and Max does not even wince.

I look to Max's dad, who is still holding Mrs. Patterson to the ground. She is not moving, but Max's dad has watched too many detective shows to let her go now. He knows that just when you think the bad guy is gone or dead, she can pop out behind an oak tree and grab you.

Still, he is smiling.

I hear sirens in the distance. The policemen are coming.

Max's mom, still holding Max in her arms, scoots over to Max's dad and hugs him even as he holds Mrs. Patterson down. Max's mom is crying rivers.

Max looks up at me from his mother's arms. He is smiling. Max is not grinning. He is smiling.

Max Delaney is smiling.

I am smiling, too. I am also crying. These are my first happy tears ever. I give Max a thumbs-up.

Through my fading thumb, I watch Max kiss his mom on her teary cheek.

sixty-one

"Do you know that you are . . ."

"I know," I say. "I've been disappearing for two days."

Teeny sighs. She does not say anything for a moment. She just stares at me. We are alone in the recess room. There were other imaginary friends in here when I arrived, but Teeny took one look at me and sent them away.

I guess everyone really does listen to a fairy.

"Does it feel . . . ?" she asks.

"It doesn't feel like anything," I say. "If I was blind, I would have no idea that I was fading away."

Actually, this is not true. Max has stopped talking to me. It's not that he is angry with me. He just doesn't know that I am around anymore. If I stand right in front of him and speak to him, he will notice me and talk back. But if I do not speak to him, he does not speak to me.

It has been sad.

"Where's Oswald?" Teeny asks. But I can tell by the way she looks down at her feet that she already knows.

"He's gone," I say.

"Where?"

"Good question," I say. "I don't know. Wherever I'm going, which probably isn't anywhere."

I tell Teeny the story of Max's escape and how Oswald the Giant broke open Max's basement prison and touched the real world one final time to slow down Mrs. Patterson and knock her off her feet, giving Max time to run. I tell her about the chase through the forest and Max's trap at the tree line and the final battle on the front lawn of Max's house. I tell her how Max's dad held down Mrs. Patterson until the police arrived, and how his father was bragging to the police officers about how his son had "matched wits with that crazy bitch and won."

Then I tell her how Oswald knew that he was dying, and how I tried to bring him back to the hospital to save him. "But he wouldn't come back," I say. "He sacrificed himself to save Max. He is a hero."

"So are you," Teeny says, smiling through her tears.

"Not like Oswald," I say. "I stood around and told Max to run and to hide. I can't touch the real world like Oswald could."

"You told Max to throw that pig through that window. And you told Max that you were imaginary so he could save himself. You sacrificed yourself, too."

"Yes," I say, feeling anger boil up in me. "And now I won't exist anymore because of it. Max is free and safe but I am dying. And when I'm gone, he won't even remember me. I'll just be a story that his mom tells him someday. How he once had an imaginary friend named Budo."

"I think he'll always remember you," Teeny says. "He just won't believe that you were ever really real. But I will."

But Teeny is going to die someday, too. Probably soon. Her human friend is four years old. Teeny will probably be gone in a year or less. Kindergarten will kill her like it kills so many imaginary friends. And when she dies, that will be it. No memory of Budo ever existing. Everything I ever said or did will be gone forever.

Teeny's wings flutter. She lifts off the couch and hovers in the center of the room. "And I will tell others," she says, seeming to read my mind. "I will tell every imaginary friend I meet, and I will tell them to tell all the imaginary friends they meet. I will tell them to keep the story going from one imaginary friend to the next, so that the world will never forget what Oswald the Giant and Budo the Great did for Max Delaney, the bravest little boy in the world."

"That's nice," I say. "Thank you, Teeny."

I don't have the heart to tell her that it doesn't make dying any easier. Or that I don't trust the imaginary friends of the world to carry our story. There are too many imaginary friends out there like Puppy and Chomp and Klute.

Not enough Teenys or Oswalds or Summers or Grahams.

Not nearly enough.

"How is Max doing?" Teeny asks, landing back on the couch beside me. She wants to change the subject and I am glad that she does.

"He is good," I say. "I thought that after everything that happened, he would be different. But he's not. Maybe a little different, but not much."

"What do you mean?"

"Max was great in the forest and even in his front yard because that was what he is good at. He has spent his life reading books about war and weapons and snipers. He has planned a thousand battles with his army men. There were no people in the woods to bother him. No one to talk to or make eye contact with. No one trying to shake his hand or punch him in the nose or zip up his coat. He was running away from a person, and that is what Max always wants to do. Run away from people. He was great out there, but it was almost like that is where he belonged."

"And now?" Teeny asks.

"When he went back to school yesterday, it was really hard for him. Everyone wanted to talk to him. It was too many people, too fast. He almost got stuck. But Mrs. Gosk saw what was happening and told all the other teachers and older kids and even the school psychologist to 'Scram!' Max is still Max. Maybe a little braver now. A little better at taking care of himself. But still Max. Still worried about bonus poops and Tommy Swinden."

Teeny furrows the spot on her face where her eyebrows would be if she had any.

"Never mind," I say. "Long story."

"How long before . . . ?"

"I don't know," I say. "Maybe tomorrow, I think."

Teeny smiles, but it is a sad smile. "I'll miss you, Budo."

"I'll miss you," I say. "I'll miss everything."

sixty-two

I was right. It is happening today. When Max turned on the light this morning, I could barely see myself. I said hello to Max and he did not answer. He did not even look in my direction.

And then I started having this feeling a little while ago. I am sitting in Mrs. Gosk's class. Max is sitting on the rug with the rest of the kids. Mrs. Gosk is reading a book called *The Tale of Despereaux*. It is a book about a mouse. I thought it was going to be stupid because it is about a mouse, but it is not stupid at all. It is great. It is the best book. It is about a special mouse who loves the light and can read and must save the Princess Pea.

Mrs. Gosk is only halfway through the book. I will never hear the end of the story. I will never know what happens to Despereaux.

Despereaux is a little like me in that way. I will never know Despereaux's fate and no one will ever know mine. I will stop existing today, stop persisting, but only I will know it. I will die a silent, unknown death in the back of this classroom, listening to a story about a mouse whose fate I will never know.

Max and Mrs. Gosk and everyone else will go on like nothing has happened. They will follow Despereaux on the rest of his adventure.

I cannot.

I feel like the there is a soft, gooey balloon in my belly. One of the balloons that float all by themselves. It doesn't hurt. I just feel like I am being pulled up, even though I am still sitting in this chair. I look at my hands and can only see them if I wave them in front of my eyes.

I am glad to be in Mrs. Gosk's classroom when I die. Max and Mrs. Gosk are my two favorite people in the whole wide world. It is nice to think that they will be my last memory.

Except I will have no memory. It is only nice to die with Max and Mrs. Gosk until the moment that I die. At that moment, nothing will matter anymore. Everything from that second on will never mean anything to me ever again. But not just everything after I die, but everything before I die, too. When I die, everything dies.

It all feels like such a waste.

I look at Max, sitting at Mrs. Gosk's feet. He loves this story as much as I do. He is smiling. He smiles now. That is the one big difference between the Max who believed in Budo and the Max that doesn't. He smiles. Not much, but sometimes.

Mrs. Gosk is smiling, too. She is smiling because Max is back, but she is also smiling because she loves this story as much as anyone else in the room. Despereaux has been thrown into the dungeon with the rats for being different than the rest of the mice, and in a way, Max is like Despereaux, too. He is different than everyone, and he was trapped in a basement, too. And just like Max, I think Despereaux will escape the dark and save the day.

The balloon in my belly is getting bigger now. It feels warm and good.

I move over and sit at Mrs. Gosk's feet. I sit right beside Max.

I think about all the people I have lost over the last two weeks. Graham and Summer and Oswald and Dee. I imagine each one standing before me. I try to imagine all of them when they were at their best.

Graham sitting beside Meghan as she faded away.

Summer making me promise to save Max.

Oswald dropping down on one knee in that doorway, hands outstretched, toppling Mrs. Patterson.

Dee shouting at Sally because she loved him like a brother.

I loved them all.

I miss them all.

I look up at Mrs. Gosk. When I am gone, she will have to protect Max. She will have to help him with the bonus poops, and Tommy Swinden, and all the other little things that Max cannot do because he lives so much of his life on the inside. That big, beautiful inside that once imagined me.

And she will. Oswald the Giant was a hero, and maybe even I was a little bit of a hero, too. But Mrs. Gosk is an everyday, all-the-time hero, even though it's only kids like Max who know that she is a hero. She will be a hero long after I am gone because she has always been a hero.

I turn to Max. My friend. The boy who made me. I want to be angry at him for forgetting about me, but I am not. I cannot be angry at Max. I love Max. Nothing will matter when I stop existing, but somehow I think I will still love Max.

Death is not scary for me anymore. It is just sad. I will never see Max again. I will miss all the thousands of days in his future, when he will grow up and become a man and have a little Max of his own. I think if I could just sit somewhere, quiet and still, and watch the little boy who I love so much grow up and live his life, I would be happy.

I do not need to exist for me anymore. I just want to exist for Max. I want to know the rest of Max's story.

My tears are warm. My body is warm. I cannot see myself, but I can see Max. His beautiful face stares up at the teacher he loves, the only teacher he has ever loved, and I know that he will be happy. He will be safe. He will be good.

I will not see the rest of Max's life, but I know it will be long and happy and good.

I close my eyes. Tears steam down my cheeks and then they are gone. The warm, wet streaks are no more. The gooey balloon in my belly grows to fill every nook and cranny of my insides, and then I feel myself start to rise.

I am no longer whole. I am no longer me.

I soar.

I hold the image of Max's face in my mind for as long as I can. Until I am no more.

"I love you, Max," I whisper as his face and everything else in the world fades to white.

epilogue

I open my eyes. I am staring at eyes. I have seen these eyes before. They are dark and warm. They know me.

I cannot place them. And then I can.

I do not understand.

I say her name.

"Dee?"

And then I know.

Acknowledgements

In the process of writing this novel, I invited about a dozen friends and family members to read along as I wrote. While their helpful suggestions, generous praise, and private counsel were critical to my success, the most important thing was the knowledge that someone was reading and anxiously waiting for the next chapter. For that, I am forever grateful.

Most important of those early readers is and always has been my wife, Elysha. Writing for me is little more than a continual, unending effort to impress the pretty girl whom I love. I am fortunate in that Elysha likes more of what I write than she doesn't and offers me the time and support to accomplish my goals. She is both the reason I want to write well and the reason I am able to write well enough.

Special thanks to Lindsay Heyer, for suggesting that my childhood imaginary friend might serve as inspiration for a novel. This book would have never happened had she not been such a good listener, confidant, and friend.

Thanks to my in-laws, Barbara and Gerry Green, for their constant support and love. Never before have I understood or experienced the sense of pride that parents can feel for a son. I am fortunate to have found this gift so late in life.

Thanks to the real-life Mrs. Gosk, who differs only slightly from her fictional counterpart. Donna is one of the finest teachers I have ever known. My desire was to give Max and Budo the best possible teacher, and I quickly realized that reality had provided me with a character much greater than any I could have ever imagined.

Great appreciation goes to Elizabeth Curione and Helen Chin, the production editor and copyeditor for this book, respectively. I believe that editors' names should appear on the cover of every book in recognition for all the work that they do in bringing a story to the finish line. Their expertise has spared me countless moments of grammatical embarrassment. Their invisible but vital imprints are hiding, much like an imaginary friend, on every page of this book.

Thanks to Laura Chasen, editorial assistant extraordinaire, who in many ways keeps the machine running on a daily basis. Laura has been generous with her time, patient with my naïveté, and was kind enough to contribute editorially to this book. I am a firm believer that there can never be too many talented eyes contributing to a book. Laura's were unexpected and appreciated.

Undying gratitude to Brenda Copeland, my editor and friend, who never fails to amaze me with her love and support for Budo and for me. I feel incredibly fortunate to have found someone as smart, as talented, and as insightful to help guide this book and my career into the future. She is fierce yet funny, capable yet kooky, and most important, a person to whom I am both honored and blessed to refer to as "Boss."

Lastly, everlasting appreciation to Taryn Fagerness, my agent and friend, who believed that I could write this story when I did not. Without her urging, Budo and his friends would remain on the heap of untested ideas that litter my hard drive. Taryn has been the invisible friend of my writing career for a long time. She is the person who makes every bump a little less jarring, every success a little more joyful, and every sentence that I place on the page a little less unfortunate. She is the Teeny of my life. My guardian angel.

MEMOIRS OF AN IMAGINARY FRIEND

by Matthew Dicks

About the Author

- A Conversation with Matthew Dicks

Behind the Novel

- "All Writers Start Out as Book Lovers"
  An Original Essay by the Author

Keep on Reading

- Recommended Reading
- Reading Group Questions

For more reading group suggestions
visit www.readinggroupgold.com

 ST. MARTIN'S GRIFFIN

A Conversation with Matthew Dicks

The first chapter of this novel is short—just half a page—but it sure packs a punch. How did you come up with the idea of starting with what is essentially Budo's bio?

This story belongs to Budo as much as it does to Max. And while most readers will be familiar with a smart kid like Max (no matter how *different* he may be), they may not be familiar with a character who's an imaginary friend. So I set out in that short page to establish who Budo is and—perhaps most importantly—what he knows.

There are many funny moments in this book. Many tender moments as well. Did you find it hard to move back and forth between the two?

I'm always immensely grateful when people mention the humor in *Memoirs of an Imaginary Friend,* perhaps because humor is difficult to pull off. So thank you. I was often called a smart ass in school (and my mother always referred to me as The Instigator), so it's probably fair to say that being funny comes naturally to me. As for the tender stuff . . . I'm a guy and I know how to be tough—when you have a last name like mine and you teach fifth graders, tough is the first thing you learn—but my students have also managed to soften me up a bit over the years. There's such love between Budo and Max I felt that I had to show it in order to accurately portray their friendship. The hardest part, though, was showing that fondness without getting maudlin or sentimental, because that wouldn't have suited Max in the least. And probably would have annoyed him, too.

How do you come up with names for your characters—real and imaginary?

I love coming up with character names, but some are easier than others. Max came to me because I

> *"There's such love between Budo and Max...I had to show it."*

wanted a name that was brisk and boyish, something that would easily fit an eight-year-old. I've also had a few memorable boys named Max in my classroom over the years, and they left a strong impression on me. Giving Max their name was a bit of a nod to those extraordinary kids. Budo is the name of a real imaginary friend. I have friends with twin boys, and their shared imaginary friend (bizarre, I know) is named Budo. I loved the name so I stole it. Chomp, an imaginary friend you meet early in the book, is also one of their imaginary friends. Oswald is a name that has always conjured fear in me, probably the result of seeing the footage of Lee Harvey Oswald being shot when I was young. Before I realized that Oswald was going to be a benevolent character, I knew that Oswald would be a perfect name for him. The character of Mrs. Gosk was easy—that's the name of a real teacher who is my mentor and friend.

I guess you could say that I like to blur the lines between fiction and the so-called real world. My daughter is named Clara after the main character in Cynthia Rylant's *The Van Gogh Café*—one of my wife's favorite books. My son is named Charles Wallace after the five-year-old boy in Madeline L'Engle's *A Wrinkle in Time*. Oh—and while we're on the subject, in England I'm published under the name of Matthew Green. I guess they figured that my real last name would cause too many jokes. Go figure.

Grown-ups use the phrase *on the spectrum* to describe Max. Is there a reason you didn't give him a definite diagnosis such as *Asperger's* or *autism*?

As a teacher I see children who are on the spectrum, and I try to understand each one as an individual. In fact, I like to understand all of my students as individuals. That was my starting point with Max.

A diagnosis can be very useful to a person and his family—it's often the first step in getting proper treatment and support. But a diagnosis can also be a label that stops the conversation, "Oh, so-and-so's got Asperger's . . ." or "She does that because she has autism," as if that can explain everything about a person. It's never that simple. I didn't want Max to be defined, or worse, dismissed.

This is your third novel. How was the experience of writing this book different from the others?

This was the first time I have ever written in the first person, and so the beginning was exceedingly difficult. Prior to writing this book, I thought that writing in the first person was foolishly limiting and wondered why any author would make such a choice. But when I sat down to write *Memoirs of an Imaginary Friend*, I realized it wasn't me who was speaking. It was Budo. So Budo would have to tell the story. But it wasn't easy.

Eventually I found myself enjoying the first-person narration, as it forced me to be more concise than I normally am. And once I found Budo's voice and understood Max, writing the story became fun.

Do you write with an outline or with the end of the story in sight?

I don't know the plot of any of my stories before I begin writing. Instead I find a character and a place to begin and start tapping keys. While a story eventually emerges, it's hard for me to take any credit since so many parts of my stories reveal themselves to me through the process of writing. I never know where a story will take me, so as new and interesting imaginary friends presented themselves to Budo, I found myself meeting them for the first time as well. And as I wrote, I came to understand that this was

"*Once I found Budo's voice and understood Max, writing the story became fun.*"

more than a book about a boy and his imaginary
friend. There is an initially unintended existential
aspect of the book that appealed to me a great deal.
Having survived two near-death experiences as well
as robbery at gunpoint, I am keenly aware of the
potential for death and for nonexistence in everyday
life. And as I wrote the book, I found some of my
omnipresent fear and sadness over the prospect of
death leaking into the story. It added an unexpected
depth to the story that I was able to later tease out in
greater detail.

Who are your first readers?

I'm lucky to have a trio of strong women who read
my work. My wife is first, my agent second, and my
editor third. My editor says she's not used to third
place and keeps lobbying to move up the chain, but
this is based on seniority, so that's just the way it is.

Why did you give the book an epilogue?

When I finished the book, it had no epilogue. I went
to bed thinking that my story was finished, but when
I awoke the next morning, those eleven sentences
were in my mind, almost exactly as they appear on
the page today. I'm glad I included them. I get a lot
of correspondence from readers commenting on the
epilogue and what it means to them.

An Original Essay by the Author

"All Writers Start Out as Book Lovers"

My love for reading began in kindergarten, with a basal reader titled *Sun Up*. I can still remember the first page:

The sun was up. Bing was up. Sandy was up. Bing and Sandy was up.

(Apparently the author cared more about Bing and Sandy than correct grammar.)

When I arrived home from school on that first day, I removed the yellow and orange book from my backpack. My brother and sister crowded around me, anxious to see what I had brought home. I read the title aloud.

"Sun Up."

My mom was so proud. At least my sister says she was. I was too focused on the book to notice. My sister says that she was proud, too. Reading seemed like magic to her.

I opened the book to the first page and attempted the first word: *the.* I sounded it out in my head: "ta-ha-eee."

"The," Mom corrected me.

The word came up again a few sentences later. "Ta-ha-eeee," I said.

Mom corrected me again. The word appeared several more times on those first few pages, and each time, I was unable to read it correctly. With each correction I could hear the frustration grow in my mother's voice.

"Why don't you take a break," she suggested, her words strained.

It took me far too long to learn to read the word *the,*

> *"I spent much of my childhood reading books that were not written for children."*

but I can remember the moment when I sounded it out correctly for the first time. When the word made sense to me for the first time. It was a big moment in my then brief existence.

The next big moment came when I was ten years old and finally able to ride my bike to the town library and check out books. My parents had never taken me to the library, so I spent much of my childhood reading books that were not written for children. I read anything I could get my hands on, and the choices were limited. Starting with the top shelf of my parent's bookshelf, I tackled our family's half-set of encyclopedias, Funk and Wagnalls, A–K. I didn't read every entry, but I read many of them—often dozens of times—and liked to show off what I knew. I remember, for example, our band leader being impressed when I was the only student to correctly identify the school's first flugelhorn. I don't remember his reaction when I asked why an instrument traditionally used in a jazz was being added to our marching band.

Behind the Novel

The depth of my A–K trivia is astounding.

Before long I had moved onto the second and third shelves, where I discovered my stepfather's World War II nonfiction (a book detailing the Japanese invasion of Wake Island was especially good), George Carpozi's account of the Son of Sam murders, and a smattering of novels including Peter Benchley's *Jaws*, which I tore into four pieces and shared with my friends at school. We would later do the same for such hard-to-find books like *Helter Skelter* and *The Lord of the Rings*.

As a parent I can't imagine letting my child read such dark and complex material, but that was how I grew up, and that was probably why my first bike ride to the public library was such a momentous occasion.

And I remember it well. My hometown library consisted of a single, poorly lit room in the lower level of the town hall, and while it contained more books than I had ever seen, there were only about half a dozen aisles of books in all. Windows ran the length of one side of the room, but they were completely obscured by a thick hedgerow, ensuring that the only light came from the humming fluorescents overhead. The carpet was industrial, the smell was government brick, and the walls were gray and bare. A single round table filled the space opposite the stacks, and the six chairs surrounding it were the only seating available in the entire space. I would often sit at this table alongside small children and the elderly, the only types of people (other than myself) who seemed to have a library card in my town. More often, however, the library was empty and always a little cold, even in the heat of August.

It was, in a word, beautiful.

I remember the first book I checked out of the library, but I can no longer recall the title, which is a shame because I've been trying to find it for years. It was a pre-dystopian science fiction story in which the tallest buildings in the world begin to liquefy, starting with the Sears Tower in Chicago. (It was the tallest building at the time.) The tip of the Sears Tower dissolves first, then, as it comes even in height with the second tallest building in the world, that building liquefies as well. And so on, and so on. Eventually all the buildings of the word liquefy at exactly the same rate, throwing the planet into terror and chaos.

If you guessed that this was the work of an alien race you'd be right. And if you guessed that this alien race felt obliged to ensure that mankind did not advance technologically beyond a point that is considered

"It wasn't until I reached high school that I fell in love with writing."

safe, that they believed that by keeping buildings no taller than six stories the technological advancement of the human race will be curtailed, well . . . you were ahead of me.

Thirty years have passed since I read that book. While I'm sure that it's out of print (it's been impossible to find), I wish I knew what the title was. When my son and daughter are old enough, I'd love to read them this book and regale them in stories about my first trip to the public library.

When I moved on from the aliens and their urban renewal I read books by Stephen King, Agatha Christie, Douglas Adams, Ray Bradbury, and Frank Herbert. Mystery, science fiction, and horror were the books that I started with, often reading two or three in a week, but I soon discovered, thanks to a kindly librarian who sought to expand my literary boundaries, authors such as Kurt Vonnegut, Robert Louis Stevenson (*Treasure Island* remains my favorite book to this day), Charles Dickens, Edgar Allen Poe, and Mark Twain.

It wasn't until I reached high school that I fell in love with writing, and only after discovering that writing allowed me to make girls laugh. But once the love for writing was real, I had an advantage, because I understood, better than many of my classmates, what made a great story. I had read many of the classics long before our teachers ever introduced them to us. I was the only kid in town to have read Shakespeare's *Hamlet*, Stephen King's *Cujo*, and Robert Pirsig's *Zen and the Art of Motorcycle Maintenance*—all in the same month. By the time I was sixteen, I had read what seemed like every book in that dingy little library, and my background in literature was wide and deep. If all this sounds boastful, well, I guess it is. Like many children who grew up to become writers, I felt myself something of an outsider and a misfit. Reading was the thing I loved to do. It was the thing that I could do well.

It was by reading that I absorbed what makes a great story. Still, I learned the hard way that knowing what makes a story and writing one are two very different things. That was okay. I'm sure that most writers can't write in the beginning. For some of us, the road is long and hard. But we still have our books when our prose falls flat and our characters fail to come alive. All writers start out as book lovers, and that does not change, regardless of our success or lack thereof. We love to read, and then we love to write. And the books are always there for us.

"All writers start out as book lovers...."

Recommended Reading

The Tale of Despereaux by Kate DiCamillo

This is a novel written for the YA audience, but honestly, it's a book for all of us. It tells the story of a brave and noble mouse who struggles to be himself in a world that insists upon conformity.

Close to Shore by Michael Capuzzo

Close to Shore is the nonfiction account of a series of shark attacks off the New Jersey shore in 1916 that later inspired Peter Benchley's *Jaws*. Capuzzo paints a brilliant portrait of this fascinating period of American history while simultaneously capturing the terror of a shark that could not be stopped.

Ballistics by Billy Collins

For those who don't like poetry, Billy Collins is for you. Collins's poems read like brief, insightful, oftentimes hilarious essays that will entertain and inform any reader.

Gone Girl by Gillian Flynn

When you finish reading *Gone Girl*, you will want to talk to everyone you know about the book and begin jamming it into the hands of friends and family members. It's an original thriller that will keep you guessing right up to the final pages of the book.

The Sparrow by Mary Doria Russell

When my friend told me that her favorite novel was about Jesuits in space, I had my doubts. They proved to be unfounded. This is an unforgettable story about what happens when a man tries to do the right thing for the right reasons and causes unspeakable disaster.

Breakfast of Champions by Kurt Vonnegut

This was the first novel I read by my favorite author, and it remains the funniest book I have ever read. I believe that this biting satire about a Midwestern car dealer's slow ride into insanity at the hands of his favorite author is Vonnegut's masterpiece.

Defending Jacob by William Landay

This legal thriller about a district attorney who finds himself defending his teenage son from murder charges will keep you guessing all the way to the story's heart-stopping final page.

I Feel Bad About My Neck by Nora Ephron

Most Americans know Nora Ephron for movies like *When Harry Met Sally* and *You've Got Mail*, but her essays are equally amusing and even more insightful. I've heard people say that she is the female version of David Sedaris, but as much as I adore Sedaris, I think Ephron is even better.

📖 *Reading Group Questions*

1. "I am not imaginary," says Budo. Do you believe him?

2. Max's mother wants desperately to understand what is wrong with Max, while his father wants desperately to believe that there is nothing wrong. Who do you side with?

3. Budo seems to watch a lot of television. How do his viewing habits shape his perception of the world?

4. Budo straddles many worlds: child and adult; real and imaginary. Could the same be said for other characters in this book?

5. Mrs. Patterson did a terrible thing. But is there any way in which her actions may have been beneficial to Max?

6. What does Budo fear most? Why does he think that Max's mom and dad are his biggest danger?

7. The author, Matthew Dicks, is an elementary school teacher. In what ways can you see the influence of this "day job" on his writing?

8. Did you have an imaginary friend as a child, and if so, which imaginary friend from the book most resembles your imaginary friend? If you didn't have an imaginary friend, do you wish you had one? Who from the book would you have chosen to be your imaginary friend?

9. What is your interpretation of the epilogue of the book?

10. Did you ever have a teacher as important to you as Mrs. Gosk is to Max and Budo? Who was your Mrs. Gosk?

*Keep on
Reading*

11. Mrs. Gosk is an actual teacher in the school where Matthew Dicks also teaches. What do you think about the idea that the author used an actual person in the novel?

12. How did you feel about Mrs. Patterson? Did you see her as a villain? Did you feel empathy for her?

13. Excluding Budo, which of the imaginary friends in the book was your favorite and why?

14. Budo describes Max as the bravest person on the planet because he has to go out into the world every day being himself even though no one likes him. Do you agree?

15. If the book is adapted for film, how do you think the role of Budo should be cast? By an actor (and if so, whom?) or through some form of animation?

Matthew Dicks is the author of two other novels, *Something Missing* and *Unexpectedly, Milo*, as well as the rock opera *The Clowns*. When he is not hunched over a computer screen, he fills his days as an elementary school teacher. He is a former West Hartford Teacher of the Year and a three-time Moth StorySLAM champion. Matthew is married to friend and fellow teacher, Elysha, and they have a daughter named Clara and a son named Charlie. Matthew grew up in the small town of Blackstone, Massachusetts, where he spent his time milking cows, mucking stalls, and managing his local McDonald's restaurant. Visit www.matthewdicks.com to learn more.

About the Author

Credit: Holly M. Williams